LISA GARDNER
Three Great Novels
The Thrillers

Also by Lisa Gardner

The Perfect Husband
The Other Daughter
The Third Victim
The Next Accident
The Survivors Club

Lisa Gardner
Three Great Novels

The Perfect Husband

The Other Daughter

The Third Victim

ORION

First published in Great Britain in 2003
by Orion Books
an imprint of The Orion Publishing Group
Orion House, 5 Upper St Martin's Lane,
London WC2H 9EA

A CIP catalogue record for this book
is available from the British Library

ISBN (trade paperback) 0 75286 004 6

Typeset at The Spartan Press Ltd,
Lymington, Hants
Printed and bound in Great Britain by
Clays Ltd, St Ives plc

Contents

The Perfect Husband

Acknowledgments

Writers have a tendency to view their craft as a solitary occupation. In fact, it takes many people to create a book and I'm indebted to quite a few. I would like to express my deep appreciation and gratitude to all the people who helped me in this process, including:

Jack Stapelton, Bristol County assistant district attorney, who generously and patiently answered a multitude of questions about crossjurisdictional investigations and arrests.

Steve Belanger, corrections officer, who shared with me enough details about life in a maximum security prison to convince me never to commit a crime.

Chris Fuss, college buddy and dear friend, who not only provided his experience in orienteering and the Revolutionary War reenactment, but also let me play with the rifles.

Aaron Kechley and Valerie Weber, two Williams alumni, who told me so much about quaint, beautiful Williamstown, I just had to use it for murder.

And to the remaining police officers, FBI agents, and other corrections officers who kindly agreed to answer my questions but asked that their names be withheld.

These people gave me their knowledge. In some cases, I did take artistic license. Any mistakes, of course, are mine alone.

Finally, special thanks to my agent, Damaris Rowland, for believing in my talent even more than I did; to Nita Taublib for being willing to take a risk on this book; to Beth de Guzman, whose razor-sharp editing made this manuscript come alive; to my family and my friends Heather, Dolly, Michele, Terry, Lori, and Betsy for their support and endless supplies of chocolate; and to my fiancé, Anthony Ruddy, for sharing it all with me and showing me a beautiful future. Words aren't enough.

Prologue

The first time he saw her, he simply knew. He watched her red and white pompoms bounce in the air. He saw the long, golden ribbons of her hair wave across the blue summer sky. He memorized her gleaming white smile as she cried her cheerleader chants and pranced with the other girls around the freshly mowed football field. Once he'd been hungry, now he looked at her and was full. Once he'd been barren, now he studied her and felt his insides burst.

He knew everything about her. He knew her parents were well respected in Williamstown, a unique position for nonacademics in this liberal arts college enclave. He knew her family came from good German stock, four generations of fair-skinned blonds running the local store, Matthews', and living out their years without ever traveling more than four blocks from their place of birth. They had a tendency to die peacefully in their sleep, except for Theresa's great-grandfather, who'd died of smoke inhalation at the age of seventy-five as he'd helped free horses from his neighbor's burning barn.

He knew Theresa rushed home from cheerleading practice every afternoon to help her parents at their store. She tidied small shelves packed with imported olive oils, spinach nutmeg pasta, and local-made maple candies molded to look like oak leaves. During late September and early October, when Williamstown was overrun by people oohing and aahing over the golden hills and scarlet underbrush, Theresa was allowed to slice Vermont cheese and fresh creamery fudge for the tourists. Then the season would pass and she would be relegated to housekeeping once more, dusting the blue-checkered shelves, sweeping the one-hundred-year-old hardwood floor, and wiping down unfinished pine tables. These were the same duties she'd had since she was twelve and he'd listened to her father tell her half a dozen times in a single afternoon that she would never be smart enough to do anything more.

Theresa never argued. She simply tightened her red-checkered apron, ducked her blond head, and kept sweeping.

She was a popular girl in her high school class of nearly one hundred, friendly but not outgoing, attractive but demure. While other seventeen-year-old girls at Mt Greylock High School were succumbing to the star fullback's urgent groping or the forbidden lure of cheap beer, Theresa came home every Friday and Saturday night by ten.

She was very, very punctual, Theresa's mother told him. Did her homework the way she was supposed to, went to church, attended to her chores. No hanging out with dopers or druggies, not their Theresa. She never stepped out of line.

Mrs Matthews might have been as beautiful as her daughter once, but those years had come and gone quickly. Now she was a high-strung woman with faded blue eyes, dirty-blond hair, and a doughy body. She wore her hair pulled back tight enough to stretch the corners of her eyes and crossed herself at least once every two minutes while clicking together her rosary beads. He knew her kind. Prayed to the Lord to deliver her from all sorts of evil. Was glad at her age she was no longer required to have sex. And on Friday night, when Mr Matthews drank a whole bottle of Wild Turkey and smacked her and Theresa around, she figured they both deserved it because Eve had given Adam the apple and women had been serving time ever since.

At fifty years of age, Mr Matthews was pretty much what he'd expected as well. Steel-gray hair, buzz cut. Stern face. Trim waist. Huge arms that bulged as he hefted hundred-pound bags of flour and seventy-pound tanks of pop syrup. He sauntered through the tiny store like an emperor in his domain. While his family worked busily, he liked to lean across the counter and shoot the breeze with the customers, talking about the falling price of milk or the hazards of running a small business. He kept a loaded gun beneath his bed and a rifle in the back of his truck. Once a year he shot one deer legally and – according to local rumors – bagged a second illegally just to prove that he could.

No one told him how to live his life, mind his store, or run his family. He was a true bull-headed, narrow-eyed, dumber-than-a-post son of a bitch.

Jim had spent just two afternoons in the store inspecting father, mother, and daughter, and he'd learned all he needed to know. The parents would never cut it in high society, but they had no genetic defects or facial tics. And their daughter, their beautiful, quiet, obedient daughter, was absolutely perfect.

Jim opened the door of his car and stepped out. He was ready.

Above him the spring sky was pure blue. Before him the Berkshire hills framed Mt Greylock High School with pure green. Below him the unbroken valley spread out like a verdant buffet, endless fields spotted by faint dots of red barns and black-and-white Holsteins. He inhaled the scents of spicy pine, fresh mowed grass, and distant dairy farms. He listened to cheerleader songs. 'Go fight win, go fight win.' He watched Theresa's long, limber legs kick at the sky.

'We're from Greylock, no one can be prouder. If you can't hear us, we'll shout a little louder.'

He smiled and stepped into the full brilliance of the spring sunshine. He caught Theresa's eye as her lithe body dropped into the splits, her pompoms victoriously thrust into the air. She smiled back at him, the gesture reflexive.

He took off his sunglasses. Her eyes widened. He unfurled his charming grin until she blushed becomingly and finally had to look away. The other cheerleaders were now glancing from her to him with open envy. A few pouted prettily and one overdeveloped redhead pushed out her perky breasts in a belated attempt to redirect his attention.

He never took his eyes off Theresa. She was the one.

He turned slightly and the sunlight glinted off the police shield pinned to his young, well-toned chest. One hundred feet from him, behind the chain-link fence, Theresa's gaze fell to his badge. He saw her instant nervousness, her innate uncertainty. Then her beautiful brown eyes swept up his face, searching his eyes.

He knew the moment he had her. He registered the precise instant the wariness left her gaze and was replaced by vulnerable, tremulous hope.

And the power that filled him was unimaginable.

In his mind he heard his father's voice, low and soothing as it had been in the beginning, before everything had gone to hell. His father was reciting a parable: There was once a tortoise and a scorpion faced by an incoming flood. Fearful, but wanting to do the right thing, the tortoise had told the scorpion he would carry the deadly creature across the raging waters to the opposite shore if the scorpion would agree not to sting him. The scorpion gave the tortoise his word and climbed onto the tortoise's back. They set out, the tortoise's short, strong legs churning powerfully, fighting to bring them to shore. The waves crashed over them, sending them reeling back. The tortoise swam and swam, struggling to bring them forward even as the water swept them back. The waves grew fiercer. The tortoise became tired. Soon, even the light weight of the scorpion began to seem like a heavy chain, threatening to drag him under. The tortoise, however, refused to ask the scorpion to jump off. He swam harder, and finally the shoreline appeared in view. It looked as if they would make it.

And then the scorpion stung him. Just dug in and jabbed the poison deep into his flesh. The tortoise looked back in shocked bewilderment, the poison burning his blood, his legs turning instantly to lead. He could no longer move. They both began to drown. At the last minute, with the salty brine filling his mouth and nostrils, the poor tortoise cried, 'Why did you do such a thing? You have killed us both!'

The scorpion replied simply, 'Because it is my nature.'

Jim liked that story. He understood. It was his nature too. He could not think of a time when he hadn't known that he was better than everyone, smarter than everyone, faster than everyone, colder than everyone.

What he wanted, he got.

Now he smiled at beautiful seventeen-year-old Theresa Matthews. He let her see the Berkshire County badge he'd worked so hard to earn. And his hand lovingly stroked the billy club hanging at his waist.

Look at me, Theresa. Look at your future husband.

In the beginning it had been that simple.

In the beginning . . .

1

J. T. Dillon was drunk.

Outside, the white-hot desert sun was straight up in the sky, bleaching bones and parching mountains. Saguaro cacti seemed to surf waves of heat while sagebrush died of sunstroke at their feet. And all over Nogales, people hid in darkened rooms, running ice cubes down their naked chests and cursing God for having saved August's apocalypse for September.

But he didn't notice.

In the middle of the cool green oasis of his ranch-style home, J. T. Dillon lay sprawled on his back, his right hand cradling the silver-framed picture of a smiling woman and gorgeous little boy. His left hand held an empty tequila bottle.

Above him a fan stirred the air-conditioned breeze through the living room. Below him a Navajo print rug absorbed his sweat. The room was well maintained and tastefully decorated with wicker furniture and sturdy yucca soap trees.

He stopped noticing such details after his first day of straight tequila. As any marine knew, true binge drinking was art, and J.T. considered himself to be Tequila Willie's first Michelangelo. Shot number one seared away throat lining. Shot number two burned away the taste of the first. Half a bottle later, no man worth his salt even winced at the sensation of cheap, raw tequila ripping down his esophagus, into his stomach, and sooner or later, out his bowels.

By the end of day one J.T. had been beyond conscious thought. The ceiling fan had become a prehistoric bird, his wicker sofa a tiger lying in wait. The toughest, meanest marine in the world had developed a bad case of the giggles. When he closed his eyes, the world had spun sickeningly, so he'd spent his first night with his eyelids propped open by his fingers, staring at the ceiling hour after hour after hour.

Now, on his fourth day of straight tequila, he'd gone beyond thought and surrendered most of his body. His face had gone first. He'd been sitting by his pool, swigging some great Cuervo Gold, and abruptly he'd realized he could no longer feel his nose. He tried to find it with his fingers – no dice. His nose was gone. An hour later his cheeks disappeared as well. No rasp of whiskers, no sting of sweat. He had no cheeks. Finally, not that long ago, he'd lost his lips. He'd tried to open them and they hadn't been there anymore. No lips.

It made it damn hard to drink, and he had twenty-four hours of serious boozing left.

He rolled slowly onto his side, discovering he still had arms and a remnant of a pickled brain. He squeezed his eyes shut and hazy images clustered behind his eyelids. He'd been a champion swimmer and percussion rifle shooter once. He remembered the welcoming smell of chlorine and the heavy weight of his black walnut rifle. He'd been a marine with 'raw talent, lots of potential' before he'd been asked to leave.

After the marines had come the stint as a mercenary, doing work he never told anyone about because then he'd have to kill them. The next image was more hesitant, still raw around the edges, as if it understood that even after four days of straight tequila, it had the power to bruise. He was back in the States. Rachel stood beside him. He was a husband. His gaze dropped to the little boy squeezing his hand. He was a father.

Now he was a drunk.

His manservant Freddie arrived, taking the silver-framed portrait from J.T.'s hands and replacing it in the safe where it would remain until next September.

'How are you doing, sir?'

'Uh.'

His iguana crawled into the room, its four-foot tail slithering across the red-tiled floor. The tequila screamed, 'Red alert! Godzilla attacks!' The sane part of him whispered through parched, rubbery lips, 'Glug, go away. I mean it.'

Glug pointedly ignored him, settling his plump body in a sunbeam that had sneaked through the venetian blinds and making himself comfortable. J.T. liked Glug.

'Water, sir?' Freddie inquired patiently.

'What day is it?'

The thirteenth, sir.'

'Then gimme another margarita.'

In the distance a phone rang. The sound made J.T. groan, and when the noise had the audacity to repeat itself, he crawled painfully toward his patio to escape.

The sun promptly nailed him like a ball peen hammer. He swayed onto his feet, squinted his eyes from long practice, and oozed straight tequila from his pores.

Dry heat, they'd told him when he first moved to Arizona. Sure it's hot, but it's dry heat. Bullshit. One hundred and twenty was one hundred and twenty. No sane man lived in these kinds of temperatures.

He'd spent enough time in jungles, pretending he didn't notice the water steaming off his skin or his own pungent odor. He'd learned to block out some of it. He'd simply inhaled the rest. The jungle lived inside him now. Sometimes, if he remembered Virginia plantations and the way his father had sat at the head of the table, clad in his full Green Beret uniform, his trousers bloused into glossy black Corcoran jump boots, his shirt pressed into razor-sharp creases and ribbons pinned ostentatiously to his chest, the jungle took up its beat in his veins.

Then J.T. would laugh. It was the one valuable lesson he'd learned from his father. Women cry. Men laugh. Whiners moan. Men laugh. Wimps complain. Men laugh.

When Marion had called to tell him the colonel was dying of prostate cancer, J.T. had laughed so damn hard, he'd dropped the phone.

Freddie emerged on the porch, austere in his neatly pressed linen suit. 'Telephone, sir.'

'Is it still the thirteenth?'

'Yes, sir.'

'Tell 'em to go away.'

Freddie didn't move. 'It's Vincent, sir. He's called four times already. He claims it's important.'

J.T. plopped down on the deck and dangled his fingertips into the pool. He'd dreamed of owning a pool like this most of his life. He half-hated it.

'Sir?'

'Vincent always thinks it's important.'

'He refuses to hang up, sir.' Freddie placed the phone on the patio. His indignant sniff indicated what he thought of Vincent. J.T. rolled over on his back. Neither Freddie nor the phone appeared to be willing to go away.

Grudgingly he lifted the receiver. 'I'm retired, Vincent.'

'No kidding, old man.' Vincent's booming voice made J.T. clutch his forehead. 'I got a live one for you, Dillon. Right up your alley.'

'It's the thirteenth.'

'All over half the globe.'

'I don't take calls until the fourteenth, and I don't take your calls any day. I'm retired.'

'Dillon, wait till you hear about the money—'

'I don't need money.'

'Everyone needs money.'

'I don't need money. I don't need business. I'm out. Good-bye.'

'Hey, hey, hey! Hold on! Come on, J.T. Hear me out, for old time's sake. Listen, I met this woman. She's really terrific—'

'Good fuck?'

'That's not what I meant—'

'Blond probably. You always were a sucker for blondes.'

'J.T., buddy, don't be such an ass. I wouldn't have called you about just anyone – I know you're retired. But this woman needs help. I mean, she *needs* help.'

'Yeah? Grab a phone book, look up St Jude, dial the number. If anyone answers, let me know. I might try dialing it myself someday. Bye.'

'J.T.—'

'I don't care.' J.T. hung up the phone. Freddie was still standing there. A bead of sweat traced his upper lip. J.T. shook his head.

'What were you so worried about?' he chided his manservant. 'That I'd say yes? That I'd give up all this for a thirty-second adrenaline rush? Freddie, I thought we knew each other better than that.'

'I'll bring you another margarita, sir.'

'Yeah, Freddie. We understand each other just fine.'

J.T. let his head fall back against the heat-proofed patio. The sun pierced his eyelids until he could see the red veins zigzagging his flesh.

Freddie reappeared with a salt-rimmed glass and set it by J.T.'s head.

'Freddie?' J.T. said.

'Yes, sir?'

'Let another call come through, and I will fire you.'

'Yes, sir.'

'Even if it's the colonel, Freddie. Do you understand?'

'Of course, sir.'

'Good.'

Freddie pivoted sharply and left; J.T. didn't bother to watch.

He tipped into the pool fully clothed. He sank all the way down. He didn't fight it, he'd never had to fight water. From the beginning, Marion had been able to do anything on a horse and J.T. had been able to do anything underwater.

His feet touched bottom. He opened his eyes and surveyed his kingdom, the sides of the pool formed by jutting red stone, the bottom that looked like strewn sapphires.

The tickling started in the base of his throat, the instinctive need to breathe. He didn't fight that either. He accepted it. The need, the panic, the fear. Underwater, he could accept anything. Underwater, the world finally made sense to him.

He ticked off the seconds in his mind, and the tickling in his throat grew to full-fledged choking. *Don't fight it, don't fight. Ease into the burn.* He passed the two-minute mark. Once he'd been capable of four, but that wouldn't happen today.

Two minutes forty-five seconds. That was it. He rocketed to the top. He broke water with a furious gasp, swallowing four gulps of air at once. His jeans and T-shirt were plastered to his skin, the tom-toms pounded against his head.

The memories were still in his mind. Rachel and Teddy. Laughing. Smiling. Screaming. Dying.

Every year he had his bender. Five days of remembering what he couldn't stand to forget.

Five days of blackness rolling over him like a fog and choking out the light.

After a minute he began to swim. Then he swam some more. Above him the air was dry, and the crickets began to sing as the sky turned bloodred.

'Are you alive?'

'Whuh?' J.T. groggily lifted his head. He'd passed out facedown on the patio. Something clammy was sticking to his skin. Wet clothes.

'Mr Dillon? Mr J. T. Dillon?'

He squinted his eyes, his pupils refusing to cooperate. Somehow everything seemed red, red and shadowed and ugly. He tried focusing harder. A human being appeared before him. She had black hair, which reminded him of an Elvis wig. He let his forehead sink back down.

'Are you all right?'

'That's always been subject to some debate.' He didn't bother to look up again. 'Lady, I don't buy Avon products or Girl Scout cookies. On the other hand, if you have any Cuervo Gold, I'll take two cases.'

'I am not the Avon lady.'

'Tough break.' He had to be dying. Not since his first day at West Point had he felt this ill.

'Mr Dillon—'

'Go away.'

'I can't.'

'Stand up, pivot one hundred and eighty degrees, and don't let the gate hit your ass on the way out.'

'Mr Dillon . . . please, just hear me out.'

He finally pinned her with a bleary gaze. She sat on the edge of a deck chair, perched like a scrawny dove and framed by the mesquite tree. Young. Really bad haircut. Even worse dye job. She tried to appear nonchalant, but her white knees were shaking. He groaned.

'Lady, you're out of your league.'

'I . . . The . . . I . . .' She stood up stiffly and squared her shoulders. Her face was resolute, but the rest of her ruined the impression. Her too-white suit was wrinkled and ill fitting. She'd lost a lot of weight recently, and the shadows beneath her eyes were too dark to speak of sweet dreams.

'Mr Dillon—'

'Freddie!' he called out at the top of his lungs. 'Freddie!'

The woman's lips snapped shut.

'He went out,' she said after a moment. She began to methodically shred her right thumbnail.

'Went out?' He moaned again, then shook his wet hair. Water sprayed out, a few drops hitting her silk suit, but she didn't flinch. He sluiced a hand through his hair, wiping long strands back out of his face, and looked at his unwanted guest one more time.

She kept a careful distance. Close enough not to show fear, but far enough to be prudent. Her stance was solidly balanced and prepared for action, legs wide apart with one foot back, chest out, arms free. It gave him a sense of déjà vu, as if he should know something about her. But the intuition came and went too fast, and he didn't feel like pursuing it.

'Your friend left,' she said. 'I watched him climb into a sedan and drive away.'

'Huh.' He sat up reluctantly. The world spun, then righted. Considering that his blood had to be ninety percent tequila by now, his vision was much too clear. How long had he been out? How much alcohol had he sweated from his pores? He was sobering up too fast.

He ripped off his T-shirt and dropped it on the deck. Then his fingers went to work on his jeans.

'I want to hire you.' The woman's voice had gained a slight tremor.

He stripped the clinging denim from his legs and tossed the jeans onto the deck. 'Better.'

'I . . . I'm not sure this is appropriate,' she said.

J.T. turned on her with a scowl, hands on his hips. Buck naked, he looked her straight in the eye and wondered why the hell she hadn't smartened up enough to disappear by now. 'Lady, does this villa look like a convent to you? This is a private residence and I'm the beast in charge. Now, get the hell out of my sight or do something useful with your mouth.'

He gave her a sardonic smile, then walked away. Freddie had left him a margarita on the poolside table. It was melted, but he didn't mind. He downed half in a single gulp.

'Vincent sent me,' the woman whispered behind him.

'That son of a bitch,' J.T. drawled without any real emotion. 'I'll just have to take him off my Christmas card list.' He downed the second half of the margarita. 'I'm counting to five. Be gone before I'm done, or heaven help you.'

'Won't you please just hear me out?'

'One.'

'I'll pay you.'

'Two.'

'Vincent did not tell me you were a pigheaded drunk!'

'Three.'

'I need a professional!'

He turned, his arms crossed over his bare chest, his expression bland. 'Four.'

Her face grew red. Frustration animated her body, bringing up her chin, sparking her eyes. For a moment she was actually pretty. 'I'm not leaving!'

she yelled. 'Goddammit, I have no place else to go. If you'd just stop feeling sorry for yourself long enough to listen—'

'Five.'

'I won't leave. I can't.'

'Suit yourself.' J.T. shrugged. He placed the empty margarita glass on the table. Then, naked as the day he was born, all one hundred and eighty pounds of muscle and sinew, he advanced.

2

Sweat beaded her upper lip. Her eyes took on a dangerous sheen. Her gaze shifted from side to side. She jammed a hand inside her purse.

J.T. pounced, hurtling his full weight upon her. They went down with a thunder, the contents of her purse spilling, a silvery gun skittering across the patio. She bucked like a bronco and attempted to scratch out his eyes with her ragged nails.

He slapped her wrist down hard. He lay on top of her, trying to keep her still while protecting the more sensitive parts of his anatomy from her lashing feet. She grabbed a fistful of his hair and yanked.

'Shit!' He jerked his head free, snapped his fingers around her wrist, and slammed it down.

She winced, but when she looked at him, her eyes still contained fire. He was bigger than her, stronger than her, and a helluva lot tougher than her. She wasn't going anywhere, and they both knew it.

She made one last futile attempt to jerk free.

'Come on,' he goaded unkindly. 'Try it again. Do you think I'll suddenly change my mind and let you go? Look at me, sweetheart. Vincent didn't do you any favors by giving you my name. I look like the devil and I am the devil. Genetics decided to play truth in advertising.'

'I have money,' she gasped.

'Who cares.'

'One hundred thousand dollars.'

'Ah, honey. That's much too cheap for me.'

'Funny, you don't look like the expensive type.'

He arched a brow at her unexpected barb. She wasn't struggling anymore, so she wasn't totally naive. He took the time to give his uninvited guest a more thorough inspection. This close, he could see that she was truly ragged around the edges. The back of her neck was whiter than the front, as if it had been recently protected by long hair, then ruthlessly exposed by desperate scissors. The roots of her dull black hair appeared blond. Her fingernails seemed to have spent quality time with a cheese grater. She had the peaked look of the anemic. For chrissake, she probably had a large target tattooed on her back.

'Little girl, don't you have enough to worry about without picking fights with me?'

'Probably,' she said gamely, 'but I have to start somewhere.'

She lashed out with her foot. He shifted and stopped the blow in time. Just as he began to grin smugly, she sank her teeth into his forearm.

He paled. His neck corded and pain shot through him, sharp and deep, as her tiny white teeth found a nerve.

Rage, primal and ugly, rose up inside him. The need to lash back. The need to return the pain inflicted upon him. He felt the jungle drums in his veins and suddenly he was hearing his father's boots rapping against the hardwood floors. His grip on her left wrist tightened. She whimpered.

'Fuck!' He yanked his arm from her mouth. Blood dewed the dark hairs and made him even angrier. With a heave he was on his feet, fists clenched, eyes black, anger barely in check. *Control, control.* He hated men who took it out on women. *Control, control.*

The silver Walther .22 semiautomatic that had been in her purse now lay just six inches from his feet. He kicked it into the pool. It wasn't enough. Once he got good and pissed off, nothing was ever enough.

'What the hell were you thinking?' he roared. She was still lying on the patio, her skirt hiked up around her thighs and revealing slender legs badly in need of muscle tone. She held her wrist against her chest. It obviously hurt, but she didn't make a sound.

He swore again and contemplated leaping into the pool. He needed a drink.

'You don't draw down on a marine,' he muttered fiercely. 'What kind of idiot draws down on a trained professional?'

'You were going to attack me,' she whispered at last. She clutched her wrist closer, the harsh red imprint of his hand staining her pale skin. It shamed him.

'I was going to carry you out of here!'

She didn't say anything.

He thrust a finger at her. 'This is my home! You shouldn't go barging into homes uninvited, unwanted and . . . and . . .'

'Untrained?' she supplied.

'Exactly!'

She didn't argue. She merely worked on getting to her feet. She swayed slightly when she stood. She didn't seem to be aware of it, smoothing down her skirt and clutching her jacket shut as if that would somehow protect her.

'I know you don't want me here. Vincent's been trying to call you, and you were never home. And I . . . I couldn't afford to wait, so I got your address and I just . . . well, I just came here.

'Train me,' she said abruptly. 'Just train me, that's all I want. One month of your time. I'll give you one hundred thousand dollars and you teach me everything you know.'

'What the hell?'

'One month, that's all I'm asking. You never have to leave the villa, you don't have to do anything other than lounge around and tell me what to do. I'm stronger than I look. I learn fast. I don't whine.'

'*Who* are you?'

She hesitated. 'Te – Umm . . . Angela.'

'Te-um-Angela? Uh-huh. Well, just for the sake of argument, why does a happy homemaker like you need training, Te-um-Angela?'

'I . . . I'm being stalked.'

'Of course. Who?'

'Who's what?'

'Who is stalking you?'

She fell silent. He shook his head. 'You don't need a mercenary, you need a shrink.'

'A man,' she whispered.

'No kidding.'

'My . . .' She seemed to debate how much to admit. 'My husband. Ex-husband. You know how it goes.'

She spoke too quickly. She glanced at him to see if he believed her or not.

He shook his head again, this time in disgust. 'You came all the way here just because of a domestic disturbance? Lady, you track a man like me down and the least you could do was have half the Medellin cartel after your hide. Jesus Christ. Go get a restraining order and leave me alone.'

She smiled wanly. 'Do you really think a piece of paper scares away a monster?'

'It beats hiring a professional. What did you do, run into Vince at a Tupperware party? You're looking at stay-fresh seals, he's hawking his connections with retired reprobates—'

'We were introduced. By a mutual friend who understands that I need real help.'

'Real help?' he snorted. 'You've seen too many Sunday night TV movies. Go to the Nogales police. I'll draw you a map.'

'The police are the ones who lost him,' she said quietly. 'Now, I'm turning to you.'

He shook his head. He tried his best scowl. She remained standing there, somehow dignified in her ugly white suit, somehow regal with her bruised wrist held against her stomach. And for once in his life, J.T. couldn't think of what to say.

The night grew hushed, just the sound of the water lapping against the edge of his pool and the lonely cry of the crickets. The mesquite tree fluttered with a teasing breeze behind her, while white rocks at her feet glittered in the porch light. The night was warm and purple-black, deceptive in its softness.

'J.T.,' she whispered, 'did you save the orphans in Guatemala?'

'What?' His heart began to beat too fast.

'Vincent told me about the orphans. Did you do that? Did you really do that?'

'No, no. You can't blame that one on me.' But his denial was too sharply spoken, and they both knew it.

'One month,' she repeated. 'One month of intensive training. Self-defense, shooting, evasion, stalking—'

'Population control, intelligence gathering. Ambushing and counter-ambushing. Sniping and countersniping. Evac and evade, infiltration and penetration. All Spec War goodies—'

'Yes.'

'No! You don't get it. Do you think killing machines are made over-night? Do you think Rambo rose up out of the ground? It takes *years* to learn that kind of focus. It take decades more to learn not to care, to sight a human being in a scope and pull the trigger as if the target really is nothing but the watermelon you used in practice.'

Her face paled. She looked ill.

'Yeah, you're just a lean, mean killing machine. Get outta here and don't come back.'

'I . . . I . . . I'll give you me.'

'What?'

'I'll give you my body, for the month.'

'*Chiquita*, you were better off sticking with the money.'

She smiled, her expression apologetic, resigned, knowing. Before he could stop her, she dropped to her knees. 'I'll beg,' she said, and raised imploring hands.

'Oh, for God's sake!' He crossed the patio and grabbed her shoulders, shaking her as if that would rattle some sense into her head.

'Please,' she said simply. 'Please.'

He opened his mouth. He tried to yell and he tried to snarl. Hell, at this point he'd settle for gnashing his teeth. But the words wouldn't come out. So many years of dirty living, and still he could be thwarted by such a simple thing as the word *please*.

'Goddammit, it's September thirteenth and I'm sober. Would someone please get me a drink!'

She took a step to comply, but then she swayed like a laundry sheet, her knees beginning to buckle.

'That's it. To bed,' he commanded, furious as hell. 'Just pick a room, any room with a bed, and lie down in it. I have a couple of hours of tequila left, and I don't want to see you again until the fourteenth unless you're bringing me a bottle and have a lime in your navel and salt on your breasts.' He pointed toward the sliding glass door. 'Out of my sight!'

She took an obedient step forward and tottered dangerously.

He had no choice. With a muttered oath he swung her up in his arms.

LISA GARDNER

She went rigid, her hands balling as if she would fight him, but her run-down state defeated her before he did. She sank into his arms like a balloon that had just had all the air let out. He could feel her rib cage clearly, as tiny as a bird's. He could smell her, the clear scents of exhaustion and fear and a warmer, mysterious odor. Then he pinpointed it – baby powder. She carried the scent of baby powder.

He almost dropped her.

He didn't want to know. He refused to know.

The closest bedroom was neat and tidy, thanks to Freddie. J.T. dumped her unceremoniously onto the double bed. 'Got any stuff?'

'One bag.'

'Where?'

'The living room.'

'Freddie will bring it in. Car out front?'

'Took a taxi.'

'Used a fake name, *Angela?*'

'Yes. And I paid cash.'

He grunted. 'Not bad.'

'I'm learning,' she told him honestly. 'I'm learning.'

'Well, learn how to sleep. It's as good a skill as any.'

She nodded, but her brown eyes didn't close. 'Are you an alcoholic?'

'Sometimes.'

'What are you the other times?'

'A Baptist. Go to sleep.'

She murmured, 'I know why you saved the children.'

'Yeah, right. Good night.'

'Because you missed your family.'

He jolted to a stop in the middle of the room and shuddered. *Rachel and Teddy and the golden days of white picket fences and four-door sedans.*

She was wrong, of course, his family had come after the orphans. And yet her words cut close. 'You don't know what you're talking about.'

'I have to.' She sighed and her eyes drifted shut. 'My daughter and I need you. You're the only hope we have left.'

'Shit,' J.T. said again, and made a beeline for the margarita mix.

Midnight. In downtown Nogales, some bars were just opening. It wouldn't be uncommon for J.T. to be heading out the door at this hour, dressed in jeans and a chambray shirt, pocket full of money and hands desperate for a beer. He'd stumble home at three or four, a couple of six-packs beneath his belt and a woman in his arms. The nights ran together.

This was the first time the man could recall a woman sleeping in the guest room with her own suitcase. The first time he knew a woman was in the house but not in J.T.'s bed. Instead, J.T. was facedown in the living room, the iguana keeping him company.

20

The house was still, quiet, almost stagnant. And yet the man knew that everything had changed. After three years, the pattern had been broken. His instructions on this point were clear.

He crept through the darkened hall. Moonbeams bathed the living room in silvery light. In one corner a small, yellow-glowing heat lamp illuminated the iguana and J.T.'s bare feet. Neither creature stirred.

The man turned away and moved carefully down the hall to the study. He picked up the telephone, years of practice making the motion soundless. He dialed from memory, already cupping his hand over his mouth to muffle his voice.

'There's a woman,' he said the moment the other end picked up.

'A woman?'

'Vincent sent her.'

'Damn.' A long pause. 'Her name?'

'Angela, that's all. Not her real name.'

'Obviously. Vital statistics?'

'Mid-twenties, five feet two inches, one hundred pounds, brown eyes, fair complexion, originally a blonde.'

'Armed?'

'A Walther .22 semiautomatic.'

'Huh. Child's toy. ID?'

'Nothing.'

'She must have something.'

'There was nothing,' he insisted. 'I checked her suitcase – the lining, hair-spray canister, hairbrush, shoe soles, everything. Plenty of cash but no ID. She has an accent. I can't quite place it. Northern maybe. Boston.'

'A professional?'

'I don't think so. She doesn't seem to know much.'

'Given the company J.T. generally keeps, she's probably an ax murderer who hacked up her husband and children.'

'What should I do?'

A frustrated sigh. 'He's back in business?'

'She's here, isn't she?'

'Damn him. Never mind, I'll take care of it. You just hold tight.'

'All right.'

'You did the right thing by calling.'

'Thank you. How . . . how is he?'

The silence stretched out. 'He's dying. He's in a lot of pain. He wants to know why his son isn't here.'

'Does he ask for me?'

'No, but don't worry. He doesn't ask for me either. All he's ever cared about was J.T.'

'Of course.' His voice was appropriately apologetic. He'd given his loyalty to a hard man a long time ago. His loyalty had never wavered; over the years he'd simply grown accustomed to his place. 'I'll call you if anything changes.'

'You do that.'

'Good night.'

'Yeah. Good night.'

He cradled the phone carefully. It didn't matter. The overhead light snapped on.

He turned slowly. J.T. lounged against the door-jamb. His arms were crossed over his bare chest. His eyes were bloodshot, but they were also intent.

'Freddie, I believe it's time we talked.'

3

Tess Williams awoke as she'd learned to awaken – slowly, degree by degree, so that she reached consciousness without ever giving herself away. First her ears woke up, seeking out the sound of another person breathing. Next her skin prickled to life, searching for the burning length of her husband's body pressed against her back. Finally, when her ears registered no sound and her skin found her alone in her bed, her eyes opened, going automatically to the closet and checking the small wooden chair she'd jammed beneath the doorknob in the middle of the night.

The chair was still in place. She released the breath she'd been holding and sat up. The empty room was already bright with midmorning sun, the adobe walls golden and cheery. The air was hot. Her T-shirt stuck to her back, but maybe the sweat came from nightmares that never quite went away. She'd once liked mornings. They were difficult for her now, but not as difficult as night, when she would lie there and try to force her eyes to give up their vigilant search of shadows in favor of sleep.

You made it, she told herself. *You actually made it.*

For the last two years she'd been running, clutching her four-year-old daughter's hand and trying to convince Samantha that everything would be all right. She'd picked up aliases like decorative accessories and new addresses like spare parts. But she'd never really escaped. Late at night she would sit at the edge of her daughter's bed, stroking Samantha's golden hair, and stare at the closet with fatalistic eyes.

She knew what kind of monsters hid in the closet. She had seen the crime scene photos of what they could do. Three weeks ago her personal monster had broken out of a maximum security prison by beating two guards to death in under two minutes.

Tess had called Lieutenant Lance Difford. He'd called Vince. The wheels were set in motion. Tess Williams had hidden Samantha safely away, then she had traveled as far as she could travel. Then she had traveled some more.

First she'd taken the train, and the train had taken her through New England fields of waving grass and industrial sectors of twisted metal. Then she'd caught a plane, flying over everything as if that would help her forget and covering so many miles, she left behind fall and returned to summer.

Landing in Phoenix was like arriving in a moon crater: everything was red, dusty, and bordered by distant blue mountains. She'd never seen cacti; here roads were lined with them. She'd never seen cactus; here they covered the land like an encroaching army.

The bus had only moved her farther into alien terrain. The red hills had disappeared, the sun had gained fury. Signs for cities had been replaced by signs reading:

STATE PRISON IN AREA.
DO NOT STOP FOR HITCHHIKERS.

The reds and browns had seeped away until the bus rolled through sun-baked amber and bleached-out greens. The mountains no longer followed like kindly grandfathers. In this strange, harsh land of southern Arizona, even the hills were tormented, methodically flayed alive by mining trucks and bulldozers.

It was the kind of land where you really did expect to turn and see the OK Corral. The kind of land where lizards were beautiful and coyotes cute. The kind of land where the hothouse rose died and the prickly cactus lived.

It was perfect.

Tess climbed out of bed. She moved slowly. Her right leg was stiff and achy, the jagged scar twitching with ghost pains. Her left wrist throbbed, ringed by a harsh circle of purple bruises. She could tell it wasn't anything serious – her father had taught her a lot about broken bones. As things went in her life these days, a bruised wrist was the least of her concerns.

She turned her attention to the bed.

She made it without thinking, tucking the corners tightly and smoothing the covers with military precision.

I want to be able to bounce a quarter off that bed, Theresa. Youth is no excuse for sloppiness. You must always seek to improve.

She caught herself folding back the edge of the sheet over the light blanket and dug her fingertips into her palms. In a deliberate motion she ripped off the blanket and dumped it on the floor.

'I will not make the bed this morning,' she stated to the empty room. 'I choose not to make the bed.'

She wouldn't clean anymore either, or wash dishes or scrub floors. She remembered too well the scent of ammonia as she rubbed down the windows, the door-knobs, the banisters. She'd found the pungent odor friendly, a deep-clean sort of scent.

This is my house, and not only does it look clean, but it smells clean.

Once, when she'd taken the initiative to rub down the window casings with ammonia, Jim had even complimented her. She'd beamed at him, married one year, already eight months pregnant and as eager as a lap-dog for his sparing praise.

Later, Lieutenant Difford had explained to her how ammonia was one of the few substances that rid surfaces of fingerprints.

Now she couldn't smell ammonia without feeling ill.

Her gaze was drawn back to the bed, the rumpled sheets, the covers tossed and wilted on the floor. For a moment the impulse, the sheer *need* to make that bed – and make it right because she had to seek to improve herself, you should always seek to improve – nearly overwhelmed her. Sweat beaded her upper lip. She fisted her hands to keep them from picking up the blankets.

'Don't give in. He messed with your mind, Tess, but that's done now. You belong to yourself and you are tough. You won, dammit. You *won*.'

The words didn't soothe her. She crossed to the bureau to retrieve her gun from her purse. Only at the last minute did she remember that the .22 had fallen on the patio.

J. T. Dillon had it now.

She froze. She had to have her gun. She ate with her gun, slept with her gun, walked with her gun. She couldn't be weaponless. *Defenseless, vulnerable, weak.*

Oh, God. Her breathing accelerated, her stomach plummeted, and her head began to spin. She walked the edge of the anxiety attack, feeling the shakes and knowing that she either found solid footing now or plunged into the abyss.

Breathe, Tess, breathe. But the friendly desert air kept flirting with her lungs. She bent down and forcefully caught a gulp by her knees, squeezing her eyes shut.

'Can I walk you home?'

She was startled. 'You mean me?' She hugged her schoolbooks more tightly against her Mt Greylock High sweater. She couldn't believe the police officer was addressing her. She was not the sort of girl handsome young men addressed.

'No,' he teased lightly. 'I'm talking to the grass.' He pushed himself away from the tree, his smile unfurling to reveal two charming dimples. All the girls in her class talked of those dimples, dreamed of those dimples. 'You're Theresa Matthews, right?'

She nodded stupidly. She should move. She knew she should move. She was already running late for the store, and her father did not tolerate tardiness.

She remained standing there, staring at this young man's handsome face. He looked so strong. A man of the law. A man of integrity? For one moment she found herself thinking, If I told you everything, would you save me? Would somebody please save me?

'Well, Theresa Matthews, I'm Officer Beckett. Jim Beckett.'

'I know.' Her gaze fell to the grass. 'Everyone knows who you are.'

'May I walk you home, Theresa Matthews? Would you allow me the privilege?'

She remained uncertain, too overwhelmed to speak. Her father would kill her. Only promiscuous young women, evil women, enticed men to walk them home. But she didn't want to send Jim Beckett away. She didn't know what to do.

He leaned over and winked at her. His blue eyes were so clear, so calm. So steady.

'Come on, Theresa. I'm a cop. If you can't trust me, who can you trust?'

'I won,' she muttered by her knees. 'Dammit, I won!'

But she wanted to cry. She'd won, but the victory remained hollow, the price too high. He'd done things to her that never should have been done. He'd taken things from her that she couldn't afford to lose. Even now he was still in her head.

Someday soon he would kill her. He'd promised to cut out her still-beating heart, and Jim always did what he said.

She forced her head up. She took a deep breath. She pressed her fists against her thighs hard enough to welt her skin. 'Fight, Tess. It's all you have left.'

She pushed away from the dresser and moved to her suitcase, politely brought to her room by Freddie. She'd made it here, step one of her plan. Next, she had to get J.T. to agree to train her. Dimly she remembered mentioning her daughter to him. That had been a mistake. Never tell them more than you have to, never tell the truth if a lie will suffice.

Maybe J.T. wouldn't remember. He hadn't seemed too sober. Vincent should've warned her about his drinking.

She didn't know much about J.T. Vince had said J.T. was the kind of man who could do anything he wanted to but who didn't seem to want to do much. He'd been raised in a wealthy, well-connected family in Virginia, attended West Point, but then left for reasons unknown and joined the marines. Then he'd left the marines and struck out solo, rapidly earning a reputation for a fearlessness bordering on insanity. As a mercenary he'd drifted toward doing the impossible and been indifferent to anything less. He hated politics, loved women. He was fanatical about fulfilling his word and non-committal about everything else.

Five years ago he'd up and left the mercenary business without explanation. Like the prodigal son, he'd returned to Virginia and in a sudden flurry of unfathomable activity he'd married, adopted a child, and settled down in the suburbs as if all along he'd really been a shoe salesman. Later, a sixteen-year-old with a new Camaro and even newer license had killed J.T.'s wife and son in a head-on collision.

And J.T. had disappeared to Arizona.

She hadn't expected him to be drinking. She hadn't expected him to still appear so strong. She'd pictured him as being older, maybe soft and overripe around the middle, a man who'd once been in his prime but now was melting around the edges. Instead, he'd smelled of tequila. His body was toned and hard. He'd moved fast, pinning her without any effort. He had black hair, covering his head, his arms, his chest.

Jim had had no hair, not on his head, not on his body. He'd been smooth as marble. Like a swimmer, she'd thought, and only later understood the full depth of her naiveté. Jim's touch had always been cold and dry, as if he were too perfect for such things as sweat. The first time she'd heard him urinate, she'd felt a vague sense of surprise; he gave the impression of being above such basic biological functions.

Jim had been mannequin perfect. If only she'd held that thought longer.

She'd stick with J. T. Dillon. He'd once saved orphans. He'd been married and had a child. He'd destroyed things for money.

For her purposes, he would do.

And if helping her cost J. T. Dillon too much?

She already knew the answer; she'd spent years coming to terms with it.

Once, she'd dreamed of a white knight. Someone who would never hit her. Someone who would hold her close and tell her she was finally safe.

Now she remembered the feel of her finger tightening around the trigger. The pull of the trigger, the jerk of the trigger, the roar of the gun, and the ringing in her ears.

The acrid smell of gunpowder and the hoarse sound of Jim's cry. The thud of his body falling down. The raw scent of fresh blood pooling on her carpet.

She remembered these things.

And she knew she could do anything.

4

J.T. was up at the crack of dawn. He didn't want to be. God knows, it was stupid for a retired man to be up with the sun, but he'd spent too many years in the military to shake the routine from his bones. Oh-six-hundred: Soldier gets up. Oh-six-hundred-fifteen: Soldier does light calisthenics. Oh-six-hundred-thirty: Marine swims fifty laps, then showers. Oh-seven-hundred: Retired man pops open a beer in the middle of his living room and wonders what the hell he's doing still getting up at oh-six-hundred.

Now it was after nine on the fourteenth of September. He'd survived another year, hung over, dehydrated, and sick of his own skin. No more tequila. He drank beer instead.

He was drinking his third when Rosalita arrived for the annual post-binge cleanup. Born into a family of eleven children, Rosalita had used her survival instincts to become one of the finest whores in Nogales. J.T. had met her the first week he'd moved to Nogales, picking her up in the usual manner. Over the years their relationship had somehow evolved to something neither of them dared to label. As a whore Rosalita had absolutely no morals and no shame, but as a business-woman she had rock-solid ethics and the aggressiveness of a tiger. She was one of the few people J.T. respected, and one of even fewer people he trusted. Perhaps they'd become friends.

She straddled his lap wearing a red gauzy skirt and a thin white top tied beneath her generous breasts. J.T. cradled her hip with one hand. She didn't notice. Her attention was focused absolutely on his face.

She'd spread an old green hand towel over his naked chest. Now she whipped the shaving cream in the small basin on the right and lathered it generously over his face. Rosalita believed a man should be shaved the old-fashioned way – with a straight razor and plenty of devilish intent.

He had enough respect for her temper to hold perfectly still.

He sat there, watching the world take on the warm, fuzzy hue he'd come to know in the last few years, and even then, even then he knew when *she* walked into the room.

Her feet were bare and silent on the hardwood floor, but she broadcasted her arrival with her scent. He'd been six when his father had taught him to air-dry his clothes, wash with odorless soap, and rinse his mouth with peroxide so the deer wouldn't smell anything as he crept up behind. In those days he'd accepted such teachings with reverent awe. His whipcord-lean, ramrod-straight, rattlesnake-tough father was omnipotent in his eyes, the only man he knew who could bag a six-point buck with a single shot. The colonel had had his talents.

Rosalita sighted Angela hovering in the doorway. Her fingers instantly dug into his chin.

'*Hijo de puta!*' she spat out.

J.T. gave her a small shrug and lifted the Corona bottle to his lathered lips.

'Angela, Rosalita. Rosalita, Angela. Angela is a current guest at our high-flying retirement resort. As for Rosalita . . . what shall we call you? An international hostess and entertainer?' He glanced at Angela. 'Every year on September fourteenth Rosalita cleans me up. You might call it her frequent flyer program.'

Angela nodded, her gaze going from him to Rosalita to him with open discomfort. The tension in the room was unmistakable. 'Nice to meet you,' Angela said at last, her voice unfailingly polite.

Rosalita froze, then began to smile. Then began to laugh. She repeated the words back to J.T. in Spanish, then chuckled harder. *Nice to meet you* wasn't something other women generally said to whores. Only a good girl would feel compelled to say such a thing, and at this stage of her life, Rosalita knew she had nothing to fear from 'good girls.'

She picked up the razor, shoved J.T.'s head back, and exposed his throat. She pressed the straight edge against his jawline and slowly rasped it down, her dark eyes gleaming.

Angela sucked in her breath nervously.

'She can't kill me yet,' J.T. volunteered conversationally. 'I'm one of the few men who can pay her what she's worth.'

Four forceful strokes, and his neck was clean. Rosalita shoved his head to the side and turned her attention to his cheek.

Angela finally entered the room; she wore an old white tank top and frayed khaki shorts that had probably fit her once. Now, they hung on her frame. In daylight, her coarsely dyed, badly whacked hair looked even worse – as if she was wearing a bad wig. For no good reason, it annoyed him tremendously.

'Your wrist?' he barked, startling Rosalita and Angela both.

'My wrist? Oh, oh, that. It's fine. Just a bit bruised.'

'I have some ice. We'll put that on it.'

'No, it's not necessary. It's not even swollen.' She moved along the side of the room, up on the balls of her feet, her back to the wall. As he watched, still searching for something to do that would make him feel better, she took a careful inventory of all the exits. Someone had at least told her a thing or two.

Her gaze fastened on his iguana, a frown marring her brow.

'Real,' he supplied.

'What?'

'The iguana. That's Glug. He's alive.'

'Oh.' She looked at Glug for several seconds. The creature didn't move.

'Where's Freddie?' she asked.

'I gave him the day off.'

'*Gave* him the day off?'

'Yep.'

'So there's no one here?'

'Rosalita probably doesn't like to be called no one.'

'But she doesn't live here, does she?'

'Nope.'

'So only you'll be around today?' She was clearly nervous. Her stance went from relaxed to prepared. Legs apart, shoulders back, hips rotated for balance. Just as it had last night, it tugged at his brain.

Abruptly recognition came to him.

'Cop.'

She froze.

'Uh-huh. I noticed it yesterday – you stand like a cop. Feet wide, chest out for balance. Left leg slightly back to keep your holster out of reach.'

She looked cornered.

He frowned, angling his head more so Rosalita could attend better to his cheek. 'You're not a cop though. You can't even hold a gun.'

'I'm not a cop,' she muttered.

'So just who are you, *Angela*? And what about your daughter?'

'What daughter?' Her voice had gone falsetto.

'Oh, give it up. You can't lie worth a damn.'

She smiled tightly. 'Then you'll have to teach me how.'

'*Idiotas,*' Rosalita interjected. She grabbed the hand towel and rubbed the remains of the shaving cream from J.T.'s face with more force than necessary. '*Hombres y mujeres? Bah. Perritos y gatitas.*'

With another shake of her head she flattened her palm on J.T.'s chest and tried to launch herself from his lap. He clamped one hand over Rosalita's wrist.

'Wait.'

He twisted her lush form on his lap, bringing her ample hips intimately against his groin. Angela had gone still, as if expecting some new form of attack.

'Look at her,' he said, pointing at Angela. 'Look at that haircut, Rosalita. We can't have her running around like that.'

Rosalita raked Angela up and down with a scathing eye. She was clearly unimpressed.

'I can't take it any more, Rosalita. With that do, she might as well pin a "fugitive" sign on her coat. Fix it for me, will you? We'll consider it my good deed for the decade.'

'You're too kind,' Angela murmured.

J.T. continued focusing on Rosalita. 'I'll pay, of course.'

Payment was the magic word. Rosalita started out asking for twenty but settled for ten. J.T. took the money from a highly skeptical Angela, pointing out that Rosalita certainly couldn't do any worse than Angela had. Moments later Rosalita had Angela positioned in J.T.'s chair, the green towel wrapped around her neck. While she washed Angela's hair and set about snipping with expert flair, J.T. propped himself up on the edge of the couch and opened a fresh beer despite Angela's disapproving frown. He could see her wrist, now on her lap. It was badly bruised.

So now you're beating up on women, J.T. Just how low do you plan on sinking?

In the disconcerting quiet of his living room he didn't have an answer. He'd never considered himself a great man, not even a good man. But he had his few principles and they gave him comfort. Don't lie and don't pretend. Don't hurt people weaker than yourself – there are enough SOBs out there who deserve it. Never, ever hurt a woman.

If Rachel could see him now, she would be ashamed.

He crossed over to the sliding glass door and watched the sunlight dance across the rippling surface of his pool.

'*Terminé!*' Rosalita announced.

Reluctantly, J.T. turned to inspect Angela's new look. He froze, too stunned for words.

Rosalita had hacked off most of Angela's hair. Now intricately layered strands darted before her ears, wisped at the back of her neck, and fringed around her eyes. The short-cropped hair should have made her look like a teenage boy, except teenage boys didn't have cheekbones that high, noses that small, or lips that full. Teenage boys didn't have saucer-shaped eyes of liquid brown, framed by thick, lush lashes.

'Jesus Christ,' he murmured. 'Jesus H. Christ.'

He started pacing. Even then he felt the tension curling up inside his belly.

'It's . . . it's a start.' Angela sounded a little stunned by the transformation herself as she gazed into the hand mirror.

Rosalita bustled away with the basin of soapy water, leaving them alone in the living room. A taut silence descended. Angela's fingers began to fidget on her lap.

'Want a piece of advice?' J.T. said all of a sudden. 'It's free.'

'Doesn't that make two good deeds in one day? I thought you'd already met your quota for the year.'

'You caught me at a weak moment. Now, do you want the advice or what?'

'Okay.'

'Dye your hair,' he said flatly. 'It's the trick of a disguise – come up with something that looks even more you than the real you. I'd recommend a dark brown or auburn, something that fits your natural coloring. Then you'll have a new look that's subtle. Right now you're too obvious.'

'Oh.'

'So there you go. Visit a pharmacy, buy some hair dye, and thirty minutes later you'll be all set.'

'Thank you.'

He grimaced. 'Advice wasn't that good.'

'J.T., about yesterday. I need to talk to you, will you—'

'Hungry?' He turned to face her. 'You need to eat more. I can make oatmeal.'

She hesitated, clearly wanting to return to the original topic. 'That makes three good deeds,' she pointed out.

'Blame it on my upbringing. I certainly do.'

'Breakfast would be nice, I guess.' She nodded toward the nearly empty beer bottle dangling from his finger-tips. 'Looks like you've already had yours.'

'Yep.'

'Do you always drink so much?'

'Only to excess.'

'Vince didn't say you were an alcoholic.'

'I am *not* an alcoholic. Prissy teetotaler.' He thumped the bottle against his thigh. She had an accent. A northern accent. Well educated. What had brought a well-educated northern woman all the way to the Mexican border, exhausted, malnourished, and obviously terrified?

His gaze fell to her thighs.

Shit.

He took a step toward her. She stiffened. It didn't matter.

He walked right up to her even as she leaned way back, sinking into the chair. Her eyes were wide and fearful. He ignored her distress, reaching out and swiping a finger down the vicious scar marring her pale thigh. Broad. Shiny. Many snaking tributaries, the kind that would be made by a bone snapping and tearing through flesh.

'He do that?'

She didn't answer.

'Dammit, did he do that?'

She opened her mouth, then gave up and simply stared at him.

'Who the hell are you, Angela?'

'A woman who needs help.'

'Your husband was that bad?'

'No,' she said bluntly. 'He was worse.'

J.T. turned away. He was angry again. That was always his problem. He was too good at getting angry and not good enough at fixing anything. *Control, control. It's not your problem, it's not your business.*

But he hated the sight of the scar on her thigh. It made him think of things he'd dedicated the last few years to forgetting. And it made him want to find her ex-husband and slam his fist through his face.

He forced himself to relax and took a swallow from his beer. He didn't speak again until he trusted himself completely.

'I'll make oatmeal.'

'Thank you.'

'Honey, you haven't tasted it yet.'

Angela followed him into the kitchen. He was proud of the kitchen – Rachel had designed it. He knew a lot about pools, and in the last couple of years he'd become a good landscaper. He didn't know much about decorating though. In the marines you stuck a girlie poster above your bed and that was considered the finishing touch.

Rachel had had a natural flair, so she'd designed the house they were going to build in Montana, where the sky was endless and they would always feel free. He was going to learn about horses. She was going to study interior decorating. Maybe they would have a second kid, give Teddy a little sister to play with. And Teddy and his little sister would be raised right, without any bad memories to keep them awake on dark nights later in life.

Those dreams were gone. J.T. just had Rachel's kitchen, a large, cool room with a red-tiled floor and eggshell-blue counter. The stove was big and accented with a wreath of jalapeños. A huge collection of brass pots and pans hung from a wire rack suspended from the ceiling. He'd placed each one just where he figured Rachel would have, having listened to her excitedly describe the kitchen night after night as they'd lain together in bed and dreamed like children.

'It's a nice kitchen,' Angela said from behind him. 'Do you cook a lot?'

'I don't cook at all.' He moved to the sliding glass door, which Rosalita had left slightly cracked. The heat seeped in like a tentacled beast. He shut the door.

'You aren't going to lock it?'

'Lock what?'

'The door.'

'No.'

There was a small pause. He contemplated the pots and pans, trying to figure out which to grab. It had been a long time since he'd tried cooking anything; that was Freddie's job.

'Do you lock your front door?'

'Nope.'

'Could . . . could I do it?'

He looked at her. She stood by the wood table, her hands twisting in front of her, and her gaze fastened on the sliding glass door.

'Sweetheart, this is Nogales, the outskirts of Nogales. You don't have to worry about anything here.'

'Please.'

He was really starting to hate how well she used that word. 'You're scared,' he said flatly.

She didn't bother to deny it.

'You think he followed you here? This big bad ex-husband of yours?'

'It's possible. He's very, very good at that.'

'You said you paid cash, used fake names.'

'Yes.'

'Then you're fine.' He turned back to the stove, but he heard her move behind him, then heard the click of the sliding glass door lock sliding home. Whatever. He didn't feel like telling her about the small arsenal he kept in a safe and the fact that even dead drunk he could shoot the Lincoln head out of a penny at two hundred yards. If she wanted the doors locked that badly, he wasn't going to argue.

He boiled water. He opened a canister of oatmeal and wondered how much he was supposed to dump in. He dumped in half and figured what the hell. If he could rig explosives, he ought to be able to manage oatmeal.

'Generally people measure it out,' Angela commented, returning to the kitchen.

'I like to live dangerously.'

'I want my gun back.'

'The water-logged .22? You'd be better off with a slingshot.'

'I want my gun.'

It irritated him. Too many people thought guns fixed things. They didn't. He ought to know. There wasn't anything he couldn't do with a rifle and yet everyone he'd ever loved had been destroyed. Guns didn't fix anything.

'First let's get through breakfast.' He dumped the oatmeal into two bowls. It had the same consistency as mud. He sprinkled the bowls with raisins for more iron and poured two glasses of milk. Angela looked at the oatmeal as if it were an unrecognizable life-form.

'Eat,' he said. 'Tough guys never turn away from a nutritious meal. Hell, if we were outside, I would've topped it with bugs. They're almost pure protein, you know.'

'I didn't know,' she confessed, and finally, gingerly, scooped up the first spoonful and thrust it into her mouth. Her eyes were closed. She looked like a little kid and he found himself thinking of Teddy again with a sharp, bittersweet pang.

'Yugh,' she said.

'Told you I wasn't a cook.' He took in three spoonfuls at once. 'Don't chew. It goes down easier.'

She looked horrified. She pushed the bowl away. Just as fast, he pushed it back in front of her. 'Eat,' he ordered. 'I wasn't kidding before – soldiers eat what they're given. And you need your iron, Rambo, so stop dreaming about room service.'

For a moment it appeared that she would defy him. But then she picked up her spoon and eyed her oatmeal as if it were a summit to be scaled.

'I can do this.' She dug in.

'It's oatmeal, Angela, not Armageddon.'

She ate the whole bowl and cleared the dishes without saying a word. Then she began washing them with the smooth movements of someone who'd done chores all her life.

J.T. wasn't used to having someone else around who wasn't Freddie or Rosalita. He felt uncomfortable and, worse, self-conscious. Virginia etiquette crept up and tapped him on the shoulder. He should put on a shirt. He should put on shoes. He should pull out a chair for the nice young lady, offer her lemonade, comment on her beauty, and talk about the weather.

'Why move to Arizona?' Angela asked. She stacked the rinsed dishes noisily beside the sink. Her bruised wrist didn't seem to bother her.

'No helmet laws.'

'Oh.' She'd run out of things to say. He'd run out of them a long time ago himself. He began ticking off the seconds in his mind. He'd hit only six when she shut off the water and pinned him with a determined look.

'I'm, not going to leave,' she announced. 'I need your help. Sooner or later you'll realize that.'

'I'm not going to realize any such thing. You're lying to me through your teeth.'

Her lips thinned. 'You don't want the truth. I know men like you. You don't want to become involved. You think you're happy living in a self-pitying vacuum.'

'Self-pity, that's what's wrong with me? First, it's drinking, now self-pity. Do you watch a lot of Oprah?'

'You think you'll be better off if you never care again.'

'Can you prove otherwise?'

'I don't need you to care, Mr Dillon. I don't need you to give a . . . a rat's ass about me. I want you to train me anyway.'

'You want me to be a lap dog,' he corrected her. 'You want me to listen to your lies, do as you ask, and never question a thing. I know how it works. I've seen Oprah too.'

He kicked back his chair and crossed the alcove. He passed the barrier of the counter. He kept advancing, his eyes dark slits. He saw her mouth open, but no word of protest emerged. She took a step back, but was brought up short by the kitchen sink. She was trapped.

He flattened her against the counter. Her breath came out more rapidly, but she didn't back down. She brought her chin up defiantly and met his gaze. He leaned into her, flattening her breasts against his bare torso, pressing his body against hers so she'd know exactly what he was capable of. He lowered his head until his breath whispered across her cheek, and she sucked in her breath in an attempt to put distance between them.

'I don't believe you,' he said softly, dangerously. 'I don't believe a woman abandons her daughter and comes halfway across the country to a mercenary's house just because her ex-husband is stalking her. And I don't like being lied to and used.' He planted his hands on the countertop.

'Why shouldn't a woman hire a trained professional?' She licked her lips nervously, then caught herself and stated more fiercely, 'Husbands, boyfriends, fathers, kill women all the time.'

'Hire a bodyguard.'

'I don't want a bodyguard! I want to know how to fight. I want to know how to protect my daughter. I am so sick and tired of running scared. You' – her finger jabbed his chest – 'you probably don't know anything about being vulnerable, being frightened. But I know. And I'm sick of it. I want my life back.'

She grabbed one of the porcelain bowls and shattered it against the sink. She raised one jagged shard and wielded it like a knife. 'I might have been slow once. I might have actually thought that if I was just good enough, just obedient enough, just *sweet* enough, it would keep me safe. Well, I don't do "sweet" anymore and I don't do "obedient" anymore. So don't mess with me, Mr Dillon. You have no idea what I am capable of.'

She pressed the sharp edge against his bare chest with enough force to line his skin. The edge ran against the scar that zigzagged furiously down his sternum. That scar had been inflicted by a man known for his sharp temper, fast hands, and utter lack of remorse. J.T. explored Angela's eyes now to see if she had that in her.

He wouldn't grant her speed. He wouldn't grant her skill. But in her gaze he found something better: dispassion.

'Jesus, you are a dangerous woman.'

'I'm learning.'

A sound split the air, startling them both. High, shrill. Sirens. Wailing sirens approaching his house. He took a step back.

His first thought was Marion, but then he noticed his house guest. She'd frozen. And she appeared terrified. Why would the cops frighten a woman running from her husband? Then he knew, positively knew, that he'd been used.

'What have you done?'

'Nothing. Absolutely nothing,' she muttered.

The sirens wailed closer. Three cars, he figured. Three police cars pulling into his driveway and shattering his peace.

'Why are you so afraid? What are you hiding?'

Her eyes were no longer so certain. She tried to push away, but his grip was too strong.

'Let me go. I didn't do anything. I just don't want anyone to know I'm here. Especially not the cops.'

'That shy, *Angela*?'

'It's not safe. He has contacts—'

'*He*? Sure, Angela, this omnipotent he. The mystery man who may or may not be stalking you, who may or may not have injured your leg, who may or may not even exist. I am tired of *he*, Angela. You want my help, you'd better do a helluva lot better than that.'

'I'm not lying! Jim wants me dead. No, he wants me to suffer horribly. I saw the pictures. I saw what he did . . .' Her voice trailed off. Then she went wild, beating at him furiously. She tried to jab his shoulder with the porcelain shard, but he deflected the blow, knocking the makeshift weapon from her hand.

'Let me go,' she cried.

The sirens came to a screeching halt on his driveway.

'Oh, my God,' she whispered. 'Maybe he's already found me.'

His hands gripped her shoulders, but suddenly he wasn't so sure. Her fear was too genuine, her panic too real. He could feel the tremors beginning now, snaking down her delicate frame.

'Talk to me, Angela, tell me the truth. Come on.'

'He was a cop! Don't you get it? He was a cop!'

He stepped back in shock, automatically letting her go. He was surprised but didn't know why he should be. There was no rule saying cops had to be good guys, just as there was no guarantee that well-respected army colonels didn't torture their families as a hobby.

Angela moved into the middle of the kitchen. Her arms were wrapped tightly around her thin waist. 'I need my gun back. Give me my gun.'

'I can't do that.'

'Oh, what are you so afraid of? Do you think I'm going to try to shoot my way out with a peashooter?'

'A gun won't help you.'

'It's the only thing that has.' She paced a dizzying circle. 'I'm leaving. Tell them what you want. I won't let them see me here. I thought confidentiality meant something in your line of work.'

'Wait—'

'I don't have time.' She kept moving.

They both heard the first of several car doors open and then slam shut.

Angela didn't turn around. Seconds later he heard the door of her room shut, then the telltale sound of the bolt lock sliding home. He had visions of little Angela flipping over the bed and hunkering behind it like the last man at the Alamo.

He was left alone in his kitchen, with the disorienting feeling that everything had slid out of control. What if this ex-husband had actually arrived? What was he prepared to do these days? How could he stand aside?

Then he heard the voice over the bullhorn. His shoulders relaxed. His lips twisted. No big, bad, evil Jim.

It was just his sister, summoned by Freddie, and riding to the rescue.

He squared his shoulders and prepared for the real war. Whoever had written that blood was thicker than water, had never met the Dillons.

5

Marion Margaret MacAllister had committed only two sins in her life. One, she'd been born the second child. Two, she'd been born a female.

She'd done her best to rectify these sins over time. In the men's locker-room world of the FBI, she could out-shoot, out-fight, and out-think her fellow agents. With her cool blond looks, she'd earned the nickname Iceman. She liked it.

Until two weeks ago, when her world had started falling apart.

She'd just turned thirty-four and had been passed over for promotion again, ostensibly because she was too young. William Walker, who did get the post, was only thirty-six – and balling the deputy director's daughter. Her father was dying of prostate cancer, a death that was taking a long time coming, and her husband of ten years had left her for a twenty-two-year-old cocktail waitress.

Then last night she'd gotten the call from Freddie. J.T. always had impeccable timing.

She motioned for the Nogales police to stay back and approached the house on her own. She wore her favorite navy blue pants suit. It was sharp and one hundred percent business. It was also too hot for Arizona. She focused on the cool feel of her gun pressed against her ribs while the dusty air stung her eyes.

'Good morning, Marion,' J.T. drawled. He lounged against the door jamb, half naked and rumpled, as if caught mid-fuck. 'How kind of you to visit.'

'We received a report of an intruder. I came to investigate.'

'All the way from DC?'

'Nothing's too good for my older brother.' She smiled with brittle sweetness and had the rare satisfaction of seeing her barb strike home. 'Step out of the way, J.T. The officers here will secure your house.'

'I don't think so.'

'Jordan Terrance—'

'Freddie call you from town?' He shifted, crossing his ankles and getting more comfortable. She knew from Freddie that he drank a lot. She'd expected the alcohol to have taken a greater toll, but J.T. had always been a lucky SOB. Not even booze had thickened his waistline or sagged his middle. He was still the lean, fit man she remembered. The kid who'd won all the swimming trophies. The son whose uncanny shooting had made their father so proud. She wanted to strangle him.

'Freddie filed the report,' she replied stiffly.

'Ah, and here I thought he and I had reached an understanding.'

'What do you mean?'

J.T. made a great show of examining his fingernails. 'I know he calls you, Marion. I know he's Daddy's little spy. You're both so afraid that someday I'll get drunk enough to speak the truth. Don't worry, I've been speaking it for quite some time now, and nobody's interested.'

'I don't know what you're—'

'I sent him away. Told Freddie to take a few days off – I didn't think my visitor wanted an audience. As for myself, well . . .' He shrugged. 'Freddie makes a fine margarita. Of course now I'll have to reconsider his return. Calling the police about an intruder – that was pretty clever. I think he's a lot more clever than either of us suspect.'

'So there *is* an intruder! Step aside.'

'No.'

'Goddammit, J.T., I know there's a woman inside. And what do you really know about her? Look at your track record—'

'Leave my past out of it.'

'We're going to search the house, J.T. I want this woman gone.'

'Got a search warrant?'

'Of course not. We're responding to a report of an intruder—'

'And I'm telling you as owner of this property, there is no intruder. Now, take your little blue men and find another party to crash.'

'You stubborn, drunken, son of a—'

'Marion, you never did learn how to play nice.'

'J.T., as your sister—'

'You're ashamed of me, embarrassed to have me in the family, and on really good days you wish I was dead. I know, Marion. These open exchanges of family sentiment always leave me feeling warm and fuzzy all over.'

'So help me God, J.T., if I find so much as a BB gun on your property—'

'It's Arizona. Lax gun laws. You gotta love that in a state.'

'I'm here to try to help you, J.T.—'

'No, Marion, you're not. You're still doing Daddy's bidding, and we both know it.' His voice grew suddenly soft. 'Why don't you ever stop by just to visit, Merry Berry? Why, with you, is it always war?'

Marion grew suffocated beneath the neck-high buttons of her suit, and for a moment she was beyond anger.

J.T. straightened away from the doorjamb.

'Send the cops away. Daddy never approved of outsiders nosing around in family business. Is he dead yet?'

'No.'

'Too bad. Well, it was nice talking to you. We should really get together more often.'

'I'm not leaving.'

'I'm sorry, Marion. You know I care about you, but I have this strong allergic reaction to federal agents. No, I'm afraid I have a strict No Cops/No FBI Agents policy for my property.'

'You are such a bastard!'

'I used to pray that was the case, but I probably have too much of the colonel in me for it to be true. What a shame.'

J.T.'s implacable grin told her he wasn't budging. He always had been a stubborn ass. But then, she could be stubborn too. And she had her orders. Straight from the colonel.

'Fine. I'll check my badge at the door.'

'And your backup band?' J.T. nodded toward the cops.

'If you can assure us that there's no intruder inside, I'll send them on their way.'

'Oh, the intruder's inside all right. I think the boys in blue should go on their way anyhow.'

He smiled at her. Then he walked inside and shut the door.

She was left standing in the broiling sun with three state troopers looking at her for guidance. She wanted to scream and she wanted to curse, but most of all she wanted to forget she'd ever met her husband.

'Go home,' she said to the troopers. 'I have the situation under control.'

Then she knocked on the door of her brother's house and prepared for round two.

Tess sat on the floor of her room, her ear pressed against the door. She'd locked it but knew from experience that the lock was too feeble to hold. She still didn't have her gun and wasn't sure what she'd do if she did. It was imperative that no one know she was there, but was she desperate enough to shoot an FBI agent to keep her identity secret?

When she found herself thinking that she could just wound the woman, she realized she was desperate enough.

She'd listened to the exchange in the front yard. Now she heard the woman's voice echo down the hall from the living room.

'All right, J.T., where is she?'

'She stepped out for a moment. I got the impression she didn't much care for the police.'

'Oh? Doesn't that tell you something right there, *brother dear?*'

'Only that she's spent some time in LA'

'Give it up, J.T. If Lizzie Borden were alive today, she'd come to you for help.'

Tess wanted to resent that comment but couldn't; too many newspapers had referred to her as the Bride of Frankenstein. The tabloids had even carried her supposed biography under the headline.

SO I MARRIED AN AX MURDERER.

The late-night talk show hosts had gotten in a few stingers as well.

She didn't like to think about Jim. She wanted definitive answers and the clarity of hindsight. She didn't have that. Even after all these years the images were murky and disjointed in her mind. The press could package her story as neatly as they wanted. She'd lived it and the truth did not allow her that luxury.

Jim Beckett had been handsome. He'd been strong. He was a highly commended police officer and a lonely man who'd been orphaned as a child. His mother had been frail, sickly, he'd told her. She'd collapsed when he was eight and his father had died in an automobile accident rushing to her side. With no surviving relatives, he'd been placed with foster parents. He'd grown close to that family, but tragedy had struck again. When he was fourteen, his foster father had been killed in a hunting accident. His foster mother had fought to keep him, only to succumb to breast cancer while he was in college. Jim Beckett was alone in the world, but then he'd seen her.

On their fourth date he sat with her on the porch swing at her father's house and took her hand. 'Theresa,' he whispered somberly. 'I know about your father, how he treats you and your mother. I understand how afraid you must be. But you're not alone anymore. I love you, baby. We're alike. We each have no one. But now we'll be together forever. No one is ever going to hurt you again.'

She believed him. She cried that night while he rocked her against his chest, and she thought, *Finally, my white knight has arrived.*

Six months later she became Jim's bride in one of the largest weddings Williamstown had ever seen. She moved from her father's house and watched Jim hang a blown-up wedding portrait above the mantel of their new home. It was the first thing anyone saw when they walked into the Beckett house: a huge glossy photo of the most beautiful blond couple in Williamstown. People nicknamed them Ken and Barbie.

On their honeymoon Jim sat her down and explained that there were a few rules she would need to follow. She was a wife now. A police officer's wife. The rules were straightforward. Always walk two steps behind him. Always ask his permission before buying anything. Wear only clothes he'd approved. Always keep the house immaculate and always cook his steak rare. Never question him or his schedule.

She nodded. She was confused, but she promised to try. She was an eighteen-year-old bride, she wanted to be perfect.

She made mistakes.

The second night after they returned from their honeymoon, Jim burned her wedding dress to punish her for buying note cards without asking. She begged him not to, so he burned her veil as well. She wasn't supposed to question him. She must remember not to question him.

She struggled to remember that. She struggled to adapt. In the first few weeks she lost most of her personal belongings to the fire. Her cheerleading outfit. Her baby blanket. Her yearbook. For a change of pace Jim cut up her childhood teddy bear into little pieces, then burned the pieces when she didn't have dinner on the table in time. Jim told her she must be stupid to lose so much stuff, so she tried harder.

She didn't want to fail the only person who claimed to love her. And he didn't hit her. He yelled sometimes. He was strict, he told her she was stupid, but he never, ever raised his hand.

She was so grateful for that.

She learned. She ran out of stuff for him to destroy. Then she discovered she was pregnant and life settled down. Jim couldn't wait to be a father. When she gave birth to Sam, he showed up at the hospital with the most ridiculously expensive strand of pearls. He told her she was beautiful. She'd done well.

And she thought everything would be all right.

Two months later Jim announced it was time to have a second child. She sat at the dinner table, breastfeeding Samantha and feeling so exhausted, she could barely keep her eyes open. She made a mistake. She forgot about the rules and said no, she couldn't handle two babies and maintain a spotless, perfect household. Jim grew quiet. He set down his fork. He pinned her with his overbright blue eyes. 'You can't handle it, Theresa? Do you think of hurting Samantha? Is that what you're telling me? Do you think of beating my baby? I know it's in your blood.'

She cried. She said no, she'd never do such a thing. She could tell he didn't believe her. Later that week she committed her first act of blatant rebellion: She bought a diaphragm and hid it under the bathroom sink. The week after that she pulled it out and discovered a pin resting delicately on top. Jim stood behind her, his face implacable. She couldn't take it anymore. She hadn't slept in two and a half months. She was exhausted, overwhelmed, and frightened she would fail as a mother. She began to sob. Jim finally moved. She cringed, but he just took her in his arms. He stroked her hair, touching her gently for the first time in months, and told her everything would be all right, he would help her. He lowered her to the bathroom floor. He pushed up her skirt. He took her while she lay there, too exhausted, too shocked, and too much in pain to move.

Afterward, he told her he wanted a boy this time. A boy to name Brian, after his father.

Jim's absences grew longer, and his returns crueler. Whatever she did, it wasn't good enough. She was a bad wife, a horrible mother. She was a stupid, stupid girl who should be grateful he'd agreed to marry her. A handsome, charming, well-respected man like him could certainly do better.

One day he sat her down in the living room and told her he was going out. He would be gone for a while. Maybe he'd return. Maybe not. He hadn't decided yet. No matter what, she was not to go down into the basement.'

'The basement? Why would I go into the basement?'

'Because I told you not to go there, so now you're thinking about it. And you'll think about it the minute I leave. "What is in the basement? Why shouldn't I go into the basement? What is he hiding in the basement?" I've planted the suggestion in your mind, you won't be able to rest until you go into the basement. I know you that well, Theresa. I can control you that much.'

'No. I won't go into the basement. I won't.'

But the minute he left, her eyes fell on the basement door. She put her hand on the doorknob. She twisted. She opened the door and stared down into the gloom—

Tess quickly cut off the rest of the memories. She pressed her fingers against her temples, already tasting bile.

Some days she could recall things objectively. She could distance herself, analyze the scenes as if they'd happened in somebody else's life. Some days she couldn't. Now she concentrated on breathing and the feel of the warm Arizona sun.

Down the hall, Marion and J.T. continued to war.

'He is dying, J.T. It's not some twisted ruse.' Marion's voice was brittle. 'Our father is dying.'

'Our father? I don't think so. I gave him to you when you were fourteen. We were playing poker, as I recall, and I was beating you quite badly. You threw a fit. So I said fine, what was the one thing you really wanted—'

'Fuck you, Jordan Terrance.'

'—and you said you wanted "Daddy" all to yourself. So I gave him to you lock, stock, and barrel. To this day I believe you got the bad end of that deal. Or tell me, Marion, did you forget that as well?'

'I didn't forget anything, J.T. I just choose to remember happier days.' There was a long pause, then Marion said, 'It's because of her, isn't it?'

A second pause. 'She had a name, Marion. She was a human being.'

'She was a lying, manipulative prostitute who caught Daddy in a weak moment. He'd just retired, he was vulnerable to . . . to female attention.'

'Mom will be happy with this analysis.'

'Mom has more bats in her belfry than a gothic church.'

'Finally we agree on something.'

'The point is, Daddy made a mistake—'

'A mistake? He got a seventeen-year-old girl pregnant. Our father, the pedophile.'

'He took care of her.'

'Is that what you call it?' J.T.'s voice dropped to a low tone that prickled the hair on the back of Tess's neck. Marion didn't recover quickly this time, but when she did, her retort was sharp.

'Oh, that's right. Daddy is the root of all evil. Hell, he was probably the one standing at the grassy knoll.'

'I wouldn't put it past him. Have you ever watched the JFK tapes closely?'

'Grow up, J.T. Daddy needs you right now, though God knows why. Maybe you don't like him, maybe you're never going to see eye to eye with him, but for chrissake, he gave you life. He put a roof over your head. He raised you and gave you anything you ever asked for – the sports car, West Point, military appointments, *cover-up* – you got it all.'

'And it still burns, doesn't it, Marion?' J.T. said quietly. 'Though Roger was hardly a shabby consolation prize.'

'Roger left me, J.T. But thanks for asking.'

'What?' J.T. sounded genuinely surprised, perhaps even stunned. 'Marion, I'm sorry. I swear to you, I'm sorry—'

'I did not come here for your pity. You utter those words one more time and they'll need Super Glue to put your face together again. No, don't say anything more. I'm sick of this conversation – it never gets any better. I'm staying seven days, J.T. Seven days for you to see the light. Then I wash my hands of this whole mess.'

'Merry Berry—'

'Don't call me that! And tell your "guest" that if I catch either one of you doing anything remotely illegal, I'll arrest both your asses. Got it?'

'You don't have to scream for me to know how much you care.'

'Oh, go knit yourself a Hallmark card.'

Tess heard the sharp, ringing sound of heels against hardwood floors. The fast, furious footsteps grew closer and Tess held her breath. But the sound passed her by. Marion stormed to the end bedroom, where her arrival was punctuated by the sound of the door slamming shut.

Tess released her breath. Her body sagged against the door. Everything was okay. This Marion was an FBI agent, but she was also J.T.'s sister and was here for reasons that had nothing to do with Tess.

She was safe, no one knew who she was, and she was still in Arizona.

She couldn't take any more. It was still afternoon, but her exhausted body demanded rest. She crawled into bed, pulled the covers over her head, and welcomed slumber.

6

It was cold in the basement. She could feel a draft but couldn't identify the source. The light was feeble, just a bare overhead bulb that lengthened the shadows. Beneath her feet she felt hard-packed dirt.

What was that leaning in the corner? A shovel, a saw, a hammer. Clipping shears and two rakes. Had she ever seen Jim use any of those things? There was a baseball bat as well. A long, golden baseball bat. She'd thought he kept his bats in the coat closet. Why in the basement? They hardly ever went into the basement.

She smelled fresh dirt and turned toward the scent. In the far corner she saw a mound of dirt perfectly shaped as a fresh grave.

No. No, no, no.

A hand clamped over her mouth.

She screamed. She screamed and the palm shoved the sound back down her throat. She was pinned against a body, struggling and squirming wildly. Dear God, help me.

Thick fingers dug into her jaw and pinned her head into place. 'I thought you wouldn't come down here, Theresa. I thought you said you wouldn't.'

She whimpered helplessly. She was trapped. Now he was going to do something awful.

She felt his arm move behind her. A black scarf slid over her eyes, shutting out the light, cutting her off from everything.

She moaned in terror.

He tied a rolled pillowcase over her mouth, the cloth pressing against her tongue and digging into the sensitive corners of her lips like a horse's bit.

He released her and she fell to the ground.

'I told you not to come down here, but you had to, didn't you, Theresa? You had to know. You shouldn't pry if you don't want answers.'

He dragged her to her feet and pulled her across the dirt floor. The pungent odor became stronger. The smell of dirt and something else, something astringent. Lime. Fresh lime to cover the scent of decaying corpses. She gagged against the pillowcase.

'That's right. You're standing at the edge of a grave. One push and you'll tumble right in. Fall into the grave. Want to know what you'll find there?'

46

He pushed her forward into empty space and she screamed in her throat. He jerked her back against him and laughed softly in her ear. 'Not quite yet. Let me show you everything else.'

His fingers dug into her hand, forcing it to reach out. She begged, her words muffled, gasping sobs behind the pillowcase. He was going to make her touch something. Something she didn't want to touch.

Her hand was buried into a glass jar. Round, firm, and moist shapes slid around her fingertips. 'Eyeballs,' he whispered. 'I saved the eyeballs from all my past wives.'

He yanked her hand back and plunged it into something else. Hair. Long and smooth and sickeningly damp at the ends. 'Scalped 'em too,' he hissed.

Again he yanked her hand back and plunged her fisted fingers into something else. Squishy and tangled and oily. Caught on her fingers, twisted around her fingers.

'Guts. Lots and lots of guts.

'And here, baby, is my crowning achievement. Her heart. Her warm, pulsing heart.'

Her hand was forcefully closed around the mass. His fingers curled around her throat. Tightening, tightening, tightening as his breathing accelerated with excitement in her ear.

'You have no idea who I am, Theresa. You have no idea.'

And just as the spots formed before her eyes, just as the abyss opened before her and she knew she could fall right in and never have to think again, his fingers let her go and the air rushed into her oxygen-starved lungs.

The blindfold was snatched from her eyes. She was staring down at blood, so much blood. She turned, too horrified to run.

She saw his face clearly. His leering, cold face.

J. T. Dillon smirking down at her with coal-black eyes.

Tess woke up harshly, the scream ripe on her lips, her heart pounding in her chest. She clutched her fist to her throat, gasping for breath. Sweat trickled down her cheeks like tears.

A pause, then she scampered out of the strange bed and turned on every light she could find. The room had hardly any lamps. She needed more light, lots and lots more to dispel the shadows lurking in the corners.

She found herself in front of the closet doors, securely blockaded by a chair. *Open the damn doors. Know that he's gone, that you won, you won.*

Suddenly with a cry of rage she kicked the chair away, grabbed the handle, and yanked the door open.

'Come on, where are you, you bastard?'

Only empty hangers stared back at her. She took a deep breath, then another, until her body stopped shaking.

You're in Arizona. You're safe. There is no blood on your hands.

It was a cow's heart. A cow's heart, linguine in olive oil, silk threads, and peeled grapes. Stuff from a gradeschool haunted house.

'Look around you, Theresa,' Jim had said after he'd snapped on the basement light. 'Look at what you're so terrified of. If you're willing to believe peeled grapes are eyeballs, no wonder you look at me and see a monster.'

She collapsed on the ground.

He squatted down until he was eye level. 'I told you not to come into the basement, but you did. You're so determined to think I'm doing something wrong. Why do you think so little of your husband, Theresa? Why are you so determined to be afraid of me?'

She wasn't able to summon an answer.

'You know what I think? I think you have really low self-esteem, Theresa. I think your father and his abusive behavior taught you to think of yourself as nothing. And now you have this handsome, charming, decorated police officer who loves you and you just can't believe that, can you? Rather than accept that a good man loves you, you wonder what's wrong with me. You obsess that there must be something wrong with me. I suggest you stop focusing on my problems, Theresa, and spend a little bit more time contemplating yours.'

He left the basement.

She remained on the floor actually wondering why she questioned her perfect husband.

Jim had been that good.

Then other memories, other images overwhelmed her. Jim's hands around her throat, squeezing, releasing, caressing, soothing, choking. The baseball bat arching up, looking like a fairy's wand in the moonlight. Whistling down. Her thigh cracking . . .

She ran for the door, undid the lock, and made it to the bathroom just in time to be violently ill.

'Was it something I said?' J.T. stood in the doorway.

Her eyes squeezed shut. She remained hunched over the sink, her arms trembling, her legs shaky. She tasted bile. She tasted despair, by far a more savage flavor.

'Please go away,' she whispered.

'Sorry, but there isn't a Virginia man alive who can walk away from a puking woman. Consider it our southern charm.'

She heard the patter of his bare feet against the bathroom floor tiles and caught the faint odor of chlorine as he approached. His torso pressed against her. She stiffened and his chest rumbled with a growl of disapproval.

He said, 'Just turning on the water. Tastes like the rusty pipe it uses to visit us all the way from Colorado, but last I checked, it was better than vomit.'

He stepped away. With a sigh she scooped the water over her face and neck, letting it pour through her mouth. It did taste metallic and rusty.

'Better?' he said after a moment.

She turned off the faucet and faced him. He wore nothing but a pair of swimming trunks, which rode too low on his hips, revealing a faint white line of untouched skin. Water trickled across his shoulders, down into the fine black hair on his flat belly.

He raised a half-filled beer bottle and looking straight into her eyes, polished it off.

'Take it.'

'What?'

'The towel, *chiquita*. You look like hell.'

Belatedly she saw the hand towel he was holding. She took it gingerly from him. He hadn't done anything, but she was scared anyway. In her experience, men – and particularly muscled men – were a clear threat to women. She couldn't picture her father without seeing his fleshy face turn beet red as he raised his thick fist. She couldn't picture her ex-husband without seeing his cold blue eyes dispassionately returning her stare as he fed her wedding gown to the flames.

But J.T. came highly recommended. Surely mercenaries didn't kill their clients. That had to be bad for business. What about a policeman murdering tax-payers? That was bad for business too.

But she'd been in J.T.'s house for forty-eight hours without incident. He fed her breakfast. He shielded her from the police. Surely if he had violent tendencies, she would've seen some indication.

Of course, it had taken her two years to recognize the violence in Jim.

Her hands came up and rubbed her forehead. She wanted to own herself, she wanted to trust herself. Two and a half years after putting Jim in prison, she still wasn't sure that had happened. She was stuck somewhere between the old Theresa Beckett and the new Tess Williams.

'Rough night for the *Better Homes & Garden* lady?'

'It's that knit one purl two,' she murmured. 'I keep having nightmares of dropping the stitch.'

'Yeah? And here I keep dreaming of blowing up churches. Come outside, the cool air does a body good.'

He turned and she realized that he expected her to follow. She looked down at her legs uncovered by her purple Williams College T-shirt. Generally she didn't follow half-naked men around while wearing only a T-shirt. Her mother had had strong feelings about women showing too much flesh. Only bad women did that, and they went straight to hell, where little devils did horrible things to them every night to punish them for being so wanton.

The image of herself as a wanton was so absurd, she had to smile. She'd never been a femme fatale, never sparked hidden flames. She'd been the dutiful, confused wife. Now she was the scared, emaciated mother. All signs indicated that J.T. found her about as attractive as an animated skeleton. She was fine with that. She just wanted him for his semiautomatics.

She followed him out to the deck, shivering as the night air hit her. J.T. didn't seem to notice. He plopped down on one of the chairs and picked up a gold cigarette case. A six-pack sat on the glass table.

Her arms wrapped around her middle as she stared up at a rich blue sky dotted with stars. The nights in Williamstown would be cool and clear by now, but the air would be scented with the rich, musty odor of drying leaves and aging pine, the refreshing tang of wind sweeping down from the Berkshires. She wondered what her daughter was doing just then. Probably fast asleep, tucked in bed with her pink flannel nightgown and her favorite talking doll. If she closed her eyes, she could almost capture the scent of No More Tears shampoo and baby powder.

Baby, I love you.

'You eavesdropped, didn't you?' J.T. asked.

'Yes.'

J.T. flipped open the slim cigarette case, banged out a cigarette, and lit it. He stared at her as he dragged deeply. 'Filthy habit. Would you like one?'

He held out the case, then snatched it back. 'Wait, I forgot. You can barely walk as it is – no cigarettes for you.'

He exhaled, leaning back and crossing his ankles.

'I didn't know you smoked.'

'I'd quit.'

'You went out in the middle of the night to buy cigarettes so you could start again?'

'Nope. I stole Marion's cigarettes. I was the one who taught her how to smoke, you know.' His lips twisted. 'At least that's what I recall. You'll have to ask her what she remembers.'

'There seems to be little love lost between you and your sister.'

'I've never been a fan of revisionist history.'

Keeping her voice neutral, she asked, 'She's really an FBI agent?'

'Yes.' Briefly his chest puffed out. 'A damn good one.'

'I heard her say she's staying for a week.'

'She is. So if you are a crook, don't tell her. She'll drag you in.'

'And you would let her?'

'If you're a crook.'

'Very good,' she acknowledged. 'You've covered all the bases. If I stay, I must be legal. If I'm gone in the morning, well, I've saved you a bunch of trouble.'

'Don't let my good looks fool you, sweetheart – I'm no dumb bunny.'

She nodded, her gaze returning to the night sky. She was cold. She wanted to go inside and sleep. She was terrified of the nightmares that would find her again.

THE PERFECT HUSBAND

'One month of training,' J.T. said all of a sudden. 'I'll do it.'

'I know.'

'Don't be so smug. We start first thing in the morning, oh-six-hundred. Physical fitness, self-defense, small firearms, the works. I'll burn your butt into the ground and turn you into a whole new woman.'

'All right.'

'Do you want to know why I changed my mind?'

'It doesn't matter.'

'But it does matter, Angela. It matters to me.' He waved his hand around the villa, the garden, the pool. 'I don't own this. Not really. Every square inch of this place, every pebble, every cactus, was paid for by my father. You could say I'm still on allowance. I can keep this, I can live this way forever in return for only two things. The first doesn't concern you. The second is that I never return to "the business." I take you on, I train you, I lose all this. Do you think I should do that for you, Angela?'

'No,' she told him honestly.

'Then we agree. I'm doing it for me. Because I want to. Because I've got the worst case of orphan envy in the whole wide world.'

He grabbed a beer, climbed off the chair, and walked toward her.

She could feel the tension in him. He was not a man who played by the rules – he probably *had* blown up churches. He had anger and dark moods she didn't understand. He was unpredictable, raw around the edges. When he moved, he didn't make any sound. And after the marble-smooth facade of Jim, he seemed unbelievably real. If this man had a problem with you, he wouldn't poison your dog or burn down your garage. He'd tell you about it to your face. He'd let you know. If he discovered a father beating his daughter, he wouldn't rig a stockroom ladder to fall, breaking the father's leg. He'd walk up to the man and slam a fist through his face.

He stopped so close, she could feel the faint heat of the cigarette.

'You dreaming about him, Angela?'

'Sometimes.'

'When was the last time you slept through the night?'

'I . . . I don't know.'

'Fixed yourself a good meal?'

'A long time.'

'Well, stop it.' He ran a finger down her arm. She flinched and he shook his head. 'There's nothing to you, Angela. You've let yourself go. Now you're just bones with shadows rimming your eyes. A good stiff wind could blow you over.'

'It's hard,' she said. 'We've . . . we've been on the run. There are problems—'

'Tough. You have to learn to compartmentalize. From here on out, you separate. You're scared, sleep anyway. You're anxious, eat fruits and vegetables. Get some mass on those bones, then we'll talk muscle. And

51

stop shredding your nails. If you won't take your body seriously, how is anyone else supposed to?'

'Strange advice coming from you.'

'I just preach, never practice.' His fingers lingered on her arm. The pads of his fingertips were rough and warm. He doodled a lazy pattern she felt down to her toes. She stepped back.

'You don't like that?'

'I . . . no, I don't.'

He chuckled. 'Liar.'

'I'm looking for a teacher, not another mistake.'

'Ah, and that's how you see men.' He tapped the beer bottle against his forearm, then lifted it for a deep swig.

'We'll start in the pool,' he said. 'Try to get you in shape without hurting anything.'

'I'm not a good swimmer.'

'I thought you said you didn't whine.'

She brought up her chin in defiance and he laughed. 'You're good. You have spirit.'

'Oh, that's me,' she muttered. 'I'm just plain *spunky*.'

He chuckled again, then his gaze grew speculative, caressing her cheek. He raised the cigarette. The end glowed red as he inhaled. Several seconds passed before he released the smoke.

She found herself watching the small O formed by his whiskered lips. She watched the long strands of his silky black hair brush his collarbone. The porch light flickered over him. She wanted to touch his skin, see if it felt as warm as it looked.

She glanced down immediately, caught off guard by her own reaction.

'Scared?' he murmured huskily, his voice too knowing.

'No,' she said instantly.

'You're shaking in your boots. And I haven't even tried anything. Yet.'

'I'm not scared!' But she was, and they both knew it. She was uncomfortable, and her thoughts were muddled. Should she trust him, should she not trust him? Should she run, should she play it tough? Should she step closer, should she step away? She was sick of the doubt.

She made her decision. Before she lost her courage, she grabbed the beer bottle and yanked it from his grasp. She crossed to the white gravel bed bordering the cactus garden and dumped the beer out.

'No more. I hired you. I want you sober.'

'A marine shoots better drunk,' he said curtly, no longer amused.

'Well, J.T., you're *not* a marine.'

'Big mistake, Angela. Big mistake.' He stalked toward her.

She stood her ground. 'You getting mean?' she said haughtily. 'Do you miss the beer that much already?'

'Not the beer. Sex.' His arm whipped out, faster than she could have imagined. One hand palmed her head, his fingertips rubbing her scalp.

'You still haven't moved. Maybe you want to kiss me. If you do something that dangerous, will you feel strong?'

He bent over her. This close she could see the feral gleam in his eyes, could see the individual hairs of his twenty-four-hour beard.

Facial hair. Genuine facial hair to go with the hair on his chest. He had no idea what those things meant to her. No idea what it was like to be confronted by a man who was anything but cold.

'Come on, Angela, kiss me. I'll show you the third thing I'm very, very good at.'

He leaned closer still but didn't touch her lips. They both knew he wouldn't. He wanted her to do it.

She reached up and carefully, hesitantly, touched the prickly rasp of his beard. It was softer than she imagined. Her fingertips tingled. He sucked in his breath. She was holding her own. She followed his jaw, learning its strong, solid line. Her fingers tangled in his hair.

'For God's sake, don't you know how to kiss a man?' He yanked her closer.

And she punched him in the shoulder.

He grunted, more with surprise than pain, and fell back a step.

'That's what I'm supposed to do, right?' she stated firmly. 'I'm supposed to take a stand. Well, I did. And while I'm at it . . .' She yanked the cigarette from his lips. 'I hate smoking.'

'Too late. You should've run, Angela, exited stage left while you had the chance.'

He caught her easily and pulled her against him hard. One minute she was standing by the cactus garden, the next she was pressed against a burning body, her legs cradled by muscled thighs, her torso clamped by sinewy arms. She opened her mouth to protest, but he merely took advantage and captured her lips.

He was not bashful or calculating. His tongue plunged in deep, hot, knowing, and tasting of tobacco. He filled her, stroked her, grazed her teeth, and challenged her. She squirmed in his arms. The kiss deepened and ripened, never painful, but insistent until she felt something unfurl in her stomach.

She wanted to melt a little. She wanted to dig her fingers into his shoulders and hold on to him.

With a harsh cry she hammered her fists against his chest. He let her go. 'Bastard!'

'Absolutely. And I warned you.'

She wiped the back of her hand over her mouth. She felt raw and exposed all over. She wanted to beat the crap out of him.

He didn't step back or come closer. He just stood there, challenging her.

She couldn't overpower him. He was stronger – men were always stronger – and she didn't know how to fight yet. Her eyes began to sting. Dammit, she was going to cry.

'Don't,' he said.

'Leave me alone.'

'Oh, come on, Angela, you were doing so much better than that. Don't give up on me now.'

'You arrogant son of a—'

'Much better. It's the spirit that will keep you alive, Angela. Don't lose the spirit. Now go to bed.'

'And yourself?' she fired back. 'Are you going to stay out here all night, ignoring your own advice?'

'Probably.'

She cocked her head to the side, sizing him up. 'I see,' she said casually. 'Your sister's only been here twelve hours and you're already falling apart.'

'Shut up, Angela.'

'Why? You can mess with my mind but I can't mess with yours? I might not be very strong and I'm probably a lousy shot, but I can connect the dots. You and your sister have some different opinions on your father. You seem to want to have a relationship with her. She seems to want to burn you at the stake. How am I doing so far?'

'Go to bed,' he warned.

'Not when I'm on such a roll. What did your father do anyway?'

'What didn't he do? Good night.'

'Did he hit you? I know about that kind of thing.'

'Your father beat you?'

'All the time,' she stated flatly. 'I still hate him for it.'

'Huh. Now, see, I think that kind of hatred is healthy. I'm a firm believer in it myself. Marion disagrees. She says our father was merely a little strict.'

'But you don't agree?'

He grunted. 'The colonel thought child rearing was a fucking blood sport.' He walked to the table, lit a new cigarette, and inhaled. His hands trembled slightly.

'Go away, Angela. Surely you got bigger things to worry about than my twisted family.'

She didn't go away. They had a connection now, and it mattered to her. 'And the woman?'

'The woman?'

'The prostitute who had your father's child.'

'My, my, you really did eavesdrop.'

'Yes,' she said shamelessly.

He continued smoking and she decided he wasn't going to answer her. Then just as his cigarette burned down to the nub, he said, 'My father took a seventeen-year-old prostitute as a mistress. He liked to do that kind of thing. She got pregnant. So the colonel tossed her out. She stood on the doorstep and begged for her clothes. He told the butler to turn the dogs loose. She left.'

'That's it?'

'Of course not. The girl tried going to Marion next. She didn't want money for herself, but for the baby.'

'But Marion . . .'

'Turned her away. Marion's whole life is about selective memory. Daddy is her darling. Whatever he does must be all right or the universe will cease to exist. If Daddy says the girl's some lying whore he's never met, then the girl's some lying whore he's never met.'

'So she came to you?'

J.T. cocked one brow. 'You mean you haven't figured it out?'

She shook her head.

'The girl's name was Rachel. Her son, my half brother, was Teddy.'

'Oh,' she breathed, her eyes wide as the pieces clicked.

'That's right,' J.T. said softly. 'I married her. And she was the best thing that ever happened to me.'

J.T. dropped his cigarette on the patio and ground it out with his heel. He saluted her mockingly and she still couldn't think of a response.

'Get some sleep. Oh-six-hundred, at the pool. And keep clear of Marion, Angie. She doesn't like you, and Marion knows how to eat a person alive, then pick her teeth with the bones. We're damn proud of her.'

He left her alone on the patio, listening to the water lap against the pool while somewhere in the distance a coyote bayed at the moon without ever getting a response.

7

This is Jim Beckett interview number one, conducted by Special Agent Pierce Quincy with assistance from Lieutenant Lance Difford of the Massachusetts Crime Prevention and Control Unit. Location is Massachusetts Correction Institute Cedar Junction at Walpole. Date is November 11, 1995. Jim Beckett has been incarcerated approximately three months. With his approval, this interview is being audiotaped and filmed. Do you have any questions?'

BECKETT: Quincy? As in the coroner on TV?

QUINCY: Medical examiner.

BECKETT: Did you watch the show as a child? Was it your favorite show?

QUINCY: I saw it a few times.

BECKETT: What did your father do?

QUINCY: He's a plumber.

BECKETT: Not nearly as exciting as a coroner. I see your point.

DIFFORD: Cut the crap, Beckett. We're not here to watch you head-shrink the FBI. Quincy's only read about you, but I know you, Beckett. Don't forget that.

BECKETT: Lieutenant Difford, charming as always. The part I enjoyed most about being a police officer was reporting to dumb fucks like you. The big bad police lieutenant whose experience and street savvy will keep everyone safe at night, when all along it's your own man who's going out there, pulling over sweet blondes, and dicing them up. How's your insomnia, Lieutenant?

DIFFORD: Fuck you—

QUINCY: All right, let's get down to business. Lieutenant Difford's right, I've never personally met you, Jim, but I know all about you. I also saw all the files you pulled from our Investigative Support Unit, so I know you're familiar with serial killer profiling techniques. As we've discussed, this interview is strictly voluntary. You don't get anything in return, except a break in what must be a very monotonous routine here at Walpole. Would you like a cigarette or anything?

BECKETT: I don't smoke. My body is my temple.

DIFFORD: Jesus Christ—

BECKETT: I want to see my profile.

QUINCY: We're not into swaps, Jim.

BECKETT: Afraid I'll be able to refute it, see all the flaws? Or are you afraid I'll be able to someday use it to my advantage?

QUINCY: You have an IQ of 145. I don't underestimate that, Jim.

BECKETT: *Laughter.* You're not half bad, Special Agent Quincy. I may just come to like you.

DIFFORD: Shit, are you two gonna exchange love letters or can we get on with it?

BECKETT: Wait a minute. I get it. You two are playing good cop/bad cop. The smooth, sophisticated FBI agent and the blue collar, illiterate street cop. Have I mentioned yet that the FBI and local law enforcement agencies haven't had an original thought since 1975?

DIFFORD: Maybe, Beckett, we're just being ourselves.

QUINCY: Jim, I'd like to start by having you describe yourself in your own words. If you were profiling yourself, what would you say?

BECKETT: I don't think so, Quincy. You're the professional here. You go first. I'll tell you if you're getting warm.

Pause.

QUINCY: All right. The FBI entered the case with the discovery of the third body outside of Clinton, Mass. Later it was determined that this was the sixth victim, but at the time there were only two other crime scenes for comparison. The victim was a twenty-three-year-old mother and cocktail waitress returning from work. Her car was found pulled over on the side of a secluded back road, the windows rolled up and the doors locked. Inside, the glove compartment was open, her keys were in the ignition, and her purse was sitting in the passenger seat. Her clothes, covered with debris from the nearby woods, were found neatly folded and stacked in the trunk. There were no signs of struggle.

A quarter of a mile from the car, the body was discovered in the ditch. The victim had been stripped naked and placed faceup, arms and legs spread-eagle. A tree branch was stuck in her vagina. Clearly the body had been arranged for shock value. The victim had been sadistically tortured and sexually assaulted. Exact cause of death was difficult to determine. The victim's own pantyhose had been tied around her neck for ligature strangulation. In addition the victim's head had been savagely beaten with a blunt instrument – later determined to be the same tree branch that was inserted in her vagina.

Bruises around the victim's breast, buttocks, and inner thighs revealed the unsub [unidentified subject] had spent a significant amount of time torturing the victim before killing her. The extensive amount of post-mortem mutilation, combined with the precise posing of the body, indicated that he'd probably spent at least an hour with the victim after the murder. The unsub had also taken the time to clean up the crime scene. There were no prints, no body hair, no semen samples, or torn clothing left behind. The victim had some defense wounds on her hands, indicating a struggle, but she'd been quickly subdued. We could find no traces of skin cells or blood beneath her fingernails.

We theorized that the unsub had utilized some credible ruse to lure the victim from her car. He'd then controlled the victim, tortured her, raped her, and killed her with particular fury. Afterward he'd arranged the body, vented further rage in postmortem piquerism, then returned to her vehicle, where he stored the clothes in the trunk and locked the car doors.

Several aspects of this crime stood out. First the fact that the unsub had lured the victim from the safety of her automobile versus using a blitz-style attack suggested that the unsub appeared to be a safe, credible person with advanced communication skills. The amount of time spent with the victim indicated the unsub was comfortable and confident in his abilities to execute the crime and escape. Lab tests revealed traces of spermicide and latex in the woman's vagina, indicating that the killer had most likely worn a condom for the sexual assault, then removed it from the crime scene. Most likely, the unsub was already at the stage where he traveled with a 'murder kit' containing such items as condoms, gloves, perhaps disguises, anything to assist him with his attack. Finally, the level of sheer violence and cruelty, combined with the vicious and shocking postmortem mutilation, indicated a man with unbelievable rage toward women.

We were dealing with a psychopath.

BECKETT: Please continue, you're finally getting interesting.

QUINCY: The unsub was most likely a white male in his late twenties to early forties. Age can be difficult to determine, but given the elaborate nature of the crime and mutilation, we estimated that the homicidal rage had been developing for quite some time. The unsub was already refining and perfecting his technique. His use of a ruse indicated the foresight and planning of a more experienced man, leading us toward an age of early- to mid-thirties. We predicted he would be outwardly charming and charismatic. A man of above-average IQ, socially adept, a capable employee, and either married or involved in a significant relationship. He was physically fit, good with his hands, and probably working in a 'macho' job. His car would be a middle-class dark sedan, possibly an old police cruiser. He had spent time in the military, but his egocentric personality and arrogance made him a poor fit – he was discharged under less than honorable circumstances. He probably has a past record of assault and/or minor sex offenses. Perhaps DWI arrests. Also, the style of ligature was similar to what you see in prison rapes, indicating that this man had probably served time.

He obviously considered himself a sophisticated killer. All three women were young, beautiful, and blond. Also, all three were risky victims for him to choose – these were not prostitutes or strippers, but mothers, daughters, and college students who had families to miss them and pressure the police for further investigation. The killer probably spent a great deal of time patiently driving around, waiting to find the right woman in the right place—

BECKETT: He's disciplined?

QUINCY: Well, as disciplined as a homicidal maniac can be.

BECKETT: It's discipline, Quincy, trust me. When the urge to kill is that strong, it takes strength and willpower to wait for the right one. You wouldn't know that. I doubt you've ever had a strong, passionate impulse in your life. What about trophies?

QUINCY: Generally serial killers take trophies. From looking at a crime scene, it's impossible to know what's missing. Maybe the unsub took a ring to give to his wife so he can experience a cheap thrill every time he looks at her. Maybe it was just a lock of hair. He'll take something though, to help him relive the crime later.

BECKETT: See, you're wrong. I didn't take anything. Why put something in my possession that would link me to a homicide? Bundy, Kemper, they thought they were smart, but they were really just animals, furious, savage animals who were slaves to their own hunger. I'm not a slave, Quincy. I controlled my impulses. I limited myself to my pattern.

QUINCY: Pattern?

BECKETT: You've never figured it out, have you?

QUINCY: Patterns are a favorite with Hollywood. Lunar cycles, numerology, astrology – they rarely have anything to do with it.

BECKETT: I agree entirely.

QUINCY: Then what do you mean by pattern?

BECKETT: You're supposedly the expert, Agent. You figure it out.

Pause.

QUINCY: What about visiting the graves of your victims?

BECKETT: Never.

QUINCY: You never visited a grave site? Not even a memorial service, a vigil, anything?

BECKETT: Discipline is the key.

QUINCY: What about returning to the crime scene? You could pretend to be there as a police officer.

BECKETT: I am a Berkshire County cop. What would I be doing at a Clinton, Massachusetts, crime scene? I insist, discipline is the key. I'm not toying with you, Agent.

DIFFORD: Bullshit. The omnipotent guise is how you get your rocks off, Beckett. If you were so fucking smart, so fucking disciplined, so *controlled*, you wouldn't be sitting in jail right now.

BECKETT: Have you ever thought of going on a diet, Difford? Look at you. You're hitting the doughnuts much too hard these days.

DIFFORD: You came back for Theresa, Beckett, just like she said you would. A smart man would've skipped town, but not you. You couldn't let it go, not after what she did. You weren't so disciplined then, were you, asshole?

BECKETT: And where were you, Difford? When I wrapped my hands around my lovely wife's neck and began to squeeze the life out of her flailing body, where was her police protection? Where was your fat, lazy ass?

QUINCY: Gentlemen . . .

BECKETT: The agent's right. This exchange of pleasantries isn't advancing science. But I have to say I'm not impressed, Agent Quincy. At this point you might as well have been reciting a textbook. Come on, *Special Agent*. Dazzle me.

Pause.

QUINCY: Your first murder wasn't planned.

BECKETT: Elementary. What killer has ever planned his first murder? You have desire, then in a fraction of a moment of time you realize that you have opportunity. You either act or you don't. That's what separates the men from the boys. Me from you.

QUINCY: You pulled her over for speeding. You had every intention of writing her a legitimate ticket. You were on duty at the time. Stop me if I'm wrong, Jim. Then you see her. She's blond, beautiful, and sitting so trustingly in her car, ready to hand you her driver's license and vehicle registration. You've been under pressure for some time. You've been drinking—

BECKETT: I don't drink.

QUINCY: But you've been under stress, even more stress than you're used to. You realize no one's around, the road is deserted, and this beautiful woman is looking up at you and smiling apologetically.

BECKETT: She wanted me.

QUINCY: You were sloppy, weren't you, Jim? You thought it was about control, but you had none. You followed instinct and the next thing you knew, you'd raped and killed a woman with your oh-so-identifiable police cruiser parked behind her car.

BECKETT: I didn't panic.

QUINCY: Your uniform was ripped, wasn't it? You'd left semen in her body and were vulnerable to DNA matching. People had probably seen you pull her over. What to do next?

BECKETT: I wrote her ticket, of course.

QUINCY: Yes, that was good. You got into your car. Gave a status report and said you were continuing on. But you didn't continue on. You hid your police cruiser, then you returned to the scene. You dressed the victim, you placed her in her car, covering her with the blanket from your trunk so it looked like she was sleeping. You needed to hide her body, but you can't drive too far away because how will you get back? So you drive her car into the nearby lake, knowing the water will do your dirty work for you. If she'll just stay in the water four, five days . . . It's hard to gather evidence from a floater.

BECKETT: Particularly after a year.

QUINCY: You got a good break, didn't you? The woman is listed as missing, your superiors call you in to ask since you gave her a ticket. You handle it cool as a cucumber, all paperwork appropriately filed—

BECKETT: I already said that half the fun was reporting to shit-for-brain lieutenants who never suspected a thing.

DIFFORD: Son of a bitch, we caught you in the end!

BECKETT: Ten bodies later . . . that you know about. But, Quincy, I'm still not impressed. So the first murder was unplanned. So the body was dumped in a lake to cover the crime. That's all logic. Tell me something cool. Tell me something that will send goose bumps up my spine.

QUINCY: The night you killed the first victim, Lucy Edwards, your wife was in the hospital, giving birth to your daughter. That was the stress you couldn't handle, Jim. The birth of your daughter.

Pause.

BECKETT: Too easy. You have the date on the ticket, so you know she disappeared that day.

QUINCY: That doesn't mean she was killed the day she was last seen. You know it's impossible to accurately pinpoint the time of death of a body that's spent a year underwater.

BECKETT: It's still just logic.

QUINCY: No, it's statistical odds, Jim. All killers have a triggering event. For disorganized killers, it's generally the loss of their job or a major confrontation with their mother. For organized killers like you, birth of their first child rates right up there. The new addition to the family, the financial strain – particularly for a police officer who was already living beyond his means. Your arrogance is your Achilles' heel, Jim. You want to think you're unique. You want to think you're the best, but really, you're just like all the others. And we can profile you the same way we profile them, by looking at what the others did.

Pause.

BECKETT: Then you don't need to talk to me, do you?

QUINCY: It's not the *what* we're trying to figure out, Jim. It's the *why*. You killed ten blond women, beautiful, loving, caring women. What drives a man to do such a thing?

BECKETT: You mean watch a woman beg for her life, snap her neck, then go to the hospital to see his newborn daughter? That was a good night, you know. Have you ever met my daughter, Samantha? She's a beautiful little girl, bright too. Tell him, Difford. You know Sam. Sam is the best thing that ever happened to me.

DIFFORD: And if the world has any justice, she'll never know who you are,

Beckett. Theresa told her you were dead. She even bought a grave marker. You have a pink marker, Beckett. What do you think of that?

BECKETT: You're bitter, Lieutenant.

QUINCY: Jim, why did you kill those women?

BECKETT: They were immoral, godless sluts who deserved to die.

DIFFORD: He's lying. He doesn't have a religious bone in his body.

BECKETT: *Laughter.* For a change, Difford's right. But I get so bored with the my-mother-toilet-trained-me-at-gunpoint excuse.

QUINCY: Did you hate your mother?

BECKETT: Which mother? Adoptive or biological? Actually, it doesn't matter. Neither of them was worth hating.

QUINCY: They told me you've been exchanging letters with Edward Kemper III.

BECKETT: Sure. Ed's a big guy. Six nine and three hundred pounds. That's a hell of a lot of psychopath. I work out everyday here, you know. I'm up to bench-pressing three-fifty. [*Beckett pulls up sleeve and flexes for camera.*] Impressive, huh? But I still got a ways to go to catch Ed.

QUINCY: Ed's IQ is also 145, did you know that?

BECKETT: He's a real Renaissance man.

QUINCY: He killed ten people as well. Is that why you decided to write to him? His victims were closer to home though – his grandparents, his mother, and her best friend . . .

BECKETT: Yeah, Ed's read a little too much Freud. All he talks about is how much he hated his mother. For God's sake, he attacked her with a claw hammer, decapitated her, then raped her corpse. It's time for him to move on. Have you heard about the larynx?

QUINCY: I read the interview notes.

BECKETT: Now, is that irony or what? Poor, bed-wetting, traumatized Ed is jamming his mother's larynx down the garbage disposal as a last symbolic act, and the disposal jams and throws the bloody voice box back up at him. Ed says, 'Even when she was dead, she was still bitching at me. I couldn't get her to shut up!' That's one of my favorite stories.

QUINCY: Did your mother bitch at you? Was she demanding?

BECKETT: My birth mother was a weak, pathetic hypochondriac without an intelligent thought in her head. When she dropped dead, she merely fulfilled her own prophecy.

QUINCY: Your father?

BECKETT: My father was a good man, don't bring him into this.

QUINCY: Would he be ashamed of you now, Jim?

BECKETT: For what?

QUINCY: I think he would be, Jim. I think you know that. I think Jenny Thomson really got to you.

BECKETT: Who?

DIFFORD: You know who the hell he's talking about, Beckett. Little Jenny

Thomson. The seventeen-year-old from Enfield. The girl whose head you cut off.

QUINCY: You didn't decapitate anyone else, Jim. Only her. You also let her get dressed after you had raped her. I think she shamed you. I think she told you that she was driving home from visiting her dying father in the hospital. That he needed her, she was his last reason to fight for life. That she loved him very much. But she'd seen your face. You had to kill her. So you did, but you didn't feel good about it, not like the others. The others you looked in the eye, but not Jenny. She was manually strangled from behind, but even then you didn't feel right about it. You were troubled and you were angry because you didn't want to be troubled. So you cut off her head, classic depersonalization. You hid it under a pile of leaves, not able to look at her. You left her body covered, not exposed like the others. But you still felt shame, didn't you, Jim? Every time you think of her, you feel shame.

BECKETT: No.

DIFFORD: You're shifting in your seat, Jim. You don't look so comfortable anymore.

BECKETT: My leg's fallen asleep.

DIFFORD: Sure, Jim.

BECKETT: I saw Jenny's father in the hospital.

QUINCY: What?

BECKETT: The nurses never put it together, did they? I went to the hospital. I wanted to see if her father was really there, if he was really dying. You can't trust what a woman says, particularly once you have her. They'll say anything if they think it will save their life. So I checked up on it.

I found him in an oxygen tent in intensive care, *Mister* Quincy. He wasn't allowed visitors, but I told the nurses I was working on his daughter's case and I had good news for him. Of course they let me in. Young nurses. One of them was quite beautiful but she was a brunette.

I leaned over until I could press my face against the oxygen tent. And I told him how beautiful his daughter was and how wonderfully she'd screamed. I told him she'd begged for her life and she'd prayed to God, but God hadn't saved her. She belonged to me and I took her. He died the next day.

You want to know what makes me, Mister Quincy? If you want to understand me, forget the mommy-hating or the bed-wetting, animal-torturing, fire-starting triad you guys developed. It's so much simpler than that. There's power in the world, and that is me.

It's the power of being alone with a woman and having her plead for her life. It's the power of having her on her knees and watching her implore God to intervene. He doesn't. She's mine. I am the strongest, I am the best. I used to not understand the Nazi officers and what they did during the Holocaust – I respected their discipline, but I didn't quite get them. Now I do. I've held a beating pulse between my fingers and I've squeezed. And it's the best goddamn feeling in the world.

DIFFORD: You're sick, Beckett. You are fucking sick.

BECKETT: Get over it, Difford. It's guys like me who keep you employed. You were just a backwater no-name county lieutenant until I came along. I was the best thing that ever happened to your career. You should like me.

QUINCY: Jim—

DIFFORD: You're wrong, Beckett. You're not the most powerful person in the world. Theresa is.

BECKETT: What?

DIFFORD: You heard me. Who brought you down, who put you in jail? Face it, you married a sweet eighteen-year-old girl you thought you could control, manipulate, and terrorize to your heart's content. But instead of simply rolling over and playing dead, she figured you out. She learned you, she fought you. She toppled the omnipotent Jim Beckett.

BECKETT: Theresa is a weak, stupid woman who couldn't even stand up to her own father. All you had to do was raise your voice and she cowered in the corner.

DIFFORD: She kept a log on you. All the times you said you were on duty when you weren't. All the times you came home with unexplained scratches and bruises.

BECKETT: She was a jealous wife.

DIFFORD: She tracked the mileage on your odometer. She kept a whole little book of evidence against you, writing in it secretly every night until she finally had enough to call the police. And you never suspected a thing.

BECKETT: Theresa is not that smart!

DIFFORD: She turned you in, Jim. You terrorized her, you traumatized her. You burned everything she owned, told her day in and day out that she was worthless, and still she stood against you.

BECKETT: I made her pay. Every time she takes a step now, she thinks of me.

DIFFORD: And every time you hear the cell doors slam shut, you can think of her.

Pause.

QUINCY: One last question, Jim—

BECKETT: Do you know what I dream of, Difford? Do you know what I think about every night? I dream of the day I see my wife again. I picture sliding my hands around her neck and feeling her hands flail against my chest. I envision choking her to the edge of unconsciousness. And then, while she's lying there, staring at me helplessly, I pick up a dull Swiss Army knife and hack off her fingers one by one. Then her ears. Then her nose. And then, then I cut out her beating heart. I'll do it someday, Difford. And when I do, I'll mail her heart to you.

*

Lieutenant Richard Houlihan walked to the front of the debriefing room and shut off the film projector. At his signal the lights came back on and sixty-five police officers and federal agents blinked owlishly. The room held the largest task force Massachusetts had ever seen. The second largest task force had been assembled two and a half years ago for the same purpose – to find former police officer and serial killer Jim Beckett.

'Now you know what we're up against,' Lieutenant Houlihan said without preamble. 'Jim Beckett has always prided himself on his superior intelligence, and last week he demonstrated again what he can do. At nine A.M. two corrections officers escorted Beckett from 10 Block at Walpole to the Multipurpose Room where he had signed up for time to conduct legal research. The corrections officers had followed proper protocol – Beckett's hands were cuffed behind his back, his legs were shackled, and they were with him at all times. Yet somehow he managed to slip free of the cuffs – we believe he may have fashioned a home made lock pick – and the moment they entered the Multipurpose Room he turned on the two officers. In two minutes he beat both men to death with his bare hands. One officer managed to activate the red alarm on his radio. When Walpole's security officers descended upon the room ninety seconds later, they found Beckett's handcuffs and leg shackles on the floor and two dead men – one missing his uniform and radio. Immediately all units were locked down, the lieutenant in charge issued a red alert, and a full-fledged search began. Somehow in this time period Beckett entered central command dressed as the guard. In full sight of the main facilities he knocked out the lieutenant and sergeant running central command, seized the master key, and unlocked the system, opening all cell doors and blocks.

'In the ensuing prison riot, Beckett simply walked away, still dressed as a corrections officer. It took eight hours to determine that he was missing.

'An eight-hour headstart. Nobody has seen him since.

'I won't lie to you, people. The weeks ahead will be the toughest weeks of your career. The Walpole's IPS [Inner Perimeter Security] Team searched the immediate area for forty-eight hours. They called in the town, county, and state police for support. The National Guard helped search for Jim Beckett. Nothing. The state's Fugitive Squad took over from there. For the last week they have combed Beckett's old neighborhoods, quizzed former associates, and turned the state upside down. The man has no remaining family other than his ex-wife and daughter, no community ties, and no friends. In the NCIC a national warrant has been listed for the man without results. In short, the Fugitive Squad found no leads and now it's up to us.

'You will work harder than you've ever worked, under more pressure than you've ever felt. The governor is watching this case. The state police colonel will receive daily briefings. Some of you have been through this before. Some of you were part of Task Force 22, assembled two and a half years ago also to catch Jim Beckett. That time he eluded capture for six months, then finally surfaced inside the house we were supposed to be protecting. Theresa Beckett almost died that night, and that, people, was our fault.

'In this room we have three task forces assigned to cover three eight-hour shifts. Do not think that because your shift is up you will simply go home. This case is front-page news – the crime hotline is currently logging two *thousand* calls a day. You do not leave until the leads generated on your shift have been recorded, classified appropriately, and followed up as indicated. Friday night Beckett will be featured on *America's Most Wanted*, and we're bringing in truck-loads of volunteers to help man the hotline. He's also listed on the FBI's Web site of America's most wanted – FBI agents will pass along any leads generated there.

'Yes, the work will be long, tedious, and grueling. Yes, morale will be low and tempers high. But we will do this, people. Beckett was once a police officer. He used his shield to lure young women away from their cars and kill them. He has attacked fellow officers, he has brutally murdered two prison guards. There is no case more personal and more important than this one.'

Lieutenant Houlihan shifted back a step, allowing his words to penetrate. When the officers began to lean forward, waiting for the next word, the plan that would catch this particular son of a bitch, he continued.

'Historically Beckett has operated in four states. Those other states have organized smaller task force teams, and they will coordinate their efforts with ours. From New York we have Lieutenant Richardson – please stand. From Vermont is Lieutenant Chajet, and from Connecticut is Lieutenant Berttelli. If you receive calls from these men or their officers, do everything in your power to assist them. They will be happy to return the favor.

'Most of the crossjurisdiction investigation will be coordinated through VICAP [Violent Criminal Apprehension Program]. This system is run by the FBI and is designed to collect, collate, and analyze all parts of the investigation through computer and communications technology. If Beckett strikes in another state, the computer will recognize the MO entered by that state into the system and notify them to contact us. You guys don't have to understand it. Your supervisors have been trained in the system and they will assist you. The big trick is, should you come up with a lead, don't sit on it. Bring it to your supervisor immediately. Speed matters.

'In addition to VICAP, the FBI is providing profiling support. Here with us today is Special Agent Quincy, who you just saw on film interviewing Jim Beckett. He's going to tell us what to look for. Agent.'

Lieutenant Houlihan stepped away from the podium. No one stirred. Police briefings could be rowdy affairs, punctuated by gallows humor and good-natured ribbing. Not this morning. Every officer sat quietly, feet flat on the floor, eyes forward. The seriousness of the matter was etched into every face and the fresh lines creasing each forehead.

Special Agent Quincy stepped up to the podium. He could identify with the officers staring back at him; he'd served as a homicide detective in Chicago and then with the NYPD before getting his doctorate in criminology and joining the Investigative Support Unit at Quantico. Now he worked over one hundred cases at a time, traveling two hundred days a year to profile unsubs, advise local law enforcement agencies on how to catch the unsub, and aid with interrogation of the caught unsub. It was stressful work. One wrong piece of advice and the investigation could head in the wrong direction, costing lives. It was hard work, logging eighty hours a week and thousands of miles. Even when he was back in Quantico, he was shut up in a windowless office sixty feet below ground. Ten times deeper than the dead, they said.

It took its toll on everyone's life. First his wife had complained about the travel. Then she'd complained about his hours. Then one Saturday, when he'd made a point of being home, she'd accidentally sliced off her finger while chopping carrots. She'd walked into the living room, carrying her index finger and appearing one step away from fainting. Quincy had looked at her bloodied hand and severed digit, and he'd thought of the Dahmer crime scene, the Vampire Killer, Kemper's victims, and he'd heard himself say, heaven help him, 'It's only a scratch, dear.'

The divorce papers had arrived last week.

But Quincy still couldn't give up his work. Jim Beckett had been wrong in the interview; FBI profilers did understand about passion, obsession, and compulsion.

Quincy began: 'Jim Beckett is a pure psychopath. Most of you out there probably think you know what that means. I'm here to tell you that you don't. Forget what you've read in the papers. Forget what you've seen in the movies. I'll tell you what to look for and we want you to focus on that. We know this man. We knew him when he killed the first victim, and we knew him when he returned six months after his first disappearance to kill his wife. We knew him in prison and we know him now. Working together, we're going to get him.

'Beckett is a master of disguise. His high IQ and natural charm enable him to blend into almost any situation. Two and half years ago he successfully hid from one of the largest manhunts in New England history for six months. We still don't know where he hid or how he did it. The bottom line is, forget what he looks like. From here on out, he's the unidentified subject, the unsub. And like any unsub, we can catch him without a physical description. We can catch him because of who he is. That's the one thing the unsub can't change.

'All right. Our unsub is a thirty-six-year-old pure psychopath. This means he is highly compartmentalized. On the one hand, he is perfectly aware of community standards and norms. He knows how to fit in, how to be successful, and how to make people like him. He's charming, outgoing, and self-assured. On the other hand, he considers himself outside of societal norms and above anyone he meets. He has no feelings of guilt, remorse, or obligation. He lies easily and is obsessed with appearance. He has a powerful sex drive and in fact, for all his outward disdain toward women, he is dependent on them for his identity and self-esteem. He can't stand to be alone. He will maintain at least one female companion at all times.

'This may not sound like much, but it gives us a lot to work with. First, this is not an unsub who will hole up. His need for companionship, sex, and interaction means he's out there right now, moving among us. He could be the security guard applying for a position at a small Vermont college or the new hire of the Connecticut Highway Department. His disguises will be "macho" – look out for firemen, construction workers, security guards, cowboys, etcetera. He lies easily, which means sooner or later he may trip up and give himself away.

'Second, he is highly materialistic and image-obsessed. Before, he maintained his perfect house, perfect clothes, and perfect car through supplementing his cop's salary with credit card fraud and theft. He'll utilize those skills now, probably stealing cars, wallets, etcetera. Remember, Bundy was first pulled over in Florida on suspicion of auto theft and stolen credit cards. If you receive calls of a middle-aged white male or pretty blond female involved in auto theft, jump.

'Third, we have Beckett's need for women. In prison he hooked up with a young blond groupie named Shelly Zane from the Walpole area. She hasn't been seen since the day of the prison break. Most likely she's his accomplice. In your files you'll find copies of all the letters he sent her. Mostly your generic pornographic prison stuff, but searching Shelly's apartment has already given us our first big break. If you'll turn to the section marked "Possible Aliases" in the binders on your desk . . .

'We assembled this list based on researching Shelly's last two weeks in Walpole. According to her phone records, she made calls to several medical supply stores, different states' motor vehicles departments, and various county records offices. We believe she was helping Beckett create a new identity by researching how to get a new birth certificate. One option, of course, is to order blank certificates from a medical supply store, then forge a doctor's signature and county stamp. That level of forgery would probably hold up to get a license and a social security card.

'However, Beckett will eventually need to leave the country, and birth certificates are checked out when someone applies for a passport. As anyone who's worked fraud here knows, there's only one good way to get a "real" birth certificate. You go to the local library and on microfiche, read the obituaries until you find a kid who was born the same year as you but died in a different county or state several years later. As long as the counties don't cross-reference birth and death certificates, the birth certificate will still be on file. You simply request a copy of that birth certificate from the county and assume it as your own.

'Sure enough, the local librarian told us Shelly had spent four days reading the microfiche of old newspapers. Going through the same newspapers, we found only four names that would fit the criteria for Jim Beckett: Lawrence Talbert, Scott Hannah, Albert McDougal, and Thad Johnson. We've notified the passport office to contact us should anyone request a passport for those names. There's a good chance Beckett will want that passport sooner or later. When he does, we got him.'

A hand came up in back. 'Why are you so sure he'll leave the country?'

'Good question. That brings us to the unsub's last major weakness: his ex-wife, Theresa Williams. As you heard on the tape, Theresa played the key role in Jim's identification and capture. He's never forgiven her for that. Each day in prison he wrote her a letter and in each letter he described exactly how he was going to kill her.

'The women of New England may be terrified now and they may be locking their doors, but frankly they're pretty safe. Beckett is going to kill again, yes. And most likely, Shelly Zane will be his first victim, once she is no longer useful to him. But his real target, his ultimate goal, is Theresa.

'He'll kill her. He'll find their daughter, Samantha, whom he seems to genuinely love. Then he'll get the hell out of Dodge. Through VICAP we track most of the United States and Europe. Jim knows that. It's our guess, given his fascination with the Nazis, that he'll head south to either Brazil or Argentina.'

A new hand went up. 'Which part of the task force is watching Theresa Williams?'

The powers that be exchanged glances. Special Agent Quincy stepped aside and Lieutenant Houlihan took over the podium. 'Ms Williams has opted against police protection.'

'What?' Murmurs broke out. Lieutenant Houlihan raised his hand to settle things down. His reaction had been the same when Difford had called him and outlined the ridiculous plan.

'She knows she's in danger. She decided her best odds lie with her being on her own.'

'We must have at least a few feds on her. He could get to her and no one would even know it.'

'People, her location is given out only on a need-to-know basis, and no one in this room needs to know.'

More grumbles. 'What about the daughter?'

'She is in protective custody with her own guards. None of you need to concern yourself with that.'

Even more grumbles. Cops hated to be left in the dark.

'What about the pattern Beckett mentioned?'

'We're working on that. Any other questions?'

Some people shook their heads. Others exchanged dubious glances. To a person, they already looked stressed.

Lieutenant Houlihan tapped the podium with his fist. 'People, that's a wrap.'

The front doors released a small flood of blue-uniformed officers. They poured into the bright fall sunlight, blinking their eyes and readjusting to daylight. Some walked in pairs, others in small groups. All walked fast, men and women with a lot of work to do.

At the end of the block, one man peeled off from the group, casually waved good-bye, and disappeared down a side street as if his cruiser was parked there.

He didn't get into a car.

He walked down that block, then another, then another. He doubled back, then finally, when it was clear no one was following him, he disappeared into the woods. He stripped off his uniform, revealing the orange construction uniform beneath it. From behind a boulder he produced the hard hat he'd hidden earlier. Shelly had been in charge of securing uniforms, following his instructions, of course. She'd done that part of her job well.

He tucked the police uniform into a paper bag and reentered civilization. His face was already expertly made up – a bit of padding here, the skin tucked there – to give himself a whole new look. After a fifteen-minute walk he arrived at the motel where Lola Gavitz had a room.

'Honey, I'm home.'

Whistling, he locked the door behind himself, then checked the curtains. He didn't bother turning on a light. He tossed the paper bag onto the single queen-size bed and walked through the gloom to the bathroom.

Shelly hung naked in the shower.

Duct tape covered her mouth. More tape bound her wrists and ankles. A small hand towel protected the tender skin of her neck from the clothesline he'd wrapped around it. The other end of the clothesline was attached to the shower head, suspending Shelly three inches off the ground. Classic autoerotic asphyxiation setup. One did learn so many useful things as a police officer.

Shelly could keep the clothesline from strangling her by looping her arms over the showerhead and holding herself up. Or she could swing her feet onto the edge of the bathtub. Of course, then she ran the risk of her feet slipping off and the sudden fall snapping her neck.

Her arms must have gotten tired though, for now she did have her feet on the edge of the tub. As he entered the bathroom, she raised her head wearily, her long blond hair sliding back from hollow eyes.

He looked at her feet. He curled one hand around her ankle. One push, that's all it would take.

She rolled her eyes in terror.

'What do you think, Shelly? Do you want to live?'

She nodded as furiously as she could with a clothes-line around her neck.

'The police predicts that I'll kill you once you're no longer useful to me. Are you still useful to me?'

More nodding.

He reached up and slowly loosened the clothesline. She collapsed into the tub like a sack of grain. He studied her for a moment, noting the silky cascade of blond hair over white skin. He stroked that hair for a bit. Then he undid his construction overalls and let them fall to the floor.

Shelly stirred in the bathtub, recognizing her cue. She lifted her face and he ripped off the duct tape with one quick tear.

'That's a good girl. Remember, you have to be useful, Shelly. You have to be useful.'

Her mouth closed around him. He let himself relax by degrees into the frantic sucking. His hands continued to stroke her blond hair, lifting it in fistfuls and releasing it. For one moment he indulged himself in the fantasy that it was not Shelly on her hands and knees in front of him, but Theresa. His stupid wife, Theresa.

He'd never made her perform like this. He'd never made her do any of the things he'd had the others do. She was his wife, the mother of his child. He'd considered her separate. Now he saw the error of his ways.

Now he dreamed of all the things he would have her do when he saw her again.

He closed his eyes and his hands curled around Shelly's/Theresa's neck.

'I'm coming for you, baby. I'm coming for you.'

8

She was fading on him. Her strokes had long since passed the fluid point. She did little more than beat at the water, and he could see her chin trembling. Twenty laps, that's all she'd done. Barely over four hundred yards, when he could swim three thousand. Jesus, they were in trouble.

He'd started her with calisthenics. She couldn't do a single push-up. Fine. Arm muscles were a problem for some women, and she had a particularly slight build. They'd moved on to stretching. Her flexibility was pretty good. She did a solid twenty sit-ups, survived twenty jumping jacks. He'd moved her on to squats, and she practically keeled over on him. No arm muscles, no legs.

The woman was beyond out of shape. She simply had no muscle mass. And skin and bones didn't fight very well.

'Another,' J.T. commanded.

'No,' Angela said, but was too tired to put any force behind her word.

He scowled at her, she turned sluggishly into another lap. 'You call that form?' he barked out. He needed a whistle.

'I told you, I'm not a good swimmer.'

'No kidding. And no push-ups, no squats. Honey, how have you gotten through life?'

'Housewives don't do the Iron Man,' she snapped. Well, it was something. If all else failed, maybe she could verbally spar Big Bad Jim into the ground.

She reached the end of the pool, and without his permission clung to the wall. Her shoulders were shaking. She placed her cheek against the patio as if finding a pillow.

She looked like a worn-out child. She looked like someone ought to pick her up, curl her in his arms, and rock her to sleep while stroking her hair.

J.T. stalked away from her in a hurry.

'Know what your problem is?'

'No, but everyone seems to have a theory.' Her lips twisted into that enigmatic, too-old smile that meant she was referring to her husband and the suitcase of secrets she wouldn't share.

'You think too much.'

'I've heard that before.'

'I mean it. You're clinging to the patio and you're thinking, I'm tired. You're thinking, My legs hurt. Tell me I'm wrong, Angela.'

Her eyes finally opened, her lashes spiky with water. 'All right. I'm tired, my legs hurt.'

'You have to find the zone.'

'The zone?'

'The zone. You ever play sports?'

'Sports?'

'Sports, Angela. You know, football, basketball, hockey, swimming, whatever. We can look it up in the dictionary if you'd like.'

'I . . . I was a cheerleader.'

'Now, why didn't I guess that?'

'It's not as easy as everyone thinks,' she retorted immediately. 'It takes a lot of flexibility and discipline. Have you ever been able to kick above your shoulder? I don't think so. We practiced very hard and it was brutal on the knees.'

'I'm not arguing. Must take some strength too, building pyramids, all that.'

'Yes. But I was one of the smaller girls. I was the top, not the base.'

'Ever fall?'

'All the time.'

'Get back up?'

'All the time.'

'Why?'

'Because that's what you were supposed to do.'

'Exactly. So you didn't think about it. You didn't say, "I hurt too much." Or "I'm afraid." Or "She'll drop me again." You just got back up because you were supposed to.

'That's what you do here, Angela. You swim and you keep swimming without a thought in your head because that's what you have to do. And you do the push-ups and you jog and you do all the things beyond exhaustion because you have to. Then one day you'll discover you're in the zone and you don't feel your legs anymore, you don't feel your arms anymore. You exist just as motion. That's the zone. Then you can do anything.'

She looked fascinated, she looked awed. He wasn't comfortable with her looking at him like that. He was just telling her the facts, not revealing the laws of the universe.

People thought soldiers and jocks were brutish men. It wasn't true. A lot of the Navy SEALs or Green Berets or Force Recon Marines looked more like accountants. Some of them were small enough to be nicknamed Mouse. Others were six four and so stringbean skinny they could barely walk through a strong wind. Extreme performance was not physical but mental. It was focus and concentration. It was finding that internal zone, where you could zero down the universe to one act, one motion, one goal. You could plow facedown through mud in the pouring rain because you were not thinking of the weight of your pack or the cold sting of the rain or the taste of the mud. You were not thinking of the two hours' sleep you'd had last night or the twelve miles you'd run this morning or the two hundred push-ups and two hundred pull-ups you'd done the minute before. You thought only of the next inch you had to crawl and then the inch after that. The world became a simple place.

And for a moment you could do anything.

SpecWar superstuds were not Arnold Schwarzenegger. They were Buddhist monks.

And former Force Recon Marines like J.T. were the men who realized the zone couldn't last forever. Sooner or later, training ended, combat ended, everything ended, and you were the same man you always were, lying on your bunk with the rage bunching your shoulders and the unrelenting memories racing through your mind.

Then you poured yourself a drink.

'I'll do another lap,' Angela volunteered. Her eyes had narrowed. His pep talk must have worked, because she looked fierce.

'You do that.'

She pushed off with more force than grace. She didn't have a swimsuit, so she wore an oversize T-shirt and shorts. The excess material created a lot of drag and quickly slowed her down. She slogged forward anyway.

Toward the end she faltered badly, and he thought he might have to drag her out by the scruff of her neck to keep her from drowning. Her flailing hands found the patio as he took the first step forward.

'No zone,' she gasped. 'God, this is horrible!'

He sat on the edge of the pool beside her and stuck his feet in the water. 'You want it to be simple. It's not.'

'Oh, how the hell would you know! Look at you!' She waved her hand at him. 'You probably catch rattlesnakes by hand. How hard has any of this ever been for you? How hard?'

'Not very,' he agreed calmly. 'I was born for this shit.'

'I hate you.' She rested her forehead against the pool edge.

He let her feel sorry for herself for a minute. Why not? There was a world of difference between the two of them. The colonel was a mean, lean bastard and he'd passed his genes to his children. In contrast, Angela had a small, slight build and no natural hand-eye coordination. She would have to fight for every lap, war with every shot. Nobody said life was fair.

'Your daughter, she's for real?'

Angela stiffened instantly, so he took that as a yes.

'Think about her, then. Don't think about yourself, focus on her.'

'What do you think has gotten me this far?'

'Huh.' They sat in silence. 'How old is she?'

Angela couldn't seem to decide how much to tell him. 'Four,' she said after a moment. 'She's four.'

'You have her someplace safe?'

'As safe as can be expected.'

'Huh.'

'Okay, it's time for another lap.'

He was surprised. '*Chiquita*, you're pretty beat.'

'I have to learn how to do this. If I'm weak, then I'd better get strong. Two more laps, all right?'

'You are stubborn.'

She appeared startled. 'I'm not stubborn.'

'Of course you're stubborn. You made it here, didn't you? What do you call that?'

'Desperation,' she said frankly.

He shook his head. 'No, trust me, you're stubborn.'

'Really?' She looked pleased. 'I'm stubborn. Good. I'm going to need that.'

She pushed off while he remained sitting there, blinking his eyes and wondering if he would ever understand her. The woman had spirit. He would've liked to have met her before the world had run her into the ground. He had the feeling that she'd been beautiful once. A petite, smiling woman with long blond hair.

Jesus, J.T. Give it up.

Behind him, the screen door slid open.

'So where's the mystery intruder?'

J.T. pointed toward the pool.

'Oh, for God's sake,' Marion said as she walked over to the edge. 'She looks like she's drowning.'

'That's her version of the doggie paddle.'

'You're kidding me.'

'Nope. Still think she's a fugitive?'

Marion finally appeared skeptical. 'I don't know,' she hedged. 'She doesn't look like much, but given the company you usually keep . . .'

'Gee, thanks, Marion. That's kind of you.'

They watched as Angela reached the end of the pool and struggled her way back. It was a long, painful process for everyone.

J.T. shook his head. 'I don't think one month is going to be enough.'

Angela finally reached J.T. and Marion, her face beet red. She clung to the edge of the pool while introductions were made. The two women showed about as much enthusiasm as could be expected.

'You can call me L.B. for short,' Angela said.

'L.B.?'

'Lizzie Borden.'

'Oh.' Marion had the good grace to flush. 'I'll confess, you're not what I expected.'

'I'm not a criminal.' Angela tried to pull herself out of the water, but her exhausted arms wouldn't cooperate. J.T. grabbed her shoulders and lifted her as if she were a featherweight. She returned her attention to Marion. 'In fact I've worked with the FBI before.'

'Whatever problems you have, I'm sure I can recommend a good law enforcement agency—'

'No, you can't. I've been through it all. I've worked with them all. And I know for certain that law enforcement can no longer help me. What I need is someone like your brother. J.T. is going to help.'

'Wait a second.' J.T. took a quick step back, waving his hands in defense. 'I'm just training you!'

'Exactly. That's the help I need. So tell me, *sensei*, what's next on the list?'

He looked at her for a moment, then at Marion. His sister was mutinous and disapproving. In fact, the only calm person on the patio was Angela.

'What's your name?' Marion prodded. 'If you have nothing to hide, you won't mind giving me your name.'

'I have nothing to hide and I do mind giving you my name. It's none of your business. Besides, if I remember correctly, you told J.T. you were here as his sister, not an agent.'

'Ignore her, Angela, Marion can't help herself.'

'I'm trying to offer help.'

'Then thanks but no thanks. Now, if you'll excuse me, I can afford only a month of J.T.'s time and I have a lot to learn. Is it time to eat yet? I'll make the oatmeal. J.T. is too dangerous with a saucepan.'

She headed for the house without another word. Marion released her pent-up breath in a low hiss. 'Jesus Christ, J.T., what have you gotten yourself into now?'

'I'm just training her on how to protect herself, Marion. How bad can it be?'

'With you, J.T., pretty bad. But that's okay, I'll keep my opinions to myself for now. Why don't you go and pour yourself another beer.'

'I can't.'

'You can't?'

He scowled. 'I agreed to stop drinking for the month.'

She arched a brow. 'Of course, J.T.'

'Dammit, I am *not* an alcoholic!'

'Of course, J.T.'

She smiled sweetly and walked away.

J.T. squeezed Angela a glass of fresh orange juice; that gave Marion her first opportunity. A cold drink created condensation on a glass, ruining fingerprints. A hot drink suffered the same due to steam. A room-temperature drink was perfect. She joined them for the end of breakfast, behaved admirably by making polite conversation, and offered to do the dishes. She set Angela's glass and spoon to the side. Later, when J.T. took Angela outside for a walk, Marion got out her fingerprint kit and went to work. One full thumbprint and two partial indexes later, she called the lab.

'The Nogales police will be faxing you some prints this afternoon. I want you to run them for me immediately. Call me here as soon as you know. Talk only to me. Are we clear? No, no, I have to go through the police – I don't have a fax machine here. It's not a big deal. They're just backwater cops, they'll cooperate. We can trust them.'

9

Nightfall. J.T. stood over the barbecue wearing a Red Hot Cajun Lover apron and grilling boneless breasts of chicken. Marion was tossing a salad and downing beers as if she were determined to pick up where her brother had left off.

Tess didn't cook anything. She didn't help with anything, and J.T. and Marion seemed fine with that. It had been seven years since she'd had someone cook for her. She found she wasn't very good at letting go. Her fingers twitched at her sides while the anxiety built in her belly. She was supposed to look perfect for dinner, hair done, makeup done, dressed to the nines. She was supposed to have Samantha fed ahead of time so she would play quietly in the bassinet, where Jim could admire his child without being bothered by her. The table had to be set a certain way, candles lit, flowers fresh, forks on the left, dessert spoon above, knife and spoon on the right. Their three-bedroom house should be spotless, the old hardwood floor smelling of lemon wax while the area rugs were freshly vacuumed and cleared of children's toys.

Jim had chosen their house because of the beautifully carved wood trim around the fireplace and windows. In other old homes, some generation always made the mistake of painting the trim white or cream or olive green. Fine old wood latexed out of existence. Not in their home. Jim had turned the original oak trim over to her like a precious gem. It had survived one hundred and twenty years. It gave their home the class and elegance befitting a decorated police officer. Nothing had better happen to the mantel or the banister or the door jambs on her watch.

When Samantha was one year old, she'd gotten her hands on a spatula covered in spaghetti sauce. She'd waved it with glee, promptly splattering red dye no. 5 all over herself, the walls, and the oak windowsill. Two drops on the hundred-and-twenty-year-old wood and Theresa couldn't get them to come all the way out. She tried Formula 409, she tried mayonnaise. She set a plant there on a lace doily and hoped Jim would never figure out that she'd failed in her mission. Two weeks later he'd dragged her out of bed at two A.M. He took her down to the kitchen. He handed her sandpaper and stain. And he stood over her until seven A.M., supervising her sanding down and restaining the window frame, his arms crossed and his face grim. Samantha began to cry upstairs.

Jim made her continue to work while her arms ached, her eyelids dragged down, and her daughter sobbed her name in the little room above.

Tess curled her fingers into the lounge cushion to get them to stop shaking. Those days were gone. She could rest if she wanted. She could wear old shorts and a T-shirt to the dinner table. She could play games with her daughter in the living room without worrying about a piece of Lego hiding under the sofa and getting her in trouble later. She could abstain from makeup. She could simply be herself.

If she could ever figure out who that person was.

She rolled onto her stomach and carefully stretched out her back. She hurt. J.T. had led her through a tough regimen of swimming and weight lifting. She figured she must have some muscle after all, because surely bone couldn't hurt that much.

J.T. had done most of it with her. He'd stretched. He'd done fifty push-ups and two hundred stomach crunches. Then he'd stood on his head with his back to the wall and lowered his straight legs until his toes touched the ground. Up and down. Up and down. Her stomach had hurt just watching.

'Take a couple of Advil before you go to bed,' J.T. advised from the grill. 'You'll be grateful in the morning.'

'If I live that long,' she muttered. She rolled over onto her side. She was sore around her ribs. She hadn't realized muscle existed there.

'Food's ready. Eat up. We'll take a walk after dinner. It's important you don't get stiff.'

She said, 'Aaaagh.'

'Remember, no whining.'

'For God's sake, J.T. Give the woman a glass of wine and ease up before you kill her.'

Tess looked at Marion with surprise, then gratitude. Marion had remained in the house most of the day. Tess could pinpoint her location by following the smell of chain-smoked cigarettes. Now the agent was dressed in fine linen slacks and a classic cream-colored silk blouse with billowing sleeves and graceful cuffs. With her hair pulled back in a French twist, delicate gold hoops winking at her ears, and more gold accenting her narrow leather belt, she belonged in an upper-class garden party. Her face, however, ruined the impression. Her delicate features were frozen into a hard look, her blue eyes perpetually narrowed into a stern, suspicious stare. When she walked, she had the fast, determined footsteps of a woman who would mow you down if you didn't get the hell out of her way.

If Marion MacAllister had met Jim Beckett, Tess was sure she would have fired her gun first and asked questions later.

They ate out on the patio. Marion served a salad with a light raspberry vinaigrette. J.T. barbecued chicken accompanied by dirty rice and beans.

She needed protein, he told her, and dumped an extra spoonful of rice and beans on her plate.

She ate everything, discovering an appetite that was powerful and foreign to her. She started out with silverware and delicate movements. Then she gave up and followed J.T.'s example, greedily tearing the chicken into strips and popping them into her mouth with her fingers.

'Is Freddie coming back?' she asked between mouthfuls.

J.T. and Marion exchanged glances. 'No,' J.T. said, his gaze never leaving Marion's.

Marion simply shrugged. She ate only the salad and half a chicken breast. After warring with herself for a full minute, Tess helped herself to the other half.

'Go easy,' J.T. commented.

'I know how to eat.'

He raised one brow but shut up. For all his words of caution, he ate two whole chicken breasts and three helpings of rice and black beans. He chewed voraciously, chasing down his food with long gulps of iced tea.

And every now and then she saw his gaze slide to Marion's beer with barely tamped hunger.

'So what did we learn in fugitive training camp today?' Marion asked at last. Done with her meal, she sat back and lit up.

'Swimming and weights,' Tess volunteered.

'She has a ways to go,' J.T. supplied.

The conversation drifted. They listened in silence to the distant sound of crickets singing in the dusk and the occasional whir of hummingbirds among the cactus.

'Do you swim?' Tess asked Marion.

'A little.'

'She rides. Dressage.' J.T. pushed his plate away. His gaze rested on his sister. 'At least she did when we were younger.'

'I stopped.'

'Hmm.'

'There was no point to it,' she said sharply. 'No one rides horses in real life. It's not a usable or marketable skill. Really, it was a waste of time.'

'You think?' J.T. drawled neutrally.

His fingers rotated the empty glass in front of him, sliding up the condensation on the side, then twirling the base again. 'I used to watch you ride. I thought you were pretty good.'

'You watched me ride?'

'Yeah. I did. Could never figure out how you managed it. Such a tiny thing commanding a twelve-hundred-pound beast around the ring. I used to think you belonged to the horse more than you belonged to us.'

'I never saw you at the arena.'

'I didn't want to interrupt.'

'Huh,' Marion said. There seemed to be a wealth of suspicion in that grunt.

J.T. turned to Tess. 'What did you do?'

'Who, me?'

'I assume you had a childhood, unless that stork story's true after all.'

The question caught her off guard. She wasn't used to anyone asking about herself. 'I did Girl Scouts,' she answered finally. 'I didn't have hobbies or things like that. I worked after school. My parents owned a general store with a small deli. Cheese, fudge, gourmet foods. It was a lot of work.'

'Working-class parents?' Marion asked. 'New England, right? You have a northern accent.' She was obviously taking mental notes.

'Down, girl,' J.T. said lightly. He offered Tess a crooked grin. 'Forgive Marion. Unlike you, we never worked as children – our father did the smart thing and married money. Now Marion is hell bent on overcoming this stigma by turning into a workaholic. We can't take her anywhere anymore. She's liable to arrest the host for income tax evasion.'

'One of us had to have follow-through. You certainly don't.' Marion stubbed out her cigarette and reached for another. She said to Tess, 'You want to know a little bit about your hero? Well, let me tell you.'

'Uh-oh,' J.T. said.

'J.T. at seventeen. He's into orienteering. Do you know what orienteering is?'

Tess shook her head. Tension swept over the table. J.T. hadn't moved, but his expression was tighter. Lines had appeared at the corners of his mouth. Marion leaned forward and plunged on.

'Orienteering is a sport from Scandinavia, developed during one of the world wars. Basically you're turned loose with a detailed topographic map of an area and thirteen controls—'

'Flags,' J.T. supplied.

'Flags to find. You have a compass, you have a map, and you have three hours to find however many flags you can find.

'It can be brutal. The courses are rated for difficulty and the truly advanced ones – the red and blue courses – aren't even forest trails, they're just flags left in the forest. You get to plow through the underbrush, hike up mountains, cross teeming rivers. People get lost. People get injured. You have to know what you're doing.'

'I knew what I was doing,' J.T. said. 'I made it back.'

'Barely!' Marion returned her attention to Tess. 'So here's J.T., seventeen years old and already arrogant. You think he's insufferable now? You should've known him then.'

'I was a saint.'

'Get over it. These competitions, class A meets, are a big deal. You compete by age group and prizes are given out. Our father always dominated the blue course, the hardest level. He always won first prize. Then we have J.T. He's still too young for the blue course. He's seventeen and the toughest course for him is the red, and he's good. Everyone thinks he'll win it and everyone's talking about how the father will take blue and the son will take red. The colonel's already choosing the spots on the mantel.'

Her jaw set, her gaze hardened. 'Morning of the meet. *Morning of the meet.* Does J.T. register for his category in the red course? No. He registers for blue. A seventeen-year-old kid registering for blue.'

'I'd already done red,' J.T. said. 'I wanted something new.'

'You would've won!'

'Trophy's nothing but cheap metal that gathers dust.'

'So what happened?' Tess demanded to know.

'Einstein here,' Marion supplied in a low growl, 'goes running off in his orienteering suit. Three hours later he's nowhere to be found. Two hours after that they're arranging the search parties, when all of sudden from the underbrush comes this huge commotion. Thrashing and cursing and swearing. Mothers are running to cover the ears of their children, and lo and behold, it's J.T. Half of his face scratched off, both of his hands mutilated, and his ankle in a twig brace. He'd fallen off the side of a hill.'

'It happens.'

'It wouldn't have if you'd stuck to red!'

'It did. And I made it back.' He turned to Tess with a wicked grin. 'Walked two miles on a broken ankle. How's that for *cojones*?'

'More like stupidity,' Marion muttered.

'The colonel was impressed.' J.T.'s voice was deceptively innocent, but Marion flinched. 'That was the kind of thing Daddy liked,' J.T. continued, his eyes fastened on Marion's face. 'Enduring pain. Having balls. Walking on broken bones. Being an m-a-n.'

Marion remained silent. Between her fingers, the cigarette trembled.

'He was wrong, you know,' J.T. said. His fingers spun away the glass in front of him. 'He should've let you compete, Marion. The orienteering, the Civil War Reenactment Society. I taught you how to read the compass, do you remember that?'

'No.'

'What about my percussion rifle? You watched me carve out the stock from the black walnut during the afternoons. Do you remember that, or did you block that out too, Marion? Did you leave all the memories behind?'

Marion remained mutinously silent.

'I remember,' J.T. said softly. 'I remember you watching me forge the barrel and locks. Took me a year to carve out that damn rifle and you watched every day. I remember you trying to pick it up – you must have been ten or eleven. But at four and a half feet long and a front-heavy twelve pounds, it was too big for you. You couldn't get the end of the barrel off the ground. So you poured the powder in it instead and rammed down the patch and ball with the rod. Then I lifted the rifle waist-high so you could half cock it, place the percussion cap, and move it to full cock. All that was left for me was to raise it to my shoulder, aim, and fire. Do you remember that, Marion? Do you remember any fucking thing?'

'You're lying.'

'Why, Marion? Why would I lie about that?'

'Because that's what you do, J.T. Invent fantasies.'

'About percussion rifles?'

'You can't stand the truth. You can't stand knowing just how much Daddy gave you, just how much Daddy favored you, and just how badly you fucked up anyway.'

J.T.'s knuckles whitened. Then abruptly J.T. pushed away. 'Sure, Marion, that's it.' He stood and began gathering dishes. 'Everything happened the way you imagined and Daddy's only crime was shutting you out. You do have follow-through. If you'd done orienteering, you would've won the trophy.'

'We'll never know, will we?'

'No, we won't. At least you have trophies from dressage.'

'Who the hell cared about dressage?'

'You did, Marion.'

Marion rose. She wouldn't look at J.T. She grabbed three plates, creating more noise than necessary, then stalked through the sliding glass door.

J.T.'s gaze remained on the door. His hands held two glasses in midair.

'You'll have to forgive her,' he murmured after a bit. 'She can be very intense.' He gathered more dishes, his movements short and choppy. 'Wanna hand me that bowl?'

'I'll help.'

'You don't have to – you must be sore as hell.' He wouldn't look at her. His gaze fixed on the table, his voice brusque. Still, she could see the darkness rolling upon him, bunching the muscles on his neck, rounding his shoulders. The patio lights washed over his face but couldn't penetrate the shuttered look masking his expression. Just his hands moved, long, callused fingers reaching, grasping, stacking. Thrusting, lifting, slamming, rapping out a staccato beat of frustration and anger that ran all the way through him and deep into the ground. 'Take some Advil,' he commanded crisply. 'Get some rest. You got a helluva lot of work ahead of you, Angie. None of it's going to be easy.'

'All right.' She still didn't move.

'Get in the house, Angela.'

'I could carry something in.'

'I don't need any help.'

She remained standing beside him, not sure what she wanted and not sure why she stayed. She studied his face, looking for something that eluded her. His expression didn't offer her any miracles. 'You . . . you and your sister, you grew up doing this stuff, didn't you?'

'What stuff?' He finished stacking all the plates and bowls. Now he gathered silverware.

'Orienteering and the Civil War reenactment. Horses and hunting. Swimming.'

'*I* did it, not Marion. The colonel was more interested in his son than his daughter. It worked for a while. Then I got too old and stubborn, stopped winning the trophies, got sick of shooting Bambi. And maybe the colonel stopped trusting me with a gun in his presence. The colonel wasn't stupid.'

Tess shivered.

'No more father-son outings,' J.T. announced. 'I joined the swim team and became the one-mile freestyle champ for Virginia instead. The colonel thought swimming was for sissies. I think he had something against men shaving their legs.' He gathered up the glasses.

'I wish I'd learned all that,' Tess said softly. 'I wish my family had been into those kinds of things. That I'd had an older brother or uncle or anyone to teach me about guns or self-defense or survival. Even how to read a compass. I wish I'd *known* it sooner.'

J.T. turned toward her. His eyes were empty and spiritless. 'Yeah, Marion and I, we're tough. We're just so damn tough.'

He carried dishes to the house. 'Tomorrow we start with handguns.'

Tess slept and, as always, Jim found her again in her dreams. In the shadows of the night she was back in Williamstown, lying in bed, the covers pulled up to her chin.

He's going to come out of the closet, she thought. Her mother had told her there was no such thing as monsters, but her mother had lied because her mother hadn't wanted to believe in such people as Jim Beckett.

He's going to come out of the closet. Run, Tess, run.

But she couldn't run. She had no muscle. She was a shapeless blob, a weak, defenseless feather pillow.

In the distance she heard a baby crying. She knew she had to move. *You must protect Sam. You have to protect Sam.*

It was too late. Her closet door slid open and he stepped into the room, grinning and golden and hefting the baseball bat.

'Did you miss me, Theresa? I missed you.'

She whimpered. She heard the plea bubble in her throat and she knew she was going to die. Samantha had stopped crying, maybe she sensed the danger. Please let her remain quiet. If she would just remain quiet long enough . . .

Jim leaned against the wall and bounced the baseball bat off his ankle. 'Where's Sam?'

'Gone,' she whispered. *Don't cry, Sam. Don't cry.*

'Tell me. I'm her father. I have rights.' He lifted the bat and stalked toward the bed.

'I am going to kill you, Theresa. Samantha will be all mine, and you're too pathetic to do anything about it.'

The bat lifted and she whimpered and she remained frozen, watching it arch.

The house was silent, her baby was silent. No more crying.

'Discipline is the key,' Jim whispered, and the bat whistled down.

Tess woke up, terrified and already reaching for the phone. She wanted to call Difford and hear Samantha's voice. Her fingers clenched convulsively around the receiver as she lay in bed, her chest heaving, the sweat rolling down her cheeks.

Slowly she forced her fingers to relax. It was dangerous to call Sam at the safe house, dangerous to do anything that would connect her daughter to her. If you really want to keep her safe, Difford had told her, you have to let her go.

So Tess let her go. Tess hugged her baby, kissed the top of her sweet-smelling head, and let her go.

And now she curled up in her bed, hugging her pillow as if it were her daughter, and thirsting for the scent of baby powder. Six A.M. Massachusetts time. Sam would be at the waking edge of slumber. Did she sleep well at the safe house, or did she have nightmares the way she sometimes did? During those times Tess would crawl in bed beside her and whisper the story of Cinderella with Sam cradled in her arms and smelling like Johnson & Johnson's No More Tears shampoo. They would both make it through the night and in the morning, like any child, Sam would smile and be happy once more.

Tess wanted so much more for her daughter than running from city to city and living in fear. She wanted Sam to grow up feeling smart and strong. She wanted her daughter to know she was beautiful and loved because Tess's parents had never told her any such thing.

She wanted Sam to be happy, and the desire made the darkness sweep over her like a wool blanket, stifling her. She wasn't sure how to give the gift of joy. She wasn't sure how to be a good parent. She had no examples to follow.

Four A.M. She crawled out of bed, shaking and shivering and feeling her leg throb. She saw Jim stepping out of the closet and heard the crack of the baseball bat connecting with her leg.

I'm going to kill you, Theresa. Sam will be mine.

Tess padded through the silent house. Not knowing what else to do, she followed J.T.'s lead. She jumped into the pool and started to swim.

Edith Magher took pride in her garden. She'd lived alone all her life, never having found Mr Right, and by the time she was forty she knew she was destined to be a childless spinster and that was that. She adopted her garden instead, each flower, stalk, and leaf becoming precious to her.

She worked outside every day, spring through fall. In the narrow six streets that served as her tiny neighbourhood, she was widely regarded as having the best yard, and even that new couple who bought the house on the corner kept their big, pawing Labradors at bay.

She was outside now, preparing her flower beds for winter. Late September was generally beautiful in Lenox, Massachusetts, the trees turning a rich gold, the sky an unbelievably bright blue. This year, however, the weather was turning cold unusually fast. On the news they were already issuing frost warnings, and even the diehards who vowed never to turn on their furnace until the first of November were beginning to think twice. Edith hadn't decided whether she was prepared to turn on her heat yet, but she was definitely tending to her garden. She believed firmly in being prepared, which was why she'd been able to retire from her bank teller job at the age of sixty instead of slaving away until sixty-five, as so many others had. This afternoon was perfect for gardening; the huge maple tree in her yard reflected a dozen shades of gold and the slowly sinking sun made the leaves even deeper. When Edith breathed in deeply, she caught the rich odors of drying leaves, fertile earth, and mulled spices. Some people worked on their gardens in the morning, but Edith had always preferred dusk.

Yesterday she'd gotten word that her dear neighbor Mrs Martha Ohlsson was finally returning from Florida. Given the news that that horrible serial killer – Jim Beckett, that was his name – had just escaped from Walpole, Edith was looking forward to Martha's return. Living next to an empty house no longer seemed safe.

Edith reminded herself every night as she locked up her tiny two-bedroom bungalow that she had nothing to worry about. Her community was a small one, a quiet one. The heart of Lenox boasted old, beautiful Victorian houses that had once been the summer homes of Boston's elite. Edith Wharton had given Lenox its claim to fame by building her mansion on the outskirts of town. Neighboring Tanglewood spread its lush green grounds and unbelievable mountain view for people who appreciated the Boston Symphony's fine music and mother nature's even finer grandeur. Between Tanglewood and the Wharton mansion, Lenox saw a fair amount of tourists during the bright summer months and brilliant fall.

Now, thanks to the unexpected cold spell, Lenox was already taking on its winter rhythms, tranquil and slow. Nothing much had happened in Edith Magher's community since a few years before, when the Joneses' oldest son had broken his arm in a car accident.

Every now and then, however, Edith had these spells. Not often – it had been years since the last one. But she was having them now, and sometimes at night she found herself lying awake just listening to the sound of her own heartbeat. She looked over her shoulder more too, as if expecting to see something awful.

Her great-great grandmother Magher supposedly had had the gift of sight. Edith didn't believe in such things. She trusted only the earth, the power of mother nature, and the beauty of her garden.

Which was why when she looked up now and saw the ephemeral image of a thin blond girl standing at the base of the old oak with blood on her face, Edith shook her head and said, 'Don't you do that to me.'

The vision politely vanished.

Edith went back inside her house and brewed a strong cup of black tea.

10

'Don't stand there.'

'Why not?'

J.T. grabbed her arm and dragged her toward him.

'Because that's a jumping cholla.'

Tess glanced at the stubby, fuzz-covered cactus then gazed at his long, tanned fingers still wrapped tightly around her upper arm. 'So?'

He shook his head, massaging his temples with one hand. His eyes were bloodshot, his cheeks thick with beard. For a change, his black hair was pulled into a ponytail and he'd donned a worn T-shirt and a pair of sandals. They were his only concessions to civility, however. He'd gone twenty-four hours without alcohol and was hell on wheels. '*Jumping* cholla, Angela. See all those tiny, furry spurs? Trust me, you won't think they're so tiny and furry when those glochids leap onto your arms and hook into your skin.'

'But it's just a plant!' As she said this, however, she was eyeing the cactus with suspicion and taking a step closer to J.T.

'It's a particularly talented plant.'

He released her arm, then stepped away. He was definitely cagey.

In contrast, she felt optimistic. She didn't care how much oatmeal J.T. made her swallow or how many laps she swam, she'd never be able to compare to a man's strength.

But a gun . . .

As J.T. lifted the small, silvery semiautomatic out of the case, she nodded. She was going to become a master marksman. That would be her advantage. Jim might be stronger than her and he might be faster than her, but not even the omnipotent Jim Beckett could outrace a bullet.

In the hot, dusty desert of Nogales, Tess was going to become the next James Bond – licensed to kill.

And she would stand there in the shadowed room, watching Jim step out of the closet like the real-life monster no one wanted to imagine. She wouldn't cower anymore. She wouldn't shake. She would not beg for her life and she would not fear for her daughter. She would stand, tall and regal, her face as cool and composed as Marion's. She would point her .22,

THE PERFECT HUSBAND

watching Jim suddenly freeze, suddenly pale, and suddenly realize that now she was the one in control.

'Can I hold it?' she asked quietly.

J.T. lifted up the gun, then froze when he saw the gleam in her eye.

'It's not a toy,' he said sharply.

'I hope not.'

'Keep the safety on, never place your finger on the trigger until ready to shoot, and don't *ever* point it at a person, even in jest. Those are the rules.'

'Yes, sir.'

J.T. shook his head. 'You just don't get it. You ju—'

'Is that the target?' She turned away from him, her veins humming with heady adrenaline. Twenty-one feet from her, two bales of straw sprouted from yellow Arizona dust. Red and white ringed targets were attached to the front of each bale by thick nails in the corner. The targets weren't that far away. They were good-sized. She thought she could take them.

J.T. didn't say anything, but she felt his gaze on her as he gave her the semiautomatic. She held it out and practiced looking down the sight. She'd held a gun a few times before. Fired one a few times. Hit a man.

She knew more than J.T. suspected. She liked it that way.

'When can I take the safety off?'

'Take the safety off? A – you're not wearing earplugs nor eye protection. B – the gun's not loaded. C – where did you learn that awful stance?'

His harsh words briefly dimmed her euphoria, but she nodded. She was there to learn. He would teach her.

J.T. tossed her earplugs and eye goggles, shoved a box of bullets in his pocket, and wrapped his body around hers.

'Here, like this.' His arms sandwiched hers, bringing her arms up straight and adjusting her grip. His groin cradled her hips and his thighs burned into her legs. Something hard and unyielding pressed into her left buttock. The box of bullets, she thought. Her stomach felt hollow.

J.T. adjusted her arms and legs as if she were a mannequin. 'We'll start with the Weaver stance which uses two hands for better control while twisting your body so you make less of a target. Face to the side, feet slightly apart for balance. Now extend your right arm toward the target, using your left to pull your arm against your chest and secure your grip. There you go. Now look down the barrel. Don't squint. You've been watching too many Dirty Harry movies.'

He withdrew. She almost fell.

'What do you see, Angela?'

'Straw?'

'No shit. Pick a ring, any ring.'

'The bull's-eye,' she said fiercely. She made the mistake of moving and lost her stance. He arranged her once more, looking impatient.

'Shoulders down, arms straight. Tuck the butt of the gun in the V

89

between your index finger and thumb. Grip it firmly. Now, see the front notch on the gun?'

She nodded.

'That's your front sight. You want to align it perfectly between the two rear sights. Then you want to aim at the target so the bull's-eye sits right on top of your aligned front sight, like a full moon. Got it?'

She nodded vigorously. 'Can I take off the safety?'

'Fine. We'll do a dry run first so you can get used to the feel of the trigger.'

'All right.' It took her four tries to push the safety down.

'Okay,' J.T. continued crisply. 'You have a Walther .22 semiautomatic pistol there, just like the one you were carrying. It's not a powerful gun and it's not super accurate, but it's small, easy to conceal, and reliable. If you're at close range, you'll hit something. So for you, that means let the attacker get in close, aim for the chest, which is the biggest target, and once you start firing, don't stop. You wing someone with a .22 and it's like grazing a charging lion – you'll only piss him off.'

'How reassuring.'

'Align your sights. Find the target. Take a deep breath, exhale slowly, then hold the rest of the air in your lungs, and pull back the trigger *steadily*. Okay. Fire.'

She squeezed the trigger. The first pull was long. Her arms bounced up and her elbows locked, but the trigger came back easier than she'd expected. The trigger mechanism clicked dully in the silence, gutless without bullets. With more enthusiasm she followed up with quick, short jerks of her index finger, all that was now necessary for the double-action pistol.

'Congratulations,' J.T. informed her. 'You just killed a cloud.'

He taught her how to load the magazine, then showed her how the gun locked open when the last shot was fired. With a push of a button the old magazine was released and she could pop in a new one. Simple. Easy. Foolproof. The gun held six bullets in the magazine plus one in the chamber, giving her seven tries to get things right.

She put in the earplugs, donned her goggles, and leveled the loaded gun at the sacrificial bales of straw. She fired the gun, then leapt like a scared jackrabbit at the noise.

'Let me be more specific,' J.T. drawled beside her. 'Before you pull the trigger, open your eyes.'

'I did.'

'Uh-huh. Try again. Hammer's already cocked back from the first pull, so you don't have to squeeze too hard. Remember to actually hold your breath while squeezing the trigger. Otherwise, your arm automatically jerks up when you inhale, and down when you exhale. You want to minimize your arc of movement. If it helps, picture my head on the target.' He smiled sweetly.

She pulled the trigger six times. She finally hit the hay bale. The target remained unscathed.

'Sugar, I didn't know you cared.'

'Shut up.' She no longer felt cocky or triumphant or ready for battle. How could anyone miss with seven shots?

She tried thinking of the zone thing. She tried picturing her daughter. She thought of that night in the basement, her hand wrapped around the cow's heart, thinking it was a real heart, a real human heart.

She swayed on her feet.

J.T. caught her elbow.

'Maybe you want to try again tomorrow,' he suggested quietly.

'No. No, I have to be able to do this.'

'It's not such a great thing to know how to do, shooting a gun.'

She pulled herself together. 'It's the only thing.'

He was silent for a moment. He shrugged. 'Suit yourself. I'm just the teacher.'

His hand slipped off her elbow. She stood alone. He rammed a fresh magazine into the gun and handed it to her.

She fired the first bullet. Her trigger pull was jerky, and she missed the hay bale altogether. Furious and frustrated, she bobbed the gun down and pulled back the trigger with vengeance. She finally hit the edge of the bale, then she hit it again.

Four more shuddering shots, each more difficult than the first, and she still didn't hit any red rings on the target.

The gun emptied. Her ears were ringing. She continued to pull back the trigger until J.T. removed the gun from her grasp. Her face was ashen, her eyes dry. She couldn't look at him. She stared at the hay bales and wondered how she could do so badly.

'*What are you going to do, Theresa? Hit me, beat me, shoot me? We both know you're not that tough. You couldn't even stand up to your father. You couldn't protect your mother. You're nothing, Theresa. Absolutely nothing, and I own you.*'

Stop it, stop it, stop it. She wanted him out of her head!

'Angela,' J.T. said sternly, 'you're thinking too much.'

'I swear I'm not thinking!'

'Find the zone. Whatever is going on in your head, block it out. Just block it out.'

'I don't have a zone!'

He shook his head, suddenly furious. 'You want to do this, Angela? Are you serious about this? Forget the damn gun, grow a backbone instead. You're tough, I've seen it. But you're an endurance tough, and that's not enough. I bet when this Jim guy hit you, you took it. I bet when anyone threatens you, you curl up in a little ball and you survive.

'Well, that's fine if survival is all you want. But you came to me. You said you wanted to do more than wait, more than endure. You wanted to fight. So learn how to fight. Stop squeezing your eyes shut and open them wide. Stop flinching at the sound and open your ears. I don't care what your mama told you, the weak will *not* inherit the earth. It'll go to the people who can run the distance and still stand at the end.'

'Like you,' she said bitterly.

'You think I'm still standing? *Chiquita*, you are *not* looking close enough.' He popped the empty magazine out of the gun and in one clean motion replaced it. His arm extended. He glanced once; one second was all he seemed to need. Then his head swiveled back to her and he pulled the trigger. She flinched at the noise, but he didn't. He kept squeezing, bam, bam, bam, bam, the concrete man in action. The gun emptied.

His hand dropped to his side.

The center red circle of the target had just been annihilated.

'My God,' she whispered.

He slapped the gun into her palm. 'Stop flinching, stop jumping. Start focussing. Maybe you gotta learn to hate. I know it works for me.'

'All right,' she said. She could hate. She hated her father for every time he pulled back his arm in rage. She hated Jim for letting her believe he would save her, then plunging her into a hell deeper than even her father could imagine. And she hated herself because she'd let both of them hurt her, because it had taken her twenty-four years to figure out she had to fight, and she still wasn't any good at it.

She assumed the opening stance. Picture Jim, she thought. Picture the police photos. Remember every single thing that he did.

She gagged. She started firing. Tears were on her cheeks.

You're blind, you're stupid. You didn't see who he was. You didn't stop him sooner.

But I figured it out before anyone else! I stopped him eventually. I fought, dammit.

Too late, not good enough. How could you have let him use you like that?

I was just a kid, a mixed-up kid, and he chose me for just that reason. Because he knew how much I wanted someone to love me, how much I needed anyone to love me.

He knew you were weak. He knew you were malleable. You didn't disappoint.

J.T. grabbed the gun from her hand. 'Stop it!' he barked. 'What the hell are you doing?'

She blinked her eyes rapidly. Slowly he came into focus. Her ears were ringing from too many gunshots. Red dust was glued to her cheeks. She looked at him. She looked at the hay bales. Straw had flown in all directions from the top of the bales; she'd finally hit the white fringe of the target with a couple of shots. The red rings remained intact.

'You're not paying attention,' J.T. raged. 'You're pulling the trigger like

Dirty Harry and your mind isn't even on it. And that's blasphemy, lady. Pure, simple blasphemy!'

'I'm trying, dammit!' She was furious, not at him, but he was available, so she chose him. She stabbed her finger against his chest. 'I hired you to teach me, dammit. If you're so great, teach me how to fire this thing.'

'Fine,' he said tersely. 'Fine.'

He stepped behind her without foreplay. She was flattened against his body, her shoulders molded to his chest, her hips against his groin, her thighs against his thighs. His chin settled on her shoulder and his breath whispered across her neck.

'Point,' he ordered.

She brought the gun up.

'Aim.'

She sighted the target.

'I said aim, Angela! What are you trying to shoot? The dirt? The sky? A cactus? Two hay bales aren't enough for you?'

'I am aiming!'

'Look down that barrel, woman. Picture your husband,' J.T. muttered in her ear. 'Picture his face as that bull's-eye, sugar. And give him hell for what he did to you.'

Her body stiffened. Her arms leveled and her eyes narrowed. Suddenly she felt very calm and very cold. She sighted the target, steadied her grip, and with a triumphant flood of adrenaline, yanked back the trigger.

The bullet sailed so far wide of the target, it was going to have to catch a train to get back to Arizona.

She stood there, shocked and appalled.

'Shit,' J.T. murmured, then shook his head and rolled his shoulder. He stepped back. 'We'll try again tomorrow, Angela. You have three and half weeks.'

She looked at the target again, then at the gun in her hand. It had betrayed her. The gun was supposed to be her advantage. If she couldn't shoot, how could she win? If she couldn't outfight, outrun, or outshoot Jim, how was she going to win?

'But I hit him once before.'

'You shot your husband?'

'I hit him. In the shoulder. It was solid.' She shook her head in a daze. 'He was moving at the time. Maybe he ran into the bullet.'

'You shot your husband?' J.T.'s brows knit into a single dark line.

'What else was I supposed to do? Let him beat me to death with a baseball bat?'

'*What?*'

She wasn't paying attention to him anymore. She threw the gun to the ground.

J.T. snapped his hand around her wrist. 'Don't do that. A gun isn't a toy. If it had been loaded, you could have shot us both.'

'Well, then at least I would've finally hit something!'

'Don't take it out on the gun and don't take it out on me, Angela. It takes time to learn these things. Did you think the money would buy you a sharpshooter's badge?'

'You don't get it,' she cried. Her gaze went to his fingers, tight and strong around her thin wrist. Those fingers could snap her bone the way Jim's fingers had wrung her neck. 'You don't know, you don't understand the things he did.'

Her voice cracked. 'I lied to you, J.T. I lied.'

He went rigid. 'I don't like lia—'

'I thought if you taught me it would be enough. But let's face it, three and half weeks won't be enough. You have to help me,' she whispered. 'You have to—'

'Don't tell me what I have to do.'

He released her wrist. One quick movement and he'd brushed her off as if she were nothing but a clinging cholla glochid.

'You don't under—'

'Shut up!'

She realized then that she'd been wrong. She'd thought him unaffected, but he was overaffected. His face contorted, his fists clenched at his sides. There was anger and there was rage, and then there was an emotion too potent to describe. Something that had been poured into him at creation and he was consumed by it from the inside out.

He took two steps forward and she shrank back.

'What is it with women? Can you tell me that, Angela? You come here, you barge into my life, and what the hell, I let you stay. I tell you who I am, I tell you what I can give. And maybe I'm hard and maybe I'm crude. Maybe I want a beer so badly I'm waking up in a sweat in the middle of the night. But I haven't touched one, sugar. I told you what I could give, you told me what you wanted, and we struck a deal. And now you want to change the rules?

'Now you suddenly want more and *I'm* the bastard for not giving more? Lady, I've been down the hero path, and let me tell you, the laurels don't fit. I know they don't fit. I don't try to get them to fit. I don't give a damn that they don't fit. I will *not* play that game again. You hear me? I will not play that game!'

His hair slipped free from its band and flew around his face. She could feel his hot breath on her cheek, the strength of his body bending over hers.

She said, 'Liar.'

He stiffened as if struck. 'What?' It was daylight and the sky stretched out blue and unchecked as only a desert sky could spread. But he squeezed her view down to just his presence, just his black, glowering, threatening presence.

She brought her chin up. She couldn't shoot a gun so she might as well talk smart. 'You can say what you want, but I know more about you than you think. You're not as cold as you pretend. You care about your sister very much. You obviously loved your wife and son.'

'Oh, those are great credentials. My sister hates me and my wife and son are dead. I'm going back to the house.'

'Wait.' Her hands reached for him. He slapped them down.

'I thought you didn't trust anyone, Angela? I thought you said you were going to take care of yourself!'

The word stung. 'I'm not as good as I thought.'

'Learn to be better.' He yanked open the gun case, stuffed the gun and spent shells back in, and walked away.

11

'Tough day at work, darling?' Marion called out with mocking sweetness as J.T. stalked back into the pool area.

'Women are the root of all evil,' he growled, then stormed into the house, tossed the gun case into his safe, and locked it up tight. That detail attended to, he walked back across the living room, unbuttoning the fly of his jeans as he went.

He thrust open the sliding glass door just in time to encounter Angela about to do the same. They both froze. He scowled first. 'Rosalita will dye your hair. Three o'clock. Go eat lunch.'

'Coward,' she said, and shouldered her way past him. He stood stock-still for a moment longer, flexing and unflexing his fingers.

'Lovers' quarrel?' Marion asked innocently, and took a long sip of an icy cold beer. One of his beers. One of his favorite beers.

'Shit.' He ripped his T-shirt off over his head in a single yank. Two quick jerks, and he kicked his jeans across the patio. Clad only in boxers, he made a beeline for the pool. He clambered up to the low diving platform and assumed a runner's stance.

'Cannonball?'

'Watch and learn, little sister.' He bolted down the slim board, energy harnessed, focused, then unleashed with the force of lightning. Bam, bam, bam, leap . . . and soar through the air like an eagle. Free, suspended, graceful. Fuck them all.

He dove clean and arrow-straight into his deep blue pool, firing all the way to the bottom.

And the crowd goes wild.

J.T. didn't come up right away. He drifted along the beautiful blue tiles, suspended like a stingray as his lungs began to burn. He rolled over on his back, fighting to remain down, reveling in the feel of oxygen-starved tissue.

Semper fidelis, baby. Once a marine always a marine.

God, sometimes he missed those days, treading freezing cold water next to his buddy as part of the hydrograph survey team. They'd do a neat over-the-horizon insert, navigate to the beach, and hide the craft. Then, while two guys directed, they'd extend the chemlight rope out three hundred meters into the ocean, a pair of marines treading water every twenty-five meters in order to analyze the gradient and consistency of the ocean floor, information that would be used for a major beach campaign. It could take eight hours to get all the info. Eight hours of dark silence, treading water and feeling your legs go numb. Basic biological functions happened in the course of eight hours. New guys got embarrassed or ashamed. Old guys simply accepted the warmth of urine suddenly passing through cold water as a kind of camaraderie, a kind of sharing that made your team-mates closer to you than your wife or mother or sister. You couldn't explain that to women. They just didn't get it.

Being a marine made you part of something, linked you to something noble. He'd gone out there with guys, good guys who did good work and never offered excuses. He'd recognized the look in their eyes because it was the look he had in his own. He'd known the set of their jaws, the sheer determination of their will. They'd sat up there on planes, prepared to make midnight jumps down to drop zones they couldn't see, and no one had bitched and no one had moaned. They'd shared their fear quietly, in the steam fogging up their goggles. Then when the command came, they'd risen as one, stood in line, and each hit the butt of the guy in front of him in the universal signal of 'Jump, and God go with you.'

He'd liked it. He'd thought he'd finally found something he could do, a place he belonged. But even marines had to take orders, and the first time he'd had to deal with a hypocritical, shit-for-brains, wife-beating senior officer, he'd lost it. He'd tried to hold his temper. He had. But then he was thinking of Merry Berry and all those nights he'd listened to his father's jump boots clip down the hall to her room. And he was thinking of all the times he tried to tell someone of what really went on in their house at night and all the times he was beaten by the colonel for 'spreading ugly, foul rumors.'

You got a problem with me, boy? You fight like a man, you take me on, hit me if you think you can. But don't go spreading lies, boy. That's the way a wuss fights, a weak, pussy-whipped mama's boy.

One night his CO had pulled back his hand to smack his wife, and J.T. had stepped over the edge. He'd beaten the man to within an inch of his life and would've beaten him more. Would've like to pulverize his head, smash the man into the ground until nothing remained. Four guys had to pull him off. And the wife called him a brute and ran back to her mushy-faced husband, throwing her arms around his neck and burying her black eye against his shoulder.

That had been the end of the Marine Corps for J. T. Dillon.

At last he saw what he'd been waiting to see – Marion peering down over the edge of the pool.

He pushed himself off the bottom and rocketed toward the top. He emerged in a flurry of water, shaking his head like a Labrador and spraying his sister liberally.

'Now, that's a dive!' he exalted, and shook his head again.

'Oh, for God's sake.' Marion took a step back and stared at him in disgust. Then she looked down at her water-spotted silk tank top. 'Look what you've done, J.T.! Christ, it's like you're six years old or something.'

'Loosen up, Marion. Wanna swim, or are agents too tough for that?'

He got what he wanted in under thirty seconds. Marion was as predictable as a wind-up doll. She might as well walk around with a sign reading

EGO – PUSH HERE FOR BEST RESULTS.

'I can fucking swim.' She jabbed the air with her bony index finger. 'Suicides.'

'Suicides? I don't know, Marion. Pretty serious for a woman.' He continued treading water and smiling at his little sister.

'Oh, you're going to pay for that, J.T. First one who cries uncle loses.'

She grabbed the bottom of her tank top and to his amusement, stripped it off. He had her mad and he had her wired. He would feel bad about it, but she was an adult; she should know better than to take up the gauntlet without thinking it through. Suicides involved swimming the length of the pool, jumping out to do five push-ups, diving back in, and repeating the process. They required serious upper body strength, giving the man the clear advantage. Not that Marion would ever admit to something like that.

Not perfect, ambitious Marion.

Her linen shorts puddled onto the deck. He discovered that even his sister's underwear was businesslike – practical pink Lycra bra and panties that were less revealing than a bathing suit. Had Roger gotten tired of efficient underclothing? Even J.T. wasn't self-destructive enough to ask his sister that question.

He swam to the end of the pool, hefted himself out, and stood.

'Ready?'

Marion had that gleam in her eye and that tilt of her chin that said she was more than ready. She was going to wipe the deck with his ass. His sister had been keeping in shape too. No fat on that body and no glimmer of weakness in that gaze.

He was looking forward to the competition.

'Go.'

They sprang in unison, firing into the pool like serious seals.

J.T. made it to the other end first, but he had length on his side. It also took him slightly longer to pull his entire six-foot frame from the water. Two steps forward and he dropped squarely onto his flattened palms. He was aware of Marion right beside him. One, two, three, four, five.

Up and into the water we go.

He was adrenaline and he was energy and he was delighted.

The first ten laps were easy. Then lungs started to burn more, motions took on a rubbery, slow-motion-like feel. He heard Marion's labored breaths as she fell down for more push-ups. Then again, maybe he was just listening to his own.

They both stumbled a bit upon rising, jostled into each other, then like punch-drunk fools exchanged glares and dove back into the pool for more.

After fifteen laps they definitely weren't seals anymore. Not even walruses. More like corked bottles bobbing in the water and reaching desperately for shore. His chest seemed to have been invaded by an army of stinging red ants and his biceps were as obedient as overcooked spaghetti. Marion's push-ups made her look like a tepee swaying in the breeze.

But she didn't cry uncle. Not Marion.

And he didn't cry uncle. Not J.T.

He decided they had more in common than they appreciated. They were both stupid beyond words, weak, ugly children determined to prove that they weren't.

Fuck you, Colonel, sir.

He hefted himself out for number twenty. His hand slipped and he went splashing back in. Marion was still in the water beside him. She seemed to be beating at the deck more than using it to pull herself up.

'You're never going to say it, are you?' he gasped.

'Bite me.'

'Such language, Marion.'

'Bite me.'

She gave a last lunge and managed to beach herself on the patio, flailing on her stomach like a dying fish. He had no choice but to follow.

'We'll say it together.'

'Youcryuncleifyouwanttocryuncle!' she expelled in one breathless rush.

'Yeah? Then let's see your next push-up, Pocahontas.'

Her eyes closed, she groaned but didn't move and didn't cry uncle. He decided two could play that game. He beached himself beside her and concentrated on enjoying the warm, solid feel of his patio.

Idly, in the hazy world of the oxygen-deprived, he thought that he felt the best he'd felt in days. Like liquid gold.

He was going to hate himself in the morning, but then, he could say that about innumerable things he'd done the night before. At least suicides weren't likely to come after him with a shotgun or give him a hangover.

Marion was moving. She planted her hands on the deck and prepared to lift her quivering body.

'You just don't quit, do you?' he asked with genuine awe.

'No.' She gritted her teeth and with a determined grunt heaved her body up. Her arms shuddered like leaves. Slowly, so painstakingly he had to grit his teeth to watch, she lowered herself to the patio and touched her nose to the surface. Even good form.

'One,' she gasped, triumphant.

So he was forced onto his arms to do five more.

Oh, well, he thought philosophically. Sooner or later one of them was bound to drop dead.

An hour later they were both collapsed on the patio chairs. Not moving. Not talking. Just lying – and lying suddenly felt like hard work.

Through the sliding glass door J.T. could see Rosalita bent over Angela's seated form, massaging suds through her short-cropped hair. Angela had changed into a pair of old khaki shorts and a white tank top. From his vantage point he could see her legs clearly, the way her thighs curved into rounded kneecaps, which gave way to slender calves, which tapered to delicate bare ankles.

He'd always loved bare ankles. Exposed ankles and bare feet. Feet could be incredibly sexy, especially small, dainty feet sporting red-painted toenails.

Rachel had painted her toenails. Sometimes, if he'd been a very good boy, she'd let him paint her toenails. He remembered late Saturday nights when she would lie back on their down-covered bed and place her small white foot on his dusky chest. She would relax, talking, laughing, giggling over inconsequential things while her long blond hair pooled around her like a halo. His job was to carefully apply the glossy red lacquer to her toenails and enjoy the sound of her happiness. He'd always liked Saturday nights.

Then there were the Sunday mornings when Teddy would crawl into bed with them, and J.T. had finally understood why people loved the smell of talcum powder.

Shit.

He didn't want to think about any of that.

That was always the kicker for him. He didn't have the stamina for the bad memories or the strength for the good.

'You want to talk about Roger?' he asked Marion, apropos of nothing.

'No.'

'I thought you guys had a good marriage, you know – other than the fact that he was Daddy's hand-picked henchman and had absolutely no redeeming qualities of his own.'

'Didn't I just say I didn't want to talk about it?'

'Yeah, but we both know I'm a son of a bitch.'

She snorted at that and they both drifted into silence. 'He left me,' she said finally, her voice flat. 'He found some young cocktail waitress and decided she was the love of his life.'

'Bastard.'

'Yeah. Guess you can say you were right, J.T.'

He nodded but didn't actually say the words. He didn't have the heart to do that to her, not to proud Marion, who he would have sworn had actually loved Lieutenant Colonel Roger MacAllister. 'I'm sorry, Marion,' he said softly. 'I . . . When Rachel died . . . It's tough. I know it's tough.'

She was silent for a moment, then turned toward him. 'I hate him, J.T. You can't imagine how much I hate him for betraying me.'

He wanted to reach over and take her hand. He was afraid if he did, she'd snap it off at the wrist. 'You're better off,' he said, but the words sounded weak. 'He wasn't strong enough for you, Marion. You need a real man, not some army bureaucrat. That's the lowest life form imaginable.'

She returned to staring at the sky. 'Maybe.'

'Have you filed for divorce?'

'I should. It would kill Daddy though. He's already furious with Roger and me for not having produced grandkids.'

J.T. read between the lines. Angry at her *and* Roger? He doubted it. He bet the good old colonel called Marion into his room on a regular basis and screamed that she was a bad wife, disobedient daughter, and an all-round failure as a woman for not giving birth. Yeah, Colonel was probably spitting mad at not having another life to ruin.

'Daddy's already dying, so I'd go ahead with the divorce. If it kills him a little faster, well, there are a whole host of people willing to pay you for that. Of course, I top the list, or I would if I had money. I've lost all that now.'

Her lips thinned disapprovingly, but for a change Marion didn't pursue the subject of the colonel.

'I think Angela is a fraud,' she said, abandoning traditional battlegrounds for new territory. 'She lies through her teeth.'

'No shit, Sherlock.'

'Why, J.T., I thought you hated liars. I thought your twisted moral code did not tolerate such behavior.'

He shrugged. 'I'm getting old, Marion. The world is wearing me down.' He turned to look at the woman in question, her shoulders covered by old towels, and her eyes closed while her hair marinated. He remembered her pounding his chest with those tiny hands that now gripped the chair arms.

She was bright, she was proud, she was determined.

She'd shot her husband. He'd tried to beat her with a baseball bat.

'I want to know who she is,' he said. 'Can you help me, Marion?'

There was a long, long silence. 'What do you mean?' his sister asked carefully.

'I mean, of course she's lying and of course Angela's not her real name. Normally I wouldn't pursue the matter. It's bad for business. But now I want to know. I want to know who she is, who's her husband, and what the hell has he done.'

'You're sure?'

'Yes.'

'You're serious?'

'Yes.'

'I already started.'

'What?'

'I took her fingerprints,' Marion said calmly. 'I faxed them in to be analyzed against the national database. It's already been twenty-four hours. Anytime now I should be getting a call telling me exactly who she is.'

His mouth opened and closed several times. He wanted to be angry but couldn't pull off the emotion. When he'd agreed to let his sister stay, had he really thought she would do anything less? Proud, ambitious, driven Marion?

And he wanted to know the answer.

'You'll tell me what you learn,' he commanded quietly, 'and no one else. If she has done something, Marion, if she is in trouble, you won't handle it—'

'Like hell. I am a federal agent—'

'No! You're my sister. You're here as my sister and that's what I want you to be. Five more days, Marion, is that asking too much? Five days, please just be my sister. I don't mind so much being your brother. I'll try not to embarrass you.'

She was silent. Stunned. He could feel it. For once, cool Marion wasn't so composed. 'All right,' she said, and seemed as shocked as he was by her answer. 'I'll tell you what I find, J.T. And it's up to you to deal with it. For five days.'

'Thank you. I mean, honestly, thank you.'

The sliding door opened. Angela appeared on the patio, looking self-conscious. Her hair had been rinsed and blown dry, though it still looked a little damp around the edges. She raked one hand through the short strands, then knotted her hands in front of her. 'Well? What do you think?'

She looked beautiful. The fading sun sparked the rich brown color, giving it fire. Her face looked pale and lovely, her eyes endlessly deep. He thought she looked nothing like the woman she'd been just hours before.

And that scared him.

He said, 'It suits you.'

'That's what a disguise is supposed to do, right? Suit you.'

'You do learn fast.'

'I do,' she assured him. 'So don't worry about me and my little outbursts, J.T. I will get tough. And I'm going to learn how to shoot that gun!'

Marion shook her head. 'You'll be sorry, J.T.,' she murmured under her breath. 'You'll be sorry.'

Dinner on the patio was a silent affair. J.T. grilled swordfish. Angela and Marion consumed it without comment. As soon as the last bite was taken, Angela rose, cleared the table, and disappeared into the kitchen.

Marion lit a cigarette. J.T. stared at all the stars and wished his throat didn't feel so dry. He could feel sweat bead his upper lip, his shoulders, his arms. He told himself it was the heat, but he was lying. He wanted a beer. He was staring at Marion's and coveting it like a man lost in the desert.

Find the zone, he told himself. Use the zone.

But the phone rang and jarred him back out.

Marion looked at him for one moment, then got up to answer it. He sat there alone with the crickets, his gaze still locked on her beer.

Just one sip; maybe two.

You gave your word.

Ah, Christ, it's just a beer. What's so criminal about a man having a beer? Men shouldn't listen to women anyway, it only gets them into trouble.

You will not be an alcoholic.

Having a beer after dinner is not alcoholism, it's enjoying a beer. Just one. I drank all the time in the service, we all did. And could we perform? We always performed. It helps take off the edge. Christ, I want to take off the edge.

Find the zone.

Fuck you, J.T. You know you're a liar, you know there's no real zone. Only time you find it is when you're in battle, and rifle shots crack the air and adrenaline buzzes in your ear. The only time you're calm, you're centered, you're at peace, is when someone's trying to kill you. And that's just plain twisted.

His hand reached out on its own. His fingers curled around the base of the cold, wet bottle.

God, he was so thirsty. His fingers were trembling. He wanted, he wanted, he wanted.

The sliding glass door slammed back and he leapt guiltily, stuffing his hand beneath his thigh.

Marion stood on the patio with the lights golden around her. The picture shook him back to other times. Marion standing at the foot of his bed in her long white nightgown, her blond hair cascading down her back, her hands twisting in front of her. Marion begging him to save her, while the colonel pounded at his locked door and demanded his children let him in.

J.T. searching for a place to hide his sister. The colonel taking the door off its hinges.

He bit his lower lip to contain the memories.

She took a step forward, then another. Slowly her face became visible. She was uncommonly pale.

'Angela isn't in the kitchen,' she whispered. 'She isn't anywhere in the house.'

J.T. nodded dumbly.

'That was the Information Division. I know who she is, J.T. And, my God, I think I may have screwed up. I may have really, really screwed up.'

12

Lieutenant Lance Difford was getting old.

He was unbearably conscious of it these days. His hair had thinned considerably; it was harder to get up in the mornings. Coffee was starting to hurt his stomach and he was actually contemplating giving up doughnuts and prime rib.

Now the weather was getting colder and yeah, his insomnia was growing worse.

He wasn't actually that old – fifty was hardly one step away from the grave in this day and age. He'd never planned on leaving the force until he was sixty. He was a good lieutenant, a decent cop, a respected man. Once, he'd thought he'd spend his days investigating death, helping the Hampden County DA prosecute homicides, and eventually retire to Florida to visit baseball's spring training camps.

Then a girl was found outside of Ipswich, her head beaten in and her own nylons wrapped around her neck. Eight months later they had another girl in Clinton and calls from the DA in Vermont wanting to compare their crime scenes with homicides from Middlebury and Bennington.

Virtually overnight Difford went from low-key police work to one of the highest-profiled cases Massachusetts had ever seen. At the end he could summon unbelievable amounts of manpower just by snapping his fingers, from county resources to state resources to the FBI. Everyone wanted to help catch the man who'd probably killed four women in three states. Except then it became five women, then six women, then ten.

Difford had aged a lot those days. Six task forces operating around the clock and the most manpower logged on a single investigation in the state's history.

What we have here, boys, is the worst serial killer New England has seen since Albert DeSalvo in '67. And you know how many mistakes he's made? Zero.

Special Agent Quincy had them staking out grave sites and memorial services without avail. They'd arranged with columnists to profile the victims, keeping their names and tragedy fresh in the public mind. Maybe the guy would contact a loved one to brag. Maybe the guy was actually the bartender at the local police hangout, pumping officers for details. They'd executed the case like a textbook study, and still more blond daughters/wives/mothers went out for a drive and never came home.

Then one night Difford had gotten the phone call, not on the hotline but at home. The woman's voice had been so muffled, he could barely discern her words.

'I think I know who you're looking for,' she whispered without pre-amble. Difford had the image of a woman crouched in a closet, her hand cupping her mouth, her shoulders hunched in fear.

'Ma'am?'

'Is it true it's a blunt wooden object? Could it be a baseball bat?'

Difford gripped the phone tighter. 'That could be, ma'am,' he said carefully. 'Would you like to make a statement? Could you come to the station?'

'No. No, no, absolutely not. He'd kill me. I know it.' Her voice rose an octave before she cut it off. Difford listened to her deep, steadying breaths as she tried to pull herself together. 'I know who it is,' she said. 'It's the only explanation. The bats, his temper, all the unexplained hours . . . The look I sometimes see in his eye. I just didn't want to believe—' Her voice broke. 'Promise me you'll protect my daughter. Please promise me that. Then I'll give you anything.'

'Ma'am?'

'This man, this killer you're looking for – he's one of you.'

Difford felt the chill shudder up his spine, and he knew then that they had him. The Hampden County DA had become involved in the case at the request of the Berkshire County DA – the minute the Berkshire County team began to suspect a Berkshire County cop might be involved.

The next morning Difford arranged with the Berkshire County DA to keep Officer Jim Beckett busy that afternoon. Then Difford paid a visit to Beckett's wife.

Difford liked Theresa Beckett. He didn't know why. He'd been prepared to hate her, to think nothing of her. If her accusation was true, then she was the Bride of Frankenstein. What kind of woman married a killer? What kind of police force gave him a job?

Maybe it was the way Theresa sat across from them, so young and scared, but still answering their questions one by one. Maybe it was the way she cradled her two-year-old daughter against her neck when the baby cried, rocking her gently and whispering over and over again that everything would be all right. Maybe it was the way she handed over her life to them. Every small, tortured detail, with her whole face telling them she would do the right thing, she needed to do the right thing.

They stripped her bare that first week. They met with her at prearranged locations every afternoon and dissected her marriage. How long had she known Beckett? Where did he come from? What did she know of his family? What was he like as a husband, a father? Was he violent? Did he ever try to choke her? What about sex? How often? What kinds of positions? Any S&M, choking, sodomy? Hard-core pornography?

And she answered. Sometimes she couldn't look them in the eye. Sometimes tears silently streaked down her cheek, but she gave them everything they asked for and then she gave them even more. She'd kept logs of his car odometer for six months. She'd noted what time he left for work, what time he came home, and listed any inexplicable scratches or bruises on his body.

She told them that Jim Beckett actually wore a wig. Shortly after their marriage he'd shaved his head, his chest, his arms, his legs, his pubic hair, everything. The man was completely hairless, like a marble sculpture. The kind of perp that would leave no hair samples behind at the crime scene.

She told them he was cold, arrogant, and without remorse. The kind of man who would poison the neighbor's dog because he objected to a Pekingese shitting on his lawn. She told them he was relentless, the husband who always got his way. The kind of person who knew instinctively how to make people suffer without even raising his fist.

And each afternoon when they tucked their note-books away, they told her they needed more conclusive information before they could move against Officer Beckett, and they left her to face her husband alone for another evening.

By the seventh day, they thought they had enough, but apparently so did Beckett. They never figured out who leaked what, but he walked into a sandwich shop on his lunch hour, tailed by two agents, and never came back out. That simply he dropped off the face of the earth.

They moved in force.

Difford still remembered the look on Theresa's face, the way her eyes widened, the way her whole body swayed that afternoon as she opened her door and investigators swarmed her house. They all wore white airpacks borrowed from the fire department, full laboratory treatment suits with hair covers to keep them from further contaminating the crime scene. They looked like creatures from a bad sci-fi flick, weighted down with equipment, moving with an eerie rustle, and descending upon her home.

Samantha had begun to cry, so Theresa called her mother to come take her daughter away.

Then she sat alone on the sofa as the men pulled up her hardwood floor, ripped up kitchen tiles, dug up sections of the basement floor, and chipped mortar from between the stones of her fireplace. They vacuumed all surfaces with a special high-powered vac that picked up hair particles and dust particles. The bags were sent to the Mass. State Police crime lab for analysis. Stains on the carpet were cut out and sent. Ditto with the kitchen tiles. Later, the police crime lab said it had never churned out so many reports on baby saliva and spit-up peaches. One patch of dirt in the basement revealed bovine blood approximately one year old.

Next they brought in the lights. The 500-watt quartz light that helped highlight unseen hair and fibers. The ultraviolet radiation light with a 125-watt blue bulb to fluoresce hair, fiber, and body fluid. The blue-green luma light also to reveal hair, fiber, body fluids, and fingerprints. Finally they even dragged in portable laser lights and infrared. All the toys the CPAC boys never got to play with, never had the resources for, that were now being offered up to them from other states, other agencies, and the FBI.

Half the state police force looked under every stone and twig for the elusive Jim Beckett while the other half dismantled his house in search of evidence of his crimes. Their first discovery was a six-month supply of birth control pills stuffed behind a piece of insulation in the attic, right over the boxes labeled

SAMANTHA'S OLD CLOTHES, TWO MONTHS.

'They're mine,' Theresa told them. Her gaze rested on Difford. 'I got them from a clinic in North Adams. He wanted a second child. I couldn't . . . I just couldn't.' She added without thinking, 'Please don't tell Jim. You have no idea what he can do.'

Then, her own words penetrating, she sank down onto the sofa. One of the officers, a victim trauma expert, sat down next to her and placed an arm around her shoulders.

In the front hall closet they found a family pack of condoms. Theresa said Jim never used them, so the condoms were sent off to the lab for the latex to be analyzed and compared with residue found in the victims. They also discovered five baseball bats and a receipt for an even dozen. Later, analysis of the fireplace ashes revealed wood compatible with the kind used in the bats, plus a chemical compound reminiscent of the glaze finish.

They also recovered four test tubes containing premeasured amounts of a blue liquid identified as the sleeping drug Halcion, as well as the *Compendium of Pharmaceuticals and Specialties*, a virtual bible of most drugs, their manufacturers, their properties, and side effects.

In the attic, tucked behind a loose board, they retrieved a stun gun and a rubber mallet. But they couldn't find any direct links between Jim Beckett and the victims. Not the trophies serial killers were liable to take, or any traces of blood or hair.

What they did find was copies of files requested by Beckett from Quantico's Training Division. The files contained the profiles and interviews of several serial killers. Beckett had gone through and marked them up with such notes as HIS FIRST MISTAKE. HIS SECOND MISTAKE. THAT WAS SLOPPY.

At the end they found one last summary comment: DISCIPLINE IS THE KEY.

And the week turned into six months without any sign of Jim Beckett.

Now Difford rose off the sofa. He looked out the window of the safe house and identified the unmarked patrol car keeping guard across the street. He checked the front door and then, because he still remembered what had happened that one dark night, would always remember what happened that night Beckett returned for his revenge, Lieutenant Difford checked the closet.

All was clear.

He walked down the hall of the tiny bungalow and opened the last bedroom door. Samantha Beckett slept in a puddle of moonlight, her face soft and smooth and surrounded by beautiful golden hair. Difford leaned against the door jamb and just watched her.

She looked so unbelievably tiny. She still cried for her mommy. Sometimes she even cried for her daddy. But she must have a lot of Theresa's blood in her, because at four years of age she was also a real trooper. Most afternoons the kid beat the pants off him in dominoes.

Difford sighed. He did feel old, but maybe these were the days for it.

'God, Theresa, I hope you know what you're doing,' Difford muttered.

He tucked the blankets beneath Samantha's chin, then finally closed the door.

'I failed your mom,' he confessed in the hush of the darkened hallway. 'But I won't fail you, kid. I swear, I won't fail you.'

He sat down in the living room, the light on, his police revolver across his knee.

He still couldn't bring himself to close his eyes.

The previous week the media had asked Difford what concerned citizens should do to safeguard their lives now that the infamous Jim Beckett had escaped.

There'd been only one thing he could think of to say. 'Lock your closets.'

13

When it grew past seven and there was still no sign of Angela, J.T. admitted to himself that he was worried. At seven-thirty he gave up memorizing the ceiling fan and pulled on a pair of jeans.

He had only one hunch, but it was a good one. It was cool outside. Fall moving into the desert and bringing some relief. The sky had expelled the sun and now a moon rose waxy and pale. Just enough light to frame the saguaros as frozen soldiers.

The desert wasn't quiet. It hummed and pulsed with the low, rhythmic chorus of the crickets, the eerie cries of the dry wind, and the faint fluttering of Gila woodpeckers whirring among the saguaros. Somewhere far off, a lone coyote mournfully howled.

J.T. left behind the oasis of his swimming pool and headed for the shooting range. He may have locked up his .22, but Angela had reclaimed hers.

He spotted her from thirty feet back, and his footsteps slowed. He didn't call out because he didn't want to startle an armed woman. Then he didn't call out simply because he couldn't think of anything to say.

He stood in the moonlight and watched her point her unloaded gun at hay bales and pull the trigger. Again and again. And then she moved and pointed, trying new stances, practicing moving and shooting.

Over and over.

He could see that her arms shook. He could tell that her fingers had grown thick and sluggish, but she didn't stop. She had set up a flashlight to illuminate her targets and she seemed intent on not wasting the light. She raised the gun and sighted the target and pulled the trigger yet again.

And he could tell that the minute she tightened her finger around the trigger, she dipped the nose of her gun, so that maybe she thought she was hitting the target, but really she was simply killing dirt.

A long time later Tess walked back to the house, her fingers too sore to curl and her arm a mass of knotted muscles. The palm of her hand hurt, her biceps hurt. Everything hurt. But she was trying.

She walked into the yard. And as her hands pressed against the sliding glass door, she knew she wasn't alone.

She turned, the gun empty against her bare thigh, and peered out into the night.

She didn't see him. She felt him.

His gaze washed over her. She felt it touch her face, then move down slowly, caressing the pulse throbbing in her throat, her breasts, her belly, her hips. It traveled back up, settled on her mouth.

A red match glowed in the dark. He brought it up to his lips, cupping it in front of him so that it briefly illuminated his jaw. He inhaled sharply until the end of his cigarette glowed. Then with two quick jerks, he shook out the match.

The darkness settled back between them, no longer calm but filled with a slow-heated pulse. She felt the throbbing rhythm in her blood. She felt the fierce feral pull of his gaze. Her lips parted.

He stepped forward.

'We need to talk.' His arm came up and he dumped a six-pack of beer on the patio table. 'They're for you, Theresa Beckett. Start drinking. And tell me everything.'

'They couldn't find him. They told me they had him under surveillance, that they knew what he was doing at all times, that I was safe. Then one afternoon he entered a sandwich shop and was never seen again. Special Agent Quincy predicted Jim would be back. Sooner or later Jim would return to kill me.'

You turned on him, Mrs Beckett, and he didn't see that coming. That's a big blow to a man like him. Now the only way he'll be able to restore his ego, his sense of self, is to kill you. He'll come back. And he won't wait long.

'I made them put Samantha in hiding. We didn't think Jim would hurt her – he seemed to honestly adore her – but we couldn't take any chances. I remained in the house, night after night. Just waiting. For six months.'

She lay in bed every night, covers pulled up to her chin, ears strained, eyes open, and heart stuck permanently in her throat. She chewed her fingernails down to raw nubs. She leapt at small noises. She forgot how to live, how to feel. And winter rolled down from the hills and blanketed Williamstown with snow.

'They searched for him everywhere, but they didn't have many leads. He rarely spoke of the past and the investigators uncovered little. His family was dead, his foster parents dead. His only friends were from the police force, and they were more like acquaintances. There didn't seem to be anyplace for him to go, and yet he disappeared absolutely, completely, as if he'd never existed. I used to wonder if he wasn't just some horrible phantom. I guess the cops began to think the same. Originally there were ten men watching my house. But then one week turned into two months.

Then four months. Then six months. Just two plain-clothes officers were still around. And suddenly Jim reappeared.'

Scratching resonated on the roof.

She lunged across her bed, yanked the receiver from the phone, and stabbed the touch-tone buttons.

Lieutenant Lance Difford would pick up, she'd murmur the code, and the police would descend if they hadn't already spotted Jim on the roof.

It would be all right.

Except the phone had no dial tone.

'Waiting for me, wife?'

She looked up.

And her husband stepped out of her closet, wearing his Berkshire County police uniform and looking like a young Robert Redford. He was hefting a baseball bat, and she could see dark smudges and loose hairs matting the end.

She leapt for the nightstand, her ragged fingernails sliding ineffectively across the smooth surface. And with agile perfection Jim lunged forward and wrapped a hand around her ankle.

'No, no!' she cried, clawing at the mattress, bruising her fingertips on the bedpost.

He yanked her onto the floor, and she landed hard, the breath escaping her in a painful whoosh. She fought anyway, trying to crawl away as his hand snaked up her exposed calf.

'Where is Sam?'

'You'll never find her!'

'Didn't they tell you what I can do, Theresa? Didn't they tell you exactly how I like to inflict pain?'

His fingers dug into her ankle. Then she felt his breath as he leaned over her back and pinned her neck against the carpet with his forearm. He spoke. His voice drifted over her like velvet, soft, heavy, suffocating her word by word.

'You helped them. Theresa. You told them things about me. Did you think it would go unpunished?'

Jim curved his hand almost lovingly around her exposed throat. Her pulse leapt like a captured mouse against the base of his palm. He slowly started squeezing the air from her lungs.

He told her to fight him. He told her he liked it when they fought him.

She squirmed, her heels searching for traction against the old carpet. She knew he would asphyxiate her slowly, then revive her and do it again, and revive her and do it again. Somewhere along the way, he would rape her and torture her. And then, when he finally tired of the sport, he would pick up the bat and she would be grateful that it was ending.

Her fingers flexed and unflexed above his grip. Her hips writhed desperately. In her mind, she kept calling for the police. She was so sure they would figure out what was going on. That any minute they'd bang down the front door. They'd save her. No one came.

Spots appeared before her eyes, white and dizzying. She felt herself spinning away, sinking into a dark, whirling vortex of nothing. She was dying and a part of her was too frightened, too overwhelmed to care.

If you don't fight now, she thought dimly, you will die and years from now your daughter won't even remember your name.

'I know what you're thinking,' Jim whispered in her ear. 'You're looking deep inside yourself, trying to find the will to defy me. You don't have it, Theresa. I took it from you. I've known you since the day I met you, and I've turned you inside out and climbed inside of you and now there's nothing left of you. Every bit of you, every last thought you have, really belongs to me. I made you. I'm inside your mind. I own you.'

The lights grew brighter behind her eyelids. The burning spread from her lungs to her whole chest. Her fingers moved feebly, then stilled.

His hands slipped from her throat. And she slammed her fist into his nose.

He fell back with a guttural cry and she didn't wait. Her flailing hand reached for the lower drawer, scrambling with the handle.

'You bitch!' He rolled off her. She heard the heavy swish of air as he raised the baseball bat.

'Please, please,' she whispered hoarsely, and ripped the drawer from the nightstand.

A sharp sound, a whistle. She ducked and rolled, and the floor shook with the force of the bat hitting the carpet.

'I'm going to kill you!'

She was crying and rolling and crying and fumbling with the damn drawer, scrambling through the contents and praying for one last miracle to save her.

Another whistle.

The bat came down on her thigh.

She heard a loud crack, then felt a red-hot bolt of pain fire through her leg. And suddenly she wasn't frightened anymore, she wasn't exhausted. She was just really pissed off.

She tried to leap to her feet, but the blinding pain toppled her. Savage, fierce, stabbing agony that ripped up her leg and brought tears to her eyes. She sensed more than saw the autographed Louisville Slugger arch and suspend.

Her head turned. She stared at him as he stood tall and majestic in an icy sliver of moon, his fake blond hair waving over his forehead, his smooth, hairless chest like sculpted marble.

And she thought that no one had ever told her the devil would be so beautiful.

The bat came down.

Her hand curled around the gun she had sought.

And she moved through the pain, screaming her terror and agony and fury as she rolled over her cracked femur bone and raised her trembling arms.

LISA GARDNER

The bat slammed into the carpet.
She started firing the gun.

'You hit him,' J. T. said at last. She was into the fourth beer now and swaying a bit. Her eyes were flat and glassy.

'Yes.' Her gaze fixed on the shimmering water of the pool. 'I hit him in the shoulder, enough to take him out. The police heard the gunshots, Difford came bursting through. They took him away. It was over.'

'But you never stopped being afraid.'

'No. He was right. I couldn't get him out of my mind. I sold the house, took Sam and we ran. For two years. New names, new towns. I go by Tess Williams now, but Samantha only calls me Mommy. She can't keep track of the names and she's always scared she'll get them wrong. So she doesn't learn names anymore, she's too frightened. It's a horrible thing to do to a child.'

'You did what you had to do.'

'It wasn't enough. I dreamed about him every night, and every night he was coming after me. A man like that . . . he shouldn't be left alive.'

'No. He shouldn't.'

'He killed two prison guards last week. Beat them to death. He's very strong, you know. I wish Massachusetts had the death penalty.'

'Angela—'

'You might as well call me Tess.'

'No, I don't think I should. You're using an alias to protect yourself. From everything you've just told me, that's an excellent idea. But, Angie, Marion took your fingerprints. She faxed them through the Nogales Police Department to the FBI. That's how I found out your real name.'

She was silent, minute turning into minute. 'Oh.'

J.T. found himself reaching out and taking her hand. It felt cold. 'She was just doing her job. She knew you were lying and she wanted to check up on you.'

'I understand.'

'She knows she screwed up. Given Beckett's background, it's understandable that you wanted to keep your identity secret even from the law. Well, that ship has sailed. Marion would like to bring you in now. She'll escort you back to Quantico personally, set up a safe house, and provide round-the-clock protection.'

'Didn't you just listen to the story I told you?'

'The police made a mistake the first time, but they're smarter now—'

'It doesn't matter!' She yanked her hand from his and stood. 'Don't you get it? He's a cop. He knows their procedures, he thinks like them. As long as I'm with them, I'm not safe because, let's face it, cops operate with rules and Jim has none. He can anticipate them, outmaneuver them, and I'm the one who ends up alone, facing a baseball bat. I won't go through that again. I won't sit around like a stupid mouse waiting for the cat to pounce.'

He looked at her silently.

'I'm staying here,' she stated. 'Even if the Nogales police know who I am, Jim has no contacts in Arizona, right? And the FBI agents in Quantico who called Marion, they can be told to keep their mouths shut, right?'

'I'll speak to Marion about it.'

'Fine, then it's settled. You don't understand, J.T. You think you do. You watch me try to swim and shoot at hay bales and you think I'm helpless. But there is one thing I'm good at. I know how to think like Jim Beckett.' Her lips twisted. Her eyes were shiny with a glaze of tears. She brushed them away with the back of her hand. 'I'm staying. If he does find me here, then I'll deal with him. Or you'll get to deal with him. You may not like it, you may not agree with me, but I was smart when I came here. If there's any person fit to take on Jim Beckett, it's an angry, arrogant asshole like you.'

Christ, she looked like something. She looked strong and she looked fierce. He wanted to yank her down onto his lap and kiss her until her fingertips gripped his shoulders and she roared his name with need. He wanted to feel her quiver as she came.

'We're back on the shooting range tomorrow, Angela. You can put your money where your mouth is then, because, sugar, from here on out, I'm going to push you *hard*.'

'Good!'

'You might want to leave now, Angela, or I'm going to rip your clothes off and take you on the patio.'

'Oh.'

'You're still not moving.'

'It's just the beer,' she assured him hastily as she remained in place. He shifted forward and she finally jolted to life. She scurried across the patio, thrust open the sliding glass door, and ran into the house. He could already picture the lock on her bedroom door slamming shut.

He remained sitting in his garden, listening to the crickets, thinking about her story, and staring at the two unopened cans of Michelob.

14

The sun was straight up, no longer fierce but having gentled through the course of the week to a kindly benefactor. It caressed Tess's cheeks and arms, trying to infuse her skin with a hint of color.

The rest of the desert, however, remained acrimonious. The saguaros looked grim and mocking, the sagebrush shuddered in the breeze. A gray roadrunner darted by. In the distance the bleached-out hills sat glumly, weighted down by rickety shanties and hundreds of lines of drying laundry.

The world was muted gold, dried-out brown, and sun-sapped green. Tess stood in the middle of it, wearing a worn white tank top with khaki shorts and feeling just as insipid and plain as her surroundings.

'Are you going to shoot 'em or sculpt 'em?' J.T. quizzed dryly. He'd stripped off his T-shirt to catch a little sun. Clad in ripped denim cutoffs and beat-up sandals, he looked more like a California surfer dude than a desperado. After two hours of watching Tess miss the targets, he also looked bored.

Marion had stopped by the first hour to lend her expertise. Like J.T., she insisted Tess needed to find the zone.

'Concentrate,' the agent had told her again and again. 'Visualize your hand extending to the target, touching the bull's-eye, and sending a bullet through the brain.'

In case that didn't work, J.T. had been modifying her .22, decreasing the trigger pressure for a smoother pull, and trimming the grip so the gun would fit more comfortably in her hand. There were six fundamentals to shooting: position, grip, breath control, sight alignment, trigger squeeze, and follow-through. Tess was now trying to focus on all of them at once. She had a headache.

Tess adjusted her earplugs and rolled her shoulders. Her hands and forearms throbbed dully. It took a lot of strength to pull a trigger repeatedly. Marion had shown off her own forearms, roped with long lines of wiry sinew. To become an agent, a cadet had to be able to pull a handgun trigger twenty-nine times in thirty seconds. A lot of female cadets couldn't do it, but lean, mean Marion could, and she had the muscles to prove it.

Tess was beginning to believe that there was nothing the Dillon children couldn't do.

She just didn't like the gun. She didn't like its weight, its feel, its noise. In her mind the gun remained inherently evil, too vicious and too powerful. And maybe she feared more than anything that once she became comfortable with it, she would turn a corner in herself and never be able to go back. She'd permanently become part of the violence. She would never escape.

You are part of the violence, she reminded herself. *Your options are to control it or be victimized by it.*

She took a deep breath. She told herself the gun was her friend. She'd used it before and it had saved her. She would master the fear and she would master the weapon.

She adapted the stance J.T. had taught her and leveled her arms.

Okay, Tess. You're a lean, mean killing machine. Align, inhale, hold it, squeeze.

She pulled the trigger. It boomed. She jumped and closed her eyes.

She was an idiot.

She finished out the clip fatalistically. When she was done, she turned to J.T.

He shook his head as he'd been shaking it all afternoon. 'Tess, why are you so afraid of an inanimate object?'

'There's nothing inanimate about a gun!'

'Then you've been watching too many Disney movies.'

He took a step forward and clasped her wrist. He ran one callused finger up her bare thigh, brushing the bottom of her khaki shorts.

She flinched. She blanched. She blushed.

'What are you doing?' she asked furiously.

'Nice scar,' he said. 'Didn't you learn anything from it?'

'Apparently not enough,' she shot back, unable to meet his gaze. He stood too close to her, and she wasn't prepared for the intense desire to lean forward and press her lips against the scar snaking down his chest.

'How . . . how did you get your scar?'

'Guatemala. I think.'

He was still standing before her. His hand was still on her thigh. 'You think?'

'Could've been El Salvador. After a bit, all jungles look alike.'

'So you were fighting?'

'Over a beautiful woman, I'm sure.'

'Of course.' She had a feeling that with him, there had truly been a lot of beautiful women.

'It's true. I think.'

'I see. After a bit, all beautiful women look alike?'

'Sure. Just taste different.'

She pulled away, trying to cover the motion by retrieving spent casings, but obviously not covering it well enough.

'I offended you?' he said after a moment, his voice emotionless, his arms crossing over his chest.

'After a week of your company? Hardly.'

'Now you're shockless? You're that tough?'

'I'm a fully functional bad ass,' she assured him.

'Good,' he said. 'Then you'll have no problem firing the gun.' He smiled at her grimly. 'Again, Tess. We're not leaving here until you get this right. The gun is a tool. Learn to use it.'

He yanked her around and she came up hard against his chest. 'We're going to try an experiment,' he murmured. His whiskered cheek nuzzled back her hair until his lips were on her ear.

'Okay,' she whispered. She was licking her lips.

'Pick up the gun for me.'

'Okay.'

'Put in a fresh clip.'

'Okay.'

'Sight the target.'

She straightened her arms and assumed the Weaver stance. He smoothed his palms down her arms, encircling her wrist with his fingers. 'Tess, you're getting some muscle tone.'

She started shivering. He misinterpreted. '*Chiquita*, you don't even have the safety off yet.'

'I'm just . . . What are you doing?'

'I'm going to shadow you. You shoot, I'll correct. Relax against me. Come on, sweetheart, relax.' He nudged her arms. She stiffened further. 'Tess,' he murmured. His teeth found her earlobe and bit down gently. 'Relax.'

'Oh, my Lord,' she said, and melted into him.

'I always knew that trick would come in handy.' His body shifted, assuming the correct stance and seeming to mold hers. She let him mold her. She could feel his leg hair and his chest hair, his raspy twelve-hour beard.

'Focus on the target,' he told her. 'Fire.'

She did as she was told. She pulled back the trigger, and her arms leapt spasmodically. He caught them right as they bobbed down and forced them up.

Finally receiving proper guidance, the bullet fired straight and true. It buried itself into the outer ring of the target.

'Oh, my God, would you look at that!'

'See,' his voice rumbled in her ear. 'It's not so hard.'

She whispered, 'Again.'

She emptied the clip. Each time, his body contracted around hers, halting her natural flinch, compensating for her mistake. They went through another clip, and the hay bale took a beating.

'Good,' J.T. said. He stepped back, but his hands remained on her shoulders. After a moment his fingers squeezed her stiff muscles, rubbing her down like a star athlete. She closed her eyes and let her head fall forward. He made her feel relaxed, he made her feel loose. He made her feel as if she could do anything.

'All right,' he said. His hands fell away. She tried not to moan. 'Now it's time to try solo. It's just like before. Stay relaxed. Point and shoot. The gun is just a tool in your hand.'

'A tool,' she repeated obediently.

'A tool. You own it, Tess, you control it. It doesn't control you.'

She took a deep breath and exhaled through her nostrils. She positioned her feet and raised the gun. She closed her eyes.

The gun was a natural extension of her hand. Her tool, for her to control, for her to use. She didn't have to pull the trigger unless she wanted to. That was strength. The power to choose.

She chose to pull the trigger. One, two, three, four, five.

And the paper target went flying.

She stared. She was so stunned, she couldn't even move. And then she turned to him, and she smiled with one thousand watts of triumph.

'Did you see that!' she cried, and pointed with her left hand just in case he'd somehow slept through the occasion. 'Did you see that!'

He smiled at her calmly and nodded. 'You hit it. All on your own, you hit it.'

And then he did something she never would have imagined him doing. He reached over and shook her hand.

She couldn't say a word. She felt his firm, reassuring grip. She returned it with one of her own. Bad ass to bad ass. She'd done it.

Then she grinned at him and whooped. 'I killed the hay bale! I killed the hay bale!'

She unceremoniously handed him the gun and raced to the long-suffering straw to inspect her work.

J.T. watched her go. She hunkered down beside the bale of straw and promptly stuck her finger in a blackened hole like a little kid. Her hair burned like copper wire beneath the sun. It matched her smile, bright, brilliant, and intense enough to make a man look twice.

She found another hole and poked her finger in that one too. God, the grin on her face!

When had she become so beautiful? She looked over at him and smiled again. Then she rested her head against her big-game trophy and he had to blink his eyes against the tightness in his chest.

In this moment she looked perfect, the way she should have looked from the beginning. She was vital and radiant, earthy and innocent.

It was the kind of moment a man should record on film and carry with him in his pocket to remember on other, darker occasions.

His mind, relentless and ruthless as always, filled in the other snapshots to come. Tess sprawled facedown on a carpet, face bruised and pulpy from a baseball bat. Body outlined in white chalk. Clothes torn and ripped.

He looked away. He focused on the dirt.

No, he thought. It won't come to that. She was tougher than that. The police were smarter than that. Hell, maybe Jim Beckett was already out of the country, sipping planter's punch in the Bahamas.

But he didn't believe any of it.

Goddamn, he wanted a drink.

He thought sobriety was supposed to be good, making a man clear-headed, sharp, focused. For him it was the opposite. He couldn't sleep at night. He was constantly edgy, and his mind was drowning beneath the weight of images he could no longer control.

Maybe a guy like him was meant to be drunk. Maybe a guy like him could only really function with the edge worn off.

He noticed things like Marion's cutting comments. He remembered things like the dreams he'd had when he'd returned to the States five years ago, and the fresh hope he'd found as a newly married man.

He remembered the first time he'd seen Rachel, holding a squalling baby and haltingly telling him she had no money anymore. The colonel had thrown her out, her savings were gone, and men didn't pay much for an exhausted mother. She'd come to him because she didn't know who else to go to. And then the first tear had trickled down her cheek, large and silent, as she'd looked away, clearly ashamed. He'd watched her try to calm her screaming baby and simultaneously wipe the moisture from her face. When he still hadn't given her a reply, she'd walked away, her thin shoulders held with more dignity than he could imagine. He'd known then that he would help her. Whatever the colonel had done to her, she was worth more. She was a better person than he'd made her.

He noticed things like when he lay down at night, the ceiling fan never stopped moving. It hummed and hummed and hummed, and stirred the air against his skin so delicately, it was maddening.

Just that morning he'd fallen asleep enraged by the air and woken up to see Rachel standing by his bed. He would have sworn it was her, and not the early Rachel but the woman who'd become his wife. So beautiful, so lovely. She had smiled at him, soft and serene. His heart had broken in his chest all over again.

Hey, babe, Teddy and I are just going to run to the grocery store. We'll be back in an hour. What would you like for dinner?

And last night he'd had more dreams. This time he was running after the

Camaro. He could see it so clearly. The kid, the stupid kid was driving in the middle of the road, swerving from side to side. Up ahead he could see the approaching headlights of Rachel's car. And he was screaming and he was running, but the damn Camaro was going too fast, he couldn't catch it.

At the last minute the kid turned his head, but he wasn't the kid anymore. He was a bald, hairless man with cold blue eyes. Jim Beckett. Beckett was grinning and then J.T. looked through the windshield of the approaching car and saw Tess's screaming face.

'Let's celebrate,' Tess said, trotting back over from the bale of straw. 'What do you do to celebrate?'

He jerked himself back to the present. 'To celebrate a successful kill?'

'Yes. A successful kill. What do you do?'

'Straight shots of Cuervo Gold followed by mad, passionate sex. I'm game if you are.'

She blushed, her breathing accelerated. 'I know,' she said brightly, no longer looking at him, 'let's buy strawberries. Can we get strawberries out here?'

'Sure.' His gaze remained on her face. Her lips had parted. Now her tongue darted out to moisten them. She had very pink lips, like rose petals.

'And fresh whipped cream,' she murmured. 'And shortcake. That's it. I'll make strawberry shortcake with dinner.'

'Tess,' J.T. said hoarsely, 'stop toying with me.'

He grabbed her hand, swung her against his chest, and devoured her mouth. He discovered those pink lips and he thrust his tongue between them, hearing her gasp, then hearing her sigh.

He kissed her deeply, like a drowning man trying to find shore. Her fingers dug into his arms and her grip was strong and urgent, just as it should be. He ate her lips, tasted her, and consumed her. And she opened her mouth for him greedily and drew him in even deeper.

Good Lord, he was drowning and he wanted to drown.

As if from a distance, he heard her moan. His hands found her ass and rotated her hips against his hardening length. Her fingernails welted his skin.

She was hungry. Her leg was already rubbing his thigh. Her fingertips danced up his arms, then his collarbone, and tangled in his hair. She pulled on his head.

'Jesus,' he muttered thickly. 'You take it wild.'

'Okay,' she said, and ground her teeth against him. She split his lip, then jerked back in shock. He touched the cut with a finger and pulled it back wet with blood.

'Didn't realize you were into that kind of stuff, Tess.' He put the finger in his mouth and licked it clean.

'I don't know what I'm doing!' Abruptly she buried her forehead against his chest and her shoulders started shaking. 'I'm sorry. I'm sorry.'

She caught him off guard with her sobs. He stood stiffly, stunned, then some old instinct flared gamely to life.

Slowly he curled one arm around her shoulders. She felt tiny against him. Carefully his other hand palmed her head. His thumb stroked her cheek once, twice.

'It will be all right,' he found himself whispering. 'It'll be okay.'

He brushed the tears from her cheek; he stroked her neck. She felt so unbelievably fragile. Images swamped him: A baseball bat arching up. A man arching the bat over her curled, defenseless body. A two-hundred-pound pumped-up giant about to annihilate his hundred-pound wife.

The rage was instantaneous. He blanked it from his mind and held her closer.

'You wanna talk about it?' he asked at last.

'I'm so humiliated,' she moaned.

'Why?' He shifted her more comfortably against his chest but kept his grip. He suspected the first time he let go, she would bolt.

'Because I'm a twenty-four-year-old mother and I don't know how to kiss. And I don't know what to do and I don't know what to want. Oh, God, it's all so messed up and crazy.' Her shoulders started heaving again.

'Your husband was your first?'

'The only one.'

'And lousy?'

'Yes.' Her arms slid around his waist and she clung to him. He hadn't had anyone hold him like that for a very long time. He'd forgotten about these things. The sweetness of a woman's touch. How much comfort she could give a man. How much she could make him feel whole.

And he felt something inside him rip a little.

He didn't want that. Oh, he didn't want that.

He took her hands in his and as fast and painlessly as possible disengaged her from his body. 'You got time now,' he said stiffly. His gaze bounced all around, landing on everything but her. 'Jim Beckett was a bastard and you left him. Now you got your whole life to figure out the rest. You're starting out fresh and twenty-four's not that old.'

'Was I that horrible?'

God, she was killing him. 'No. No, Tess, you weren't. You just . . . it's like your shooting. You were trying too hard and bringing too many things into it with you.'

'Oh.' Her lips twisted. 'So there's a zone for kissing too? I should've figured that.'

'Yeah. You know those zones.'

'I bet you have them all down.'

'Not all of them. But shooting, swimming . . . fucking. Yeah, I guess I have my strengths.'

She fell silent. He used the opportunity to clear his throat. It felt too dry.

He suffered another pang of longing for a beer. Any beer. Dirt-cheap beer, he didn't care.

'We should get back to the house.'

'What are we going to learn this afternoon?'

'Hand-to-hand combat.'

'Not hand to baseball bat?'

He winced. 'We'll cover that too.'

More silence. Then she pulled away. 'All right.'

He heard her footsteps as she moved over to the gun case. Heard the sharp *clack* as she popped it open, then the tinkle of brass casings being poured into their container.

He tried to pull himself together.

He kept seeing that damn Camaro. And his father walking down the hall.

He shook his head. *Push it away, J.T., just push it away.*

It didn't work. He needed a beer.

15

'I know where Jim Beckett is.'

'Yes, ma'am?'

'I've seen him in my dreams. He's with a blond woman and there is the sound of dripping water. Slow dripping-water. Drip . . . Drip . . . Drip . . .'

'Ma'am?'

'I smell fresh snow and pine trees. Yes, he has gone to the mountains. The beautiful, beautiful mountains. There, he will be reborn.'

'Uh . . . yes, ma'am. Which mountains?'

'How should I know that, silly girl? You are with the police. I have given you direction, now you must follow!'

The phone clicked. The operator sighed. 'Yes, ma'am,' she whispered. She hit the reset button on her keyboard and her terminal immediately lit up with a fresh call.

'I've found Jim Beckett!'

'Where, sir?'

'He's living across the street from me. I spotted him last night, through the window. I broke my leg, see, but that doesn't mean I'm helpless. Sitting at my window, I see all sorts of things. And last night I saw him, standing in the window, arguing with a woman. I think he may have killed her.'

'May I have your name, sir.'

'Jimmy Stewart. That's J-i—'

'Jimmy Stewart? As in Jimmy Stewart?'

'That's right.'

'Do you watch a lot of Hitchcock films, sir?'

'Why, yes, yes, I do.'

'Thank you, sir.' She disconnected that call on her own. Her terminal immediately lit up again. Five thousand calls a day and still going strong.

'Jim Beckett is my next-door neighbor!'

'Of course, sir.'

'He just moved in last week. I was suspicious right away. The man's bald, you know. What kind of self-respecting man goes around looking like a bowling ball? He's Irish, isn't he? You can't trust the Irish.'

'May I have your name and address, sir?'

'My name? Why do you need my name?'

'We just need a contact, sir. A police officer will follow up with you and take an official statement.'

'I don't want a cop coming to my home.'

'We can do it by phone, but we need your name.'

'Hell, I don't want a cop coming here. Everyone will think I'm a snitch. I'm not a snitch!'

'Of course, sir, but—'

The caller slammed the phone and the operator winced a little, but there was no time for contemplation. Her terminal lit up again, and with a tired sigh she hit the enter key and started over.

Across the room Special Agent Quincy ran down the log sheets, seeing if anything leapt out at him. He'd been in Santa Cruz working on a series of grave robberies and mutilations. Since many disorganized serial killers started with corpses before graduating to living victims, the local law enforcement had gotten the FBI involved early. The hope was they could catch the guy before young women suffered the same fate as the dead. Unfortunately they weren't having much success. At eleven P.M. Quincy had caught the red eye to Boston. He was exhausted, rumpled, and unshowered. He was used to it by now.

He moved on to the tenth page of the log sheet, but still nothing leapt out at him. Operators took each call, logging the caller, their address, return phone number, and tip. The police officers on duty then sorted through the log sheets, scratching off about eighty percent as worthless, eighteen percent as worth calling back, and two percent as worth checking out in person. From 'Jim Beckett is really Elvis' to reports of grand theft auto, the officers got it all.

Quincy abandoned the log sheet and poured himself a second cup of coffee. Instant. He hated that crap. There would be justice in the world the day police officers had cappuccino machines.

Lieutenant Houlihan spotted him from across the room and approached.

'You look like hell,' the lieutenant stated.

'Thanks. It's part of the new Bureau regulation. All agents must look overworked or they're being paid too much. So how's it going here?'

'The bad news is we still have no sign of Jim Beckett. The good news is we may have found Jimmy Hoffa. Oh, and we've averted two attacks of aliens looking to overrun the US government.'

'Not bad.'

'How's the coffee?'

'Pretty damn awful.'

'Thank you, we take a great deal of pride in that. Notice the economy-size jug of Tums sitting next to it.'

Quincy nodded and finished off the cup. He couldn't help wincing at the end, but at least it was caffeine. He set down the cup, rolled his neck, shook out his arms, and worked on feeling human. He nodded toward the gold medal Houlihan wore around his neck. He didn't remember having seen it before.

'New good luck charm?'

Lieutenant Houlihan shifted from side to side, looking suddenly sheepish. 'My wedding band.'

'Really?'

'Well, it meant a great deal to my wife that I wear a band. I kept telling her, in my line of work you don't want to give that much personal info. Three days ago was our one year anniversary. She had my band melted into this medallion and gave it to me. Now we're both happy. Maybe it is lucky. Luck wouldn't hurt these days. You married?'

'Recently divorced.'

Houlihan pointed to his necklace. 'Third wife,' he confessed. 'She's a trauma nurse, it works out much better. I come home three hours late saying I'm sorry but there was a traffic accident and it took us two hours to find the driver's arm, she just nods, tells me she was held late with a drive-by shooting, and dinner's on the table.'

'I see your point.'

'But I imagine with all the traveling you do, it's still rough. Nothing spells cop – or agent – like d-i-v-o-r-c-e.'

Quincy shrugged. The breakup of his marriage still bothered him. 'Yeah, and then guys like Bundy are getting married and fathering children from death row. I'll never understand women.'

'Not that you're bitter.'

Quincy laughed reluctantly. 'Not that I'm bitter,' he agreed.

'So, Agent, do you have any good news for me?'

'I have news,' Quincy said with a sigh. 'But I don't think it's good.'

He led Houlihan over to the small working space he'd managed to claim. His laptop was already open and running. 'Okay, so Beckett has a pattern.'

'You solved Beckett's pattern?'

'We did, and you're going to like this. We've been looking at numerology, astrology, lunar cycles. I had a friend of mine from the CIA – a decoder specialist – looking up longitudes and latitudes of crime scenes and trying to crack an encrypted message. Computers have been chewing away on this stuff, all because we know how clever Jim can be. And you want to know the answer? I'll show you the answer.'

Quincy turned his computer so Houlihan could see the screen.

'Shit,' the lieutenant said.

'Absolutely. Strictly grade-school stuff. You know how hard he must have been laughing over this in his prison cell? He's so clever, he makes stupid look good.'

Quincy shook his head. It was all there on the screen and he'd discovered it purely by accident. He'd been listing all the female victims in order in one column. Then he'd listed the crime scenes in order in the next column. He'd glanced at the column. If you took the first letter from each city and scrambled them, they read: Jim Beckett. The bastard had spelled his name in dead women.

'Help me out here, Agent. What does this mean?'

'It means there's method to his madness. It means his talk of discipline isn't completely smoke and mirrors. And, Lieutenant, it means he isn't done.'

'Sure he is, he spelled his name. No letters are missing.'

'These are the dead women, Lieutenant. His past work. Then he attacked his wife in Williamstown—'

'He didn't kill her.'

'Nope, he didn't. But he was sent to jail, and there he killed two prison guards. At MCI Cedar Junction in *Walpole*.'

Lieutenant Houlihan fell silent. Then, 'W. He wanted the letter *W*. *Jim Beckett w*. What does that mean?'

'It means he has more to say. Maybe *Jim Beckett was something or Jim Beckett wants* something. I don't know. But there's a phrase in his head and he won't stop until he's gotten it out. He's not done, Houlihan. He's not done.'

'Lieutenant,' a voice called across the room. 'I have Lieutenant Berttelli from Connecticut on the phone for you.'

Houlihan and Quincy exchanged glances. Houlihan took the call at a nearby table. It lasted just a few minutes.

'They found Shelly Zane. You coming?'

'Yes. What city?'

'Avon. Avon, Connecticut.'

Quincy added it to his column.

It took three hours to drive to the cheap roadside motel outside of Avon. The crime scene photographer had just finished up, and now the Connecticut task force officers were bagging the evidence. Two officers were trying to figure out how to move the queen-size bed, which was bolted to the floor. Finally they decided severing the bolts would disturb the crime scene too much, so they instructed a rookie to crawl beneath the bed and retrieve the victim's fingers.

When Quincy walked in, that was the first thing he saw – some rookie's butt sticking up from beneath the bed as he reached for Shelly Zane's fingers. Those were the games Beckett liked to play. He liked to mutilate his victim's hands and he liked to mess with cops. Somewhere right now Jim was probably driving down a highway and chuckling at the thought of some rookie on his hands and knees recovering bloody fingers and trying not to retch.

Quincy walked into the bathroom, where Shelly Zane's body lay splayed out on the cracked blue-tiled floor between the toilet and the bathtub. Her arms were over her head, her mutilated hands palm up, as if she were caught in the act of surrendering. A pair of nylons were tied so tightly around her neck, they'd almost disappeared into the flesh. Quincy had already spotted the empty package of Hanes Alive Support hose in the wastebasket. Bundy had bragged that they had superior tensile strength, making them the garrote of choice for ligature. Apparently Beckett had paid attention to that part of the Bundy interview notes.

Postmortem lividity was most pronounced in the head, above the ligature line, and in the arms and lower legs, indicating that she'd been hanged. Around the knotted nylons, ruptured blood vessels had turned her neck black and blue. Petechial hemorrhages had darkened the whites of her eyes bloodred.

The back of her head was thick with blood and gray matter. The walls bore the spray pattern. Beckett had strangled her to death, dropped her down, then beaten her with a blunt wooden instrument. Typical homicidal overkill.

Thirteen victims later, Beckett's rage was only growing worse.

Shelly Zane's body was already outlined with chalk, unusual for this early in the evidence-gathering process. Behind him, Lieutenant Berttelli was raking a young officer over the coals for it. Probably the officer who'd arrived on the scene first.

'What the fuck were you thinkin'?' the lieutenant was screaming. 'Didn't they teach you to *never* mess with the crime scene until the photos are taken? What am I supposed to tell the DA now? I got a bunch of fucking photos of a fucking outlined corpse that no fucking judge is gonna admit as evidence.'

'I swear, I didn't do it—'

'Well, it wasn't the fucking chalk fairy.'

'Beckett,' Quincy said calmly. Lieutenant Berttelli shut up long enough to pay attention. 'Beckett knows the rules of evidence,' Quincy continued. 'And he likes to mess with our minds.'

Quincy's gaze came to rest on the note pinned to Shelly Zane's stomach. 'The officers left it for you,' Lieutenant Houlihan supplied.

The note had his name on it. It said in simple block letters: SHE WAS NO LONGER USEFUL TO ME.

Quincy rose. 'He's on the move.'

'You think he's going after Tess?'

'Yes.'

'We should call and warn her.'

Quincy eyed him sharply. 'I thought you didn't know where she was.'

Lieutenant Houlihan shifted. 'I don't personally know where she is, but I know who does.'

'And you would contact this person and he would contact her?'

'Yeah, something like that.'

Quincy nodded. 'Lieutenant Houlihan, absolutely, positively, do *not* do that.'

'What?'

He gestured at the note, and for the first time Houlihan caught the anger simmering in his eyes. 'Don't you recognize those words? Do you think it's mere coincidence that he's using the same phrase I used in the briefing one week ago?'

Houlihan blanched. 'Holy shit.'

'Do you see now how much he's toying with us? That note is a lie, Lieutenant. Because Shelly Zane is still useful to him. You react to her murder. You break the silence, you contact the person, who contacts Tess—'

'Which is exactly what he's waiting for us to do. He's watching us, hiding wherever the hell he hides. The minute we break silence, he'll have her. Holy shit.'

Houlihan looked as if he'd gained ten years in ten seconds. Quincy figured he looked the same.

'Tess was right to go out on her own. We are absolutely, positively, dangerous to her. Beckett's too close for us to see, he hides in our wake. And he's not going to stop until he finds her. He's got his message in mind, but his ultimate target, his ultimate goal, is killing Tess.'

Houlihan looked at the blond corpse on the bathroom floor. He stared at the note piercing her skin. 'God, I hate this job.'

'Me too, Lieutenant. Me too.'

The young, somber-faced man walked into task force headquarters, went straight to the officer on duty, and flashed his badge. 'Detective Beaumont,' he introduced himself. 'I'm from Bristol County and I have an urgent message for Lieutenant Houlihan.'

'I'm sorry, Detective, but Lieutenant Houlihan is currently unavailable.'

'Officer, you don't understand. This is urgent, I mean *urgent*. I just drove up forty minutes from Bristol to make sure Houlihan gets the news. I need to speak with him.'

The officer wavered. Detective Beaumont leaned forward.

'Please. We think we may know where Jim Beckett is. I have to get word to Tess Williams or Lieutenant Difford immediately. Help me out here, Officer. Speed matters.'

She caved in with a sigh. 'See that man standing over there? That's Sergeant Wilcox. He's in charge of the safe house. He can probably help you.'

'Sergeant Wilcox?'

'Yes, that's him.'

'Thank you, Officer. You've been very helpful.'

Edith smoothed a hand over her old blue flannel shirt and tried not to shift too much on the front porch. Last night she'd received a call from Martha, stating that she would arrive first thing this morning – the poor woman had been driving up all the way from Florida over the last few days. That was Martha for you. At sixty years of age, the woman was as proud and independent as they came. She'd moved into the neighborhood only a few years earlier, but the first evening she'd knocked on Edith's door and offered a pint of scotch. The two women had sat on Edith's patio, opened the fifty-year-old bottle, discovered a mutual love of cigars, and spent two hours agreeing that there hadn't been a decent president since Eisenhower.

Edith appreciated such relationships. She was too old for foo-fooing or fussiness. Most women her age started off talking about Jell-O salad and soon fled from the premises when Edith stared them straight in the eye and declared, 'Who the hell cares about Jell-O? It's the rapid proliferation of assault weapons that keeps me awake at night.'

She didn't want platitudes or shoulder-shrugging. Everyone should say what they wanted. It saved time.

Martha spoke tersely. At times she could be imperious, but Edith figured that's what came from living your whole life head and shoulders above the rest. Martha was tall, and that was an understatement. Of Swedish descent, she had her father's impressive height and shoulders, though neither was so attractive on a woman.

Most men were too intimidated to come anywhere near a woman of Martha's impressive bulk, but apparently she'd met an equally impressive Swede in her youth and before he'd died, they'd had one sizable blond son. Edith had never met the son. From the few things Martha had casually mentioned, he was a salesman of some kind and moved a lot. Martha didn't see him often and generally didn't go on and on about him the way some mothers did.

Edith appreciated that. Having spent all her life childless, she got impatient with endless stories about whose son was being promoted to what position and whose daughter was giving birth to how many grand-children. Good Lord, the world was already overpopulated and over-extending the earth's resources. Didn't people give the matter any thought?

An old brown Cadillac turned down the street like an unwieldy boat. Martha had arrived. Minutes later Edith was pumping her neighbor's hand vigorously.

'Lord, Florida was good for you!' Martha's faded blond hair had lightened to a snowy white, which looked natural with her sun-darkened skin. It had been years since they'd last seen each other, but after one glance Edith could tell that Martha was Martha. She still had the same startling blue eyes and smooth complexion; Swedes aged so nicely. Martha's taste in clothes hadn't changed either. Today she sported a huge pair of brown polyester pants and a man's oversize red flannel shirt. A wide-brimmed straw hat perched precariously on her head, smashed there at the last minute.

Martha patted her generous waistline. 'The food was too good,' she drawled huskily, her voice still carrying a hint of Swedish mountains. 'But the weather was too hot. I missed snow.'

Edith shook her hand again. 'It's good to have you back,' she repeated. And it was good. She tried to pretend she didn't see things. She tried to pretend she didn't feel things. But the air in their community was different these days. Edith didn't like it.

And more and more often Edith found herself staring next door and thinking that now was not a good time to live so close to an empty home.

'Let me help with your luggage,' Edith volunteered, already moving toward the trunk and shaking away the shivers creeping up her spine. She had no use for 'feelings' or 'visions.' A person couldn't act on a feeling. 'You travel light.'

'At my age, who needs things?' Martha pulled out two suitcases. 'And the house?'

'Just the same as you left it.' Edith had agreed to take care of the house when Martha had announced she was going to visit Florida for a spell and try her hand at golf. Edith had a key to the place and gave it the once-over every month. Martha called every few months to ask about the house, though generally the discussion turned quickly to politics. Martha didn't like Clinton. Edith couldn't stand Newt. They both enjoyed the conversations immensely.

Edith turned to the front door, already tugging on the suitcase. But then she froze, the hair on the back of her neck prickling up.

The girl stood in front of the door perfectly naked. This close, Edith could see the butterfly tattoo above her left breast. Nothing big or vulgar. The butterfly was small, dainty even, a light flickering of color that spoke of a lonely wish for flight. Blond hair cascaded down her shoulders, of course – all the girls were blondes.

Edith raised her gaze even though she didn't really want to see more. There was nothing, no message, not a plea to give her a hint. The girl just stood there, naked with blood on her face, and her eyes were faintly apologetic, as if she knew she was as unwanted dead as she had been alive.

'Go away, child,' Edith said softly. 'There's nothing I can do for you.'

The girl remained, stubborn. Edith squeezed her eyes shut, and when she opened them again, she'd won and the girl was gone.

Belatedly she became aware of the quizzical look on Martha's face. 'You all right?'

Edith didn't answer immediately. 'Did you hear that serial killer got loose?'

'Huh?'

'Jim Beckett, that's his name. Killed ten women and now two prison guards. Got outta Walpole. That's not far from here.'

Martha didn't say anything, but for one moment Edith saw something flash across those bright eyes. It looked like fear, bone-deep fear. The big woman composed herself quickly, squaring her broad shoulders.

'This is a small community, Edith, a quiet place. Someone like him wouldn't have any cause to come here.'

Edith watched Martha awhile longer, but Martha's expression was blank.

'I'm sure you're right,' Edith said at last.

She didn't believe either one of them though. And it bothered her that they'd each told their first lie over a man such as Jim Beckett. It bothered her a lot.

16

J.T. was on edge.

By nightfall, he paced the living room with enough energy to power a small city. Marion took one look and returned her beer to the refrigerator. She reentered the room with two glasses of water, handing one to her brother.

J.T. downed it wordlessly. He wiped his mouth with the back of his arm. Then he resumed pacing.

'Oh, for God's sake,' Marion said at last, 'you're giving me gray hairs. Sit down.'

He pivoted and headed the other direction. 'Don't you feel it?' he asked.

'Feel what?'

'Tess, go to your room.'

'What?'

'Lock the door. Knit a sweater.'

'Oh, no. If there's something going on, I want to know.'

J.T.'s gaze locked on his sister. Marion shook her head. 'I walked the grounds just half an hour ago, J.T. There's nothing out there but your own dark mood. Stop panicking Tess.'

'She wanted to stay.'

'Would someone start speaking English?' Tess demanded. Her belly had knotted.

'I don't like it,' J.T. repeated. 'Air's different. Something. Shit, we're outta here.'

'What?'

J.T. strode across the room. 'You heard me. Grab your purses, girls, we're blowing this joint.'

'J.T., this is stupid—'

J.T. halted. 'You got friends in the Nogales Police Department, right, Marion?'

She nodded warily.

'Call them. Tell then we're going out for a few hours. Tell them we're worried about the "intruder" returning. Ask them to send a patrol car to cruise around a bit, say half-hour intervals.'

'I don't know . . .'

'Marion, what can it hurt?'

That got her. Marion placed the call while Tess found a light jacket. Tess returned to the living room quickly; she no longer felt like being alone.

Wordlessly they piled into Marion's car, three people staring out at a black landscape, trying to see what was out there.

'A bar?' Tess declared twenty minutes later, staring incredulously at the neon-clad, rock'n'roll-blaring joint. 'J.T., this isn't a good idea. Why don't we go to a movie?'

He kept walking. 'Crowds are good, Tess, and so is a place with five exits.'

Marion and Tess exchanged dubious glances. J.T. strolled inside, obviously no stranger to the establishment.

Located on a busy street in downtown Nogales, it advertised itself aggressively with loud music and rowdy patrons. At the moment Bruce Springsteen was blasting everyone new eardrums with the loudest rendition of 'Born to Run' that Tess had ever heard. Above, a seventies disco ball swirled madly, casting a dizzying array of diamond dots onto a dance floor filled with people who truly knew how to move. The light disappeared at the corners, leaving gaping pools of blackness where she could dimly see couples in various stages of drinking and displaying public affection. Everyone looked Latino.

J.T. cut a clean path through the madness, his gaze watchful. Tess and Marion kept close to him. J.T. raised his hand and pointed to a corner, his lips moving but his words lost in the thundering music. Tess and Marion moved quickly to follow, fading deeper into the hallway, the music receding behind them. New odors assaulted their senses: beer, urine. Sex.

Finally J.T. came to a doorway guarded by tendrils of orange and red glass beads. He held the curtain back and motioned for Marion and Tess to enter. His gaze swept the hall behind them, then he let the curtain drop.

'A video arcade?' Marion huffed. 'You brought us here for video games?'

'They're better than the beer, Marion. Or are G-men too tough for pinball?'

Tess stared. They weren't alone in the room by any means. It was filled with a huge crowd and electronic sounds. She heard a coin machine dispensing change and the glug-glug of some animated character dying. Several men looked up when they entered, appeared a little surprised, then went back to what they were doing before. There were few women in the room. One of them, scantily clad in a crimson skirt and halter top, looked like hell on wheels sitting at a car game. She'd attracted several onlookers and didn't seem to mind.

J.T. went straight to a row of older pinball machines and selected one. DEAD MAN WALKING, it said.

Tess shuddered.

'Come on, ladies. It's hand-eye coordination.'

'I don't have any, thanks,' Tess volunteered.

With another scowl and frustrated sigh Marion gave up on protesting and sized up the machine. 'All right. You're on.'

'Two out of three?'

'Four out of seven. You're obviously not new here.'

'High score is mine.'

'Oh, really? How drunk were you at the time?'

'Stone cold sober,' J.T. drawled. 'Down here, Marion, pinball's serious business.'

'Yeah, well, so is cotton,' she muttered.

'Tess,' J.T. said calmly. 'Watch the doorway, will you? If anyone white walks in, let me know. I don't think we were followed, but it's been a bit since I played cat and mouse.'

J.T. popped two quarters into the machine. Marion cracked her knuckles and stretched out her arms. The two of them got down to the obviously serious business of pinball, but Tess didn't relax that easily. Her gaze kept darting back to the doorway, just in case Jim Beckett magically appeared.

J.T. was no slouch. He hit five digits before his turn was up, and gave way only after delivering a mocking bow. Marion took over with narrowed eyes and thinned lips. She looked as if she'd gone to war.

She moved too fast, and the first silver ball escaped through the paddles before she'd made much progress. She slapped the machine, earning a tilt sign.

'Relax, Marion. It's just a machine.'

'Fucking machine,' she supplied.

'Have it your way.'

She attacked the second ball, and since she had phenomenal hand-eye coordination and a wicked learning curve, she made the machine sing. A light began to burn in her eyes. And for a moment she looked exactly like J.T.

'She's something, isn't she?' J.T. murmured.

Tess nodded. 'What did your parents feed you?'

'Lies. Pure lies. Taught us the truth of the world early on.' His lips curved into a ghost of a grin. 'See any sign of trouble at the door?'

'No.'

'Huh. Maybe Marion was right. Maybe I just need a drink.'

'J.T.—'

'Shit!' Marion yelled, and hit the machine. 'Piece of junk!'

J.T. jostled his sister aside. 'Easy, honey. Machine can't help it if I'm better than you.'

Marion leaned against the wall next to Tess, but she no longer appeared relaxed. J.T. settled in at the pinball machine, looking like a captain at the helm of his ship.

'Face it, Marion, you should've joined the marines.'

'No, thanks. I figured one Dillon punching out COs was enough.'

J.T. pulled back the handle and sent the silver ball flying. 'I suppose I could've just enrolled him in the Communist Party, but beating the crap out of his own wife seemed to warrant something more personal.'

'Communist Party?' Tess asked. She wasn't sure she wanted to understand this conversation.

'West Point,' J.T. supplied. 'I enrolled the director in the Communist Party. I *hated* West Point.'

'And that got you kicked out?'

'Nah. That was considered a boys-will-be-boys prank. When he came to call me on it and found me in bed with his daughter, *that* got me kicked out.'

'You seduced the director's daughter?'

'He's a pig,' Marion said. 'Absolutely no self-control.'

'How do you know I was the seducer?' J.T. quizzed innocently.

Marion shook her head. 'Give it up, Jordan. If you were turned loose in a nunnery, by the end of the day they'd all renounce God.'

'Thank you. I try.' J.T. gave Tess a look that was blatantly wolfish. 'Did I scare you?'

'When?' She was having trouble concentrating.

'Earlier. When I asked Marion to call the police.'

'I guess. I have a lot to be scared of.'

'You have both Marion and me here, Tess. It's even legal for Marion to shoot to kill.'

'He's right, you know,' Marion said. 'At least this time. It's not easy to become an FBI agent, and it's even harder for a woman. I'm good. I'll make sure nothing happens to you, Tess.'

Tess didn't answer; she'd been told such things before, and none of the assurance had helped her when Jim had stepped out of her closet and hefted a bat to his shoulder. She said, 'That was a nice thing you did – putting away the beer. Teetotaling is really getting to him.'

'Yeah, I guess it is. I knew about the annual tequila binges, but they're only once a year and, well, given the circumstances . . .'

'His wife's death?' Tess guessed.

Marion nodded. 'Teddy died instantly. But Rachel . . . She was in a coma for five days. J.T. just kept sitting there in the hospital, holding her hand. He seemed so certain that she would open her eyes and be with him again. He just couldn't let her go. He's weak that way.' Marion pushed away from the wall. 'You have to be able to cut your losses, to move on. But J.T. can't seem to do that. He wants to go back and fix things way after the fact. It's a waste of time.'

J.T. lost his turn and Marion strode forward, leaving Tess to digest this unexpected burst of information. J.T. came to lean against the wall beside her, stretching out his legs and crossing his arms. He already appeared much more relaxed. She moved a little closer to him and joined him in a comfortable silence.

It wasn't until the seventh game that the trouble happened.

Tess never did know who started it. One moment she was watching J.T. volley the silver ball back into the megapoints zone, the next she heard a scream followed by a crash.

Everyone turned at once.

A man, obviously drunk, was towering over the woman who'd been playing the car game. He pointed at her and cursed her in voluble streams of Spanish. Though only half his size, the woman didn't give an inch. She stood to her full height and screamed right back.

The man pulled back his arm. He slapped the woman hard, snapping her head around. She crashed against the machine, falling bonelessly to the ground.

'For God's sake, no!' Marion cried. She lunged for J.T.'s arm, but she was too late. J.T. plunged into the thick of it.

Like a massive tidal wave, the crowd of people surged, some eddying out the door to escape and others moving in closely. More people – muscle-bound, testosterone-pumped men – flooded in, looking for action. Tess saw the woman try to rise, then flounder and fall back. Something dark and wet matted the woman's hair. Blood.

'Damn,' Marion said. She shook her head, then seemed to lose the war with herself and stepped forward.

Tess looked at J.T. He was raising his left arm to block one blow and pulling back his right arm to deliver another. She looked at Marion, striding purposefully ahead.

She took a deep breath.

She set her sights on the fallen woman and stepped into the whirlpool.

It was hot. Sweat-soaked flesh pressed against sweat-soaked flesh until the air seemed to steam. It was loud. She couldn't distinguish any single voice or cry, she just heard the dull roar building to a crescendo. It was thick. She was too short to see over and too small to shoulder her way through. So she pushed and pawed, as if hacking her way through a dense undergrowth, trying to remember where she'd last seen the woman and head in that direction.

She burst into a small clearing and drew in a huge gulp of air. Then, like a swimmer, she held it in her lungs and plunged back in.

An arm caught her in the shoulder and she stumbled. Another arm caught her and tossed her back onto her feet. She lurched forward, her hands fisted at her sides, her jaw clenched. Someone jostled her, and in a spurt of terror she used some of her newly developed muscle to push back. The body gave way instantly. She was amazed.

She pushed herself through and found the fallen woman, who was moaning and clutching her head. Tess hunched down, eyeing the woman anxiously.

A crash resounded above them. Tess and the woman swiveled their heads simultaneously to find the new threat. A man stood beside them, looking not at them but at another charging man. The first man wielded the jagged half of a broken beer bottle in front of him.

'Damn,' Tess swore. Out of the corner of her eye she caught Marion bursting from the crush, her hair disheveled, her blouse ripped. She didn't even glance at Tess or the fallen woman. She went straight after the man with the broken bottle. He tried to bring up his arm to fend her off.

He didn't have a chance. Two smartly delivered chops, and Marion had him writhing on the ground, holding his twisted arm and screaming curses. The charging man hesitated, not sure what to do with a woman. Marion decided the matter for him. Her foot hooked him neatly behind the ankles, and with a fierce yank she toppled him to the ground. A new cry rose up from the crowd.

Tess stopped thinking. She offered her hand to the fallen woman and helped her to her feet. The woman clutched her bloody head.

'Look out!' Marion cried.

Tess froze. The man who'd started it all was there, towering above them, his eyes bright with rage. He carried a chair leg in one hand.

Tess stared at the rounded wood. And she thought, It's not nearly so sturdy as a baseball bat.

The chair leg was raised up into the air.

Then Tess shivered, her gaze locked onto the images suddenly in her head. The baseball bat swinging down. The crack of her thigh. The burning pain. The scent of blood. The knowledge of all the other times the bat had whistled down and connected with human flesh and bone.

How did a head sound when hit by a bat? Like wood cracking? Or more like a melon going *splat?*

A dull roaring filled her ears.

Dimly she heard the chair leg whistle down. Dimly she saw the man tossed forward and J.T. standing in his spot. Then, as if from far, far away, Marion said, 'God, J.T., she's going to faint.'

'Shit.'

Suddenly strong arms were around her, swinging her up. She went wild, fighting and clawing, and she couldn't even remember what she was fighting. She just had to fight.

J.T.'s hand caught hers, trapping them against his chest. 'Shh, *chiquita,* I have you. I have you.'

She buried her face against his shoulder and prayed he wouldn't let her go.

J.T. carried her out of the building and into the cool, night air.

'Are you all right?' J.T. asked half an hour later as he set her down on the sofa.

Marion had dragged the wounded woman out of the bar, entrusted her to the care of the few people in the parking lot, then they'd escaped the scene. Now J.T.'s thumb brushed Tess's cheek, then feathered through her hair. His gaze was intent as he searched for wounds.

'Yes. Yes, I'm fine,' Tess murmured, too embarrassed to meet his gaze. J.T. and Marion had been ready to take on the place. She'd seen one raised chair leg and almost fainted. Some bad ass she was.

'That wasn't how the evening was supposed to turn out.'

'I suppose it's a bad sign when your star pupil almost loses her lunch during her first brawl. Maybe next time Jim shows up, I can vomit on him for self-defense.'

'Tess—'

Marion returned from checking the grounds, snapping on the living room light. She'd already spoken to the police; they hadn't seen anyone lurking in the vicinity.

J.T. moved back. For the first time, Tess noted the scratch running down his cheek and his bruised knuckles.

'You're hurt.'

He glanced at his hands idly. 'It's nothing.' He turned to Marion. 'And you?'

'I'm fine.' Marion leaned against the doorjamb, her silk blouse ripped and linen pants beer-stained. Her hair had come undone, golden waves now rippling down her shoulders. The style took ten years off her age.

'You should leave your hair down,' Tess blurted out. 'You look beautiful.'

'Gets in my way.' The agent was already braiding the strands.

'Forget it,' J.T. told Tess flatly. 'She likes the feminazi style.'

'I prefer the word *professional*. Would you like some ice for your knuckles?'

'Whatever.'

Marion rolled her eyes but went after the ice.

An awkward silence filled the room. Tess didn't know how to break it. She examined her hands. She wished she had bruised knuckles.

'I'm sorry,' J.T. said abruptly.

'For what?'

'Uh . . . the bar fight. They aren't so unusual at that place.'

'You wanted a fight?'

A pause. 'Maybe.'

'All the swimming,' Tess murmured, 'all the weights, the jogging, the shooting, it's not enough for you, is it?'

'I'm an intense kind of guy.'

She looked at him, then she stared at the doorway that led into the kitchen. 'J.T., why are you always so angry?'

'Who, me?'

'Marion has that anger too.'

'Marion has ice in her veins. She likes it that way.'

'Versus you—'

'Who has tequila. It's been a long night, Tess. We all need some sleep.'

'Did you really think someone was watching the house tonight, or was that just an excuse?'

'No,' he said immediately, but then looked troubled. 'I don't know. Maybe Marion was right. Maybe it's just withdrawal. I'm . . . I'm a little on edge these days.' He looked her in the eye. 'Tess, when it comes right down to it, Marion is the one you can count on. I have raw talent, she has follow-through. I get in trouble, she gets things done. Remember that, all right? If push comes to shove, go to Marion. She'll take care of you.'

'You're wrong,' she told him. 'When push comes to shove, you're the one who's going to help me, J.T. You're the only one I know who's intense enough to take on Jim.'

He silenced further declarations with a finger over her lips. Wordlessly he took her hand and drew her off the sofa.

There was no light on in the hallway. It loomed dark and endless, as hushed as a sanctuary. Her footsteps slowed. So did his. When they arrived at her room, she didn't open the door. She leaned against it and stared at his face.

She traced the fresh scratch marring his cheek. 'Does that hurt?'

'No.'

Her fingers curled around his chin, then brushed his lips.

'What are you doing, Tess?'

'Nothing.' She touched his nose, his cheekbone, his eye. Her hand curved around his neck, rubbing the taut, corded muscles there, and she heard his indrawn breath leave him hoarsely.

She liked touching him. She could feel his power, electric and tantalizing and held precariously in check. She had done the right thing in coming to him.

She'd found the right man.

And she wanted him.

She knew so little about desire. She thought he was the kind of man who could teach a woman all about it. The kind of man who could draw a woman in and wring her out with passion.

She leaned forward.

'Don't.' He grabbed her shoulder and pinned her back. 'Don't.'

'Why not?'

'It's not what you really want, Tess.'

'I'm stronger than you think.'

'Yeah. But maybe I'm not.' He let her go. 'Good night.'

'But—'

His gaze stopped her. It washed over her and stripped her bare. He moved closer. Then closer still. His head dipped. She held her breath and opened her lips, prepared to meet him all the way.

He twisted his head to the side at the last moment, and his teeth caught her earlobe delicately. 'Go to bed, Tess. And lock your door.'

Then he was gone.

17

'¡*Mierda!* You are not even trying!'

'Jesus, lady, you're demanding!' J.T. rolled off Rosalita, lying on his back and staring up at the swirling ceiling fan.

Rosalita propped herself up beside him. 'You are not yourself.'

He cocked a brow. 'You get off twice and you're still so pissed you speak gringo? Rosalita, you are the Antichrist.'

She didn't scowl, she didn't sulk. She looked worried instead. He hated that. God almighty, someone deliver him from the women in his house.

Tentatively she ran one finger down the scar on his chest. He barely resisted the urge to bat it away. 'It's *la chiquita*, no? You like her.'

'I don't like anyone, Rosalita. It's part of my charm.'

No, he was not himself this evening. He was taut and aching. He was screwing the best whore in Nogales and thinking of another woman.

Christ, he wanted her. He wanted to take her until she couldn't walk, she couldn't stand, she couldn't breathe, until all she could do was scream. Then he wanted to take her again.

And afterward? his mind whispered. *What could you give a woman like that out of bed, J.T.? What could you offer a woman like her?*

She was changing, becoming strong, capable. He knew, because he'd seen it before. Seen a woman come into herself and realize that she didn't have just arms and legs but that she could run, fight, give, take. She could reclaim all the pieces of herself that had been stolen by stronger, cruel men and do whatever she wanted.

Rachel had chosen to give herself to him. And he had loved her for that unbearably.

He reached for the nightstand, found a crumpled pack of cigarettes, and pounded one out. He brought it to his lips and lit it. The tobacco seared ten years off his lungs. Gotta hate it. Gotta love it. It was just his style.

Rosalita was still watching him. Now she pressed her body next to his. He could roll her over and thrust into her again and she would only sigh her contentment. He could guide her head down and she would swallow him whole. If he could think of it, she would do it, and she could probably do a few things that defied his imagination as well.

He simply lay there, exhaling smoke and watching it drift languidly up to the whirling fan blades.

'I'll bring you a drink.' Rosalita climbed out of bed, wrapped the sheet around her body. 'You'll feel better then.'

'You should get married,' he said lightly. 'Find yourself a husband and raise a few kids instead of hanging out with the likes of me.'

The look of concern on her face grew. If he did or said one more thing out of character, the woman was going to check his forehead for fever and fetch him a doctor.

She opened the door and trailed down the hall.

Who was she most likely to run into tonight, Tess or Marion? The woman he didn't want to save but seemed to think that only he could save her? Or the woman he'd once tried to save but now seemed to think that he was the devil?

'God does have such a sense of humor,' he muttered to the ceiling. 'Even a worse sense than mine.'

The cigarette burned down to his fingers. He let it drop to the floor, pressing it out with the pad of his thumb. He gave up smoking every morning and started again every night. And tonight it wasn't even dulling his brain the way it was supposed to.

He was still thinking of Tess and thinking of Tess made him remember Rachel. J.T. had married Rachel because he understood that she was an eighteen-year-old mother who wanted the best for her son. He'd married her because if she was as corrupt, twisted, and manipulative as Marion said, then it was the colonel who'd molded her into that shape.

His father had come up to him after the ceremony, pumped J.T.'s hand, and stated, 'Now Teddy will have the family name and I'll get my second son into West Point to redeem my first son's mistakes. I knew you'd do the right thing, Jordan.'

And J.T. had said, 'You touch Rachel or Teddy ever again, and I will kill you. Understand, *Daddy?*'

It was the only time J.T. ever saw the colonel pale.

For the first six months he and Rachel lived together like awkward acquaintances. She had her room in the apartment. He had his. When they talked and interacted, it was about Teddy. But sometimes, late at night, they would sit at the kitchen table, drinking beers and revealing little bits and pieces of themselves.

She told him about the stepfather who made it impossible for her to remain at home. He talked about the first time his father had whipped him and how sure he'd been that he deserved it. She recalled trying to find a job, then realizing homeless fifteen-year-olds couldn't get one. He spoke of the jungle and the endless hours of sitting in steam, waiting for the right moment to pounce and destroy.

One night she told him about the first time she'd sold her body. She'd recited Dr Seuss rhymes in her mind to block out the act. Afterward she hadn't cried. The man had paid her well, so she hadn't cried. She'd just rocked herself back and forth and tried not to remember the life she'd dreamed about as a little girl.

Neither of their lives made much sense, but somehow, sitting up together late at night, they made the warped, jagged pieces fit. They offered each other the forgiveness they couldn't offer themselves. They planned a future. They built a new life.

Until the little kid who'd been beaten by his father loved her, and the adolescent who'd been rejected by his younger sister loved her, and the man who'd gone off to fight wars because he no longer cared if he lived or died loved her. Until every single deranged, hopeful, frightened part of him loved her.

Then Rachel had gone and gotten herself dead.

J.T. reached over to the nightstand, retrieved another cigarette, and started destroying his lungs all over again.

Rosalita drifted back into the room. She paused at the foot of the bed and smiled.

And just for a minute, in the twisted corridors of his mind he saw Marion, young, vulnerable Marion. And his baby sister's hands were clasped and her face terrified as she ran from the monster they both knew too well. *'Hide me, J.T. God help me, please, please, please!'*

'Shh,' he whispered to his own mind, and squeezed his eyes shut.

When he reopened them, Rosalita was by his side, no longer concerned but triumphant. She held out the icy glass.

Tequila on the rocks with a twist. He looked up at her, and she smiled at him, happy. 'You will be yourself,' she said simply.

'You are the Antichrist,' he whispered.

His fingers curled around the glass.

Marion entered the living room just as a woman in a white cotton sheet disappeared into her brother's room. For a moment Marion thought she'd seen a ghost. She shook her head and crossed to the phone.

She liked the living room late at night. Sometimes she went out there just to sit and watch the moon slide through the open blinds and sift over the wicker furniture. In one corner the iguana slept by a heat lamp. Otherwise she was alone.

She contemplated lighting a cigarette but knew by then that J.T. might appear. Sometimes, as she sat in the shadows, he would emerge from the hall and head straight for the patio. Minutes after he'd slipped through the sliding glass door, she'd hear the muted splash of a perfect dive.

Marion took a deep, steadying breath, picked up the phone, and dialed. 'How is he?' she asked.

'Marion?' Roger's voice was groggy with sleep. It was two A.M. his time.

Was he sleeping with his new toy? Had she interrupted something? She hoped so.

'How is he?' She gave up on her earlier good intentions and found a cigarette. Her hand was trembling.

'Marion, it's two in the morning.'

'Thank you, Roger, but I can tell time. Now, how is he?'

Roger sighed. She thought she heard the low murmur of a woman's voice. So the cocktail waitress was there. It hurt. It hurt more than she thought it would.

I loved you, Roger. I honestly loved you.

'He's dying, Marion. Jesus Christ, what the hell do you want me to say? The doctors have given him medication for the pain, but at this point not even that's enough. Maybe another week, maybe two. Or maybe tomorrow he'll die. For his sake, I hope so.'

'Not a very charitable thought about the man you considered your mentor, Roger. But then, we both know just how highly you regard loyalty.'

He was silent. In her mind she could see the way his lips would be thinning right now and his high brow creasing into lines of tension. She'd been married to him for almost ten years. She knew him inside and out. She knew he was slightly weak and spineless. She knew he was smart and ambitious. She knew everything about him – she'd thought that was what marriage was all about.

'All right, Marion,' he said quietly. 'Be bitter if you want to. But you're the one who called me. I'm just the messenger telling you that your father is still in the last stages of cancer. He's in pain, he's delusional. He moans and sometimes he cries out for Jordan and sometimes he cries out for Teddy. If you want him to live like that, fine. I think it's a helluva way to die.'

J.T. and Teddy. She wasn't surprised that the colonel hadn't called her name. He'd never had any use for a daughter.

'And Emma?' she threw in, referring to her mother. Marion didn't like Emma. She considered her a weak bitch more content with fantasy than being a good wife to the colonel. But Roger had always had a soft spot for the demented old bat.

'I worry about her too,' Roger said predictably enough. 'She's quoting Sophia Loren's lines from *El Cid*. I'm half afraid she might actually stick his corpse on a horse one of these days. You know she's always worse under pressure.'

'Pressure? The woman cracks under the strain of what shoes to wear in the morning.'

'Marion . . . why did you call?'

'I wanted make sure nothing had happened.'

Another lengthy silence. This time she knew he was not frowning. Instead, he was painstakingly choosing his words. Roger was a very diplomatic man, a born spin doctor. She imagined his career would continue to advance nicely in the army.

'Marion . . .' His voice was soft. She automatically stiffened her spine. 'I know this is a tough time for you. I know I hurt you—'

'Hurt me? *Hurt me!* You walked out on our marriage!'

'I know, Marion. But—'

'But what? We had respect, we had friendship. We had ten years of history. My God, Roger, we had a solid relationship.'

'Except that you froze every time I touched you.'

She went rigid, the cigarette burning down to her lips. She couldn't breathe, she couldn't speak, she couldn't move.

'I'm sorry,' Roger said. 'God, I'm sorry, Marion. I know that hurts. But how was I supposed to take that? How was I supposed to live like that? I have needs—'

'It's my job, isn't it? You've always been jealous, haven't you? Thought it took too much of my time, kept me from being the perfect army wife and hostess. And my career is a good career too, one as good as yours – and I'm stronger than you. I shoot better than you. You're . . . you're just an army bureaucrat and I'm the one out there actually making a difference!' Her voice was harsh. It kept her from falling into a million pieces.

'Well, I wouldn't have minded a wife who came home on occasion. A wife who didn't compare me to her boss or to her darling father. Is that so much to ask for?' The carefully crafted words were spinning away from him. She took sublime satisfaction in that.

'You're weak!' she spat out into the phone. 'You're spineless and only half the man the colonel is. You're not a real lieutenant colonel, you just know how to play political games. I'm glad you left. It's better this way. You play with your little child. At least you finally found someone you can be better than!'

'Dammit, Marion! Don't do—'

She didn't hear the rest. She slammed the phone down so hard, Glug flinched. She stared at the lizard, willing it to move so she'd have an excuse to tear it to pieces.

The iguana wisely played dead. She lit a fresh cigarette and inhaled the acrid smoke until tears stung her eyes. Her body was trembling and she hurt, way down deep inside.

For just one moment she wanted to curl into a ball and weep. She wanted to hold out her arms and have someone wrap her in a strong embrace and whisper soothing words in her ear.

It'll be all right, Merry Berry. I'll save you. I'll save you.

The words came out of nowhere, as faint as a dream. She rubbed her cheeks with her fists, swallowing through the tightness in her chest.

To hell with Roger. He was a weak man consoling himself through his midlife crisis with a twenty-two-year-old. She was tougher than him. She was tougher than most men she met. It unnerved all of them. Even in the nineties, men expected a little simpering, a little need. They told her she would have equal opportunity as a female agent, then tried to hide dead bodies from her sight as if she might faint. And then when she bent down and investigated the scene, they exchanged glances over her head as if she were some dyke in disguise.

They told her they didn't mind independence, then looked wounded the first time she didn't cry in their arms because she'd seen a murder. They said they understood her strength, then resented it when she outperformed them on the shooting range.

She was not the one changing the rules. She was not the one saying she was comfortable with one thing and expecting another. She'd married and she was faithful. She'd taken a vow of fidelity, bravery, and integrity, and she was a good agent. She'd promised the colonel she would make him proud and she would be at his side holding his hand when he died. And she'd see to it that he got the best sendoff any man had ever had.

She brushed off her shirt. She patted her hair, which was pulled back into a French twist. She told herself she was composed and together and the strongest thing this side of hell.

Then she walked down the hall to her bedroom.

Her feet slowed by J.T.'s door. The urge welled up so strongly, her hand actually curled around the doorknob. *Open the door. Go inside. He'll help you, he'll help you. Jordan will save you.*

Then she remembered that day at J.T.'s orienteering match, when their father had come back and he hadn't. She'd stood there while the adults had conferred, holding her stomach against the anger knotting her belly. Jordan had gone and done it. He'd escaped, he'd run away. He'd left her.

Then he was crashing through the underbrush. And instead of being relieved, she hated him all the more. Because he had come back, the dumb bastard, and for just one moment she'd thought that he was free, that J.T. had at least escaped and she wouldn't have to be scared for him anymore.

While the colonel had patted J.T. on the back for walking on a broken ankle, Marion had leaned into the woods and vomited until she dry-heaved.

'I hate you,' she now whispered, the words choked with tears.

She stormed into her room. 'Goddamn everyone in this house,' she muttered. 'Goddamn them all.' She slammed the window open, found a fresh pack of cigarettes, and tapped out one.

That was it. She'd had enough. She'd given J.T. his one week to decide. Tomorrow she would give him his last chance to see the light. Then she was getting out of this hellhole.

The cigarette trembled between her fingertips. She couldn't get it to light. She broke it in half in disgust and stared out the window. She found her arms wrapped around herself, and for an uncanny instant she suffered the sensation she was being watched.

She bolted from the window, grabbed her gun, and returned to the window with it already cocked. Eyes sharp in the night, peering this way, peering that way.

Shit, Marion, what are you doing? Jumping at shadows, ready to shoot at cacti. When did you become so fucked up?

She lowered the gun and hung her head between her shoulders. 'Get some sleep,' she ordered herself. 'Close the window and get some fucking sleep.'

She crawled into bed. The night was quiet and still. Just the crickets, the relentless crickets, murmuring through the night. She wrapped her arms around her pillow, and the exhaustion crashed over her. In two breaths she was asleep.

Merry Berry had some dreams.

The first two were nightmares, making her toss in bed and her lips move in soundless prayer. A tall, dark figure strode into her room. She heard the sound of jump boots against hardwood floors, and the ringing nauseated her.

Then that image spiraled away and she'd arrived in Arizona. She was running around the hacienda, calling J.T.'s name. She had to protect . . . she had to find . . . She rounded the corner and there he was: Jim Beckett's face pressed against the window, his tongue licking the glass.

She murmured in her sleep, trying to push the dream away. She was so tired and she was so afraid. There was never anyone to comfort her anymore. Never anyone who cared.

Sleep took pity on her and dragged her into a softer embrace.

She was little, little and strong. She rode the big gelding effortlessly, feeling his muscles bunch and flex at her command. 'Faster,' she whispered to him. 'Faster.'

Her hair flew behind her, the wind brushing tears from her eyes. Around and around they went. Faster and faster. Until she saw the jump. The big, huge jump looming ahead. They were going too fast, they would never clear the hurdle. Frantically she pulled back on the reins, but her horse fought the bit, his massive head twisting.

J.T.'s voice called out, soft but clear. He'd been there all along, out of sight, but she'd known he was there. She had depended on it.

'You can do it, Merry Berry,' he shouted. 'You can do it.'

She took the jump. She heard him clapping his hands.

And for just one moment she was free.

Jim was ready.

In the dark hours right before dawn he sat naked in the shuttered room and finished his preparations.

On the floor he had lined up two plastic eggs filled with neon purple Silly Putty, a box of clear sandwich bags, two bags of pillow stuffing, four packages of women's nylons, eyeliner, and a fairly expensive black wig guaranteed to make him appear 'ten years younger,' according to the salesman. Last was a large-size Middlesex County police uniform, stolen out of the police locker room from an officer who obviously spent most of his time at Dunkin' Donuts.

Beneath the harsh glare of a bare-bulb desk light, Jim labored over the uniform, his long, lean fingers meticulously ripping stitches and pulling off patches.

In the majority of situations, just the appearance of a uniform was enough; to an inexperienced eye all cops looked alike. But in fact, different departments, cities, and counties had their own distinct patches. Rank was indicated by the colored stripe running down the trouser leg as well as the bars or patches on the collar. Different counties also had different styles – from straight trousers to balloon trousers – and different colors – from brown to navy blue to black. These were all things to consider, since in the next twenty-four hours this uniform would have to withstand the intense scrutiny of people who knew better. Having made it this far, Jim had no intention of being screwed by such a simple thing as the wrong patch or an insignia he couldn't explain.

Beside him, he had a full-color book illustrating all the different uniforms of different state and county law enforcement agencies. He also had a book on police patches as well as his own personal collection he'd compiled during the seven years he'd served as an officer. Some he'd purchased, some he'd stolen. All were useful.

He pulled off the last patch and held the huge dark blue uniform up to the light. It would do.

He set aside the uniform and turned to the items on the floor. He selected the Silly Putty first, pounding it out, molding it, and inserting it into the plastic sandwich bags. When tucked inside the mouth, the pouches would give the appearance of jowls. He cut off the legs of the nylons, filled them with pillow stuffing, and closed the top with a few quick stitches. Instant thunder thighs and Buddha belly. The wig and makeup would be applied at the last minute.

He pulled out an old shoe box and sorted through his collection of badges and name tags until he found what he wanted. He's started stealing badges five years before. Detectives and rookies were the easiest – detectives because they were so arrogant they never thought anyone would rifle their jacket pockets, rookies because they were stupid. Jim had realized such things as authentic badges would always come in handy. He'd built his stockpile carefully. Then, two and a half years ago, when he'd realized his activities were suddenly being monitored and two plainclothes officers were following him, he'd made his final preparations. He'd found the perfect lair. He'd stashed his badges, a fake ID, a ton of cash, and, yes, two passports.

His diligence had paid off. The police never found his cover and he spent two years in prison, knowing that sooner or later opportunity would present itself, and he could pick up right where he left off.

He selected the appropriate badge and went to work sewing on the name patch. God was in the details.

His conversation with Sergeant Wilcox had gone well, particularly once he'd taken the man out to lunch and pumped him full of Halcion. The good old sergeant had slept like a baby as Jim had driven him out of the city, tied him to a tree, and prepared his Swiss Army knife. It hadn't taken long to get all the information he required.

He'd called the sergeant's wife and explained that Wilcox's assignment now required absolute secrecy. Her husband would not be home for a few days, nor would he be allowed to call. By the end of the week they would be able to tell her more.

Then he called the task force, spoke to the officer in charge, and said he was Wilcox's doctor. Wilcox had come down with an extreme case of food poisoning and would be out for the next twenty-four hours. Of course he'd return to duty immediately after that.

Sooner or late the authorities would ask more questions. That was fine. Jim just needed twenty-four hours. It would all be over then.

He rose, stretching out his long, toned body. Three hundred push-ups, five hundred sit-ups a day. Not an ounce of fat on him. Ed Kemper might be bigger, but in an arm-wrestling match, Jim was confident he would win.

He shook out his arms and legs. Four hours of sleep was all he needed nowadays. A deep calm had settled over him. Tonight his plan entered phase two and he was prepared. He had thought of everything, accounted for anything. He was invincible not because that's what he wanted to be; he was invincible because he worked at it.

Two years he'd rotted in Walpole. Two years of living in a six-by-eight cell in maximum security, allowed out for only one hour a day, Monday through Friday. Even then he was placed in handcuffs and leg shackles before being escorted by two guards to the maximum security rec area – really just a new six-by-eight cell outside, enclosed in wire mesh and nicknamed the dog cage. No more than two maximum security prisoners were allowed outside at once, and then they were put in distant cages so even conversation was difficult. Not that it mattered. Walpole was run by the Latin Kings these days. Like he wanted to mingle with a bunch of fucked up, coked up spics.

They'd wanted his ass. He had seen it in their eyes sometimes as he was escorted by their cells. He could smell their hatred and blood lust sluicing off their skin, flung toward him with their gang signs and low hisses. He liked to look them in the eye, stare them down, because they thought they were so bad when really they had no idea what it was all about. They clung to each other like weak-kneed bastards, passing drugs in hand-shakes, murdering over imaginary slights, and figuring it made them men. It meant nothing. The correction officers cracked down. Walpole went to the highest level of security and became a no-contact prison. And Jim found himself sitting across from Shelly in the visiting center with soundproof, bullet-proof glass between them because the guards finally figured out girlfriends were swapping more than spit in all those passionate kisses.

Two years of wearing orange. Two years of sitting alone on a cot, listening to stone walls reverberate with unbridled hatred and poorly thought out politics. Two years without sex.

Never again. He'd made his plans carefully, he'd tended to all the details. He would not be going back to jail. And he would have his revenge.

He curled up naked on the bare cot. He slept and dreamed of the feel of Shelly's mouth sucking him dry. And the feel of his hands wrapping around her neck, squeezing, squeezing, squeezing.

'I'm coming for you, baby,' he murmured in his sleep. 'I'm coming.'

18

Tess was ready.

She woke up with the first rays of the sun, stretching out slowly. Newly formed muscles pulled and contracted. She could identify baby biceps, emerging triceps, and infant quads. She ran through a warm-up drill in the middle of her room and was pleased by the smooth, graceful flow of stance into stance.

She was getting there.

Her gaze went instantly to the phone. She wanted to call Sam. She wanted to hear her daughter's sweet voice and tell her everything was going to be all right. Did Difford tuck her in each night, did he read the right stories? Did he watch her eat her fruit, or was she managing to drop it under the table?

God, she wanted to hear her little girl's voice.

And tell her what, Tess? That you'll come home? That you'll save her from her daddy? That you're putting her in jeopardy just by calling?

She turned away, her hands fisted at her sides. Just a few more weeks, then she should be ready to hunt down Jim. The nightmare would end. She would reclaim her daughter. Would they live happily ever after?

Tess wasn't sure she believed in such things anymore.

She got ready for her morning swim. But when she walked into the living room, she froze.

J.T. and Marion faced off with the Navajo rug as their arena, so intent on each other, they didn't notice her. They circled like warring destriers, nostrils flaring, chests heaving, and flanks quivering. Glug served as an unwitting and unlikely centerpiece for the exchange.

'That's right, J.T.,' Marion muttered furiously. 'Daddy's really Darth Vader and I'm Princess Leia. Now step over to the dark side so we can get this show on the road!'

'I already told you I'm not going.'

'I gave you over a week, J.T. How long are you going to carry a torch for a mythical past?'

'Forever is a nice round number.'

Marion threw up her hands in disgust. 'Stop it! Just stop it! What is it with you? No matter what, you have to make a mess of things. Don't you understand that this is your last chance? You walk away from Daddy now, and that's it. He's dying and you will *never* get to wrap up loose ends.'

'You make life sound like an Italian opera.'

'And you like hating him, don't you, J.T.? He's an excuse for you. You get yourself thrown out of West Point, blame Daddy. You punch out your CO, blame Daddy. You drink too much, whore too much, try to kill yourself in godforsaken jungles for causes no one cares about, and what the hell, you blame Daddy. Well, this is it. Tomorrow morning I return to D.C. You can come and redeem yourself, or you can stay here and rot.'

A muscle twitched in J.T.'s jaw. He shook his head. 'I have to train Tess. Even if I was stupid enough to contemplate the trip, I still couldn't go.'

'Coward. You're just using Tess as an excuse.'

'Excuse? What the hell, Marion? Aren't you the one who keeps telling me just how dangerous Jim Beckett is? First you tell me how much help Tess needs, then I'm supposed to just walk away to attend such mundane matters as the colonel's death?'

Marion's face turned several shades of outrage. 'Bring her.'

'Bring her?'

'You heard me, J.T. You don't want to leave her alone, you need more time to train her. Then bring her with you. Take her to D.C. – it's not rocket science.'

'Oh, that's just a great idea, Marion. You're right. I'll bring Tess to D.C. I'll introduce her to the man who beat my sister and raped my wife. And just to see if he's really dead, I'll leave her alone in the room with him. We both know nothing brings the colonel to life like a beautiful, young, defenseless woman.'

'You delusional son of—'

'I hope he's dead!' J.T. declared. Then his voice dropped low. 'Then I *will* go to D.C. just so I can dance at his burial. I'll build a champagne waterfall in the middle of the front lawn and dance around it, singing "Ding-dong, Daddy's dead" for the whole world to hear.'

'You are hopeless! But most of all, you are drunk!'

Tess stared at J.T., waiting for him to deny the accusation, to state once again that he was a man who always kept his word.

Instead, he said, 'I beg to differ. I've had only one drink. That means I am merely myself.'

'But you drank, J.T. And you swore not to. You violated your own twisted moral code. Christ, look at you. Just look! You can't follow through on anything, you can't commit to anything. You are actually a talented human being and yet your life is nothing but a string of failures. And now you're selling whatever future you might have had to the worm in the bottom of the tequila bottle.'

'It was only one drink, Marion.'

'One is all it takes.'

His jaw clenched. 'And you?' he whispered. 'The perfect daughter to the father who beat us as a hobby. And he did worse than that, didn't he, Marion? You can live your life in denial, but I was there too. I know what he did. I heard his footsteps in the hall every night, I saw him go into your room. Don't you think I tried to stop him? Don't you think I . . . I . . . God. I wanted to *kill* him.'

Marion's face had turned to stone. 'Leave me out of your lies, J.T.'

'I'm not the one whose life is a lie. If anything, my life is too honest.'

'Forget it.' Marion threw her hands in the air. 'I wash my hands of you, J.T. You're sick and beyond help. You've destroyed our family, you know that? All of Daddy's hard work, all of his respect, *ruined* because of you. That's it. You're a waste of my time, and I'm outta here.'

She whirled and stepped toward the hall. J.T.'s hand snaked out fast, wrapping around Marion's wrist.

She looked down. 'Keep your hand there one minute longer and you will lose it.'

His grip tightened anyway and he said, 'Don't go.'

'*Don't go?*'

'Stay. Stay right here, Marion. Don't go back to D.C. and don't go back to him. Let him die. Let the colonel just die. And then maybe you and me . . . maybe we can start over again. For God's sake, Marion, you're my little sister.'

Marion glanced up at his face, at eyes that pleaded.

And in a flurry of movement she pivoted, chopped his forearm with her left hand, and yanked her arm free.

'You're a weak, self-pitying bastard, J.T. And there's no way you're dragging me down with you.'

She thundered down the hall like a Sherman tank, pushing Tess aside. Seconds later, the sound of the slamming door registered her departure.

J.T. slowly rubbed his arm where a red welt was rising to life. He looked lost, as if he didn't know what to do with himself.

Tess took a step forward.

'Going to jump in as well? Extract your pound of flesh while the meat's still fresh?'

'No.'

'Why not?'

There was no mockery in his voice. No sarcasm, no challenge. She hadn't thought there would be a time when she would miss that in him.

'It's not fun to kick a man when he's down?' she offered weakly, searching for some reaction in his face.

At long last his lips quirked. 'Yeah, I suppose that's true.'

She took another step forward, but he moved away to the table next to the sofa. He picked up Marion's gold cigarette case, then pulled out a quick ticket to cancer.

'Go away, Tess.' The match flared to life. He brought it to the end of the cigarette and inhaled deeply.

'I can't.'

'Haven't we had this conversation before?'

'Yes, and I won it then too. It's one of the only things I do well – argue with you.'

'Doesn't count. Everyone seems to win at that.'

'You really love Marion, don't you?' She wanted to touch his hand. She wanted to wrap her arms around his shoulders and hold him tight.

It took J.T. a long time to reply. 'Yeah. But I'm getting older and wiser every day.'

'Your iguana,' she reminded him. He always told Marion she couldn't smoke in front of Glug.

His gaze went from her to the pet to her. She could practically see the darkness suddenly bloom in his eyes. The wild self-derision that had been beaten into him by his father and stoked by his sister's rejection. The self-destructive rage that knew his sister was right and he had failed at everything. In fact, he had planned his life just that way.

The darkness scared her. It touched her. It brought goose bumps to her arms and shivers down her spine. Jim's rage had terrified her because it had been so cold. J.T.'s anger moved her because it was so real.

'J.T.,' she whispered, and reached out her hand to him.

'You're right,' he said abruptly.

He lifted the cigarette from his lips. He admired the glowing red tip with mock exaggeration.

He held out his left hand.

'Don't,' she cried, but it was too late. As she watched, he ground out the red tip in his palm.

'What are you doing?' His pain was in her voice.

'What I was taught.'

'J.T.' She took a step toward him.

'Don't do it,' he growled. 'I am a bastard and I am a son of a bitch and I am so on edge, I don't know myself anymore. You step into this room and I *will not* be held responsible for my actions.'

'I'm not asking you to!' she cried. Then she took another step and another step.

She planted herself in the middle of the living room. 'I have seen evil, J.T. I've seen bad and I've seen worse. You are not it, J.T. You aren't.'

'Goddamn you,' he said. 'Goddamn you.' He threw the cigarette case across the room in a fury, and it landed with a ringing thud.

She held her ground.

He flung out his arm and swept the side table clear. The porcelain lamp shattered. The clay coasters cracked.

She held her ground.

'You'll wish you never met me,' he warned. Then right on top of that, 'Goddamn us both.'

He stalked toward her and she was ready.

His hands wrapped around her waist like a vise. Not soft. Not gentle. She didn't murmur one sound of protest as he shoved her back and pinned her against the wall.

If she was going to run, she should've done it earlier. Now she was committed and there would be no stopping.

He lifted his hands and planted one on each side of her face.

'You think I won't take what you offer? You think I'll come to my senses at the last minute and walk away? You think I'm good? You think I'm decent? You haven't listened to a word of what Marion said.'

He caught her lower lip furiously, pulling on it with his teeth.

She wrapped her arms around his neck and bit back. It was rough and crude. He attacked her mouth, she fought back. Her life had been passivity and coldness, fright and rejection. Now she met passion head-on.

His body pressed against hers, his hips showing her exactly what he wanted and exactly what she would give him, because the time for no had come and gone and baby, this was it.

He sank his teeth into the tender flesh above her collarbone. She cried out and he stuck his finger in her mouth like a plug. She bit it, sucking it, rubbing her tongue along its length.

'Christ, you're greedy.'

His fingers slipped up her shorts, dipped into her panties, and thrust into her.

She cried out again, shocked in spite of herself. Unprepared, in spite of him. He slowed. His head came up. He looked at her with glittering eyes.

'You really don't know anything, do you?' he whispered thickly.

'No,' she confessed. 'No.'

'You're too late,' he muttered. 'You're too late.'

'I know, I know.'

His finger slid deeper, penetrating, stretching, seeking. His palm pressed against her, rubbing rhythmically, giving her a tempo she instinctively understood.

She felt the mysteries press against her. She closed her eyes and saw unspeakable colors building behind her lids.

'J.T.' she groaned. 'J.T.'

'Open your eyes. Look at me. I want to see it. I want to see everything.'

Her eyes cracked open, glazed and vulnerable. His finger moved faster and faster. There was no tenderness, just raw, primitive need.

She bit her lip.

And he whispered hoarsely, 'Now.'

She climaxed, screaming and shuddering and melting from the inside out.

She was barely aware of being dragged to the floor. He tore off their clothes, then he was on her, his hands impatiently parting her legs. He rubbed against her, one last second of tantalizing pressure, then he whispered, 'Hold on to me, Tess. This is gonna be rough.'

He thrust inside her, and she was filled. She was annihilated.

She grabbed his shoulders and hung on for dear life.

He pulled back, his arms trembling with the strain. He flirted with her again, rubbing against her, making her squirm. Her legs wrapped around him tightly, and she stopped simply receiving, instead arching to meet each demanding blow.

The climax slammed into them both, screeching through their blood for a long, suspended moment when they could not breathe, could not move, could not feel even the pounding of their pulse.

He pulled away abruptly, the way she knew he would. He rose quickly, as she'd expected. He looked down at her, his face an unreadable mask.

'You don't have to say anything,' she told him. She felt bruised and battered, used and abused. And unbelievably satiated. Wise with the power of the mysteries and sense of her own self.

He strode away from her, already heading for the pool.

'I guess I don't have to ask if it was good for you,' she called out proudly.

He paused, his hand on the sliding glass door. 'Did I hurt you?'

'No.'

'I was rough.'

'I wasn't complaining.'

'Maybe you should have.'

'Already blaming yourself, J.T.? Adding me to the long list of things you beat yourself over the head with late at night? I know you better than you think. I believe in you more than you do. So don't bother hating yourself for showing me the wonders of animal sex. Really, I accept full responsibility for my actions.'

'Tess—'

'J.T., if you apologize now, I'll never forgive you.'

He stiffened. 'Fine.' He walked out the sliding glass door and jumped into his pool.

'Remember, Tess,' she whispered to herself, 'you are strong. You are very, very strong.'

It was a seedy place. Beat-up old trucks and battered blue Chevrolets dotted the parking lot. There might have been painted yellow lines once, but now they were obscured by dust and tumbleweeds. Removed from the nicely paved streets of central Nogales and the all-American McDonald's, the bar sat back in the desert, framed by a distant hill covered with run-down shanties. No smooth adobe walls or cheery red roof. This was wood, gray, beaten wood haphazardly stuck together with gnarled nails and sheer determination. Rusted tin formed a brown-spotted roof. When it rained, the place sounded like a bongo drum.

Now faint sounds of salsa leapt from the cracks, as if even the music was desperate to escape the dreariness. Smoke wafted out, ghostly tendrils curling up to the sky.

A flickering red neon sign pronounced the joint MANNY's. Just Manny's. Tired. Dusty. Forgotten.

Marion thought it was perfect.

Her sleek blue rental car looked out of place, but then, so did she. She pushed open the door without apology, entering the joint like the proverbial new gun in town. The music didn't stop for her, but the patrons did. Two men to her left, hunched over a threadbare pool table, looked up from their game. Behind the bar, a short, bald man in a sleeveless denim vest that showed off his serpent tattoos stopped pouring beer from the tap. To her right, small clusters of men and a few women glanced up once, then did a double take.

Marion pushed her way to the bar. 'I want a whiskey. Straight up.'

Serpent man stared at her. She stared back. He still didn't move. 'You got a problem with dollars?' she asked coolly.

'No.'

'Then I think we can be friends.' She pulled out a crisp twenty and slapped it on the counter.

The bartender fetched a bottle of whiskey. As if it had been a signal, the crowd returned to its business.

Marion didn't turn. She didn't look. She sat alone at the bar, listening to the murmurs. She couldn't speak Spanish, but she understood it well enough.

When the bartender gave her her drink, she thanked him with a mocking toast. She raised the glass. She parted her pink lips. And she tossed back the whiskey in one gulp.

She slammed the glass down. She swallowed through the pain in her gut. Then delicately she touched the corner of her mouth with a single French-manicured nail.

'Give me another.'

'*Sí, señorita.*'

'Exactly.'

19

'I want the Apple Jacks.'

'Okay, okay,' Difford muttered, pushing open the door with his foot and balancing four grocery bags with his arms, fingers, and hips. Samantha went barreling in, unmindful of his precarious juggling act. Decked out in her pink winter coat with the hood pulled tightly around her face, she looked like a strawberry version of Frosty the Snowman. Her blond hair peered out around the white furry trim of her hood. Her cheeks were a healthy, happy red. It was probably still too warm for full winter gear, but Difford had never dressed a kid before, so he liked to err on the side of caution.

'Apple Jacks, Apple Jacks,' Samantha sang at the top of her lungs.

Difford grunted, wondered how mothers ever learned how to cope with children, and managed to kick the door shut with his foot. A bit more juggling, and he made it all the way to the tiny brown kitchen, dropping only two oranges.

Samantha chased the fruit down the hall, then came trotting back with the oranges clutched in her mittened hands like trophies. She beamed at him triumphantly. At that moment, despite his best intentions, his chest tightened and he did understand exactly why mothers coped with children.

'Thank you,' he said with somber politeness, and accepted the oranges.

'Okay, the cereal now!' Her smile grew. She was perfectly delighted with herself and her persistent efforts that had finally yielded the sugar-coated cereal. He'd been so careful to buy only healthy things. Tess had given him a list of appropriate grocery items and he'd been plugging Samantha with bowl after bowl of Raisin Bran. But today at the store she'd noticed the Apple Jacks on special display at the end of the aisle and that had been that. She wanted Apple Jacks! Difford discovered he could command a whole police department but not one determined four-year-old. They bought the Apple Jacks. Two boxes. Buy one get one free. He was such a sucker.

'Lunch first,' he insisted. Her face fell, her lower lip jutting out suspiciously. He suffered an immediate burst of panic. 'Oh, no, you don't,' he said, shaking his head. 'Nutrition is important. We have turkey or ham.'

Samantha looked at him, her bright blue eyes keenly intelligent. Her head cocked to the side, and by now he could read the signs. She was determining how hard to push him. This was his own fault; the first few days, he'd given her heaven and earth every time she cried. Samantha had quickly internalized that lesson and become hell on wheels.

He forced himself to stand firm. Think of her as a new recruit, he reminded himself. A cadet who needed a strong guiding hand.

After a minute he won the battle of wills. 'Turkey,' she decided.

Difford grinned, feeling ridiculously proud of himself. He didn't win often. Tess hadn't warned him of a small child's capacity for deviousness.

'Okay,' he said, and put away the groceries. He then laid out the bread, mustard, and mayonnaise. Samantha was in charge of adding the turkey, which she did with true flourish. They sat at the simple wood table and ate in silence.

He figured they'd play dominoes afterward. The kid still kicked his butt, but he was getting better.

He sent her to go get the game while he finished cleaning up. Minutes later he wandered into the living room, where they generally played, sitting cross-legged on the floor. His knees were getting sore.

He was about to push back his reclining chair, when he noticed the pillows. Yesterday he'd tucked them behind his back for comfort as he'd leaned against the sofa. He wasn't much of a pick-up guy. He'd thought he'd left them on the floor.

Now one sat neatly in each corner of the couch.

Samantha walked into the room, carrying the box of dominoes.

Difford said in as calm a voice as he could manage, 'Sam, I want you to go to your room.'

'But I didn't do anything wrong!'

'I know, sweetheart.' His eyes darted around the room as he reached beneath his jacket for his gun. 'We're playing a new game, honey. I just want you to go to your room for a few minutes, okay? I'm . . . I'm preparing a surprise for you in the living room.'

She looked troubled. 'I don't like this game!' she cried, dropped the dominoes on the floor, and ran sniffling for her room.

Difford didn't waste any time. Looking across the street, he could see an old green car parked at the corner. He raised his hand. Both of the officers waved back. Okay, his cover car was still present and it was broad daylight. If someone had tried to approach the safe house, the officers would have noticed.

He searched the house anyway, gun drawn and eyes sharp as he went from room to room. Living room was clear. Bathroom, including the shower, was clear. He entered his bedroom slowly, sweeping the space with a steady, level arm, pointing his gun in all corners. Then he pressed himself against a wall and slid the closet door open with his foot. Quick step and pivot, and he faced off against his clothes. Nothing moved, nothing stirred. He brushed his gun through the hangers. Empty.

He started to breathe a little easier. Nerves, he told himself, just nerves. The news of Shelly Zane's murder had gotten to him. The knowledge that Beckett was out there somewhere, gunning for Theresa, was definitely keeping him up at night.

But Beckett was just a man. Tess had stood up to him before. Lieutenant Houlihan and Special Agent Quincy were doing their best to make sure she would never have to again. A lot of good people were working this case. Sooner or later they'd get Beckett.

He finished the sweep of the house, telling Sam it was part of the game as he checked her room, her closet, beneath her bed. He could tell she didn't believe him.

But the house was clear. All was still well. Maybe he'd just forgotten about picking up the pillows. Maybe Sam had done it.

He replaced his gun in his holster. He offered Samantha his hand. She took it without question.

'Dominoes?' he tried.

'I want my mommy.'

'I . . . I know.'

'Do you know where my mommy is?' Her lower lip had begun to tremble.

'Yeah, honey, I do.'

'Make her come home.'

Difford squatted down. 'She wants to come home, Sam, she really does. No one loves you like your mommy does. But she has to take care of some things first. She's, uh, making everything safe, you know? And once it's all safe, she'll come get you and you'll always be together.'

'I want her now,' Sam whispered.

'I know, Sam. I know. Come on, kid, let's play dominoes.' He led her into the living room, not knowing what else to do.

Samantha didn't sit across from him as she usually did. Instead, she sat right beside him, her little shoulder against his side. After a moment he put his big arm around her and patted her awkwardly.

She braved a tremulous smile and opened the domino box.

'My mommy will come home soon?'

'Right.'

'And then we'll always be together?'

'Yeah, honey. Everything will be all right.'

'Can we watch *Jurassic Park* again tonight?'

'Okay,' he said, but couldn't quite stop the sinking feeling in his chest. He patted her shoulder again. 'Okay.'

Tess went to find J.T. The patio was empty, the pool flat. She felt the pinprick of unease.

Gravel crunched. She whirled toward the sound with her hands already fisted.

J.T. emerged from the side of the house, buck naked and wielding his gun. He didn't even glance in her direction. He disappeared around the left side, his gun leading him forward.

She was still standing there stupidly.

J.T. rematerialized on the patio, his gun down by his naked thigh.

'I thought I heard somethin',' he muttered.

'I – I didn't see anything.'

'Yeah, well, you were staring at my butt.'

Her cheeks flushed crimson. 'Just admiring the view.'

'Huh.'

He took two steps forward, one step back, and finally stood still. 'Guess I'm just edgy.'

She contemplated him silently for a moment. 'Did you really drink last night?'

'Yeah. One shot. Tequila. Lord have mercy on my soul.'

'I think it's a little late for that.' She contemplated berating him. She contemplated calling him a fool. She decided in the end that neither was necessary. No one had ever been harder on J. T. Dillon than J. T. Dillon.

She said, 'I need you.'

'Don't.'

'Too late. You know what I'm up against, J.T. Marion's told you enough about Jim. He's going to come after me, and I have to be ready. We've done so well this last week. I can swim farther, I have some muscle tone. I can shoot a gun—'

'Barely.'

'Exactly! I need to learn more. I need you to teach me more. Be there for me, dammit. It's only a few more weeks.'

'I can handle it,' he said stiffly.

'Are you sure? It's not weak to call AA, J.T. It's not weak to admit that you need help.'

'I'm fine! Don't you have any hay bales to shoot?'

'None of them are as much fun as hounding you.' She walked right up to him. She could feel the heat and tension radiating from him, and it made her hot.

'Greedy,' he whispered.

'I learned it from you.'

He was growing hard. She could get him to want her again, get him to take her again. Here on the patio, or maybe beneath the mesquite tree, or maybe on a glass table. Maybe all three.

And then what?

She pushed herself away. His breath exhaled with a hiss.

'Get back on the wagon—'

'I stopped with one,' he interrupted tightly.

'Good. Don't take it any further. Now go after Marion.'

His eyes widened incredulously. 'What?'

'She needs you, J.T.'

He held up his forearm and pointed to the red welt. 'Tess, open your eyes.'

'I have. And I'm telling you she needs you. Why do you think she ran away, J.T.? So that you would follow. So that finally someone would follow.'

'Marion could chew up an armored tank for breakfast, then spit out perfectly formed nails the rest of the day. End of story.'

He strode toward the sliding glass door. 'You still want a teacher, right?'

'Yes.'

'Then stop standing there, yapping at me. This isn't Club Med; get in your damn swim clothes. We'll begin with weights, end in the pool. You got five minutes.'

'She's scared,' Tess whispered behind him.

He said to them both, 'Stop kidding yourself.'

'Can I buy you a drink?'

'I'm not stopping you.' Marion leaned over the pool table, where she was slowly and methodically annihilating all the men in the bar. The sun had gone down. The interior was darker and smokier than before. Her eyes had adjusted hours before, and now she didn't notice the changes.

'Eight ball, left corner pocket,' she called. She lined up the shot, pulled back the stick, and slammed it forward with more force than necessary. The cue ball nailed the eight ball, ramming it into the faded green lip of the edge and forcing it to rocket into the corner pocket with a sharp clatter.

She straightened and raised her cigarette to her lips. Inhale. Exhale. 'I believe you owe me twenty bucks.'

The man grumbled. She hadn't caught his name. She didn't care. He'd been better than the others, but still no match. He coughed up the money. She added it to her stack.

She turned and scanned the bar. She had the tickling in the back of her neck, that sensation of being watched. Of course, the whole damn bar was staring at her. She turned back to the pool table.

Fresh meat arrived with her drink. He smiled at her, trying to be charming, but she wasn't so drunk she couldn't see the predatory intent behind his smile. She accepted the glass, leaning her slim hip negligently against the table and blatantly eyeing him since he was blatantly eyeing her.

He was tall, over six feet. Beneath his red baseball cap, tufts of dishwater-blond hair stuck out like straw. He had a mustache and stubbly beard, and the broad shoulders and muscled arms of a workingman. His stomach wasn't flat anymore though. He'd been a stud once. Now he was going to seed.

'So what's your game?' he asked with a wink.

'Eight ball,' she said coolly, 'I'll give you three-to-one odds. Betting starts at twenty.'

He crossed his arms so that his biceps bulged.

'You really that into pool?'

'You really think you can pick me up with one drink?'

His face reddened. She kept staring at him. Men couldn't stand up to that stare. They all fled like dogs with their tails tucked between their legs. Then they called her a bitch.

'All right,' he said, surprising her. 'I'll play. But I'll warn you now, I'm better than what you're used to.'

'I'll be the judge of that.' She slammed back her whiskey and picked up the cue stick. Her gun was nestled beneath her arm, hidden by her jacket. She liked the feel of it there, comforting and cold.

They got down to business.

Do you miss me, Roger, do you think of me at all? Or am I just a cold bitch to you, one you married for Daddy's connections? How can a cocktail waitress make you so damn happy?

She bent low and broke the balls with a fury. Two solids went in. She inhaled another cleansing gulp of tobacco and contemplated her next shot.

And you, Daddy? Why don't you ever call my name? Wasn't I a good daughter? Didn't I do whatever you asked?

She sank three more, then scratched.

Her opponent took over with a swagger. She was unimpressed.

Then there's you, J.T. Running off and ruining the family name. You're nothing but a drunken loser and then you say I'm like you. I am nothing like you. I am strong.

Her opponent cleared the table. She looked at him, mildly shocked.

'Told you I knew what I was doing.'

'I suppose you did.'

He set down his cue stick while she counted out three twenties and handed them over. He shook his head.

'Haven't you had enough foreplay? Aren't you ready to get down to the real business?'

She contemplated acting outraged. She contemplated feigning ignorance. She set down the money and with a shrug of her shoulders said, 'All right. What did you have in mind?'

'Come with me, darling. I'll fuck your problems right out of your head.'

She stared at him. He was past his prime, but his arms were still lean and hard. He knew how to play pool and was more man than anything else that had walked into the room.

She should tell him no. She was the good daughter who'd only ever slept with Roger. She was the good agent who knew better than to leave with a strange man.

She said, 'All right.'

She picked up her purse and accepted his heavy grip as he led her to the door.

'And you froze up every time I touched you, Marion!'

She still couldn't shake the feeling that someone was watching her, that if she turned around now, she'd find one pair of eyes a bit too sharp, a bit too knowing.

She didn't turn around.

Outside, the air was cool and crisp and her nostrils flared, almost offended by the sweetness after the reeking bar. The sky was pitch black, good for midnight doings.

Her stud led her to his truck. No one was around in the parking lot, but she wasn't worried.

He held open the passenger door for her. She wasn't sure if that was a positive sign or not. She didn't ask where they were going, she didn't contemplate the events at hand. She lit another cigarette and rolled down the window to smoke.

He drove to the middle of nowhere. Had he taken other women there before? Was he married and that's why they didn't go to his apartment? She didn't care. None of it was her business. She was just along for the ride.

'No one comes out here,' he said, looking at her for the first time. 'But it's nice on nights like tonight. You can smell the creosote, look at the stars. Thought you might like it better than some trailer that stinks of beer and socks. I don't clean much.'

'It's fine.'

He opened the door. 'I have a blanket in the back. Ground's soft.'

So he'd come here before. A regular lovers' lane. She watched him in the side mirror. He pulled out a square army blanket and unfolded it on the ground. No iron pipes. No handcuffs. Just a Don Juan after all. She opened her door and stepped out.

The night was chilly, penetrating the haze pressed over her conscience. Then he stepped forward and grabbed her, pushing her against the truck. His mouth swooped down and he stabbed his tongue into her mouth.

The taste hit her hard, the intrusion shattering her apathy until she almost gagged. Then she remembered this was what she was supposed to want. She forced her body to relax. She wound her arms around his neck and tried not to wince as his meaty chest crushed her breast.

He sank to his knees, began to unbutton her jacket.

'Wait,' she said. She didn't want him to find her gun. 'I'll do it. You take off your shirt.'

His eyes were dark with lust. His thick fingers went instantly to his shirt. 'Turn around,' she told him.

'Why?'

'Because I'm fucking shy. Turn around.'

He shrugged and did as he was told. She stripped off her jacket, then unfastened her shoulder holster and placed it on the ground beneath her jacket.

He turned back around and attacked her, tearing off her silk shell. He pressed his teeth against her neck. He spanned her waist with his hands. He brought his fingers up and kneaded her small breasts as if he could force them to be larger, more voluptuous. She stood still, her hands at her sides.

His hands found her bra clasp and undid it, baring her breasts to the night wind. The briskness made her nipples harden and peak. He took it personally, crowing his satisfaction. Hot and wet, his mouth fastened upon a nipple and sucked voraciously.

She looked down. She watched his head bob up and down at her breast. She heard slurping, grunts and groans. His hips were beginning to rock insistently.

He switched to her other breast, his jaw working furiously.

She shivered. She thought in the back of her mind that the stars were very beautiful and that she was very small beneath them.

His hands fastened on the waistband of her slacks and pulled them down along with her sensible panties. She didn't protest.

'Man, baby, you are hot,' he said. 'A real fucking piece of ass.'

She looked at him blankly, wondering if he was even looking at her body. She was not hot. She had flat breasts and almost no hips. She was too thin and wiry. Roger had often complained that there wasn't a single soft spot on all of her body. She was muscle and sinew. There were young boys more feminine than her.

The stud pushed off his pants. His dick sprang out, huge and purple, alien and grotesque. At least Roger had been small.

She took a step back. It was too late.

He dragged her down to the blanket, already snuffling between her breasts, his fingers kneading them painfully.

'Baby, baby, baby,' he muttered thickly. 'Oh, baby, baby.'

She tried to shut her ears against the sound.

'Kiss me. Come on, darling, don't be shy. Kiss me. Touch me. Go wild.'

He placed his lips on hers as if he knew she needed the encouragement. Then he grabbed her hand and wrapped it around his dick. She flinched at the feel of it throbbing between her fingers. It was alive. She should want it, she should revel in it. She should cry, Oh, yes, fuck me.

She wanted to run.

He took her head between his hands. 'Do you nibble? Come on, don't be shy. Swallow me whole, baby. You'll like what I give you.'

Before she could react, he forced her head down. Now his dick was pressing against her cheek, smelling overpoweringly of musk.

'Come on, what are you waiting for?' For the first time, his voice was impatient.

Kiss the willy. Come on, Marion, you know what I want. Be a good girl and open your mouth. Kiss the willy. Kiss Daddy's willy.

She raised her head and vomited all over his lap.

'Jesus fucking Christ!' He sprang back, batting at her furiously. She fell to the side, still vomiting rancid whiskey. Her shoulders trembled. She hunched her small, naked body over her knees and shut out the world until the black void was complete, the memories pushed back and locked up.

She reached frantically for her clothes.

The stud came after her, angry and enraged. She didn't think, she wasn't composed. She fought instinctively, and five moves later he was writhing on the ground without even the breath to curse. Throwing on her clothes, she grabbed his truck keys and told him he'd find his vehicle back at the bar.

Then she climbed in the truck, started the engine, and roared back out onto the long, empty road.

Run, Marion. Run and don't look back. You don't want to know what's behind you. You never wanted to know what was behind you.

20

J.T. woke up instantly, lying on his back amid the tangled sheets. He stared at the ceiling blankly, blinking his eyes and trying to pinpoint what had woken him.

Then slowly his gaze drifted to the foot of the bed.

She stood there, pale and ethereal once more. Long blond hair tumbled down her back in fat, loose waves. Small hands knotted and unknotted in front of a flowing white nightgown. Her expression tore at him, begging him to save her.

His breath caught in his throat. He told himself again and again that it was only memory: living, breathing memory standing at the foot of his bed. He squeezed his eyes shut, his mind screaming for the demon to go away. He couldn't save her. He hadn't saved her. He was nothing.

He opened his eyes.

She was still there.

And he realized for the first time that she wasn't a child. This wasn't little Merry Berry, stepping from his mind into his bedroom. This was Marion, grown-up, alive, and real.

His hand lifted from the sheets on its own accord, stretching out to her. 'Marion . . .' His voice cracked.

'I came,' she whispered. 'I wanted to see . . . if I'd ever stood here. If it felt . . .' Her eyes squeezed shut. 'No. It never happened! It never, ever happened!'

She grabbed the skirt of her nightgown and fled.

His hand fell to the sheet in shock. He couldn't breathe, he couldn't move. He was suspended someplace between the past and the present and his chest was on fire with pain.

He swung his legs over the side of the bed. He reached the door in two steps, flung it open, and caught a flash of white as she disappeared into her room. He gave chase. He had to. Just once he had to get this right.

Her door slammed shut forcefully, rocking the still house and locking with a definitive click. J.T. beat against it frantically.

'Marion, let me in! Can't we talk about this? Christ, Marion. Just once can't we talk about this?' He pressed his cheek against the wooden door, knowing he was begging and beyond caring.

From the other side of the door he heard a rough, choking sound. She was crying. Cold, perfect Marion was sobbing.

He sank down to the floor.

'Marion,' he called hoarsely. 'Marion, Marion. I tried. I tried so hard to save you. God, I tried . . .'

But there was no reply, just the hoarse sound of his little sister sobbing.

He pressed his cheek against the door. He closed his eyes. Then he banged on the door helplessly with his fist, needing her to let him in, desperate for her to let him in.

Marion, I know I failed you. But I came back. I came back and you'd forgotten everything – all the good moments, as well as the bad – and that failed me. How could we fail each other? How could we serve the colonel like that?

Marion didn't come to the door, nor did she answer his pleas. So he switched to cursing the colonel instead. Thirty-six years old, he cursed his father and wondered how a grown man could feel such fear.

Minutes passed. Her sobbing stopped and silence took its place, reigning in the dark, shadowed house,

'Marion?'

There was nothing. She'd come. She'd left. He was right back where he started except for the pain devouring his chest, the dark, enraged beast screaming and gnashing in his belly.

'It's okay.'

He looked up. Tess stood in the gray-filled hallway, her gaze understanding. She took his hand.

'Give her until morning. She isn't ready to listen to you now.'

'I tried,' he whispered dumbly. *Failure, failure, failure. Pussy-whipped mama's boy.*

'I know.' She touched his cheek. 'It's okay. You were just a little boy, J.T. It wasn't your fault.'

He buried his lips against her hand, squeezing his eyes shut against the unbearable darkness that had lived inside him for so long. He wanted to hate someone; for a moment he even wanted to hate her. But he hadn't enough energy left inside him. He was wrung out and empty.

He felt her guide him to his feet. She led him to his room and tucked him into bed. He simply lay on his back, staring at the ceiling and going insane with the memories. He wanted a drink. Wouldn't someone give him a drink?

Push it away, push it away, Rachel whispered in his mind.

But he couldn't. The memories had been seared into his head and he couldn't get them out of his mind.

Tess pulled out a chair and sat down.

'I'll stay. You shouldn't be alone on a night like tonight. Not with tequila in the house.'

'Stop it,' he muttered. 'Go away. Isn't a psychotic ex-husband enough for you? Can't you just leave the rest of us alone?'

'I've been inside the darkness too, J.T. I know that sometimes the light seems too far away. We all get lost in the dark, and it's such a scary place. Such a lonely place.'

Her words hurt him, looked inside him, and laid him bare. He was thinking of all those nights, listening to the colonel's jump boots ring against the floor. With no one to tell, no one who would help him or Marion.

Night after night, lying there, wanted it to stop, needing it to stop. And always facing it alone.

He gave in with a groan. He grabbed Tess by the hand and yanked her into bed. She fell against him easily, already whispering his name.

'I know,' she murmured against his hair. 'I know.'

He buried his face against her neck.

'I won't leave you,' she whispered. 'I won't leave you.'

His hands dug into her back and brought her closer.

Difford was uneasy.

Long after the sun went down, he and Sam are their macaroni and cheese dinner. They watched *Jurassic Park* and saw the children survive the monsters. Difford checked out Samantha's room, but there were no demons beneath the bed or in the closet. He tucked her in, brushing back her hair and retrieving her fancy talking doll that did more things than any doll he'd ever heard of. Tonight she had him read her 'Snow White.'

She went to sleep. He prowled the living room and wondered why his nerves were on edge.

The phone rang. He almost jumped out of his skin. He lunged across the living room and caught it before the second ring – he didn't want it to wake Sam up.

'Lieutenant?'

'Yes.' Difford's voice was wary. He waited for the security phrase.

'It rains upon the plains in Spain,' the caller said. 'Difford, it's Sergeant Wilcox. Listen closely—'

'I heard you had some kinda stomach bug.'

'No. I had a bad case of Halcion poisoning.'

'What?' Now Difford paid attention.

'We don't have much time, all right? Some guy calling himself Detective Beaumont showed up yesterday, claimed to be from Bristol County with an urgent message for you. The man spiked my coffee while I was questioning him in the interrogation room.'

'Beckett.'

'Yeah, it was Beckett. He rifled through my notebook, he asked me some questions. Lieutenant, we're pretty sure he knows where you are and that he has a copy of the house key. We have to get you out of the house now.'

Difford was silent. And then, finally confronted by a danger he could act against, he felt calm. 'What is the plan?'

'Okay, the minute you hang up with me, look out your window. Officer Travis is going to get out of the back-up vehicle – he's a big guy, you can't miss him. Just drift casually toward the front door, okay. No sudden moves. Beckett might be watching. Why don't you have a cup of coffee in your hand for the officer. It'll look like the man is just getting his caffeine fix. The minute he's in, shut the door. He'll help you round up Sam. You'll take the car in your garage—'

'Wait.'

'What?'

Difford felt the first beads of sweat pop up on his brow. 'If he, uh, if he has the key to the house, he can get into the garage. I haven't checked the garage recently. I just hadn't thought of it. He could be . . .'

'Shit.' A tense pause. 'All right. I'll tell Officer Travis. Once he's in the house, he'll check the garage, you cover him. If all is clear, the three of you exit the garage. Evasive maneuvers, then come straight to HQ. Clear?'

'Clear.'

Difford hung up the phone. He crossed to the window and pulled back the curtains. The hairs on the back of his neck were up. His breathing had gone shallow.

He saw the car light come on across the street as the door opened. He saw a big, heavyset officer climb out of the front seat. Briefly he saw the second man bent over, as if picking something off the floor. The door shut and the light went out. Officer Travis now looked around. Difford saw the man's hand rest on his unsnapped holster.

'Stay calm,' he murmured to the junior officer. 'Remember, you're just coming for coffee.'

But he could feel the young man's tension from here. Suddenly, in this quiet neighborhood, it seemed the whole world was watching them.

Officer Travis advanced across the street. Belatedly Difford moved to the kitchen to pour a hasty mug of coffee. His eyes were on the garage door.

Beckett turned off the cellular phone and set it on the floor. He'd spent an hour that morning practicing Sergeant Wilcox's voice. The effort had paid off.

He turned, his movements a bit awkward in the heavily padded uniform. His 'partner' had been reclining in the passenger seat, a blanket pulled up to his neck so it appeared that he was sleeping. Knowing the car light would illuminate his form, Beckett leaned over the dead body, straightened the seat, and slumped the man over. Rigor mortis was beginning to set in, so it wasn't easy. Then again, Beckett had gotten used to maneuvering dead bodies. The trick was to bend the man at the bullet hole in his waist.

Beckett looked up. Sure enough, Difford stood in the living room window, waiting for Officer Travis to step out of his car.

'Happy to be of service,' Beckett murmured, and opened the car door.

The knocking echoed through the safe house quietly. Good, Difford thought. Officer Travis was at least thinking of Samantha. Difford approached the door, the steaming coffee clutched in one hand. He had to resist the urge to glance over his shoulder at the garage door.

Keep cool, keep cool.

'Password,' Difford demanded through the dead-bolted door.

'It rains upon the plains in Spain.'

Difford checked out the officer through the peep-hole. The kid looked young, but then, they all looked young to Difford. He was a big guy who obviously needed to work out more. Christ, how had the Pillsbury Doughboy end up as his back-up? Difford cracked open the door, not amused.

He gave the junior officer another scathing inspection with the chain still on. Difford wasn't about to act stupid now. The uniform checked out, though the kid had no awards to speak of.

'ID?'

Officer Travis dutifully produced his shield. Fine.

Difford unfastened the chain and held out the coffee mug. 'Take it and act calm. Remember, you just came over for a cup of coffee.' His gaze swept the block. The streetlights created puddles of darkness; he'd always hated streetlights. So far, nothing moved.

'All right, come in.'

Officer Travis stepped into the house, looking tense and uncomfortable beneath Difford's scrutiny. 'How long have you been with the force?'

'Two years.'

'Two years and you got this duty?'

'Manpower shortage. The Camarini shooting and this are sucking us dry.'

'Huh. Ever secured a house before?'

'I was part of the Gingham bust. That's why they signed me up.'

Difford finally relented. The Todd Gingham deal had gone badly. They'd thought they had the nineteen-year-old arms dealer holed up in his house in New Bedford. The neighbors had seen him wielding a handgun and looking high as a kite. A SWAT team had been called in. Shot the hell out of the house. Kid escaped out the back and opened fire on a few squad cars. It had taken six officers and a flying tackle to finally neutralize the threat. So Officer Travis had been in the line of fire. He'd functioned beneath gunpowder, adrenaline, and screaming men.

Difford began to relax. He cocked his head and led Officer Travis to the garage door.

'Set the coffee on the table. Take the lead. I already checked out the rest of the house. If he's here, he's in there.'

'No, Difford. He's right here.' Officer Travis moved faster than Difford would have thought a fat man could. He whirled, his arm arched up, and Difford saw his eyes right before the man's fist snapped back his chin.

He went down hard, but his hand got around his gun. *Don't panic, don't panic.*

He pulled his gun out of his holster. *Shoot, dammit, shoot.*

The baton caught him square on the forearm; dimly he heard the crack of his arm breaking. Fingers went numb. Gun flew across the room and hit the wall.

Get his feet. Kick out his feet. Get him down.

His ankle hooked Beckett's. He pulled hard. The baton caught him across the cheek as Jim toppled. Ringing filled his ears. He tasted something rusty in his mouth, blood. Shit, it was pouring down his chin. What had happened to his teeth?

He planted his good arm on the floor and started crawling for his gun. *Faster, faster, faster.*

Tess, I'm sorry. I'm sorry.

He heard the rustle of nylon and knew Jim was beginning to rise. He picked up the tempo, forcing himself to move. The gun was so close, twenty feet, ten. If he could just get his hand out—

Beckett sat on his back hard, slamming Difford to the floor. The breath left him in a giant whoosh and he couldn't get it back. Hands wrapped around his throat and began to squeeze. He fought, he squirmed against the floor. The world spun away and he sank into the blackness.

The void didn't hurt.

And it lasted only a minute. Then the pressure was gone. His lungs instinctively inhaled, his eyes fought to see. Vaguely he felt Beckett rise. He saw his gun kicked far away. Beckett picked up a kitchen chair. He strode down the hall and jammed it beneath the closed door of Samantha's room.

And Difford knew what was going to happen then. The chair told him clearly what Beckett didn't want his daughter to wake up and see.

Beckett walked back down the hall. Difford tried to pull himself away, but his broken arm refused to move and blood and teeth were already pooling in his throat. He shimmied three more feet, then Beckett's hand curled around his ankle, pinning him in place. He couldn't quite stop his own whimper.

'I have a few questions for you,' Beckett whispered in his ear.

A sliding rasp. A knife appeared before Difford's gaze.

'Sergeant Wilcox was too easy,' Beckett murmured. 'Have you ever noticed that cops have the lowest threshold for pain? They spend their whole life studying it and thinking that because they have, they're immune to it. It will never happen to them.'

'Son of a bitch,' Difford gasped.

'Shh. Don't wake Sam.'

Difford's eyes shut. He felt something trickle down, his cheeks. It might have been tears.

'Make it hard, Difford. Give me a challenge. I want a challenge.'

Jim Beckett went to work.

Beckett moved in the moon-shrouded living room. First he picked up the phone and dialed in to the officer on duty.

'Bravo Fourteen,' he intoned. 'Checking in, all's clear.'

'Roger, Bravo Fourteen.'

'Talk to you in an hour.' Officer Travis signed off.

It was now one A.M. At two A.M., the new shift would arrive. Jim had to keep on schedule.

He opened the garage door. He arranged Difford's body in the trunk. Returning to the kitchen, he attended to the mess with paper towels. Blood was oily, harder to clean up than people expected. He'd read of a couple in the Midwest who'd opened a business cleaning up after death. Homicides, suicides, they took care of everything and made a lot of money. While in prison, he'd been tempted to write to them for tips.

Now he didn't have time to be too neat. He got the worst and arranged furniture over the rest. Then he quickly stripped down to the jeans and T-shirt he wore beneath the bulky uniform, tossing the uniform in the washing machine next to the kitchen. He would turn on the washer before leaving. Removing his wig, he also took the time to scrub the makeup off his face – he didn't want to scare Sam. Following that same vein of thought, he found one of Difford's old baseball caps to wear over his bald head.

He'd forgotten Difford's affection for baseball. Had he remembered, he would've killed the lieutenant with a bat just for irony's sake.

One twenty A.M. Jim scrubbed his arms and hands in the sink, then placed the coffee mug inside. He'd left prints everywhere. It was the nice thing about being him now – he no longer had to hide. He could leave fingerprints, hair, blood, wherever the hell he wanted. As an escaped convicted murderer, his job was even easier.

Finally he stood in the hallway before the closed door of Samantha's room. His stomach fluttered with nervous butterflies, a unique sensation. He felt like he was about to ask out a girl for the first time.

He rubbed his hands on his thighs and decided he was ready.

He removed the kitchen chair, not hearing any movement on the other side of the door. Difford hadn't made much noise. Jim had counted on Difford wanting to protect Samantha as much as he did. He twisted the doorknob and very carefully eased the door open.

And the silvery moonbeam illuminated the bed like a spotlight, accentuating her white-blond hair and spilling over her cheek.

Jim Beckett stared down at his little girl with awe, and his love for her bloomed in his chest.

Her eyes fluttered open, sleepy and innocent. Then they widened with shock. He silenced her impending scream with a single finger pressed gently over her lips.

'Sam,' he whispered.

Her eyes widened more at the sound of his voice. 'D-d-daddy?'

'Yes, baby.' He smiled. She looked unbearably lovely. She looked perfect.

'You came back.'

'Of course I came back, Sammy. I came back for you. And we'll never be apart again.'

J.T. slipped out of bed and into the pool before sunlight. He swam one hundred laps, twenty-five butterfly, twenty-five backstroke, twenty-five breaststroke, and twenty-five freestyle. The chlorine stung the scratch on his cheek.

At last he pulled himself out of the pool and wiped the water from his skin with his hands. The sun was just beginning to peer over the horizon. He stood there for a moment, watching the rays gently weave into his mesquite tree and illuminate his garden.

He knew what he had to do next. He walked to Marion's room.

Her doorway was open, as he figured it would be. The room was empty, as he'd known would be the case. He sat down on the edge of the bed. He ran his hand over the pillow she must have hugged as she sobbed herself to sleep.

Merry Berry, I am so sorry.

'I should've killed him,' he said in the silent room. 'I should've just killed him.'

He found himself in front of the open refrigerator, staring at four bottles of beer. Corona Extra Gold. Cold and smooth going down. *Takes the edge off – isn't that what you want, J.T.? Something to take the edge off.*

Something to make you forget, because you never mastered denial like Marion did.

His hand reached in. He curled his fingers around the cool neck of elixir. So easy to pull it out. He could be drunk before the sun even got high in the sky.

He thought of Tess, still sleeping in his bed. He thought of the way she'd cradled his head between her breasts and stroked his hair. He thought of the feel of her lips, brushing his temple.

She was a fool, he thought angrily. Hell, maybe they were both fools.

His hand slid away from the beer bottle. He stalked back out to his pool and swam a hundred laps more.

*

As he walked back to the house towel-drying his hair, he heard the phone ringing. He didn't pay it any heed. Tess emerged from the hall, her footsteps fast and urgent. She'd obviously been searching for him.

Once she spotted him outside, her shoulders immediately relaxed. He didn't smile, but he didn't scowl. He just looked at her in her big, oversize Williams T-shirt. Goddamn, he wanted to hold her.

The phone was still ringing. She finally reached for it.

He stepped into the living room in time to hear her say 'Yes' in a wary voice.

Her knuckles whitened, her body began to sway. Her gaze swept up and her beautiful brown eyes were dilated with horror.

'My baby,' she whispered. 'My baby!'

The phone clattered to the floor as down she went.

He caught her as she fell and wrapped her against his chest.

21

Special Agent Quincy rubbed the back of his neck. It was just after ten A.M. and he'd spent most of the night at the Difford crime scene. In the last three days he'd slept only eight hours and lost five pounds, and he felt it.

'Tell me something good.'

'The Red Sox finally won a game.'

Quincy gave Houlihan a blurry glare. 'Try again.'

'Sorry, that's it. When Officers Campbell and Teitel arrived for their two A.M. shift, they found Harrison shot dead in the car and the safe house empty. Traces of blood on the kitchen floor indicate violence, but we haven't located Difford's body or his car. Samantha and all of her belongings are gone. Also, the gun cabinet was forced open and emptied. We're not sure what all Difford had in there, but he formally checked out a Mossberg 12-gauge shotgun, a Smith & Wesson 9mm, his police issue .357 Magnum, and probably a Smith & Wesson .38 Special. Difford may have kept a few surprises in the inventory as well. Maybe a sawed-off shotgun. You know how cops can be about guns.

'We have Beckett's latent and patent prints at the crime scene, paper towels with makeup residue, a state police uniform, and a state police badge issued to an Officer Travis four years ago. Beckett also left us his wig, nylons stuffed with padding, and yes, two plastic bags filled with neon purple Silly Putty. Then we have his note.' Lieutenant Houlihan's voice grew somber. He said softly, 'Beckett wrote: "Sergeant Wilcox sends his regards." Wilcox has been missing for twenty-four hours now. His wife thought he was on special assignment, we thought he was out sick. There, uh, there hasn't been any sign of his body yet.'

Quincy squeezed his eyes shut and pinched the bridge of his nose where the tension had gathered like a hard knot, pressing against his eyeballs, trying to force them out of their sockets. 'The neighbors? Did they see anything?'

'Saw two cops sitting in an unmarked car most of the evening. One of the officers appeared to be asleep.'

'Estimated time of death for Harrison?'

'Six P.M. Beckett probably shot him beginning of shift, when Harrison first climbed into the car.'

'And you last heard from the watch car at one A.M.'

'Exactly. Difford called in a little after midnight. So sometime between midnight and two A.M.. . . .'

'Wonderful. You call in the National Guard?'

'Are you kidding? If a person can dress himself, I have him looking for Jim Beckett. We've cordoned off a fifty-mile area. Samantha Williams's picture has been sent to every TV station and newspaper in the nation. Soon her picture will be plastered on every milk carton in the goddamn free world.'

'It's a start.'

'We're going get him, Quincy. How the hell is he going to hide a four-year-old girl? No, he finally screwed up and we're going to nail his ass.'

'Humph.' Quincy wasn't convinced. He leaned back and studied the cheap white ceiling, the kind that could double as a dart board and on slow nights, probably did. The inset lights increased the pounding behind his temples. Some days the pressure made him want to flush his whole head down the toilet and yet he still wouldn't give up his job. What kind of sick bastard did that make him?

'Want a few more ideas?' He phrased it as a question because the task force fell under Houlihan's control and Quincy didn't want to appear as if he were taking over. Crossjurisdictional coordination was never easy during the best of conditions, let alone when everyone had been up all night and the case seemed to be unraveling before their very eyes.

'Well, you're the Einstein. If you know the secret formula for catching Jim Beckett, cough it up. Our department can't afford any more fucking nights like this.' Houlihan's voice contained a bitter, rusty edge that they both felt. In Quincy's career, he'd seen eight officers go down and two damn good agents. How many times had he listened to the guns firing their grim salute? It never got any easier. It never got less personal.

'Okay, we know Beckett loves his daughter. We don't believe she's in any danger. So you're right, let's exploit this for all its worth. You have a four-year-old girl to keep happy. What do four-year-olds want?'

'I'm the proud father of two Dobermans, Quincy. What the hell do I know about kids?'

'Hmm, and I can't even handle goldfish.'

'Hold on a sec.' Lieutenant Houlihan opened the door of the office and shouted, 'Rich, get in here!'

The middle-aged homicide detective materialized a few seconds later. He'd also been up half the night, but he didn't comment on it. Like all the task force members, his face was haggard and his shoulders drooped. In the last twenty-four hours they'd seen Lieutenant Difford and Officer Harrison brutally murdered. Most likely Sergeant Wilcox had met the same fate.

They were angry. They wanted justice, they wanted revenge. Beckett's chances of being brought in alive were diminishing exponentially – much to Quincy's regret. They still had a lot to learn from a man such as Beckett. Except that the price was becoming too high.

'You got two kids, right?' Houlihan pressed the detective.

'One girl and one boy. Ages three and five.'

'Good. Think like a four-year-old for us.'

'Jesus.'

'You've been woken up in the middle of the night,' Quincy supplied. 'You're tired and cranky. Beckett probably had to look for a hotel, right?'

Rich shook his head. 'He took Difford's car, yeah? Kids sleep great in cars. We used to drive Shawn all night long when he was teething. It was the only thing that put him to sleep.'

'Shit. So Beckett, with possibly one hour's head start, can drive straight through. What about the morning? By the time she does wake up, she's going to be scared, uncertain, cranky . . .'

'Happy Meals,' Rich supplied without hesitation.

'What?'

'Greatest form of bribery on the planet. Kids are unhappy or whining, take them to McDonald's. Is Beckett a cook?'

'No, he's a chauvinist pig.'

'Well, kids aren't really into restaurants, especially four-year-olds. Check all the fast-food places. She'll need to eat, and any kid worth her salt will want to eat at McDonald's or Burger King or a place like that. Those commercials really brainwash the little guys.'

Quincy nodded. 'There you go. Let's get a map, plot out just how far he could get in one night of driving, and canvas fast-food joints with her picture. I can get the field office to help.'

'Works for me,' Houlihan said curtly. Rich was excused. 'I want the airports on alert too. LaGuardia, Logan, JFK, etcetera. Can you arrange it?'

'He won't try to leave the country yet.'

'How can you be so sure?'

'Tess is still alive. He won't leave until he's gotten her.'

'Come on. How's he going to track down Tess with a four-year-old?'

'I imagine he has a plan.' Quincy leaned forward. 'Airports are alerted, Lieutenant. The international departure gates have had Beckett's picture ever since he escaped. We can get them Sam's picture too, but I don't think he'll fly the coop yet. Sam was step one. Killing Tess Williams will be step two.'

'Then he'll leave?'

'I don't know.'

'You don't know? You're the expert and you don't know?'

Quincy remained silent for a moment, giving Houlihan a chance to take a deep breath and pull it together. When the lieutenant had succeeded in fisting his hands down by his sides, Quincy tapped his computer. 'Remember the pattern—'

'For chrissake, screw the pattern! He's doing it personal now, not by the numbers.'

'He's doing both. Think, Houlihan. He uses the first letter from the place he leaves the bodies to play his little games. Two guards in Walpole, W. Shelly Zane in Avon, A. Harrison and most likely Wilcox in Springfield. S, Was. Jim Beckett was . . .'

'The best.'

'Number one. Here. Supreme. It could be many things. The point is, the phrase is unfinished. And we still haven't found Difford's body. My guess is that he'll drop it somewhere else for another letter. Perhaps he's done the same with Wilcox's body – we won't know until we find it. But Beckett is still engaged in his little game, and he finishes what he starts. Maybe he'll complete it out of the country. Maybe he'll take a year off and then do it. But he'll kill again. Until we find him, he'll pursue Tess Williams and he'll pursue others.'

The silence stretched out long. Houlihan's jaw was so tight, Quincy could hear the lieutenant's teeth grind with frustration. Quincy didn't say anything. Any comment now would merely light the lieutenant's fuse. He sat back and waited it out.

'I offered her police protection,' Houlihan said abruptly, his voice tight. 'She turned me down. She won't come in.'

'Tess Williams?'

'Yeah. Difford left her contact number in a safety deposit box. That way if anything happened to him, we could notify her. Difford liked to think of all the angles, plan for all contingencies.'

'Beckett probably knows where she is,' Quincy said quietly. 'He must have gotten the safe house information from Wilcox. He'll have used the same tactics on Difford.'

'Yeah. What a way to go.' Houlihan swallowed thickly, then made a big production of squaring his shoulders. 'I gave it to her straight. I offered her what I could. She told me the police had done quite enough already—'

Quincy winced.

'She would handle things her own way.'

'Oh, God.'

'She's been training with a mercenary.'

'You're kidding.'

'Nope. She's gone vigilante.' Houlihan tried to force a laugh. 'Can you blame her?'

Quincy shook his head tiredly. 'Let's just hope she doesn't do anything stupid.'

'This is stupid.'

'You don't have to be here.'

'Tess, think about it a minute. Beckett kidnaps your daughter. So what do you do? You return to his backyard. What do you think he intended?'

Tess stared stubbornly out the window. It was after midnight and they were on the Mass Pike, headed toward Springfield. Few cars were on the road. The moon was weak and further obscured by a steady drizzle. The windshield wipers offered a rhythmic, *thump thump, thump thump,* otherwise the rental car was quiet.

J.T. was tired and grim at the wheel. He already missed the sun and the desert. Six hours ago he'd been wearing a T-shirt and admiring his garden. Now Rosalita tended his villa and Glug while he and Tess landed in a state so damn cold, it was inhospitable.

J.T. didn't like Massachusetts. Boston had strong ethnic populations from all over the world – Irish, Italian, Chinese – but everyone still had to answer the same three questions to consider themselves a true Bostonian: Did their ancestors get off the *Mayflower*? Did they go to Harvard? Did their family personally know any of the Kennedys?

Fail that and forget it. You could live in Boston until you were a hundred and fifty and you still wouldn't be a Bostonian.

'You said Beckett loves Sam, right?' J.T. continued pressing. 'So she's not in immediate danger.'

'Not in immediate danger? For God's sake, she's been kidnapped by a sadomasochist serial killer who rapes and strangles women as a hobby. How safe can she be? He'll never hit her, but he's on the run. What if the police corner him? What if there's a shootout? Dear God, what if there's a shootout?'

'Tess—'

'No.' She shifted away from him. 'I don't want any platitudes.'

'Oh, dear, what will I say now? Listen to me and pay attention. By your own admission, you are Big Bad Jim's prime target. And you've just traveled within striking distance.'

'The police think he knows how to locate me in Arizona anyway.'

'Yeah, but with a four-year-old girl, it's going to be a little difficult for him to get there. Dammit, Tess, you're doing exactly what he wants.'

Tess simply shrugged. 'Jim's a resourceful man. He would have found a way. Now we do it my way.'

'You're not ready for this.'

'Oh? And at what point is someone ready to take on Jim Beckett? After they've been a homicide cop for ten years, twenty years, thirty years? Oops, I'm sorry. He killed them too.'

J.T.'s grip tightened on the wheel. She'd been withdrawn, sarcastic, and bitter ever since getting the news. So far she'd been everything but afraid. That was a bad sign. Fear served a purpose; it helped keep people safe.

'Let me drop you off at a hotel,' J.T. tried again. 'I'll check out the safe house and see if there's anything to be learned. If there's a trail, I'll find it. We'll go from there.'

'No.'

'So eager to be part of the action?'

'My daughter, my ex-husband, my problem.'

'Your death.'

Her jaw clenched.

'Tess,' he said quietly. 'How long do you plan on punishing yourself?'

'What?'

He took the exit for Springfield. 'You heard me. There's more on your mind than Jim Beckett, and, honey, you'd better get it out. Because you take him on with a chip on your shoulder and he will eat you alive.'

'I don't know what you're talking about.'

'You're angry.'

'He murdered my friend! He kidnapped my child!'

'Not at him. You're angry with yourself.'

'And why would I feel that? Because I left my daughter alone to be taken? Because I left the state so Difford could get killed instead of me?'

'Because Samantha was kidnapped while you were screwing a former mercenary and playing family counselor to siblings only Manson could love?' he finished for her. 'Come on, Tess. Get it out, get it all out. Hit me if you want. Hit yourself. Then pull it together. Because I'm not letting you out of this car until I know your mind's one hundred percent on the matters at hand. You're worthless otherwise.'

'Dammit!' she cried. Then she did hit him. In the shoulder, hard. Next she hit the dash. Three times. He could still feel her frustration and rage.

'I should've stayed with Sam,' she whispered miserably. 'I should've stayed with my daughter.'

'Then you'd be dead too. You wanted change, Tess. This is it. Stop being the martyr and learn to be the cavalry.'

Neighborhoods appeared around them. He knew they were getting close. In a low voice Tess directed him to the former safe house. Most of the neighborhoods appeared older, comprised of one-story ranch-style homes with two token windows, one token chimney, and not much else. Like growing up in a cereal box, J.T. thought.

He turned down another street. This late, there was no one around. Cars slumbered in driveways. Houses hunkered down on their foundations. Not even a porch light offered a ray of comfort.

He looked over at Tess. She was very pale.

'I can still take you to a hotel.'

'Fuck you.'

'Oh, yeah, Tess. You're tough.'

She scowled, then pointed to a house tucked between two others. Yellow crime scene tape encircled it like a garish boa.

J.T. parked the car next to the curb. He looked down the block just in case an unmarked car was watching. Nothing. Of course the action here had already come and gone. The crime lab chemists had probably spent a solid day here, analyzing the scene, dusting for prints, cataloguing evidence. Dogs had been brought in to locate Difford's body, which Tess said they still hadn't found. Now the real police work would be performed in the lab, the house just an old monument to the violence.

J.T. and Tess had come for that testimony. They needed a starting point to track Beckett, and his last crime scene seemed as good as any. Maybe it would tell them something, maybe it wouldn't.

J.T. opened the door and stepped out into the stunningly cold fall night. 'Christ,' he muttered. 'Give me a cactus any day.'

He jammed his bare hands into his front jeans pockets and hunched lower in his leather bomber jacket. Tess was already climbing out of her side of the car, much more suitably attired.

'Stay here.' He stepped up onto the sidewalk.

'No.' She closed the car door and squared her shoulders.

He didn't feel like arguing. He walked right over to her and pinned her against the car with his body. His dark eyes bore into hers, harsh and impatient.

'I'm the professional.'

'I'm the client.'

'Tess, you'll only make a mess of things. Now, get back in the car.'

She stared at him mutinously. 'He already has Sam. How much messier could it get?'

'A lot,' he said bluntly. He pinned her in place and leaned closer. She didn't shrink or cower. Her brown gaze remained steady. God, she'd learned. A regular hellion these days. Marion would be proud. He said, 'Beckett isn't a hay bale, Tess.'

'I know. I felt some pity for the hay bales. I don't feel any toward Jim.'

She pushed against him hard, but his body didn't budge.

'In the car.'

'Nope.'

She pushed again, and while he was steeling his body against that feeble effort, she ducked beneath his arm. Step, twirl, and she was free, striding beyond his reach with a grim smile.

'You have to admit, I'm getting a lot better.'

He scowled. 'It's not a game.'

He wanted her in the car. He wanted her someplace where he wouldn't have to worry about her.

She headed toward the front door. 'Do you really think he's here? He already has what he came for.'

'I don't feel like taking any unnecessary chances.' He briefly debated knocking her out cold and stuffing her into the trunk until it was over. It would serve the fool right.

'He has Sam,' she said flatly. 'He'll have to stay with her in the evening.'

'Or find a beautiful blonde to watch her for him.'

She paused. He caught a slight tremor racking her frame. But Tess brought her chin up stubbornly. The wind stirred behind her, bringing him the scent of China Rain. The moon highlighted her sable hair and caressed her heart-shaped face.

'Christ,' he muttered, and turned away. She looked beautiful, precious, and he didn't want to see that – not knowing what he did to beautiful, precious things. Thirty-six years old and his life was still locked in the same old patterns, spiraling toward the same bitter end. He hated that. 'You got your gun?'

'Yes.' Now she sounded shaken.

'Get it out.'

'You think he's in there?'

'Get out the damn gun. You wanna play soldier? Soldiers do not question orders. You do as you're told when you're told. Is that clear?'

'Yes, sir.'

'You'd better believe it.' He took out his gun and removed the safety. Cocked, locked, and ready, the only way a marine made an entrance. 'Follow me and do what I say. Don't make any noise, don't leave my side. Disobey me once and I'll shoot you myself.'

'Yes, sir.'

'You know what a clock is?'

She gave him an exasperated look that clearly stated she knew what a clock was.

'Good.' He ignored her attitude. 'Anything happens, this is how it works. You're responsible for the six to twelve position, I'll cover twelve to six.'

'You mean . . . you mean shooting, don't you?'

'Well, you can shake his hand if you want to, but I wouldn't recommend it.'

'Okay, okay,' she said hastily. Her uneasiness had returned. Then she cleared her face and set her shoulders, the good little soldier. She was killing him.

'The car,' he attempted one last time.

'No.'

'Stubborn ass.'

'Yes. Are we going to talk all night, or do this?'

'Fine.' He sounded angry and couldn't help it. 'But don't say I didn't warn you.'

'Don't worry, I give you full permission to engrave "J.T. was right" on my tombstone.'

'Gee, thanks. I look forward to that.'

He looked back at Tess one more time. Her hands were trembling slightly, but she was holding the gun the way he'd taught her.

J.T. gave up on indifference.

Okay, God, he bargained shamelessly in his mind. *You got Marion. You got Rachel. You got Teddy. The colonel's prostate cancer was a nice poetic touch, but thirty years too late. Give me Tess. Just give me this one.*

Then I'm willing to call it even if you are. It's a helluva deal.

He received no answer but then he never had. He smiled grimly.

'We're going in. *Semper fi.*'

J.T. entered first, his back pressed against the entryway wall, his arm making smooth, level sweeping motions as he pointed his gun at each shadow. His left arm was cocked back, beaming a small flashlight into the entryway. He looked like Rambo.

She felt like the halfhearted understudy.

J.T. slid around the corner and she followed quickly, focusing on taking quiet, shallow breaths. The hallway was long and dark and seemed to bisect the house as a main artery. Her nose twitched. She recognized the scents from years before. The pungent odor of chemicals sprinkled and sprayed onto carpets, the oily residue of fingerprint powder clogging the air. The distant rusty scent of something she didn't want to contemplate. Crime scenes had their own distinct fragrance of old violence and fresh chemicals. It made bile rise in her throat. She swallowed it back down.

J.T. turned right and led them straight into a tiny kitchen. Dishes were still stacked in the sink and a newspaper was open on the kitchen table, giving the eerie feel of life interrupted. The vinyl floor, however, no longer looked like a kitchen floor. Huge sections had been ripped up, cut out, and sent off to the state crime lab. Most likely they were being analyzed for blood.

J.T. opened the lower cupboards and swept the dank depths with the penetrating flashlight beam. The light came up, washing over an old countertop, now coated in luminescent chemicals.

The beam continued relentlessly. The walls glittered as the light picked up various residues. As he glanced up, he saw the flashlight illuminate dark dots arching across the ceiling like a rainbow. The spray pattern. Indicating a beating with a blunt wooden instrument. Like a tree limb or mop handle or baseball bat.

She was having a much harder time breathing. She squeezed her eyes shut and pictured Sam. *You're doing this for your daughter. You will be strong for your daughter.*

'Hold it together,' J.T. growled in her ear. He moved into the living room.

After another deep breath she followed. There was less disturbance here. The furniture looked like it had been hastily rearranged by cops looking for evidence. Random squares of carpet had been cut up and sent off to labs. It was obvious, however, that the main action had happened in the kitchen. The living room just got the residue.

'Stay here,' J.T. said curtly. 'I'll check out the rest of the house.'

'What about my six-to-twelve responsibilities?'

'The wall is the only thing holding you up. Let's not push it.'

He slid down the hall without another word, taking his flashlight with him. She gripped her gun tighter in her sweaty palms. Carefully she eased away from the wall. She wasn't going to be sick, she wasn't going to faint, she wasn't going to be scared. She was going to be strong, she was going to be tough.

Jim walked up right behind her and popped the plastic bag over her head.

'Theresa,' he whispered in her ear. 'I see you answered my invitation. And it looks like you brought me your mercenary to kill.'

J.T. had just opened the last dresser drawer in the spare room when he knew he was no longer alone. Tess? She couldn't move that quietly. These were the steady steps of a professional.

Beckett. How?

He tightened his finger around the trigger of his 9mm and rolled up on the balls of his feet just in time to hear the telltale whistle of a bat whizzing down. He leapt to the side and fired twice. The bat crashed into the dresser.

J.T. pivoted, tried to aim, and received two sharp blows to his kidneys for his efforts. His gun went flying. He lashed out with his foot and heard the grunt of Beckett receiving the blow.

Whirling his head around, J.T. spotted his gun. He lunged. Simultaneously Beckett lifted the bat.

Roll and fire, just like a shooting drill, except Beckett wasn't a cardboard target and the stakes were real.

His finger pulled back sharply, one, two, three, and through the ringing in his ears he heard Beckett's sharply indrawn breath. The bat, however, rose again.

J.T. moved but not fast enough; the bat caught him with a solid crack against his forearm. His fingers went immediately numb, then flared red hot with pain. The gun dropped from his lifeless hands.

'Shit.'

The bat rose.

There was no more time for thinking. Now it was about adrenaline. It was about rage. And J.T. felt a whole lot of it well up inside him.

His lips curved back in snarl. He held his wounded arm against his ribs and kicked hard with his left leg. He connected solidly with Beckett's kneecap, hearing the other man's winded grunt and feeling the blood lust grow.

He lashed out again, stomping a rock-hard stomach. Quick pivot and turn, and he smashed his foot into Beckett's upper arm. The bat dropped to the floor. J.T. closed in for the kill.

Just as he lunged forward, however, Beckett hooked his feet and he flew through the air. He landed hard, his hands too numb to catch him. The oxygen left his lungs in a painful whoosh, his chest filled with fiery red ants. His eyes saw spots and his bruised hip roared with pain.

He kept moving, instinct yelling *roll roll roll or die.*

He staggered to his feet, trying to sight Beckett. The world spun sickeningly. He couldn't get his balance. He couldn't find his gun.

Shit, he was in trouble. *Focus, dammit, focus.*

His blurry gaze finally found Beckett, a tall, pale shadow that looked alien and ghostlike. It took J.T. a minute to understand why. Beckett was hairless, no head hair, no eyebrows, no nothing. His eyes seemed to have receded in his face, smaller and more penetrating without brows to highlight and soften. A serpent's head, that's what it looked like.

The two men stared at each other.

J.T. held his arm against his side. Blood trickled down Beckett's shoulder.

Beckett moved. He clenched his teeth in blatant frustration and leapt for the window. J.T. lurched after him.

At the last minute, however, Beckett turned, one foot swung over the windowsill.

'Theresa,' he said simply. 'By now I wouldn't think she has any oxygen left.'

J.T. halted.

Beckett smiled. 'You fool. I had her for years. I can tell you, she's not worth it.'

'You're dead.'

'She's mine. Help her and you become mine too. Just ask Difford when you see him again.'

Beckett slipped out the window, and there was nothing J.T. could do that wouldn't cost Tess her life. He recovered his gun from the floor, and with his left arm clutched against his ribs raced for the living room.

Tess was handcuffed to the coffee table with a plastic cooking bag plastered against her skull.

J.T. unsheathed the knife from his ankle, slit the plastic bag, and peeled it back from her face. Her head lolled to the side, her pale skin tinged with blue.

'Tess, Tess, come on, come on!'

Her head fell to her chest.

He slapped her hard and was rewarded by a sharp intake of breath. She was alive. He'd screwed up, but somehow she was alive. He rocked her against his chest. He cursed his own stupidity. He got down to business.

They had to leave. Now.

'Jim,' Tess whispered hoarsely. Her eyes were glazed.

'He left. But he might come back. Can you walk?'

'I tried to shoot him. I raised my gun, but—'

'Shh, pull yourself together. Come on, Tess.'

He raised the coffee table, slid the other half of the handcuffs free, and dragged Tess to her feet. She leaned against him heavily, still gasping for air.

'Okay. You breathe. I'll run. Here we go.'

He pulled her out the front door, and the night slapped them like a vengeful woman, cold and stinging against their cheeks.

Run, it seemed to hiss in their ears.

J.T. didn't argue.

'He's dead.'

Marion glanced up from the fire, her cheeks unusually rosy from the mesmerizing flames. She sat on the edge of a white leather stool. Italian leather, very good. She'd picked it out herself and the couch and recliner that went with it. They fit the living room well, a minimalist motif of white leather and frameless glass. She'd always liked this room in her upscale Virginia town house.

After the warm earth tones and vivid greens and reds of Arizona, however, she suddenly found the white overwhelming. And she resented that fiercely.

'Did you hear me?' Roger stood stiffly in the doorway, as if he couldn't decide whether it was safe to enter or not. She looked at him coolly, not giving him the slightest expression that might aid his decision.

She knocked back the last of the brandy she'd been sipping. 'I heard you.'

'I thought you were going to be by his side.'

'Obviously I didn't make it.'

'Are you all right, Marion? You don't seem . . .' His voice trailed off. His face held genuine concern. She hated that.

'Go back to your cocktail waitress, Roger. I don't need you here.'

For a change, he didn't listen to her. Instead, he stepped into the room.

She arched one fine brow. 'Why, Roger, did you grow a spine while I was away?'

His face spasmed, revealing the direct hit. 'I know this has been rough for you, Marion,' he tried valiantly.

'Spare me.'

'I know you must hurt a lot right now. I can't be your husband anymore. I'm sorry. But I thought . . . I thought I might still be your friend.'

'Why would I need a friend?'

'I know you loved him,' Roger whispered hoarsely. 'I loved him too,

Marion. He was my friend, my mentor . . . I already miss him. I can't imagine how much you must hurt.' The emotion welled up in his face. Before he controlled himself, she saw the glint of honest tears in his eyes.

She stared at him blankly. She should be crying too. She should feel sadness, grief. But she felt nothing, just ice, flowing through her veins and freezing like a solid mass in her stomach. Ever since two nights ago, ice was the only emotion she could find.

Because sometimes when it cracked, she glimpsed things she didn't want to know.

Roger stepped forward. He looked handsome and distinguished in his suit, the crystal chandelier reflecting off his fine light brown hair and elegant patrician features. He'd been born with a silver spoon in his mouth and was the epitome of grace, refinement, and class.

The first time she'd seen Roger, she'd been dressed in a flowing white gown and slowly descending the grand curving staircase of her parents' house to make the dramatic entrance for her eighteenth birthday party. Roger had been standing by the colonel's side in full military dress uniform, looking at her mesmerized while the chandelier glinted off the medals on his chest. Her gaze was supposed to sweep the whole room like a duchess granting royal privilege. Instead, she'd simply stared at Roger. She'd thought he was a prince coming to carry her away.

If he put his arms around her now, could he make the images go away? Could he save her from the ice that was consuming her?

I am lost inside myself and no one can hear my cry.

'Marion—'

'Go home, Roger. I don't want you here.'

'You shouldn't be alone—'

'Go home, goddammit! Go home or I will call your sweet little cocktail waitress and tell her just how strong and brave you really are! Get out of my home. Get out of my living room. Play the grieving protégé on your own time!'

He looked stricken. She took a step forward and he shrank back. His face became shuttered, his eyes accusing, and he didn't have to move his lips for her to know what he was thinking.

Cold Marion, unfeeling Marion, frigid Marion.

And for her part she remembered life after the storybook wedding. She recalled the time she'd been in the bathroom, washing her face, and he'd slammed open the door, stepped into the bathroom, and in front of her startled gaze lowered his zipper and pissed in the toilet. He'd stared at her mutinously. '*After five years of marriage, we ought to be at least comfortable enough to take a leak in front of each other, Marion. I want that kind of closeness!*' She'd just stared at him, unable to keep the horror and disgust from her face. He'd never done it again.

'All right,' he now said stiffly, retreating to the door. 'I'll leave, if that's what you want.'

'How many times do I have to say it?'

He opened the door, then paused long enough to shake his head. 'You've always been remote, Marion,' he said quietly. 'But I don't remember you as being so cruel.'

'I'm just getting wiser.'

'Don't get too wise, Marion. You don't have that many friends left – just Emma, whom you despise, and J.T., whom you hate.'

'Emma is insane and J.T. is a drunk. I don't give a flying fig for either of them.'

'J.T. is a drunk?'

'Absolutely,' she said coolly. Goody Two-shoes Roger always had been fascinated by her brother and even more fascinated by J.T.'s obvious disdain.

'Is that why he didn't come back?'

'I'm sure of it. You'll have to come to terms with it, Roger. My brother is no longer some dashing rebel. He's just an alcoholic. And wherever he is right now, I'm sure the tequila is golden.'

22

The motel room was brown, shit brown. Brown floor, brown beds, brown curtains. Not even a traveling salesman would like the room. Tess thought it was fitting.

J.T. was fetching ice. She stood alone in the middle of the room with her arms wrapped around her middle. She could hear a faint ringing in her ears. When she inhaled, her throat felt scratchy and raw.

She'd called Lieutenant Houlihan and told him what had happened. The APB had been updated with the information on Jim's recent sighting, and local search efforts intensified. The lieutenant wanted her to come in. She didn't see what that would accomplish. They would put her in a house. She'd sit and wait as she'd waited two and a half years ago. The mouse pinned by the cat, living day in and day out waiting for him to finally pounce. She just couldn't do it anymore.

You were going to be so tough. Instead, you walked right into Jim's trap.

She found a thick wool sweater in her bag and pulled it out. Her hands were trembling so badly, it took her a few tries to get it on. She could still hear her teeth chattering with the unrelenting chill.

Where is Samantha? Is she asking for you right now? Is she curled up, wondering why you haven't come to save her?

Why didn't you save your daughter?

The night was too dark. The room was too empty. The truth came crashing down on her and there was no way to escape it: She had failed her daughter.

J.T. walked into the room. The slamming of the door sounded loud in the silence. 'You okay?'

'No.' She sounded raw.

'Have a glass of water.' He stuck the plastic cup into her hand without waiting for her argreement. 'Drink it up. Pull yourself together. We need a new plan.'

She looked at him at last as he sat down by a warped brown table. He'd bought cigarettes while fetching the ice and now he lit one up. He used only one hand. The other remained tucked against his ribs.

'You're hurt.'

'I'm fine.'

'Your arm.'

'You know how to set a bone fracture?'

'Not really. My father always took my mother and me to the emergency room so we could tell naive interns that we'd fallen down the stairs.'

'Well, we're not going to any emergency room. I'm fine.'

She looked away. The acrid smell of cigarette smoke stung her eyes. She could feel the hot, salty knot of tears in her chest, but she couldn't cry.

Samantha. Difford. How much are you going to let Jim take from you?

'I shot him,' J.T. said at last.

Her eyes widened.

'Jim and I had a little get-together in the back bedroom. He brought his bat, I brought my gun. Next time I'm leaving the 9mm at home and bringing an AK-47.'

'Is he seriously wounded?'

'No.' J.T. sounded furious. 'Probably just a flesh wound. He sure as hell didn't slow down much.'

'I don't understand why he was there,' she murmured. 'Why did he come back and where was Sam?'

'He came for you, Tess. He planned it like a two-for-one sale – get his daughter, kill his ex-wife.'

'Where did he come from?' she whispered. 'One moment I was all alone, and the next . . .'

J.T.'s jaw tightened. 'I screwed up,' he said tersely. 'Didn't secure the perimeter, didn't scope out the full house before leaving you behind. I didn't really expect . . . Well, I screwed up. It's that simple.'

'You didn't know.'

'I should've.'

'What do we do now?'

'Sleep. Eat. Regroup in the morning.'

The room drifted into strained silence again. She snapped on the TV to fight it. The first image she saw was Sam's.

'Samantha Williams was kidnapped late last night from a police safe house in Springfield. Two officers were killed by her father, convicted serial killer Jim Beckett, who is considered armed and dangerous. Samantha is four years old, wears a pink winter coat, has long blond hair and blue eyes. Anyone with information on Samantha can call the hotline listed below.

'Once again, Jim Beckett is considered armed and dangerous and should *not* be approached. He frequently disguises himself as a police officer or security guard. Police are currently combing the area with the aid of the FBI and the National Guard. Beckett escaped three weeks ago from the maximum security block of Walpole after killing two corrections officers . . .'

Tess couldn't stop staring at the screen. It showed one of Samantha's preschool pictures. She was looking over her shoulder with a toothy smile, her blue eyes bright, her blond pigtails curly. Tess fell to her knees.

'Let it out,' J.T. said quietly behind her. 'Let it all out.'

She couldn't. She couldn't cry. She couldn't yell.

What are you going to do, Theresa? Fight me? We both know you're too weak for that.

'Pull it together, Tess,' J.T. said more sharply. 'Take a deep breath. Focus on the carpet if it helps.'

You're weak, stupid. You couldn't even stand up to your father. What did you do when he hit your mother? Watch? And what did you do while he hit you? Wait?

'Tess! Dammit, don't do this!' J.T. grabbed her shoulders and shook her hard.

For a moment she lolled like a rag doll. She couldn't find her strength. She had no mass, no muscles, no bones. She had no spirit.

'Tess?' J.T. whispered roughly. 'Sweetheart, please . . .'

The dam broke. She began to sob, her throat burning, her shoulders heaving. So many tears. J.T. sat down beside her on the ugly rug. He wrapped his good arm around her shoulders and cradled her against his chest. She cried against his T-shirt, big, messy tears that soaked through to his skin and made her feel worse. He stroked her hair.

'Shh. Shh. I'll help you. We're going to find Sam, sweetheart. I promise you, we'll find Sam.'

She cried harder. He rocked her against him.

'It's okay, honey, it's okay. I know. I know.' He kept murmuring against her hair. She pressed her shivering body against him.

Hold me, hold me, hold me. Don't ever let me go.

'I know,' he whispered. 'I know.'

'We should ice your arm.' It was an hour later. She'd sobbed, J.T. had smoked. Now they both sat on the edge of the too-soft bed, looking worse for wear. 'Can . . . can I look at it?'

He shrugged and pursed his lips around the thin white cigarette. The pungent smoke stung her eyes.

'Can you stop smoking?'

He arched one dark brow.

'In return for my health services,' she negotiated.

'I thought you didn't know much about first aid.'

'I know better than to smoke, so I'm obviously more qualified than you.'

He didn't give in right away, but after a few moments he ground out the cigarette. 'Self-righteous Tess,' he murmured.

She ignored his comment and sank to the brown carpeting before him.

His knees parted, allowing her closer. His thighs brushed her shoulders. She placed her fingers on his arm and heard his harsh breath.

She had told him the truth earlier. She had no idea what she was doing. In her mother's house she'd learned to put makeup over scrapes and bruises, not Bactine. She'd learned to mend broken bones with carefully scripted lies to health care professionals. She'd learned how to pretend most of the beatings didn't hurt.

Now she examined J.T.'s injured limb helplessly. His left forearm appeared furious – beet red, swollen, and hot to the touch. She risked a glance up, her fingers still resting delicately on his skin. His face had gone pale. Sweat beaded his upper lip. She could tell he was biting the inside of his cheeks to keep from making a sound.

'I think you need a real doctor,' she said quietly.

'Do what you can, Tess. Or I'll fix it the old-fashioned way.'

'Amputation?'

'Bourbon.'

'Oh.' She poured ice into a towel and placed it to bring the swelling down. He could wiggle his fingers a little, but not a lot. Did that mean it wasn't broken, just badly sprained, or did that mean something worse? She had no idea.

Finally she gave him a couple of aspirin from her purse.

'Two? My arm's been pulverized by a baseball bat and you hand me two aspirin?'

'You're right.' She doled out six. He swallowed them as a single handful.

She sat on the edge of the king-size bed, her knees not far from him. They had been through a lot, but neither of them knew how to put it into words. She'd slept with him, but she didn't know how to ask him to hold her. She'd cried on his shoulder, but she didn't know how to offer him comfort.

'Are you going to stare at me all night?'

'Maybe.'

'You're giving me the jitters.'

'Why did we come to a hotel? Why didn't we go straight to the police?'

J.T. was silent for a moment. 'Because they're the police.'

'You don't trust them?'

'No, I guess I don't. Big Bad Jim seems to know how to run circles around them. We're better off on our own.'

'Your arm is busted, I almost died. Care to say that again?'

'And we both lived to tell the tale. So far that puts our records way ahead of the police.'

'J.T., he has my daughter.'

'We'll find him.'

'How?' She could hear the hysteria in her voice. 'Place an ad in the yellow pages? Read tea leaves?'

'I don't know.'

'*You don't know?*' She was screaming at him now. She didn't mean to scream.

'Tess, I'm not fucking Superman! I don't have all the answers. I'm making it up as fast as I can.' J.T. slammed out another cigarette and promptly snapped it in two. 'Shit,' he said, and reached for another. 'What time is it?'

'Three A.M.! He has had my daughter for over twenty-four hours. Twenty-four hours and we have nothing!'

'We know he's in the area. We forced him to take a risk returning to the crime scene. Sooner or later he'll screw up.'

'Oh, that's a fine strategy. The police have been using it for the last three years with such success as well.'

'Fine, Tess.' Now his voice was cold. 'What do you suggest?'

'I . . . I . . .' She didn't know. She just wanted Jim dead. And she wanted to hold Samantha in her arms again.

She closed her eyes. She took a deep breath and raked her hand through her hair. Suddenly she was too tired to think. The pain ran too deep, sapped all the strength from her until she was simply a hollow husk. Her daughter was out there alone. She was sitting in a cheap roadside motel, not knowing what to do. Her head hurt unbearably and J.T. was right, he was not Superman. She was foolish and silly to expect so much from him.

You have to learn to stand on your own. You have to be strong. You have to pull it together and get your daughter back.

She stood and held out her hand. 'Come to bed.'

J.T. snarled, 'Well, sweetheart, I do try hard to be accommodating, but even my talents are limited by the loss of an arm.'

'I didn't ask you to fuck me,' she said bluntly. 'I know you're not angry enough to do that.'

His black eyes widened, then narrowed dangerously. 'If I screw you out of anger, what makes you so hot for me?'

'Lust. Pure lust. Isn't that what you want to hear?'

He didn't reply. And he didn't accept her outstretched hand. She shook her head, disgusted with them both. Why couldn't he understand that for a woman like her, there was no such thing as simple lust. Even when she wished there was.

She grabbed his right hand because she knew he'd never take hers, and with a fierce jerk she brought him to his feet.

He towered over her, his face no longer passive and no longer unreadable.

'I changed my mind,' he murmured. 'I'm angry enough after all.'

'Like hell.' She pushed him back on the bed. 'You're going to lie there, keep that ice on your arm, and do exactly as I say.'

She placed both her knees on the bed, the mattress sagging dangerously.

J.T. was still watching her through heavy-lidded eyes. She reached across to the bedside lamp and snapped it off.

'I prefer seeing,' he commented.

Her breasts were brushing his chest. She drew back carefully, not wanting to prolong the contact but not wanting to disturb his arm. 'Sleep.'

'Sleep?'

'It's as good a skill as any, remember?'

'Only until eight A.M.'

'Fine. Only until eight.'

'He's gotta have someone watching Sam,' J.T. was insisting. 'A relative we don't know about. An old friend. An unwitting accomplice. He couldn't just leave her alone to return to Difford's house.'

'I don't know,' Tess said. She was straddling his lap, examining his arm. It looked even worse in the morning light. Now he couldn't move his fingers at all.

'Think, Tess.'

'I have thought about it! I'm telling you, his family is dead, he never had friends, just associates, and now there's no logical person for him to turn to. On the other hand, he picks up women like that.' She snapped her fingers. 'Maybe he has a steady girl these days. I don't know.'

'Where did he hide last time?'

'I don't know.'

'He disappeared for six months and the cops still don't know how?'

'I'm sorry, J.T., but once he was caught, he didn't exactly volunteer all the information. That only happens in the movies.'

'Where did they search last time?'

'In the beginning, everyplace, just like they're doing now. His picture was posted, a hotline established. They issued a warrant throughout New England. As time wore on, however, the task force grew smaller, the effort less intense. Police departments don't have the budget to maintain that level of manpower and diligence for six months.'

'Which Jim knows. So he waited, the number of officers working the case slowly dwindled down, and soon there's you, sitting in your old house with only a couple of cops working each watch shift.'

'We weren't even sure he'd come back,' she whispered. 'Quincy just thought it was probable.'

J.T. was silent. His skin was an unhealthy color. His forehead felt like he was running a fever. 'He could do that again, you know.'

'He has Samantha.'

'Exactly. An even better reason for him to lie low. He has a place – maybe a person. Let's just assume that for now. He used it last time he disappeared and he's using it now. You're right. He keeps a low profile, and six months from now the task force will be half the size. They'll start thinking he slipped through the net unseen, men will get called onto more active cases. Yeah, if he can be patient, it can work.'

'Then we find him,' Tess said simply. 'I'm not leaving Samantha in his possession for six months or a year.'

'I'm not arguing. But we have to have a starting point. We need information.'

Tess took a deep breath. 'You're absolutely right, J.T.'

The tone of her voice gave her away. He was immediately shaking his head. 'You can lead a horse to water, Tess, but you can't make him drink.'

'I'm not playing with a horse. I'm talking about you and your sister and my daughter, who needs you both!'

'Trying to play matchmaker?'

'I'm trying to do what's best for Samantha.'

He stiffened, letting her know she'd struck deep. He rolled off the bed and stood, putting plenty of space between them. 'Marion might not be willing to help. Not given the way she feels about me right now.'

'She doesn't hate you any more than you hate her.'

'Get that out of your crystal ball?'

She walked up to him and placed her fingertips on his collarbone. She wasn't willing to accept his distance, and she wasn't willing to let him push her away. 'You were just a little boy, J.T. She must understand that you couldn't have saved her any more than you could have saved yourself.'

'Save her? Tess, she won't even admit it happened.'

'I know. It's not uncommon for incest survivors—'

He flinched at the word, his face shuttering.

'You can't even say it, can you?' she whispered.

'I don't . . . I don't . . . It's an ugly word.'

Her gaze remained on his face, her fingers rubbing his shoulders.

'I still see it all so clearly,' he muttered. His shifted beneath her touch, his body wired with tension. 'She tells me it never happened, but I can still remember every detail of it. All the times he beat us. All the times she stood at the foot of my bed and begged me to save her—'

He pushed away from Tess.

'J.T.—'

'Stop it!' His right hand raked his hair. 'It happened. We grew up in spite of him. And I hope he rots in hell.'

'But you still love your sister,' she said softly.

His hand balled into a fist. His jaw worked. 'Yeah,' he said, staring out the window. 'And she still thinks I'm a loon.'

'I don't think so, J.T. I think she's beginning to think you're right, and that's what scares her so much.'

She took a step toward him, reaching out. He flinched. 'Don't.'

She faltered, stung by the rejection. She forced her hand down to her side, her gaze never leaving his face. He hurt, she knew he hurt. She could see it in the remoteness of his expression. *Let me in, let me help a little bit if I can.*

But he remained unyielding. She didn't know anyone who could be as hard as he could be hard.

She took a deep breath. Her eyes stung.

'All right,' she said quietly. 'I'm going to shower. You do . . . you do what you think is best.'

'Yeah, I'll do that.'

'You're the professional.'

The minute the bathroom door closed behind Tess, J.T. retrieved a cigarette. He paused long enough to open the window and get hit by the solid New England chill. Then he brought the cigarette to his lips, lit it clumsily, and inhaled gratefully.

The open air was cold, the sky gray but bright enough to hurt his eyes. He stood there anyway, squinting, exhaling out the window and smoking the first cigarette down to a nub. Then he lit a second.

And then he picked up the phone.

His finger shook when he punched the number. He told himself it was the nicotine. Marion picked up on the third ring. For a minute he couldn't find his voice.

'Hello? Hello?' She already sounded angry and she didn't even know it was him. He contemplated hanging up, but didn't.

'Hello, Marion,' he said at last.

She was silent. He used the opportunity to drag deeply on his cigarette. On the other end of the line, was she doing the same? That was a pretty picture – a brother and sister who couldn't carry on a thirty-second conversation, but boy could they smoke.

'Are you speaking to me or not?'

'Give me one reason why I should.'

'It's about Beckett.'

'Beckett?' She sounded suspicious. 'What do you want, J.T.?'

'I'm not asking for me, Marion, I know better. Tess is asking. And let's not forget that this is the kind of case that could build a career.' He couldn't keep the edge out of his voice.

'You have two minutes to state what you need, or I hang up.'

'Information.'

'Information?'

'Beckett returned to Mass. He killed the cop who was watching Tess's daughter and kidnapped her.'

'Oh, shit.' For a change, Marion's voice was soft. Her shock sounded genuine.

'I think he has Sam stashed with some friend,' J.T. said quietly, 'but Tess can't think of anyone. The FBI are the ones who've been tapping phones and handling surveillance. Maybe there's something there that will tell us where he's gone, who might be helping him.'

'Maybe.' She was silent for a moment. 'Why come to me, J.T.? Why not just contact the special agent in charge? I could get you a name if you want.'

'Is that what you want me to do, Marion? Contact the SAC?'

This time the period of silence was long. He forgot about his cigarette until it burned down far enough to singe his fingers.

'I'll come,' she said abruptly. 'Where are you?'

'Outside of Springfield in a motel.' He rattled off the phone number, careful to keep his voice neutral. He wasn't sure how to feel yet. Or if he should feel anything. 'Ah . . . give us a call when you land at Logan. I'll give you directions from there.'

'The shuttle flights are steady. I imagine I can be there by midday.'

'All right.'

He waited for her to say good-bye and hang up the phone. Or say she remembered something, maybe the good times. The hot summers they'd spent perfecting cannonballs into the swimming pool, or early evenings when he would watch her ride, thinking she must be the most graceful girl in the world to sit so perfectly on that huge horse.

She said abruptly, 'Daddy's dead.'

'Okay.'

'The funeral will be next Friday. He's being laid to rest in Arlington with full military honors.'

'Huh.'

'Will you come, J.T.?'

'No.'

'Your hatred is that pure, then?'

'Isn't yours, Merry Berry?'

She hung up the phone and the dial tone filled his ear.

He interrupted her shower. She halted, her hands shampooing her hair, her gaze questioning. He took in the sight of her body covered delicately with soapsuds. Her arms had freshly defined muscles, her legs too. He couldn't really remember what she'd looked like that first day anymore. He just saw her now and she was beautiful to him.

His gaze rested on the harsh red line encircling her neck. The ligature line from the plastic bag.

'What are you doing?' Her voice was husky, uncertain.

'Looking for someone to scrub my back.'

'What makes you think I'd do a thing like that?'

'I'm an invalid. You'll help me.' He pulled the shower curtain all the way back, unmindful of the hot water that sprinkled his chest. He placed his right hand on his fly and rapidly undid the buttons.

She remained standing beneath the shower spray, openmouthed and watching as he stripped. He joined her in the tub, his legs cradling hers.

Without asking, he took the soap from her hands. He ran it over her breasts, her flat belly. He felt her skin quiver beneath his touch. Wordlessly he brought the soap up and slid it over the red welt encircling her neck, as if he could erase it. As if any man had that kind of power. Christ, he wanted it. He wanted to make the world better for her, he wanted to give her everything he hadn't been able to give Marion, everything he hadn't been able to give Rachel and Teddy. He'd failed so many times. It scared him to death to try, and scared him even more to leave Tess alone at the mercy of a man like Jim Beckett.

His fingers massaged the red line again. He thought that when he saw Jim Beckett next, Beckett's death would be painful and a long time coming.

Goddammit, let me keep one person safe. Let me help Tess, let me help Samantha. Let me stand up at the plate and finally be a man.

She said quietly, 'You called her, didn't you?'

His thumb brushed again, slow, his silence answering for him.

'J.T., I'm proud of you.'

'I don't need you to be proud of me.' He let the soap go. He looked into her eyes, searching for something he was too afraid to put into words. Her eyes were so large and so clear. Trusting. God help him. God help her.

His fingers slid into the brown thistledown of her curls and found her. She was moist, hot, ready. She arched into him, her hands digging into his shoulders. She whispered his name; the sound alone toppled his control.

She gave him hope. And maybe something more.

She pressed her forehead against his chest as his fingers started to move. 'I know,' she whispered against his skin, 'but I'm proud of you anyway.'

'I want Mommy.'

'I know.' He touched her blond hair lightly where it pooled over the plain white pillowcase. She sank deeper into the pillow, not quite cringing but not quite wanting the contact. After the first big shock of seeing him, she had become worried and anxious. She didn't fight him, but she didn't cling to his hand the way she used to. He accepted that. It had been two years since she'd last seen him, and he hardly looked like his old self.

He continued smoothly. 'As I told you, Mommy's not coming back.'

Sam's lower lip jutted out. Blue eyes became liquid. 'But she *promised*!'

He didn't respond to the whine in her voice. If you reward such behavior with attention, the child never learns. Instead, he said bluntly, 'Theresa lied to you, Sam.'

'Mommy wouldn't do that!'

'Yes, she would. She told you I would never come back, correct?' Samantha nodded miserably. 'She lied, Sam. She lied, but it's okay, because I'm here for you now.'

She cried a little, as if that would refute his words. He remained sitting there patiently. Finally she wiped the moisture from her face, then sighed with a little girl's broken heart. He didn't console her or hold her. He just waited. Within a few weeks Theresa's image would begin to fade in Sam's mind, within a few months her mother would seem like a distant shadow, and within a few years Theresa wouldn't be recalled at all. Starting over again tabula rasa was the glory – the privilege – of youth.

When Samantha was tearless and composed once more, he tucked the covers beneath her chin and patted her shoulder. 'I have a surprise for you,' he said lightly, giving her a reward for handling her new circumstances so well.

'A surprise?' She mused over the matter for a bit. 'Is it *Toy Story*?'

Her eyes were so bright, he felt a pang of regret that he hadn't thought to buy her the movie. He didn't have time to attend to such things now. Last night's unfortunate rendezvous with Theresa had already added days he couldn't afford to his master plan. Also, beneath his long-sleeved black turtleneck, his shoulder throbbed from the bullet wound. He moved stiffly and resented it fiercely.

'It's not *Toy Story*,' he said, his voice tighter.

Samantha cringed and he forced himself to smile. He'd forgotten just how sensitive children could be. The minute he relaxed, so did she. Her eyes grew contemplative once more.

'Did . . . did . . .' Her face grew very bright. 'Did you get me a new brother or sister?'

In spite of himself, Jim blinked his eyes in shock. 'No,' he said slowly. 'Has Mommy talked about getting you a new brother or sister?'

Sam shook her head glumly. 'No, but I've always wanted one.'

He smiled, and for a change the gesture was genuine on his face. From the moment he'd first seen Samantha nestled against Theresa's breast, he'd been enraptured by his daughter. She was half him, half his genes. He could see himself in her bright blue eyes. Already she showed promise of great intelligence and great resilience. Even as a baby she hadn't cried as much as other babies cried. She was better than all that. Sweet, genuine, and strong. She was the better part of him.

'Daddy,' she demanded, impatient now.

That made his smile grow. He was pleased that she'd called him Daddy. 'It's better than a brother or sister. I got you a new grandma.'

'Grandma? You mean Grandma Matthews is here?' She looked very puzzled.

'No, a new grandma. Now you have two.'

She slowly nodded. '*Two* grandmas. When do I get her?'

'In the morning.' He brushed back her hair. 'I have to go away for a while, but you'll meet your grandma when you wake up. She's tall and heavy, and speaks with a light accent I'm sure you'll find funny. Do what she says, Sam. She'll take good care of you.'

Sam didn't look convinced.

His thumb brushed her cheek. 'Do you trust me, Sammy?'

More slowly this time, she nodded.

'Good. I'll take care of everything. In just a few days I'll be back. And then we're going to leave. I think we'll go someplace very warm, what do you think of that?'

'Will Mommy come with us?' she whispered.

'No.'

'Grandma and Grandpa Matthews?'

'No.'

'The . . . the new grandma?'

His eyes grew unreadable. 'Maybe,' he said at last. 'I haven't decided yet.'

Edith had just sat down on her patio with her morning cup of tea and a wool blanket, when Martha's front door opened. For a moment Edith was startled. It was still dark out; Edith had always been an early riser, and these days her insomnia had her up before even the sun. In the first hours of dawn the air in the community was almost normal again, almost peaceful.

But the door opened, and the air was shattered. Edith felt goose bumps rise on the back of her neck. She clutched her warm mug tighter.

Martha stepped out and looked at her from across the way.

There was tension between them. It had been growing ever since Martha's return, taking shape and substance from the myriad small lies that had inexplicably fallen from their lips. It had gained permanence yesterday, when Martha had simply disappeared. Edith had gone over for their nightly cigar and found the house empty. Just empty. Martha didn't owe her an explanation, of course. The woman was responsible for her own life, but the mysterious absence, the undefined disappearance, had dealt the final blow to the fragile friendship between them.

It made Edith think of just how little she knew Martha, just how little the woman spoke of herself. She'd moved into the neighborhood two years earlier, been around for a bit, then hightailed it to Florida with barely a by-your-leave. The phone calls in between had made the absence less conspicuous, but Edith was paying attention now. She was realizing she really didn't know her neighbor at all.

Martha stepped off her patio and crossed to Edith's yard.

Abruptly the hair rose on Edith's arms. The air howled around her ears. She knew without turning that the visions were back, the poor, tortured girls hovering around her patio as if there was something important they had to tell her but death had robbed them of their voices.

The tea mug trembled violently in her grasp, splashing her hands with scalding hot liquid.

'Edith,' Martha said, coming to a halt at the bottom of the steps.

Edith didn't say anything. She just looked at her neighbor.

This close, she could see the subtle changes. Martha's eyes were now dulled by exhaustion and strain. She moved differently too. She walked stiffly, as if her age had caught up to her suddenly and now weighed on her heavily.

'Martha,' Edith acknowledged at last.

'I apologize for intruding.'

'No need.'

Martha squared her shoulders. 'I have a visitor,' she announced. Her gaze met Edith's. It was a touch defiant.

'A visitor?' The hair still danced up Edith's arms with wild electricity. Her chest was beginning to tighten with a familiar pain.

'My granddaughter.'

'You have a granddaughter?'

'From the boy. The salesman who travels.'

'I see.'

'I had to meet him, unexpectedly. Something came up; he needs me to watch my granddaughter.'

'Uh-huh.'

Martha looked at her again. In this dark moment before dawn, her gaze appeared flat, as if she were dead. 'Will you meet her this morning?'

Edith wasn't certain. Finally she nodded. 'If you'd like.'

'If . . . if something should happen to me, will you take care of her, Edith? I would trust you with her.'

Again there was that stare. That only-half-alive gaze. There was no pleading in Martha's voice, not even fear. It was strangely matter-of-fact, and that scared Edith more.

'Yes,' she agreed softly. 'I suppose. But I'll need the address and phone number of your son.'

Martha shrugged. She said, 'Don't worry. He'll find you.'

23

They met at a small diner, one of those places where people bring their children because the ice cream sundaes are better than the hamburgers, and senior citizens laid claim to corner booths to enjoy the 'two eggs, two strips of bacon, two pieces of toast for $2.22 special.'

Against an unlikely backdrop of a swirling sea of red and blue floral carpet, Marion perched on the edge of a brown vinyl booth and waited impatiently for her brother and Tess to arrive.

One long, slim leg was carefully crossed over the other. Her back was ramrod straight. She hadn't dressed for her surroundings, but had donned a navy blue pants suit trimmed with gold braid around the cuffs and collar. The outfit inspired enough awe to halt a two-year-old, who stared up at her icy, perfect posture as if maybe he should salute. Even her hair was obedient, pulled back harshly into its usual French twist with not a single strand escaping to curl delicately around her cheeks.

She glanced down at the toddler, her blue eyes cold and impenetrable. With a startled squeal he bolted on stubby legs. Marion simply raised her cigarette to her pale pink lips and inhaled.

'Scaring off another admirer, I see,' J.T. drawled, walking across the restaurant to her with Tess in tow. A moment later he leaned against the booth, hip thrust out. A homemade sling decorated his arm.

She exhaled into his face. 'It's a gift.' She looked at him steadily, waiting to see who would draw first blood.

Tess positioned herself between brother and sister. Marion flicked her a cold glance. 'And you're playing ref?'

'Apparently,' Tess said, but didn't sound happy about it. She had just started sliding into the booth, when Marion shook her head.

'Not here. Too public.'

The cool agent collected her cigarettes and led them toward the back, where the banquet rooms were open and unoccupied. She commandeered the smallest one, closing the door behind them and gesturing to the collection of empty tables.

Tess selected one in the middle of the room. J.T. sat next to her, while Marion took the seat across.

'Nice,' Marion commented, nudging her chin toward J.T.'s sling. 'Making a fashion statement?'

'Beckett.'

Marion arched a brow, stubbed out the remains of her cigarette, and consulted her pack for a second. 'Found him already? Then why do you need me?'

'He found us. Last night.' He recapped events briefly, Tess filling in portions. Marion smoked, nodded, and smoked some more.

When they were done, she split her disapproving gaze between the two of them. Law enforcement never looked kindly on civilians taking matters into their own hands, and Marion was no exception.

'Do you know what happens when you hook up a psychopath to electrodes and tell him he's going to receive a shock?' Marion asked.

'Not really.' J.T.'s tone was laconic. Tess could tell that he already had all defenses up.

Sensing the same, Marion turned her attention toward Tess. She said, 'Nothing.'

'Nothing?'

'Nothing. His heartbeat does not accelerate, he will not sweat. There is absolutely no response, no fear of pain. That is the nature of the psychopath – impenetrable, cold, and immune to fear.'

She said the words quietly, but Tess already knew what Marion was driving at.

Marion stubbed out her cigarette. 'I pulled Beckett's files as you requested, J.T. I read them myself on the plane. I'm only going to tell you this once – you're in over your head.'

'Thanks. Now tell me what's in the file.'

Her gaze remained on Tess. 'Jim Beckett is a pure psychopath. You survived him once, now you've survived him twice. Be grateful for that, Tess. And let the police handle it – let the FBI handle it – because you won't be so lucky the next time. Beckett isn't someone who's made a lot of mistakes.'

'I don't plan on asking him to dance,' J.T. said curtly. 'And I'm too old for lectures. Trust me just once, Marion. I know what I'm doing.'

Her tight lips said she doubted that.

J.T. gave up with a disgusted shake of his head. 'Fine, we'll skip the foreplay. Tell me where he is.'

Marion lit a fresh cigarette. 'Oh, dear me.' She drew out the words, matching his mood inch for inch. 'I meant to bring the magical map to his hiding place, but I must have left it on the plane. Whatever will we do?'

'Smart ass.'

'I learned it from you.'

'And I'm so damn proud.' His gaze narrowed, pinning her in place. 'His friends and associates. You said he escaped with the help of some prison groupie.'

'Dead.'

'Dead?'

'So he killed the prison groupie. Then he broke into the safe house?'

'No, then he kidnapped Sergeant Wilcox and tortured and killed the man. Two kids found the body early today in the woods. Beckett had covered everything but his hands with rocks. Of course, wildlife had taken its toll on the man's hands.'

'He likes to mutilate people's hands,' Tess whispered.

Marion looked at her curiously. 'It's true. Quantico isn't sure why. Maybe because hands are so personal. Or maybe simply because it makes the process of identifying the body that much more difficult.'

'Have they found Difford's body?' J.T. quizzed.

'No. But they found his car. Twenty miles from Difford's house, so Beckett probably had another vehicle parked there for the exchange. The trunk of Difford's car was soaked through with blood. We're pretty sure he's dead. We're not so sure why Jim has kept the body.'

'Sam?' Tess asked. She couldn't keep the plea from her voice.

Marion looked away. 'Nothing. I'm . . . I'm sorry.'

'He told me we'd see Difford again.'

'What?' Both Marion and Tess stared at J.T.

'Back in the bedroom he said, "When you see Difford again, you can ask him about it." '

'So you think Difford's still alive?' Marion prodded.

J.T. shook his head. 'Too risky, particularly with Samantha around. But Big Bad Jim doesn't do things randomly. He kept the body for a reason. We just have to get better at anticipating him. After all, he does such a nice job of anticipating us.'

'The pattern,' Tess muttered. She felt frozen and numb. They sat in such an ordinary banquet room in an ordinary restaurant in an ordinary town. And they spoke casually of murder, torture, and the best way to use a corpse. This was why Jim played games. Because more than killing, he enjoyed tormenting. Somewhere right now she was sure he was thinking about what he'd done to her life and enjoying every minute of it. She didn't want to give him that satisfaction.

'Pattern?' J.T. quizzed.

'*Was*,' Marion supplied. '*Jim Beckett was* . . . ? Quincy has some theories. Jim Beckett was number one? Jim Beckett was here? Jim Beckett was the best? Whatever. What's relevant is that Beckett forms his pattern based on where he leaves the bodies. Obviously that's why he took Difford's.'

J.T. frowned. 'In other words, he's running out of time.'

Marion looked at him with a puzzled expression. 'How do you get from A to B?'

'Well, he's been killing at each location, right? Now, however, he's . . .

206

recycling bodies, so to speak. Instead of leaving Difford in Springfield with the others, he took the body to a new city, gaining a new letter. Obviously he wants to finish his statement, but he realizes he doesn't have unlimited time. Maybe since he took Sam he's decided he has to wrap things up and get on with it. I thought he would hole up.'

Tess began rubbing her temples. She still couldn't get the pictures out of her mind. Her four-year-old daughter being driven around in a car with Difford's corpse in the trunk.

'Look, Marion, the man must have a hiding place or accomplice,' J.T. continued. 'Surely you guys are looking into it.'

'Oh, no, J.T., we thought we'd just sit back and see how many cops he kills. Of course we're looking into it! But you know as well as I do that the logical starting place for any investigation is friends and relatives. Beckett has none.'

'How can you be so sure?'

'I read the reports, of course! His family is dead—'

'Did they check for death certificates?'

'They're not stupid, J.T.! Yes, they checked.'

'Death certificates can be forged. How thorough was the check?'

For the first time Marion faltered. 'What do you mean?'

'Did they actually call the doctors or hospitals that signed the certificates? Come on, it's one of the most elementary ways to start a new life. Forge your own death certificate, then assume someone else's birth certificate.'

'I . . . I don't know. I'd have to ask.'

'Ask.'

'Well, yes, sir! Even then, J.T., it's hard to believe a member of his family faked their own death so they could hide a killer. Far more likely is that he found a new friend. The man is good with women.' Marion's glaze flicked to Tess.

Tess bowed her head with shame. Yes, she was the Bride of Frankenstein. She'd fed and clothed a killer. She'd even borne his child. Some nights she watched Samantha sleep so sweetly and she wondered if evil could be inherited. No one knew what caused a psychopath. Were they born? Were they made? Could they pass on that cruelty to their children?

J.T. took her hand. 'If he was to find someone else, Tess,' he asked softly, 'what should we look for?'

Tess shrugged. She felt weary again, but she forced herself to function. This was what it was all about. Not giving up. Not letting him win. 'She'll be blond, pretty, no older than early twenties. She won't be a professional or college educated. She could be a waitress, a stewardess, the woman working at the dry cleaner's. Maybe a police receptionist. He would like that.'

'It's tough search criteria,' Marion murmured. 'Not that some police officer wouldn't love the assignment of cataloguing all the young, beautiful blondes in the area.'

J.T. shook his head, then rubbed the back of his neck with his one good hand. 'In other words, we have no leads. How can a man kill sixteen people, kidnap a child from beneath the police's nose, and leave no trail?'

'It's his specialty. He's studied it. He's careful.'

'Discipline is the key,' Tess whispered. Her eyes squeezed shut. She felt so much horror, because she knew the truth. It didn't matter that he had their daughter. It didn't matter that he'd brutally savaged Difford. Jim still wasn't done. 'He'll strike again. He always finishes what he starts. He'll finish the pattern. He'll come after me.'

She saw Difford, telling her everything would be all right. She saw Sam, asking her why she had to go away, why they couldn't stay together.

She saw herself, standing at the altar, saying I do.

'Tess, are you all right?'

She turned her head slowly. She stared at J.T. She wondered if Beckett would kill him too.

'I . . . I need some fresh air.'

Marion and J.T. exchanged glances.

'Please. I'll be back . . . in a minute.' She pushed herself away from the table.

'Tess—'

She shook her head, ignoring J.T.'s outstretched hand. She made it to the banquet room doors, pushed them open, and plunged herself toward the daylight. The sun streamed through stained glass trim of blue and red.

She saw the reflection on her hands as she leaned against the hallway wall. She thought it looked like blood.

'She doesn't look like she's doing so well.'

'She's tough. She can handle it.' He wanted to sound firm, but he didn't. Offering comfort wasn't his strong suit. And watching Tess suffer tore at him in ways he didn't want to be torn.

He glanced at Marion. She wasn't as calm as she pretended either. Every time she raised her cigarette, he could see her hand tremble. After a moment she held out her pack of cigarettes to him. He accepted, lighting one quickly. They sat there and smoked.

'How are you doing?' he asked at last to cover the silence.

'Just dandy. I'm thinking of suing Roger for all he's worth, and he's worth a lot. Old money. What more can you ask for?'

'Physical harm,' J.T. suggested lightly. 'I'll help you burn down his place if you'd like. I know a thing or two about setting explosives.'

'Really? Hmm, blow him up. Why not? It could be fun.'

'You're a trained professional, Marion. Think of how well you could stalk him. It would be an example for hundreds of women with traitorous husbands.'

The corners of her mouth lifted briefly. J.T. kept his hand on the cigarette so he wouldn't do something so stupid as reach out and take her hand.

'I'm glad you came,' he offered abruptly.

'Why did you ask me to?' Her smile was gone. Now she was cool, but perhaps also a bit nervous.

'Because I needed the information and I knew you could get it.'

'No other reason?'

'No other reason. Why did you come?'

'Because I want to get Beckett.'

'No other reason?'

'No other reason.'

'We're both bad liars, Marion.'

She turned away, but not before he caught the flash of vulnerability in her eyes. The tension in his body increased.

'Next time Beckett will kill you, J.T.' She motioned her head toward his arm. 'Two-handed you couldn't take him on. What are you going to do with one?'

'Fire the gun faster.'

'Don't be stupid. Take Tess and get out of Massachusetts. Special Agent Quincy is one of the best. He'll take care of things.' She paused for a moment. 'I think I may try to volunteer my services. The FBI still balks at putting its female agents on violent crime cases, but my caseload is relatively light right now. I know they need more manpower. Perhaps something could be arranged.'

'You think you can take on Beckett?' He kept his tone indifferent.

'I'm a trained professional.'

'Yeah, Marion, and so am I. But you've been trained to follow rules. Where I've been, there were none. Beckett knows law enforcement. He can anticipate you guys, think like you guys. On the other hand, he's never met the likes of me before.'

'Oh, yes, J.T. You're just tough shit, and you have the arm to prove it.'

'Both Tess and I walked away alive. That's more than anyone else can say lately.'

Marion shook her head furiously. 'You're so damn arrogant. If you ever met God, the first thing you'd say is What are you doing in my chair?'

'And as long as She got up and handed it over, we'd do just fine.'

'Drop it, J.T. Get out. You're good at running, why quit now?'

His face darkened. 'No.'

'Why?'

'Because I have nothing better to do than piss you off, why do you think? Marion, I took the job, dammit. I'm trying to follow it through. Isn't that what you're always telling me to do? Isn't that what you've always wanted?' He leaned forward abruptly. 'And I *want* Beckett. I want him dead.'

'So you'll know you're the biggest, baddest, toughest thing around?'

'No,' he said, angry enough to lash out with the truth. 'So Tess can sleep at night. So she can have her daughter back. So two people can get on with their lives, because we sure as hell aren't doing a great job of getting on with ours.'

'I don't know what you're talking about.'

He hit the table with his fist. 'Yes, you do, Marion. I know you do. I can see it in your eyes. And I know it's the real reason you came, just like it's the real reason I called you.'

Her face fired to life. It filled with a venomous rage that froze the breath in his lungs. He knew that kind of anger. He knew that kind of hate.

'He left everything to you, you son of a bitch!' Marion hissed. 'He left everything to *you.*'

J.T. couldn't think, couldn't respond. He sat there and took it.

'You hated him. You walked away from him, tossed everything in his face, blackened the family name, and became a first-class loser . . . and he left the bulk of the estate to you! Emma gets a trust fund to keep her shopping until she finally cracks up completely. My *child* gets a trust fund. You get the rest. You bastard. You bastard, you bastard, you bastard!'

Her face was no longer icy, it was haggard and unbearably tortured. J.T.'s hand began to shake. It was out in the open now. And it hurt more than he'd thought.

'I don't want the money. I won't accept it. Take it all.'

'He left it to you, goddammit. The least you could do is accept it!'

'No. He was the bastard, Marion, the fucked-up will only proves it. Take everything. You . . . you deserve it.'

'Don't you mean I *earned* it?'

The world stopped spinning. He couldn't quite grasp all the memories, emotions, and reactions that flooded his head. He whispered faintly, 'So you do remember. You really do remember.'

'No!' she declared immediately. Neither of them believed her.

'Marion . . .' He reached out his hand. She immediately shrank back. 'What he did to you was so wrong,' J.T. whispered. 'My God, he raped you—'

She flinched, but he couldn't stop. It had to be said. He didn't know any other way to move on.

'It wasn't your fault, Marion.' The words tumbled out. He said them almost desperately, not sure how long she would allow him to speak, and having so many things that he just *needed* to say. 'You have to understand that it wasn't your fault. It *wasn't*. He was a sick, twisted man who ruined us both for sport. But he's dead now. He's dead and we're alive and we can get through this. We'll stand together, you and me. Don't you remember?'

He tried to take her hand, but she still wouldn't let him.

'Leave me alone,' she whispered. 'I am nothing like you, J.T. I'm not some drunken failure.'

'When we were kids, Marion, I used to wish I was a girl. You want to know why?'

She stared at him dubiously.

He continued. 'So he would've left you alone. I figured if I'd been born the girl, at least he would've left you alone.'

He looked at her openly, no more wisecracks, no more defenses, no more protection. He couldn't be more honest.

And he saw the ice crack. Marion was gone and Merry Berry sat before him, and she looked so unbelievably lost and so unbelievably alone that tears stung his eyes. *Oh, God, what had the colonel done to them? And why now, even after the man's death, couldn't they make it right?*

'I remember the pillow forts,' he whispered with a voice so hoarse it couldn't be his. 'Tell me you remember the pillow forts. Tell me you remember how we used to throw socks at the maid and she'd throw them right back and we would screech and howl and laugh.'

She shook her head. He could see the tears in the corners of her eyes.

'You would come into my room at night, and we would huddle beneath the sheets with a flashlight to read GI Joe comic books. You liked the character Snake. You thought someday he'd come and rescue us.'

'No.'

'And we were always moving and there were new cities and new schools and new kids, but at least we had each other. You used to hold my hand the first day of school and I would tell you everything would be all right.'

'No.'

'And once I told a school principal that the colonel hit us. And I told the man that the colonel went into your room every night—'

'*No!*'

'And he told me I was a liar and gave me detention for spreading rumors. The colonel beat me so hard, I couldn't sit for a week, and you wouldn't even talk to me. I had no idea what he'd told you or why no one ever believed me. Why someone like Snake didn't come at night and save us.'

'Damn you, damn you, damn you.'

'I hated him, Marion. But I never hated you. You were the only good part of my childhood. The only person who gave me hope. The only one I loved.'

'Shut up!' The tears escaped and trickled down her cheeks. He wanted so badly to touch her. He wanted to wipe away her tears and hold her close, because he could feel the tears in his own eyes and the rage that never quite went away because so much had been taken from them and they couldn't get it back. Now there was only emptiness and rage and an unbelievable hurt he'd never known how to mend.

'I don't want to hear any more!' she whispered brokenly. As he stared at her, she drew the cigarette back up to her lips with a hand that shook so badly, it took her three times to actually thrust the cigarette between her teeth.

'Marion,' he said urgently, 'we have to talk about this.'

'I . . . I can't.'

'Merry Berry—'

She leaned over, her blue eyes desperate and pleading. 'Jordan Terrance, if you ever loved me, then you will swear to me now that you will never bring up Daddy again. Swear to me!'

He shook his head.

'Swear to me!' she demanded fiercely.

'And that will make it go away?'

'*Swear!*'

He shook his head again. It didn't deter her. He pleaded with her. It didn't matter. She was adamant, and he felt too much guilt to fight her. She won. 'All right, Marion. All right.'

She released her breath, leaning back with a shaky sigh.

'I'm not like you,' she said at last. 'You did the right thing, J.T. Leaving him. Hating him so purely. I . . . I can't. It's all twisted inside me and . . . I can't make head or tail of any of it. I used to think I was so strong, but maybe I'm not strong at all. Maybe I just can't handle it.'

'You've made it this far. Talk to me. Trust me that much—'

Her head turned slightly. Her eyes were filled with guilt and anger and pain. He began to understand just how much he'd failed her all those years ago.

Oh, God. 'Marion . . .'

She looked away. He heard the sound of Tess's footsteps behind them, and with a blink of an eye Marion's expression shuttered. His sister was gone and only the cold, composed FBI agent remained. They'd grown up in a household filled with masks and where everyone was a quick-change artist. Some habits couldn't be broken.

'You swore,' Marion reminded him under her breath. 'I'll hold you to your word.'

Tess arrived at the table. She stated without preamble, 'I have a plan.'

She planted her hands on the table. 'We'll take it back to where it all started. Williamstown, the old house. We're going to give Jim what he wants more than anything. We're going to give him a second shot at killing me.'

24

'Mr Dillon, this is going to hurt a bit.'

'No kidding.'

The doctor gripped the fingers of J.T.'s injured hand and tugged hard. Tess heard the grind, then crack, as the bone snapped into place. J.T. paled, the pain blinding, but he didn't say anything. His eyes remained expressionless on the far wall as Tess winced for him.

The doctor finished inspecting the freshly aligned bone while Tess and Marion waited in metal chairs. Marion wouldn't look at her brother. She stared at everything else in the tiny room – the mechanical bed, the tray of tools, the X ray of his left arm lit up on the wall, the countertop covered with swabs, tongue depressors, and a blood pressure cuff. When the doctor forcefully aligned her brother's arm, Marion flinched. Otherwise she sat quiet and motionless, as if she weren't even in the room.

Tess recognized the signs. Marion felt her brother's pain and resolutely shut it out. J.T. felt his pain and her pain and resolutely shut them both out. Tess wondered how many times they'd gotten to practice this drill growing up and figured it was more than a few. She had her drills too, the distant place in her mind she hid in so she wouldn't hear the sound of her father's hand smacking against her mother's cheek, or feel her husband's body laboring above hers.

The past crept in on people in the most insidious ways.

The doctor finished drying the special polymer blend that now wrapped from beneath J.T.'s elbow to his palm. J.T.'s fingers stuck out ludicrously from the white prison. The polymer substance was waterproof so he could swim. Other than that, his arm was pretty much out of commission. The doctor finally handed him a sling.

'Give it six to eight weeks to mend, then you'll be good as new.'

'Uh-huh.'

'You don't have to wear the sling, but I'd use it the first couple of days to keep your arm fully immobilized so the fracture can begin to heal.'

'Uh-huh.' J.T. tossed the crumpled sling onto the floor and let it lie.

The doctor frowned. 'No running or undue activity until that cast is off. Fall or jar that arm again, and you'll have a serious break.'

'Uh-huh.'

The doctor looked even more uncomfortable. 'Any questions?'

J.T. stared at the man for the first time. Tess saw the doctor recoil instinctively. She didn't blame him. J.T. looked demonic.

'Treat a gunshot wound in the last few days?'

'Pardon?'

'Treat a gunshot wound? Probably to the shoulder. Man's bald, doesn't even have eyebrows. He would be hard to forget.'

The doctor glanced over to Tess and Marion as if pleading for help. Marion flashed her FBI creds.

'Answer his question.'

'Ah . . . no. Honestly, no. I can ask around though, if you'd like.' The combination of Marion's coolness and J.T.'s fierceness made him suddenly eager to please.

'You're telling the truth?'

'Mr Dillon, I'm a doctor, not a felon.' The doctor sat up a little straighter, reclaiming his dignity.

J.T. shrugged and hopped down. 'If you say so. How much do I owe?'

While the doctor continued blinking his eyes, J.T. unclipped a thick wad of bills from his pocket and began counting out the hundreds.

In the parking lot of the doctor's office Marion said good-bye. She'd agreed to talk to Special Agent Quincy about Tess's idea, though Tess could tell the blonde had her doubts about the wisdom of Tess serving as bait.

Tess wanted her to run it by Quincy. Maybe he'd take it more seriously if he heard it from a fellow FBI agent.

Marion crossed to her car. Her gaze flicked to J.T. twice before she finally opened the door.

'Remember,' J.T. said tersely. 'You can call – anytime.'

Marion hesitated, then nodded.

Tess heard J.T. release the breath he'd been holding. He watched his sister drive away, his eyes hooded.

'You okay?' she asked quietly.

'Just fucking dandy.'

'I thought as much.'

He climbed into the passenger side of their rental car. Tess got into the driver's seat and started the engine. She wondered if he would offer any information, or make her pry it out of him with a crowbar. She suspected the latter.

'You're sure you're all right?'

'I don't want to talk about it.'

'Maybe you should.'

'Lay off, Tess.'

She couldn't though. 'I want to be there for you, J.T. The way you're there for me.'

'When Marion becomes a serial killer, we'll talk.'

'That's not funny.'

'No, I suppose it's not.' His gaze went out the window. 'Just drive, please. I appreciate your offer, but for now, just drive.'

She gave in. Thirty minutes later she pulled into the motel parking lot, turned off the engine, and got out of the car. She'd made it two steps across the parking lot when he finally spoke.

'I'm going for a drive.'

'J.T., that's a lousy idea.'

'Tough. I'm doing it anyway.'

She turned on him. 'And what am I supposed to do? Sit around and knit? Wait for Jim's next attack all alone? Some bodyguard you are!'

'You're right. Get in the car.'

'What?'

'Get in the car. Or get left behind.'

He was already sliding behind the steering wheel. Clearly the matter was no longer open for discussion. She stalked over to the passenger side, sat down hard, and glared at him mutinously.

'You can't drive, you have only one arm!'

'You're probably right.' He started the engine. He looked at her long enough to smile grimly. 'Fasten your seat belt,' he drawled, then slammed the car into gear. He roared the car through intersection after intersection while she gripped the dash with both hands.

'Slow down! For God's sake, slow down!'

'Scared, Tess?' he murmured, turning and staring at her as a sharp curve appeared in the narrow back road. 'Hell, you're planning on taking on Beckett. My driving oughta be boring compared to that.'

'The corner, the corner!' she screamed.

He smiled at her and jerked the wheel, sending her careening against the door. 'No problem.'

Her heart beat rapidly in her chest. She could taste the sweat beading up on her upper lip. She understood what he was doing now, and that he wouldn't slow down. He was angry, and angry J.T. could be juvenile, selfish, and dangerous.

'I'm not going to change my mind, J.T. And I'm really tired of games.'

He didn't reply. His jaw set, his biceps bulged as he corralled the speeding fury of the automobile and bent it to his will. A dirt road appeared to one side, looking bumpy and forgotten. Maybe meant for tractors or heavy pieces of equipment that traveled at five miles per hour.

Tess squeezed her eyes shut.

Pedal to the floor, J.T. attacked the road. The car hit a bump squarely and for three seconds they were airborne. The vehicle hit the dirt hard, shocks groaning, car doors rattling, trunk heaving. Tess felt her teeth grind and her bones crunch. Beside her, she heard J.T.'s breath and knew it had hurt him as well.

She opened her eyes and whirled on him.

'Enough!' she cried. 'Stop this idiocy now! Right now!'

Just like that he slammed on the brakes.

The car came to a heavy halt. Unprepared, Tess landed harshly against the dash, but J.T. didn't apologize. He yanked open his door and rocketed from the vehicle.

Tess scrambled to follow, having no intention of backing down now.

Dust still swirled around their feet, the crisp fall chill immediately bracing their skin. She saw no house, no vehicles. Just flat, barren fields that were beginning to frost over, and the distant promise of mountains.

J.T. stalked around the car, his eyes boring into hers.

'You won't serve as bait,' he declared. 'I forbid it!'

She opened her mouth to argue, but he stormed right up to her, backing her up against the car, trapping her with his body. He smiled, but it wasn't pleasant.

'So eager to die, Tess?'

'No,' she said breathlessly. Her hands were pinned to her sides by his body. She jerked them free and planted them against his chest. If he wanted to fight, she'd fight. She'd learned to give as good as she got.

'You're not going to do it,' he said curtly.

'Yes, I am.'

'There's a flaw in your plan, Tess – a man like that isn't afraid of pain. If he attacks, the only way to stop him will probably be to shoot him. And then what, Tess?'

'He'll be dead.'

'And Sam? What about Sam? With him dead, how are you going to find your daughter?'

'I . . . I—' She didn't know. 'I'll make him tell me where she is,' she said stubbornly. 'I will.'

'Dammit!' he roared. 'I won't let you do this!'

'Like hell!' She heaved with her hands, trying to push him away.

He pushed in closer, his eyes dangerous. 'Attacking an injured man, Tess?'

'Whatever works.' She wiggled her hips, determined to break his hold. It was useless.

'This injured man is trying to save your life!' he snarled, leaning closer, his breath hot against her cheek.

'Save my life? What do you care about my life? You haven't even acknowledged its existence for the last two hours!'

'Feelings hurt? Because I didn't flatter you or gaze longingly into your deep brown eyes?' Abruptly his right hand slid down her sweater and cupped her breast. He knew her body too well. One flick of his thumb and her nipple grew hard. She resented him doing that to her. She arched helplessly into it anyway, wanting him to touch her again.

'I thought of you,' he whispered. 'I thought of your breast in my mouth. Your hands in my hair. I thought of bending you over backward and fucking you. Is that what you want to hear? Is that romantic enough for you, Tess?'

His hips rotated against her suggestively. She bit her lower lip, hating him for making her want him and treating it as if it were nothing.

'Damn you,' she whispered.

For his reply he caught her lower lip and sank his teeth into it. Her hands uncurled on his chest. Her fingers dug into his shoulders, drawing him closer while her mind screamed white-hot fury and called her a fool.

She yanked her head. 'Stop it. I'm not your toy!'

'Could've fooled me.' His thumb began a more insistent pattern around her taut nipple. Her back arched into it.

'It doesn't matter,' she said hoarsely. 'I'm still going to set the trap. I'm still going to do exactly as I planned. If you want to be angry, fine. If you want to torture me until then, fine. But I know it means nothing to you, and it changes nothing!'

He swore. Then he kissed her hard. It was an eating kiss. His tongue plunged in, hot and thick and filling her. She accepted it greedily, her hips pressing against his groin, feeling his growing hardness. He ground into her and she met him halfway.

Then abruptly he pulled back. She cried out her disappointment shamelessly, her hands reaching for him. In a smooth movement he grabbed her shoulders and spun her around. She landed facing the hood with his breath hot against her ear. His hips rotated suggestively against her buttocks.

'Unbutton your jeans,' he whispered. 'Do it for me now.'

She shook her head but her hands were on her zipper. His fingers curled around the thick denim and tugged it down the minute she unzipped the fly.

She felt the cold winter air against her exposed hips. She felt him push up her sweater, her hands planted on the trunk of the car.

He thrust his foot between hers, parting her legs, pulling her hips closer. It was crude and coarse and she arched her back, her eyes already shut as the anticipation swelled in her veins.

'I'm not going to let you bait Beckett,' he growled.

'You can't stop me,' she murmured, and parted her legs farther.

'Goddammit,' he swore, and thrust hard. She cried out as he penetrated. 'I'm going to save you,' he ground out, his hips already moving. 'Dammit, I'm going to save you. I'm going to save you!'

'You can't,' she whispered, but then she couldn't think. The air was cold and crisp, his body hard and hot.

The tempo increased and her ears knew only the sounds of her thundering pulse and his grunting breaths. The feel of him sliding inside her, deeper and deeper. The joining of him with her. The realization that it might mean little to him, but it meant everything to her. It would always mean everything to her.

'Goddamn the colonel!' he whispered abruptly. 'Goddamn Jim Beckett. I won't let them destroy another. I won't let—'

His voice broke into a garbled cry. He thrust hard, pouring into her just as she cried out her release.

Then she whispered his name and knew in her heart it was too late for sanity. She understood his anger, she understood his fear. She understood his need. She'd gotten under his skin and seen all the good he couldn't acknowledge, the fear he tried to hide, and the loneliness he pretended didn't exist.

She loved him.

Much later, when the sun was gone and a fresh moon flirted with the sky, they checked into a new motel room. J.T. was silent, as he'd been all afternoon. After dropping her bag on the floor, Tess handed him her bottle of aspirin. He shook out eight and popped them at once.

Tiredly he began to strip off his clothes. She watched, wordlessly.

'You're making me self-conscious,' he muttered.

'I'm just admiring. Has anyone ever told you that you're beautiful?'

'The stress has fried your brain.'

'I mean it, J.T. You're beautiful to me.'

He turned away and climbed into bed. She removed her clothes and joined him. They'd already spoken to Lieutenant Houlihan. There was no sign of Jim, no sign of Sam. Somewhere out there her daughter slept alone. Was she well cared for? Had she been fed? Did Jim read her stories before tucking her into bed?

Tess couldn't stand the distance anymore. J.T. was the one who played tough. Tess knew she was overwhelmed and frightened and near despair. She curled her naked body spoonlike around his, though she knew he resented the contact.

He stiffened. She held on anyway, pressing her cheek against him.

'She's starting to remember,' he said abruptly.

Tess stilled, then stroked her fingers down his shoulder in silent comfort. 'You'll help her.'

'She made me promise never to mention him again.'

'Give her time. Sooner or later she'll need to talk about it. She'll come to you, and you'll be ready.'

'Rachel used to tell me that I had to let things go. That I held on too tight.'

'Maybe.'

'I failed her, Tess. You should've seen the look in her eyes . . . I didn't even know how much I'd failed her until I saw her memories in her eyes.'

'Shh . . .'

He didn't say anything for a long time. Then abruptly he rolled onto his back. She couldn't see his face in the darkness, but his fingers touched her cheek softly.

'Don't do it.'

'I have to. Everyone has fought the battle but me. Everyone has paid the price but me.'

'So that's when you'll be happy? When he finally kills you?' His voice was tight, his muscles tense to the touch.

She opened her mouth, then closed it again. 'I don't want to talk about it anymore.'

'Well, I do. Go away, Tess. Go hide out in some hotel in Arizona and I'll pretend to be you in the house.'

'You're injured.'

His muscle spasmed and she knew she'd inflicted an immeasurable blow to his masculine pride. 'Don't you trust me, Tess?'

She pressed her cheek against his shoulder. She threaded her fingers through the dark hair on his belly. 'It can't be just you, J.T.,' she whispered, 'trying to save the world. No one is that strong. It will be you and me together in the house. I'll be bait, you be ready to catch the rat.'

'I won't have you die on me.'

'I won't.'

'I'm so tired of them dying on me.' His voice was hoarse.

She held him closer. 'I love you,' she whispered.

Neither of them spoke.

Edith sat in the living room of Martha's house, holding a cup filled with black tea and watching Martha's granddaughter read a book on the couch with Martha sitting beside her.

The living room really wasn't much. The sofa was old and threadbare and had probably been purchased from Goodwill. Like the other few pieces of furniture, it reminded Edith of the clothes Martha selected – old, eclectic, and mismatching. There weren't even pictures on the walls. Edith had never noticed that before. In the whole house there wasn't a single picture or framed photograph.

Edith forced her gaze back to the little girl. Her name was Stephanie, and she seemed to be a somber, quiet child. She wore a thick sweat suit with a baseball cap covering her hair and eyes. Her face nagged at Edith mildly, as if she'd met Stephanie before. Of course, little kids had a tendency to all look alike to her.

She focused on examining her tea as Stephanie continued reading the story of Cinderalla out loud.

Edith was just picturing the pumpkin stagecoach in her mind, when the chills swept up her arms.

She looked up and wished she hadn't.

Girls, so many girls. She'd never seen so many at once before. Here in this living room their features were so clear, she thought she could reach out and touch them. How could Martha not see them? How could Stephanie talk of mice turning magically into footmen while a dozen ethereal shapes swarmed around them, naked and ashamed?

Her chest hurt, the pressure squeezing her ribs like a vise. She opened her mouth. She tried to yell at them to leave her alone; she was just an old woman and she didn't know what they wanted.

Then she realized that they weren't looking at her, not pleading with her with their tortured eyes. Instead, they stared at Martha and Stephanie, and their distress was plain.

Edith bolted upright. She spilled her tea across her lap, not noticing the burn.

'Martha!' she gasped. 'You're in danger! Horrible, horrible danger!'

Stephanie stopped reading and looked at Edith with wide blue eyes. Martha raised her head more slowly.

'Stephanie, please go to your room.'

Stephanie got up quickly, looking relieved to escape. Then Martha turned to Edith.

'How do you know?'

'I see things,' Edith confessed in a rush. She'd never said so out loud before. It eased the pressure in her chest. She said more firmly, 'I see the dead.'

Martha's eyes widened. Edith waited to see shock, disgust, or even a faintly repelled look. Instead, Martha's gaze grew sharp and intensely curious.

'You see the dead?'

'Yes.'

'Do they talk to you?'

'No, they just appear, so tortured, as if there's something they need me to understand.'

Martha leaned forward and clutched Edith's hand. Her grip was surprisingly strong.

'Tell me,' she whispered. 'Tell me everything.'

In the bedroom Samantha took her ear away from the door. She'd been trained how to dial 911 and give her full name, address, and phone number. But she didn't have a phone in this room and she no longer knew her address or phone number. She wasn't sure what she was supposed to do now.

Finally she walked over to the bed she'd been given just a few days ago.

She sat on the edge and stroked her dolly's hair. 'It's all right,' she told her baby. She patted the pretty pink doll again. 'Mommy will come. Mommy will come and everything will be all right.'

25

The police were trying to make up for past mistakes. Now the officers filing in for the briefing had to show their badges at the door. All three task force leaders stood next to the receptionist, personally identifying each man. With this system it took forty-five minutes to assemble the group.

Tess sat at the front of the room, J.T. beside her. Marion sat toward the back and Tess was still trying to decide if the distance was intentional. For the past twenty-four hours Tess and Marion had hammered away on Special Agent Quincy and Lieutenant Houlihan until they agreed to Tess's plan. Last night Tess felt triumphant; finally something would happen. This morning she watched the news, saw her daughter's picture flash across the screen once more, and simply felt terrified.

'All right, people,' Lieutenant Houlihan said, 'listen up.'

Quincy strode into the room, looking harried, and Houlihan scowled. Quincy did a small double take, and instead of walking to his chair in the front of the room, promptly took a seat next to Marion. Houlihan got on with it.

'As you know, we have formulated a new strategy for catching Jim Beckett. In the front of the room here, we have Beckett's ex-wife, Tess Williams, whom many of you know from before. Two and half years ago she agreed to sit in her house and wait for Jim Beckett's return. We agreed to protect her and catch her husband. We didn't fulfill our end of the deal so well. Now she has volunteered to do the same once again, and, people, this time we're going to get it right.

'We have three teams in this room. I've already briefed your supervisors, who will cover the details with you later. This is what you need to know now. Task Force A will continue canvassing for Samantha Williams and Jim Beckett. I know the hotline is still getting hits. Plus, it has been suggested that you follow up on the validity of Beckett's family's death certificates. You're moving from an eight-hour to a twelve-hour shift—'

There were a few tired moans.

Houlihan continued ruthlessly. 'Yes, people, your life sucks. Next, Teams B and C are assigned to Tess Williams with everyone rotating eight-hour shifts. You have three main objectives: Scout and secure Williamstown, watch the safe house, and remain mobilized for a full-fledged assault. Officers will be deployed in pairs. Some of you will walk beats, others of you will keep watch from unmarked cars. We will have ten officers deployed at all times. The FBI will coordinate surveillance and wiretapping. Also aiding you will be the SWAT team. We can't keep them on full alert indefinitely, but they have agreed to give us three snipers to cover the rooftops. As you will read in your reports, that's how Jim Beckett entered the house the first time around. This time we're not going to give him that chance.'

A hand came up in back. It was an older detective who'd worked the task force two and half years before. 'With all due respect, Lieutenant, we can't maintain this forever. Last time we also started out ultra alert and ultra ready. But six months later we were down to two men watching the house and no SWAT support. How's this going to be any different? We got budgets, we got constraints. And Beckett knows it.'

Houlihan nodded. 'Good question. We might as well cover it now. Special Agent Quincy . . .'

Houlihan stepped aside and Quincy walked up to the front of the room. He didn't look at J.T. or Tess. In his dark blue suit he appeared composed and distant. Tess had spoken to him numerous times; now, as before, their lives were intimately intertwined. But he still refused to call her by her first name, and he rarely spoke to her about anything outside of business.

His job had taught him dispassion well. The things that horrified her were commonplace to him. The questions she found intrusive were merely business. His job took him outside the world of civilized people, and she didn't think he could find his way back anymore. She respected him immensely and worried about him frequently.

He began as he always began, without preamble. 'We don't believe we'll have to wait long for Beckett's attack. We believe he is beginning to decompensate.'

'English, please,' Lieutenant Houlihan muttered. 'We're not the ones with the PhD.'

'Jim Beckett's beginning to fall apart,' Quincy said bluntly.

Disagreeing murmurs broke out. The man had killed three officers in twenty-four hours. That didn't fit their definition of someone falling apart.

Quincy held up a silencing hand. 'Hear me out. A psychopath is a complex creature. In many ways, however, we can compare him to a particularly bad child.'

More grumbles. Quincy remained patient.

'You've heard the tapes. You know Jim Beckett considers himself to be a man of unprecedented control. "Discipline is the key," that's what he likes to say. However, he's wrong. He is driven by a compulsion that not even he can explain. On the one hand, he considers himself outside the boundaries of society – that is his neurosis. On the other hand, deep down, like any person, he has a need for limits. As he gets away with murder, he tries even more daring and dangerous stunts. Not just because of ego, but because some part of him *wants to be caught*. Like the child who evolves from petty tantrums to small crime to get a parent's attention, Beckett will commit riskier and riskier murders seeking that barrier.

'That is the psychological component of his decompensating. Research also indicates there is a physiological component, but we don't understand it as well. The act of murder appears to release chemicals in the brain. Murderers talk about a feeling of euphoria similar to a runner's high. Before a murder they are tense, wound, overwrought. Afterward they are relaxed, calm, and settled. Over time, the desire, the *need* for this euphoria begins to drive the killer. We see shorter periods of time between killings, cycle times going from six months to *six days* to, in the current case of Jim Beckett, *six hours*.'

The room grew quiet.

'In most cases the organized serial killer begins to demonstrate more and more of the traits we associate with a drug addict. One, he's no longer so composed or calm. Physical health deteriorates. The chemicals released in the brain and constant adrenaline rush interfere with his ability to function. Like someone mainlining cocaine, he stops sleeping, foregoes food, and neglects personal hygiene. Second, his murders become more rash and desperate, the junkie needing his fix. They also become more brutal; the killer goes from carefully orchestrated murders to a blitz style of attack – hit and run. Third, the use of alcohol and drugs generally increases as the killer seeks substitute highs.

'In short, the killer becomes thoughtless and vulnerable. We have seen the pattern in Kemper, Dahmer, Bundy, and numerous other killers. And we are seeing this pattern in Beckett. Observe.'

Quincy waved his hand and the lights dimmed. He turned on an overhead projector and a time line appeared on the wall. It was marked with red lines, then blue. The blue lines leapt up uncontrollably at the end of the graph.

'Before going to prison Beckett killed ten women over sixteen months. This is indicated by the red lines, starting with the birth of his daughter, and ending eight months before he was caught. The blue lines indicate postprison behavior. He's now killed six people in less than four weeks. First he killed two corrections officers. He was quiet for three weeks. Then suddenly, in four days, four people died.

'Not all these deaths were necessary. Shelly Zane was his accomplice and would've continued to aid him. His penetration of the safe house could've been done with less violence. Originally his pattern was one body per letter. For example, he killed one woman in Clinton, Massachusetts, for the letter C. Now he's killing multiple people at a location. Two corrections officers in Walpole for the letter W. Both Wilcox and Harrison in

Springfield for the letter S. Basically he's gone into a mode of extreme overkill.

'Also, he's no longer sleeping. Observe the last four days and the distances between the crime scenes. First he killed Shelly Zane in the early morning, dumping her body in Avon, Connecticut. Then he drives up to the Springfield area. He kidnaps, tortures, and kills Wilcox eight hours later. Now he must drive to his hiding place, probably outside the Springfield area, as we've turned the immediate vicinity upside down. He has to steal a police uniform, buy his disguise. Then he must assemble everything. Make the phone calls to cover his tracks, etcetera. Then he has to drive back to Springfield as Officer Travis. By six in the evening the next day he surprises and shoots Harrison. Then he has to stay awake in the unmarked police car. One A.M., after thirty-six hours without sleep, he attacks Difford. Then he kidnaps Sam. Now he must run all night. He's carrying around Difford's corpse, and Difford is not a small man. Maybe he does get to sleep a few hours in the early morning while Sam sleeps. But soon she's awake and now he must entertain his daughter. He's gone over forty-eight hours on minimal sleep, and instead of going to bed that night, he returns to the Difford crime scene. He attacks Ms Williams and Mr Dillon, and he sustains a shoulder wound. Once again he must drive back to his hiding place, wounded and having gone fifty-six hours on almost no sleep. Samantha will be awake soon, keeping him up for another day.

'He still has Difford's body, and he still has some sort of plan.'

Quincy looked at Tess. 'I believe it's all aimed at getting you, Ms Williams. His rage is getting high, his blood lust outweighing his control. If he can find you, he'll move. Your idea to serve as bait is most likely the best we can do. Sooner or later there is going to be a confrontation. It's better that it be on our terms than on his.'

The room remained hushed. Tess felt that silence echoed inside her. She nodded slowly.

Abruptly a phone rang. People looked around, shaken and confused. After a moment it became apparent that the ringing was from the back of the room.

'My cell phone,' Quincy murmured. His briefcase was sitting back there. He nodded toward Marion, who picked up his phone and answered it.

She frowned, then covered the receiver with her hand.

'It's a Lawrence Talbert requesting "Coroner Quincy."'

Quincy froze. He didn't say anything, and then Tess understood. It was him. It was Jim. Holy Mother of God, it was Jim.

Suddenly Quincy was gesturing wildly and officers scattered from their seats. Trace the call, trace the call, she watched their mouths cry silently.

Marion walked slowly to the front of the room and handed the phone to Quincy. Her face was calm, controlled. Tess's fingers dug into J.T.'s thigh.

'Hello? Who is calling, please? Dammit, I know it's you.'

Quincy's gaze went to the ventilation grate high up in the wall. 'No, wait, I don't understand, tell me more. I don't have tools—' His voice was growing frantic, urgent. His knuckles had gone white on the phone. 'Give me a minute. I just need to get a screwdriver. I'm an agent, not a handyman. Wait, I didn't hear you. Can you repeat that? There seems to be interference on the phone—

'Goddammit!' Quincy cried. Beckett had hung up, and in a rare display of rage Quincy hurled the phone across the room. It hit the far wall hard and shattered.

'Son of a bitch, son of a bitch,' Quincy was murmuring. His head was down between his knees. He was breathing hard, as if he'd run a long race. Sweat beaded his face.

He straightened slowly and looked at the faces staring back at him. Then he turned toward the ventilation grate.

'Would somebody get me a screwdriver, please.'

Nobody moved. They just stared up at the grate in the high wall. Tess felt the hysteria bubble up in her throat. No place was safe. No place could remain untouched. Jim went anywhere. He contaminated everything, like a pestilence. She felt the contamination in herself, way down deep. She understood that like Quincy, she'd traveled too far outside the bounds of the civilized world and she'd never find her way back.

'Look at me.' J.T. was before her. He'd stood, and now his hands gripped her shoulders. She managed to bring her gaze up and meet his hard, dark stare. 'Come on. I want you out of the room.'

Someone had handed Quincy a Swiss Army knife with a screwdriver. He stood on a chair before the grate.

'No,' Tess told J.T.

'Dammit, don't subject yourself to this. It's what he wants.'

'I can't leave.'

'Tess, dammit—'

'What if it's . . . Sam?' Her voice was so hoarse, she barely recognized it. She hadn't realized her true fear until she spoke the words out loud. Now the rushing filled her ears and she thought she might faint.

The grate came off. She remained sitting there, transfixed.

'Focus on me, Tess. Focus on me.'

The smell hit her first. She gagged. Spots appeared before her eyes. There were tears on her cheeks.

Dimly she heard Quincy say, 'Well . . . we've found Lieutenant Difford's head.'

One of the officers led them to the main room. J.T. went off to fetch them both cups of coffee. Tess remained standing in the middle of the room, letting the reassuring noise of talking people and jangling phones sink into her.

The room had high ceilings and not many windows. Once there must have been cubicles, but they'd all been taken down and replaced with long tables. Operators sat elbow to elbow at computer terminals, logging calls on the hotline and jotting down notes. The phones never stopped ringing.

Someone had posted black-and-white copies of Samantha's picture along the wall. Her smiling, innocent face ringed the room and reminded them why they were there, why they were keeping the hours they were keeping.

Tess wanted to touch the photographs, stroke her fingers down the pale cheek, as if that would bring her daughter back to her.

It was odd to stand in the middle of such activity and yet have nothing to do with it. Once Tess had thought all this was focused on her. Now she knew better. If she ceased existing tomorrow, Jim would still kill and the law enforcement bureaucracy would still churn, trying to catch him.

J.T. returned and shoved a lukewarm cup of coffee into her hands. Quincy was on his heels with Marion.

'Why don't we go into one of the interview rooms,' Quincy suggested. 'Lieutenant Houlihan will join us shortly.'

He ushered them back to a small room with a two-way mirror. It held a single card table and two metal folding chairs. With a murmured apology he went off to find three more chairs.

'How are you holding up?' J.T. asked.

She took a sip of coffee before replying. 'As well as can be expected.'

'He does it just to rattle your cage.'

'Then he's good at rattling cages.'

He stood close. She knew he was waiting to see what she wanted. Did she need to wrap her arms around him? Maybe press her cheek against his shoulder. She thought about it, but she didn't think there was any comfort that he could offer that would blot the picture of Difford's severed head from her mind.

It'll be all right, kid. I'll take care of Sam. Houlihan and Quincy will catch Beckett. It'll be all right, kid.

Quincy returned with the chairs and they all took seats. Moments later Lieutenant Houlihan joined them. His face was still gray and his forehead lined with frustration, anger, and pain.

'No blood,' he said without preamble. 'The head was cut off immediately after death, frozen to slow decomposition, then left in the ventilation shaft. You can access the shaft via the roof. Son of a bitch must've crawled in the morning we were all still at the crime scene and left his little present.' Belatedly he glanced at Tess and Marion. 'Sorry,' he muttered.

'It's okay,' Tess said as she gripped her cup more tightly. 'I'm getting used to these conversations.'

'How did he get Special Agent Quincy's cell phone number?' Marion was eager to establish that she was part of the law enforcement group and not some weak-kneed female observer. 'Surely your number is unlisted, sir.'

'Difford had it,' Quincy said. 'Wilcox too. Beckett either found it on their persons or asked them for it.'

That made everyone in the room visualize just how he would 'request' information, and they all shifted uncomfortably in their chairs. Tess found herself looking at J.T. again. His gaze was locked on the far wall, but she could see that his jaw was tight. He wouldn't worry about himself, it wasn't his nature. But she imagined he could vividly picture Jim Beckett attacking either her or Marion. She had made that horror part of his world. It seemed so blatantly unfair.

'Why just the head?' she asked after a moment.

'I don't know,' Quincy replied.

'Scare tactics,' J.T. stated. 'Demoralize the troops.'

Quincy frowned but didn't argue. It was obvious the straitlaced agent didn't approve of a mercenary.

'He still has Difford's body,' Marion pointed out.

'Perhaps,' Quincy shrugged. 'No one's checked the trunks of their cars.'

They all fell silent, and the air was heavy and strained.

'Do you think you should also be under watch?' Tess spoke up softly. 'You keep saying I'm the target, but he's focused on most of the people who helped catch him before. That was me, Difford, and you, Quincy.'

'It bears consideration.'

'What if he uses the safe house as a ruse? The police are watching me in it, so he seizes the opportunity to get you. That would be something he'd do.'

'Absolutely.' Quincy thrummed the table with his fingers. 'I'll be in the surveillance van with Lieutenant Houlihan for most of the watch. They can guard my back.'

'Snipers?' J.T. quizzed. 'Three's nothing for a town.'

'Williamstown is small,' Lieutenant Houlihan interjected. 'You can walk from one end of it to the other in just twenty minutes. Basically it's a collection of old buildings that make up Williams College, with some historic storefronts for the tourists. Tess's house is on Elm Street, ten minutes from Main Street. The whole block is old, restored row houses. We'll position the snipers on the corners, providing aerial coverage of the street.'

'One corner will be uncovered.'

'True, but visibility is pretty good. We'll put one guy mid-block on the right with the other two on the left-hand corners, forming a triangle around Tess's house. It should keep the roof clean.'

'And the officers on duty?' J.T. persisted skeptically. It was obvious he didn't think much of the police or their efforts.

'We'll have a main surveillance van, two unmarked cars, and three pairs of cops walking the city. It's a college campus with a lot of young coeds. We'll warn everyone of the danger and maintain a strong police presence throughout the campus. Williams College security and the local police will also provide regular patrols.'

'Uh-huh. Won't a surveillance van parked outside the house be a bit obvious?'

'It won't be on Elm. Arnold, Hall, Maple, and Linden all intersect. We'll pick one of the streets as a starting point and move around between them.'

'Why are you so sure he'll come?' Marion pressed no one in particular. 'It's the way you caught him the first time, so he knows it's risky. Two, it doesn't fit his pattern. JIM BECKETT WAS HERE or JIM WAS NUMBER ONE makes sense. JIM BECKETT WAS W? I don't see how it can fit.'

'He'll come,' Tess said.

'Because he's deteriorating?'

'Because he always finishes what he starts,' Tess murmured. 'Always.'

Marion sat back. 'I guess I just don't understand that kind of anger.'

'You can't,' Quincy spoke up. 'You're a woman.'

When Marion tried to protest, Quincy waved her down tiredly. 'I'm talking statistics, not chauvinism. Most serial killers are male. Maybe part of it's hormones, but certainly it's also behavioral. When men get angry, they are taught to lash out at others. When women get angry, they are taught to turn in on themselves. Quite simply, your mothers torment you and you become alcoholics or anorexics or suicide risks. You don't become killers.'

His gaze slid to Tess. He spoke matter-of-factly.

'Beckett will come, Ms Williams. And when he does, it will be bloody.'

Marion waited for her brother and Tess to return to their motel before she made her move. It was after six, but the war room showed no sign of slowing down. Phones were ringing, operators answering. Lieutenant Houlihan was yelling at some young officer while simultaneously crunching Tums. The mood in the building was stark.

She kept walking, looking for a vacant interview room or forgotten corner. Instead, she ran into Officer Louis, a straw-haired kid who looked too much like Richie Cunningham for his own good. He spotted her coming, froze, and gulped noticeably.

She'd run into him earlier that day. Perhaps someday he'd be a good police officer, but personally she thought he had the spine of a jellyfish. In turn, he seemed to view her as the human equivalent of a black widow spider, waiting to seduce him into answering her questions, at which time she would calmly bite off his head to complete the mating.

'I'm looking for Special Agent Quincy.'

Officer Louis couldn't get the words out. He backed against the wall and pointed down the hallway. Shaking her head, Marion walked past him. His sigh of relief was audible.

She found Quincy sequestered in his own little space, surrounded by crime scene photos. He didn't look up right away. She used the opportunity to glance at the color photographs. They didn't appear to be from Jim Beckett's files. Most of these victims were middle-aged women. They'd been carved up brutally by a serrated knife.

Quincy sifted through them one by one, as though he were shuffling a deck of cards. At long last he sighed, shook his head, and finally set them down, clearly not having found what he was seeking.

'Another case, sir?' she asked respectfully. She'd automatically assumed a cadet's stance, legs apart, shoulders square, hands behind her back.

'Santa Cruz,' he muttered, his gaze still on the photos. 'Can you believe that at one time Santa Cruz was the serial killer capital of the world with three active murderers? Now we have another there. It makes you wonder what's in the water.'

He pushed back from the rickety table. Marion could see the exhaustion deeply stamped into his face. His hand was rubbing the back of his neck.

'And her?' Marion asked, suddenly feeling too unnerved to state her real purpose for finding him. She gestured to the framed portrait of a smiling brunette.

'Oh, her? My wife. I mean ex-wife.' He smiled ruefully. 'Divorce came through a few weeks ago. I guess I'm still adjusting. I've always traveled with her picture, you know. Set it up in every cheap motel and overheated police station in the country. Now I find I can't work without it. Silly, isn't it?'

Marion shifted, even more discomfited by this personal insight. 'Not really, sir. My . . . uh, my husband and I recently split as well. After ten years. It's a big adjustment.'

'Hard to be married and be an agent.'

'That's what everyone says.'

He smiled. 'It is a platitude, isn't it?'

'I don't know, sir.'

They drifted into silence, but it was too unsettling for both of them. 'What can I help you with, Agent?' Quincy asked briskly.

'I . . . I want to speak with you about my role in this case.'

'Your role? You're not even officially on this case, Agent. So far your involvement is due to circumstance, not assignment.'

'I understand. I would like to change that if it's possible. I've been interested in this kind of work for a long time.'

'I pulled your file.'

Marion waited patiently.

'You have a good record. Seems that you can be rigid at times, but you keep a cool head and have above-average analytics.'

'Thank you, sir.'

'But from what I could tell, your experience is in white-collar crimes, mostly bank frauds—'

'There have been some homicides,' she interjected. 'Deals gone bad, informants who were found out, that kind of thing.'

'But always in conjunction with a fraud case.'

'Dead is dead, sir. They were connected with our work, crime scene came under our jurisdiction, and we got to figure out who killed them.'

'The Investigative Support Unit is different, Agent. It's all we do. A typical cop may see a gruesome murder two or three times a year. They might see a serial killer once in their *career*.' Quincy gestured to the pictures spread out on the table. 'This is all I see. One hundred and fifty cases of killing, rape, child molestation, and kidnapping. I deal only with the extremes, day in, day out. On the road, in the office, this is it.'

'I understand.'

'I would be lying if I said it didn't get to you.'

Her chin came up. 'I think I can handle it, sir.'

'I don't think you know what "it" is.'

'Is it because I'm a woman?'

'Don't insult me, Agent.' His voice held clear warning. She persisted anyway.

'You talk statistics, sir. Well, the Bureau statistics show that female agents are disproportionately assigned to white-collar cases and not homicides.'

'That's the Bureau. We have female profilers in the Investigative Support Unit – and they're damn good. And you're not them, Agent. They paid their dues. They served as cops, forensics pathologists, or criminologists. They all joined with extensive homicide experience. If you're serious about the ISU, talk to your director about getting on some different cases. Prove yourself in the kiddie pool before you jump into the ocean.'

'I have this opportunity now.' Her voice was steady but her eyes burned. She was being put in her place and she hated it. Sometimes it seemed her whole life had been spent being put in her place by men who should've known better. Who should've trusted her more.

'I have some ideas,' she persisted.

'Agent—'

'Just hear me out. I looked at Jim Beckett's file. I've spoken to Tess Williams at length. I think it's clear, I think it's obvious, Jim Beckett must have an accomplice. You said he can't go long without female companionship. Tess also stated that he charms and seduces women as a hobby. I think there is someone helping him with everything, someone who helped him two and a half years ago, when he disappeared for the first time. And I think I may know how to find that person.'

Quincy appeared skeptical but he didn't interrupt.

She kept talking before she lost her courage. 'Let's assume for a moment that the woman isn't a random stranger but someone he's known for a while. That means he would need to maintain the relationship even while in prison.'

'Shelly Zane was his only visitor ever logged.'

'Yes, but what about *called?* I checked with Walpole. Beckett was a model prisoner. He didn't have any disciplinary tickets written up, and as a "ticket free" maximum security inmate, he was entitled to four phone calls a month, up to thirty minutes apiece.'

'I know, Agent. And as you must have found out from Walpole, those calls are monitored. Prisoners must file all numbers with security to be approved. They don't even get to dial. The guard brings the phone down to the cell, plugs it in, places the phone call, and then passes the phone through the window for the inmate to pick up. A four-digit security code has to be entered for any number to go through, so the prisoner can't try to covertly hang up and dial a different number. Any sign of two-way calling, and the phone automatically disconnects. The system is pretty rigid, and we checked Beckett's numbers. He called Shelly Zane about twice a month and his lawyer for the other calls.'

'I know, sir,' Marion forced herself to say patiently. 'I did look into the matter. I know two-way calling shuts off the phone, but what about call forwarding?'

'Who would forward a call for a prisoner?'

'Shelly Zane.'

Quincy was silent for a moment. Then he blinked his eyes. 'I don't know if Zane has call forwarding.'

'She does. I checked. She used it a lot. In the last two years calls were forwarded to two hundred and forty-seven different numbers. I compiled a list.'

Slowly Quincy nodded. 'We should look into that. We can ask Houlihan to have Task Force A start in on it immediately. They could use a few good leads.'

'Thank you, sir.'

'You can sit in the surveillance van with Houlihan and me,' he said abruptly. 'If there's action, you'll see it.'

'What about assisting Team A?'

'That would be stepping on the team leader's toes, Agent. First thing you learn in crossjurisdictional investigations – don't step on local law enforcement's toes.'

Marion knew a lecture when she heard one. 'I would like to sit in the van. Thank you, sir.'

'Then it's settled. You may not agree, but even being invited to take part in surveillance on this kind of case is a huge responsibility. Don't blow it.'

His tone was curt and dismissive. His attention was already returning to his gruesome stack of photos, and it was clear he didn't want to speak to her anymore.

She nodded her head once and left. Her throat was thick with frustration. She had wanted more. More praise for her ideas, more inclusion into the male-dominated world of violent crime. More recognition that she was smart, savvy, and capable. Instead, she'd been dressed down as thoroughly as any rookie, then tossed a bone to keep her from whining too much.

She thought Quincy was wrong. She had her own opinions, her own ideas. And she was suddenly sick of spending her life playing by other people's rules.

Opportunities were not given. They were made.

She knew how she would make hers.

The phone rang in the motel room. Tess snatched up the receiver.

'Yes?' Her voice was hopeful. Lieutenant Houlihan had told her he would call if they learned anything about Sam. Tess had been staring at the phone for the last two hours as the sun had sunk, the room had darkened, and she and J.T. had become too weary to even snap on a light.

'Oh, hi, Marion.' Her shoulders slumped. 'No, we're fine here. It's just a motel, you know how motels are. It does have a pool, so J.T. got to swim. I don't think it helped much. He's about to wear a hole in the carpet. Do you want to speak to him?'

J.T. halted mid-stride. The look on his face was wary and torn.

Tess held out the phone to him. Marion's answer had equaled his expression. At least they were both trying.

'Hello?' J.T. said carefully. 'No, it's fine. Tess is playing solitaire, I'm going insane. The usual.' He nodded his head and just listened for a bit. 'He wasn't the right one for you,' he said finally. He sounded awkward. 'You'll . . . you'll find someone else. Someone better. It's tough. I know. But there are other fish in the sea, you know?' His gaze rested on Tess.

After another few minutes he said good-bye and hung up. He resumed pacing immediately.

'Is she okay?' Tess asked quietly.

'The divorce papers arrived today. Her housekeeper called her with the news.'

'Oh,' Tess said with feeling. 'That must be very difficult. Especially now, with everything else going on.'

J.T. nodded, but she couldn't read his expression.

'It was good that she called, J.T. She's reaching out to you.'

'Yeah.' He was silent for a moment. 'I'm not good at this.'

'You're doing fine.'

'I don't know what I'm supposed to say.'

'No one does. Have you ever tried explaining to a four-year-old that her father's an ax murderer? In the end, we all make it up as we go along.'

'Huh.' He still didn't sound happy. She got up off the bed and went to him.

The moonlight slashed across his face, shrouding his eyes in shadows. She touched his shoulders, then his cheek. She moved until her body was brushing his. His face was hard, his chin and jaw sculpted with resolute lines. He looked strong, and suddenly she needed that strength.

She wrapped her arms around his waist. 'Hold me.'

'I'm not . . . I'm not . . .' His arms went around her. He held her, but a part of him remained out of reach.

She drew back and took his hand. 'Let's go to bed.'

He simply stood there.

'J.T., this is our last night together. Tomorrow we're in Williamstown. I know you want me to do it differently, I know you're worried the worst will happen. I made my decision. I accept that risk. And I know I have this night and I would like to spend it with you. Can you give me that much?'

He couldn't find an answer.

Her face was pale and ethereal, her eyes huge, luminescent, and knowing. He thought if he remained silent and distant long enough, she'd give up and storm away. He'd forgotten just how well she'd learned to fight. She wrapped her arms around his neck. She pressed her slender body against his.

He wanted to be cold. He wanted to be unfeeling.

Her lips feathered over his gently, and he succumbed. He slanted his mouth and devoured her.

She haunted him and he didn't want to be haunted. She consumed him and he didn't want to be consumed. The emotions rolled over one another, churning his blood. He kept hearing Marion's voice, the thin thread of vulnerability beneath her dispassionate words, the unspoken need he didn't know how to address. He kept seeing Tess, her eyes dilated with horror as the ventilation grate came off and revealed once more what Jim Beckett could do.

Marion and Tess. The women he loved, the women he was so sure he would fail. The women he wanted to hold close and the women he wanted to push away because he couldn't stand his own weakness. He couldn't stand the fact that Tess was right and he couldn't save the world all by himself or make it a better place.

Tess pulled herself closer to him, fragile and strong, needy and giving. He kissed her senselessly, trying desperately to overpower his desire, to crush true emotion beneath the leaden weight of pure lust.

He dragged her down onto the bed. He tasted the sweetness of her skin and inhaled the soft, secret scent of her body. He felt her rose-petal skin and unending warmth.

She thought he and Marion were the tough ones – she didn't understand. The fire that had forged them had made them too brittle. Tess was the one who'd emerged as true steel.

He gave in to the pull of her fierce embrace and the whispered urgings of her lips.

Suddenly their lovemaking became urgent and fierce, a war fought amid tangled sheets. She rolled him onto his back and straddled him shamelessly.

'I love you, J.T.,' she whispered. 'I love you.'

Finally she moved. Tears glittered on her cheeks. She cried and she rode him and she let him see her cry as she did so. He couldn't look away.

'Don't do this,' he muttered. 'God, don't do this to me.'

She kept moving. Suddenly his right hand was at her hip, his fingers digging into her flesh, his strong arm setting a furious pace. His heels dug into the mattress, giving him leverage as his hips thrust up hard. She had wanted to consume him, but now he consumed her because she was killing him with her silent tears and he didn't know what to do.

Her head fell back, her climax long and racking and ripping his name from her lips. He didn't relent, moving, moving, moving, and spiking her back up. He thrust harder, sweat building, teeth bared.

The climax eluded him. Fine tension corded his neck and rippled his body with unbearable pain. He wanted, he needed.

He didn't know anymore. The emptiness was endless and he was dying and she was the only person who could save him and he didn't even know how to say the words.

He rolled her over harshly, his body still joined with hers, and fucked her hard. She gasped. He couldn't stop. The release was so close, but he couldn't find it. He couldn't embrace it, he couldn't welcome it, because he knew when it came it would be like a spring rain and smell of the roses that reminded him of her.

'I love you,' she whispered against his sweat-soaked torso. 'I love you.'

And he climaxed with a primal yell, his semen ripped from him and pouring into her.

He collapsed over her, shaking and trembling and fallen apart. She held him close, then stroked his hair.

'I know,' she whispered. 'I know.'

Later, the sheets tangled around their legs, the sweat drying on their bodies, he said, 'I loved Rachel.'

'I understand.'

'She died.'

'I know.'

'I never told her that I loved her.'

'I'm sure she knew.'

'But no one ever told her. Not her parents, not the colonel. Not me.'

'But you showed it to her, J.T. That matters more.'

His head turned toward her. His fingertips brushed her arm. 'Sometimes I hate you.'

'I know,' she told him honestly. 'That's how I know that you care.'

In the morning the thin rays of a weak sun rapped at the window, illuminating the room in shades of misty gray. Tess crawled out of bed first, entered the bathroom, and closed the door without looking back.

He waited until he heard the scouring sound of the shower. Then he reached over to the nightstand and found his pack of smokes. His hand was trembling, making it difficult to get one out. Finally he dragged a cigarette to his lips, lit it with a plastic lighter, and inhaled deeply. He leaned back onto the bed, staring at the ceiling and watching the rolling smoke slowly dissipate as it rose through the early morning air.

Alone, he had no more pretensions. He hadn't been the kind of brother he should've been. He hadn't been the kind of husband he should've been. His life had started with pain and he'd been adding layers ever since.

Tonight a new layer would be spread. He wanted to get this one right. He was afraid the beast in his belly would keep that from ever happening. He had too much anger in him. He wasn't good at leaving it behind. He understood all that and wondered if understanding it really made a difference.

His lips formed the words soundlessly three times before he trusted himself enough to add voice. Finally he whispered, 'I love you too, Tess.'

And a second later: 'Jim Beckett is a dead man.'

26

'Well, here it is,' Marion announced. She gestured to the house Tess had lived in for four years, her entire married life. The house had been sold two years earlier, but the police had commandeered it. The owners had been forced out with their furniture and the house hastily filled with garage-sale rejects.

Tess found the decor as dismal as her mood.

In the living room to her left, a sloping blue love seat had been stuck in the middle of the brown carpet. Dark brown shelves had been hastily erected and stuffed full of used paperbacks. An old TV sat on a coffee table with a more modern-looking VCR. The metal desk lamp perched on the fireplace mantel provided the only light. Stairs were straight ahead. The small brown kitchen to her right. Upstairs was the master bedroom and two extra rooms. She hated to think what kind of furniture was in them.

'The kitchen is fully stocked,' Marion said. 'You also have a TV, bookshelves, and so forth. It'll be just like before—'

'Solitary confinement,' Tess stated.

Marion glanced at J.T. 'Not quite solitary.'

J.T. didn't look at either of them. He prowled the living room perimeter, peering through the front bay of windows.

'We've been talking on and off over the police scanners,' Marion continued. 'Not too many conversations, but enough to give the general idea that a "special package" is arriving in Williamstown and should be "handled with care." Quincy is confident that Beckett monitors the police scanners. Sooner or later he'll hear the chatter and make his plans.'

'Which roofs have the snipers?'

Marion pointed them out for J.T. 'One across the street with a clean line of fire on the front door. Other two on the corners of this side of the block.'

'Lots of chimneys and fancy archways. What are the chances of a clean shot?'

Marion shrugged. 'Depends on where Beckett stands. Either way, they'll see him coming and the rest of us will mobilize.'

'Huh. Windows wired?'

'All wired. Bug in every room.'

'The bathroom?' Tess asked. Now she was beginning to remember all the details her mind had conveniently blanked from the last time. She'd hated last time.

'*Every* room. This is your life, right?'

'Lucky me.'

'You need anything, just speak up loudly. We'll be monitoring you from the van at all times.'

'I guess this means no sex,' Tess said. She was struggling for control.

'Only if you want an audience,' Marion said expressionlessly. 'Any questions?'

'Did you pull sewage maps of the area? What about manholes, any underground systems?'

'J.T., we know what we're doing.'

'I don't want to see any utility trucks in the area. No cable company, no phone men, no electric company. Call and tell them to keep out or I'll personally give their driver the message. It's too easy for Big Bad Jim to use something like that.'

'We won't even permit door-to-door encyclopedia salesmen,' Marion assured him.

'Huh.' J.T. turned to Tess. 'Fine with you?'

'Just dandy.' She forced a smile to take the sting from the words. It didn't work. She still felt like a rat in a trap.

She glanced at Marion. 'Any news about Sam?' she whispered, though she knew there wasn't.

'Not at this time.'

'Difford's body?'

'Nothing.'

J.T. shook his head. Marion scowled. 'The task force is working very hard, goddammit. We'll let you know as soon as we get a break. Now, if you'll excuse me, I have some loose ends to attend to. I'll return by sundown.'

Marion headed for the door. J.T. followed, catching up with her in the doorway.

'How are you?' he asked before he lost his courage.

She didn't answer right away. 'Fine.' She glanced toward Tess, then looked at him. 'Congratulations.'

'For what?'

'She's a strong woman, J.T. I'm happy for you.'

He scowled, then gave it up. 'Yeah. She is. Thanks.' He looked away for a moment. The sky had become unbearably bright and clear. 'She deserves better,' he said.

'You're not so bad.'

'Not so bad?'

'Not so bad.'

'Marion . . .' His throat constricted. He couldn't say the words. It wasn't the way things worked between them. He settled for brushing her arm lightly. 'Keep me posted about the stuff with Roger, okay? I'm not the best at saying the right things, but I know you loved him, Marion. I'd like to help. You know, if I can.'

Marion looked at the floor. 'J.T., you know those mean things I said about Rachel?'

He nodded. He remembered each and every one of them.

'I sent her to you,' she confessed in a rush. 'She came to me looking for help. And I – I just couldn't help her. I looked at her, and I wanted her to just go away. I couldn't even bear to look at her. Just this poor slip of girl, and I couldn't even look at her. Stupid, wasn't it?'

She shrugged. He began to hear the things left unsaid.

'I gave her your name. I told her you would help. I knew . . . I knew you would have the guts to do what I couldn't.'

'You did the right thing, Marion. Thank you.'

'Good,' she said quietly. She sounded better. 'I wanted you to know.'

'I'll be there for you, Marion. When you're ready.'

She smiled again, faint and tremulous. Briefly she touched his face.

'I know.'

She left.

He turned back to Tess.

She still stood in the middle of the living room, looking ragged from her sleepless night. Her thumbnail had gone to work on her other fingers. She didn't seem to notice.

He walked toward her and brushed her mangled fingernails. She flinched, looking chagrined.

'Got your gun?'

'Yes,' she said, clearly startled.

'Want to practice now? We can do some shadow targeting without bullets.'

Her relief was palpable. 'All right.'

He nodded, already reaching for the 9 mm holstered against the small of his back. He had a .22 around his left ankle and a hunting knife strapped against the inside of his left forearm cast.

He was ready.

Tess retrieved her gun from her purse.

'We're ready, Tess. We'll get him.'

Tess just smiled. 'That's what Difford used to say.'

'Yes, I understand the doctor is dead. We just need some way of verifying this death certificate. Yes, ma'am, twenty years is a long time ago. Do you have copies in the hospital files? Or maybe a nurse or someone else in attendance at the time still works at the hospital. Yeah, I'll hold.' Detective Epstein rolled his eyes. He hated this kind of grunt work.

Jim Beckett's foster parents had been dead less than ten years, so verifying their death certificates hadn't been tough. They'd gotten lucky with his birth father – a police officer who'd arrived at the traffic accident twenty years ago was still on the force. He confirmed James Beckett had been DOA, a victim of a four-car pileup.

Verifying the death certificate for Mary Beckett was more difficult. The doctor who'd signed the original certificate was dead and the hospital bureaucrats had bigger matters than hunting down records on someone who'd died twenty years earlier.

The person came back on the line. Detective Epstein stopped twirling his pencil.

'Archives? What do you mean by archives? In a *separate* storage facility. Well, sure I understand the volume of records you must have. Is there a system? Can you send some exhausted intern to search? Well, ma'am, I'd send an officer, but you're not really going to let us paw through your records unattended, are you? That's what I thought. So what time is good for you? Yeah, an hour it is.'

He hung up the phone and rubbed his eyes. Technically his shift had ended two hours ago. It was about to extend for several hours more.

Night was falling soon. The first night with Tess Williams in her old house, and Team A was feeling the pressure. If they could find Jim or Samantha Beckett ahead of time, they'd save everyone a lot of trouble. There were twelve of them working now. Epstein had taken over confirming the last death certificate. Four officers were hunting down the numbers Shelly Zane had forwarded calls to over the last two years. Eight officers still reviewed the hotline logs, following up leads, chasing down ghosts. Shit, this case was killing them all.

Epstein had known Difford. He'd respected the lieutenant very much. Once they'd gone to a Red Sox game together. Difford had been one of the few locals who'd remained loyal to the Red Sox even in the rotten years – the long, long periods of them.

Epstein picked up his jacket. 'Andrews, you available?'

'Only if I have to be.'

'You have to be. Grab your coat. We have an appointment.'

'Where to?'

'A storage facility. We have a haystack to search for a needle.'

'Jesus, Epstein. You sure know how to show a guy a good time.'

Marion sat in the middle of the floor in the office she'd borrowed. She was surrounded by a sea of maps, all wearing different shades of pastels. She had New England maps, Massachusetts maps, Berkshire County maps, and Williamstown maps. They frolicked around her, holding the secret to long life.

She'd been staring at them all day, and now her vision was blurred. She was also having difficulty concentrating.

For no good reason she remembered being seven years old and ducking with J.T. behind a sofa cushion as Melhelia, their maid, launched another sock grenade over the defensive perimeter of decorative pillows.

J.T. was laughing. Merry Berry was giggling. It defied the imagination.

She shook her head. She blinked her eyes three times, then popped them open and focused on the maps. She didn't want to think of herself or long-ago days. She didn't want to think of the shadow that hovered behind the laughing Merry Berry, the dark shadow that tinged the edges of all her memories, even the good ones.

She wanted to think of Beckett. She wanted to crawl behind his eyes.

'We have more in common than you can imagine,' she muttered. 'Ice. It's all about ice.'

No empathy, no compassion. Just the cool practicality and efficient ruthlessness of immoral genius. No restraints, no boundaries. If you could think of it, you could do it.

She stared at the maps harder, willing the dispassion in her blood. Focus, focus, focus.

A knock sounded on her office door, making her flinch. She scowled, rubbed the back of her neck, and pulled herself together.

'Come in.'

A secretary cracked open the door. 'Roger MacAllister on line one for you.'

'Tell him I'm not available.'

'He's called several times now, Agent.'

Marion turned to the Williamstown map. 'Tough.'

She ran her finger down the streets, trying to see the small, quaint town the way he saw it. Trying to know it as he knew it.

Jim Beckett was number one. Jim Beckett was here. Jim Beckett was *here*.

She stared at the map harder and at Tess's house, which she'd marked with an X.

'Oh,' she said at last, the pattern clicking in her mind. '*Oh*.'

Eight p.m. The sun was down, the streetlights on. In the generic white van Lieutenant Houlihan and Special Agent Quincy sat in silence. The snipers were in place on the roof, woolen mittens pulled over their hands for warmth. At the end of the block a young college girl in black tights, black boots, a short red skirt, and beige barn jacket arrived home with her backpack, opened her front door, and stepped inside.

At six o'clock the tiny residential block had showed signs of life. Now things were settling down. The few families who lived there were eating dinner. The college students had already departed again, heading for a

Friday night of college entertainment. Houlihan didn't imagine they'd see much more traffic until one or two A.M.

Linden Street was a quiet place.

The radio crackled briefly to life. Patrol teams Alpha, Beta, and Omega all reported in. So far, no signs of Jim.

'Get ready for a long week,' Houlihan muttered.

'Where's Agent MacAllister?' Quincy asked.

'I don't know. She's your agent.'

Quincy looked at his watch again and frowned. 'I wouldn't have thought she'd blow it this early on,' he murmured. He went back to staring out the window. He hated stakeouts.

Houlihan finally picked up the cell phone and checked in at headquarters. 'Any news?' he asked the sergeant in charge.

'No, sir.'

'What about Team A? Have they found any leads on Jim or Samantha?'

'No, sir.'

'All the death certificates are confirmed?' Houlihan pressed. He was damn tired of hearing 'No, sir.'

'Yes, sir.'

'I thought they had a lead?'

'I just spoke with Detective Epstein himself. Hospital archives revealed a copy of Mary Beckett's death certificate. His family is dead, sir. If someone is helping him, it's someone we've never heard of. They're still working on the phone list.'

'Just wonderful.' Houlihan grumbled a bit more, then hung up the phone. Quincy remained silent.

They stared down the street. Waiting.

Marion changed clothes. She pulled on a pair of designer jeans, a peach silk turtleneck, and a cardigan of hand-woven Irish wool. She left the cardigan unbuttoned so she could reach easily for her gun.

The clothes were much nicer than what a college student would normally wear, but at a glance they would do.

She pulled the first pin out of her hair. Then the second, then the third. The pale gold locks uncurled slowly, as if they were afraid of the unexpected freedom. She picked up a brush and worked on her hair until it gleamed.

She had no bangs and no natural wave. Just fine flaxen strands that reached the small of her back. She added a headband and thought she looked like Alice in Wonderland. Perfect.

The clock glowed 8:30 as she pulled on her gray wool overcoat. Her shoulder holster fit comfortably. Around her ankle she had a .22.

She took out her FBI shield and studied it one last time. Fidelity, bravery, integrity, it said. *I do solemnly swear that I will support and defend the*

Constitution of the United States against all enemies, foreign and domestic . . .

She placed the shield on the middle of the bed. There was one last matter to attend to. She kept the note simple:

J.T.
  I do remember the pillow fort and the GI comic books and the night we cried because Snake still hadn't come to take us away. Sometimes I still dream of the colonel and he is always standing amid the flames of hell while little demons flay his skin. I watch from outside the intense heat and I always think, it's not enough. There is nothing that would ever be enough.
  You were right to remember, but I need to forget.
  Remember me young, for both of us.
  Merry Berry

She left the pad sitting next to the phone. She added two extra clips to her coat pocket.

Head high, shoulders square, she left the room and didn't look back.

Edith sat on her front porch, hugging her old hunting coat closer to her. It was cold, colder than it should be.

She'd thought that after telling Martha about her visions, everything would get better. They'd spoken of it frankly. Martha was afraid of her son. She thought he may have done some bad things and that's what the dead girls were trying to tell Edith. Tonight Martha would bring little Stephanie over to Edith's while she went to the police.

Edith had agreed. They were taking action. They had a plan. The visions should go away.

But as she stood on the front porch, her chest had that too-tight feeling and goose bumps were already prickling up her arms. As she stood on her front porch, she knew that she was scared. Very scared.

Martha appeared in her driveway again. She was loading up the trunk of her car. She'd been loading it for a while with luggage and bags of supplies. Edith had no idea how Martha had ended up with so much stuff.

Martha disappeared back inside her home. She no longer moved stiffly. Now her strides were long and purposeful, almost jaunty. Their plan had had a euphoric effect on Martha. Edith suspected it would only be temporary. Thick shadows circled Martha's eyes and her gaze had that too-bright look of someone who wasn't sleeping at night.

Edith felt another chill and rubbed her arms again. The girl drifted back in front of her – the one with a butterfly tattoo. Edith shook her head. 'I'm doing what I can. Now go away. Find the light, do whatever it is you people do.'

Martha reappeared, Stephanie's hand tucked in hers. They crossed the yard, then Stephanie's small hand was ceremoniously transferred to Edith's age-spotted grip. The little girl didn't appear happy, but she didn't complain. Beneath the brim of her everpresent baseball cap, she wore the resigned expression of someone who'd gone through all this before.

Edith thought she was very strong for a four-year-old.

'If all goes well, I'll have a restraining order by morning,' Martha said.

'How will a restraining order protect you from Jim Beckett?' Edith grumbled.

Martha instantly stilled. She looked at Edith very carefully. 'How do you know about Jim Beckett?'

'I—' Edith's mouth worked soundlessly. It was one of those things she hadn't known she'd known until she'd said the words out loud. 'I just . . . I just do.'

Martha nodded, but there was something new in her expression. Something that made Edith stand very still. Beside her, Samantha had stopped breathing, also sensing the danger.

The old woman and child stood together very quietly.

Slowly Martha nodded. Slowly she stepped back.

She finally climbed into the car and shut the door with a bang. The shakes hit Edith in a rush; suddenly her whole body was trembling.

She looked down at Stephanie, subdued Stephanie, whose hair was as golden as any of the faded girls haunting her porch. She looked at the old brown Nissan now pulling out of the driveway.

And suddenly the visions cleared her porch. They leapt into the car, crowded into the car with their long blond hair and silent, somber faces. They were crying and keening, tearing at their hair, spilling out of the car. Begging for help.

Edith dragged her eyes away, feeling the pain once more in her chest. Needle-sharp pain. Horrible pain.

Her gaze went to the back of the car, pulling down the street. Her gaze landed on Martha's too-white hair, and she knew. She knew why the visions had started appearing. She knew why they grew worse when Martha was in the room. She knew why Martha's face was too smooth and her hands too strong and her shoulders too broad.

Martha wasn't Jim Beckett's mother. Martha was Jim Beckett.

The brake lights suddenly glowed bright red. The beat-up car halted in the middle of the street.

And she knew that Jim Beckett knew that she knew.

She grabbed Samantha's hand tightly.

'Run, child, run,' she commanded, and yanked her off the patio. 'Run with me!'

*

Tess pulled away from the window. She turned toward J.T., who sat in the reclining chair, twirling his hunting knife around his fingers.

'You all right?' he asked.

She said simply, 'Nightfall.'

27

Marion walked down the streets of Williamstown without fear.

She'd scouted them out earlier, matching buildings to the street map she'd burned into her mind. Houliban hadn't lied – Williamstown was small. Settled in 1753 as West Hoosuck, the town was nestled in the Berkshires with a 450-acre campus. Land sprawled around the town, undulating green fields broken up by impressive gothic churches built from stone. White-trimmed brick buildings added prestigious touches. The mountains towered in the horizon.

The heart of Williamstown, however, contained no more than a few square miles. From Marion's location off central Hoxsey Street, she could walk to Tess's house on Elm in twelve minutes. She could run there in six. The centralized collection of shops, dormitories, and houses made it the ideal setting for a hit and run. And the steady traffic of bundled-up college students and tourists made it easy to blend in.

She could understand why Jim Beckett would allow himself to be lured back to this town.

She lingered on Hoxsey Street. The science compound loomed to one side, a dark mass of shadowed buildings where old pine trees sheltered a zigzagging maze of walking paths. The other side of the street began with the beautiful redbricked Spencer House, one of the many fraternities lining Main Street. The rest of the street was occupied by old, traditional homes that had been subdivided into apartments for the Williams students. The student infirmary marked the end.

It was only nine-thirty, and the street witnessed steady traffic flow. Students traced the walking paths that began one block over on pulsing Spring Street and carried them through the science compound, across Hoxsey Street, and down the row of fraternities. Tonight students walked briskly and in groups. Obviously they'd paid attention to warnings of a possible escaped murderer in the area.

Marion urged them on mentally. *Run and run fast. You don't want to meet Jim Beckett tonight.*

Jim Beckett was here.

She turned the phrase over in her mind again and again, and that was the only one that made sense. 'Jim Beckett was the best' was pejorative; he'd say 'Jim Beckett *is* the best.' Same with 'Jim Beckett was number one.'

Jim Beckett was here. The statement was as arrogant and childish as the man. It fit him.

Tonight – or maybe tomorrow night, or the one after it – he would come after Tess. But he would also finish his pattern. He always finished what he started. He didn't have time to do it anymore with city names. But he could use street names.

Tess lived on Elm Street. That supplied one of the *Es* in *here.*

But to start he would need the letter *H.*

Marion pivoted and walked down the other side of Hoxsey. It would end here.

She veered away from the main street, following one of the footpaths through the science compound. Gravel crunched beneath her feet as she walked.

A group of four students passed by her and faded away.

A blue-suited security guard approached, gray hair protruding from beneath his cap. His generous middle jiggled like Jell-O.

She shook her head, tucking her chin against her chest for warmth as she trudged on. Another retired policeman who'd become a rent-a-cop. Slow, out of shape, and absolutely no match for a man like Jim Beckett.

Out of the corner of her eye she saw the guard's head come up. His face was lined heavily. He had jowls.

Less than twelve inches away from him, she finally noticed his eyes.

Bright blue eyes.

Ice.

She reached for her gun. And he lunged forward.

'Where's Marion?' J.T. grumbled. He paced back and forth in the kitchen, where Tess was trying to keep busy by making chili. She was stirring the beans obsessively and adding chili powder with a heavy hand.

He glanced at the clock for fourth time in five minutes.

Only 9:35. And they were already going nuts.

'Maybe she's still at the office.'

'Maybe.' He could feel the tension rising inside him. Jungle drums with a jungle beat. He couldn't stop pacing.

He picked up the phone and called in. Lieutenant Houlihan picked up the secure line on the first ring. 'What?' the lieutenant demanded sourly.

'I thought Marion was coming back to the house one more time.'

'She seems to have changed her mind.'

The statement irritated J.T. beyond reason. 'Put her on the phone.' His tone was curt.

'Can't.'

'Can't?'

'She's not here. I don't know what the deal is. Last we heard, police team Alpha saw her walking down Hoxsey Street. She must have had some last-minute things to do. It's going to be fun watching her try to explain it to Quincy. He really doesn't look happy.'

J.T. frowned harder. 'Why would she be walking around? That's not like her.'

'Don't know. It's been a tough week.'

'Yeah, well, Marion isn't exactly weak in the knees.'

'J.T., she's not under my jurisdiction. She was supposed to be here by seven. It's now 9:38, and last we knew she was walking through Williamstown in an overcoat and casual clothes. The officers said they almost didn't recognize her with her hair down.'

'*What?*'

Warning bells were already going off in his mind. He didn't want to believe them. 'She was wearing jeans and her *blond* hair was down. Would you say she looked like a college student? Like a young blond coed?'

There was a stunned pause. Then, 'Oh, shit.'

'You idiot,' J.T. swore, and suddenly he was so angry and so terrified, his hand shook on the phone. 'Can't you see what she's doing? Damn you! *And damn her!*' He didn't wait for a reply. He slammed the phone down and grabbed his gun from the small of his back.

Tess was staring at him, her hand frozen on the wooden spoon protruding from the pot of chili.

'Lock the door behind me,' he ordered curtly. 'Don't move, don't blink, don't open the fucking door for anyone. For *anyone*. Do you hear me!'

'Y-yes,' she whispered. He was already running toward the door. 'Wait! You can't—'

It was too late. He was gone.

'Damn!' Houlihan grabbed the van door. Quincy's hand shot out and stopped him.

The radios were crackling to life around them. The snipers reported J.T. running from the house. Team Alpha was responding to reports of a disturbance at the Student Union.

Things were heating up.

'Stay smart,' Quincy warned. His grip relaxed a fraction, but not his gaze. 'Team Alpha will check out the disturbance. Can we move Team Omega to the last reported sighting of Marion?'

Houlihan made a fist, then released his breath with a sigh. 'Yeah. Yeah, we'll do that.'

'Can you handle surveillance alone?'

'What?'

'The van, can you handle it alone?'

'Sure I can—'

'Good. Ms Williams is alone in the house now, Houlihan. That's not acceptable. I'm going over.'

Houlihan gave it some thought. His nerves were strung too tight. Hell, all of their nerves were strung too tight. And now they had an agent going AWOL and her mercenary brother following suit. Everybody wanted to know what the hell was going on and what the hell to do. Now was not the time for panic. Beckett was right, after all. Discipline was the key. Houlihan took a deep breath and said, 'Remember, Beckett has the guns he stole from Difford's safe house. You got a vest on?'

'Yes. I'll watch from inside the house. You keep control from the outside.'

Quincy pulled out his 9 mm and took off the safety. From the drawer in the specially equipped van he pulled out two more magazines and slipped them into his pocket. He nodded to Houlihan one last time, then stepped out of the van.

Houlihan closed and locked the door behind him. He was now alone. His eyes chased down all the shadows. He sat down lower in his seat.

It was 9:41 P.M. and his team was fractured.

It wasn't good.

In the war room an operator waved her hand for the sergeant. She put the caller on hold and said to him, 'I have a woman on the line who insists she knows where Jim Beckett is.'

'And where is that?'

The police operator sighed. In the last few weeks she thought she'd heard it all. By the time this gig was up, she would have no more faith in man's intelligence. 'The woman claims her next-door neighbor is Jim Beckett. Her next-door neighbor, the sixty-year-old retired woman from Florida.'

'A sixty-year-old retired woman is Jim Beckett?'

'Yes, sir.'

'Of course, what was I thinking? Why are you wasting my time with this?'

'Because the woman also claims she has Samantha Williams with her right now. She says she's calling from a gas station, Martha is going to hunt them down at any time, and she's scared for herself and for Samantha. I can hear sounds of traffic in the background and what sounds like a child crying. She says she's not hanging up until we send over the cavalry, and I believe her.'

The sergeant motioned for the headset. He put it on and took the caller off hold. 'Hello? This is Sergeant McMurphy. Who am I speaking to? Edith? Edith Magher? How can I help you, Edith?'

He was frowning. Edith Magher. Why did that name sound familiar? He glanced at the log sheet while she babbled in his ear about dead girls haunting her porch and her sixty-year-old neighbor who liked to smoke cigars and was too big and too strong and had too blue eyes. . . .

He didn't see her name listed on the log sheet. He flipped the next page, going back a few days. He could hear a child sobbing quietly in the background. The woman kept telling her everything would be all right. And then she started talking about the dead girls climbing into a brown Nissan and Martha/Jim Beckett driving away. But Martha/Jim knew that Edith knew. Sooner or later Martha/Jim would come get them.

The sergeant's gaze fell on the list of phone numbers Team A was tracking down. Suddenly the name blazed out at him. Edith Magher. Shelly Zane had forwarded calls to her seven times in the last two years.

The sergeant grabbed the operator's shoulder so tightly, she winced. He pointed furiously at the screen. 'Where's the location of the caller listed on this damn thing? I need the location and I need it now!'

Beckett trapped her arm first. Marion didn't panic and she didn't struggle too hard. She let him drag her behind the trees, where they were further isolated, while her mind formulated her best plan of attack. He thought she was helpless. She wasn't. But she didn't want to give away the game too soon. With a man like Beckett, surprise was everything.

She raised her foot and slammed it down hard on his toes. He jerked away, but the motion unbalanced him. With a quick twist she slipped out of his grip, leaving him holding just her coat.

She spun to face him, bringing her gun out of her holster, but he caught her squarely on the chin with a single fist formed by knitting together his two hands. Her head cracked back.

Move through the pain, she ordered herself. She drew out her gun and he nailed her forearm with the billy club. Her fingers went numb. The gun dangled, and for a moment she thought she was going to lose it. The gun would fall and she would be helpless.

Don't drop your weapon.

She grabbed it with her left hand and got off three awkward shots.

He dropped low, then rushed her. He plowed her back against a hulking tree, knocking the air from her gut. She responded instinctively, hammering down on the back of his neck with the butt of her gun. He grunted and squeezed harder, two years of weight lifting in a prison rec room giving him incredible strength. His shoulder pressed into her diaphragm, squeezing her lungs, killing her.

She couldn't shoot him. She couldn't get her hands to function. White dots were appearing before her eyes. She tried to bring up her knee. He blocked it effortlessly. She pulled at his hair and the wig came off in her hand.

The world began to spin. Her chest burned. Her body cried out for oxygen. Tree bark dug into her back. There were so many ways to suffocate a person. She'd forgotten about that. What a thing to forget.

J.T., I'm so sorry.

With her last sane thought she fired the gun again, alerting the world to her position. Then she clawed at Beckett's shoulder, searching for his old gunshot wound.

It didn't matter.

Beckett counted off eight more seconds, then her body went limp.

He let her slip to the ground, stepping back and staggering drunkenly for a moment. The back of his head continued to throb from her blows. When he tried to focus on her, he saw double.

He didn't have time for such weaknesses. Discipline is the key.

He raised his baton and got it over with. One two three. After a bit of practice a man became efficient about these things.

He ran, stripping off his guard's uniform as he raced through the trees. Act one was over. On to act two.

J.T. heard the gunshots as he raced down Main Street. He veered onto Hoxsey, rushing through students, who were suddenly stopping, eyes wide.

'Move, dammit!' he cried. 'Outta my way!'

He knew the minute he'd found her, because people mingled around the entrance to the shadowed footpath, not quite sure what Bad Thing had happened and not quite willing to step forward and find out. They craned their necks from the relative safety of the lit sidewalks.

J.T. swung his cast-covered arm like a bat, forcing his way through.

'Cop!' He lied baldly. 'Someone dial 911!'

'Some guy went crashing through the trees,' a kid volunteered.

'He looked like a campus guard.'

'Stupid campus guards,' another student murmured. 'Probably shooting at a rat.'

'Or his big toe.'

J.T. raced forward. Passing the fifth tree he saw her, her long, golden hair spilling out from behind the tree trunk. Darker red strands were slowly mingling with the gold.

'No! No no no no no!' He fell to his knees. He grabbed her hand. Then he grabbed her shoulders and clutched her against his chest. Her head rolled lifelessly forward, her lashes still against her cheek, pine needles tangled in her hair.

So much blood. Her skull fell apart in his hands. He tried to hold it together. To put her back together again. And he willed her to survive as he'd willed her to survive every day when they were children.

Pillow forts and GI comic books.

Live, live, live.

Horseback riding and swimming suicides.

Don't leave me don't leave me don't leave me.

Standing at the foot of his bed, begging him to save her.

Don't let me fail you a second time.

'*Damn you!*'

Beckett moved fast through the shadows. He came at last to a thick hedge and stopped to regroup. His breath was coming out in sharp gasps, forming puffs of steam in the cold night air. He could feel blood on his cheeks, and the back of his skull was swollen and tender.

These things were not supposed to happen to him.

The euphoria was dimming. Beneath, exhaustion threatened to crash his system. He shook his head, fighting it.

He had the letter *H*. He was fulfilling his plan.

Some adjustments would have to be made. Edith knew his true identity and had Samantha. He'd debated giving chase, but couldn't possibly kill an old woman in front of his daughter, so he'd let them go for now. Later he would show Edith what happened to women who crossed him. Then he would simply reclaim his daughter from the police. He'd done it before, he could do it again.

Theresa was still in the area, and that's what mattered. They'd buzzed about her enough on the police scanner and he understood that he was invited to join them.

He was looking forward to seeing her again.

He smoothed a hand over the navy blue suit he'd worn beneath the guard's uniform. From the pocket he produced four towelettes and used them to wipe the thick makeup from his face, wincing a little as the soap stung the scratches along his jawline. Next he pulled out a pair of glasses and a short dark wig.

Then he unbuckled the sawed-off shotgun he'd strapped beneath his arm. Difford's gun cabinet had been a gold mine.

He was ready.

Tess turned to Quincy. 'Ten o'clock,' she whispered. 'Where is he?'

'Any sign?' Quincy asked over the walkie-talkie.

'Unconfirmed,' Houlihan answered. 'There's a report of another disturbance on Hoxsey, the sound of gunfire. Team Omega is almost there—' Crackling interrupted. A new voice came on.

'This is Sniper A. It's ten o'clock-check time. I have visual of B, but no reports on C. Please confirm.'

Houlihan's voice crackled again. 'Sniper C, come in. Sniper C, come in.'

The radio was quiet.

'Sniper C?'

More silence. Tess and Quincy exchanged glances.

Houlihan's voice was strong. 'Do we have visual of Sniper C?'

'This is Sniper B. I'm looking across the street now. I see Sniper A standing in the west corner. I do *not* see Sniper C in the east. I repeat, I do *not* see Sniper C in the east. Please confirm, Sniper A.'

'This is Sniper A. I don't have visual, sir. Requesting permission to check it out.'

'Permission denied,' Houlihan said flatly. 'Hold your position. I'm calling in SWAT. I repeat, stay at your points, I'm calling in SWAT. We are now in status red. I repeat, status red.'

As Tess watched, Quincy calmly took out two extra clips of bullets and placed them on the table beside him. He raised his 9 millimeter and pointed it at the door. 'Do you have a gun, Ms Williams?'

'Yes.'

'Now is the time to take it out. Please remember, he's here to kill. There will be no negotiating on his part and there will be no leniency. Do you understand?'

'I understand,' she said. 'I won't hesitate.'

'Good.'

'Sir, let us take her. Sir, you have to let go now.'

J.T. stared at the man dully. He was wearing a paramedics uniform and holding a red medical kit. Behind him sirens whirled red and garish.

'I'm holding her together,' he said hoarsely, not relinquishing her.

'I know, sir,' the young man said gently. He could tell that the woman was dead. 'That's our job now. Someone said you were a cop.'

Slowly the words penetrated. J.T. looked down at Marion. Her head lolled against his arm. The loss inside him was too great. He couldn't measure it. He couldn't put it into words. He couldn't feel it, because when he did, it would bring him to his knees.

He placed his baby sister in the paramedic's arms. 'I have to go. Take good care of her for me, please. Just . . . please.'

He began to run.

Behind him the paramedic shouted at him to stop. He didn't listen.

The darkness in him had grown a voice. And now it screamed at the top of its lungs, *Kill Jim Beckett, kill Jim Beckett, kill Jim Beckett.*

He ran like a man possessed, and blood lust lit his eyes.

'Sir, sir!' The walkie-talkie blazed to life. 'This is Team Omega. We have a hit on Hoxsey. I repeat, a woman is down on Hoxsey, same MO. Beckett is in the area!'

Tess put her head between her knees and started taking deep breaths. Quincy's radio seemed to dance with a hideous cacophony of reports.

'This is Team Alpha. Repeat, Team Alpha. We are on the roof, east corner. There is no sign of Sniper C—'

'This is Team Omega. Officer down, officer down. Repeat, Agent MacAllister is down—'

'Shit!' Quincy's fist hit the table. Tess jumped.

'Suspect is reportedly dressed as a security guard. Last seen headed north. We are in pursuit. Requesting full mobilization—'

'SWAT team has been mobilized. They are in transit—'

'Officer down, officer down! This is Team Alpha, from the east corner. We have found Sniper C. Dear God, sir, we have found Sniper C—' From the background there came the sound of retching. 'Requesting backup, requesting immediate backup. He's on the roof. Shit, I think I see him. He's on the fucking roof! The roof, the roof!'

Over the airwaves Quincy and Tess heard the sound of men running.

'Hold positions, hold positions!' Houlihan screamed. 'I said, hold your fucking positions!'

Gunfire exploded across the radio. The sound of a man's hoarse cry. 'Difford. OhmyGod, ohmyGod! Jesus fucking Christ!'

Houlihan was now yelling at the top of his lungs.

'What is going on out there?' Tess cried.

'I don't know,' Quincy said.

His face had gone pale. His gaze settled on the ceiling.

J.T. rounded the corner. He heard shooting and drew his gun. He heard a man's cry. He was still too far away to see anything. He just heard the sound of all hell breaking loose. Three blocks to go, two.

The doorbell rang, followed by immediate pounding.

'Ms Williams, open up. Detective Teitel, Massachusetts State Police. I've been sent to stand guard.'

'Stand back,' Quincy told Tess.

He didn't have to convince her. She clung to the wall, her .22 held before her in a shaky hand.

Quincy approached the door, keeping to the side. 'I want to see your badge,' he called out.

'Okay.'

Quincy stepped up to the peephole.

The shotgun blew the door apart and hurled him across the room.

Screaming filled the room. It took Tess a moment to realize it was her own.

J.T. rounded the corner. Black-clad men swarmed the rooftop, screaming at the top of their lungs. Sirens split the air behind him. An ambulance roared toward him and he barely jumped out of the way.

He twisted his ankle and went down hard.

More gunfire split the neighborhood. A shotgun blast.

He staggered up and continued running.

Kill Jim Beckett. Kill Jim Beckett.

'Hay bales, hay bales!' Tess cried. She pointed her gun and tried to remember her stance.

Jim pointed his shotgun at Quincy, slumped on the floor.

'I'm going to kill you, Theresa,' he said calmly. 'The question is, how many police officers will you take out with you?'

Tears streaming down her cheeks. *Don't hesitate. Don't hesitate.*

Quincy moaned. There was blood on his face, pieces of wood embedded in his skin. But she knew he was wearing a bulletproof vest, which would have spared him the worst.

Jim pumped the chamber.

J.T.'s form filled the doorway. Tess couldn't stop her gaze from flickering there. Jim turned and calmly pulled the trigger.

'*No!*'

The shotgun blast burst her eardrums. J.T. fell back into the sidewalk. Down he went, arms splayed like a cartoon character's. Because the violence never ended. For her it just went on and on and on.

She pointed her gun, squeezing the trigger. Jim grabbed the .22 from her hand and pistol-whipped her hard. She fell to her knees, clutching her cheek.

'We do it my way.' Grabbing her arm, Jim dragged her upstairs.

Fresh blood stained his shoulder red. Had she hit him? She couldn't think anymore. Her cheek was on fire from the blow, and ringing filled her ears. The madman was winning. Jim had gotten control.

No! Goddammit, no!

She kicked out at the back of Jim's legs, aiming for his kneecap. He twisted away. She knitted her fingers of her free hand into a shovel and went after his kidneys. He slapped her across the face. She bit his shoulder, then tore into his ear.

'Fuck!' He flung her from him so hard, she hit the wall and fell to the floor. Even then she staggered up and aimed a kick toward his groin.

Fight, fight, fight. She fought.

And Jim Beckett rose in front of her as an enraged beast. He threw aside the shotgun. He grabbed her shoulder and yanked her toward him. She hit his clavicle with the heel of her hand. He grunted with pain.

Then he wrapped his hands around her throat and squeezed.

She fell to her knees. She struck out futilely. She thought she heard groaning downstairs and she struggled to buy time. She didn't want to die. White lights appeared in front of her gaze, but she refused to give in.

She'd fought too hard, come too far to fall to Jim now. She would win, goddammit. She would win.

Jim smiled cruelly. His hands tightened their grip.

J.T.'s chest was on fire. When he drew in a deep breath, his insides burned beneath his Kevlar vest. He was pretty sure he was dying. The stars looked too bright above him and the pavement was too cold beneath him.

He kept thinking he was supposed to ask for Merry Berry, then memory hit him hard.

He struggled upright. He heard the smack of flesh hitting flesh. He hated that sound. Tess . . .

Furious, he staggered to the shattered doorway, his left hand barely holding his ribs together. He grabbed the doorway for support, and wooden slivers drove into his palm.

He used the pain to anchor him.

The colonel had raised a son who could walk two miles on a broken ankle. That's a man. Be a man. Fight like a man.

He found the hunting knife strapped inside his cast and advanced for the stairs.

Sirens wailed behind him. Men were still screaming. Someone was yelling about the front door.

Let them all come. Let them all fucking come.

Beckett saw someone out of the corner of his eye. He dropped Tess and reached for the shotgun. He didn't see the knife hurtle through the air, until it drove through his shoulder.

He stared at it without comprehension. J.T. had arrived on the landing.

With a roar he charged.

He caught Beckett around the middle, and they went down with a crash. Something warm filled J.T.'s mouth. He opened his lips, and blood spilled down his cheek. The rusty flavor made him angrier.

Beckett fisted his hands and drove them into the small of J.T.'s back. J.T. got a fresh mouthful of bloody bile. He reared back and caught Beckett beneath the chin with his head. Then he reached up for the handle of his knife and gave it a twist.

Beckett staggered back with a sharp cry of pain. Vaguely J.T. was aware of the thick shadows beneath the man's eyes, the gaunt lines of his chin. Beckett had lost twenty pounds since his prison break, and he looked it.

He didn't feel it though. He felt only the heady thrum of adrenaline in his ears. The sirens, the screams, the noise. It fueled him.

He grabbed the baton he'd strapped inside his arm and started swinging.

J.T. leapt out of the way the first time. He rolled the second. The third swing cracked him on his already cracked ribs. The pain rocketed through him beyond description or color. He fell to his knees.

Above him the baton rose again. He could hear the whistle. Feel the draft.

He commanded his body to roll. One more time, closer to the stairs. His muscles took a long time responding.

The baton whistled down.

And the shotgun blast sent Beckett halfway across the second-story landing. Tess stood with the gun in her hands and the powder staining her cheeks. She pumped in another cartridge.

A low, wet groan escaped Jim's lips. As J.T. lay there, his eyes barely able to focus, he watched her walk over to him. There were no tears on her cheeks. No emotion in her eyes. Her face was pale, her face was calm. He thought of Marion as Tess pointed the shotgun at Jim's fallen body and pulled the trigger.

Through the haze of dissipating smoke, her brown eyes met his.

'It's over,' she whispered hoarsely, shotgun against her shoulder. 'Massachusetts might not believe in the death penalty, but I do.'

Jim didn't move again. Tess let the gun slide to the floor. She cradled J.T.'s bloody head on her lap and waited for the police to make it up the stairs.

Just south of Lenox, the cop turned his wailing car into a gas station. A backup patrol car came to a screaming halt behind him.

The woman who was about to pay for her gas stared at them. The man who was unscrewing the gas cap of his Mercedes stopped. The two young kids who were out looking for a good time hunched down lower and wondered if they'd hidden the marijuana far enough beneath the seat.

The cops searched for the pay phone.

An older woman with a somber face and liver-spotted hands appeared from around the side. A little blond girl clung to her neck. She looked at the policemen somberly.

'Edith?' one of the officers asked.

She nodded and he approached the pair slowly, since the girl was obviously scared. The girl perfectly matched the posters all over the war room. He knew. For the last few nights, the officer had gone to bed so tense, he'd dreamed of that face.

'I want my mommy,' she whispered in a tiny voice.

'I know, sweetheart. You're Samantha Beckett, aren't you?'

She nodded slowly, her grip still tight around Edith's neck.

He gave her a reassuring smile. 'It's okay. We're gonna take you to your mommy, Sam. We're gonna take you home.'

Epilogue

The new arrival caused a bit of a stir.

She stood in the doorway of the Nogales bar with the long, slender lines of a beautiful woman. Male heads turned instantly, some ancient instinct coming alert. Cue sticks halted before cue balls. Beer mugs paused before parted lips. Predatory gazes cut through the thick miasma of cigarette smoke and lingered on the simple white cotton dress that brushed down her figure and flirted with the tops of her knees.

She stepped into the bar.

Her steps did not invite interruption. She had a target and headed straight for it. Observant gazes plotted the trajectory and ran ahead of her to see who the lucky man was. The minute they figured it out, the gazes quickly hurried away.

If she could tame him, she was welcome to him. The rest of them had already learned to get out of his way – and they'd each learned that lesson the hard way.

He was hunched over a tumbler of amber liquid. His blue cotton shirt was rumpled and hung over faded jeans. His black hair had gone a long time without being cut. His lean cheeks were thick with unshaved whiskers.

Some of the women had found him handsome. He hadn't appeared to find them to be anything at all.

He came day in and day out. He drank. He played pool. Then he drank some more.

Now the mystery woman arrived beside him. She slid onto the ripped vinyl stool. She gazed at him quietly. He didn't look up.

She said matter-of-factly, 'I love you.'

He raised bleary eyes. They were bloodshot and shadowed enough to indicate he hadn't slept in weeks. It had been a month since she'd last seen him. The police had brought her Sam. Beckett had been carted off to the hospital and pronounced DOA. J.T. and Quincy had been hospitalized for broken ribs, and in J.T.'s case a punctured lung. She'd visited the hospital every day for a week. He'd lie there silently the whole time, not responding to her voice or her presence. He'd looked half dead, and at times she wondered if he wished that he were.

Then one day she'd shown up and he was gone. He'd dressed himself in his bloody clothes and walked out the front door. There had been nothing the hospital staff could do to stop him, and nobody had seen him since.

Difford's body was recovered from the rooftop, where Jim had placed it as a decoy after he'd killed the sniper. A store mannequin's head had been attached to Difford's neck. Tess had attended the memorial service for the lieutenant and the sniper. Following Difford's wishes, his body was cremated and his ashes scattered over the Atlanta Braves spring training field in Florida.

Two days later Tess had attended Marion's funeral, where Marion was laid to rest next to her father in Arlington. J.T. still hadn't shown up. It was as if he'd fallen off the face of the earth. That's when Tess had known he'd returned to Nogales.

'What are you doing here?' His voice sounded hoarse, either from whiskey or tobacco or disuse. Maybe all three. His fingers picked up a cigarette case. He didn't open it, he just twirled it between his fingers. It was the cigarette case that had belonged to Marion.

'You shouldn't be here,' she said.

His gaze slid down her body, then dismissed her. 'Too virginal. I'm not interested.'

'I'm not in the sinning business.'

'Well, I am.'

'Come home, J.T.' She touched his cheek lightly. His beard was so long, it was silky. She reacquainted herself with the line and feel of jaw, the fullness of his lips. She ached for him. She looked at him and she hurt. 'Tell me how to help you.'

'Go away.'

'I can't.'

'Women are always trying to change a man. You think there's something more inside us, and frankly it's just not true. I am what I am.' He jerked his hand around the bar. 'Honey, this is me.'

'You are who you are. But this isn't it. This is you drunk. I've seen you sober. I care for that man an awful lot. I think that man is one of the best men I know.'

His gaze fell to the table and the tumbler full of amber liquid. Shame stained his cheeks.

'I'm haunted,' he said abruptly. 'Like an old house. I close my eyes and I see Rachel and Marion again and again. Sometimes they're happy. Sometimes they're sad. There's nothing I can do about it. I reach out my hand to them and *poof*, they're gone.' He opened his palm on the counter and flung the emptiness into the air.

Tess didn't know what to say. She wasn't an expert on how to heal. She did the best she could. She kissed him. And he didn't taste of whiskey or cigarettes. He tasted suspiciously of apples.

Her gaze went from him to his glass to him. He sat stiffly while she sniffed the contents.

'Apple juice?'

'Yeah.' Shame infused his cheeks again. 'I tried whiskey. I truly, truly did. And every time I raised the glass, I just saw Marion shaking her head at me. Christ' – he hung his head – 'I'm a teetotaler!'

'It's okay,' she assured him, stroking his hair. 'It'll get easier. It will.'

He didn't look convinced. Her fingers traced the beard on his cheeks, the purple puffiness beneath his eyes, the fullness of his lips. 'J.T., I love you.'

He groaned like a trapped beast. His eyes closed. 'Why can't you just go away? Why can't you just leave me alone? You killed him, you survived, isn't that enough for you?'

'I don't want to live in the past.'

'I can't escape it.'

'You can, it's just going to take a while.' She gave up sitting beside him and slid onto his lap. In this bar few people noticed. His thighs were hard and masculine beneath her, the denim of his jeans soft and worn. She kissed his lips, then his cheek, and then the scar on his chest.

She rested her head against his shoulder, and after a heartbeat she felt his arms slide around her waist. He buried his face in her hair.

And after a ponderous moment his broad shoulders began to shake.

'Tell me,' she commanded softly.

'I love you. Christ, I love you.'

And he was dying and there was nothing for him anymore. No place he could go where he didn't see Marion lying in the dirt, no room to sit in where he didn't see Rachel waving to him and blowing a kiss as she got into her car, and Teddy's little arm waving in the backseat. He wanted to find them each again. He wanted to hold them in his arms and whisper, Please, please be happy. I love you, I just wanted you to be happy. I love you.

Remember me young, for both of us.

He raised his head. There were tear tracks on his cheeks. He didn't care anymore.

'Make me whole. I want to be whole.'

She pressed his face against her throat and stroked his hair. She smelled of roses. He inhaled deeply and felt the scent finally soothe his shattered senses.

'Come on. It's time to go home and meet my daughter.'

He kissed her. He held her close.

And he let her take him home.

Later, almost twelve months after that bloody night, he had the dream for the first time. Marion and Rachel were in a field of wildflowers, wearing white dresses and whimsical summer hats. Teddy picked daisies at their feet, his chubby hand filled with the flowers. They were talking and laughing, enjoying the day.

J.T. stood at the edge of the field, invisible to them and unable to touch. They spread out in the field and opened their arms to the sun.

It was a ridiculous dream, he thought upon waking. But he held it in his mind anyway.

He liked to remember them laughing, he liked to remember them happy. In the end maybe that was the most any of us can do – remember the ones we loved the way we loved them.

He rolled over and curled his arm around his wife's supple waist.

'Bad dreams?' she murmured sleepily.

'No.'

'Okay. Stop hogging the covers.'

She drifted back to sleep. He pulled the covers over her shoulders, then settled her against him. She whispered his name and even in her sleep returned his embrace.

The Other Daughter

Acknowledgements

As always, I'm indebted to quite a few people for their expertise and patience in helping make this book a reality. Being myself, I took artistic license with a great deal of the information but tried to keep things as rooted in the real world as possible. All mistakes are mine, of course. Special thanks to:

Special Agent Nidia C. Gamba and Supervisory Special Agent John C. Ekenrode of the Boston Federal Bureau of Investigation healthcare fraud squad. I know I didn't have the space to do your job justice, but I hope you'll appreciate the fact that I tried.

Bob and Kim Diehl, former corrections officers for the Texas Department of Corrections. Not just anyone will answer e-mails from a total stranger, particularly a stranger inquiring about proper protocol for the electric chair.

Larry Jachrimo, custom pistolsmith and true artist. I've never liked guns, but you helped me appreciate them.

The Arthritis Organization for the general information on AS and to my brother, who is living with it. The older we get, Rob, the more you are my hero.

Jennifer Carson, R.N., my dear roommate from college and one of the few healthcare professionals who doesn't mind answering all my inquiries about poisons. You've got a devious mind, Jenn, and I love you for it.

Finally, to my agent, Damaris Rowland, for riding this roller coaster with me, and to my new husband, the love of my life. I couldn't do this without you.

Author's Note

Fans of the death penalty in Texas will notice an immediate discrepancy in my novel – that a man is sent to the electric chair in 1977. In fact, Old Sparky was retired in 1964 after the execution of 361 men, and the death penalty was not carried out again until 1982, when Texas got lethal injection. Never let it be said that historical accuracy got in the way of a writer.

For the record, the Huntsville Prison Museum does exist and is an excellent source of information on the colorful world of the Texas Department of Corrections. Bonnie and Clyde are among the most famous prisoners documented there, though I like to think that Russell Lee Holmes would be worthy of similar notoriety. The Captain Joe Byrd Cemetery also exists in real life, and, yes, the day I visited it, there was a freshly dug grave just waiting for the next recipient – I was told there was another execution planned that night.

And the owl did hoot while I was there, and there was one helluva thunderstorm, and I do so solemnly swear I will never commit a crime in the state of Texas.

Prologue

September 1977
Huntsville, Texas

At six A.M. the Huntsville 'Walls' Unit went to full lockdown.

Outside the redbrick walls, protesters were already gathering for Texas's first execution in thirteen years. Inhumane, picket signs read. Cruel and unusual. The 'Texas thunderbolt' should never have been brought out of retirement. The death penalty was capricious and irresponsible.

An equal-sized crowd begged to differ. Cruel and unusual was still too good for Russell Lee Holmes. Send him to the chair. Let him fry. Execution candidate number 362 was worth bringing back the electric chair – in fact, they should bring back hanging.

Inside the Death House, where he'd been brought just the night before, Russell Lee Holmes settled his sparse frame more comfortably on the lone bunk in his cell and ignored them all. He had watery blue eyes, a thin face, and a hunched, lean frame. After thirty years of chewing tobacco and drinking soda, his teeth were crooked, stained, and half-rotted. He liked to pick them with his thumbnail. He definitely wasn't a pleasant man or a brilliant man. What he was was quiet and, for the most part, indifferent. Sometimes it was difficult to remember just what his small, finely boned hands had done.

In January, when Utah had ended the Supreme Court's moratorium on executions by throwing Gilmore in front of the firing squad, there hadn't been any doubt that Texas would reenter the death business. And there hadn't been any doubt that Russell Lee Holmes would be the first man up to bat.

Maybe that's because when the sentencing judge had asked him what he had to say about kidnapping, torturing, and murdering six small children, Russell Lee had said, 'Well, sir, basically, I can't wait to get me another.'

The warden arrived at Russell Lee's cell. He was a fat, barrel-chested man, nicknamed Warden Cluck due to jowls that reddened and shook like a rooster's when he was angry or upset. Russell Lee knew from experience that it didn't take much to get Cluck upset. Now, however, the warden seemed kind, even benevolent, as he unrolled the warrant and cleared his throat so the other four men in the Death House could hear.

'Here's your sentence, Russell Lee. I'm gonna read to you your sentence. You listenin'?'

'They're gonna fry my ass,' he said casually.

'Now, Russell Lee, we're all here to help you today. To get you through this with less fuss.'

'Go to hell.'

Warden Cluck shook his head and got to reading. 'It is the mandate of this court, that you, Russell Lee Holmes, shall be executed for the following crimes.'

He ran down the list. Six counts of murder in the first degree. Kidnapping. Rape. Molestation. All-round sadistic bad ass deserving to die. Russell Lee nodded to each charge. Not a bad list for the kid his mama had simply called Trash, as in 'filthy white trash,' as in, 'no betta than yer father, that piece of no good, filthy white trash.'

'You understand the sentence, Russell Lee?'

'It's a little late if I don't.'

'Fine, then. The Father's here to meet with you.'

'I only want to speak with you, my son,' Father Sanders said soothingly. 'To be with you in this time of crisis. To allow you to unburden your soul and understand this journey you are about to take.'

Russell Lee, always cordial, said, 'Fuck you. I don't want to meet no pussy God. I'm looking forward to meetin' Mr Satan. I figure I can teach him a thing or two about how to make babies scream. Don't you got a kid, Warden? A little girl . . .'

The warden's pudgy face had suddenly turned beet red. He stabbed a thick finger in the air while his jowls started shaking. 'Don't start. We're trying to help you—'

'Help fry my ass. I'm no fool. You want me dead so you can sleep at night. But I think I'm gonna like being dead. Then I can go anywhere I want, be like Casper. Maybe tonight I'll find your little girl—'

'We ain't gonna bury your body,' the warden yelled. 'We're gonna put it through the chip machine, you son of a bitch. We're gonna dice you into dust, then dump the dust into acid. Won't be no trace of your sorry ass left on the face of this earth by the time we're done with you. No fucking molecule!'

'Can't help myself,' Russell Lee drawled. 'I was born to be bad.'

Warden Cluck hiked up his gray pants, jerked his head at the priest to join him, and stomped out of the cell.

Russell Lee lay back down on his cot and grinned. Time for a good nap. Nothing more to look forward to today. Nothing more to look forward to period, Trash.

His grin faltered when in the corridor, the four dead men took up the chant.

'How do you like Russell Lee? Baked, crisped, or fried? How do you like Russell Lee? Baked, crisped, or fried?'

Three-thirty P.M. Russell Lee got up, his last meal of fried chicken, fried okra, fried sweet potatoes finally arriving. With it came an uninvited guest, reporter Larry Digger – the warden's way of punishing him for his morning display.

For a moment the two men just stared at each other. Larry Digger was thirty years old, his body trim, his face unlined, his dark hair thick. He carried the wind of the outside world with him like a special scent, and all the men stared at him with sullen, resentful eyes. He breezed into Russell Lee's cell and plopped down on the cot.

'You gonna eat all that? You'll burst your intestines before you ever get to the chair.'

Russell Lee scowled. Larry Digger had been latched on to him like a leech for seven years now, first following his crimes, then his arrest, his trial, and now his death. In the beginning Russell Lee hadn't minded so much. These days, however, the reporter's questions made him nervous, maybe a little scared, and Russell Lee *hated* being scared. He fastened his gaze upon the meal cart and inhaled the oily scent of burnt food.

'Whaddya want?' Russell Lee demanded, digging into the pile of fried chicken with his hands.

Digger tipped back his fedora and adjusted his trench coat. 'You seem calm enough. No hysterics, no pledges of innocence.'

'Nope.' Russell Lee ripped off a bite of chicken, chewed noisily, swallowed.

'I was told you'd sworn off the priest. I didn't think you'd take the Jesus route.'

'Nope.'

'No purging of sins for Russell Lee Holmes?'

'Nope.'

'Come on, Russell Lee.' Digger leaned forward and planted his elbows on his knees. 'You know what I want to hear. It's your last day now. You know there won't be a pardon. This is it. Final chance to set the record straight. From your lips to the front page.'

Russell Lee finished the chicken, smacked his greasy lips, and moved on to the charcoaled okra.

'You're gonna die alone, Russell Lee. Maybe that seems okay to you now, but the minute they strap you into Old Sparky, it won't be the same. Give me their names. I can have your wife flown in here for you. And your baby. Give you some support, give you *family* for your last day here on earth.'

Russell Lee finished the okra and plunged three fingers into the middle of the chocolate cake. He collapsed a whole side, excavated it like a tunnel digger, and started sucking the frosting from his palm.

'I'll even pay for it,' Digger said, a last-ditch effort from a man who was paid jack shit, and they both knew it. 'Come on. We know you're married. I've seen the tattoo and I've heard the rumors. Tell me who she is. Tell me about your kid.'

'Why does it matter to you?'

'I'm just trying to help you—'

'You gonna bring 'em here and call 'em freaks, that's what you're gonna do.'

'So they exist, you admit it—'

'Maybe they do. Maybe they don't.' Russell Lee flashed a mouthful of chocolate-coated teeth. 'I ain't telling.'

'You're a stubborn fool, Russell Lee. They are going to fry you, and your wife will never have benefits and your kid will get raised by some other junkyard dog who'll claim it as his own. Probably become a loser just like you.'

'Oh, it's all taken care of, Digger. It is, it is. Matter of fact, I got me more of a future than you do. That's what they call irony, ain't it. Irony. Good word, goddammit. Good word.' Russell Lee turned back to his cake and shut up.

Larry Digger finally left in a rage. Russell Lee tossed his leftover food, including most of the cake, onto the concrete floor. He was supposed to share his dessert with his fellow death row inmates; that was protocol. Russell Lee ground the cake into the cement floor with the heel of his right foot.

'Let them all share that. Let the motherfuckers share that.'

Abruptly a loud *crunch* rang down the corridor, the noise growing, swelling, into a fierce, angry crescendo. It paused, dipped low, then soared high, going from a whine to a snarl.

The executioner was warming up the chair, testing his equipment at 1800 volts to 500 to 1300 to 300.

Suddenly the moment was very real.

'How do you like Russell Lee?' the corridor pulsed. 'Baked, crisped, or fried? How do you like Russell Lee? Baked, crisped, or fried?'

Russell Lee Holmes sat down quietly on the edge of the cot. He drew in his shoulders, thought of the nastiest things he could think of. Small, soft throats, big blue eyes, shrill little-girl screams.

I won't say a word, baby. I'll keep it to my grave. 'Cause once there was someone who at least pretended to love Trash.

Boston, Massachusetts

Josh Sanders trudged down the brightly lit halls. A first-year resident, he was going on hour thirty-seven of a supposed twenty-four-hour ER shift and he functioned purely on autopilot. He wanted sleep. He must find an empty room. He must sleep.

He came to the door of room five. No lights were on. Dimly he recalled that the boards listed five as unoccupied. Slow night in the ER.

Josh entered the room and yanked back the curtain surrounding the bed, ready to collapse.

A whimper. A hoarse, strangled wheeze. A moan.

The freshman doctor caught himself and snapped on the overhead light. A fully clothed little girl lay magically sprawled on top of the bed.

And she was clutching her throat as her eyes rolled back into her head and her whole body went limp.

The death team was well trained. Three guards snapped Russell Lee Holmes into leg irons and a belly chain. He informed the warden he could walk out on his own, and everyone fell into position.

The guards flanked Russell Lee. Warden Cluck led. They marched down the forty-five-foot corridor, where the green door that had greeted 361 men now held Russell Lee's number.

At five the barber had shaved his head, sculpting a perfectly bald crown for the electrode plate. Then there'd been one last shower before he'd donned the execution whites. White pants, white shirt, white belt, all made from cotton grown on the prison farms and cut, spun, and sewed by prison inmates. He was going to his death looking like a fucking painter and without a trace of the outside world upon him.

The door swung open. Old Sparky beckoned. Rich burnished wood, over fifty years old and gleaming. High back, solid arms and legs, wide leather straps. Looked almost like Grandma's favorite rocker except for the face mask and electrodes.

The executioner took over and everything happened in a blur. The guards were strapping Russell Lee to the golden oak frame. One thrust a bite stick between his teeth, the other swabbed his left leg, head, and chest with saline solution to help conduct the electricity. The executioner followed up with metal straps around his calves, metal straps around his wrists, two diodes on each side of his heart, and finally a silver bowl on top of his shaved head. In less than sixty seconds Russell Lee Holmes had been crowned king.

The executioner taped up his eye sockets so there would be less mess when his eyeballs melted, and stuck cotton balls up his nose to limit the bleeding.

Eleven-thirty P.M. The death squad left the room, and Russell Lee's 'torture time' began. He sat, strapped to his death chair, surrounded by blackness and waited for the phone on the wall to ring, the phone connected directly with the governor's office.

In the three viewing rooms across from him, others also waited. In room one were the witnesses – Larry Digger and four relatives of Russell Lee's victims who could afford to attend. Patricia Stokes had lost her four-year-old daughter Meagan to this monster's handiwork. Her husband was on duty at his new job, so she'd brought along her fourteen-year-old son instead. Brian's young face was immobile, but Patricia was sobbing quietly, her thin arms wrapped tightly around her tall, gaunt frame.

In room two, the executioner stood ready. This room contained the second phone connected directly with the governor's office. It also boasted three large buttons, an inch and a half in diameter, which jutted out of the wall. One main inducer and two backups. The state of Texas always got the job done.

Room three was for family and friends of the inmate. Tonight its only occupant was Kelsey Jones, Russell Lee's beleaguered defense attorney, who was wearing his best suit – a mint-colored seersucker – for the occasion. Kelsey Jones had a special assignment. He was to watch. He was to report back, Russell Lee's last consideration to the woman who had loved him.

Then Kelsey Jones was to forget all about Russell Lee – a task he would gladly accept.

Eleven thirty-one P.M. The countdown began, and the many subterfuges and manipulations that had started more than five years before finally came to a head. All rooms were quiet. All occupants were tense.

The man who was responsible sat in the chair with tape over his eyeballs and ground his teeth into the bite stick.

I AM POWERFUL. I AM HUGE!

His bowels let loose. And he gripped the end of the armrests so hard his knuckles turned white.

Love you, baby. Love . . . you.

'Code Blue! Code Blue!' Josh simultaneously shouted orders and checked the little girl's pulse. 'I need a cart, stat! We got a young female, looks to be eight or nine, barely breathing. Somebody call peds!'

Dr Chen rushed into the room. 'Where did she come from?'

'Don't know.'

Staff and crash cart arrived at the same time, and everyone fell into a fast, furious rhythm.

'She's not on the boards,' Nancy, the head nurse reported, grabbing a needle. The IV slipped in, followed by the catheter. Immediately they were drawing blood and urine.

'She's running a fever! Oh, we got hives!' Sherry, another nurse, had finished snipping away the cotton sweatshirt to attach the five-lead heart monitor and revealed the little girl's inflamed torso.

'STAND BACK!'

The chest X ray flashed, and they fell back on the patient, working furiously. The girl's body was covered with a sheen of sweat and she was completely nonresponsive. Then her breathing stopped altogether.

'Tube!' Josh shouted, and immediately went to work to intubate.

Shit, she was small. He was afraid he was hurting something as he bumbled his way around her tiny throat like a water buffalo. Then the tube found the opening and slithered down her windpipe. 'I'm in!' he exclaimed at the same time Sherry whirled out of the room with vials of fluid for the CBC, chem 20, and urine drug screen.

'Pulse is thready,' Nancy said.

'Assessment, Josh?' Dr Chen demanded.

'Anaphylaxis reaction,' Josh said immediately. 'We need one amp of epi.'

'Point-oh-one milli,' Dr Chen corrected him. 'Peds dosage.'

'I don't see any sign of a bee sting,' Nancy reported, handing over the epinephrine and watching the doctor administer it through the breathing tube.

'It could be a reaction to anything,' Dr Chen murmured, and waited to see what the epi would do.

For a moment they were all still.

The little girl looked so unprotected sprawled on the white hospital bed with five wires, an IV, and a bulky breathing tube sprouting from her small figure. Long blond hair spilled onto the bed and smelled faintly of No More Tears baby shampoo. Her eyelashes were thick and her face splotchy – smudges under the eyes, bright red spots staining her plump cheeks. No matter how many years he worked, Josh would never get used to the sight of a child in a hospital.

'Muscles are relaxing,' Josh reported. 'Breathing's easier.' Epinephrine acted fast. The little girl's eyes fluttered open but didn't focus.

'Hello?' Dr Chen tried. 'Can you hear me?'

No response. He moved from verbal to tactile, shaking her lightly. She still did not respond. Nancy tried the sternal rub, pressing her knuckles against the tiny sternum hard enough to induce pain. The little girl's body arched helplessly, but her eyes remained glazed.

'Hard to arouse,' Nancy reported. 'The patient remains nonresponsive.' Now they were all frowning.

The door burst open.

'What's all the ruckus about?' Dr Harper Stokes strode into the room, wearing green scrubs as if they were tennis whites and looking almost unreal with his deep tan, vivid blue eyes, and movie-poster face. He had just joined City General Hospital as a hotshot cardiothoracic surgeon and had already taken to striding the halls like Jesus in search of lepers. Josh had heard he was very good but also seemed to know it. You know what the difference between a cardiac surgeon and God is? God doesn't think he's a cardiac surgeon.

'We got it,' Dr Chen said a bit testily.

'Uh-huh.' Dr Harper sauntered over to the bed. Then he spotted the little girl sprouting tubes and drew up cold, looking honestly shocked. 'My God, what *happened*?'

'Anaphylaxis reaction to unknown agent.'

'Epi?'

'Of course.'

'Give me the chest X ray.' Dr Stokes held out a hand, peering at the girl intently and checking her heartbeat.

'We got it under control!'

Dr Stokes raised his head just long enough to look the younger MD in the eye. 'Then, why, Dr Chen,' he said somberly, 'is she lying there like a rag doll?'

Dr Chen gritted his teeth. 'I don't know.'

Midnight. The doctor entered the executioner's room and took up position against the back wall, his hands clasped behind him. The executioner picked up the phone connected to the governor's office.

He heard dial tone.

He recradled the receiver. He counted off sixty seconds.

He stared at Russell Lee Holmes, who sat in the middle of the death chamber with his lips peeled back from his scarecrow teeth in an idiot's grin.

'He's too dumb to know what's going on,' the doctor said.

'Don't matter now,' the executioner said.

His watch hit 12:01. He picked up the phone. He still heard the dial tone.

He hit the main inducer button and 440 volts/10 ohms of electricity surged through Russell Lee Holmes's body.

The lights dimmed in the Death House. Three inmates roared and clapped while one curled beneath his cot and rocked back and forth like a frightened child. The relatives of the victims watched stoically at first, but when Russell Lee's skin turned bright red and began to smoke, they turned away. Except for Brian Stokes. He remained watching, as if transfixed, while Russell Lee Holmes's body convulsed. Abruptly his feet blew off. Then his hands. Behind Brian, his mother screamed. He still didn't look away.

And then it was simply over.

The doctor entered the death chamber. He'd wiped Vicks VapoRub beneath his nose to block out the smell. It wasn't enough, and his nose crinkled as he inspected the body.

He looked at the middle window, into the executioner's room. 'Time of death is twelve-oh-five.'

'I got drug screen results!' Sherry plowed through the door, and Josh grabbed the reports, just beating out Dr Harper Stokes.

'She's positive for opiates,' Josh called.

'Morphine,' Dr Stokes said.

'Narcan,' Dr Chen ordered. 'Point-oh-oh-five milli per kilo. Bring extra!' Sherry rushed away for the reversing agent.

'Could she be allergic to morphine?' Josh quizzed Dr Chen. 'Could that be what caused the anaphylaxis reaction?'

'It happens.'

Sherry returned with the narcan and Dr Chen quickly injected it. They removed the breathing tube and waited, a second dose already in hand. Narcan could be repeated every two to three minutes if necessary. Dr Stokes checked the young girl's pulse again, then her heart.

'Better,' he announced. 'Steadying. Oh, hang on. Here we go . . .'

The little girl was moving her head from side to side. Nancy drew a sheet over her and they all held their breath. The little girl blinked and her large eyes, a striking mix of blue and gray, focused.

'Can you hear me, honey?' Dr Stokes whispered, his voice curiously thick as he smoothed back her limp hair from her sweaty forehead. 'Can you tell us your name?'

She didn't answer. She took in the strangers hovering above her, the white, white room, the lines and wires sticking out of her body. Plump and awkward-looking, she was not a pretty child, Josh thought, but at that moment she was completely endearing. He took her hand and her gaze rested on him immediately, tearing him up a little. Who in hell drugged and abandoned a little girl? The world was sick.

After a moment her fingers gripped his. A nice, strong grip considering her condition.

'It's okay,' he whispered. 'You're safe. Tell us your name, honey. We need to know your name.'

Her mouth opened, her parched throat working, but no sound emerged. She looked a little more panicked.

'Relax,' he soothed. 'Take a deep breath. Everything is okay. Everything is fine. Now try it again.'

She looked at him trustingly.

This time she whispered, 'Daddy's Girl.'

1

She was late, she was late, oh, God, she was *so* late!

Melanie Stokes came bounding up the stairs, then made the hard left turn down the hall, her long blond hair whipping around her face. Twenty minutes and counting. She hadn't even thought about what she was going to wear. Damn.

She tore into her room with her sweatshirt half pulled over her head. A strategic kick sent the heavy mahogany door slamming shut behind her as she shed the first layer of clothes. She toed off her tennis shoes and sent them sailing beneath the pine bureau that swallowed nearly a quarter of her bedroom. A lot of things came to rest beneath the battered dresser. One of these days she meant to clean it out. But not tonight.

Melanie hastily shimmied out of her ripped-up jeans, tossed her T-shirt onto the sleigh bed, and hurried to the closet. The wide plank floorboards felt cool against her toes, making her do a little *cha-cha-cha* along the way.

'Come on,' she muttered, ripping back the silk curtain. 'Ten years of compulsive shopping crammed into one five-by-five space. How hard can it be to locate a cocktail dress?'

To judge by the mess, pretty hard. Melanie grimaced, then waded in fatalistically. Somewhere in there were a few decent dresses.

At the age of twenty-nine, Melanie Stokes was petite, capable, and a born diplomat. She'd been abandoned as a child at City General Hospital with no memory of where she came from, but that had been a long time ago and she didn't think of those days much. She had an adoptive father whom she respected, an adoptive mother whom she loved, an older brother whom she worshiped, and an indulgent godfather whom she adored. Until recently she had considered her family to be very close. They were not just another rich family, they were a tight-knit family. She kept telling herself they would be like that again soon.

Melanie had graduated from Wellesley six years earlier with her family serving as an enthusiastic cheering section. She'd returned home right afterward to help her mother through one of her 'spells,' and somehow it had seemed easiest for everyone if she stayed. Now she was a professional event organizer. Mostly she did charity functions. Huge black-tie affairs that made the social elite feel social and elite while simultaneously milking them for significant sums of money. Lots of details, lots of planning, lots of work. Melanie always pulled them off. Seamless, social columnists liked to rave about the events, relaxed yet elegant. Not to mention profitable.

Then there were the nights like tonight. Tonight was the seventh annual Donate-A-Classic for Literacy reception, held right there in her parents' house, and, apparently, cursed.

The caterer hadn't been able to get enough ice. The parking valets had called in sick, the *Boston Globe* had printed the wrong time, and Senator Kennedy was home with a stomach virus, taking with him half the press corps. Thirty minutes ago Melanie had gotten so frustrated, tears had stung her eyes. Completely unlike her.

But then, she was agitated tonight for reasons that had nothing to do with the reception. She was agitated, and being Melanie, she was dealing with it by keeping busy.

Melanie was very good at keeping busy. Almost as good as her father.

Fifteen minutes and counting. Damn. Melanie found her favorite gold-fringed flapper's dress. Encouraged, she began digging for gold pumps.

During the first few months of Melanie's adoption, the Stokeses had been so excited about their new daughter, they'd lavished her with every gift they could imagine. The second floor master bedroom suite, complete with rose silk wall hangings and a gold-trimmed bathroom, where she needed a stool just to catch her reflection in the genuine Louis IV mirror, was hers. The closet was the size of a small apartment, and it had been filled with every dress, hat, and, yes, gloves ever made by Laura Ashley. All that in addition to two parents, one brother, and one godfather who were shadowing every move she made, handing her food before she could think to hunger, bringing her games before she could think to be bored, and offering her blankets before she could think to shiver.

It had been a little weird.

Melanie had gone along at first. She'd been eager to please, wanting to be happy as badly as they wanted to make her happy. It seemed to her that if people as golden and beautiful and rich as the Stokeses were willing to give her a home and have her as a daughter, she could darn well learn to be their daughter. So she'd dressed each morning in flounces of lace and patiently let her new mom cajole her straight hair into sausage curls. She'd listened gravely to her new father's dramatic stories of snatching cardiac patients from the clutches of death and her godfather's tales of faraway places where men wore skirts and women grew hair in their armpits. She spent long afternoons sitting quietly with her new brother, memorizing his tight features and troubled eyes while he swore to her again and again that he would be the perfect older brother for her, he would.

Everything was perfect. Too perfect. Melanie stopped being able to sleep at night. Instead, she would find herself tiptoeing downstairs at two A.M. to stand in front of a painting of another golden little girl. Four-year-old Meagan Stokes, who wore flounces of lace and sausage-curled hair. Four-year-old Meagan Stokes, who'd been the Stokeses' first daughter before some monster had kidnapped her and cut off her head. Four-year-old Meagan Stokes, the real daughter the Stokeses had loved and adored long before Melanie arrived.

Harper would come home from emergency surgeries and carry her back to bed. Brian grew adept at hearing the sound of her footsteps and would patiently lead her back to her bedroom. But still she'd come back down, obsessed by the painting of that gorgeous little girl whom even a nine-year-old girl could realize she was meant to replace.

Jamie O'Donnell finally intervened. Oh, for God's sake, he declared. Melanie was Melanie. A flesh-and-blood girl, not a porcelain doll to be used for dress-up games. Let her pick her own clothes and her own room and her own style before the therapy bills grew out of control.

That piece of advice probably saved them all. Melanie left the master bedroom suite for a sunny third-story bedroom across from Brian's room. Melanie liked the bay windows and low, slanted ceilings, and the fact that the room could never be mistaken for, say, a hospital room.

And she discovered, during a clothing drive at school, that she liked hand-me-downs best. They were so soft and comfortable, and if you did spill or rip something, no one would notice. She became Goodwill's best customer for years. Then came the trips to garage sales for furniture. She liked things banged up, scarred. Things that came with a past, she realized when she was older. Things that came with the history she didn't have.

Her godfather was amused by her taste, her father aghast, but her new family remained supportive. They kept loving her. They grew whole.

In the years since, Melanie liked to think they all learned from one another. Her well-bred southern mother taught her which fork to use for which courses. In turn Melanie introduced her depression-prone mother to the reggae song 'Don't Worry, Be Happy.' Harper instilled in his daughter the need to work hard, to consciously and proactively build a life. Melanie taught him to stop and smell the roses every now and then, even if just for a change of pace. Her brother showed her how to survive in high society. And Melanie showed him unconditional love, that even on his bad days – and Brian, like Patricia, had many of those – he would always be a hero to her.

The doorbell rang just as she unearthed her shoes. Jesus, she was cutting it close tonight.

Hair and makeup, quick. At least her pale features and baby-fine blond hair didn't require more than the lightest touch of color and a simple stroke of the hairbrush. A little blush, a little gold eye shadow, and she was done.

Melanie took a deep breath and permitted herself one last assessment in the mirror. The event was coming together in that crazy way each one did. Her father had volunteered to greet the guests, a definite overture of peace, and her mother was appearing more composed than Melanie had expected. Things were working out.

'It's going to be a great evening,' Melanie assured her reflection. 'We got rich patrons, we got a blood donor room. We got the best food money can buy and a stack of rare books to collect. Your family is doing better, and to hell with Senator Kennedy – it's gonna be a great night.'

She gave herself a smile. She pushed herself away from her bureau. Took a big step toward her door. And suddenly the world tilted and blurred in front of her eyes.

Black void, twisted shapes. Weird sense of déjà vu. A little girl's voice, pleading in the dark.

'*I want to go home now. Please, let me go home . . .*'

Melanie blinked. Her cluttered room snapped back into view, the fading spring sun streamed through the bay windows, the hundred-and-ten-year-old floor felt solid beneath her feet. She discovered her hands pressed against her stomach, sweat on her brow. She glanced around immediately, almost guiltily, hoping no one had noticed.

No one was upstairs. No one knew. No one had seen or suspected a thing.

Melanie quickly descended the stairs where the sounds of gathering people and clinking champagne glasses beckoned gaily.

Four spells in three weeks. Always the black void. Always the same little girl's voice.

Stress, she thought, and walked more briskly. Delusions. Neuroses.

Anything but memory. After all this time, what would be the point?

The Boeing 747 touched down badly, bumping and skipping on the runway. Larry Digger was in a foul mood to begin with, and the botched landing did nothing to improve it.

Digger hated flying. He didn't trust planes, or pilots, or the computers that were installed to imitate pilots. Trust nothing, that was Larry Digger's favorite motto. People are stupid was his second favorite.

Gimme a drink was probably his third. But he wasn't about to say it then.

Time hadn't been kind to Larry Digger. His trim frame had turned soft at pretty much the same rate his promising investigative reporter's career had turned sour. Somewhere along the way his mouth adopted the perpetually dour look of a hound dog, while his cheeks developed jowls and his chin got too fleshy. He looked ten years older than his real age. He felt about another ten years older than that.

At least he had until the phone had rung three weeks earlier. Within days he'd hocked his stereo equipment for a first-rate tape recorder, then sold his car for a plane ticket and traveling cash.

This was it for Larry Digger. Twenty-five years after he'd started the search for the Holy Grail, he was in Boston, and it was boom or bust.

He hailed a cab. It had taken him a week to track down the address in his fist. Now he handed the piece of paper to the tired-looking driver who was paying more attention to the Red Sox game on the radio than to the other cars on the road.

Digger was traveling light, just clean underwear, a couple of white shirts, the tape recorder, and a copy of his own book, published fifteen years before. He'd started writing it soon after Russell Lee Holmes's execution when most nights he woke up with the scent of burning flesh polluting his nostrils. The other guys had gotten a break that night. Blowing an inmate apart had given the anti-death penalty liberals all the ammunition they'd needed. Texas had gotten to hastily re-retire Old Sparky, not entering the execution business again until 1982, when the state got lethal injection.

It hadn't helped Digger though. He'd thought Russell Lee would be the big story for him, finally break him out of Pisswater, USA, and move him to national news. They'd kept him in Huntsville, covering the retirement of Old Sparky, covering the debate. Then he got to cover the setup of the lethal injection, and way before he was ready, he was back to watching men die.

He had started needing a drink before going to bed. Then he started needing two or three. Most likely he was on his own slow road to dying, when lo and behold, the phone had rung.

Two A.M., May 3. Exactly three weeks ago. Larry Digger remembered it clearly. Fumbling for the ringing phone on the bedside table. Swearing at the thundering sound. Pressing the cold receiver against his ear. Hearing the disembodied voice in the dark.

'You shouldn't have given up. You were right about Russell Lee Holmes. He did have a wife and child. Do you want to know more?'

Of course he did. Even when he knew he should've given up, when he knew that his obsession with Russell Lee Holmes had cost him more than it had ever given him, he hadn't been able to say no. The caller had known that too. The caller had actually laughed, a weird, knowing sound that was distorted by some machine. Then he'd hung up.

Two days later the caller was more specific. This time he gave Digger a name. Idaho Johnson.

'It's an alias. Russell Lee Holmes's favorite alias. Track it down, you'll see.'

Digger had tracked the name to a marriage certificate. He'd then traced both husband's and wife's names to a birth certificate for a child listed as Baby Doe Johnson. No sex or hospital was listed, but there was a midwife's name. Digger found her through the Midwives Association, and there he'd struck gold.

Yes, she remembered Idaho Johnson. Yes, that picture looked like him. A slight hesitation. We-ell, yes, she understood that his real name was actually

Russell Lee Holmes. Not that she'd known it then, she informed Digger crisply. But when the cops had arrested Russell Lee and the papers had carried his picture, she'd sure figured it out. Then the midwife thinned her lips. She wasn't willing to say another word. Baby Doe Johnson was Baby Doe Johnson and she didn't see any reason to infringe upon the privacy and rights of a child simply because of what the father had done.

Digger had tried tracking down the child and mother on his own, only to hit a wall. The woman's name on the marriage certificate also appeared to be an alias, having no social security number, driver's license, or tax history to back it up. Digger had combed through old records, old files. He'd hunted for photos, property deeds, any damn kind of paper trail. No sign of Angela Johnson or Baby Doe.

Digger had gone back to the midwife.

He'd begged. He'd pleaded and argued and browbeat. Offered money he didn't have and glory he'd never known. The best he could get out of the woman was one last grudging story, a small incident that had happened to her after Russell Lee's arrest. Really, it had probably been nothing.

But to Larry Digger it had been everything. Within seconds of hearing the midwife's little tale, he thought he knew exactly what had happened to Baby Doe Johnson. And it was a bigger story than any dried-up, washed-up, half-drunk reporter had ever dared to dream.

But why dredge it up twenty years later?

He'd asked his three A.M. caller that question, actually. And he still recalled the weird, high-pitched answer.

'Because you get what you deserve, Larry. You always get what you deserve.'

The cab was slowing down and pulling over. Digger glanced around.

He was in downtown Boston. One block from the Ritz, one block from the landmark Cheers, limos everywhere. This was where the Stokeses now lived? The rich did get richer.

God, that pissed him off.

Digger slapped ten bucks in the cabbie's hand and crawled out of the taxi.

The sky was clear. He sniffed a couple of times, wiped his hand on his rumpled trousers. Air definitely smelled like flowers. No exhaust fumes here. Rich folks probably didn't stand for such things. Some big park loomed behind him, filled with cherry trees and tulips and, of all things, swan boats. He shook his head.

He turned away from the park and inspected the row of buildings. They were all stone town houses, three stories high and rail thin. Old and grand. Nestled shoulder to shoulder but still managing to appear aloof. Built by blue bloods, he figured, one hundred years ago, when everyone was still tracing their lineage to the *Mayflower*. Hell, maybe they still were.

He checked the addresses. The Stokes home was the fourth in. It was currently lit up like the Fourth of July, with two red-coated valets guarding the doorway like matchsticks. As he watched, a Mercedes-Benz pulled up and a woman stepped out. She'd draped purple sequins and white diamonds all over her plump body and looked like a moldy raisin. Her husband, who was equally portly, waddled like a penguin in his tux. The couple surrendered their keys to a valet and sauntered through heavy walnut doors.

Digger looked down at his old trench coat and rumpled pants.

Oh, yeah, he could just stroll right in.

He walked into the park, took a seat on an old wrought iron bench beneath a vast red maple tree, and contemplated the Stokes house once more.

As the reporter who'd tagged Russell Lee Holmes to the grave, Larry Digger had gotten to know all the families of the murdered children. He'd met them when their grief was still a raw, ragged wound, and he'd interviewed them later, when the horror had leached away and left only despair. By then the fathers had a vengeful gleam in their sunken eyes. They fisted their hands and pounded already beat-up furniture when speaking about Russell Lee Holmes. The mothers, on the other hand, clung to their surviving children obsessively, and stared at all men, even their husbands, mistrustfully. By the time the state got around to killing Russell Lee, most of the families had imploded.

Except the Stokeses. From the very beginning they had been different, and from the very beginning the other families had resented them for that. Except for Meagan, Russell Lee's victims lived in poor neighborhoods. The Stokeses had lived in a mansion in one of the newly rich neighborhoods of Houston. The other families had had that worn, mongrel look of two working parents. Their kids had had torn clothes and uneven teeth and dusty cheeks.

The Stokeses belonged on the cover of *Better Homes and Gardens* – the strong, noble doctor-husband, the slender, classy, former-beauty-queen wife, and their two golden children. Gleaming blond hair; perfect white teeth; pink, rosy cheeks.

They were the kind of people you half *wanted* something bad to happen to, and then, when it did . . .

Digger had to look down at the grass. Images from that time still shamed and confused him.

The way Patricia Stokes's clear blue gaze had softened when she spoke of her daughter, trying to describe to reporters the perfect little girl who'd been kidnapped from her family, begging them to help her find her daughter. Then, the way her face had broken completely the day Meagan's body had been ID'ed. Her blue eyes grew so bleak that for the first time in his life, Larry Digger would've given up a story, hell, Larry Digger would've given up his *soul* to give this perfect woman back her daughter.

Right after the execution, when Patricia had been overcome by grief and horror, Digger followed her to the hotel bar. Her husband hadn't come. Work, Digger had heard. According to the rumor mill, since the death of Meagan Stokes, all Dr Harper Stokes did was work. The man seemed to have some misguided notion that saving other lives would make God give him his daughter back. Rich men were stupid.

So, the fourteen-year-old Brian had gone to Texas as his mother's escort. He'd even followed his mother into the bar as if he owned the place. When the bartender tried to protest, the kid gave him a look. A don't-you-mess-with-me-after-the-things-I've-seen look. The bartender shut right up.

Christ, what kind of kid attended an execution?

Right about then Digger figured that the Stokeses weren't so perfect or golden after all. There was something there, something beneath the carefully manicured surface. Something dark. Something sinister. In all the years since, he'd never shaken that impression.

Now here he was, twenty years later. The Stokeses had a new daughter, and this one had gotten the chance to grow up. But somehow the demons couldn't all be settled, because someone had called up Larry Digger and invited him over to play.

Someone still thought the Stokeses hadn't gotten what they deserved.

Digger felt a chill.

He finally shrugged. He spared one last thought for the other daughter, wondering what she was like, if she'd found any happiness there on Beacon Street. He decided he didn't care.

This was his shot and he was going to take it. He'd done his research. He had his information. And he knew by then how to make his opportunity.

Ready or not, Melanie Stokes, he thought indifferently, *here I come.*

2

By nine-thirty, guests were filling up the Stokes home like glittering jewels. White-tuxedoed waiters cut clean lines through the expensively dressed crowd, offering silver trays heavy with champagne flutes or sizzling garlic shrimp or wild boar with blueberry demiglaze. Baccarat chandeliers threw sparkling lights over carefully coiled hairdos and captured handsome men whispering to beautiful young ladies.

Rushing down the stairs, Melanie waved merrily at the Webers and the Braskamps and the Ruddys, then exchanged nods with the Chadwicks and Baumgartners. Lawyers, deans, chiefs of surgery, and management consulting VPs. Investment bankers and a few politicians. Boston was full of new money and old money, and Melanie had shamelessly invited it all. Everyone brought a rare book to donate for literacy, and if they were all jockeying to give the best book, the most priceless donation, even better. When it came to fund-raisers, Melanie was a true hussy.

She exchanged smiles with her father, who stood by the door, looking elegant in his favorite satin-trimmed tux. At nearly sixty years of age, blue-eyed, golden-haired Harper was in his prime. He worked like a dog, jogged religiously each morning, and was an avid golfer who'd finally gotten down to a nine-handicap. More important, *Boston* magazine had just named him the best cardiac surgeon in Boston, a long overdue triumph. Tonight Melanie thought her father appeared happier than she'd seen him in months.

Satisfied, she went in search of her mother. Parties had always relaxed Melanie, hence her job. She felt comforted by the throng of milling people, the flutter of multiple conversations. In her mind, hell was solitary confinement in a room that was cold and stark and unending white. Fortunately with her job, her volunteer work at the Dedham Red Cross Donor Center, and her family, she didn't have much time to waste on worrying about being alone.

Melanie finally spotted her mother across the room and altered course straight for her.

Patricia Stokes was tucked in a corner, standing next to one of the sterling silver juice carts, and chatting with the young male server. This was a sure sign that she was nervous. A tall, striking blond who had conquered the hearts of most of the men in Texas by the time she was eighteen, Melanie's mother had grown more beautiful with age. And when scared or unsure, she had a tendency to migrate toward men, as they inevitably gushed over her every word.

'Melanie!' Patricia had spotted her daughter. Her face immediately lit up, and she waved enthusiastically. 'Darling, over here. I've spoken with catering and the juice stations are all set.'

'Wow,' the waiter exclaimed. 'Your daughter looks just like you!'

'Of course,' Patricia declared breezily. Melanie rolled her eyes. She didn't look like her mother any more than a yellow buttercup resembled a yellow rose.

'Are you harassing the help?' she asked her mom.

'Absolutely. Charlie here was just pouring me a drink. Orange juice. Straight up. I figured that would keep the room buzzing. "Does she have vodka in that or doesn't she?" "Does she/doesn't she?" You know I love to be the life of the party.'

Melanie squeezed her mother's hand. 'You're doing fine.'

Patricia merely smiled. She knew people still whispered such things as *They found her first daughter murdered. Just four years old and her head was cut off. Isn't that horrible? Can you imagine?*

And these days they were adding *Her son just announced he was gay. You know he's always been, well, troubled. And get this – she's started drinking again. That's right. Fresh out of rehab . . .*

'Everything looks great,' Patricia said too cheerfully. Two women walked by, then whispered to each other furiously. Patricia's grip on her crystal glass grew tight.

'They'll get over it,' Melanie said gently. 'Remember, the first public outing is the worst.'

'It was my own fault.' More hesitation now, genuine remorse.

'It's okay, Mom. It's okay.'

'I shouldn't have been so weak. Fifteen years of being sober. Sometimes I don't know myself . . .'

'Mom—'

'I miss Brian.'

'I know,' Melanie murmured. 'I know.'

Patricia pinched the bridge of her nose. She had worked herself up to the point of tears, and Patricia Stokes did not cry in public. She turned, giving the room her back until the worst passed.

The waiter looked reproachfully at Melanie, as if she should be doing something. Melanie would love to do something. Unfortunately the rift between her father and brother was old, and there was little she or her mother could do. Harper looked in good spirits tonight, so maybe the end would soon be near.

'I'm . . . I'm better now,' Patricia was saying. She had pulled herself together, adopting that firm smile she'd learned in some finishing school umpteen years earlier.

'You can go up anytime you want,' Melanie said.

'Nonsense. I just need to get through the first hour. You're right – the first public outing is always the hardest. Well, let the windbags talk. I've certainly heard worse.'

'It's going to be okay, Mom.'

'Of course, it is.' Patricia was back to her overbright smiles, but then she leaned over and gave her daughter a genuine hug. Her arms were strong around Melanie, the scent of Chanel No. 5 and Lancôme face cream comforting. Melanie looped her arms around her mother's too-thin waist the way she had been doing since she was nine and let the embrace last for as long as her mom needed it to.

When they drew back, they were both smiling.

'I have to get to the kitchen,' Melanie said.

'Do you need help? I'm really not doing much.'

'Nope. This show is on the road.' She was already stepping away, but then her mom caught her hand. She looked intent.

'William coming?'

Melanie shrugged. 'He *is* dad's favorite anesthesiologist.'

'Nervous?'

'Never. What's one ex-fiancé among three hundred people?'

'William's a jerk,' her mom said loyally.

'And you are the best.' Melanie gave her mother's hand a squeeze, then plunged into the crowd.

A sudden movement caught her eye. She turned just in time to see the flapping tail of a brown overcoat disappear into the kitchen. That was odd. Who would be running around in a soiled overcoat?

She was about to follow up, when she heard a commotion from outside. The valets were fighting over whose turn it was to park a Porsche. By the time Melanie sorted it all out, the matter of the out-of-place overcoat had completely slipped her mind.

An hour later Melanie realized she still hadn't checked in on the blood donor room that her friend Ann Margaret had set up in the front parlor.

'I'm so sorry!' she apologized immediately, bursting into the wood-paneled room that now boasted four blood donor stretchers instead of the usual leather sofas. 'I wanted to see if you needed anything, but it's been so crazy!'

'Completely understandable,' Ann Margaret drawled as she finished rubbing iodine on the exposed skin of a man's arm and in the next heartbeat slid in the needle. 'As you can see, life here is just fine.'

'Hey, gorgeous,' the man said. 'I've been wondering where you've been hiding.'

Melanie burst into a smile. 'Uncle Jamie! Here you are. I should've known my godfather would fly all the way from Europe just to hole up with a beautiful woman.'

'Can't help myself,' Jamie informed her. 'It's the gift of being Irish.'

Melanie shook her head. She'd heard it all before but didn't mind hearing it again. A longtime friend of her parents from their days in Texas, Jamie O'Donnell was one of her most favorite people in the world. He jetted all over the globe tracking down rare items for his import/export company, then blazed into town twice a year to spoil her rotten with imported chocolates, exotic toys, and larger-than-life stories.

Now he was sprawled on the raised donor bed, looking just off the docks even in a three-thousand-dollar tuxedo. It was probably the single diamond winking in his left ear, or the mischievous look on his face.

'They take your blood, Uncle Jamie? Somehow I figured with the life you've led . . .'

'Ah, I'm a saint, lass. A pure, angelic sort, I swear it.'

'Hardly,' Ann Margaret murmured, and snapped a rubber band around an empty donor bag.

Melanie looked back and forth between her godfather and best friend. Maybe it was just her, but she would swear there was a light blush on Ann Margaret's face, a reluctance to meet Jamie's direct gaze. Very interesting.

Melanie climbed onto the stretcher next to Jamie's and offered up her arm to donate while she and her godfather caught up.

Jamie didn't waste any time. 'Brian really thinks he's gay?'

'I don't think he merely "thinks" it.'

Jamie sighed. 'And your dad, being the open-minded fellow that he is, tossed him out on his arse.'

Melanie grimaced. 'Brian didn't exactly help matters with his method of announcement. I mean, one minute Harper is serving duck à l'orange to the hospital's head of surgery, the next his own son is bolting up, yelling he's tired of the goddamn lies and he's a goddamn homosexual and Harper had better goddamn deal with it. I don't think I've ever seen Dad hold a duck leg in midair for so long. If the whole thing hadn't been really happening, I think it might have been funny.'

'Brian always lets things build too much,' Ann Margaret stated knowingly, having followed the family saga for the past ten years. 'Wasn't he seeing a therapist?'

'He stopped. I believe his lover is the therapist's brother, or something like that.'

'You're kidding!' Both Ann Margaret and Jamie managed to be aghast.

'Well, at least tell me your brother is doing okay,' Jamie said to Melanie.

But Melanie couldn't. 'I don't know. Brian . . . Brian isn't speaking to me.'

'*No.*' Jamie shook his head. 'Stupid young fool. He and Harper have always gone head to head – they're both too damn thick, that's the problem – but the boy's crazy about you. I used to tease your parents that he mistook you for a puppy, the way he'd run around feeding you toys and feeding you chocolate. He's got no good reason to be taking out this newest tiff on you.' Jamie paused, then asked carefully, 'He *doesn't* have any reason to be mad at you, right, lass? I can't see you caring about his sexual orientation or whatever the hell they're calling it these days.'

'I don't,' Melanie said. 'Neither does Mom. But I don't know . . . Brian's always been moody. He has his spells, kind of like Mom, his blue periods, even his angry periods. When I heard him shout that he was a homosexual, some part of my brain clicked. I thought, oh, well, that's why. And now we know, and it's all out in the open, so everything will get better.

'But it didn't get better. Something went off in him. I mean, *went off*, and suddenly it's like he hates us. All of us. I don't know why.'

Her godfather looked troubled. 'You try talking to him?'

'I left six messages, then went over in person. He wouldn't answer the door.'

'That kid just tries your patience.'

'He probably needs more time.'

Jamie didn't look convinced. 'He shouldn't need time to know to treat his mom and sister with respect. Well, what's done is done. Has Harper said anything more about it?'

'You know this isn't the kind of stuff he talks about.'

'Harper needs to pull his head out of his ass,' Jamie declared, one of his favorite opinions about Harper. He said it without vehemence though. The two men went back too far to be hotheaded about their differences now.

'Dad's just conservative,' Melanie said. 'I imagine not too many of his aging Republican cronies have ever had to deal with sons announcing that they're gay.'

'Your son is still your son.'

Ann Margaret placed two fingers over the gauze pad covering the needle on his arm. 'So says the man who doesn't have one.'

Jamie actually flushed. 'Just mind your own business, you nosy little—'

Ann Margaret yanked the needle out of his vein. He made a silent O with his lips, then, every inch a chastised schoolboy, obediently lifted his arm above his head and held it there.

'You're doing great,' Ann Margaret declared merrily, and Jamie gave Melanie a long-suffering look that declared he knew he'd met his match – but he still didn't want to hear about it.

Ann Margaret moved on to Melanie next, removing the needle, applying a Band-Aid.

'I think Harper is going to give soon,' Melanie confided when both she and her godfather were allowed to sit up. She moved to Jamie's stretcher, where they sat side by side.

'You think?'

'I found him crying,' she said quietly. 'Late last week, on the sofa downstairs, when he thought no one was around.'

Jamie glanced down at the floor, completely subdued. After a moment Melanie looked at him curiously.

'What do you want from him, Jamie? Dad was raised in the fifties, when men were men, women were women, and gays were freaks. I'm not saying that's right, but it's hard to undo a lifetime of thinking.'

'You always were a good diplomat, Mel.'

'It's not world politics, Jamie. It's *family*.'

They both drifted into silence, and after a while their gazes turned to the glittering crowd.

Melanie picked out her father. He now stood in the left corner of the living room, sharing a laugh with his rival at Mass. General. William had arrived and waited at her father's heels. Like Harper, William Sheffield, MD, prided himself on his perfect appearance. Tonight, though, he looked tired, worn around the edges.

Maybe trying to keep up with three women was finally taking its toll on him.

Melanie quickly pushed that thought away. Not her business anymore, not her problem.

She looked for her mother and found her at nearly the opposite corner of the room from her husband. Melanie's parents rarely kept each other company at parties, and not at all these days, with the situation with Brian causing a rift between them.

They were never the type to argue in public, however. They never even disagreed in front of their children. Discussions took place discreetly, late at night, when they thought Brian and Melanie were asleep, and a united judgment was then passed in the morning. For the most part, Melanie regarded her parents' marriage as solid, if stale. Even now she didn't worry about them. After all, they'd weathered far worse crises.

Presently Patricia set down her orange juice glass and started moving. She passed right by where Harper was standing. Melanie thought her mother would simply keep going, but her father reached out and stopped her with a touch of his hand to her bare elbow. It was hard to say who was the most surprised by the unexpected contact, Patricia or Melanie.

Harper's mood was definitely softening, for whatever he said to his wife, it made her smile. He murmured something more, his blue eyes sparkling, and she actually laughed, looking startled, looking pleased. She turned toward him fully. His long surgeon's fingers skimmed her collarbone before coming to rest on her slender waist, and she leaned toward her husband in a way Melanie hadn't seen in a long, long time.

Jamie shifted beside Melanie, and she realized he was watching her parents as well, his expression hard to read.

'It's going to be all right,' Melanie murmured with renewed confidence. 'See, the worst is over.'

'Your mom looks great,' Jamie said softly, and behind them Ann Margaret bound their pints of blood more briskly.

'She's attending her AA meetings diligently. She's a tough one, you know.' Melanie glanced at her watch, then hopped down from the stretcher. 'You in town a bit?'

'Coupla weeks, love.'

'Tea at the Ritz?'

'Wouldn't miss it for the world.'

'It's a date. Take good care of him, Ann Margaret. I'll catch you both a little later.'

Melanie had no sooner turned down the back hall to the kitchen than she bumped into another guest. She glanced up to apologize and found herself looking at a short, balding man in rumpled streetclothes. She'd seen his overcoat earlier, she realized, heading down the hall, disappearing around the corner.

'Who are you?' she asked sharply.

The man grinned, but it wasn't friendly. 'Larry Digger, ma'am. *Dallas Daily.* Unh-unh. Don't turn away from me, Miss Stokes. I've spent all night long waiting to catch you alone. Goddamn, you are one busy lady.'

'You don't belong here, sir. This is a private function, and if you don't leave right now, I'm calling security.'

'I wouldn't do that if I were you.'

'Well, you aren't me,' she said firmly. She opened her mouth to summon help. Suddenly the man's hand snapped around her wrist and he stared at her with an intensity that was startling. Melanie couldn't breathe.

Something was stirring in the back of her mind. Ripples in the void. *Not now, not now.*

'I know about your father,' the man whispered intently.

'H-Harper Stokes?'

'Nah, Miss Stokes. I know about your real father, your *birth* father.'

'What?'

He smiled. A smile of supreme satisfaction. 'Follow me, Miss Stokes,' he said calmly. 'I'm gonna tell you a story. A little story about Texas and a serial killer named Russell Lee Holmes.'

3

Larry Digger tugged Melanie into the foyer. The Duvets, about to depart, gave them a curious look, and Melanie's lips formed an automatic smile. She was still turning the reporter's words around in her head.

I know about your real father . . . your birth father . . .

Digger twisted them away from the guests and headed down the back hall. Two servers burst through the swinging doors at the end. 'Jesus Christ, this place is overrun. How many rich people do you know?'

'Do you want money? Is that what this is about?'

Digger jerked her toward the back patio, but it was also filled with guests who gave them startled glances. 'Fuck this!'

He gave up on the house altogether and pulled her across the street to the Public Garden.

The night was warm and humid, the air fragrant with cherry blossoms and hyacinths, the gas lamps soft. May was a gorgeous month in Boston, and people took advantage of it. Melanie could see young couples nuzzling beneath maple trees, older couples herding their children, other people walking dogs. The park was active and well lit, so Melanie wasn't afraid.

Mostly she was confused. A dull throbbing had taken root behind her left eye, and she was thinking Russell Lee Holmes, Russell Lee Holmes. Why did that name sound so familiar?

Larry Digger stopped beneath a tree, shoved his pudgy hands in his trench coat pockets, and squared off against her.

'Russell Lee Holmes murdered six children. They ever tell you that?'

'What?'

'Yep. That's what he did. Mean son of a bitch. Liked his children young and with curly blond hair. Kidnapped poor children mostly, white trash like himself. Took them to dump yards and messed them up like you wouldn't believe. I have photos.'

'What?'

'Come on,' Digger said impatiently. 'Stop playing stupid. Russell Lee Holmes. Killed your parents' first daughter. Raped her and cut off her head. What was her name again?'

Oh, God, that's where she knew the name. Brian must have told her, or Jamie. Certainly her parents never spoke of that time.

'M-M-Meagan,' Melanie whispered.

'Yeah, Meagan, that's it. She was the worst one, all right. Four years old, cute as a button. Your parents doled out a hundred thousand bucks for ransom, and all they got to bury was a headless corpse. Enough to drive a mother to drink—'

'Shut up!' Melanie had heard enough. 'What the hell do you want, Mr Digger? Because if you think I'm going to just stand here and listen to you take potshots at my family, you got another think coming.'

'I want you!' Digger moved in close. 'I've been following you, Melanie Stokes. For twenty-five years I've been trying to find proof of your existence, trying to find out if Russell Lee Holmes really did have a wife and child, because that son of a bitch wouldn't tell a soul, wouldn't even tell me on his execution day, the bastard. But I've kept looking. Russell Lee Holmes was front-page news when they got him, and he was front-page news when they fried his ass. And he's gonna be front-page news again when I announce that I've found his daughter. You know what, Miss *Holmes* – you got his eyes.'

'Look, I don't know what your game is, but I was found in *Boston*. I don't have anything to do with some guy in Texas.'

'I never said you grew up in Texas, just that your daddy died there—'

'After fathering a child in Boston? I don't think so.'

'Oh, but I do. See, Russell Lee may have lived in Texas, but once he was arrested for murder, it was probably best for his wife and child if they got out of town. The newspapers were overflowing with accounts of what he did, you know – particularly the Stokes girl.' Larry Digger rocked back on his heels. 'He kidnapped her right from the nanny's car, sent a ransom demand, and raped and killed her even as your parents were struggling to raise the money. Very ingenious of him, you have to admit. I mean, there he was, coming up with ways to get *paid* for his work—'

'Goddammit.' Melanie had definitely had enough. 'I am *not* Russell Lee Holmes's daughter. You, on the other hand, are a crackpot. Good-bye.'

Melanie took a step. Larry Digger snapped his hand around her wrist and held tight. For the first time Melanie was afraid. When she turned, however, the reporter said calmly, 'Of course you're Russell Lee's daughter.'

'Let go of my arm.'

'You were found the night Russell Lee Holmes died,' the reporter continued as if she hadn't spoken. 'They ever tell you that? Yep, Russell Lee goes to the chair in Texas, and a little girl without a past suddenly appears in Harper Stokes's hospital. Awfully coincidental if you ask me. And then you gotta wonder – why was Harper even working that night? The man who killed his little girl is being executed, and he stays home to work? Kind of strange if you ask me. Unless he knows he has a good reason to stick around the hospital.'

'I was drugged and abandoned in the ER,' Melanie said slowly. 'My father is a cardiac surgeon. That he came downstairs at all was purely a fluke—'

'Or good timing.'

'Oh, for heaven's sake, how many men die a day in the US anyway? A few thousand? A few hundred thousand? Want to tell me I'm their daughter too?'

She gave the reporter an exasperated glance and simultaneously yanked her arm free. Digger appeared unconcerned, fishing out a crumpled pack of cigarettes and pounding out a smoke.

'Come on, Miss Holmes. You honestly never wondered where you came from? You're not the teeniest bit curious?'

'Good-bye.'

He smiled. 'I know your family, Melanie. Your mom, your dad, your brother. I covered their story when Meagan was kidnapped, and I was with Patricia and Brian the night they fried Russell Lee Holmes. You don't want to listen to me, fine. You go inside and tell your mother that Larry Digger is here to see her. Didn't she just get out of rehab? I understand that since the death of her first daughter, her nerves have never been the same.' Digger exhaled a plume of smoke right into Melanie's face. 'What do you think?'

'You are a piece of shit.'

'Ah, honey, I've been called worse.' Digger flicked ash off the end of his cigarette. 'How's Brian anyway? I remember him pressing his face to the glass in the witness room – you know, back then. When they fried Russell Lee, it was gruesome, just plain sick. Everyone closed their eyes and covered their ears. But fourteen-year-old Brian Stokes pressed his face against the glass and stared at Russell Lee dying as if he was trying to sear it into his brain. *Sear it*, mind you.

'I hear Brian's gay now. Do you think watching a man die could affect a man's sexual preferences? Just asking.'

The last comment, so cruel in its casualness, struck Melanie like a blow. She had to close her eyes, and then she was so angry she couldn't speak. She wanted to hurt him. The intensity of the desire balled her hands into fists. But she was no match for him, fat and all, and they both knew it.

'I want you away from my family,' she said finally. 'Whatever it is you have to say, you say it here. If you honestly have a story, I'm sure a quote from a killer's child is worth enough to you to stay the hell away from them. Deal?'

Larry Digger pretended to consider it. He took another deep drag from his cigarette and looked at the park around them, but his beady eyes were already gleaming triumphantly.

'I like you,' Digger said suddenly. 'I don't like most people, Miss

Holmes. But I like you. You not only have Russell Lee's eyes, you got his spine.'

'I'm just so darn flattered,' Melanie spat out, and Digger laughed.

'Yeah, you're a fine piece of work. So tell me, sweetheart, what's it like to suddenly get to live with so much money?'

'Oh, it's just as good as you dreamed, Larry, and everything you'll never have.'

'Yeah? Too bad I'm going to ruin it for you.' Larry Digger stubbed out his cigarette on the tree trunk and got serious. 'The hospital,' he said. 'I think that's the key. Over a hundred hospitals in this city, and you just happen to end up at Harper's?'

'Coincidence.'

'Maybe, but they all start to add up after a while. First we got the timing, Miss Holmes. You just happened to appear the night Russell Lee is fried for killing little kids. Then we got location. You just happened to be dropped at Harper's hospital and he just happened to have blown off an execution to be there. Then we got you. A little girl. Found perfectly clothed and in good health but nobody ever claimed you? All these years, not a single whisper from the people who must've taken care of you for nine years, bought you clothes, fed you, put a roof over your head, hell, even made sure you were found at a hospital, where you'd be in good hands. And then there's the matter of your amnesia. A healthy little girl who couldn't remember *anything* about where she came from, not even her own name. And all these years later, two *decades* later, you *still* don't remember. Seems strange to me that a nine-year-old child could appear out of nowhere, remember nothing, and be claimed by no one. Strange. Or planned.'

'You know what they say, truth is stranger than fiction.'

'Oh, that's a good one, Miss Holmes. Harper ever take you to a hypnotist? What about regression therapy or aromatherapy or whatever else quacks are dreaming up these days?'

'The doctors who checked me out said I was physically fine and that I'd remember when I was ready to remember.'

'Come on, Miss Holmes, surely the great Dr Harper Stokes had a few opinions on this subject. He coulda taken you to a hypnotist anytime and what would anybody have done about it? What would have happened? You would've remembered, that's what. And your family, sweetheart, doesn't want you to remember.'

'Oh, this is *stupid!* All you have supplied are a bunch of coincidences. And your little scenario has holes you could drive a truck through. Plain and simple, my parents *loved* Meagan. No way would they knowingly have adopted the child of her killer. That doesn't make sense.'

Larry Digger was looking at her curiously. 'You honestly believe that, don't you?'

'Of course I do. What the hell do you mean?'

'Huh.' He nodded to himself as if she'd just answered a very important question. Melanie shook her head, starting to feel more confused now, as if she were at the top of a very steep precipice and she'd just taken her first misstep.

The throbbing in her head was growing. Black voids were appearing in front of her eyes. She hadn't suffered from a serious migraine in years, but now she had the faint realization that she was dangerously close to vomiting.

'Maybe you had to know Harper and Patricia in Texas,' Digger was murmuring. 'Maybe you had to see them sitting up in their rich palace no fourth-year resident should be able to afford. Maybe you had to see them in Texas with their two kids, one so sweet, everyone loved her, and one already so troubled, half the moms on the block wouldn't let him play with their children. I'm getting the impression, Miss Holmes, there's a helluva lot about your family you just plain don't know.'

'That's not true. It's not.'

'Ah, Miss Holmes.' Larry Digger sounded sympathetic, almost pitying. It confused her more than his vicious comments had. 'Let me tell you something, Melanie, for your own sake. I didn't find you on my own, kid. I got a tip. An anonymous call in the middle of the night. Needless to say, reporters don't like anonymous tips, not even washed-up pieces of shit like me.' His teeth flashed, then his voice turned horribly somber. 'I had the caller traced the second time, Miss Holmes. Right back to Boston, Massachusetts. Right back to Beacon Street. Right back to *your house*. Why do you think that is, Mel? Why is someone from your house calling *me* about Russell Lee Holmes?'

'I don't . . . It doesn't . . . None of this makes any sense.' The world tilted suddenly. Melanie sat down on the ground. She heard herself whisper, 'But that was so long ago . . .'

Larry Digger smiled. 'You get what you deserve, Melanie Stokes. By the caller's own words, you get what you deserve.'

'No—'

'How much of a person's temperament is genetic, Melanie Holmes? Are junkyard dogs born or raised? Are you really as polished and refined as your uptight adoptive parents, or does a little Texas white trash lurk beneath that surface? I already know you can be tough. Now, what about *violence*? Ever look at a little kid, Miss Holmes, and feel *hungry*?'

'*No!* No. Oh, God . . .' Her head exploded. Melanie grabbed her temples, pressed her forehead against her knees, and rocked on the grass.

From far away she heard Larry Digger chortle. 'I'm right, aren't I? Twenty-five years later, I'm finally getting it ri—' His words suddenly ended in a yelp.

Melanie turned slowly. A white figure had joined them in the park. He seemed to have his hand clamped on Larry Digger's shoulder.

'She asked you to leave,' the newcomer said calmly.

Larry Digger tried to push the man away. 'Hey, this is private. Don't you got horse d'oovers to serve or something?'

'No, but I'm thinking of sharpening my knives.'

The man tightened his grip even more, and Digger held up his hands in surrender. The minute he was released, he backed up. 'Okay, I'll go. But I'm not lying. I do have proof, Miss Holmes. I have information, not just about your father, but your *birth mother* as well. Ever think of her, Miss Holmes? Bet she could actually tell you your real birthday, let alone your real name. Midtown Hotel, sweetheart. Pleasant dreams.'

The man took a quick step forward at the sarcastic tone, and Larry Digger hightailed it out of there, his stained coat flapping behind him.

Melanie's stomach heaved. She celebrated Larry Digger's departure by spewing shrimp all over the grass and the man's glossy black shoes.

'Shit!' he yelped, leaping back awkwardly. He didn't seem to know what to do.

That made two of them. Tears of rage streamed down Melanie's cheeks. Her head was throbbing, and images added to the chaos in her mind. Blue dress, blond hair, pleading eyes. *I want to go home now. Please, let me go home.*

'Are you going to be okay?' A hand draped back her hair. 'Jesus, you're burning up. Let me call an ambulance.'

'No!' Melanie's fear of hospitals outweighed her fear of pain. She snapped her head up and promptly winced. 'Give me . . . a minute.'

Her savior was not impressed. 'Jesus, lady. You go walking with a seedy-looking stranger – what were you thinking?'

'Nothing, obviously.' Melanie pressed the heels of her hands against her eyes. The man was absolutely right, and she resented him for it. With no other choice, she finally risked opening her eyes.

It was hard to see in the dark. The gas lamp caught the man's features only in half wash, illuminating a square jaw, lean cheeks, and a nose that had been broken a few too many times. Thick dark hair, cut conservatively short. Lips pressed into a grim, unyielding line. She recognized his uniform. Great, she'd just been saved by one of her own waiters.

She closed her eyes again. Nothing like being caught at her worst by someone who could spread stories.

'Are you going to live?' the waiter asked sharply.

'Possibly. It would help if you'd lower your voice.'

He seemed contrite for a moment, then ruined the impression with his next words. 'You shouldn't have let him drag you off like that. That was a stupid thing to do. Did he want money?'

'Who doesn't?' Melanie staggered to her feet, needing to move, to just . . . move. Unfortunately the ground shifted beneath her, the trees bobbed.

The waiter had to grab her arm. 'You keep trying to stand and we're going to have to start a suicide watch for you. Vision?'

'White dots.'

'Hearing?'

'What?'

'Prescription meds, right?'

'In the house,' she murmured, and tried to take a step. Her legs collapsed. The waiter caught her. She floated limply on his arm, suddenly beyond caring.

Please, please let me go home!

No, honey. You don't want to go home. It's not safe . . .

The man muttered something about foolish women, then swung her up in his arms. She leaned against his shoulder. He felt solid and firm and strong. He smelled like Old Spice.

Melanie buried her face against his neck and let the world slip away.

Special agent David Riggs was not happy. First, because he wasn't fond of rescuing damsels in distress. Second, because he was going to take a lot of heat for rescuing this particular damsel.

'We're eyes and ears only at this stage. This is a very delicate investigation. Don't fuck it up.'

Riggs was pretty sure Supervisory Agent Lairmore would consider following, intervening, and now carrying Melanie Stokes to be a fuckup. He was supposed to be shadowing her father. He was supposed to be overhearing Dr Harper Stokes's confession of healthcare fraud that he would casually drop at his daughter's black-tie event, high on vodka tonics and friends. Uh-huh.

David shifted Melanie more comfortably in his arms and crossed the street. She was smaller than he would've guessed, having watched her dart around the house all evening like a firefly. She never slowed down and hardly even seemed to need a gasp of air. He'd watched her do everything from heft boxes of mangoes to mop up a spill. He'd also noted that she circled back to the living room half a dozen times to discreetly check up on her mother.

Now she was leaning her head against his shoulder in a way a woman hadn't done in a long, long time.

He didn't know what to make of that, so he turned his mind sharply to the file he had on the Stokes family and the few things it told him about Melanie Stokes. Daughter, adopted at the age of nine after being abandoned at the hospital where Dr Stokes worked. A bit of a media buzz portraying her as a modern-day Orphan Annie. She'd graduated with a BA from Wellesley in '91 and was active in various charitable organizations. One of those I-want-to-give-something-back-to-the-world kind of people. Nine months earlier she'd become engaged to Dr William Sheffield, her father's favorite right-hand man, then ended it a mere three months later without ever giving a reason. One of those my-business-is-my-business kind of people. She helped take care of her mother, who, as Larry Digger had pointed out, had never been the same since the murder of her first daughter. One of those you-mess-with-my-family-you-mess-with-me kind of people. Whatever.

Nothing in the files indicated that Melanie Stokes was the daughter of a serial killer, though David had found the reporter's list of coincidences extremely interesting. Then again, David couldn't decide what he thought of the reporter. For all his bluster, Larry Digger's hands had been shaking toward the end. The man had probably skipped his nightly pint of bourbon to make contact. No doubt he was drowning in it now.

Melanie moaned as the house lights hit them both.

'Don't throw up on me again,' David muttered.

'Wait . . .'

'*Are* you going to be sick?'

'Wait.' She gripped his jacket. 'Don't . . . tell anyone,' she muttered intently. 'Not . . . my family. I'll pay you . . .'

Her eyes were clear. Big and earnest and a startling color, somewhere between blue and gray.

'Yeah, well, sure. Whatever you want.'

She sank back down into his arms, seemingly satisfied. David pushed into the foyer and everyone spotted them at once.

'What's going on here?' Harper Stokes immediately strode toward them, William Sheffield in tow. Then Patricia Stokes came flying, sloshing orange juice on her designer dress.

'Oh, my God, Melanie.'

'Bedroom?' David asked, and ignoring everyone's gasps and questions, headed up the stairs. 'She mentioned having a migraine.'

Harper swore. 'She should have Fiorinal with codeine in the bathroom. Patricia?'

She darted ahead three flights and burst from her daughter's bathroom, pills and water in hand, just as David laid Melanie down on a rumpled bed. Immediately he was pushed aside by her family, Harper anxiously picking up his daughter's hand and checking her pulse. He took the water and held it to his daughter's pale lips to wash down the pills. Patricia followed with a damp towel, gently bathing Melanie's face. That left William Sheffield, who hovered self-consciously in the doorway. It wasn't clear to David why the former fiancé was even in the room.

'What happened?' Harper demanded. He checked his daughter's pulse again, then took the towel from his wife and positioned it across Melanie's forehead. 'Where was Melanie? How did you end up with her?'

'I found her in the park,' David said. Apparently the answer sounded as vague to Harper as it did to David, because the surgeon shot him a look. David returned the stare.

Of all the people in the room, David knew the most about Dr Harper

Stokes – he'd spent the past three weeks compiling a file on the man. Considered a brilliant surgeon by many, he'd recently been anointed the top cardiac surgeon in a town known for its surgeons. Others alleged he was an egomaniac, that his zealousness to heal had more to do with the recognition it brought him than honest interest in his patients. Given the growing Hollywoodization of hospital surgery, David found that a tough call to make. Most cardiac surgeons these days were after fame or fortune. After all, there were NBA athletes courted less aggressively than a good, charismatic surgeon who could bring in the bucks.

The only thing different David could find out about Dr Harper Stokes was his background. In a day and age when a surgeon's career track started at the age of eighteen with enrollment in an Ivy League college, Dr Stokes's academic career was mediocre at best. He'd graduated from Texas A&E at the middle of his class. He hadn't gotten into any of the top twenty medical schools, having to settle for his local 'safety school,' Sam Houston University. There, he'd been known more for his upscale wardrobe and dogged work ethic than for a gift for surgery.

Oddly enough, the single event that seemed to transform Harper Stokes from average resident to surgeon extraordinaire was the kidnapping of his daughter. His personal life had disintegrated, and he had turned to work. The more chaotic the Stokeses' world became, the more time Harper spent in the hospital, where he did have the power to heal and redeem, and, what the hell, play God.

Russell Lee Holmes may have destroyed a family, but in a strange way he had also created one topnotch surgeon.

Recently the FBI had received three phone calls on the healthcare fraud hotline about Boston's number one cardiac man. Someone thought Harper's pacemaker surgeries were questionable. At this point in the investigation, David had no idea. Could be just a jealous rival blowing smoke. Could be that the doctor had come up with a way to make a few extra bucks – God knows the Stokeses lived high enough on the hog.

So far the only dirt David had found on the man was his penchant for beautiful women. Even that didn't seem to be much of a secret. He went out with his pieces of pretty young fluff; his wife kept looking the other way. Lots of marriages worked like that.

'But why was Melanie in the park?' Harper was asking with a frown, jerking David's attention back to the cramped bedroom.

Melanie answered first. 'I wanted some fresh air. I was going to step out for only a moment.'

'I happened to notice her leaving the house,' David said. 'When she hadn't returned for a while, I decided to see if everything was all right. I heard the sound of someone being ill across the street and found her.'

Harper remained frowning, then turned to his daughter with a mixture of genuine concern and reproach. 'You've been pushing yourself too hard, Melanie. You know what stress can do to you. You have to remember to monitor your level of anxiety. For heaven's sake, your mom and I would've helped you more if you'd just said something—'

'I know.'

'You take too much upon yourself.'

'I know.'

'It's not healthy, young lady.'

Melanie smiled wryly. 'Would you believe I get it from you?'

Harper harrumphed but appeared honestly sheepish. He glanced at his wife, and the two of them exchanged a look David couldn't read.

'We should let her rest,' Patricia said. 'Honey, you just get some sleep, relax. Your father and I will handle everything downstairs.'

'It's my job,' Melanie tried to protest, but the pills were getting the better of her, making her eyelids droop. She made an effort at sitting up in the bed, but didn't even make it past halfway. Finally she curled up in a little ball in the middle of a big sleigh bed. She looked frailer than she had standing up to the reporter. She looked . . .

Patricia covered her with a quilt, then ushered everyone out.

'You just happened to notice Mel leaving the house,' William Sheffield said as David brushed by him.

David calmly responded. 'Yes, I did. Did you?'

The ex-fiancé flushed, glanced quickly at Harper for support, and when he got none, slunk away.

'Thank you for helping our daughter, Mr—' Patricia paused in the doorway long enough to place a light hand on David's shoulder.

'Reese. David Reese.'

Patricia kept her hand on his shoulder. 'Thank you, Mr Reese. Really, we are indebted—'

'Not a big deal.'

She smiled, an expression that was sad. 'To me it is.'

Before David had to summon another reply, Jamie O'Donnell burst up the stairs, demanding to know what had happened to his Melanie. A trim woman with graying Brillo-like hair and nurses' whites was hot on his heels. Ann Margaret, David heard Patricia exclaim.

David used the opportunity to exit, then paused on the second story landing to eavesdrop. O'Donnell was adamant about being informed. Ann Margaret insisted upon seeing Melanie. Harper uttered something sharp and low under his breath. David didn't catch it, but all four adults immediately hushed up. No more conversation from upstairs, just the sounds of four adults easing into Melanie Stokes's bedroom.

The hair was prickling on the back of David's neck. He hadn't felt this way in a long time. Not since that day he'd sat in the doctor's office, waiting for the final news, then saw the look on the MD's face when he walked back into the examining room. At that moment David had known that life as he knew it – as his father knew it – was coming to an end.

There was no good reason for him to feel that way here. So far he had just a doctor, a family, and a drunken reporter. Nothing that sinister, nothing that promising as an investigative lead.

And yet . . . What was it Larry Digger had said?

He'd received his tip on Melanie Stokes's alleged parentage from an anonymous caller who declared that everyone gets what they deserve.

That was odd. Three weeks earlier, when the Boston field office had received an anonymous tip regarding Dr Stokes's alleged illegal surgeries, the caller had also insisted that everyone gets what they deserve.

And David didn't believe in coincidences.

4

Three A.M. David Riggs's shift as a waiter for the reception finally ended and released him into the streets of Boston. He was limping badly, his back feeling the strain even more than usual. Playing waiter was hard work. It meant he got to serve drinks, replenish hors d'oeuvre trays, and scrub his knuckles raw cleaning up. It meant he got to run all over hell and back, trying to be both a decent server and a diligent agent. Next time Lairmore asked him to go undercover, Riggs would nominate Chenney. Let the rookie lead the glamorous life.

Beacon Street was deserted now, the rich folks asleep in their town houses. Farther down, however, he heard the telltale rattle of a grocery cart on city sidewalks. Not all of Boston's residents were wealthy.

David kept walking, cutting across the Public Garden, where hours earlier he'd eavesdropped on Larry Digger and Melanie Stokes. He should probably call Chenney, see how the rookie was holding up. The new kid in the Boston healthcare fraud squad was a serious body builder, one of those guys who look like a giant slab of meat. Big square head on top of a big square neck on top of a big square torso. When he walked, his bulging arms arced out to the side, like an ape. He was hard to take seriously, particularly when he introduced himself as a former CPA.

David still wasn't sure what he thought of the kid. It didn't help that Chenney had no training. The academy gave agent wanna-bes only a sixteen-week basic intro to white collar crime. The real plunge into the fun-filled world of MDRs, HMOs, unbundling, uploading, Part A versus Part B claims wouldn't happen until time and budget permitted Chenney to take specialized training through the National Healthcare Antifraud Association. Until then it was sink or swim, the Bureau's favorite way of seeing what rookie agents were made of.

Tonight Chenney was supposed to be trailing Dr William Sheffield, but David had caught the anesthesiologist leaving the party after two A.M., and Chenney hadn't been anywhere in sight.

Either he was very, very good, or asleep on the job. David knew where he'd cast his vote.

He grimaced in pain, caught sight of an on-duty cab, and made his decision. At this stage of the investigation, nothing was moving that urgently. He and Chenney could catch up in the morning.

The ride home was long, and by the end David was curled up on the floor, his nostrils filled with the rancid odors of sweat and tobacco while his lower back convulsed and he writhed helplessly. He stumbled out of the taxi as soon as it pulled up to his Waltham apartment complex, shoved money into the cab-driver's hand, and staggered to his feet. He walked around the parking lot. Had to work the muscles, had to get them to relax. Movement was important, exercise the only way to keep what flexibility he could.

Your sacroiliac joints are inflamed, Mr Riggs – that's the joint where your spine is connected to your pelvis – and that inflammation will start to spread up your back, causing increased discomfort. Exercise, ice, and nonsteroidal anti-inflammatory drugs are the key.

I was an athlete! I was supposed to be a major league pitcher! I know how to ice down. I know pain!

There's not much else we can tell you, Mr Riggs. Ankylosing spondylitis symptoms vary intensely from person to person and are systemic. You may experience fever, fatigue, and digestive problems, and sometimes AS attacks organs such as your eyes, heart, and lungs. We can't predict how it will affect you personally. All we can tell you is that arthritis is chronic and those people who promise you a miracle cure are only trying to make a quick buck. You can still lead a full, satisfying life with AS, of course, Mr Riggs, and there are many organizations out there to help you, but you will have to be more creative. Figure out the lifestyle that best works for you.

I have no life. I have no lifestyle. I am so damn tired.

The worst of the spasms finally passed. He kept walking anyway, though he wasn't sure why. Maybe because he'd gone so long without sleep, he'd forgotten how to do it. Maybe because he'd come to dread his bed, where he would start out in slumber and end up clutching his throat, gulping for air. He hadn't experienced that until two weeks ago. He didn't know if it was some kind of phase or if his arthritis had gotten worse.

And he didn't ask, because he was never sure if he wanted to know the answer.

He thought of baseball, the heady days of sweet sixteen.

Saturday afternoons, playing ball with his dad and his younger brother, Steven, talking about 'the show,' because Bobby Riggs had been a pretty good pitcher in his day – made it to the minors – and now looked at his sons with hope. Then out of the blue Heather Riggs had been diagnosed with breast cancer, and her husband and sons had come to the field just to take a break from the pain. Then young, beautiful Heather Riggs had died from the breast cancer, and they'd come out to the field because it was all they had left.

A father and his two sons whacking balls and sliding around bases, learning to communicate with each throw, hit, and catch. Cancer could take a loving mother and wife and rip a family apart. But baseball would never let you down. Baseball was as good as gold.

And so was David's arm.

David's arm had been the best of the best. David's arm could take him to the show.

At seventeen he'd been a Mass All-Star pitcher, and the pro-team scouts were already knocking on the door. He and his dad would stay up late talking about which major league teams had the best pitching programs for him, which place *they* would choose.

Then the nagging pain in his lower back wouldn't go away. He had problems running. Bruised tendon, they thought. Maybe he was out-pitching his arm, needed to give it a break. David had to ease up. Steven took over for a while.

But David's back got worse and his shoulder got worse, and one day he was in a doctor's office being told his joints were too inflamed for him to continue pitching while Steven was throwing his first no-hitter.

The Riggs men had never been quite the same since. David gave up serious baseball – pro teams didn't recruit young studs with health problems – and went to college instead. He didn't play baseball anymore. He left that to Steven, who did get a college scholarship but was never scouted by the pros. Steven had an arm, but he didn't have *David's* arm, and they all knew it.

Steven was now an assistant baseball coach at UMass Amherst, happily married with two great kids and maybe the next major leaguer. And since David couldn't be an all-star pitcher for his father, he'd offered up federal agent instead. He'd put away murderers, catch a serial killer, get a movie of the week. When he'd been assigned to the Boston office, he'd fantasized about exposing Boston's Mafia. He'd work undercover to expose the prominent crime families and have a showdown with the head don.

First year out of the academy, a chiropractor finally diagnosed David as having AS. His 'bad back' would never get better.

The Bureau assigned him to white collar crime, where the biggest field danger was paper cuts from sorting through hundreds of boxes of sub-poenaed files. David got good reviews each year for his 'analytics,' the Bureau's euphemism for being adept at speed-reading large quantities of gibberish while downing take-out Chinese. And he watched his academy classmates break up drug rings, foil terrorism plots, and get promoted first. Those were the breaks in the Bureau.

His back felt much better now. Did that mean it would let him sleep? Nearly five in the morning. Steven probably had a game today. He should drive over and watch. His father would be there.

David would probably go in to work instead. The cleanup at the Stokes house wasn't finished yet, and David needed the excuse to be around. It would give him a chance to learn more about Dr Harper Stokes and Digger's strange allegations about his adopted daughter.

David walked into his apartment as the first rays of sun began to lighten the sky. Only two pictures decorated the walls. Fenway Park lit up at night. Shoeless Joe Jackson. Not much about the place to call home.

David cast off his clothes without turning on the light and slid into bed. Two more hours until the alarm clock would go off. He needed to sleep.

He stared at the portrait of Shoeless Joe instead.

'Remind me life isn't fair,' he muttered to his idol. 'And tell me it's okay, dammit, it's okay.'

Shoeless Joe didn't reply. After a moment David rolled over and pretended to get some sleep.

5

At four A.M. Melanie bolted awake, a scream ripe in her throat and images blazing in her mind. Little Meagan Stokes chasing her with a bloody head. Little Meagan Stokes chanting *'Russell Lee Holmes. Russell Lee Holmes. You're just the brat of Russell Lee Holmes.'*

Melanie climbed out of bed. Her breathing was hard, her hands were shaking. She could taste blood. She finally realized that in her instinctive effort not to make any noise, she'd bitten her tongue.

She rubbed her damp cheeks, took a deep breath. A minute more and she slid to her feet. Downstairs, she could hear the grandfather clock ticking. Other than that, the three story house was perfectly still.

Melanie moved quietly. Driven by an impulse she didn't care to examine just yet, she headed downstairs.

The living room was empty, the furniture reassembled, and the whole room cast in a soft glow from the gas lamps on the street.

She drifted toward the fireplace, feeling lonely.

Since her breakup with William, she'd had too many nights like this one, when she woke up to silence and roamed the house, looking for something she couldn't name.

Until he'd proposed to her, she actually hadn't thought too much about a family of her own. She had her parents to take care of, her brother to worry about. Her life was full enough. But then William had asked for her hand in marriage. She'd never been sure why. She'd said yes. She'd never been sure why. Maybe because at that moment she had a vision of herself as Cinderella living happily ever after with Prince Charming, and that vision had seduced her.

The hard facts of reality had emerged soon enough.

She didn't miss William though. What she missed, she supposed, was the dream.

She came to a halt in front of the fireplace. And her gaze turned automatically to the huge oil painting of little Meagan Stokes.

'First we got the timing, Miss Holmes. You just happened to appear the night Russell Lee is fried for killing little kids. Then we got location. You just happened to be dropped at Harper's hospital and he just happened to have

blown off an execution to be there. Then we got you. A little girl. Found perfectly clothed and in good health but nobody ever claimed you? All these years, not a single whisper from the people who must've taken care of you for nine years, bought you clothes, fed you, put a roof over your head, hell, even made sure you were found at a hospital, where you'd be in good hands. And then there's the matter of your amnesia. A healthy little girl who couldn't remember anything about where she came from, not even her own name. And all these years later, two decades later, you still don't remember?'

'No,' she whispered to Meagan. 'I don't remember. I swear I don't.'

But she wasn't sure anymore. The stirrings in her mind, the recurring black voids, the little girl's voice. How many times now? She'd tried to pretend it wasn't happening, that her mind wasn't beginning to open up and show her things she didn't want to know.

She already had a family. She didn't want to know about a serial killer or her birth parents or her first nine years. None of that mattered. The only thing that did was that when she'd been abandoned in a hospital without even a name, the Stokeses had stepped in and rescued her.

For God's sake, she would be *nothing* without the Stokeses. Nothing.

Twenty years ago, she'd been a little girl waking up alone in a hospital ER. The white, white walls. The scary needles and tubes. The bewildering, frightening faces of strangers.

Everyone assured her she would be all right. Everyone told her that her parents would show up at any time and set everything straight. She was well fed, well taken care of. Someone out there most certainly loved her.

A couple of days passed. Time spent in the peds ward listening to other little children whimper and be comforted by their parents. Melanie would roll over in her high, white hospital bed and stare at the blank wall, trying desperately to picture the mommy who would come one day soon to comfort her.

Social services took over, transferred her to a nearby hospice. No more talk about the return of her loving parents. Now everyone murmured about finding a good foster home instead. What about adoption? It would be one thing if she were a baby, she heard someone say, but since she wasn't . . .

Night after night, alone in a plain room, realizing more and more that no one was going to magically arrive for her. No one was going to take her home. No one could even give her a name.

Then Patricia Stokes came.

She appeared in the doorway in a pretty pink suit, saying she'd come to read Melanie a story. Melanie didn't say a word. She looked at the thin, beautiful woman with her sad, lilting voice, and had thought almost viscerally, *I want her.*

She'd thrown her arms around the pretty lady. She'd buried her face against her fragrant neck. *Tell me everything is all right now. Tell me I have a home.*

The beautiful Mrs Stokes had read her a story about a fairy-tale princess. For reasons Melanie hadn't known, she'd cried at the end. Then she'd hastily dried her tears, given Melanie a yearning look, and quickly left the room.

Later, one of the social workers explained to Melanie that Mrs Stokes had lost her four-year-old daughter years ago in Texas. It had been very tragic. Now the Stokeses were starting over in Boston and Dr Harper Stokes and his wife were among the most generous people in the community. Really, a lovely couple. So sad what had happened, of course, but sometimes God knows best.

Melanie got it. The Stokeses were missing a little girl the way she was missing a family. Apart, they were all lonely. Together, they would fit.

The next time Patricia arrived, she thrust out her arms. In an instant Mrs Stokes folded her into her embrace. She began to cry again. This time Melanie patted her back.

'It's all right now,' she whispered solemnly. 'I'll be your little girl and everything will be all right.'

Patricia had cried harder.

Six months later the Stokeses brought Melanie home.

By the time she was twelve, Melanie was the only one who could make her overworked father laugh. She was the one who understood Brian and his black moods.

Then there were the really dark nights, when her brother stayed out late and her father worked late, when Melanie would go downstairs and find her mother staring up at the oil portrait of the four-year-old daughter who would never be coming home. The little girl Patricia had brought into the world and lost. The little girl who, even though Patricia had Melanie, she still couldn't forget.

On those nights Melanie would lead her mother upstairs and into bed. Then she would sit with her mother in the silence and hold her hand, trying to help her simply get through.

It's okay, Mom. I'll take care of you. I will always take care of you.

Five o'clock. The grandfather clock chimed again, rousing Melanie from her memories.

She was still staring at Meagan Stokes, who beamed as she held out her favorite red wooden horse to whoever was watching her. Little Meagan, with the perfect blue ruffled dress, big blue eyes, and golden sausage curls. Bright Meagan, who, just three weeks after the painting was completed, would be dead.

And twenty years later the Stokes family were still trying to get over it. Melanie understood now that there were some wounds not even an earnest new daughter could mend.

She finally turned away. She curled up on the sofa and whispered, 'But they're my family too, Meagan. I earned them. I did.'

The man hummed softly to himself in the dark room. Making a list, checking it twice . . .

Twenty-five years he'd waited. Thought about what he'd do, turned it over in his mind, refined it until it was absolutely right. Three weeks earlier he'd started the ball rolling with a single phone call. *First get everyone in the same town.* With Larry Digger's arrival just a few hours ago, the last of the players had arrived. *Now let the games begin.*

Twenty-five years ago such crimes had been committed, both big and small. Twenty-five years ago such sins had been tolerated, both big and small. He had always thought human nature would take care of everything in the end. Someone would break, someone would talk, maybe even Larry Digger would finally put the pieces together.

But year had passed into year, and everyone did absolutely nothing. Told nothing, asked nothing, remembered nothing, learned nothing. Everyone got away with it.

He had had enough. Now he was taking matters into his own hands. Starting with the list – the complete compilation of the crimes committed by each.

The crime of not telling. The crime of not knowing. The crime of not remembering. The crime of unconditional love. The crime of unrelenting cowardice.

The crime of never being enough of a man.

Then there came the worst crime, a crime so big, he could not come up with a name that could capture its full nature. It was hypocrisy and greed and selfishness all rolled into one. It was taking what other people had simply because they had it. It was heartlessness and it was worse – it was ruining people's lives and not losing a moment of sleep.

It was the one Real Sin, for he had often thought that the true heart of the devil was contempt.

He had not come up with the price for this sin. It needed to be special, it needed to be simple, and it needed to be horrible.

He returned to what he did have. Candles and feathers and ancient art. A child's toy and a child's dress. Cow tongues and pig hearts and a bushel of apples. An object that bobbed in a glass jar and was so gruesome, not even he could stand the sight.

A phone number.

His preparations were complete.

Time for the opening gift. He studied his list. He studied his pile. He made his decision: Melanie. Melanie, who had actually found happiness as the Stokeses' other daughter. Melanie, who, in all these years, had never done him the favor of remembering.

He got out his butcher's knife. He sharpened the blade.
He was ready.
Do you know the perfect crime?
I do.

6

Sunday was a beautiful day, bright spring sun, gaily chirping birds. Melanie woke up to discover herself on the camelback sofa with waiter David Reese peering down at her. She sat up in a hurry.

'What the hell are you doing in my living room?'

'My job. What the hell are you doing sleeping here?'

'None of your business!' Melanie blinked owlishly. It was bright. Too bright. And noisy too. Screeching cars, shouting pedestrians, honking horns. She suddenly had a bad feeling.

'What time is it?'

'One-thirty.'

'*Oh, my God.*' Melanie never slept past eight. Never. And now it was all coming back to her. The scene with Larry Digger, David Reese carrying her home, the bad dream, the long night in front of Meagan Stokes's portrait. And now David Reese again, still smelling like Old Spice and rattling her nerves.

He'd traded in his white waiter's tux for an old Red Sox T-shirt and jeans. In daylight she saw that he had brown hair with hints of red. Deep brown eyes with hints of green. A face closer to forty than thirty, weather-beaten and hawkish. Intense, she thought immediately.

He took a couple of steps away from her, and she noticed a limp. He winced but covered up by pressing his lips into a thin line.

'I take it you're here for work,' she said finally.

'We're dismantling the juice carts. It's a laugh a minute.'

'I'm sure it is. Now, is there something in particular that dragged you out into the living room?'

'Tools. Harry was in charge and all he brought was a ball peen hammer. Not too bright, Harry.'

She said briskly, 'The tool kit is in the utility closet in the kitchen. Go look there.'

David merely stuck his hands in his back pockets. 'We searched the kitchen area already. No tool kit. Nice collection of lightbulbs though.'

'Oh.' She frowned. 'Well, my father might have taken it out for something. Go ask him.'

'Can't. Dr Stokes left first thing this morning.'

'What about María?'

'That the maid? Haven't seen her.'

'Well, maybe my mother knows what my father did with it.'

'Mrs Stokes is gone too. She didn't want to be late for her spa.'

'Oh, I forgot.' Sunday was AA day. Her mother wouldn't be home until at least five. Which meant it really was up to Melanie to find the missing tool kit.

She rose to her feet, but David didn't seem to be in the mood to move. In fact, he appeared to have something on his mind.

She looked at him curiously.

He asked abruptly, 'How are you?'

'Fine.'

'Spending the night on the couch?'

'It's a very comfortable sofa.'

'With a clear view of Meagan's portrait?'

'I came for the sofa, not the view.'

'Uh-huh,' he said. 'Just because a man showed up last night and alleged that the murderer of Meagan Stokes was really your father. That your adoptive parents aren't as good or kind as you believe—'

'Oh, my God, you heard everything!' She had thought he'd arrived only toward the end. She hadn't realized . . . He'd never said . . .

She jabbed a finger at his chest. 'How dare you! You stood there and *eavesdropped* on my life. What the hell did you think you were doing?'

'Checking to see if you were all right—'

'Dammit, *why did you follow me last night?*'

David shook his head, his voice ringing with disdain. 'You walked out the door in the middle of your own party with some suspicious man administering a death grip to your arm, and you have to ask why I followed? Chrissakes, you looked like you were setting yourself up to get killed!'

'I can take care of myself.'

'Lady, go tell that to my shoes.'

Melanie flushed. Shit, she had thrown up on him. It was hard to argue with that. Before she could summon some smart retort anyway, just for pride's sake, he said, 'I got a job to do. When you find the tools, yell for Harry.'

'Fine.'

'Fine.'

He headed down the hall and Melanie thought good riddance. It was late. She needed to get on with her day. Then a fresh thought struck her and made her call him back. 'Wait!'

Halfway down the hall, David halted grudgingly, giving her an impatient stare.

'Since . . . since you did hear everything . . .'

'Uh-huh.'

'What . . . what did you think of Larry Digger?'

'I think he's probably a drunk,' David said matter-of-factly.

She breathed easier. Yes, this was the opinion she wanted – assurances that Larry Digger was full of shit. 'It's a preposterous story.'

'Lot of holes, like you said.'

'Really.' She waved her hand dismissively. 'No parents in their right mind would give the child of their daughter's murderer a home. That's outrageous.'

David nodded again, but now his gaze was hooded and hard to read.

'He's probably just after money,' she said. 'Thank you, Mr Reese. I'll get those tools to you shortly.'

'There was one interesting thing he did bring up,' David said.

Melanie paled. 'What?'

'Why now? If it's all about money, why didn't Larry Digger approach you or your parents years ago?'

Melanie suddenly had a chill. She rubbed her arms to chase it away. 'It could have taken him a long time to come up with a story. Or maybe he didn't need money before.'

'The phone call's interesting too. Why say that he'd traced the tip to your house? Why add that particular detail?'

Melanie couldn't answer. Would Larry Digger really try to be exact if he simply wanted money? Cons could be elaborate. But why now? Not earlier, when she would have been more vulnerable, more interested in the past.

She was still churning the questions over in her mind when David said, 'I could help you with this.'

'Pardon?'

'I used to be a policeman, all right? I got arthritis. Took me off the force, but I still have contacts. If you want, I could check out Larry Digger.'

The limp, the twinges of pain he tried to hide, must be from the arthritis. And his having been a cop would explain why he had followed her last night. Everything about Larry Digger would have triggered his instincts. So he had followed and looked out for her.

Melanie found herself warming toward David Reese. But then she shook her head. 'It's okay, I can take care of it.'

'With all due respect, what do you know about a man like Larry Digger?'

'Well, for starters, I know I can check his story about the anonymous tip by looking through our phone bills.'

David narrowed his eyes. 'What about a full background search?'

'I'll call his employer. Newspapers in Texas.'

'Know how many newspapers there are in Texas?'

Melanie smiled at him sweetly. 'Then I'd better get right on it, shouldn't I?'

315

'Don't give an inch, huh? Don't ever ask for help?'

'Welcome to the Stokeses, Mr Reese. We take care of our own.'

'Yeah?' David gave her a hard stare. 'Then why, when some tired old reporter was dragging you out of your own home, was a waiter the only one who noticed? What do you think of that, Miss Stokes?'

Melanie didn't have an answer.

Two cups of coffee later, alone in the dining room, Melanie watched the afternoon sun sift through lace curtains as she picked on a blueberry muffin.

'Maybe you had to see them in Texas with their two kids, one so sweet, everyone loved her, and one already so troubled, half the moms on the block wouldn't let him play with their children. I'm getting the impression, Miss Holmes, there's a helluva lot about your family you just plain don't know.'

Why didn't she know more about Meagan Stokes or her family's life in Texas? In spite of her bold words to both Larry Digger and David Reese, that fact was beginning to trouble Melanie.

She'd always assumed that the subject of Meagan was too painful for her parents to discuss. Also, it was probably not a topic of conversation they wanted to share with their adopted daughter. In spite of what people liked to say, families with adopted children had different dynamics. The beginning was not natural or smooth, but held a closer analogy to dating – everyone wore their nicest clothes, practiced their best manners, and tried not to do anything that would make them look too foolish. Then came the honeymoon phase, when parent and child could do no wrong, since everyone was just so gosh darn happy to have one another. Then, if the adoption was successful, the family finally eased into the fifty-years-of-marriage stage. Comfortable, well-adapted, knowing each family member's strengths and weaknesses, and loving them anyway.

Melanie liked to think her family had achieved that final stage of familial nirvana, but now she had to wonder. If they were so comfortable with one another, why hadn't they ever spoken of Meagan? Why hadn't Melanie asked? Even if it had been painful once, it had been *twenty years* ago. Surely after two decades . . .

It's the past, she told herself firmly. It shouldn't matter.

But now she was no longer certain. Larry Digger's insinuations were taking root. The reporter was starting to win.

Melanie gave up on the muffin. She crossed the hall into her father's study, where she was immediately greeted by the sight of books piled everywhere. On the cherry-wood desk, on the red leather swivel chair, and on the floor.

Apparently, while she'd been out dealing with Larry Digger, the literacy ball had turned into quite a success. She should catalogue the books that afternoon, prepare them for inventory by the rare-book dealer on Boylston Street. There was a lot of work to get done.

Melanie opened up the mahogany file cabinet and looked for a file marked Nynex. The good news was that her predictably anal father did keep the phone records each month. The bad news was that they had not yet received the new bill covering three weeks ago. Tomorrow she would call and request an early copy of the bill.

That would take care of Larry Digger.

But what about her own past? Why *hadn't* her parents pressed to find out more? In the beginning they had probably been scared. If they found her real parents, those parents could potentially take her away from them. But it had been twenty years and they had never once asked her if she had remembered anything. They had never even asked her if she wanted to pursue things further. What about hypnosis or regression therapy or things like that? Surely her father, as a doctor, had thought about it.

But nothing was ever said, and Melanie was left with the uncomfortable thought that for all the closeness in her family, there was a strange, unspoken rule. Don't push too hard, don't say too much. Don't look back.

'*I'm getting the impression, Miss Holmes, there's a helluva lot about your family you just plain don't know.*'

And if you told them the same, she thought bluntly, what would they say? She was no better, she liked her privacy too. She'd never told her family the details of what went on with William. She'd never talked about the perfect first date, when he'd taken her walking along the Charles and they had discussed greedily, almost feverishly, what it was like to grow up knowing you'd been abandoned by your birth parents. She'd never talked about the weekend three months later, the perfect weekend when they had made love until four in the morning. Later, getting dressed, her body all languid and flushed from sex, Melanie had spotted the lace bra stuffed beneath the mattress, the bra that wasn't her own. She'd gone home knowing her engagement would have to end but never mentioning a word of it to her parents. When the deed was finally done, she'd simply told them it hadn't worked out. No more, no less. Her parents seemed to understand, though she could tell her father was hurt. William had been his idea, after all.

No one spoke of it again, and Melanie liked it that way.

She had her past, her parents had their past. The more she thought of it, the less she found it sinister and the more she considered it basic human nature. Little secrets, little moments of privacy. That was all. Just because people needed their space didn't mean they'd conspired to adopt the daughter of a killer. That was absurd.

Larry Digger was absurd.

Tomorrow she'd get the phone bill. It would reveal no calls to Texas. Then they could all get on with their lives.

And the voids? The little girl's voice and cries to go home?

Melanie didn't have an easy answer for that one. She was twenty-nine years old. She liked her work, enjoyed her community, loved her family. Did she really care about where she came from anymore?

Was there ever a point in your life when you didn't?

Melanie sighed. She wasn't going to get much done in her current state of mind. What she needed was a good jog.

She went upstairs, her footsteps slowing as she saw her bedroom door. It was ajar; she could see the reflection of tiny flickering lights on the wood panel. Then the smell hit her. Gardenias, thick and cloying.

Melanie didn't own anything that smelled like gardenias.

Something . . . something was beginning to stir again. Shadows shifting in her mind. Ripples in the void.

She pushed open her door. Her bed came into view. She'd left it rumpled in the middle of the night. Now the yellow sheets were drawn up, the handmade blue and purple quilt perfectly smooth. Melanie's bed was never made.

'María?' she whispered.

No answer.

Her gaze fell to the foot of her bed.

And all of a sudden the images exploded.

Little girl holding the red wooden pony. Little girl on the floor of the crude wood cabin, clutching her favorite toy to her chest.

'I want to go home,' she whimpered.

'Give me the toy, sweetheart. If you give me the toy . . .'

'I want to go home.'

'Meagan, stop pouting.'

'P-p-please?'

'GIVE ME THE PONY.'

'I want to go home, I want to go home, I want to go HOME. No. No, no. NOOOOO!!!!'

Melanie ran into the hall. She was crying, falling to her knees, pressing her forehead against the floor, trying to get the images to go away. She didn't want to know. She didn't want to see.

Then she inhaled the scent of gardenias again, and the pictures resumed rolling.

Vaguely she heard footsteps pounding up the stairs.

'Hello? I thought I heard a cry . . . Melanie!'

She couldn't get her head up. She couldn't tell David Reese to stay away. It wasn't his business. No one's business but hers.

She lay there with her head pressed against the floor and distorted pictures flashed like lightbulbs in her mind.

Meagan, pony, cabin. Meagan, pony, cabin.

Who is in the doorway? Who is standing in the doorway?

What am I doing here?

I don't want to know, I don't want to know . . .

'Oh, God,' David said.

Melanie looked up. He was staring into her room with an expression on his face she couldn't read. Maybe it was shock. Maybe it was pity.

She had to turn away, and then she whispered, 'Don't let my parents see. My brother . . . my brother will know what to do.'

She closed her eyes again.

Who is in the doorway? Who is standing in the doorway?

I don't want to know . . .

7

Brian Stokes had always known he was destined for a difficult life. From earliest memory, his moods had been cynical and bleak. His childhood was defined by endless gray nights, his father always working at the hospital while his mother sat stiffly on the sofa, regal in her loneliness. Sometimes Brian would play little games, cuddling up to his mother, giving her his most charming grin until she would finally smile and pull him into her sweet-smelling embrace. Other nights he was cruel, smashing vases and furniture, running screaming through the house until his mother would break down into tears, sobbing and crying and begging to know why he hated her so much.

At the age of six he didn't have an answer. He didn't know why he made his mother laugh or why he made his mother cry. He was mostly aware of a sense of guilt and insecurity. That something in the household just wasn't right. They would all hate him in the end, he thought. His father, his mother, his baby sister, Meagan . . .

Probably the only person he'd been good to in his life was Melanie, and lately he'd been mean even to her. He'd ignored her phone calls and other overtures. He'd removed himself to his South Boston condo, where he could hone his self-loathing to a razor-sharp edge.

Three months ago he'd lain in bed, wondering why he didn't just slit his wrists, then had thought of Meagan. Precious, beautiful Meagan. The way she used to hold out her arms and beg for piggybacks. The nights he used to run to her room just to watch her sleep, to keep her safe though he hadn't known from what. Not until it was too late.

Meagan, Meagan, I am so sorry.

He'd gotten out a box of razors.

And then he'd thought of Melanie. The way she'd looked the first time he'd seen her, the way she'd thrown her arms around him, the way she had loved him, simply loved him.

Melanie had brought life back into the Stokes family, and Brian could not fail her. If he didn't want to live for himself, then he would have to live for her.

He'd joined a support group. He was learning that he carried too much rage. He was learning that he had 'conflicted' views of his family and 'issues with real intimacy.' He was learning he needed to figure out once and for all who he wanted to be. Not what his father wanted, not what his family wanted, but what he wanted.

Brian Stokes needed to learn to love himself. And he was realizing more and more that had less to do with his confusion about being a homosexual and more to do with his guilt over his baby sister's death. Twenty-five years later all those days in Texas were suddenly haunting him with a vengeance. Some nights he'd wake up in a cold sweat. Other times he'd wake up screaming.

Then there was the night Brian dreamed his own parents' death, and it made him happy. These days he did not trust himself to go home.

Then this morning, Jamie O'Donnell had called. Melanie was looking too pale, too worn around the edges, Jamie said flatly. She'd had a migraine last night and she had migraines only under extreme stress. Did Brian know what the hell was going on?

He didn't. He was concerned.

Then he got the call after two P.M. Some man who wouldn't give his name curtly stating that Melanie needed him. Brian didn't argue. He ignored his father's specific declaration that Brian Stokes was no longer welcome at Beacon Street and ran through two red lights in his haste to get there.

He still wasn't prepared for the scene in Melanie's room. He took one look at the old red wooden pony and the altar of lit votive candles and said, 'Don't let Mom see that.'

'Are you kidding? For God's sake, get in here and shut the door.'

Brian entered the bedroom and shut the door. His sister stood across the room, still wearing pajamas though it was extremely late in the day. Her arms were wrapped around her waist. Tears stained her cheeks. The sight of her so obviously frightened undid him. Melanie was never frightened. Never.

'Melanie—' He took an automatic step toward her, then hesitated. She looked unsure of him, conscious of the gulf that had grown between them. That was fair, he decided. He was standing in this room and he was unsure.

Another awkward moment passed. She finally broke the silence.

'Brian, meet David Reese.' She pointed to the only other person in the room, who was moving around with purpose. 'David Reese is a former police officer,' she explained. 'He has contacts—'

'Former police officer?'

'Arthritis,' David said curtly. Brian nodded; he'd noticed the limp. 'I called in a friend, an active detective, someone who knows how to be discreet. Your sister is real hung up on being discreet.'

Melanie was looking at Brian questioningly. He finally nodded his approval. He didn't know what he thought of David Reese, but he didn't know what else to do. He'd never seen anything like this before, and he didn't have any connections in law enforcement.

'Jesus Christ, what *is* this?' Brian finally burst out. 'I mean . . . who would? How? Why?'

'Don't know yet,' the ex-cop said. 'We'll start with the what, which is forty-four votive candles scented with gardenias. One red wooden pony, a scrap of old blue fabric, some bloodstains. Note the arrangement of the candles. Someone's sending a message.'

Brian turned slightly and gazed at the arrangement straight on. Shit. The flickering candles spelled one word. Meagan.

A distant memory returned to Brian. Baby Meagan on the floor. Brian grabbing her doll and ripping it apart. Meagan crying, not understanding. Brian shaking the stuffing all over the floor. '*You gotta be tough, Meagan, you gotta be tough.*'

The distance between them yawned again.

'I got up in the middle of the night,' Melanie said quietly. 'I went downstairs. When I came back up . . . well, here it was.'

'You were up in the middle of the night?' Brian asked sharply. 'Melanie, it's been years . . .'

'Do you sleepwalk?' David Reese asked her.

But Melanie was gazing at Brian, and in her eyes he saw what he'd been most afraid of: hurt. He'd hurt her. When Melanie got up in the middle of the night, Brian was supposed to be there for her. He was the one who always woke up, always followed her downstairs to keep guard as she stared at Meagan's portrait. He was her older brother. It was his job.

'I don't sleepwalk,' she said after a while. 'Sometimes, I'm just . . . restless.'

'Melanie . . .'

'Later, Brian. Much later.'

David Reese cleared his throat, forcing their attention back to him. 'Your mother could return home at any time, so we gotta get working here.' Without waiting for an answer, he continued brusquely. 'Let's start with the horse. It's the one from the oil portrait downstairs, isn't it? Meagan's horse.'

'The chipped ear,' Brian murmured. 'I did that. I threw it against the fireplace. I was . . . angry. She had it the day she was kidnapped, but it was never recovered. At the time the police said Russell Lee kept it as a – what did they call it? – as a trophy.'

'You never saw the horse again? Not even when they arrested Holmes?'

'No. Never.'

'And the fabric?'

'I don't know.' Brian studied it for a moment, not touching it but looking down at it. 'It could be from her dress,' he decided at last. 'It's blue. But that was a long time ago, you know, and it's so . . . stained now.'

'Was she found with her dress on?'

Brian glanced at his sister, hesitating. 'Wrapped in a blanket.'

David nodded. Meagan had been found in *only* the blanket.

'How did someone get in?' Melanie interjected finally. 'We have an alarm system.'

'Was it set?' David demanded.

'Of course it was set!' She looked at him dryly. 'Come on, you're dealing with a family who knows exactly what can go wrong. You'd better believe my father sets the alarm each night.'

'Huh.' David mulled this over for a minute. 'Who stayed the night?'

'Myself, of course,' Melanie said. 'Mom and Dad. María, the live-in. Also, we'd planned for Ann Margaret, my boss and friend from the Red Cross Center, to stay in the guest room – it's a long drive back to Dedham that late at night. I imagine that she did, but we'd have to ask María to be sure.'

'Does your dad search the house before setting the alarm?'

'Why would he do that?'

'You had three hundred people in your house last night. Any one of them could've slipped unnoticed upstairs, and—'

'And simply waited,' she finished for him.

'Shit,' Brian said.

'There's got to be a connection between Larry Digger and this,' Melanie said. 'Maybe he sneaked in after we spoke. Maybe he found this stuff when he was following Russell Lee Holmes.'

David shook his head. 'Too subtle. How could a man dressed like him – smelling like him – slip unnoticed upstairs?'

'He got into the house the first time—'

'Wait a second!' Brian broke in. 'Larry Digger? The reporter from Texas? Larry Digger was at *our house* last night?'

His sister smiled thinly, smiled tiredly, and then she told him.

Brian sat through the whole story stony-faced. He thought he should have a reaction. He didn't. The best he could come up with, staring at forty-four candles arranged in his dead sister's name, was fatalism. Texas was already back in his dreams, already messing with his mind. They couldn't move on, that was the problem. None of them had ever learned to move on, and now Russell Lee Holmes was going to get them in the end. Had they really thought something as simple as death could conquer a man like Russell Lee Holmes?

'Brian?' Melanie asked quietly. 'Brian, are you okay?'

He touched his cheeks. Shit, he was crying. 'And you didn't even call and tell me,' he whispered.

'I called you today.'

'Things have changed that much, have they, Mel?'

She looked at the floor. 'You were the one who went away, Brian. You were the one who decided to hate all of us.'

She was right. Brian wanted to take her hand, squeeze it gently, remind her of the old times. He couldn't.

'Forget about Larry Digger,' he declared rashly. 'I'll take care of everything, Mel. I promise.'

'No! That's not what I want, Brian. I can handle the situation.'

'There is no situation! Larry Digger was a sleazy half-rate journalist then, and he's a sleazy half-rate journalist now. You are not the daughter of Russell Lee Holmes, and I will not tolerate someone approaching my baby sister with this kind of bullshit. This has nothing to do with you, Mel, nor should it.'

Melanie's eyes turned hard. '*Nothing* to do with me? *Why?* Because I'm not a real Stokes? Because even after twenty years you still treat me like a guest—'

'Dammit, that's not what I meant. You know me better than that, Mel.'

'No, I don't anymore! So you'd better explain what you meant, Brian, because as far as I'm concerned, all developments, attacks, and threats on our family – on *my* family – have everything to do with me!'

'It does not,' he roared back. 'With all due respect, you weren't part of this family when Meagan was kidnapped. Do you know that BOLO means Be On the Look Out for? Do you know that local postal companies will deliver hundreds of thousands of copies of a missing child flyer for free? That major airlines will carry them to airports all across the United States?

'*Do you know* how it feels to deliver ransom money and then just wait? Or what it's like when the police stop talking about recovery and show up with cadaver dogs? Or even better, what it's like to go to a morgue viewing room to identify the remains of a child? You don't, Mel. You don't know, because Meagan had nothing to do with you and that's the way we want to keep it!'

'Too late,' she said crisply.

His sister stormed away from him toward David Reese. He was the older brother, dammit. He should be allowed to protect his sister if he wanted to. *And he did not want Melanie involved with Meagan.*

'It gets worse, Brian,' his sister said. 'I'm seeing Meagan Stokes, and I don't think the images are dreams.

'I think I'm finally remembering, Brian,' she told him quietly. 'And what I'm remembering is the last days of Meagan Stokes's life. When she was kept in a wood cabin. When she clutched her favorite wooden toy. When she still believed she would get to go home alive.

'And there's only one way I could know that, Brian – if I was also there. If I was with her. If I was *Russell Lee Holmes's daughter.* I'm sorry, but I think Larry Digger just might be right.'

Brian suddenly started to laugh.

'Of course, of course,' he heard himself gasp. 'Evil never dies. It just becomes part of the family. Welcome to the real Stokes family, Mel. Welcome *home.*'

8

A pager went off. Brian returned the call, then announced he had to go to the 'goddamn' hospital to see a 'goddamn' patient. David took that to mean that he was still a little bit upset.

David and Melanie walked him down to the front door. Brian was muttering that everything was screwed, Melanie was murmuring that everything would be all right, and David was wondering when Chenney was going to show up. They'd just gotten Brian out the door with promises to keep him posted and blood oaths not to mention anything to his mother, when Chenney came trotting up the stone steps, juggling four heavy evidence kits and looking wired for action.

'You need to change,' David stated brusquely to Melanie.

Melanie nodded, looking subdued. The exchange with her brother had obviously taken its toll, robbing her eyes of the fierce spark that had entertained David just hours before and leaving her looking bruised. Tough day for Melanie Stokes.

'I'll grab some clothes, change in the guest room,' she murmured.

David's voice came out gentler this time, almost soft. 'Well, sure. We won't be up for a few minutes anyway. You know. Take your time.'

He shrugged a bit, feeling awkward now for no good reason. Chenney was staring at him in disbelief, while Melanie flashed him a grateful smile that unnerved him a bit more. He wasn't that prickly, was he? He had manners. He'd even been raised to hold doors, pull out chairs, and chew with his mouth closed. He could be charming.

He scowled. He was losing focus.

Melanie disappeared upstairs; he turned to Chenney.

'What am I doing?' the rookie said in a rush. 'What do I say? What's my cover? Do I need a badge?'

Christ, where did the academy get these kids?

'Chenney, you're passing as a cop. Use your real name and, for God's sake, real procedure when bagging the crime scene. Got it?'

Chenney nodded. 'Got gloves, got bags, got finger-printing kit, got vacuum. It'll be clean.'

'You're golden.'

'That's all? That's all I'm doing?'

'I know, it's not like the full-color brochure. You'll get used to it.'

'I don't understand what this has to do with healthcare fraud,' Chenney mumbled.

'That's why they pay us the big bucks.'

'Lairmore know about this?'

David stiffened. 'Not yet.'

Chenney looked at him squarely, showing the first real spark of intelligence that David had seen. 'He's not going to like this. Your position is becoming involved, now you have me running around impersonating a police officer, and none of this seems directly pertinent to the case. If this blows up . . .'

'I'll be sure to say none of it was your idea.'

'That's not what I meant,' Chenney protested, appearing honestly injured.

'Whatever. Upstairs, Chenney. We need to finish before the parents come home.'

'Why?'

'Work now, debrief later. That's the drill.'

David led the way up the stairs, knowing the kid was right about Lairmore and feeling even more tense. He needed to get Melanie talking about her family, particularly Dr Harper Stokes. He needed to start tying this stuff together in a nice, clean case analysis.

Behind him Chenney lugged the heavy vacuum cleaner and fingerprint kit. 'Well, if they're paying us the big bucks, why can't he afford a personality?'

Things smoothed out upstairs. David had to give the junior agent some credit. At the first sight of the altar with the now-extinguished candles and child's toy, Chenney settled right down, donning a pair of latex gloves and looking all business. By the time Melanie walked into the room clad in a nubby wool sweater and ripped-up jeans, he'd already started documenting the scene.

David made the introductions. He was aware of how young and fresh Melanie looked with her un-made-up face and clipped-back long blond hair. They caught Chenney up on the situation. He took a lot of notes, then they took a little field trip across the hall to Brian's room.

It seemed very dark, decorated in shades of forest green and deep burgundy. Brian hadn't lived in the house for ten years, but the big captain's bed carried the clear imprint of someone having sat on it.

'So the subject sneaked up here after the party, made himself comfortable, and waited for lights-out,' Chenney deduced, then ruined the professional image by looking to David for approval.

'You're the cop,' David reminded him with a bit of an edge. The rookie stood straighter, then looked at Melanie Stokes.

'Well, at least he wasn't trying to hurt you, ma'am,' Chenney said.

Melanie was startled. 'What do you mean?'

'If the guy was here all night, he could've come into your room anytime. But he waited until you left to make his move. Just look at the candles. Votives are good for about eight hours. They were nearly burned down to the base by two P.M. So we can assume he entered your room after four A.M. – when you had vacated the premises.'

'Thank God for small favors,' Melanie muttered.

Chenney shrugged. 'The perp definitely didn't want to have a confrontation with you, ma'am. At this stage, he just wants to do his little displays. So you figure he sets it up while you're gone. Forty-four candles, the horse, the fabric. I'd say it took him at least an hour. So maybe he departed the house around six—'

'He couldn't depart,' Melanie interrupted with a shake of her head. 'That would set off the alarm system. Any opening of an external door, whether from the inside or outside, activates the system.'

They all looked back at the bed. 'So he set it up, lit it, and went back into hiding,' Chenney said.

'Waited until someone got up and deactivated the alarm.' David filled in the picture in his head and liked none of it. 'Then he just sauntered out the front door.'

Melanie was looking shaken again.

'There's another consideration,' David mused out loud. 'The subject was already in the house. He/she/it could've chosen any room for the display, but he went to Melanie's room, not her parents'. I'd say that makes you the target, not them.'

Chenney seemed a bit taken aback by this blunt disclosure, but Melanie simply nodded. David hadn't thought she'd mind. From what he could tell, Melanie worried a lot more about her family than she did about herself.

'It's getting late,' she said at last. 'I'm surprised my mother hasn't come home as it is, so . . .'

Chenney took that as his cue. 'I'm gonna need an hour or so. You start thinking of a plausible excuse for my presence, I'll start working through the scene.'

'Thank you, Detective.'

'No problem, ma'am!' Chenney left.

Melanie and David were suddenly alone. She crossed over to the large bank of windows, looking out over the Public Garden, where the cherry trees were in bloom and young lovers were walking hand in hand. With the fading sunlight catching her profile in shadows, she looked at once vulnerable and pensive. She looked lovely, David thought. Then he shook the thought away.

'We have a few more questions. You ready?'

'I made my brother cry.'

'He's a big boy. He'll get over it.'

'There is a shrine to a murdered child in my bedroom.' Her voice rose a notch. 'It's in my head, David. Dear God, it's in my head.'

She pressed her forehead against the window, as if the contact might chase the images from her mind. She took a deep breath, then another. Her hands were shaking. David watched her weather the storm and didn't do a thing. After another minute she pushed herself away from the window and squared her shoulders.

'Well,' she said briskly in that tone of voice he'd come to know well, 'what's done is done. Detective Chenney will take care of everything and let me know what he learns?'

'He'll send the evidence to the lab. See what comes up.'

'Like fingerprints, right?'

David arched a brow. 'There won't be any fingerprints.'

'You don't know that—'

'Come on. This guy spent hours staging a scene. He's not going to make a mistake that obvious.'

She looked deflated for a minute, then bounced back stubbornly. 'Well, the detective will learn something.'

'Maybe. Look, if you want answers, let's start right now. Lab work isn't everything. Most info comes from interviews, and we have just a few questions for you.'

'You mean Detective Chenney has some questions.'

'Sure, you can wait for Chenney, but he's gonna be in your room for at least an hour. By then it'll be six, your mom could be home anytime . . . I don't think you want to have this discussion then.'

'Oh.'

David pushed the advantage, not wanting to give her time to think. He strode forward brusquely. 'We'll start with the standard drill. Get through it all in a jiffy.'

Melanie still looked hesitant, but in the face of his curt determination, she finally nodded.

'We got a pretty good idea how the person got into the house,' David stated. 'Now we need to know why and we need to know who.'

Melanie shook her head. 'Other than Larry Digger, I have no idea who would connect my family with Russell Lee Holmes after all these years. My parents don't discuss Texas much.'

'Why not?'

She gave him an exasperated look. 'I imagine because it hurts like hell.'

'Twenty years later?'

'Hey, Mr Reese, when your daughter is kidnapped and murdered, you can get over it in twenty years. My parents haven't.'

David grunted sufficiently chastised. 'Fine. Let's start with the altar, then

– it tells us a few things. For starters, this was an intimate act. Not just in your house, but in your bedroom. Not just in your bedroom, but at the foot of your bed. Then there are the items themselves. The pony and scrap of fabric that appear to be from Meagan Stokes, the first daughter. That seems to be a very deliberate slight against you, the second daughter. Then there is the use of scented candles. Do you know much about the olfactory senses, Melanie?'

'You mean other than to smell?'

'There's more to it than that. The sense of smell is directly wired to the limbic system, which is one of the oldest parts of the brain. An important part of the brain too. It's the part that helps you love and helps you hate. And'—he looked her in the eye—'it helps you *remember*. Exposing someone to a strong fragrance linked with a certain time or place is one of the most effective ways to evoke a memory.'

He saw that Melanie grasped his meaning immediately, because she sat down hard on her brother's bed. 'The gardenias, the flashbacks. It was planned, wasn't it? Shit. It was *exactly* what the person wanted.' She suddenly sounded furious. 'I will not be manipulated in my own house. I will not!'

David regarded her curiously. 'Did you say flashbacks? As in more than one?'

She looked cornered. 'Fine, fine, I'd been starting to see little things. Not much. A black void, a little girl's voice. Nothing substantial.'

'Uh-huh. When did it start?'

'I don't know. Six months ago.'

'Six months ago. Of course.'

'Of course?' Now she was scowling. 'What do you mean, of course?'

'I mean six months ago was right about when your brother announced he was gay. Six months ago was right about when Boston's most perfect family started to fall apart.'

'How do you know all this?'

'Caterers gossip,' David said offhandedly. 'Think about it. The Stokeses move to Boston, adopt a new daughter, and for the next twenty years life is just grand, right? Then comes Brian's announcement and things around here start to fall apart. Your father isn't speaking to him, right? Your mom is distraught over the situation and starts drinking again. And you suddenly start having flashbacks.'

'It's not like that,' Melanie protested. 'One son coming out of the closet doesn't cause all that.'

'Maybe not in most families,' David said matter-of-factly, 'but in a family with the Stokeses' history? Come on. You're a bright person, you can put this together. Your mom and dad have already lost one child. You have already lost a whole family. When your father practically disowned your brother, don't you think it hit all the same triggers? Didn't you and your mom and probably your dear old dad start to feel like everything was falling apart again? Old insecurities, old fears . . .'

Melanie looked haggard. 'Jesus Christ,' she whispered. 'Why don't you just fucking cut out my *heart?*'

'I'm not trying to cut out your heart. But someone is trying to get you to remember.'

'*But why? Who?*'

'Someone who knows what happened to Meagan,' David said. 'Someone who could recover the toy she had with her the day she died. Someone who knows enough about you, Melanie, to realize that the scent of gardenias would trigger a memory of Meagan.'

Slowly Melanie nodded, following his train of thought. 'Larry Digger,' she said savagely.

'No. Larry Digger doesn't know shit. If he had proof, he'd already have written his story and sold it to the highest bidder. He wouldn't be messing around with votive candles.'

'Russell Lee Holmes?'

'Executed and buried. Come on, you know who I'm talking about.'

She was immediately defensive. 'No, I don't! My family has nothing to do with this!'

'Larry Digger alleged that there was more to them than met the eye—'

'Larry Digger is a drunk!'

'Larry Digger knew them in Texas, which is more than you can say. Why was your father in the ER the night you were found? How is it that you can remember Meagan Stokes? You gotta have some connection with Russell Lee Holmes, and according to Larry Digger, your parents know that. Your parents didn't adopt a random little girl, but the daughter of Russell Lee Holmes.'

'*That makes no sense!*' She'd risen off the bed. She was nearly nose to nose with him now, and neither one of them backed down. 'My parents loved Meagan! They would not adopt the daughter of her killer!'

'*How do you know?* How *do you know?*'

He thought she was going to hit him. Maybe she thought she would too. The air had gotten too hot and too tense. Then her gaze dropped to his lips, and the air became tangled with other, unwanted emotions. Her lips thinned. She drew back furiously.

She said in a cold voice, 'All right, David. Let's do it your way. My beloved parents really conspired to adopt Russell Lee Holmes's daughter. Maybe in a sick and twisted way they felt he owed them a child. I was drugged so I wouldn't remember where I had come from, and my father stayed in the ER, and *voilà*, everything went as planned. I got my new family, they got a new daughter. Everyone's happy. Right?'

'Yeah?' David was suspicious. He didn't think for a moment that she believed any of this.

'Then,' she continued relentlessly, 'twenty years later, they magically do what? Suddenly announce the truth? Or even more outlandish, plant an altar in my room in the dim hope that I'll remember and figure out who I am and what they did? Come on! First you're saying they conspired to adopt a killer's daughter, then you're saying they conspired to reveal their conspiracy. Give me a break.'

David frowned. He said grudgingly, 'That doesn't make much sense.'

'No kidding.'

'Unless—'

'No!'

'Unless it's just one person trying to reveal the truth. Think about it. Six months ago this whole family was turned upside down. There's a rift between your father and brother, a rift between your mother and father, and even tension between you and Brian. It seems to me that family loyalties and dynamics are shifting as we speak. Maybe that's the key. Maybe the last six months finally gave someone incentive to come forward with the truth of what happened all those years ago. It gave someone incentive to call Larry Digger. How about that?'

Melanie looked mutinous, she didn't have a quick retort. The last six months had changed everything, and she knew it.

'We should run through all your family members,' David said.

'No.'

'You do it with me or you do it with Chenney. Your mom could come home at any time.'

'You know, you can be a real son of a bitch.'

'Yeah, but I'm the son of a bitch who noticed when you were being dragged out of your own house by a seedy-looking stranger. And I'm the son of a bitch who came running when you passed out in your hallway. Not too bad for a son of a bitch.'

His voice sounded more belligerent than he'd intended, and Melanie turned away, looking troubled.

'No,' she said at last. 'You're not bad.'

He shifted from foot to foot, slightly mollified but also self-conscious. Popularity wasn't in his job description. Results were.

'We're a very private family,' Melanie said after a moment. 'My parents have suffered enough. I don't want you to think of them as criminals.'

'I know, I promise to bear that in mind. Now let's start with your father and brother. It's common knowledge that your father has cut your brother from his will. Maybe that made your brother angry, gave him an ax to grind?'

'Brian would not do this. I won't pretend that he and my father have an easy relationship, but if Brian wanted to hurt Dad, he wouldn't use Meagan Stokes – it hurts *him* too much. You saw Brian when he walked into my room. He's even more shaken up than I am. For God's sake, he just saw his little sister's toy from twenty-five years ago. The little sister I know he thinks he failed.'

'He's an intense guy.'

'David, his younger sister was *kidnapped* and *murdered*. He was nine when it happened, which is old enough to understand what's going on but not old enough to do anything about it. Meagan's murder was a traumatic chapter for this family, okay? If they were all perfectly well adjusted after that, *then* they would be odd.'

David didn't comment. Personally he thought the Stokeses were a little beyond odd.

'What about your mom? Sounds like she didn't care for Harper's dismissal of her son. She resumed drinking—'

'Yes, which is a problem that started when Meagan was kidnapped! Meagan's murder hurt her worst of all, David. She's still trying to get her life together. There are nights I find her downstairs, touching that oil painting as if she can feel her daughter's cheek. There are weeks you can just see it in her eyes, that endless wondering of what she could've done differently or how she could've been a better mother. I know there are times she looks at Brian and me and is simply terrified. Don't pin this on my mother, David. She's already paid her dues.'

'Seems the whole family's always looking out for her, a grown woman.'

'We love her! We worry about her!'

'And you don't love your dad?'

'That's different. My father is capable of taking care of himself. My mom—'

'Is troubled,' David supplied flatly. 'Depression, drinking. Anxiety attacks. Patricia Stokes may be a great mom, even a loving mom, but she's not going to win a most stable person of the year award.'

'My mom is a good woman, David. She loves us very much. She just . . . she just misses Meagan.'

David arched a brow, holding Melanie's stare for a long time. So she meant what she said about her mom. David continued down the list.

'And your father? How does he feel about all this?'

'Oh, Dad is Dad.' For the first time, Melanie relaxed. 'He's a man's man, laughs when he feels like crying and would never go to the hospital himself unless the bone was protruding from the skin. Takes his role as a family provider very seriously and is positively intense about looking after our welfare – you know, the man's turf. You probably understand him better than I do.'

'Does that include him disinheriting his own son?'

Melanie grimaced. 'Dad's not good at admitting he's wrong.' Then in a level voice, she said, 'My father is a fixer, David. He fixes people, he fixes problems. Unfortunately, it's hard to fix emotions like grief and remorse and guilt. I know there are many things about my mom he just doesn't get, and Brian's announcement caught him totally off guard. In my father's world, your firstborn son *does not* announce he's gay. He just needs time to accept it. He really is a good father.'

'He prides himself on his income.'

'He does very well.'

'Does he support the family too well?'

Melanie frowned. 'I don't know what you mean.'

David made a show of shrugging. 'What does a Beacon Street town house like this cost? One million? Two million? And then there are the furnishings, the cars, the vacation homes. The artwork, the antiques, the silk curtains. Awfully nice life even for a doctor.'

Melanie's guard was up now, her face shuttering. 'I don't think my family's finances are relevant.'

'Most crimes are committed for love or money. And Larry Digger commented that in Texas, your parents lived better than they should've.'

'Larry Digger is jealous,' Melanie said firmly. 'That's all.'

David waited, let the silence drag out. She didn't budge. Who knew what the Stokeses were really like? But David decided they had a helluva daughter in Melanie.

Or was that toughness courtesy of Russell Lee Holmes?

Shit. David had just given himself the chills.

He returned to the Stokes family members and friends. 'What about William Sheffield? How did you two meet?'

'He works with my father. Dad brought him home for dinner.' Her lips curved dryly. 'Oh, the conspiracy.'

'I heard him talk last night,' David commented. 'Sounded like he was from Texas, which makes a lot of former Texans in this house.'

'Sure. That's why he and Dad originally started talking. Two expatriate Texans in a Boston hospital. If you ever moved to Texas, you'd probably befriend the first Bostonian you met.'

'Yeah, but would I marry him off to my daughter?'

Melanie stiffened. 'That's ancient history.'

'Does that mean he ended it and not you?'

'The ending,' she said in a steely voice, 'was mutual.'

'How mutual?'

'I found him in bed with another woman, David. That pretty much seemed a hint.'

David was startled. Weasely William Sheffield cheating on Melanie Stokes? Christ, he was even dumber than he looked.

'Bitter?' he asked more intently than he'd wanted.

'Nope. The ending was inevitable. We never should have become engaged to begin with.'

'Then why did you?'

She shrugged. 'He was an orphan too. I thought that gave us something in common. Or maybe it was simply because he asked, and if you've been abandoned once, having someone say they want to spend the rest of their life with you is irresistible. We both realized our mistake soon enough, particularly once he started telling me I didn't count as an orphan.'

'Huh?'

'I had been adopted,' Melanie said dryly. 'I had been given a family, a rich family. After a while it became clear that that ate away at William. Of the two of us, he'd been more wronged by life, so life, and especially me, owed him something. Let's just say I'm not very good at owing anyone anything.'

David almost smiled. Yeah, he couldn't see her answering to William Sheffield's beck and call. The stupid little prick. He cleared his throat, struggling once more to get back to business.

'Did anything seem off to you with William last night? Did he seem pale? Preoccupied?'

'He works hard.'

'Any harder than usual lately?'

Melanie took a minute to answer. 'I don't think so. Generally he's assisting my dad and my dad's workload hasn't been heavier than usual. But I did think William looked as if something was bothering him.'

'Then maybe we should check into it.'

'He doesn't have anything to do with Meagan—'

'He's involved with your family now. He spends time in your house. Maybe he learned something from your father and hopes to capitalize on it.'

Melanie sighed, but she didn't argue. He could tell that doubts were beginning to wear her down.

'What about the Irishman who was here? Jamie . . . Jamie . . .'

'Jamie O'Donnell. He's my godfather. He wouldn't have anything to do with this.'

'What's his connection to the family?'

'He and my parents go way back in Texas. They've known each other for forty years. He was best man at their wedding.'

'He's business partners with your father?'

'They do some deals every now and then. To tell you the truth, I'm not sure how Dad and Jamie first met. I know Dad's parents lived in the suburbs, whereas Jamie pretty much grew up alone – in cardboard houses, he likes to say. They both built themselves up, Jamie as a businessman, my father as a surgeon. I think they respect that about each other.'

'And O'Donnell knew Meagan?'

Melanie's gaze softened. She clearly had a soft spot for her godfather. 'The situation with Meagan broke Jamie's heart. You want to know why my parents love him so much? Because he viewed the bodies for them, David. He told me about it once. When a child is missing, someone in the family must take responsibility for viewing bodies that match the age and general description of the child. That was Jamie's job. He went from morgue to morgue all over the South, viewing remains of four-year-old girls that fit the description of Meagan Stokes.

'He told me once that he still sometimes dreams of all those little girls, wondering if they ever did find a home, ever ended up buried by people who loved them. Or if they all just ended up in potter's field with only a number for identification. Sometimes I think losing Meagan affected him even more than my father. Most likely they just show it differently.'

'And the other woman?' David pressed. 'She came up with him, wearing nurses' whites.'

'Oh, that's Ann Margaret.'

'She spent last night here too, you thought.'

'Yes. She's my boss at the Dedham Red Cross Donor Center. I've been volunteering there for ten years now, so she's come to know all of us.'

'Sounded to me like she had a Texas drawl too.'

Melanie rolled her eyes. 'Yes, she lived there decades ago. She's been in Boston forever now. And that's totally random. She wouldn't even have been in the house if I hadn't started volunteering at the Red Cross Center.'

'Huh. I kind of thought there was something between her and your godfather.'

Melanie faltered. 'Actually I kind of thought there might be something too. They've seen each other many times at the various functions I've organized. They could be *involved*, I guess. I don't see how it's anyone's business but theirs.'

'Why wouldn't they tell you if they were seeing each other? What do they have to hide?'

Melanie shook her head. 'Since when does exercising the right to privacy mean hiding something? Ann Margaret of all people has nothing to do with Meagan Stokes. None of the Stokeses even knew her back then. Let's not be too ridiculous here.'

'Are we being so ridiculous?' David asked bluntly. 'What exactly was the situation with Meagan Stokes? Do we really know what happened twenty-five years ago? There is the red wooden pony in your room along with a scrap of fabric that, according to your own brother, shouldn't still exist. Larry Digger is claiming he got phone calls about Russell Lee Holmes from your own house. *You* are starting to remember Meagan's last days. Seems to me that everything right now is up for grabs. Whatever we thought we knew about Meagan Stokes, we don't. Whatever you thought you knew about your past, you don't. And whatever you thought you knew about your friends and family, you don't.'

Melanie's face had paled.

'Someone's leaving a murdered girl's toy in your room. Now is not a good time for assumptions.'

'Do you believe in ghosts, David?'

'Not at all.'

'What about fate or karma or reincarnation?'

'Nope.'

'Do you believe in anything?'

David shrugged. It wasn't a question he'd contemplated in a long time, but he found he did have an answer. 'I believe Shoeless Joe Jackson should be in the Baseball Hall of Fame. And I believe what's going on here has nothing to do with Russell Lee Holmes. Instead, it has to do with your family. And you, Melanie, need to be careful.'

She smiled wanly, her finger plucking at the edge of her brother's bedspread. She looked like she was going to say something, then she just closed her mouth.

After a moment she looked up at him. 'Thank you.'

David hadn't expected gratitude. He didn't know what to say. He studied the floorboards. Old. Thick. Solid. Chenney was probably almost done, he thought. They should both get moving. He remained standing where he was. Then his hip locked up on him and he had to shift position, rubbing absently at his lower back.

'Does it bother you a lot?'

'What?' he asked distractedly. *Someone tips the Bureau about Dr Stokes committing healthcare fraud, while also tipping Larry Digger that Dr Stokes's adopted daughter might be the child of Russell Lee Holmes. What's the connection?*

You get what you deserve.

So which one of the players feels that the Stokeses had not gotten what they deserved? And why do something about that now?

'The arthritis.'

'Huh?'

'You're rubbing your back.'

'Oh.' He immediately dropped his hand to his side; he hadn't realized what he'd been doing. 'I don't know.' He shrugged self-consciously beneath her steady stare. 'Some days are fine, some aren't.'

'Are there things you can do for it? Exercises, medication, ice packs?'

'Sometimes.'

'But it cost you a dream, didn't it?' she asked softly. 'Of being a cop.'

He was not prepared for her to come so close to the truth, and then he was struck with something akin to claustrophobia. He felt the sudden need for space. The sudden need to retreat. Hell, to hide in some deep, dark cave where no one could look at him too closely and see that he was afraid these days. He was afraid of everything – his future, his health, his career – and it shamed him.

'I need to get back to work,' he stated emphatically. 'You know caterers. Job's never done.'

'Sure.' Melanie rose off the bed. The room was nearly pitch black now. Night had fallen on them so quietly, they hadn't even thought to turn on the light.

She was regarding him steadily. Too steadily, he thought.

'David,' she said. 'Would you be willing to do one last favor for me?'

'I thought you didn't accept favors—'

'I want to see Larry Digger. First thing tomorrow.'

Shit. David shook his head. 'He's not a reputable source.'

'But he's the best I have and you're the one who just said I have to start questioning everything. I want to speak with him, David. If need be, I'll go alone.' She spoke in that level tone of voice again. That non-negotiable tone of voice.

'All right,' he said heavily. 'Ten A.M., out front.'

Melanie smiled. She crossed the room. She brushed his hand briefly, a small token of gratitude, nothing more. Then she disappeared down the hall, where the sickly scent of gardenias remained thick.

9

By seven P.M., David and Chenney had cleared out of the Stokes household and headed in their separate directions. Night had fallen, warm and lush, a perfect spring night in a city that weathered such long, cold winters, it knew how to appreciate spring. So far David was spending his beautiful spring evening parked on the east end of Storrow Drive, waiting for petrified tourists to battle their way to Faneuil Hall. He'd headed home to shower and change his clothes. There, he'd consulted Shoeless Joe, who didn't have any stellar advice. Shoeless was best at baseball and dry cleaning. Healthcare fraud, cool blondes, and twenty-five-year-old homicide cases were out of his league.

David had decided he'd do more research on the Stokes case at the office. Not that he had big plans on a Sunday night.

Not that he could get the image of Melanie Stokes out of his head.

Now his twenty-minute commute was turning into a sixty-minute Boston marathon. On Storrow Drive, the out-of-towners were paralyzed, hunched over their steering wheels with the nervous looks of scared jackrabbits. The taxi drivers, on the other hand, were cutting in front of every Tom, Dick, and Harry, blaring their horns and turning the four-lane traffic jam into an even larger snarl. They didn't call Boston drivers assholes for nothing.

David should just get an apartment downtown. Agents made good money, and it wasn't like he had a wife, two point two kids, and a black Lab to support. He could get a decent place on Beacon Hill. Save himself a commute that most Boston drivers turned into blood sport. Be able to walk to work whenever he wanted. End up in the office all the time.

Oh, yeah, that's why he stayed in the 'burbs. 'Cause otherwise he'd be living in One Center Plaza.

A cab that was twisted across two lanes finally decided to give up one and they all eked forward.

The in-line skaters were still out, joggers too. In the pedestrian river park that ran along Storrow Drive, soft city lights illuminated college students in cut-off shorts playing night Frisbee while J. Crew-clad yuppies walked overbred golden retrievers. Behind them flowed the Charles River, which hosted Harvard's crew team as well as many other pollutants. One year, former governor Weld dove into that water during the election race to prove it really wasn't as bad as it looked. They'd be testing him for cancer for years to come.

It took Riggs another twenty minutes to make it the last two miles to the office. Another lovely evening spent driving Boston-style.

The FBI occupied floors four through eight of One Center Plaza in downtown Boston. Visitors got to enter at the midpoint – floor six – and the healthcare fraud squad got to go straight to the penthouse suite on floor eight. The view wasn't half bad.

David walked through a sprawling turquoise space that had been remodeled more times than most agents could count. City lights glimmered through the wall of windows, the only illumination in the dark, empty space. Caseloads must be very light right now if David was the only one burning the Sunday-night oil.

He finally came upon the wall panel, snapped on the overhead lights, and blinked owlishly. Dark, crouching beasts metamorphosed into tongue-shaped desks rimming the perimeter. Hunched backs became computers sitting on top of desks. Monsters transformed into piles and piles of subpoenaed records. Welcome to Riggs's world.

He headed to his desk, automatically avoiding the holes in the floor where pipes had been ripped out in yet another expansion of the limited office space. The Boston field agency was among the fastest growing in the Bureau, having gone from old-fashioned offices to compact cubicles to the current one big turquoise-carpeted space where they could all openly and freely exchange ideas. On slow days agents amused themselves by dropping pennies down the old pipe holes and listening for the landing.

His message light was blinking. David popped up the receiver while rubbing his lower back and dialed in. He had received two messages since checking in at noon.

'David, it's your dad. Thought we'd see you today. Guess you had to work. Steven's team did well, won four-three though not through any help from his pitchers. Bad batch this year, he's at his wits' end. I think he should make his starter sit out altogether – the boy's a head case – and bring up this freshman, James, who has a superb arm. They'd pay for it this year, of course, but in the long run—'

David fast-forwarded through that message until he came to the second one, left by Chenney.

'I'm at the lab. They're PO'd we didn't use an official forensics team and snarling that we probably contaminated evidence. I told them to get over it. Hey, we gotta catch up. I'm confused as hell 'bout the case. Plus, I never told you about my morning surveillance. I started at the hospital watching Sheffield like you said, but he left with the flu. Then I spotted Harper leaving the hospital with Jamie O'Donnell. . . . I did try to call you first,

Riggs, but you never turn on your beeper, you know. So I made a judgment call, whether you like it or not. Call me when you get a chance.'

Shit. David would bet money that Chenney had gone with Harper and Jamie O'Donnell because watching them seemed more exciting than sitting outside the house of a sick man. The kid still had so much to learn about what constituted 'real' work. It's not the glamour, Chenney. It's results.

He dialed the rookie's cell phone. No answer, so David left a message to meet him at the Massachusetts Rifle Association at ten P.M. That gave David ninety minutes to kill.

He requested a copy of the Meagan Stokes case file from the Bureau field office in Houston. Then he called the Houston PD for a copy of their case file as well, as they had had primary jurisdiction. The Bureau case file would focus on the kidnapping aspects and any profiling if it was done. The PD case file would have the nitty-gritty, including the evidence trail. David wanted to find out if Meagan's red pony really had been recovered and had been sitting in an evidence locker all these years. That still wouldn't explain the full magnitude of the scrap of blue fabric, but David hadn't even told Melanie or Brian about that yet. He wanted more time to think about it himself.

David journeyed down to the Bureau's research center and booted up the machine. It took a few minutes for the computer to warm to life. He used the time to prop up his leg awkwardly on the desk and bend over it to stretch out his back. The Bureau had research agents who could look up anything an investigator was willing to write down on the forms, but David liked to do it all himself. Skimming files, narrowing searches, made him think. And sometimes the information he needed in the end wasn't what he'd started out looking for, but what he'd found along the way.

He started his search with Melanie Stokes. September 1977 was the magic date. The *Boston Globe* carried a small human-interest story on a girl, approximately nine years old, who'd mysteriously appeared in City General's ER. The girl had been drugged with morphine and had suffered an allergic reaction. To date, no one had come forward to claim her.

A week later, he found a small update. The girl, who could identify herself only as Daddy's Girl, had been given a clean bill of health and turned over to Child Services. She was in good condition and showed no evidence of abuse. She had no memory, however, and an extensive picture campaign had yet to yield results. A black and white newspaper photo appeared beside the text. Young Melanie Stokes looked plump, her hair was straight and limp, her features undistinguished. Certainly not the most beautiful little girl in the world, but there was something about her face – something yearning, he thought.

A few months later a significantly larger story appeared. 'Real-Life Orphan Annie Finds Daddy Warbucks.' The *Boston Globe* carried a feature article on 'Daddy's Girl' going home with Dr Harper Stokes and his wife,

Patricia, who had started formal adoption proceedings. A social worker reported that Patricia had given Daddy's Girl a new name.

'The little girl asked Mrs Stokes why she didn't have a name. And Mrs Stokes said of course she had a name, they just had to find it. Then our little sweet-heart asked Mrs Stokes if she'd give her a name. Mrs Stokes became very teary-eyed. It was really touching. She said, "How about Melanie? It's the most beautiful name I know, and you're the most beautiful girl I know." Ever since, Daddy's Girl will reply only to Melanie so that's what we call her. I think it's really great that she finally has a name. Of course, now she wants a birthday.'

Another source, who wished to remain anonymous, disagreed that Melanie was such a great name. 'Personally I think it's a little sick. I mean, it's just so close to Meagan. It can't be healthy for any of them.'

David thought that woman might have a point. Melanie got a name, Melanie got a great house, but she'd also gotten to grow up literally staring at a portrait of the first daughter. The murdered daughter.

Seemed spooky to him.

David switched to looking up Russell Lee Holmes. Here he found some information that was much more interesting. He read so intently, he was almost late to his meeting with Chenney.

'Why are we meeting at a gun club?' Chenney asked a little after ten as David unlocked the doors leading to the cavernous indoor shooting range.

'Because I think better shooting.' David shoved the doors open and they walked into the empty room.

'Oh,' Chenney said as if he understood. The kid was addicted to weight lifting, so maybe he did.

David had been a member of the MRA all his life, first through his father, then on his own. For most of his childhood, if he wasn't playing ball, he was sitting in the club lounge, listening to cops talk about the screwed-up legal system and the age-old rule to shoot first and ask questions later because it was 'better to be tried by twelve than buried by six.' By the time David was sixteen, he knew almost as much about police procedure as he did baseball. And he was just about as good with a gun. In the club's trophy case were a few plaques and honors that were his own.

'Holy shit!' Chenney said as David opened his gun case and started unpacking. 'They told me your father was a custom pistolsmith, but I had no idea! Can I hold it?'

David shrugged, handing over his Beretta to Chenney while he dug out eye gear and a box of bullets. People had been shooting earlier in the day. The air was acrid with the lingering odor of gunpowder and oil.

'My God, this sucker has radioactive sights! I've only ever heard of them.'

'My dad,' David said simply, and pulled on his goggles. His gun was a souped-up hot rod these days, ready for a shootout with several AK-47-

carrying drug lords. He kept telling his father the customization wasn't necessary. His father kept saying 'uhhuh' and doing it anyway.

'Oh, my God, you have . . . everything!' Chenney was twisting the gun all around in his hand. 'Check out this hand-metal checkering. Forty lines per inch. Gorgeous! He had to use a magnifying glass for that, huh?'

'Dad's an artist.'

'Ambidextrous safety, dehorned, custom sights. Sheesh.' Chenney pointed it down the shooting gallery and dry-fired. 'Five-pound trigger, accurized, I'd bet. Now, that's a gun.' Chenney handed over the semi-automatic with reluctance. He gazed at his own Glock with the expression men got in rest rooms when they realized the other guy's penis was bigger than theirs.

Then he seemed to get over it. Both of them slid out clips and loaded. 'Oh, yeah,' Chenney said after a second, 'your brother was a pitcher, right?'

David stilled, then pushed the third bullet in. 'Yep.'

'I know he's a coach now, but he must still keep his arm up.'

'Yep.'

'Cool. I belong to a league, see. Bunch of guys, mostly feebies, bureaucrats. I'll tell you honestly, our pitcher sucks. If we don't find a new guy, we're in for a rough summer. So I heard from Margie that your brother was this great pitcher. Pitched for UMass, led them to a division title. He must be pretty damn good – that's a tight division.'

David focused on getting the fourth bullet in. 'It's a tight division.'

'We want him!' Chenney exclaimed. 'He's just what we need – a ringer to strike out a bunch of over-the-hill cops who spend way too much time at Dunkin' Donuts. Will you set it up for me?'

'A ringer, huh?'

'Yeah, the best pitching arm around.'

'Sure,' David said. 'I'll set it up for you.'

David finished loading his clip. He slid it into place. He swallowed twice. Then he peered down his finely accurized sights and said, 'You left Sheffield today, didn't you? This morning. You abandoned your target for a more interesting party on the block.'

Chenney flushed. 'You'll be glad I did. I overheard some interesting stuff.'

'Chenney, don't ever leave your target. If you're following someone, you're following someone—'

'He was sick! I watched him stagger out of the hospital looking pale as a sheet. Shivering and sweating. He told the unit head he had the flu and they sent him packing. Trust me, once Sheffield made it home, he wasn't going anywhere.'

'Chenney,' David repeated firmly, 'don't ever leave your target. If you're following someone, you're following someone. Got it?'

'All right, all right.' Chenney put on his goggles, not looking happy at the dressing-down. By mutual agreement they set up the first targets the customary twenty-one feet back and ran through one clip.

The rookie shot aggressively. He lined up fast, fired fast, and screwed his face into an ugly expression that would've made Clint Eastwood proud. He put most of his bullets through the inner two rings, but when they brought in their targets, Chenney could barely pass a pencil through the single hole made by David's twelve shots.

'Twenty-one feet's too easy,' he grumbled. 'Average distance for a law enforcement conflict, my ass. You ought to be prepared for anything.'

David shrugged, tearing down the paper and clipping up fresh targets. 'So what did you learn, Chenney? What made Harper Stokes and Jamie O'Donnell seem so interesting?'

'Hey, something's up,' the rookie stated immediately. 'I followed Harper and Jamie O'Donnell to some ritzy golf course. With a bit of encouragement, management let me hang out at the bar, where I could hear everything O'Donnell and Harper were saying over their lemonades. Harper, he downs an entire glass without saying a word. Then he simply turns to O'Donnell and out of the blue states, "I got a note." '

'A note?'

'Yeah, he told O'Donnell he found it on his car this morning. It said, "You get what you deserve." He looked O'Donnell right in the eye, rather intense like, and asked him what he thought it might be about.

'O'Donnell looked at him for a minute, also real quiet, like they were having some kind of subtle pissing war, then said, "Annie's been getting phone calls." '

' "Annie's been getting phone calls?" '

'Yeah. He said someone's been calling this Annie person and hanging up. She assumed it was some prankster. But you could tell they weren't so sure. Then Harper said, "Larry Digger's in town." O'Donnell seemed a little surprised. He shrugged. And Harper said, "Josh gave me a call. Apparently Digger contacted him with a few questions about Melanie. Why do think that is?" O'Donnell just shrugged. He said, "Who knows why Digger does anything? Maybe the whiskey dried up in Texas."

'Harper grunted. You could tell he didn't buy it. But he didn't say anything more and neither did O'Donnell. A few minutes later they started playing golf, but I'll tell you, something wasn't right. They were tense and pretty quiet the whole nine holes. And they played *fierce*, you know what I mean? This wasn't two guys out having a leisurely Sunday tee time. They went after each other as if out for blood. Really weird relationship there. I don't think they're going to donate kidneys to each other anytime soon. Do you think this has something to do with the scene in Miss Stokes's room this afternoon?'

David looked at the rookie incredulously. 'Yeah. I think it does.'

'I knew it.' Chenney beamed. 'So it's not such a bad idea that I left

Sheffield, huh? I learned something in the end. I did.' He faltered. 'So what did I learn, Riggs? What the hell is going on?'

'Ain't that the question?' David muttered. He sent the targets back fifty feet, donned his earplugs and goggles, and started firing. After a moment Chenney joined him.

Spent shells gathered on the shooting bench and bounced on the floor. Nine-millimeters spit a little fire from the side vents, making it hot, making it loud. Chenney went after his target like hell on wheels. David was slow and rhythmic, performing a motion he'd done so many thousands of times, it was as natural to him as breathing.

Harper and Jamie O'Donnell. And Annie? Ann Margaret, most likely. Ann Margaret getting phone calls, though Melanie swears she has no real ties to the family. So what's the thread through all of this? What the hell is going on?

It came to him as he cleared the last shot. He ejected his clip, opened the chamber, and set his gun down with the barrel still pointed along the shooters alley. As he drew off his plastic goggles, Chenney retrieved the targets.

At fifty feet David's cluster had expanded slightly within the bull's-eye. Chenney's was getting ragged, his last few shots dropping down due to his haste. While Chenney scowled, David calmly filled him in on the events from last night, starting with Larry Digger and the reporter's allegation that Melanie Stokes was the daughter of Russell Lee Holmes.

'That's nuts,' Chenney declared at the end. 'No parents are going to knowingly adopt the kid of a murderer. And even if they did, there's no motive for them to alert someone to that fact now. You know what I think it is?'

'I'm almost afraid to ask.'

'A smear campaign!'

'A smear campaign?'

'Yeah, against Harper Stokes. Think about it. First we get an anonymous tip that Harper is committing healthcare fraud, allegedly inserting pacemakers into healthy people. So far we haven't found evidence of anything, so who knows? Then Larry Digger gets a call, allegedly from the Stokes house, that Harper's daughter is the child of a murderer. Harper Stokes has a bit of an arrogance rep and he's successful. Maybe some underling is out to get him, or a rival cardiac surgeon. They're striking Harper where it would hurt most – his reputation.'

'I don't think so.'

'Why not?'

'Because of Harper's reaction to the note. He didn't just dismiss it the way you would if it was some random thing you found on your windshield. Instead, he asks O'Donnell about it, and O'Donnell doesn't have anything to do with Harper as a surgeon. Then Harper's next words are that Larry Digger is in town – Harper himself is connecting the note to some petty journalist he knew twenty-five years ago. And how does O'Donnell react to all that? He comments that Annie is getting phone calls.'

'Who is Annie?'

'Ann Margaret, I believe. Melanie's boss at the Dedham Red Cross Donor Center.'

'What does she have to do with all this?'

'She's from Texas.'

'Texas?'

'It's the common denominator,' David said patiently. 'All these people are from Texas, and we know what happened in Texas.'

'We do?'

'Meagan Stokes, Chenney, four-year-old Meagan Stokes. That's what Harper Stokes and Jamie O'Donnell were talking about. Harper's first response: *Larry Digger is in town . . . asking about Melanie.* And O'Donnell trying to dismiss Digger but obviously not completely convinced himself as to what Digger is up to. Well, Larry Digger is in town looking for dirt about what happened twenty-five years ago. No matter which way you spin it, we come back to the homicide of a four-year-old girl.'

'But that's a closed case. They fried the guy. End of story.'

'So you'd think. But here's a news flash. I pulled up some information on Russell Lee Holmes before I came, and you know what? Good old Russell Lee was never *convicted* of murdering Meagan Stokes.'

'Huh?' Chenney was confused.

'Russell Lee was convicted of killing six children, but Meagan wasn't one of them. The police didn't have enough physical evidence to make the case. It was only later that he admitted to Meagan's killing, a confession he made to Huntsville beat reporter Larry Digger.'

'Shit. You don't think . . .'

'I don't know what to think yet. But I got a lot of questions about what happened to Meagan Stokes. And I have a lot of questions about exactly who is sending these little messages, and what it is the sender thinks everyone deserves.'

'We're beyond healthcare fraud, aren't we?' Chenney pressed. 'Meagan's toy, the scrap of fabric, the notes that these people need to get what they deserve. We're looking at homicide, aren't we? A twenty-five-year-old homicide.' Chenney didn't sound glum about this development but excited.

'Yeah,' David muttered with less enthusiasm. 'Maybe.'

He reloaded his gun, his mind still preoccupied. He got ready to shoot, and he said quietly, 'Did you notice anything weird about the scrap of blue fabric in Melanie's room, Chenney?'

'Not really. It was old and bloodstained. Probably twenty-five years old. The lab will sort it out.'

'The fabric probably is old,' David informed him. 'But that blood was not. As a matter of fact, I'd say the blood was about eight hours old.'

'Huh? That doesn't make any sense.'

David turned toward him, the hard lines of his face even harsher beneath the fluorescent lights. 'You ever play games, Chenney?'

'Yeah, baseball, basketball, football.'

'No, strategy games. Chess, bridge, hell, D&D.'

'Well, no.' The rookie looked bewildered. 'What does that have to do with anything?'

David turned back to the targets. 'We are in a game now, Chenney. The anonymous tipster, he dragged us in for some purpose only he knows about. Then he dragged Larry Digger in the same way. And now here we all are, players on the board, while he tosses the dice. Sends notes to some people, an altar to someone else, phones still others.'

'But why?'

'I don't know yet. Off the top of my head, I'd say something more happened twenty-five years ago. Something that affected a key group of people, something they've all done a great job of hiding. But this tipster, he's upset now, he's tired of the quiet. He wants everyone finally to get what they deserve. And he seems willing to go to great lengths to make sure it happens.'

Chenney pondered this in silence. 'Are we talking some kind of nut?'

'I don't know.'

'The altar, that seems to be the work of a nut.'

'Maybe. But why would a nut call the FBI? What would a fruitcake want with the Bureau?'

'A job,' Chenney said with a ghost of a smile. But then he sobered up again. 'Yeah, I don't like the call to the Bureau. The crazy ones want vengeance, not justice. You think this tipster really is telling the truth? That Harper Stokes is committing fraud, and he and his wife knowingly adopted the daughter of a serial killer?'

'I don't know.'

'Riggs, what the hell are we supposed to *do?*'

David donned his ear protection again, then the goggles. 'First thing tomorrow, pull all the files on William Sheffield, going back to Texas. Then do the same with Ann Margaret and Jamie O'Donnell. I want to know exactly how each person got involved with the Stokeses. I want to know exactly how or if they met Meagan Stokes and if they were questioned by the Houston police twenty-five years ago. I want to see *financials* going back as far as your little heart can imagine. You cover the friends and I'll do the same with the family. We shake the tree hard enough, something will fall out.

'And then we move on it.' David finally smiled, but it was savage and grim. 'I fucking hate games.'

He picked up his gun. Adopted the target pistol stance, sighted the red rings twenty-five yards away. His hand shook slightly; the 9mm was heavier than the .22 target pistol that earned him the NRA ranking of distinguished expert back in the days when everything he touched had turned to gold. Back in the days when there had been nothing young, virile David Riggs couldn't do.

He thought of Melanie Stokes again, the way she'd touched his hand.

He thought of Chenney, *So I heard from Margie that your brother was this great pitcher . . .*

He thought of the pain in his back that was slowly and steadily getting worse. He thought of the illness that had no cure.

He fired off three shots, fast and smooth. Chenney drew in the target. The single hole through the bull's-eye was nearly perfect.

'Shit!' Chenney said in awe.

David just turned away and began picking up the spent shells.

10

Eleven P.M. While David Riggs picked up spent shells in the shooting range, Melanie roamed the three stories of her home, looking for anything that might give her peace of mind. She'd opened all the windows on the third story and turned on a fan to air out the cloying scent of gardenias. She'd cleaned her room, hanging up clothes, tending her plants, straightening her drawers. She'd showered, letting the water pummel the tight muscles of her neck.

By the time she emerged from the bathroom, it was easy to believe the afternoon had never happened. The altar had been a figment of her imagination. The images in her head merely a particularly bad dream.

She was in her home. She was the beloved daughter of Patricia and Harper Stokes. Nothing could touch her.

Melanie sat on the edge of her bed and had a good cry.

She wasn't prone to sobbing. She hadn't cried when she'd ended her engagement with William. Tears embarrassed her, made her feel weak, and she didn't like that. She was strong, she was capable, she was in control of her life.

But tonight she cried hard. It finally dissolved the horrible knot in the pit of her stomach and eased the ache in her chest. It cleared her mind, and that allowed her to consider the afternoon objectively for the first time.

She discovered that she was frightened and rattled after all. She wasn't afraid of the altar or the person prone to such petty acts. She was frightened, however, of the consequences. What if she truly was the daughter of Russell Lee Holmes? If her father had dismissed a birth son for his sexual preferences, what in the world would he do to an adopted daughter who turned out to be the child of a killer?

She was not so strong and noble after all, Melanie decided. She wasn't keeping Digger's allegations from her parents to protect them. She was keeping them from her parents to protect *herself*. Because she had no intention of doing anything that might alienate her family. Because even at the age of twenty-nine, abandonment issues were a bitch.

Melanie finally trudged downstairs, entering the sterile world of the stainless steel kitchen and brewed herself a cup of chamomile tea. She added a bit of honey, a squeeze of lemon, then retreated to the dining room. The grandfather clock in the foyer chimed once to signal half past the hour.

Eleven-thirty P.M. Her mother should have been home hours ago. Her father too. David was right. Her family was fractured, her father disappearing more and more, her mother battling the gin, and her brother AWOL. Whom was she trying to kid? The Stokeses were a mess.

She thought to hell with it all, and headed for her father's study. The books were there. She needed to catalogue them. She should've done it hours before. She was being lazy and remiss. Now it was time to focus, time to get to work.

She pulled out a piece of paper from her father's desk and got busy. One book down, a hundred more to go. She got up, headed into the foyer, and checked the alarm. It was set and tested active.

She returned to the study, made it through five more books, then had to check the windows. The alarm system would tell her if any zones were trespassed, of course. But she had to make the inspection anyway before she could convince herself to return to the study.

She finished her chamomile tea and settled into work mode. Title, author, publisher, date of copyright. Number, catalogue, move on. Work was important, and she was good at her job.

Larry Digger. Why approach her now? What did he really want from her? A story of the year or a quick buck?

The altar in her room. Who would do such a thing? What message was being sent? That she wasn't Meagan Stokes? That she couldn't replace her parents' first child? She knew that well enough herself, thank you very much.

David Reese. Waiter, former cop. Fascinating hands. She'd noticed them earlier. Long, deft fingers. Broad, calloused palms. Hands you could depend on. A face, however, that needed to learn how to smile.

'What are you going to do, Mel?' she murmured to herself in the empty house. 'What are you going to do?'

She didn't know. When she'd first inhaled that scent of gardenias and the images had exploded in her mind, they had seemed so real, so genuine, that a part of her had thought, this is it, I am Russell Lee Holmes's child. But in the aftermath she found it easier to retreat behind doubts. There could be another explanation. Maybe she just had weird associations with gardenias. Maybe she was simply too susceptible to Larry Digger's innuendo.

But the altar in her room, with Meagan's toy, a bloody scrap of old fabric, and forty-four gardenia-scented candles arranged to spell a dead child's name . . .

Melanie didn't have an explanation for it. According to her brother, Meagan's toy should not still exist. According to her own desires, she should not be able to remember a shack inhabited by a murdered child.

According to her world, a trespasser should not wait in the bedroom across the hall from hers late at night, simply to mess with her mind.

But the altar existed. It was real. Someone was trying to send a message about something, and she had to take that seriously. She should ask questions of Larry Digger, she supposed. Do research on her own. See what the police found out. Maybe someone was just angry with her and her parents and trying to shake things up. She would have to get to the bottom of it, if not for her family's sake, then for her own.

The house security system sounded a warning chime. Melanie stilled, then heard the telltale beep of someone entering the entry code into the front alarm box. Another beep as the alarm was rearmed. Seconds later footsteps sounded down the hall, then her mother poked her head into the study.

Patricia wore a long, black wraparound coat and a pillbox hat. The makeup was smudged around her eyes, and she looked as if she'd had a very long day. Generally she returned from her AA meetings looking flushed and revitalized, armed with her twelve steps and ready to take on the world. Not tonight.

She stepped into the room with her fingers nervously fiddling with the top button of her wrap and her gaze studiously avoiding her daughter's.

'Hey,' Melanie said at last. 'You're home late.'

'Hi, sweetheart.' Her mother smiled belatedly, struggled harder with the top button of her coat, and finally got it undone. She draped the wrap over a pile of books by the door, plopped her hat on top of it, then finally crossed to Melanie for a brief kiss on the cheek. Her lips felt cool. Melanie caught the scent of stale cigarette smoke mingled with Chanel No. 5, and stiffened.

Her mother smelled as if she'd been in a bar.

Automatically, helplessly, she started searching for signs. The smell of mouthwash used to cover gin and tonic. A slight swaying. Overbright eyes, anxious chatter.

Her mother's hands were shaking, her expression tremulous. Other than that, Melanie couldn't be sure. It could be just one of those days for her mother, or it could be worse. In the past six months it had become so hard to tell.

Her mother pulled back, seeming to inspect the piles of books.

'Is your father already in bed?' she asked brightly.

'He's not home.'

Patricia frowned, picked up an old book. 'Well, he's out rather late for a Sunday. Probably checking up on some important patient.'

'Probably.'

Her mother set down that book. Picked up another. Her back remained to her daughter. 'How is your migraine, honey?'

'Fine.'

'Relaxing day?'

'Sure,' Melanie said quietly. 'Sure.'

Patricia turned. She dropped the book she was holding almost forcefully, almost angrily, and the sudden display of emotion sounded Melanie's alarm bells once more.

Patricia's chin was up. Her blue eyes were beginning to glow. She appeared defiant, and that made Melanie's heart sink. Oh, God, so she'd been out after all.

Her mother simply wasn't that strong. Her life had so many demons, so many dark moments . . .

And then Melanie found herself wondering why. It had been twenty-five years and yet she was still so troubled. *Just what had she done?*

'I'm not drunk,' her mother announced abruptly. 'Oh, don't bother to deny it, Melanie. I can see in your eyes that you think I've been drinking. Well, I haven't. It's just been . . . it's just been one of those days.'

'So you had only one drink instead of four?' Melanie's voice came out sharper than she intended. She bit her lip but couldn't call the words back.

'Sweetheart, I'm telling you, I didn't have a drink—'

'Then where have you been all day? It's nearly midnight!'

'I've been out.'

'Out where? Come on, Mom, out to what bar?'

Patricia drew herself up haughtily. 'I wasn't aware that I had to explain myself to my own child.'

'That's not what I meant—'

'Yes, it is. You're worried, and when you worry, you mother all of us. And we let you, don't we, Melanie? I've been thinking about that tonight. How much your father and I depend on you to take care of things. How much *I* depend on you. For God's sake, we let you work yourself to a point of vicious migraines. What kind of parents do that?'

Patricia crossed the room, taking Melanie's hands and looking at her with an urgency that confused Melanie, caught her off guard.

'Oh, God, Melanie,' her mother cried. 'If you could've seen yourself last night, having to be carried back into your own home by some stranger. You looked so pale, so fragile, and I realized for the first time what I'd been doing to you. I've been so lost in my own confusion, my own pain over Brian, I'd never thought about yours. You just seem so strong, I take it for granted. So I turn to you, pile it on. And you're such a good girl, you never complain. But it's not fair of me, and at my age I ought to know better. For chrissakes, when am I going to take care of myself?'

Melanie opened her mouth. She had the strange sensation of being in quicksand.

'I . . . I don't mind.'

'Well, you should.'

'Well, I don't. I honestly don't.'

'And I'm telling you that you should! Melanie . . .'

Patricia took a deep breath. For a moment she appeared impatient and almost furious. Then she looked frightened and, at last, fatalistic, as if something else had happened, something she wasn't prepared to share yet but they would all know about in the end.

Jesus Christ, what was this all about?

Patricia said more quietly, 'Melanie, have you ever had a turning point in your life? I know you're only twenty-nine, but have you ever felt yourself at a crossroads, when suddenly all of life was murky, and even though you can't see the landscape and you're not sure where you're going, you know you must take a step. And that this will be an important step. This will be The Step.'

Melanie thought of the past twenty-four hours. She said, 'Yes.'

'Good.' Her mother clutched her hands more tightly, her eyes beginning to burn again. 'I had a turning point today, Melanie. I've had them before – I'm fifty-eight years old after all – and to tell you the truth, I've blown all of them. Stepped the wrong way every single time. Gone back instead of forward. But I think I finally did it right, Melanie. Because I thought of you.'

'Mom?'

'I found myself in a bar tonight.'

'Oh, God, I knew it. Why? What happened?'

'It doesn't matter. I went to a bar. I contemplated ordering a drink. I was so rattled, I was thinking, why not? Once you've fallen off the wagon the first time, it just doesn't seem so far to fall. We all have our patterns, and this one's mine. When I'm frightened, I head for the booze. I'm over-whelmed, sad, depressed, I head for the bottle. But then I thought of you, Melanie. How you looked last night, flattened by a migraine and still not wanting to worry us. How much you take inside yourself when you shouldn't have to. How you love me even when I do all the silly things I do. How much you love all of us when I know there are times we are far from lovable.

'And I thought . . . I thought I couldn't have a drink and still face you. I just couldn't.' Patricia's voice grew soft. 'Melanie, do you even know how much I love you? How you are such a godsend to me? The last six months, you have held me together. I don't think I could've made it without you. I want you to know that. I want you to know, to really know, how much I care.'

Melanie couldn't speak. She held her mother's hand, feeling touched, but, heaven help her, also suspicious. Her mother never spoke like this. None of them did.

She was thinking of Larry Digger again, wondering if he had gone back on his word and approached her mother, if that was what had rattled Patricia Stokes. And then she was thinking how odd it was that they were having a conversation about how much they cared while both of them were purposefully keeping huge chunks of their day to themselves. It was like exchanging compliments on hairdos while wearing hats.

And then she wondered how much of the Stokes family was based upon that, lies of omission carrying back to the sunny days of Texas.

Her mother let go of Melanie's hands. She picked up a pile of books and set them on the floor. Now that she'd said what she wanted to say, the intensity had drained out of her face. She looked more settled. Whatever need she'd had, she'd fulfilled it, at least for then.

'Here,' she said firmly. 'Now that I've filled your head with too much stuff, let me help you. Your father's right – you're working too hard.'

'Mom?'

'Yes, darling?'

'I love you too.'

'Thank you,' Patricia whispered softly, and smiled back, looking happy. She picked up a book and got to work.

Thirty minutes later the front door banged open. The alarm chirped. Both women jumped, then flushed self-consciously, sharing a nervous laugh neither cared to explain. Harper came striding into his study in green hospital scrubs, one hand tucked behind his back, the second hiding a yawn. He halted and regarded them both curiously, clearly not expecting to find either awake.

'I thought I saw the light on. What are you two ladies still doing up?' He gave his wife a kiss on the cheek, then hugged his daughter. 'Sweetheart, feeling better?'

'Right as rain,' Melanie said. He checked her forehead and pulse anyway. After migraines, he always tended to her as if she were a patient.

'Better,' he finally declared, 'but you still need to take it easy. Here, maybe this will help. I was going to give these to you and your mom in the morning, but as my two favorite women are still up . . .'

Harper pulled out his hidden hand and produced a small bouquet of flowers and a box of chocolates. Four sunflowers, treated with purple dye until they were a rich magenta color. Very striking, and offered at only one of the more tony florists on Newbury Street. He handed them to Patricia and she flushed, giving her husband almost a shy glance.

Her father was definitely working hard at making up for past mistakes, Melanie thought approvingly. Not bad at all. She got a small box of champagne truffles. Teuscher. Flown in from Switzerland twice a week. She approved of that peace offering as well and promptly helped herself.

Her father pretended to check the pulse on her wrist again, then swiped a chocolate. She had to laugh. On impulse, she hugged her father again, and even more unexpectedly, he held the embrace.

'You should get upstairs,' he said after a minute, his voice a little gruff. 'You need rest, young lady.'

'Why don't we finish up tomorrow,' her mother said lightly. 'I can help you out in the evening, and we'll get through them in no time.'

Melanie was tired. But then she found herself thinking of her room again. Her room and the altar. Her room that had been entered in the dead of night while the rest of the house slept.

Melanie gazed longingly back at the books.

Her father would have none of it. Ever the fix-it man, he took her arm and led her and her mother upstairs.

Nighttime rituals came smoothly. Her father set the alarm from the second floor landing. Her mother kissed her cheek. Her father gave her a hug. Melanie murmured good night. Her father told her to sleep in. She said she had a meeting at ten. Her father said he had surgery at eleven, her mother commented she was due at the children's hospital to read at eleven as well. The beginning of a new week at the Stokes household.

Her parents disappeared inside their bedroom. Melanie just caught her father asking her mother how her day was. Patricia did not say anything about turning points. She simply said, Fine. And yours? Fine. She imagined them climbing into their separate sides of the bed, continuing the same polite conversation until both fell asleep.

Then she thought of David Reese and wondered if he would stick to his side of the bed. She doubted it. He struck her as the intense, silent type. Sex would be hot, slick, and fierce. Few words before and after, but what a ride in between. Something twisted low in her stomach, made her sigh. Yearning. Hunger. Pure sexual frustration.

She was lonely these days, she thought, and smiled wryly. Why else would she spend so much time trying to convince herself she had the perfect life?

Melanie reached the third floor. She inspected Brian's empty bedroom from the door. Tonight, no intruders lingered. Only then did she finally, reluctantly, go to bed.

Her dreams were the standard anxiety dreams. She was in her first year at Wellesley, sitting down to take a final exam and realizing at the last minute she'd forgotten to study. She didn't understand the questions. Oh, God, she couldn't even fill in her name.

Then she was in an elevator shaft plummeting down.

Then she was suddenly in the hospice where she'd stayed when she was nine years old, eagerly waiting for the Stokeses to take her away. Except this time they walked right past her. This time they picked up a new girl with perfect sausage curls and walked out the door.

No! No! she cried in her dream. *You're my family. My family!*

At the last minute, fourteen-year-old Brian Stokes looked at her. 'Did you honestly think you couldn't be replaced? Just ask Meagan.'

The hospice spiraled away. She ran through black voids, utterly lost, calling and calling for someone to see her, to tell her her name. She couldn't bear not to know her own name. And the blackness went on and on and on . . .

Suddenly she was cocooned in a warm embrace. Solid arms, low, gentle voice. *Shh, it's okay, love, it's okay. I'm here for you. I will always be here for you. Even if you never remember . . .*

Melanie stirred. In her sleep she whispered a name.

It was the closest to the truth she ever came until it was too late.

11

Monday morning Patricia watched her husband read the *Boston Globe*. After all these years, she knew exactly how Harper would read the paper – starting with the business section, where he would check his stocks and on a good day smile and on a bad day frown but never actually announce anything because he always kept the financials to himself. Then he would move on to the local section, first skimming it for any articles pertaining to himself or City General, then reading the articles in depth. After Boston news, he moved to national, then international, slowly expanding his circle of interest to include the things not immediately relevant to himself.

He had once told her that it was important to be well read on all subjects so you could make intelligent conversation at work. Though he'd never expanded upon that statement, she'd understood all the things that were left unsaid. Harper came from blue collar stock. People who did not debate national news or attend black-tie parties or hobnob with political movers or shakers. People whose biggest dream was someday landing a government job that would provide enough of a pension to support fishing in their old age.

Harper, of course, had dreamed big. From the very beginning he'd bought the right clothes, trimmed the calluses from his hands, and done his best to appear even more upper class than the people who were born into it. Even though he'd been a struggling med student, no one had questioned his roots.

Patricia suspected that Harper also thought this facade was important to her, because she'd grown up in the lap of Texas oil luxury. He would never have it be said that she married beneath her or that he provided less for her. Love and money were intrinsically tied in his mind.

Patricia respected that. She admired it. Harper fit the model of man she'd come to know so well: conservative, hardheaded, firm. She supposed that's why she loved him so much. No matter what he did, he was familiar to her. His shortcomings were her father's shortcomings, his strengths her father's strengths. His brand of caring, her father's brand of caring. There were never any surprises, and in her later years she appreciated that.

Once, when she'd been just a child, she'd thought marriage would be about roses and candlelight and never-ending romance. Her husband would always be dashing and passionate. She would always be beautiful and sweet sixteen. Life would be taken care of for her; she would never be lonely or frightened.

Of course marriage didn't work that way. Sometimes, on the bad days, when it required effort just to open her eyes and swing her legs out of bed, she wondered what she was still doing with Harper. What kind of woman stayed with a man who first pursued her with obsession and now hadn't touched her in years? What kind of woman stayed with a man who'd looked at her the way Harper had looked at her the day Meagan's body was identified, as if she was the worst form of life on earth, as if she'd done something even crueler than kill her own child?

On her strong days, however, she acknowledged that this was simply what marriage was about – perseverance. She and Harper had survived the grueling demands of a surgeon's career even as Harper's fellow residents divorced in a giant tidal wave. They had endured the loss of their child when the divorce rate for such couples was over seventy percent. Long after their friends had remarried and divorced for the second time, they were making the decision to adopt a little girl. They had raised their children together. Gotten them through college. Seen them ensconced in their chosen careers.

Their marriage may not be a honeymoon anymore. It may even be more about companionship – which she knew her children, even Melanie, didn't understand – but it was also about having a history. Knowing each other so well. Growing together. Accepting each other.

Weathering life together. Simply weathering it.

The past six months had certainly put that to the test. Since the scene with Brian, Patricia had found herself unhinged in ways she couldn't discuss with her husband, or even with Melanie. She would find herself lying in bed, listening to Harper's snores far away, and thinking of the bottles of gin that beckoned in the parlor, the sweet oblivion she often remembered as a lush, ecstatic dream. Other times she would find herself going downstairs and staring at Meagan's painting, beautiful, happy Meagan, who'd trusted her mother to banish the monsters that hid beneath the bed.

Then, in the brief period when she had given in to the lure of gin and tonic, she'd reached some new level of being permanently off kilter, where she would wake up at four A.M. and race to Brian's room, convinced he must be there though he hadn't lived at home since he was twenty-four. She would yank out drawers like a woman possessed, searching for old clothes she could hold against her and inhale the scent of her son's skin. And when she failed to find any trace of him still imprinted in the room, when it began to seem that Harper had wiped her firstborn child from the face of the earth, panic would rear its ugly head, and aided by alcohol, devour her alive.

Suddenly she would be desperate to find Meagan. *Meagan darling, where are you? Come home to Mommy. Please, come home.*

The cop would materialize beside her in Brian's darkened room. 'At least she didn't suffer, ma'am.'

Her head was cut off – she suffered!

Next, the blue-suited FBI agent would step through the window. 'There was nothing you could do, ma'am.'

I shouldn't have left her with Nana. Why did we hire so much help?

Finally, the burly sheriff would slide from beneath the bed, chewing a big plug of tobacco to cover the fact he'd just been ill. 'Well, ma'am, at least now you know. It's better to know.'

My baby is never coming home. My baby has no head. Would you look at what he did to her hands? Oh, God, Oh, God, why am I still alive? Why couldn't you just kill me? Please, please just kill me . . .

Curled up on her son's bed twenty-five years later, she would imagine herself sitting on the grass outside the woods where the cops were working. She would hear the buzz of the flies and smell the overripe scent of decay. She would open her mouth to scream and laugh instead. Just laugh, laugh, laugh.

'*It will get better, lass. Somehow, it will get better.*' Jamie had told her that.

But it had gotten worse. For the next five years her life simply spiraled away.

From pushing a new life from her body to picking out the tiny white coffin for a closed-casket funeral, because there wasn't enough left of her four-year-old daughter for a viewing. From active mom to screaming, raving lunatic, turning away from her son, refusing to acknowledge his existence because children just broke your heart. From dutiful wife to frozen, inconsolable human being, refusing Harper's tentative overtures, knowing he blamed her for what happened to their daughter, knowing that he was despite that making amends. Realizing she no longer cared.

A chill had moved over her, until she didn't belong to herself. She shut down, picked up the bottle of gin, and embraced the fog that blanketed her like the softest caress. She lived for the fog, she loved the fog. It was the best lover she'd ever had, and she fell graciously into its arms, smoothing it like a handful of rich soapsuds over her bare, aching breasts. She rolled languorously through the days, not thinking, not feeling, not existing, because then the pain would be too much.

Just kill me, just kill me. Why aren't I dead?

Her father had demanded she stop drinking. Her husband had checked her into a rehab ward, seeking as always a scientific solution to her emotional ills. None of it mattered. She hadn't cared what they thought, she hadn't cared what they wanted or that her son was turning into a somber, hard little man, incapable of smiling. She hadn't cared about anything.

Then Harper, dazed, overwhelmed, workaholic Harper, had done the unexpected. He'd moved them all to Boston, where images of Meagan could no longer torture her or Brian in the halls. And in a single defining moment, the kind of moment that gave her faith in him and hope for their marriage, Harper had brought her to see 'Daddy's girl.'

Patricia had taken one look at Melanie, small, earnest, blue-eyed Melanie, and everything in her had given way.

She fell in love again. The ice cracked, the fog receded. She wanted to hold this little girl so badly, it was a physical ache. She wanted to take care of her troubles, she wanted to tell her it would be all right. She wanted beyond all reason to keep her safe.

She loved little Melanie for being little Melanie. She loved the way she endured the unknown, the way she tried to make people smile. She was strong. She was spirited. She was earnest. She was everything Patricia had always wanted to be but had never quite managed. She was Patricia Stokes's hero.

For Melanie, Patricia had pulled herself together. For Melanie, she'd started to love Brian again, to give him the attention he desperately needed, to give him back his mother. For Melanie, she'd even started loving her husband again, because just when she'd thought there was nothing left between them, he'd given her this most precious gift: a second daughter and a chance to make things right.

The night Melanie came home, Patricia had slowly stripped off her clothes and for the first time in five and a half years, she'd crawled into her husband's arms. Harper had even accepted her, though she knew there had been other women in between and she knew his heart had not completely melted like hers.

When the short physical period ended, she understood. Harper would never love her the way he once had. He would not worship her or pursue her as he'd done in the very beginning. He would not look at her with the same urgent passion.

He would accept her. He would take care of her. But he would not forgive. In Texas, forgiveness was women's work.

Now Harper set down the business section. He picked up the metro news. For a moment she had a glimpse of the face she'd known for thirty-eight years, his eyes still as blue, his jaw still as square, his hair still as thick and golden.

Even at the age of fifty-eight, he looked like the man who had turned her head away from Jamie O'Donnell and swept her off her feet.

She sectioned out another bite of grapefruit.

And unbidden, the memories came back to her – of Texas nights, hot and humid, when the three of them had thought they could take over the world, Jamie so strong, Harper so charming, and Patricia simply so beautiful.

Harper's nothing but a handshake and a smile, lass. He's obsessed with image, not substance. You can do better than him.

He understands me, Jamie.

Why? Because he wears the right clothes, gets a good manicure? Because he'd sell his own mother for an invite to the right party?

Exactly, my love. Exactly.

'I'm sorry, Meagan,' she mouthed to her grapefruit. 'I am so sorry.'

Harper lowered his paper. 'What?'

'I'm worried about Melanie.'

Harper promptly set down the paper. 'She's been working too hard,' he said seriously. Health was his domain, and he'd always been very worried about Melanie's, especially her migraines. 'She's got to learn to slow down.'

'I've been trying to help her,' Patricia said, then shrugged delicately. She couldn't get her daughter to slow down any more than she could her husband.

As if reading her mind, Harper said, 'What if we all went on a vacation?'

'Pardon?'

'I mean it, Pat.' He leaned forward, sounded earnest. 'I've been thinking about it for weeks now. I've always said someday, when I retire, we'll travel everywhere. Well, hell, I'm not getting any younger. None of us are. Maybe it's time to finally be impulsive. Take our children and cruise the world. What'd you say?'

Patricia couldn't say a word. With shaking hands she set down her silver spoon. Cruise the world. Just like that. In her wildest dreams her husband never said such things.

She searched his gaze warily, looking for something she couldn't name. She wondered if her husband knew that even after all these years, she loved him. Even when he put his job before the family. Even when he went out with those silly young twits, then came home and kissed her dryly on the cheek. She wondered if he knew how patiently and quietly she was waiting for the day he did retire and he would belong to her again. Then maybe they could recapture what they'd shared so briefly in those first hot days of Texas. Then maybe they could finally leave all the mutual mistakes, and mutual sins, and mutual regret behind, and start fresh.

Didn't people always say it's never too late for new beginnings?

'Would you . . . would you leave the hospital?'

'Well, not *leave it* leave it.'

Patricia ducked her head so he wouldn't see her disappointment. 'A vacation, then? Like a week or two?'

'Longer. Maybe four months, six months. Hell, maybe I could be really wild and take a leave of absence.'

A leave of absence. That got her attention again. She didn't know whether to be thrilled or suspicious. She did her best to sound interested. 'Really? When?'

Harper said matter-of-factly, 'I was thinking next week.'

In the sudden quiet of the patio, Patricia was certain her husband would be able to hear the pounding of her heart. Next week. Harper never moved that fast. He never did anything as dramatic as take a leave of absence from his career.

Oh, God, it wasn't about Melanie or romance after all. He knew. Her husband knew.

The note, sitting in her car after the AA meeting. Inside her locked, alarmed Mercedes, placed on the driver's seat.

Five words, cut out of a magazine. Simple. Knowing. Chilling to the bone.

You get what you deserve.

In the cold moment that followed after she read the note, her heart beating like a trapped bird in her chest, Patricia had experienced a horrible instance of prescience, where the past blended with the future and there was no way she could stop it. Don't hurt her, she'd found herself silently begging. Don't hurt Melanie. I was good this time. I swear, I swear, I have been so good.

'Pat? Come on, I thought you would be pleased.'

'Six months,' she murmured, keeping her gaze on the table. 'Somewhere far away. Would we take Melanie?'

'Yes.'

'Would we . . . would we take Brian?'

Harper hesitated, then slowly he nodded. 'But not any lovers. I'm trying, Pat. Jesus, I'm trying. But I'm not ready to go that far.'

'The whole family,' she murmured. 'Going away. Someplace far. They would need more notice than a week, sweetheart. That's awfully short.'

He remained firm. 'Hey, if I can find a way to get out of the hospital, so can they.'

'So next Friday?'

'Yes. Next Friday.'

She should push more, she thought. Demand to know why. She was too afraid of the answer. She whispered, 'All right, darling, all right.'

María appeared in the doorway. 'Dr Sheffield here for Dr Stokes.'

Harper looked surprised, but then he rose and placed a quick kiss on his wife's cheek. Patricia had placed the sunflowers on the patio table that morning. He touched one magenta petal. 'It'll be all right,' he told her softly. 'You'll see.'

He strode out of the room. Patricia was alone with her half-eaten grapefruit. She wasn't sure what had just happened. The spur-of-the-moment vacation for no good reason. Her own desperate willingness to play along.

Secrets, she thought. Hers. His. And last night she suspected Melanie had them too. There had been too many long pauses in her daughter's speech.

Too many guards on her eyes. Melanie always had kept too much to herself. Did she really think her parents hadn't figured that out?

You get what you deserve. You get what you deserve.

Oh, Jesus God.

Patricia felt exhausted. She could barely lift her spoon or summon the energy to eat. Life was spiraling away on her again. Her breath was coming too quick and fast. An anxiety attack. At her age you would think she would know better. She didn't.

She went in search of her daughter. If she could just see Melanie, just know that her little girl was all right, not kidnapped, not murdered, not dead, it would help. If she could reassure herself that this was the present and the past was truly the past and long dead . . .

But Melanie was nowhere in sight. At ten-thirty in the morning Patricia Stokes crawled back to bed.

She knew she should be stronger. Today she wasn't.

Melanie woke up late again, then had to scramble to be ready by ten. She yanked a dress over her head while dialing Ann Margaret to tell her she wouldn't be at the donor center today. She wasn't feeling well. Maybe a touch of the flu. Ann Margaret was sympathetic. Don't worry, dear. Get lots of rest, dear. You know how much we worry about you.

Melanie went downstairs feeling about two inches tall. She hated lying and was doing too much of it these days.

She burst out the front doors eight minutes after ten. David Reese was waiting across the street, leaning against a cherry tree, his legs crossed, his hawkish face showing impatience. He looked as if he hadn't slept a wink the previous night, and the moment he spoke he sounded in a sour mood.

'Was that William Sheffield who just walked into your house?' David asked as a form of greeting.

'Yes. He probably has some meeting with my dad.' She was fidgeting with the strap of her purse, trying to get it to stay on her shoulder, but apparently David had had enough of waiting. He pushed away from the tree and immediately started walking.

'Do they always meet at your house?'

'Well, no, not always.'

'Why this morning?'

'I don't know. I just caught the tail end of things as they walked into the study, but William was upset. Sounded like his house was broken into last night.'

David came to an abrupt halt. '*His house* was was broken into? Like yours the night before?'

Melanie saw where his thoughts were heading and immediately shook her head. 'I'm sure this has *nothing* to do with our house. William has a slight *bingo* problem, you know? No doubt he got a little over his head again and a few creditors decided to help themselves. That's what Dad was grumbling when he showed him into his study. "Well, William, what do you expect?" I guess the intruder even left a note.'

David grabbed her arm. The intensity in his eyes caught her off guard. 'A note? What kind of note?'

'I . . . I don't know. I didn't hear that much.'

'Did you hear William say something was actually taken?' David demanded. 'Did he actually complain about losing money?'

Melanie tried to remember. She honestly hadn't paid that much attention. 'I think he did deny it; he said he'd won last night. But my father didn't believe him. Said his record spoke for itself.'

'What about the note?'

'He just kind of went, Well, if it was just a creditor, why the hell would he leave a note? Creditors take money, not write poetry.' She paused. 'Basically, William was upset and my father was trying to calm him down. End of story.'

David was still frowning, but he finally let go of her arm. 'I'd like to know what the note said.'

'*Why?* What could possibly be so important?'

' "You get what you deserve," ' David said. 'Isn't that what Digger's caller told him?'

'Oh.' Melanie had forgotten about that. She considered it for a moment, then shook her head. 'William's just an associate of my father's. He has enough problems of his own.'

David let the matter drop. They both resumed walking.

The morning was bright and sunny, not a cloud in the sky and not a tourist-free space on the tree-lined street. Men in double-breasted blazers window-shopped at Armani's, while college coeds with pierced navels walked into Ann Taylor and coffee shops. She and David wove their way through the throngs. The hotel was only fifteen minutes away by foot.

Melanie finally looked at her silent companion. David had dressed up for the occasion in black slacks and sports jacket. Brooks Brothers would be her guess. Looked nice on him. Very nice.

They went four blocks down Newbury before Melanie's nerves couldn't take the silence anymore.

'Did you have a relaxing evening?'

'Dandy.'

'You're limping less today.'

'Lucky me.'

'You're not much for conversation, are you?'

'I grew up in a household of men. Mealtimes were for chewing.'

'I bet. So what happened to your mother?'

'Cancer.'

'I'm sorry.'

'So was she.'

Melanie refused to be fazed. 'So then it's just your father and . . .'

'One brother. Younger.' He added, 'Steven. Currently married, two children, baseball coach at Amherst. Good pitcher. Better?'

'A regular speech,' she assured him, and thought he might have smiled.

They crossed over to Boylston Street, passing the Pru Center, where the Stokeses did all their shopping, then turned at the Shari Theater, where Melanie had watched the re-released *Star Wars* trilogy in a single afternoon. The hotel was nearly in sight.

'You didn't call Larry Digger, right?' David checked.

'Of course not—'

'Good. I want to catch him off guard, before he has a chance to perfect his story. What about your parents? What did you tell them last night?'

'Nothing—'

'And your brother? Hear anything more from him?'

'No.'

'He didn't even call?' David seemed surprised by that. 'So much for the protective-older-brother act.'

'Brian's one of those people who require a lot of space. He'll call when he's ready. He will.'

'Always the diplomat, huh?'

She looked him in the eye. 'Don't knock it until you try it.'

'Touché,' he said. 'Touché.'

They arrived at the First Church of Christ, Scientist, just a block from the hotel. Melanie watched shouting children splash in the long reflecting pool. God, it was a beautiful day.

A moment later she followed David into the Midtown Hotel.

There weren't many people in the lobby. One man was buried behind a newspaper in the corner, while an exhausted mom tried to rein in two racing children. The counter was manned by a short, pert redhead whose eyes lit up at the sight of David. She managed to ring Larry Digger's room while giving David a blatantly suggestive glance.

Melanie decided she didn't like the redhead much.

David himself barely seemed to notice her. A mood had swept over him upon entering the hotel. His face was shuttered, but his hooded eyes were observant. He stood differently, up on the balls of his feet with his left leg back for balance. He was on alert, Melanie finally realized. Studying the lobby, its occupants, its exits. He was preparing for Larry Digger.

The redhead got off the phone with Larry Digger and pointed them down the hall, giving David a last generous pout. He turned away without a backward glance.

They found Larry Digger waiting for them at the door to his room, his face smug, then faltering when he saw David.

'Who the hell are you?' Digger demanded.

'Your helpful hardware man,' David said. He led Melanie inside, then kicked the door shut with his foot and stood, arms across his chest.

'Shit, you're the waiter.' Digger turned to Melanie. 'Why the hell did you bring him? This is between us.'

'I want to see your proof, Mr Digger. Mr Reese offered to escort me. Now, do you want to talk, or should I leave?' She sat on the edge of a chair, making it clear she was ready to get up again at any time.

Digger looked at David unhappily. 'Can't you at least wait in the hallway?'

David did Melanie the favor of answering. 'No.'

Digger gave up, pacing the small room. He was wearing the same pants from last night but a fresh shirt. There was no evidence of a suitcase in the room, just one worn duffel bag and a pile of notebooks on the bedside table. A tape recorder rested in the middle of the bed, the top open and gaping hungrily.

'You can start talking anytime,' Melanie prodded him. 'That is, if you have anything useful to say.'

Digger stopped pacing and gave her a belligerent gaze. 'Oh, no, that's not the way this is going to play out. You want your proof, you have to answer *my* questions first. That's the way it works.'

'Why? At this point I'm still not sure you're telling the truth. Maybe you're making this all up for money.'

'And that's such a sin? Jesus, what would you know? Living in that town house, every need taken care of, every wish fulfilled, and what did you do for it, sweetheart? What did you ever do to deserve the life you lead?'

Melanie's lips thinned; his comments struck too close to home. 'I was lucky,' she said stiffly. 'So far, much luckier than you have ever been.'

'Well, doesn't that just make you special? Hey, for your information, I don't even need you anymore. I've talked to the intern who found you at the hospital. I've gotten in touch with the social workers assigned to your case—'

'What about Harper and Patricia Stokes?' David asked from the doorway. 'Did you contact them?'

'Not yet, but since Melanie's not cooperating . . .' Larry Digger made a show of shrugging, but his gaze was shrewd. He leaned against the bureau and eyed them both.

'I figure I can write this up by end of week,' he announced. 'Auction it off to the highest bidder, with or without a quote from Miss Holmes. Welcome to journalism in the nineties.'

'Then it is about money. When all is said and done, you are simply after a buck. Well, that answers my question. Good day, Mr Digger, and good riddance.' Melanie shook her head in disgust and stood.

Digger grabbed her arm. Bad move. David immediately strode toward him.

'Oh, what are you gonna do, gimpy?'

David's face turned to stone, and Melanie felt the hair prickle at the nape of her neck. David Reese was angry, a deep anger that made him dangerous. At that moment Melanie had no doubt he could inflict as much or as little damage as he intended.

The reporter was not a dumb man after all. Very slowly he brought up his hands. 'Hey, hey, hey, we've gotten off track here. We all want the same thing. I'm sure we can work it out.'

David relaxed just slightly, but his gaze held a warning. Digger tried to plead his case to Melanie instead.

'It's not about money,' he said sourly. '*It isn't.*'

'Sure it is.'

'Goddammit! Don't you think I'm tired of chickenshit tabloid journalism too? I have a *real* lead, Melanie Stokes, whether it violates your precious little world or not. And I intend to write a *real* story whether you like it or not.'

'Tell me the truth,' Melanie said curtly. 'Tell me something convincing.'

Digger crossed to the bedside table and picked up a handful of ragged papers. 'You want your truth, here it is. *This* is the story of Russell Lee Holmes and the woman who bore his child.'

'How do you know?' Melanie pressed. '*How do you know?*'

Digger was silent for a moment. He seemed to be contemplating his options. Maybe his greed was warring against what appeared to be his genuine pride in a job well done. Maybe he just wasn't sure how seriously to take her. Then he spoke.

'Russell Lee Holmes had a tattoo on his upper arm. This was all documented when he was arrested. The tattoo said "Trash loves Angel." Now, Trash is Russell Lee's nickname. He wouldn't tell anyone who Angel was, just said he wasn't "no fuckin' virgin." But, unfortunately for him, Russell Lee sometimes spoke in his sleep. He liked to say the name Angel. And every now and then he'd have these little conversations with his baby – with his own kid.

'Even before they brought him to the electric chair, I started looking into it, trying to find his wife and child. I wanted to know what it was like to be married to Russell Lee. You know anything about child molesters, Miss Stokes?'

She shook her head.

'There are several types. You can be either a preferential child molester – meaning you really do prefer children – or a situational molester, which means you'll turn to children if they happen to be around, but adults will do just as well. Make sense?'

Melanie nodded, though she wasn't sure something so horrible could make sense. Larry Digger continued more enthusiastically now, warming to his subject, pleased to show off his research.

'Most child molesters are situational offenders,' he said. 'They fall into four categories – repressed, morally indiscriminate, sexually indiscriminate, and inadequate. A repressed guy will molest his own children versus risking approaching anyone else. He's not only a sick son of a bitch, he's basically a spineless bastard as well. The morally indiscriminate, on the other hand, is a true equal opportunity monster. He'll rape his children, he'll rape his neighbor's children, and then to top it all off, he'll rape his wife and his neighbor's wife. He has no conscience at all, and preying on kids is just part of the fun. Then we got the sexually indiscriminate. He'll prey on anyone too, but for a different reason. He's sexually bored, likes the risk, the sense of adventure. What do you think is worse, Melanie? Preying on your kids because you can or preying on your kids because you have nothing better to do with your time?'

He didn't give her a chance to answer, which was just as well. Melanie suddenly had a feeling where the reporter was going, and it was a freight train straight to hell.

'The fourth type is the inadequate,' Digger announced. 'He's a loner, probably has no adult relationship to fulfill his needs, and in the end lures children he knows or has easy access to, because they are nonthreatening and he knows he's a wimp and not capable of much. So there you go, four types of sickos. Wanna cast your bet as to which type fits Russell Lee Holmes?'

'Morally indiscriminate,' David said without hesitation. 'Has no conscience or sense of remorse about his actions. He didn't even repent when sitting in the electric chair.'

Digger nodded approvingly. He looked Melanie in the eye.

'There's another defining characteristic of the morally indiscriminate offender, a neat little twist that'll just chill your heart. He'll not only turn on his own children, but he'll have children *just so he can have them to turn on.* So he has property at home. So he has all the access a godlike creature such as him is entitled to. I want to find Russell Lee Holmes's wife because I want to ask her what it was like to realize she'd been used by her own husband to produce his next victim.'

Digger's voice turned soft. 'Do you understand yet why you were given up by your own mother, Miss Holmes? Why you might have been spirited as far away from Texas as possible? Why your birth mother has never made any attempt to claim you or acquaint you with your past? Do you understand yet why you had been brought into this world?'

Melanie was having a hard time breathing. A fresh migraine was taking root behind her eye. The shadows were shifting in her mind again, revealing glimpses of a time and place she didn't want to know. The wooden shack. The little girl, clutching her favorite toy and staring right at her, not knowing yet what her fate would be.

'You still haven't given any proof,' she said roughly. 'You've only established that Russell Lee Holmes was evil. I got that. So his wife had motive to give her child up for adoption. I got that too. But you still haven't said anything to convince me that I'm that child. Come on, how in the world would some poor woman in Texas get her child to a Boston hospital ER?'

'Honestly, I don't know. But I can still give you your connection. See, I tracked down the midwife who had the honor of delivering one Baby Doe to none other than Russell Lee Holmes and his wife. Of course, she didn't know who they were then. Interestingly enough, Russell Lee used aliases for himself and his wife even before he began his dirty deeds.

'But when Russell Lee's pictures suddenly became front-page news, the midwife figured it out. And then, when she's still trying to figure out if she should say something about it or not, a man appears in her doorway.

'He offers her a large sum of money to forget all about Russell Lee Holmes's child. He tells her if she ever says a word, there will be con-sequences. *Dire* consequences. Now, this is the kind of man you don't mess with. So the midwife agrees. She doesn't take the money – she's got a little bit of an attitude about pride in her job and all that – but neither does she ever say a word. The identity of Russell Lee's kid remains safe with her long after Russell Lee goes to the chair.'

Digger smiled. It was the only warning Melanie got. 'Hey, Miss Holmes, the man who approached the midwife was Jamie O'Donnell. Now, if this has got nothing to do with you, why does your godfather care about Trash's first kid? Why is he showing up on the porch of some little old midwife and threatening her life if she can't keep a secret? You wanna tell me?'

Melanie's stomach plummeted. She didn't have an answer.

'Did you . . . did you contact Jamie? Did you ask him that?'

'Jamie O'Donnell? Shit, you're a few cards short of a full deck. The man runs guns, for God's sake. He knows people, he's hurt people. No way in hell I'm going near him.'

'*What?*'

Larry Digger blinked at her shocked tone. 'Lady, don't you know *anything* about your family?'

Melanie was dazed. Her godfather imported small gift items. Wooden boxes from Thailand, figurines. He traveled a lot. That's all.

'What about this Angel?' David asked. 'You found her?'

Digger shook his head. 'No. Like I said, the woman used an alias and the midwife knew only the fake name. I asked for a description, but it was too generic to help. Russell Lee didn't leave any personal documents behind, and even his lawyer is a tight one on the subject. Client–lawyer privilege carries to the grave and all that crap.'

Digger stared at Melanie. '*You* must have lived at least a few years with your birth mom. Now, I know your memory isn't all it's cracked up to be, but a mom is a mom. She's gotta be in your mind somewhere. A little bit of hypnosis, regression therapy, whatever, I can reunite mother and child. Now, how is that for a story? What'd you say, Miss Holmes? Wanna meet your *real* mom? Wanna hear your *real* name? It'll be fun.'

Knocking sounded at the door. 'I ordered breakfast earlier,' Digger said. 'Never come between a man and his fried eggs.'

David stepped toward Melanie. Digger opened the door. Two sounds emitted – short, popping crackles, like potato chip bags bursting open. And Digger collapsed where he stood, blood bubbling from his chest.

Melanie found herself looking at a dark-haired man wearing a poorly fitting hotel uniform and a very large gun.

He took aim again.

'Get down!' David roared, leaping toward her and sending them sprawling behind the bed. Two more pops. Bullets sailed just above their heads.

As she watched, David reached beneath his nice sports jacket and pulled out a gun.

'FBI,' David Reese yelled. 'Drop it!'

12

Thunder erupted suddenly from David's gun. Three pops followed, sending one bullet flying past Melanie's ear. She cringed, and then David's gun roared once more.

'On the count of three,' David commanded.

'What?' She couldn't hear through the ringing in her head.

'On the count of three, *run.*'

Pop, pop.

'One. Two. THREE!' David sprang up firing. '*Now, now, now!*'

Melanie crawled two feet before she could get her legs beneath her. Still firing with one hand, David pushed her, and she bolted out from behind the bed.

The shooter was fleeing down the hall, carrying Digger's notes and leaving a trail of blood behind him.

Melanie took off in the opposite direction. David Reese was right behind her.

'Everyone down! Shooter in the building! Press the alarm, press the alarm!'

People flattened like pancakes. Two women screamed. Melanie kept running through the lobby and the doors into bright blue sunlight and Copley Street.

She made it halfway up the block before a strong arm whipped around her waist and snapped her to a halt. She screamed, he stuffed a hand in her mouth and yanked her into a doorway. She started fumbling for her mace.

'It's me, goddammit, it's me. Calm down!' David's skin was pale, his hair spiky with sweat. She couldn't see any sign of a wound, but he was breathing hard and he looked as if he was in a lot of pain. Maybe ducking up and down and shooting firearms weren't good for his back. If he did have a back problem. If his name was David Reese.

She tried to shove away from him. He locked his arm around her waist more firmly.

'Who the hell are you? What the hell are you doing?' she yelled, still pushing hard.

'Trying to keep you out of the line of fire,' David bit out. 'Do you think a guy like that has qualms about shooting you in the back?'

She almost wiggled free. He caught her again. 'I don't know what I know about a guy "like that." I've never been shot at before!'

'Well, neither have I, so shut up and let me think.'

Sounds had erupted on the streets. People shouting. Cars honking, then screeching to a halt. The shooter was probably bolting from the back exit of the hotel. After another moment David loosened his grip and looked out into the street.

'Shit.' He turned on her angrily. 'Don't you realize who that was?'

'No,' she spat out. She took advantage of his relaxed grip to yank away. 'Dammit, let me go!'

'Jesus Christ.' He half released her, half covered her mouth. Bad move. She bit him. This time he let go, but his eyes were burning.

Down the street, sirens finally split the air, and two cop cars came barreling into view.

'That was the guy reading the paper in the lobby,' David growled. 'The guy who watched us walk into Digger's room, and instead of turning away, came in after us. Now, why the hell would someone do that?'

'Are you really with the FBI?'

'Yes.'

'You lied to me!'

'Well you got your revenge, because that guy wasn't firing blanks and he wasn't shooting for show. Now would be a good time for you to answer more questions, starting with the complete list of everyone who would want you dead!'

Later, David Reese took her back to the hotel room which was now swarming with police. He introduced himself as Special Agent David Riggs of the Boston office FBI and promptly launched into a steady stream of questions, as if caterers turned out to be undercover agents every day.

Melanie stared at Digger, unable to look away. He had a large hole in his chest and his blood was everywhere. It carried a warm, rusty scent and was underscored by the smell of feces and urine. David explained that death caused the bowels to relax and release their contents. Melanie hadn't known that.

A Boston homicide detective arrived. Clad in a dapper double-breasted suit, his pitch-black hair slicked back and his face freshly scrubbed, he introduced himself as Detective Jax. He looked like he ought to be in a one-hour cop drama. He gave Melanie a slow once-over, offered her a seat and a cup of water, then got down to business.

'Nine millimeter,' the detective told David as he dug bullets out of the drywall with his pocket knife. He dropped them into a plastic bag.

'A Beretta,' David said. 'Can't mistake the sound.'

Jax pointed at the floor, where a trail of dark red drops led toward the hall. 'His?'

'Got his hand. Slowed him down a bit, but not much. Tough son of a bitch. I hate that trait in assassins.'

Jax grinned. He finished collecting bullets and moved on to Digger's open duffel bag. 'Two pairs of underwear, both dirty. Two white shirts, not really white. *Three* brand-new bottles of JD. A man with priorities, I see.'

'He didn't seem that bad when we talked to him. Tox screen will tell the story.' David nodded at the cleared bedside table. 'The shooter grabbed Digger's notes before taking off. Not an easy maneuver with shots being fired, so my guess is that was part of the deal. Two dead people and all the reporter's information.'

'Two dead?' Melanie spoke up. 'Why two targets? Only Larry Digger was shot.'

David answered her. 'The receptionist said the shooter was here all day yesterday. She simply assumed he was a friend of one of the guests. Then he showed up again this morning with the newspaper. So the guy is on day two of a stakeout when we showed up. He watched us head for Digger's room, then, according to the receptionist, he got up, made a call from his cell phone and disappeared to the basement, where he must have snatched the uniform.'

Melanie's eyes widened. The Boston detective shared her concern.

'This guy walked into the room with a silenced Beretta, knowing *all three* of you were in it?' Jax said.

'No one knew I was Bureau,' David stated matter-of-factly. 'And no one knew I was coming. My guess is, that's what the phone call was about. Whether the shooter should proceed with an unexpected *third* person present.'

'Versus the original targets of Larry Digger *and* Melanie Stokes.'

'You figure the shooter was told it would only be a matter of time before Melanie met with Digger. So he waits – two for the price of one. Harvard MBAs aren't the only ones worried about efficiency in the workplace anymore.'

Detective Jax shook his head, working a toothpick in the corner of his mouth as if it were his last cigarette. 'That guy had to be bumming when he realized you were a Feebie. So much for quick and easy.'

David finally cracked a ghost of a grin. 'I'd like to think so. It may be the only good thing to come out of this day.'

His gaze flickered to Melanie. She got it. Good ol' David Riggs was lamenting the loss of his cover. Now he'd have to explain why a G-man was posing as a caterer. That would be an interesting conversation. She was already sharpening her claws for it.

'Well, hope you don't have any travel plans, G-man,' Detective Jax said, ''cause this is our jurisdiction and we're going to have *lots* of questions for you.'

'I got my case to run too.'

'Which will be my first question—'

'Detective, don't bother.'

'Sooner or later—'

'Then find me later.'

The two men exchanged steely glances. Finally Detective Jax granted David the first round of the pissing war, shrugging a little and switching the toothpick to the other corner of his mouth.

They decided to notice Melanie again, leading her out of the room so the photographer could shoot another roll of film. Someone in a white coat was running a tape measure between Larry Digger's body and the open door, while the medical examiner arrived and began a preliminary examination of the scene. The business of death, Melanie discovered, took a lot of people to complete.

'We want you to come downtown now, ma'am,' Detective Jax said. 'We have a sketch artist we'd like you to work with so we can start circulating a picture to local doctors. Maybe the guy went in search of a little love and tenderness for his hand.'

'I want to go home,' Melanie said flatly.

The two men exchanged looks. 'We'll talk about that downtown,' David said, reaching for her arm.

'I don't think so. Last I knew, I wasn't under arrest, *Special Agent*. Which means I can do whatever I want. At this point I'm going home.'

'Melanie, just listen to me for a minute—'

'Listen to you? *Listen to you?*' Her control began to unravel. 'I don't even know who you are! Why were you at my house Saturday night. Did you know about Larry Digger ahead of time? Did you think he would show up? Or does this have to do with more than him? *Oh, my God.* Who are you really investigating? You used me!'

David managed to grab her arms. 'Downtown, Melanie.'

'No, I will not—'

He snatched a raincoat, covered her head, and dragged her toward a patrol car. Suddenly she was bombarded by the sounds of snapping cameras and four TV personalities competing for a story.

'Officer, Officer, do you have any leads?'

'What's the motive? Is this Mafia related?'

'Is she a witness? Or a suspect? Come on, give us a statement.'

'Duck your head,' David said calmly. 'In you go.'

He stuffed Melanie into the backseat, and seconds later the car was pulling away. The cameras continued frantically snapping last shots in preparation for the eleven o'clock news.

Larry Digger had finally gotten his dream, Melanie thought. The aging reporter was officially front-page news.

13

'I just need to change clothes and grab my things,' David announced nearly five hours later as he walked into his apartment and tossed his keys onto the couch. Melanie remained standing in the doorway, still so angry, she didn't trust herself to speak. She wanted to skin David Riggs alive. She wanted to stake him to a hill of red fire ants and cover him with honey.

If she wasn't so angry, she would be afraid.

'You're the target of a hired hit, Miss Stokes. Furthermore, you've seen the assassin, so he definitely can't let it go. We simply can't guarantee your safety if you return to your residence at this time.'

Special Agent Riggs, who seemed to have taken personality lessons from a brick wall, had announced that he would watch her. They'd go to his apartment and pick up his things. They'd buy her some things. He'd take her to a hotel for the night. Problem solved.

Detective Jax hadn't even looked at her. Said if the FBI had the resources to spare, it was fine by him. So nice to finally learn her place in the world.

'It's not exactly Club Med,' David muttered now, snatching up various items of clothing strewn across the floor. 'I'm not home much.'

'No kidding,' she said sourly.

The color of David's apartment was hard to determine as most of the space was covered by clothes, magazines, and paper. Wadded napkins had been tossed on the parquet floors. A pile of unopened mail lay on the dining room table. Mounds of paperwork nearly obscured the laptop on an old oak desk. The place didn't have a stick of furniture that looked new or a plant that required care.

At least he'd hung two pictures. One was of Fenway Park at night, while the other was of some guy in an old-fashioned baseball uniform. There was also a line of baseball caps hanging on one wall and at least two baseball bats. Then there were the four movies piled on the floor next to the VCR: *Bull Durham, The Natural, Field of Dreams, Eight Men Out.* Apparently, the apartment had a theme.

Melanie sniffed suspiciously and turned back toward the sidewalk. 'I'll wait outside.'

'I wasn't expecting company.' David scowled, then swiped up another towel. 'Close the door, gimme a minute. It's not as bad as it looks.'

'I don't think that's possible.' But Melanie returned to the foyer and shut the door. Not a good move. The room was instantly cast in darkness. Her stomach rolled. Images of bloody Larry Digger pressed against her mind, and she felt suddenly very tired.

She pulled back the vertical blinds, seeking the reassurance of sunlight. David crossed the room and jerked the blinds shut.

'You're not really getting this whole notion of protective custody, are you?'

'There's nothing back there but woods.'

'Someone can climb a tree and shoot you.'

'Open your blinds, *Agent Riggs*, or I'm going to puke.'

David pinned her with an intent gaze, but then it softened. 'You all right?' he asked roughly, as if he wasn't used to being kind.

'Stop it,' she ordered immediately. 'No playing nice.'

'I'm not playing—'

'Of course you are! You lied to me. You still haven't told me what's going on and you're keeping me from going home.'

'I'm not the enemy. Jesus Christ, I just dodged bullets for you!'

'*For me?* Hah. You've been following me with your own agenda the whole time.' She jabbed a finger into his chest, her temper building dangerously. 'Give me some answers, David Riggs. Why were you at my house Saturday night? Who really was *Detective* Chenney? What the hell are you investigating and *what is going on?*'

'I don't know, goddammit. I don't.' A warning gleam had come into his eye.

Melanie ignored it, leaning closer, angling up her chin. She wanted a fight, she realized. She wanted something other than helplessness and fear. And she wanted some reaction from him. Because she'd *liked* David Reese the waiter. He had seemed an ally of sorts, and it was pitifully true that these days she didn't have very many of them.

'*If this has nothing to do with you, Melanie, why does your godfather care about Trash's first kid?*'

David turned away. 'I want out of these clothes,' he announced curtly. 'You probably need to change as well. Then we'll eat, and *then* we'll talk.'

'Will you answer my questions?' she called after him.

'Only if you ask nicely.'

'I reserve the right to be as nasty as I want—'

'No fucking kidding,' David muttered, and disappeared into his bedroom. Two minutes later he was back in the hall, having exchanged his slacks and jacket for jeans and a gray sweatshirt, its sleeves pushed up. His dark hair was tousled, and he sported a five o'clock shadow to go with his glower.

He no longer looked like an FBI agent but like a red-blooded man. Dark hair smattered the backs of his hands, tendons wrapped around his forearms. Broad chest, narrow hips, grimly set jaw. A man used to control. A man who did things on his terms. Few friends. Fewer loved ones.

And, dammit, *that* was a type she knew too well. Her father running her life, Brian trying to protect her, William hoarding his secrets. Her godfather too.

David took a step forward and she caught a glimpse of the limp he was trying to hide. His expression remained shuttered. His hands fisted at his sides. Even in pain, he gave nothing away. Even in pain, Special Agent David Riggs shut her out.

He tossed her a pair of sweats.

'You change, I'll order the pizza.'

Melanie nodded. Then, much to her horror, she burst into tears.

David fetched a large pepperoni pizza and two dinner salads from Papa Gino's on the corner. He was back in his apartment in less than five minutes, and they sat down at his recently cleared dining room table.

Melanie seemed to have shrunk while he'd been away, her petite frame nearly swallowed by his old black sweat pants and red T-shirt. And she looked pensive.

The crying jag had obviously embarrassed her. It had scared the crap out of him. He didn't know what to do when women cried. Hell, he didn't know where to look. He'd felt out of his league, the way he'd felt since he'd driven Melanie to his apartment and realized he couldn't remember the last time he'd brought a woman home. It had been a long time ago. Back in the days when he could sleep through the night without his muscles locking up and making him gasp for air. The kind of experiences a man really didn't need to share.

They ate in silence for ten minutes.

Then Melanie said, 'All right. Begin.'

David took his time to finish chewing a bite of pizza. 'You ask first. I'll see if I can answer.'

'Oh, well, that certainly promises clear and coherent communication.'

He grinned. 'I'm a G-man. We're famous for clear and coherent communication.'

Melanie thinned her lips disapprovingly. 'Are you really with the FBI?'

'Yes.'

'Do you really have arthritis?'

His jaw tightened. 'Yes.'

She gazed at him curiously. 'They don't mind?'

'I can fulfill the duties required of the job.'

'But aren't there physical tests—'

'I passed.'

'And wouldn't other agents worry about being partnered with someone who—'

'I like to think that my sparkling personality more than compensates for such concerns.'

Melanie rolled her eyes. 'So what do you do?'

'White collar crimes.'

'Like fraud cases, banking, money laundering?'

'There you go. The glamorous life.'

'I see.' She gazed at him levelly, and he suddenly saw the killer instinct spring to life in her eyes. 'So that story about how you were a cop and then got arthritis . . . That was just a load of crap designed to earn my sympathy and make me easier to manipulate? Wasn't it?'

'I needed a credible reason for you to let me help—'

'Why not the truth? Or are agents famous for lying as well?'

'Yes, ma'am,' he said in a steely voice. 'We sure as hell are.'

She leaned closer. 'What about *Detective* Chenney? Bureau as well?'

'Yes.'

'And the whole display of bagging the scene in my room? The candles, the toy horse, the questions you made me suffer through—'

'Bags are at the crime labs, information is being processed. It's a real investigation, dammit. I am trying to help you.'

She nearly laughed in his face. 'Then tell me what you were doing at my house, Agent. Finally give it to me straight.'

David took another bite of pizza. Then he helped himself to a drink.

'I was investigating Dr William Sheffield,' he said, gambling that William's betrayal would have cost him Melanie's loyalty. 'His *bingo* problem has led him to take loans from some very questionable sources and gained our interest.'

Melanie looked suspicious. 'Then how did you end up following me?'

'You have a history with the man. I couldn't be sure what your exact involvement with him might still be. Then you left the party with someone who obviously didn't belong.'

'You thought I was making a payment for William? Oh, please, I wouldn't give him water in a desert.'

'Of course.'

Melanie sat back. He supposed he'd passed round one, because the intensity had drained from her face. Now she looked confused, then troubled. 'If William was your subject, why get involved in my case?'

'I think your life is in danger.'

'I think you're right. But why?'

'I started researching Russell Lee Holmes. I also requested the Meagan Stokes case file just out of curiosity. I haven't received the full case file yet, but I've gotten to read enough newspaper accounts to realize that there are a lot of unanswered questions about Meagan Stokes. For example, did you know that Russell Lee was never convicted of murdering Meagan Stokes?'

'What?'

'He confessed only after he was already convicted of six counts of first degree murder. The police never made the case because they never had any physical evidence tying him to the crime. Your brother is right, that horse, that scrap of fabric in your room – they were never found twenty-five years ago. So where did they come from? Who would still have a toy last seen with a murdered child?'

Her eyes, those startling blue-gray eyes, went saucer wide.

'You think someone else murdered Meagan Stokes.'

'Maybe, maybe not.' He shrugged, but then his hunch got the best of him again. He leaned forward. 'There was a ransom demand in Meagan's case, did you know that? Russell Lee didn't do that with anyone else. And it doesn't fit with him or his MO. How would an illiterate, uneducated man fashion a ransom note? That alone suggests that either it wasn't him, or there was someone else involved. An accomplice. Maybe someone close to the family who would know its schedule.'

'You think someone in my family helped Russell Lee Holmes kidnap and murder Meagan Stokes!'

'I think something really bad happened twenty-five years ago, and it wasn't the fault of Russell Lee Holmes. That's what I think.'

Melanie looked like she was going to hit him, and then for a minute she simply looked scared. She picked up her soda and took a long sip, her hands shaking.

David got up and cleared the pizza box from the table. When he sat back down, she'd composed herself once more, her face still pale but her shoulders square and her expression resolute. She said, 'All right, Agent. Tell me your theory. Tell me exactly what you think is going on.'

So he did. 'Something bad happened twenty-five years ago to Meagan Stokes, something that involved more than Russell Lee Holmes. That's why the police never found more physical evidence. That's why it's possible that Meagan Stokes's toy and dress fabric appeared in your room. And whatever it is that occurred, it involved your family and friends. For twenty-five years they've kept quiet. They let Russell Lee Holmes go to the execution chamber and got on with their lives. But now someone else has entered the picture. Someone who's suddenly shaking things up.

'This person calls Larry Digger with a tip on how he can finally find Russell Lee Holmes's child. This person creates the altar in your room, sending a message about you trying to replace Meagan. This person is also sending notes.'

'What notes?'

David hesitated, forgetting she hadn't known and worried he'd just tripped himself up. 'Ah . . . your father got a note.'

'When?'

'At the party. After you had your migraine. I overheard your father and Jamie O'Donnell talking. Your father said he found a note on his car. It said the same thing Larry Digger's caller said. *You get what you deserve.*'

Melanie was staring at him incredulously.

'Your father also knew Larry Digger was in town,' David continued rapidly. 'He mentioned it to O'Donnell, who said that someone named Annie was getting phone calls. Now, who do you think Annie is?'

'Ann Margaret? You think he means *Ann Margaret?*'

'She's from Texas, just like the rest of them. Now we know your father knows something and O'Donnell knows something and Ann Margaret knows something. Who else is from Texas, and who else is talking about receiving notes?'

'William,' she whispered.

'There you go. That just leaves your brother and your mom. Your brother seemed as shocked as you were about the altar in your room. But what about your mom? Notice anything unusual with her?'

Melanie sighed. David took that for a yes.

'Last night. She came home late, nearly midnight. She said she'd been to a bar, told me how much I meant to her. But . . . but I could tell she wasn't actually saying what had rattled her so much. And she was speaking too urgently, as if it was suddenly extremely important I understand how much she cared about me. You know, the way someone might speak if they thought something bad was about to happen. Something . . . final.'

David nodded. 'So there's theory number one. Something more happened to Meagan Stokes. It involves all of your family in one way or another. And somebody else knows now. This person is rattling everyone's chains, bringing out all the skeletons. Which brings us to theory number two.'

He said quietly, 'You are theory number two. Whatever happened twenty-five years ago, you hold the key.'

'My amnesia. The lost nine years . . .'

'Exactly. Larry Digger couldn't find Russell Lee Holmes's wife on his own, but he was betting you could help him. If we assume that you are Russell Lee Holmes's child, think of what could be locked up in your mind. Certainly someone seems to believe you know something important. Hence, the scented candles and objects you might know in your room, put there to trigger a reaction—'

'But I didn't remember anything clearly.'

'Not yet, but you might. Therefore, you, like Larry Digger, have become a threat.'

'Larry Digger was getting too close,' Melanie said slowly, filling in the pieces. 'He honestly did have a lead, he was making progress. So someone, still trying to cover tracks, orders him killed. I might remember, so I'm a target too. But that makes no sense. If someone is pushing people to get at the truth, why order assassinations on Larry Digger and myself?'

'It's not the same person who ordered Larry Digger and you shot. It was someone else. This person wants the truth exposed but for whatever reason can't just announce it on his own. Maybe he has no credibility, maybe he's ashamed, mentally disturbed, I don't know. So he's trying to get at things in an underhanded way. However, he's also scaring the shit out of everybody. Think about it. Your family and friends have done very well for themselves. If the truth about the past came out now . . .'

He let the words trail off meaningfully, and once again Melanie understood.

'You think someone I know hired that hit man. Hired the hit man to kill Larry Digger, swipe his research, and eliminate me as well. Extinguish whatever clues might be locked in my mind. Erase, once and for all, any trace of what happened to Meagan Stokes. Christ . . .'

Melanie grew silent, grew haggard. She whispered, 'It's a war, isn't it? Someone is trying to expose a secret no one else wants exposed. And I'm just the person in the middle, the adopted child who might hold the key to the truth behind a little girl's twenty-five-year-old murder. Oh, Jesus Christ, at this point, whatever is in my head, I don't want to know!'

'I don't think you'll have a choice.'

'I always have a choice,' she said firmly. She got up from the table, wiped it, washed her hands, paced, then sat down.

'I probably am the child of Russell Lee Holmes,' she murmured. 'The memories of the shack. The notes . . .'

'We could look at having Holmes's body exhumed and do a DNA test. That would resolve it once and for all.'

She nodded absently. 'There are just so many inconsistencies. Why would my parents knowingly adopt Russell Lee's child—'

'Maybe they don't know. Maybe Jamie O'Donnell arranged it.'

'How, by dumping me at a hospital and assuming Patricia and Harper Stokes would magically adopt me?'

'Whose idea was it to adopt you, Melanie? Did they ever tell you who suggested it first?'

'My mother,' she said instantly. 'She and I . . . we just sort of *clicked*.'

'There you go. And it wasn't a random dumping. Your father did work there and was in the ER. Seems a fair bet that he'd hear about you, come see you for himself, maybe bring his vulnerable wife, who is hungering for a little girl . . .'

'Still leaving a lot to chance,' Melanie muttered.

'Fine. Spin it the other way. Your parents did know you were the daughter of Russell Lee Holmes. They agreed to adopt you for reasons we still don't understand, and provisions were made. The night Russell Lee was executed, you're dropped off at the hospital where Harper Stokes just happened to be on duty while the rest of his family was in Texas watching an execution you would think he'd also want to see.' He paused. 'Larry Digger had a point about the coincidences. One or two is happenstance, but three or four?'

Melanie's gaze dropped to the table. She rapped on it with her fingers many times. But then she looked up, and there was a clearness in her eyes David hadn't expected. It nailed him in the solar plexus, made him conscious of her golden hair and citrusy perfume and those haunting eyes . . .

She said quietly, steadily, 'But even then . . . I still don't believe it, David. I don't. My parents didn't just give me a home, they've been *good* parents. Not reluctant, not grudging. Whatever I've needed, whatever I've desired they've given it to me. If you assumed they were in on "it," whatever it might be, wouldn't they be resentful? Wouldn't human nature dictate that every time they saw me, they saw the man who killed their daughter? I don't care what that damn altar was trying to imply. I'm not a second-rate daughter. *My parents* have never let me *be* a second-rate daughter. That's the kind of people they are, David. That's my family. It must be relevant that I love them so much, and they love me.'

'Hey, family is family,' he tried. 'Sure you care—'

'Somewhere out there I have a birth mother,' Melanie interrupted. 'I have a real name, a real birthday. If you believe Larry Digger, I could be on the verge of what every adopted child dreams about – discovering her birth parents. But I don't care. I'd give it all up, David, just to have my family back the way it was. I love them. I have always loved them. I will always love them. That is how I feel about my family.'

David didn't answer right away. Faced with Melanie's earnestness, a trait he himself lacked, he studied the floor and the scuff marks made from all the long nights he'd spent pacing it.

'Loving wives take home abusive husbands all the time,' he said finally, quietly. 'They get strangled for their trouble. Loving parents bail their troubled kids out of jail and give them a second chance. Then they take a bullet to the head while they're sleeping one night. Love doesn't have anything to do with it in the end. It can't save a person's life. Just ask Meagan. I'm sure she loved your parents too.'

He strode to the bedroom door, intent on grabbing his duffel bag, but Melanie caught his arm. He stopped but didn't look at her. He didn't want to see tears on her pale cheeks. For all his big speech, he wouldn't be able to handle that, and he knew it. He suddenly hated the fact that he always sounded so harsh.

'I gotta pack a bag,' he grumbled. 'We should go.'

And she whispered, 'My family is all I have, David. Please don't take them away from me. Please.'

He pulled his arm free and walked away.

14

After David disappeared into his bedroom, pointedly closing the door behind him, Melanie wandered the living room, rubbing her arms. Ever since the shooting of Larry Digger, she couldn't seem to get warm.

Now her head was filled with conflicting images. Her big, burly godfather whom she adored. Her strong, silent dad who'd always been there for her. Her fragile, tremulous mom, whom she loved beyond reason. Brian, her hero. Ann Margaret, her friend.

A person capable of harming Meagan Stokes. A twenty-five-year-old cover-up.

She tried to tell herself it was all a crazy mistake. Logic gone awry, conspiracy theory run amok. But her mind was too rational for her own good. She couldn't dismiss the altar and the pieces of evidence in her room. She couldn't dismiss Larry Digger's body and the shooter who had aimed right at her. She couldn't dismiss David's point that the police had never found any physical evidence tying Russell Lee Holmes to Meagan Stokes.

Melanie didn't know what to do. She was tired, frustrated, and overwhelmed. She longed desperately for the comfort of her own home, and for the first time feared it as well. She wanted to hear her mother's reassuring voice. She had no idea what she would say. She wanted her family. She was beginning to feel as if they were all strangers.

What were they so afraid of?

Nine o'clock on a Monday night. Melanie didn't have answers, so she took the low road and sought distraction instead. David's apartment boasted a bookshelf crammed full of cheap metal trophies. One had a plastic guy on top that seemed to be pointing a gun. The dust-covered brass plate declared the owner to be the Junior Champion, .22 Target Pistol 25 feet.

Tucked between it and six others were a collection of well-thumbed gun magazines and patches and bars still in their wrappers. Marksmen, Distinguished Expert, one said. So David Riggs was not only a loner but a gun aficionado as well. That didn't surprise her.

But the largest trophy turned out not to have a thing to do with guns. It was pushed all the way in the back, as if David couldn't decide whether to be proud of it or not. A baseball player was poised on top, bat positioned on its dusty shoulder. The brass plate at the bottom was worn, as if thumbed over and over again. The letters faintly proclaimed: Mass All-Star Champion.

She moved on to the picture of the baseball player on the wall. *Shoeless Joe Jackson* was scrawled across the lower right-hand corner. The name sounded vaguely familiar to her.

She looked at the picture of Fenway Park, then returned to the bookshelf and found a scrapbook.

The first picture was old, the edges crinkled, the color yellowed. The woman was young, dark hair neatly curled under at her shoulders, warm, intelligent gaze looking straight into the camera. David's mother, Melanie realized; she had passed on her rich hazel eyes to her son. She looked like a strong, sensible woman. The kind who ran a tight ship.

She disappeared from the scrapbook much too soon. The split-level ranch house with its olive colored carpet and brown linoleum disappeared as well, the family portraits becoming a thing of the past.

David's mother died, and his scrapbook became about baseball.

Here was David Riggs, age eight and decked out in a Little League uniform. Here was ten-year-old David with his whole team. Here was David, with Steven and Bobby Riggs posed on a baseball diamond. Here was Bobby Riggs tossing balls to his sons, who were now taller, leaner.

Certificates appeared in the scrapbook, announcing pitching achievements. First no-hitter. Lowest number of hits allowed in a season. Best ERA. Then came the newspaper articles: 'Promising Young Pitcher in Woburn' 'Woburn High Grooming Best Ever' 'The Major League Recruiters Arrive in Town – All Know They Are Eyeing the Riggs Boy.'

And the pictures . . . Pictures of Special Agent David Riggs Melanie would not have thought possible. No grim expression or lined face. He beamed in color photos, posing enthusiastically with his glove, then in mid-pitch. He played with the camera. He winked at the crowd. He was the hometown hero and the photographs documented it diligently. Young David Riggs, who was going to go to the pros and make Woburn proud.

Young David Riggs, arching up on the pitcher's mound to catch a ball his face so earnest, so intent.

Next shot. The ball in his glove, his body descending from the sky, and his face beaming with joy.

Next shot. David holding up the ball, showing it to his father, who was screaming on the sidelines. For you, Dad, his expression announced. And Melanie could read Bobby Riggs's reply in his exulted look, his parted lips. *That's my boy*, the father was screaming, *that's my boy!*

Melanie hastily closed the scrapbook. She had intruded too far. These were private photos of a private time that had come and gone. This was David with his family, and David with baseball, which seemed to be an even more personal relationship. She should've let it be. Everyone deserved their walls.

Of course, she opened the scrapbook and looked again.

God, he was magnificent when he was happy. The passion, the fire. She could see how that would make him a good federal agent, but as a baseball player . . . wow.

And then Melanie entertained the worst of all female fantasies – she wondered if she could make him smile like that, if she could fill his eyes with such primitive joy. If she could heal a man and make him feel whole.

This time she closed the scrapbook more firmly, then tucked it back in its place on the bookshelf. The images were emblazoned in her mind. She did her best to tuck them away as well.

The bedroom door was still closed. She passed by closely enough to realize that he was talking in there. Phone call. To whom? Then she had another thought. Whatever he was saying, it probably had to do with her case. Which was her life. Which was her business, dammit.

Melanie cupped her ear against the wood. She could hear every word.

David was giving someone a thorough dressing-down. 'Sheffield did not just stay home all night, dammit. He told Melanie's dad he won last night, which means he was out gambling. And apparently while he was out gambling, someone broke into his house. We're not even sure if anything was taken, but they left a note. Now, I want to know what the note said!

'Yeah, Chenney. Do you understand now why sticking to your target is so important? Is this getting through to you yet? Just because people go home sick doesn't mean they stay home sick.

'Look, I wasn't sure what I thought of this either in the beginning. The case did seem far-fetched. But we've moved way beyond coincidence at this point. We know Harper Stokes got a note. Melanie believes her mother may also have gotten a note. Now, I can't be sure, but I'm willing to believe someone played a game at Sheffield's house as well. We need to know exactly what happened there.

'No, don't break into his house. Go through his trash. It's much simpler.

'Okay, it's also messier, but that's the glamorous life. Sheffield works tonight, right?

'Yes, I want you on his tail. And stick this time, even at work. I'm getting very curious about the hospital angle. So far our anonymous tipster seems to know exactly what he's talking about, so we may have much more of a fraud case than we thought.

'Yeah, yeah, yeah, I know you don't know anything. God, they gotta start getting you guys more training. Well, do you have a pen and paper? I'll give you a lesson for the day.

'Okay, pretend for a moment that our tipster is correct and they are installing pacemakers in healthy patients. Now, no single doctor or healthcare professional, no matter how brilliant, can summarily recommend a pacemaker. A cardiologist would have an opinion. The cardiac surgeon too. Then there's the ER docs who admitted the case, the nurses who attended the patient, and the anesthesiologist who would be monitoring all the patient's vitals and administering meds during surgery. All these people examine the patient, update the chart, and know what is going on. And that's assuming the patient never asks for a second opinion. Lots of people do, which means a whole new round of doctors reading charts and offering opinions.

'So first off, it can't be as simple as faking a chart or misdiagnosing. Hospitals are set up exactly so that kind of situation can't happen. Given that, our suspects are going to have to find someone who at least exhibits symptomology. Probably a patient who comes into the ER as a "chest pain – rule out MI" admit, which means a person suffering from chest pains that they want to make sure isn't a myocardial infarction. A heart attack, Chenney. Myocardial infarction equals heart attack.

'Now, following protocol, most ERs will slap an EKG on the patient, snap a chest X ray, as well as draw six to seven vials of blood to test for cardiac enzymes. But some of these enzymes can take twelve to thirty-six hours to show up, so even if the chest X ray is clear and the EKG good, a hospital will generally keep the patient for a day or so for observation, particularly if there is a history of heart problems in the family and the person appears at risk – overweight, high blood pressure, and so on. Now, City General has a notoriously aggressive cath lab, so their ER does also send the patient to the cath lab to shoot the coronary – check for blocked arteries.

'In the cath lab they have to feed a catheter through the femoral artery to inject the patient with dye. They'll heavily sedate the patient for the process, then send the patient to ICU for recovery and monitoring. They're also going to keep the patient under sedation because they don't want him or her to wake up in the middle of the night and pull out the catheter. So that gives us our first "opportunity" for nefarious deeds right there.

'At night in the ICU, the nursing staff is generally spread thin and focusing on the more critical cases. You have a recovery patient who is drugged and certainly not going to notice what's what. Someone could easily slip into a room, inject a patient with a drug or tamper with the EKG, and probably escape with no one the wiser.

'Ask around, Chenney. Have people seen Dr Sheffield roaming the ICU a lot? That might tell us something right there.

'No, I don't completely understand what healthcare fraud has to do with Meagan Stokes, only that our tipster seems to know more than we do. Anything back from the lab yet?

'Two types of blood? Really? Jesus.' David sighed. 'This case just gets weirder and weirder. Other findings?

'Yeah, I know it's too soon, I'm being an optimist. Okay, have them do a

DNA test. I imagine one kind of blood is probably Meagan Stokes's. As for the other, I haven't a clue. Has the Meagan Stokes case file arrived from the Houston field office yet?

'What do you mean, they said the case file is unavailable? It's a twenty-five-year-old closed file. It's gotta be sitting in the archives.

'A case file can't be just "out." The Bureau isn't a library, for God's sake.

'Shit, someone is yanking our chain. Okay, what about the Houston PD? Did they fax over their case file? Uh-huh. Give me a rundown.

'Life insurance. On two children. One million apiece. Shit. What kind of parents insure their children for a million bucks? Then again, it does explain a town house on Beacon Street.

'No evidence from Meagan ever found? Yeah, that's what I thought. Okay, when I get to the hotel tonight, I'll give you another call and have you fax the file over. Don't worry about Lairmore. I'm the lead agent, so I'll take the heat. Most likely he'll chew my ass tomorrow morning sharp, then we'll all get on with our lives. You all set with Sheffield tonight in the ICU?

'I know you're tired, Chenney. So am I. Unfortunately, whoever the hell is doing this seems to be in a rush to make up for lost time. We had Larry Digger showing up on Saturday, the altar assembled for Sunday, and a paid assassin appearing on Monday. God knows what's happening right now as we speak. We're just going to have to deal for a bit.

'I'm watching Melanie Stokes tonight.

'I know, I get all the great jobs. Enjoy tagging Sheffield. Bye-bye.'

Melanie scurried for the sofa. The bedroom door swung promptly open and David came striding into the room, scowling and looking preoccupied.

'The lab hasn't had enough time for in-depth analysis,' he stated without preamble, 'but we do know there were two types of blood on the scrap of blue fabric in your room. They'll run some more tests.'

Melanie nodded. David didn't offer anything more. He was standing in the middle of the room with his hands on his hips and his mind a million miles away. He was tired too, Melanie realized. There were fresh lines around his mouth and at the corners of his eyes. His skin was drawn too tight, making him look especially harsh and stern.

He crossed the room to his answering machine. The message light was blinking and he punched play. Then he strode back into his room for his duffel bag while the tape rewound. He'd just returned to the living room when the first message began.

'Hello, David, this is your dad. Still haven't heard from you. I guess the Bureau is keeping you busy? I'm reading now about some new methods for accurizing. Want to bring your Beretta in? I have some things I want to try out.' Bobby Riggs's voice petered out awkwardly. Melanie could hear the man swallow. 'Ah, well. Just thought I'd see if you were in. No big deal. Give me a call if you have a chance. I got tickets to the Red Sox – or . . . ah, hell. It's been a while, David. Just call sometime.'

Melanie looked at David. His face was still a mask.

The next voice came on.

'Riggs, check your goddamn voice mail. I have a message that you've been involved in a shooting. I got a Boston police chief talking to me about homicide. What the hell happened to eyes and ears only, Riggs? And what happened to procedure? When one of my agents discharges his weapon, I *do not* expect to hear about it from Boston PD. In case you're still ignoring the voice mail, I want you in my office oh-seven-hundred tomorrow! And bring a damn report with you!'

The call ended abruptly. David merely smiled.

'That was my boss,' he said easily. 'Guess I won't be getting that corner office after all.'

A clipped professional voice came over the tape. 'This is Supervisory Special Agent Pierce Quincy from Quantico. Sorry to call you at home, Agent Riggs, but I was notified today by the Houston field office that you were requesting the Meagan Stokes case file. I would like to know why you are requesting this particular case file. You can contact me at . . .'

He rattled off the number. Melanie looked sharply at David, who had gone perfectly still.

'Shit,' he said after a moment, belatedly scribbling down the phone number. 'What the hell is this all about?'

'He said you requested the file.'

'Well, no kidding. But first Houston tells me the file is unavailable, now I have Quantico calling me at home to follow up on my request in less than twenty-four hours. Why does everyone suddenly care so much about a closed case file? And, especially, why Quincy?'

Melanie looked at him blankly. 'Would you like to translate for those of us who are merely personally at risk and not the trained professional?'

David shook his head. He still looked confused. Actually, he appeared nervous. He finally walked into the kitchen, grabbed a bag of frozen carrots, and slapped it onto his lower back. 'You haven't heard the name? He was involved in the Jim Beckett case last fall.'

'The serial killer who escaped from Walpole?' Melanie had heard of that case. There was probably no one in New England who hadn't locked their doors and windows when the former police officer and killer of ten women had broken out of Walpole. In his brief time of freedom, Beckett had managed to cut a broad, violent swath. She didn't even remember how many people he had killed in the end. It had been a lot.

'Quincy did the original profile,' David muttered. 'Served as the FBI consultant when the case team reassembled and was instrumental in plotting strategy. Beckett murdered an FBI agent, you know. There was some question about her role at the time, but Quincy stated she died in the line of duty, and if Quincy says she died in the line of duty, then trust me, all the bureaucrats have her listed as dying in the line of duty. After helping catch Beckett, he's violent crimes official expert *du jour* and about as politically untouchable as one gets in the Bureau. Basically, God himself just called about Meagan Stokes.'

15

'Why would this expert call about Meagan?'

'There's only one way to find out.' David held up the number.

Melanie faltered. Her chin was up, her shoulders square. Some part of her wanted to be strong enough. This was her family, and she would do anything for her family. She *owed* it to them.

The rest of her was feeling bruised and battered. She wanted the truth, but she feared it just as much. The truth did not always set you free. Sometimes it bound you to dark, bloody deeds and cost you the people you loved.

'Why don't you go into the bedroom,' David suggested. 'You can rest while I handle the phone call.'

'No. I'm ready.'

'You've had a long day.'

'It's my family, David. I want to.'

He was quiet for a moment, then he shrugged. But his look was different. More understanding, she thought, and that undid her a little. Heaven help her, but if David Riggs turned kind now, she would most likely fall apart.

He turned away before the moment became something neither one of them was prepared to handle.

He set up the speakerphone on the dining room table and they both took a seat. Though it was after hours, they got Supervisory Special Agent Pierce Quincy on the first try.

'This is Special Agent David Riggs returning your call.' David hit a button on his phone base. 'Just so you know, you're on speakerphone and Melanie Stokes is also in the room.'

'Good evening, Ms Stokes,' Quincy said politely, then added to David, 'Why is she part of this call?'

'I'm in the middle of a case that concerns her,' David said tersely, 'and it was for her that I requested information on Meagan Stokes. Why are you involved? Isn't this a closed case?'

'Yes. Thus, I was equally surprised to find a field agent from Boston requesting this information. According to your file, you work with white collar crimes.'

David tensed and Melanie got the distinct impression she was in the middle of a pissing war where information would be doled out only in hard-to-earn pellets. As the junior agent, David got to go first.

'My complete involvement in the case isn't something I want to discuss right now,' he said curtly. 'But to get the ball rolling, Melanie Stokes is Harper and Patricia Stokes's adopted daughter. Two nights ago a reporter named Larry Digger—'

'The *Dallas Daily* reporter?'

'That's the one. He showed up and alleged that Ms Stokes was the daughter of Russell Lee Holmes. Yesterday she found a shrine at the foot of her bed. It contained one red wooden pony, presumably Meagan Stokes's toy, a scrap of blue fabric presumably from Meagan Stokes's dress, and forty-four gardenia-scented candles spelling out the name *Meagan*. Then today Larry Digger was shot and killed. Now, why do you have the Meagan Stokes file?'

'Forty-four candles?' Quincy murmured. Melanie could hear scratching sounds as he made notes. 'Confirmation on the toy and fabric scrap?'

'At the lab now. Brian Stokes, the brother, has made an initial ID.'

'Interesting. I don't see any mention of the police ever finding the red wooden pony or the blue dress. On the other hand, many items from the other victims were recovered from Holmes's cabin.'

'Why do you have the file?'

'Down, Agent,' Quincy said lightly, earning a fresh scowl from David. 'I'm sorry if I sounded too intense on the message, but I just started researching Russell Lee Holmes as part of an internal project to develop our intellectual capital—'

'What's that?' Melanie whispered to David.

'He's researching Russell Lee Holmes to add his profile to the violent crimes database of information,' David translated. 'The Beckett case must have been something else, because the Bureau usually encourages internal projects only when they decide an agent's one wick short of melt-down.'

'The more you deal in death, Agent,' Quincy said quietly, 'the more you learn the value of stopping and smelling the roses.'

It sounded to Melanie as if the older agent spoke less out of wisdom and more out of regret. She began to like Supervisory Special Agent Quincy.

He said, 'Special Agent Riggs is correct. In the violent crimes division, we maintain an entire database of information we've gathered from mur-derers, rapists, all the people you wouldn't want to invite over to your mother's for dinner. It is by analyzing and comparing these cases, these offenders, that we have been able to come up with the common traits and behavior characteristics we use to profile.

'As part of my project, I proposed that we go back and analyze famous historic cases. Last month I turned to Russell Lee Holmes. Imagine my surprise when halfway through this process I received a call about one of the files.

'Do you know much about the Meagan Stokes case, Ms Stokes?' Quincy asked.

'It's not something my family talks about.'

'Do you have any theories as to why Larry Digger approached you?'

'I was found in the hospital when I was nine. I don't have any memory of where I came from. That makes me an easy target.'

'We've covered this ground,' David said impatiently. 'There are some reasons to believe Larry Digger's allegations. That's not why I requested the Meagan Stokes file.'

'Then why did you request the file?'

'Because I'm not blind, deaf, and dumb,' David snapped. 'Because I can read between the lines, and just as you've probably concluded in the last few weeks, there are a lot of reasons to doubt that Russell Lee Holmes killed Meagan Stokes.'

Even though she'd heard this theory once before, Melanie still found it jarring. Hundreds of miles away, however, Quincy did not seem startled.

'Very good, Agent. I have spent two weeks trying to figure out what to do. After all, there is no statute of limitations on homicide, and I am almost one hundred percent certain that Russell Lee Holmes did not kill Meagan Stokes.'

'He was innocent?' Melanie asked.

'I would not say he was innocent,' Quincy calmly corrected her. 'I believe he did kill six young children. I doubt, however, that he kidnapped and murdered Meagan Stokes.'

'Russell Lee Holmes was never tried for Meagan Stokes,' David reviewed. 'He was convicted of killing six other children, and confessed to Meagan's murder only later, after he'd been found guilty. He made that confession to Larry Digger.'

'Why do you believe he made the confession?' Quincy asked David like a teacher quizzing a student.

'Because he was already sentenced to death. What was one murder more?'

'Hold on,' Melanie protested. 'Even if it didn't cost him anything, why would Russell Lee Holmes do someone a favor by confessing? He's not exactly a nice guy.'

'I don't think he did it for nothing,' David said, and for the first time, he wouldn't meet her eye. 'I think he may have been given an offer he couldn't refuse.'

She didn't understand. They had just had this conversation. Why hadn't he said this then? What new warped theory was cooking in that head of his?

'I think,' David said slowly, 'we just figured out why your parents may have knowingly adopted the child of a murderer. He covers their sin.'

Melanie stopped breathing. She had the strange sensation that David's apartment was tilting and she was plunging headlong into the abyss.

'Melanie?' David asked quietly. She managed to turn her head. He was looking at her with genuine concern. It turned his eyes gold. Both gentleness and anger brought out the gold. Why had she never realized that before?

She suddenly wanted him to hold her, to feel those arms around her again the way he'd done the first night, when he had carried her away from Larry Digger, and the scent of Old Spice had made her feel safe.

Melanie looked down. She worked hard at getting the next breath, then the one after that. Slowly the knot eased from her chest, the pressure easing slightly.

'Why don't we take this one step at a time,' Quincy said reasonably. 'You've drawn some interesting conclusions, Agent Riggs, but you're new at this and don't have all the information yet. Ms Stokes, are you certain you want to be part of this discussion?'

'Yes,' she said hoarsely. 'Yes.'

Quincy began almost gently.

'In 1969, when Russell Lee Holmes kidnapped his first child, Howard Teten was just beginning to outline the techniques we call profiling. Without a framework for approaching such crimes, the local police and FBI handled the Russell Lee Holmes case merely as a murder investigation. They focused on *how* the crimes were committed, the modus operandi, instead of *why* the crimes were being committed – what need was driving the killer's behavior. This is an important distinction, Ms Stokes, for a serial killer's MO can change over time. Maybe he switches from binding to drugging victims, but a killer's need, *control and domination of women*, will not change. This is called the killer's "signature." It will be the same at every single killing, from the first to the thirtieth, even if everything else about the crime seems different.

'In 1969, however, the police did not understand this principle of a killer's "signature." They mistakenly attributed a murder to Russell Lee Holmes based on a superficial MO, since they lacked the tools to analyze deeper, more significant issues of his pathology.

'Russell Lee Holmes hated poor white children. Are we clear on that?'

David nodded. Melanie managed a small yes.

Quincy continued. 'Russell Lee Holmes never advanced beyond the fourth grade and was illiterate. He held a slew of menial jobs, was known for his nasty temper, and his last job review simply stated: "He likes to spit." Most likely Russell Lee Holmes hated poor white children because a very deep, very real part of Russell Lee Holmes hated himself. And he acted upon this hatred pathologically, picking out small, vulnerable girls *and* boys because in the most elemental way, he was trying to destroy his own roots. Russell Lee Holmes did not suffer from a conscience. He did, however, possess a great deal of rage.

'Now, as an illiterate, unskilled man, Holmes could not exercise his rage in a sophisticated manner. The six murders were clearly blitzkrieg attacks. Holmes entered poor areas, which were undoubtedly familiar to him and in which he undoubtedly blended in, and simply snatched whatever child was easiest. Later, the police identified the shack he used to perform the worst of his crimes.'

'It was out in the woods, wasn't it?' Melanie whispered. 'Single room. Tightly constructed, not even a draft. The windows are dusty though, I can't see out. And cracked halfway across. I watched the spider walk along that crack.'

'Ms Stokes,' Quincy said carefully. 'I happen to have pictures of the shack in front of me, full-color crime photos. I'm not sure what you are describing, but Russell Lee Holmes's shack had no windows. It was a simple, handmade structure, and I assure you, it had plenty of drafts. Several of the floorboards even came up. Beneath them was where the police found his stash of "trophies."'

Melanie stilled. 'It's not . . . I'm not picturing Russell Lee Holmes's shack?'

'Absolutely not.'

She looked at David. 'Then maybe, maybe I wasn't there. Maybe I'm not—'

'Or Russell Lee Holmes kept Meagan someplace else.'

'Or Russell Lee Holmes was not involved,' Quincy said.

'Then why would I be in the room, seeing Meagan?' Melanie addressed David.

'I don't know. Maybe Meagan was kept in a different location, and for some reason you were also held there.'

'Ms Stokes,' Quincy said, 'when you say you can picture Meagan Stokes, what exactly do you mean?'

Melanie couldn't bring herself to answer. She looked to David for assistance.

'She's recently started to remember things. That's one of the reasons we believe Larry Digger may have been telling the truth. Melanie seems to have some memories of being shut up in a one-room cabin with Meagan Stokes.'

'What else do you recall?'

'That's all.'

'But you've just started remembering, correct? Think of the images that must be in your mind. There are so many things we could learn from you, particularly about the Meagan Stokes case. Would you be willing to come here? I know some expert hypnotists who could work with you.'

Melanie almost laughed. 'Oh, yes, everyone seems quite fascinated by the "potential" of my mind.' Her lips twisted. 'Except me, of course.'

'Hypnotism, Ms Stokes. In a controlled environment. I promise we'll take good care of you—'

'No, thank you.'

'Ms Stokes—'

'I said no thank you! For God's sake, it all happened twenty-five years ago, and I *do not* want to remember dying children!'

Quincy was silent, probably disappointed.

'Of course,' he said at last. 'Then let's review what we know based upon the police notes. So Russell Lee Holmes hated poor white children. He kidnapped them, he tortured them in his private cabin, and when he was done, he strangled them with his bare hands, another symbol of someone performing a deeply personal act of violence. He disposed of the bodies randomly, dumping them naked in ditches, drainpipes, and open fields. Again this fulfilled his need to denigrate the children, to cast them aside as proverbial rag dolls not worthy even of protection from the elements.

'In short, in every act he performed, he revealed his hatred of youth, poverty, and weakness. He revealed his hatred for himself. And then we get to the Meagan Stokes file.'

'She wasn't poor,' David said. 'There was a ransom demand. And her body was buried in a forest, not dumped. It was decapitated.'

'She was in the nanny's car,' Melanie murmured, 'parked in front of the nanny's mother's house. I thought that was considered a poor neighborhood.'

'It was a lower income neighborhood,' Quincy said carefully, 'but I would still categorize it as up from Holmes's usual hunting grounds. And then, the victim profile doesn't fit. Meagan was well dressed, well groomed. She sat in a nice car and played with an imported toy. She was bright and well spoken. If Holmes was acting out a primarily self-destructive act, there should've been nothing about Meagan Stokes to trigger his blood lust. There should've been nothing about her that would've reminded himself of him.'

'Maybe it was revenge,' Melanie said. 'The other children he hated because they were like him. He killed Meagan because she was above him.'

'Possible, Ms Stokes, but not probable. That is a distinct change in motivation, and it's rare to see a change in a serial killer's pathology. Now, in some cases, a killer may snatch a different type of victim because the desired target is not available. He prefers young, twenty-something blond women, but when the blood lust got too high, the killer "settled" for a thirty-something brunette. But in that case the killer's need, hurting women, was not that particular and thus it was still fulfilled. For other killers, however, the victim profile is intrinsically tied with their signature. They don't want to just hurt women. They need to hurt "loose" women, so the killer would never substitute a mother of three for a prostitute, even if the mother of three was more convenient. That crime wouldn't fulfill their need. For these men, finding the right target is like falling in love. They describe spending weeks, months, years, looking for the "right one." They start with the physical – in Holmes's case, young, undersized, dirty, and poor. And then they simply see her. The one who moves something in their chests. The one who makes their palms perspire. And they know – this one will be their target.

'Russell Lee Holmes falls into this group of men, and looking at the victim profile, I am not convinced there was anything about clean, vibrant, upper-class Meagan Stokes to evoke blood lust in Russell Lee Holmes. To put it colloquially, she was not his type.'

'There are all the other factors,' David interjected, looking at Melanie. 'Such as how did an illiterate man fashion a ransom note?'

'Excellent point, Agent,' Quincy said approvingly. 'I have a copy of the ransom note in front of me. As the police argued in 1972, it is a very crude note with the words cut out of newspapers and the grammar incorrect. It was hand-delivered to the hospital where Harper Stokes worked, which was clever but simple. All of this fit their image of Russell Lee Holmes. However, if you break the note down, that argument does not hold. The words are too precisely placed for an uneducated, angry young man. There is no glue leaking from the edges, indicating a great deal of precision. Finally, there are no prints, no postmark, not even saliva used to seal the envelope. Whoever created this note was patient, intelligent, and very savvy about police procedure. None of that fits with what we know about Russell Lee Holmes.'

Melanie got up and shakily ran a glass of tap water in the sink. 'Then why can I picture Meagan in that shack? If she wasn't kidnapped by Russell Lee Holmes, why would she be there?'

'I'm not sure, Ms Stokes. I'm honestly very curious about your "memories" and what they might mean for the Meagan Stokes case. My overall impression is that it was a copycat crime deliberately set up by someone who knew something of Russell Lee Holmes's activities and who set out to emulate them, not out of neurosis, but out of a rational desire to cover up his or her own crime. When Meagan was kidnapped, it was already suspected that the children were kept alive and hidden away, so perhaps a shack was chosen to ensure that the crime fit as much "physical evidence" as possible. In 1972 that was certainly enough to fool the local police and FBI.

'But as I mentioned before, profiling takes us beyond mere physical imitation of crimes to the underlying motivations and behavior. Once again, the Meagan Stokes case does not fit with Russell Lee's motivation. Which brings me to the final, overwhelming factor in my mind – the disposal of her body.

'All of Russell Lee Holmes's victims were stripped naked and dumped. Except for Meagan Stokes. She was naked, but her body had been wrapped in a blanket. She was not dumped, but carefully buried. She was also mutilated, her hands and head cut off. Are you familiar with decapitation, Agent Riggs?'

'What do you mean?'

'Decapitation generally happens for two reasons. One is logical. The cleverer criminals, generally psychopaths who are actively seeking ways to cover their footsteps, will remove the head of their victim to make identifying the body difficult. They will also cut off hands in some cases.'

David said, 'But we've already established that Russell Lee Holmes isn't exactly clever or logical. So what's the second reason?'

'Emotional. Sometimes, if a murderer feels guilty about a victim, suffers remorse or shame, he will mutilate heads or hands to depersonalize the crime. Decapitation can be an indication that the victim was close to the killer.'

'Oh, God,' Melanie said, already knowing what was coming next.

'In conclusion,' Quincy said quietly, 'the body was covered by either someone who was very careful, or by someone who truly cared.'

'The parents,' David filled in, then added almost savagely, 'for the money, right? The million bucks.'

Melanie looked at him, startled. 'What?'

'Harper and Patricia Stokes had million-dollar life insurance policies on both of their children,' Quincy provided calmly. 'In fact, before Russell Lee Holmes confessed, the police were actively investigating Harper Stokes. The seventies were a tough time for him. He had lost quite a bit of money on various speculative deals, and without that life insurance policy he may have been forced to declare bankruptcy.'

'You do not murder your own child for money!' Melanie shouted. 'Not . . . not even for a million dollars! And if both of them were insured, why Meagan? Why not Brian? Oh, God, why not Brian?' She bowed her head, even more horrified. Of course Brian had probably thought of that before. Most likely her moody brother had spent most of the last twenty-five years thinking *Why not me?* And he had always been resentful toward their father, almost hateful. Had he known? Had he suspected? *Oh, Brian . . .*

'Wouldn't you just fake the kidnapping?' she cried. 'Couldn't they have just faked Meagan's disappearance, held her in a shack, and collected the ransom money from the bank or whatever? That would fit with what I know—'

'Except how would they explain the money,' David said softly. 'If Harper and Patricia Stokes suddenly had a hundred thousand dollars, people would get suspicious. If they had lost their daughter, however, and received the life insurance, then everything was explained.'

'Except their daughter is dead. They wouldn't do that. I know them, David. They are my parents and I swear to you they couldn't do something as sick as murder their four-year-old daughter for money.'

'Ms Stokes,' Quincy interjected somberly. 'I know you don't want to hear this, but based on what I've seen here, I think Meagan Stokes was decapitated out of guilt. She was buried out of remorse. And she was wrapped in a blanket out of love. Ms Stokes, in only three other cases have I seen a child's body so carefully swaddled and buried. In all three of those cases, the killer turned out to be the child's mother.'

'Oh, God.'

'Serial killers do not have a need to cocoon their corpses in soft blankets. Protecting a child, however, even when it is too late, even when it is out of guilt, is a trait that is distinctly maternal. At this point, based on what I have read, I would reopen this case, Agent Riggs and Ms Stokes. I would look at the family members very carefully. I would examine everyone's motives and exactly what was going on with the family in the summer of 1972, including all friends and relatives. And I would start with Patricia Stokes.'

16

The Waltham Suites was a decent hotel. The two-bedroom accommodation was decorated in shades of blue and mauve with that fake cherry-wood furniture so many New England hotels favored. One bedroom was upstairs in a loft area, the other was downstairs across from the kitchenette. David placed his duffel bag in the lower bedroom – closest to the door – while Melanie roamed the living room, her complexion still the color of bone.

At the drugstore by David's apartment they'd gotten her some basic toiletries. The pharmacy chain didn't carry any clothes, so Melanie remained stuck with David's old T-shirt and oversized sweats. They made her appear small, particularly now as she stood at the dark window with her arms around her waist and her gaze focused on a moonless night. Outside, cars raced down the interstate. Headlights washed over her face briefly, illuminating her eyes.

'Well,' David said at last, 'what do you think?'

'It's fine.'

He waited for her to say something more, but she didn't. David wasn't sure what to do. Ever since the discussion with Quincy, Melanie had slid deeper and deeper inside herself. Her eyes had taken on the flat look of a war veteran, her lips compressed into a bloodless line. She'd hit the wall, he figured, and now would either bend or break. Unfortunately, he couldn't figure out which, and it was beginning to scare him.

She turned on the TV. A brightly dressed anchorwoman gazed somberly at the camera while reporting, 'Shots broke out in downtown Boston earlier today.' Footage of the outside of the hotel filled the screen. People were gawking at the door. A few tourists were taking pictures. Little was known, and the ten-second report wrapped up without saying much of anything.

Melanie turned off the TV. She picked up a magazine, flipped through it, set it down. Next, she picked up an ashtray. Her hands were trembling. Christ, she had small hands. He couldn't imagine her shut up in some shack with the likes of Russell Lee Holmes.

David set his laptop down on the dining room table. He planned on working most of the night, doing more research, catching up on his paperwork. At seven A.M. sharp he and Chenney had to meet with

Supervisory Agent Lairmore. The discussion wouldn't be pretty. Lairmore liked things neat and clean, investigations run like paint-by-number kits. That his healthcare fraud agents were now chasing a twenty-five-year-old homicide would not amuse him.

David walked into the kitchenette, tossed his supply of vegetables into the freezer, then hesitated.

His back hurt. Shit, it *throbbed*.

He wasn't sleeping enough, and he was under stress. He was shooting guns again, and recoil always did him in. Truth of the matter was, the Bureau had done the right thing by assigning him to white collar crime. He couldn't go racing down dark alleys in the heat of the moment. He couldn't leap tall buildings in a single bound. He did have a medical condition, and it was growing worse.

His life now boiled down to three fun-filled options each night: carrots, cauliflower, or broccoli?

He went with cauliflower, stuffing two bags in the back waistband of his jeans. When he walked out of the kitchen, he looked like an idiot, and he knew it.

Melanie was no longer on the couch. She'd returned to the window and had her hands pressed against the glass. There was something about her profile, haunted, stark, resigned, that sent him reeling.

David had a crazy flashback. He was nine years old, and his mother had finally come home from the hospital. She was lying on the couch in the living room with him and his dad and Steven around her. His dad and brother were smiling rigidly. Dad had explained it to them earlier – their mom was dying. Nothing more to be done. Now they must be strong for her. As strong as strong could be.

His mom ruffled his hair. Then she stroked Steven's cheek as if he were still a baby. Then she looked away, her gaze steady, accepting, and so racked with pain, it had socked the breath right out of David.

They were all trying to be brave for her, he'd realized at the age of nine, when really his mother was the brave one. They were trying to be heroes, when she already was one. Oh, God, his mother was a magnificent woman!

And a heartbeat later the cancer took her away.

David snapped back to the hotel room. Grown man, not a kid. Frozen vegetables strapped to his back. That familiar ache tightening around his ribs.

He wished he could stand more like a man for Melanie Stokes. *Goddammit . . .*

'You should get some sleep,' he said tersely.

She turned toward him, her face expressionless. 'What are you going to do?'

'Work. Tomorrow I got a meeting with my boss, then I'll follow up with Detective Jax. It'll be a busy day.'

Melanie frowned. 'And what am I supposed to do?'

'Stay outta sight, of course. Relax a bit. Sit back and smell the coffee.'

'Sit back and smell the coffee?' She arched a brow, her voice picking up, her cheeks turning red. Maybe he shouldn't have sounded so flippant. '*Sit back and smell the coffee*. Oh, sure. In the last two days I've learned I probably am the *fucking* child of a *fucking* murderer, adopted by other *fucking* murderers to cover their own *fucking* tracks. Sure, let me spend the day with Juan Valdez. That sounds *fucking great!*'

David leaned back. Then his own temper sparked. So he didn't know all the right things to say. He was just a guy. An overworked, unappreciated, sexually frustrated guy.

'I'd take you to the office,' he informed her coldly, 'but the Bureau doesn't have day care.'

Her eyes went wide. The pulse point on her neck began to pound. Her hands formed into tight fists, and the frustration ripped down her spine in a long, violent tremor.

He was suddenly breathless.

Melanie wanted to fight, he realized. She wanted to yell, she wanted to scream, she wanted to run. He could feel it all there, broiling, clouding her eyes.

Saint Melanie. Charitable Melanie. Perfect daughter, perfect sister Melanie. For the first time he got it. All the little bits of her – the angry parts, the resentful parts, the fearful parts – she swallowed back down because she was the adopted daughter and she couldn't afford to make waves. She couldn't afford to be less than Meagan.

Shit, he suddenly wanted to kiss her. He wanted to close the space between them, take her lips, and feel all those emotions explode beneath him. Wild Melanie. Hurt Melanie. *Real* Melanie. Fuck. He wanted the *honesty* of it, and that was the biggest lie of all.

'I want to be alone,' she said abruptly.

'Still hiding? Still going to smile and pretend it's all right?' He took a step toward her.

'You're one to talk,' she said, bringing up her chin. She was trying to look blasé, but he could tell she was pissed. Her cheeks were red and her eyes overbright. She looked gorgeous.

He took another step and she shook her head.

'No,' she said fiercely. 'Dammit, just *no*. I don't care how you look or if you smell like Old Spice. I don't care if it's been months since I've had sex. I don't care if fucking you would be a helluva lot better than thinking about Russell Lee Holmes—'

'So you've thought about it.' His tone was blatantly triumphant, unforgivably smug. She looked mutinous.

'Of course I did. You picked me up that first day. Carried me. Made me feel safe.' Her voice faltered. She made a wistful sound, and it lured him closer, made him hold his own breath. Then her lips thinned and she recovered herself with a vengeance. 'But that wasn't real, was it, David? Not an act of kindness at all, but a federal employee doing his job. And you *lied* to me. I am so *tired* of everyone lying to me!'

'I did my job by covering my identity. Not all lies are created equal.'

She laughed harshly. 'Splitting hairs, that's what it boils down to. Splitting hairs. Oh, my God, my mother.'

She sat down on a chair. David said to hell with it and went over to her.

She was stiff, resistant. He curved one arm around her, figuring if she belted him, it was his own fault. But she didn't hit him. She made a sound, the sound of surrender, then strong, capable Melanie Stokes buried herself in his arms.

Ah, Christ. She was so small, hardly made a dent against his chest. And all that silky blond hair and the soft citrusy scent. He did want to keep her safe. Lord help him, he wanted to be her hero.

He pulled her onto his lap and rocked her against him.

She did not cry. He figured she wouldn't. Instead, she fisted his sweatshirt, burying her face against his throat. He placed his cheek on the top of her head and wrapped his legs around her.

'I love them,' she whispered. 'They're my family and I love them. Is that so bad?'

'No,' he said roughly. 'No.'

'They gave me everything I ever wanted. They played with me, they loved with me. They went to *garage sales* with me, for heaven's sake. The Stokeses at a garage sale. Surely that couldn't all be a lie. Surely.'

'I don't know. I don't.'

She gripped him tighter. And a heartbeat later she murmured, 'I'm nine years old again, waking up in the hospital with all these lines and needles sticking out of my body, and this time there is no one to bail me out, David. This time there is no one there.'

'Shh,' he told her again and again. 'Shhhh.'

She started to cry. After a minute he kissed the top of her head. Then he kissed her harder, smoothing back her hair, kissing the tears from her cheeks. And then he was kissing her neck, her forehead, the curve of her ears. Anything but her mouth. He knew, they both knew, he couldn't kiss her mouth. Don't cross the line, don't cross the line.

She angled her head up and he grazed the corner of her lips, the tip of her chin, the point of her nose, the dimple of her cheek.

'More,' she whispered, 'more.'

So he kissed her throat, small, nuzzling kisses, like they were hormone-enraged teenagers necking on the sofa. He drew her lobe between his lips and sucked. She sighed and shifted restlessly on his lap. He nipped her ear. She wriggled against his erection, and now they were both breathing very fast.

Her neck. She had a long, sexy neck. Her cheeks, smooth as silk. He followed the line of her jaw, and then, as if drawn by a magnet, his lips were at the corner of her mouth again. He could feel her breath coming hard. Feel her tension, the tight moment of total anticipation. A slight turn, by either one of them, and the kiss would be had. Her lips beneath his. Her mouth opening hungrily. The wonderful, satisfying flavor of Melanie Stokes.

He could feel her shuddering. God, she was tearing him apart.

Slowly, very slowly, David drew back. They both sighed and it said enough.

He was the agent building a case against her father. He still hadn't told her the complete truth, and he'd been raised better than that. Even if he couldn't be the baseball player his father had wanted, he could still be the man.

'You all right?' he murmured after a moment.

'Better.'

Her hips were still resting against his groin. She didn't seem to mind, so neither did he. It was one of the advantages of being an adult, David thought. You really could just hold someone.

He looped one long strand of her hair around his hand. She had beautiful hair. It smelled good too. He would like to bury both his hands in it and rub until she sighed.

His erection got a bit more uncomfortable, and he had to shift.

'You wear Old Spice,' Melanie murmured. 'I didn't think anyone wore Old Spice anymore.'

'My dad,' he said absently, and moved on to examining the shell-like curve of her tiny ear.

'You're close to him, aren't you?'

'Used to be.' Melanie Stokes even had pretty ears. Probably had cute toes as well, he thought.

'Used to be?' She looked up at him.

'Things change. They just do.'

'The arthritis?' Her gaze narrowed shrewdly. 'Is your father the same great communicator as you?'

'I learned it all from him.'

'Ah. And your mother isn't alive anymore to run interference. What a shame.'

'I suppose.' He'd never thought about it that way, but Melanie probably had a point.

'Tell me about your mother,' she murmured intently. 'Tell me what it was like to grow up with people you knew were your parents and would always love you.'

David couldn't answer right away. The pain beneath her words tightened his throat too much.

She said, 'Please?'

'I don't know. I don't remember much. You know kids. You inherit the world and you take it for granted.'

'Did your mom bake cookies? When I was in the hospital, I always imagined a mom in a white ruffled apron baking chocolate chip cookies. I don't know why that image was so strong for me.'

'Yeah, my mom baked cookies. Chocolate chip. Oatmeal. Sugar cookies with green frosting for St Patrick's Day. God, I haven't thought of that in a while.' He rubbed his forehead. 'Uh, she read us stories too. And made us clean our rooms. She even laughed at my father's stories from work. And she was very pretty,' he said. 'I remember thinking as a little kid that I'd gotten the prettiest mom on the block.'

'She sounds wonderful.'

'Yeah,' he whispered softly. 'She was. I remember . . . I remember her and Dad coming home from the hospital, sitting us down. I remember they were holding hands and my dad was crying. I'd never seen him cry before. Then they said "Cancer." Just "cancer," as if that explained everything.'

'I can't imagine explaining that to a child.'

'Neither could they, I guess. Dad told us Mom would need more help around the place, so Steven and I cleaned it up pronto that first afternoon. We actually tried to clean the bathrooms for the first time as a surprise. For the record, hand soap doesn't clean stainless steel very well. Then you should've seen us with the vacuum cleaner. Oh, boy.'

'Made a mess?'

'Sucked up half the drapes. Who would've thought?'

Melanie smiled. 'It was sweet, though, both of you trying.'

'Yeah. Mom went to chemo, we stripped the kitchen floors. Radiation treatment started, we did the windows. She relapsed, we shampooed the rugs. People in the neighborhood were always dropping by with casseroles, pot roasts, you know, because surely with the little wife feeling "blue," the husband and sons would starve. They'd comment on how great the house looked, how great Steven and I looked. What brave little troopers we must be.

'My mom went back to the hospital. We stripped beds and soaped down furniture and beat out drapes and polished silver and she came home. She came home and lay down in our perfectly spotless living room and died. Because that's what cancer does. It kills you even when you have perfect little boys and a perfect loving husband doing everything they know how to do to keep you alive.'

'I'm sorry,' she whispered.

He shrugged awkwardly. His voice had broken more bitterly than he'd intended. He couldn't find a good flippant retort to break the mood. He never thought about this stuff. He just didn't. Now he felt overexposed.

He untangled Melanie from his lap, climbed off the chair, and put some space between them. He could tell she was a little hurt, but he couldn't find it in himself to go back.

'It's . . . uh . . . it's not easy to talk about it,' he said.

'I know.'

'I just, um, need some space.'

'David, I know.'

'Jesus Christ, how much bad luck can one fucking family have!'

Melanie didn't say anything this time, and he exhaled in one angry rush. Time to get a grip, Riggs. Time to pull it together. He settled his hands on his hips and looked around.

'It's getting late, Melanie. What do you say?'

'Yeah, I guess it is time for bed.' She suddenly flushed. 'I mean to sleep. In our own rooms. In our own beds.'

'You take the loft. I should be close to the door.'

'You really will be gone all day?'

'I have to go to this meeting. My boss is a little excited about me firing my gun. In contrast to what you might think, it doesn't happen every day, particularly when you work fraud.'

'You did well,' she said, looking impressed. 'Got me out. Wounded the guy.'

David grimaced. 'After all the times I've fired at paper, I should've put it where it counted.'

'He was a human being, David. Not paper.'

'Well, we'll see if we both still think that when he comes around again. I'll try not to be in the office too long. Why don't you sleep in, order up a big breakfast. Take a day to relax and catch your breath again.'

'Maybe,' she said at last. Then, 'I should call my mother.'

'No—'

'Yes. I can't just stay out all night without even a phone call. You have no idea how much she worries.'

David gave her a look. 'Don't tell her what's really going on. Until we know who is involved and why, it's too dangerous. Got it?'

'I'll say I'm spending the night at a friend's.'

'Don't go into details. Details will only get you into trouble.'

'So says the master,' Melanie muttered. She turned toward the stairs. The minute she saw shadows gathering upstairs, her shoulders sagged.

'Why don't I leave the lights on?' he said.

'It's okay. I'm a grown woman. I know better than to be afraid of the dark.'

'Yeah, but I'm an FBI agent, and frankly, we're all a bunch of wusses. There isn't an agent alive who doesn't sleep with the light on. I swear.'

She smiled. It was filled with just enough gratitude to tighten his chest.

'Thank you,' she whispered.

Melanie climbed upstairs. David watched her, feeling the cold water trickle down his back as the cauliflower melted in his jeans.

He turned on his computer. Fetched the fax sent by Chenney earlier in the evening. Started poring over a twenty-five-year-old case file, courtesy of the Houston police.

His back throbbed, his eyes blurred with exhaustion. He made some instant coffee and kept going.

'I'm gonna get you,' he muttered. 'Whoever you are, after what you did to little Meagan, I'm gonna get you good.'

17

Patricia was asleep when the phone rang. In her dreams she was Miss Texas again, walking the runway with her Vaseline smile and beaded gown. Look at me, look at me, look at me.

And they did. The men roared their approval. The women cried to see such beauty. She had captured the hearts of her home state. She had made her father proud, and as they placed the diamond tiara on her head, she wished it would last forever.

Fairy tales should never end.

She walked backstage and Jamie O'Donnell wrapped his arms around her.

'Beautiful lass, beautiful lass.'

She giggled and kissed him passionately.

She looked beyond his shoulders and saw her daughter's headless body.

'Bad Mommy, bad Mommy, BAD MOMMY!'

Patricia jolted awake with a scream.

Blackness, thick blackness. The phone rang for the second time, and she fumbled for it. She could read the clock now. Just after midnight. Harper was still not home.

She put the phone to her ear.

'Mom?'

Patricia was so disoriented, she almost screamed again.

'It's Melanie,' the voice continued, and Patricia, rattled beyond words, just nodded. Then she gripped the phone tighter and commanded herself to pull it together for her second daughter. 'Yes, Melanie love? Where are you calling from? It's after midnight – are you all right?'

There was a pause, too long a pause. Patricia felt the first whisper of unease. 'Honey, is everything all right?'

Did you find a note too? Did someone slip into your locked car? Threaten you, snatch you, kill you? Oh, God, please, baby, please, baby, tell me you're all right. I swear I never meant—

'I've just had a long day,' Melanie said. 'I met up with a friend. We went to a few bars. I'm going to stay here for the night.'

Patricia frowned. Her daughter never did things like meet an anonymous friend for drinks and then spend the night.

'Are you sure you're all right? I can come get you. It's no bother. Really.'

'I'm fine.'

'Are you having another migraine? Your father and I have been worried about you.'

'You have?' She sounded genuinely surprised.

'Of course. Melanie, I don't know what's going on. You're calling me in the middle of the night, and you don't sound like yourself. Please, sweetheart, if you need to talk, if you've done something and now you need a shoulder to cry on . . .'

Her voice ending pleadingly, maybe desperately. Suddenly she had that same tightness in her chest she'd gotten the day she'd come home to police cars surrounding her house and a man she'd never met before calmly telling her they were doing everything they could to find her daughter.

'Melanie?' she whispered.

'Do you remember the first day you came to the hospital?' her daughter asked suddenly. 'Do you remember the first time you saw me?'

'Of course I do. Why—'

'When I looked at you, Mom, I remember thinking you were so beautiful, so lovely. I desperately wanted to be your little girl. I don't even know why. I just did. What did you think when you looked at me?'

'I . . . I remember being very impressed, Melanie. You were such a small child, abandoned, no name, no memories. You should've been terrified, but you weren't. You smiled bravely. You told little jokes and made other people laugh. You looked . . . you looked strong, Melanie. You looked like everything I had always wanted to be.'

'But why adopt me? Had you and Dad spoken about adopting a child before?'

'Well, no . . .'

'Then why change?' Melanie's voice had gained urgency. 'Why suddenly adopt a nine-year-old girl?'

'I don't know! It was like you said, I suppose. The minute I saw you, I wanted you too.'

'Why, Mom? *Why?*'

'I don't know!'

'Yes, you do, dammit! I want to hear it! Why me?'

'It doesn't matter—'

'Yes, it does! You know it does. Tell me. Tell me right now. *Why did you adopt me?*'

'*Because you looked like Meagan!* All right? Are you happy? Because when I saw you I thought of Meagan, and then I had to have you. I just had to have you . . .' Patricia broke off. She realized what she had said. The silence on the other end confirmed it. Oh God, what had she done?

'Meagan,' her daughter said quietly. 'You looked at me and you saw Meagan.'

'No, I didn't mean that! Melanie, please, you confused me, you badgered me.'

She didn't seem to have heard her. 'I got a family because I looked like a murdered little girl. The house, your love . . . All along you just wanted Meagan back.'

'No!' Patricia cried. 'No, that's not what I meant—'

'Yes, it is, Mom. Finally we are getting to the truth. Why is it so hard in our family to get to the truth?'

'Melanie love, listen to me. I am human. In the beginning . . . in the beginning maybe I was confused. Maybe I did see what I wanted to see. I *know* you are not Meagan. Remember when I dressed you up in those lacy dresses and did your hair? Remember what that did to you? And I saw it, Melanie. I realized how much I was hurting you. And I let it go. I realized I wasn't looking for Meagan after all. She was gone, but through God's good graces, I had gotten another little girl, a different little girl, Melanie Stokes, who likes used clothes and garage sale furniture. And I discovered I genuinely *loved* Melanie Stokes. You healed me, honey. You are the best thing that ever happened to me, and I swear to you, Melanie, your life has not been a lie. I love you. I do.'

There was no answer. Just more chilling silence that signaled her daughter's doubt, her daughter's hurt.

Patricia closed her eyes. A tear trickled down her cheek. She didn't wipe it away.

'Melanie?' she whispered.

'Did you really love Meagan?'

'Oh, heavens, child. More than my own life.'

More silence. 'I . . . I have to go now.'

'Melanie, I love you too.'

'Good night, Mom.'

'Melanie—'

'Good night.'

The phone clicked. Patricia was alone in the darkness.

She thought of those warm, sunny days in Texas with the first daughter she had loved so much. She thought of the note in her car. She thought of her son, no longer speaking to his father. She thought of Jamie O'Donnell and all the sins that never could be undone.

She whispered, 'No more, Lord. This family has paid enough.'

Dr William Sheffield slept on the empty hospital bed the way he'd learned when he was an intern. Then the hand on his watch hit three A.M., and the tiny bell began to chime.

He sat up smoothly, going from deep slumber to instant wakefulness the way only a doctor can. He felt a faint hammering in the back of his skull. The whiskey, of course.

He'd brought a pint into the hospital with him earlier, finding a back room and spending hours bolstering his courage, fingering the gun he now wore beneath his white lab coat. He wasn't thinking of what he'd found in his house last night – piles of healthy pink organs and a shiny red apple on his bed, and on his bathroom mirror the words *you get what you deserve* scrawled in blood. The whiskey warmth had carried him to his special place, where he was the golden boy, the perfect anesthesiologist, the man who always won at the roulette table with his lucky number eight.

'*Just a few more,*' Harper had repeated earlier in the day.

It's too risky, William had insisted.

Nonsense, Harper had said briskly, but William could tell he was scared too. The last few days, calm, controlled Harper Stokes hadn't seemed so calm or controlled. William had even caught him glancing over his shoulder from time to time, as if he expected to find something bad behind him.

'*Three more, tops,*' Harper had finally said. '*You can handle it, William. Your credit card debts will be clear and you can start over, clean slate. Still making over half a million as an anesthesiologist. As long as you don't resume gambling, you should be able to live a very good life, without anyone being hurt or anyone being the wiser. That's what you've always wanted, isn't it?*'

That was what William had always wanted. The fancy house, the fancy car, the fancy clothes. Every symbol of success dripping from his wrist, his feet, his body. So William had agreed. He'd had his whiskey, and an hour earlier he'd walked into the ICU, and in plain sight of God and everyone, he'd injected a vial of propranolol into the candidate.

Now he dug into the pocket of his lab jacket and fingered the second needle.

He stepped out into the hall.

At three in the morning the hospital had adopted a quiet, somber state. Lights were dimmed for patients. The nurses talked softer. Machines pulsed rhythmically. There was no one in the halls as William slipped into the ICU.

The candidate had been admitted that morning. That's how William categorized them in his mind: Candidates.

Tonight's candidate was a sixty-five-year-old male. Healthy. Active. History of heart disease in the family – he'd watched his father drop dead of a heart attack at fifty – so at the first signs of chest pains, the man had dialed 911 and hopped a ride to the ER.

He'd gone through the whole medical process, including a fluoroscopy, which had revealed he didn't have any blocked arteries. Now he was drugged in the ICU to keep himself from pulling out the catheter. His heart monitor looked good. They still weren't detecting any dangerous cardiac enzymes, and most likely he'd be released in the morning, none the worse for the wear.

Except an hour ago Dr William Sheffield had injected him with the beta blocker propranolol, causing temporary heart failure that had been reversed only by the nurse administering .5 milligrams of atropine. That had been round one. Now it was time for round two, and the overworked nurse was once again out of the room, checking on someone else.

It was the fault of budget cuts, William thought dully. The fault of stupid nurses who didn't protect their charges from people like him. The fault of paranoid candidates who thought they could still eat pepperoni pizzas and garlic bread without repercussions.

The fault of everyone else but him. He was just a lonely, abandoned kid trying to make his way in the world. The rest of them should know better.

William grabbed the T-injection port on the IV and stuck in the second needle.

The candidate's heart rate plunged to below thirty beats per minute and the heart monitor screeched red alert.

William hightailed it for the door. He was just about to pass through, when he spotted the nurse racing down the hall, a second just coming around the corner behind her.

Shit, they would see him. How to explain leaving the room? What to do?

Hide. William dropped to the floor and rolled beneath a pile of soiled sheets just as one of the nurses rushed into the room.

'Come on, Harry, come on,' the nurse was saying. 'Don't you do this to me again.'

The second nurse arrived on the scene. 'I got a pulse.'

'He's still breathing, what's the blood pressure?'

The rasping sound of the blood pressure cuff. The nurse cursed at the reading while the blood monitor alarm still screeched because Harry's heart refused to speed up.

'We need atropine,' the first nurse declared. 'Second time tonight. Come on, Harry, what are you trying to do to us? We like you here, I swear it.'

She rushed out, then returned moments later. William heard her tap the needle to remove air pockets.

The atropine, he guessed. Please, please, don't let her drop the needle and bend down to pick it up.

'Come on, come on, come on,' the first nurse muttered. Abruptly the beeping stopped. The atropine had successfully stimulated the heart rate back to normal.

'Well, he's stable for now,' the first nurse said with a sigh.

'Have you called Dr Carson-Miller?'

'Not yet, but I'll give her a buzz now. This is Harry's second attack in just three hours. That's not good.'

'Anything you need me to do?'

'No, I'm all set. Thanks, Sally.'

'Anytime. M&M's at four, right?'

'Wouldn't miss it for the world.'

Sally exited. The first nurse picked up the phone and called the on-duty cardiologist.

Once again everything proceeded as planned.

Harper had explained it to him two years ago. '*What is the weakness of a hospital? The fact that it's all routine. Each crisis has a process. Everything we do is planned and predictable. In the end, medicine is much more cookie-cutter than doctors care to admit, and we can exploit that.*'

'He's gone bradycardic twice now,' the nurse was explaining to Dr Carson-Miller, no doubt having woken her up from her sleep in another empty hospital room. 'I've administered atropine both times to restore rhythm.'

William knew the cardiologist's response. 'Twice, huh? Keep Harry NPO. We'll have his doctor check him out again in the morning, and bring in Dr Stokes for a consult. Glance at his day, all right? Good night.'

The phone clicked. William managed to breathe again. Everything was done. He still felt hysterical but wasn't sure why. After all, it went just like all of them went, smooth as glass. Inject twice, giving the candidate two bradycardic episodes. Cardiologist does the sensible thing and recommends the installation of a pacemaker to regulate the heart, Dr Harper Stokes agrees, and it's done.

Why wouldn't the nurse leave now? William needed her to leave now.

He heard footsteps, loud, ringing footsteps coming down the hall. Men's shoes appeared in view. Brown suede Italian loafers.

'I'm sorry, sir,' the nurse said immediately. 'But you can't just walk into the ICU.'

'Um,' the man said. 'I know . . . this is for family only—'

'During visiting hours,' the nurse said firmly. 'These aren't visiting hours.'

'Ah, yes, um, I know. But I'm with the FBI . . .'

William bit his lower lip.

'I'm a friend of this guy. I mean, he's an old friend of the family. I understand he had some chest pains today and was rushed to the ER. We'd heard it was nothing, but then I found out he was in the ICU. I promised my pop I'd check in on him. Of course, my job doesn't let me come during normal hours. I was just gonna glance in, but the lady at the desk said he'd been having problems. Can't you at least tell me what's happening.'

The man was lying, of course. Even a four-year-old could tell the man was full of shit. FBI agent appearing in the hospital at three A.M. to look in on a 'friend'?

And then William understood. That's what the note had said – *You get what you deserve.* And the organs, of course, the organs were a symbol of what he and Harper were doing. Someone knew. Someone had sent the agent for him. At any minute the agent would make a pretense of dropping his gun, bend down, and shoot William.

You've been a bad boy, a very bad boy. Bad Billy.

'Oh, dear,' the nurse said. 'You really can't be in here. I'll have to ask you to step outside.'

'But is he all right?'

'Mr Boer has had a rough night, I'm afraid. Most likely he'll have surgery in the morning, but his doctor can tell you more about that.'

'He needs open heart surgery!' The man sounded both stricken and triumphant.

'Well, he might.'

'Please, nurse, tell me exactly what happened.'

The feet started moving. The nurse was ushering the man to the door. But she was also beginning to explain.

William lay transfixed.

You get what you deserve.

Slowly he reached beneath his arm and pulled out his gun. He took off the safety.

He was ready, he promised himself. He wasn't some scared, spineless kid anymore. He'd learned a lot growing up as an undersized boy in a Texas orphanage.

Time to start thinking, William. Time to take control.

You get what you deserve.

William made his decision. If that's the way this thing was going to be played, he'd play it. Dr Harper Stokes might think of William as harmless, maybe even a fall guy, but Dr Stokes hadn't seen nothing yet.

18

In a dark suite of the Four Seasons, just across from the Public Garden, just across from the Stokeses' Beacon Street town house, Jamie O'Donnell sat on a blue velvet sofa, brandy snifter in one hand, TV remote in another.

An old goat like him shouldn't be surfing the channels with the lights out. He should turn off the TV, go to bed. Snuggle up with Annie and savor the soft sound of her breathing. Beautiful woman, Annie. The best thing that had ever happened to him.

He remained in front of the TV, flipping the channels.

In many ways Jamie considered himself a simple man. He'd worked hard all his life, fighting his way up from poverty tooth and nail. He'd killed men and he'd seen them die. He'd done things he was proud of, and he'd done things he knew better than to think about late at night. You did what you had to.

He'd arrived in Texas at the ripe old age of thirteen. He started working the oil fields when he was just fourteen. By the time he was twenty he'd developed the broad shoulders and thick neck of a day laborer. His face was generally stained black, his nails too. Definitely not a pretty boy, but he'd never let it get in his way.

Come sunset, Jamie was always the first person off the fields, into the showers, and then into town. College campuses, that's where he liked to go. College campuses were where he could dream. And that's where he'd met Harper Stokes.

Introduced by mutual friends, they'd sized each other up immediately. Shrewd Harper had recognized that Jamie didn't fit in – no way was this thick, dark man a student. In turn, Jamie had known that Harper didn't fit in – no way was this thin, overdressed Poindexter really an aristocrat. They were the outsiders, and they both knew it. So they spent the next few months competing against each other to see who would break into the golden clique of old money. They schemed against each other and ridiculed each other and somehow, along the way, they ended up friends.

Harper liked to talk of money even back then. He was obsessed with what other boys wore, what other boys drove. Jamie understood. He'd spent enough time in the oil fields to know he wanted to be someone someday too.

Harper lectured him nonstop about the power of education, the proper way to talk and dress. Jamie figured he might have a point. He cleaned up a little. Then he taught Harper how to throw a proper right hook. Now, that was something every man ought to know.

And then on Friday nights, the mutual education delved into deeper grounds. Bookish Harper, desperate for the perfect upper-class wife, couldn't even get a date. Jamie, on the other hand, went through women by the dozen. He adored them, and they sure as hell adored him. So every now and then he'd try to send one Harper's way. It seemed the least he could do.

Then Patricia walked into both their lives.

Ironic that the things men would do for love could be so much worse than the things they'd do out of hate.

Life worked itself out. Jamie knew that now. In many ways he and his old friend had gotten exactly what they wanted. Harper lived in a Boston town house. He had his showcase wife, his golden children, his glowing rep-utation. No third-generation blueblood would question the great Dr Stokes these days.

And Jamie couldn't complain either. He jetted around the globe, he built a business empire. He stayed in all the right places, met with all the right people. Sure, not all his friends belonged in polite society. But he had power now. No one was getting rich off his sweat but him.

Two old men. So many years the wiser.

Perhaps when all was said and done, the biggest lesson of all was that familiarity did breed contempt.

One hour earlier Harper had called him on the phone, rousing him from his slumber. Harper's voice had been too calm. His anger too quiet.

'What are you doing, O'Donnell? It's been twenty-five years, I've kept my end of the bargain, and we are much too old for this shit.'

Jamie had yawned. 'Harper, it's two in the morning. I don't know what you're talking about, and I don't feel like playing guessing games—'

'The note in my car, dammit. This little vendetta against William. Breaking into his house to plant a pile of pig organs? Classy, O'Donnell. Just plain classy.'

'Someone left a pile of pig organs in William's house?' Jamie laughed. 'Did the poor boy get sick? I bet he did. I would've paid to see that, you know. I've always hated that spineless bugger.'

'Oh, cut the crap. I want to know why you're doing this. Dammit, we all have too much to lose.'

'You got it all wrong, sport. I don't know what the hell is going on or who the hell is doing it, but as of tonight, I also joined the club.'

'*What?*'

'I got a present too. Hand-delivered to the concierge downstairs. Wrapped nicely, I have to say. The ribbons even made those pretty little curlicues. You'd like it, Hap, you would.'

'What was it?' Harper sounded perplexed. He'd never liked the unexpected, and it was stealing his headwind of righteous rage.

'I got a canning jar. And floating in it, in some kind of shit I just don't want to know, is a cock and balls. A penis. A pickled penis.'

There was a moment of horrified silence, then Harper laughed. Then his voice grew cold. 'A castrated penis, how charming. Tell me, Jamie, do you still dream about her? Do you still lust after my wife?'

'For God's sake, Hap, I'm telling you again, I'm not the one responsible for what's going on. It's been decades, man. I've moved *on*.'

'Ah, decades, of course. I suppose even beauty queens don't look quite the same after thirty years—'

'You're an idiot, Harper.'

'That's what you'd like to think. But I'm the one who won the girl in the end, aren't I? And *I know* that still galls you, O'Donnell. You just can't handle that you've never understood Pat any more than you've understood me.'

'Hap, you're missing the point.'

'What point?'

'Somebody knows, Harper. After all these years, somebody knows about Meagan.'

Harper shut up. He turned his attention to business, and together they ran through the facts. It wasn't encouraging. Harper had received a note. William had gotten a pile of organs and a note, and Jamie now had a pickled penis. Plus there were the hangups Annie had been receiving. Finally, Larry Digger was in town after all these years.

'It could be him,' Jamie said after a moment.

'He doesn't have the imagination. Never did.'

'What about Patricia? Has she received anything?'

'Hasn't said a word to me.'

'She wouldn't say anything, Harper, at least not to you.'

Harper didn't argue the point. No matter what he liked to say, his marriage had fallen a long way from being a love match over the years, and they both knew it. 'She'd tell Brian though,' he said at last. 'And Brian would be angry enough to tell me.'

'Even now?'

'I think you know as well as I do, O'Donnell, that my own son hates me more than ever. I would think that would make you happy.'

'No,' Jamie said honestly. 'It doesn't.'

Harper cleared his throat. He was shaken up about his son. Handling it badly, in Jamie's opinion, but genuinely shaken up. That made Jamie feel something he wasn't prepared to feel after all these years – pity.

Sometimes he hated Harper Stokes. He saw all the things Harper did that his family knew nothing about, and at those times he thought Harper Stokes could very well be the devil. Then there were moments when he confused even Jamie. Harper did seem to love his son. He had been honestly betrayed by Brian's little announcement.

'Melanie's migraine,' Harper suddenly said.

'What about it?'

'I assumed it was due to stress, but what if it's not? Melanie hasn't had a migraine in ten years, not even when she split with William. So why now? Unless it's more than just stress. Unless it's her memories.'

'It could be. It could be.'

Jamie couldn't say anything more. He could tell Harper was equally spooked. Her memory was the wild card, the one thing that could undo it all. In the beginning they'd obsessed about it constantly. But after twenty-five years, all of them, he supposed, had grown comfortable.

'The truth has a life of its own,' Jamie said at last. 'Maybe the only real surprise is that it took it this long to find us again.'

'Who the hell could be doing this?' Harper exploded.

'I don't know.'

'What about you? Or maybe Brian?'

'What would we possibly have to gain, old man? How could we come out ahead? Melanie would hate our guts, and maybe you don't care, but I know I do. And I'm sure as holy hell that Brian does.'

'It's too late, O'Donnell. All of us have gained too much to lose it all now. I'm taking the family to Europe, that's it.'

'Europe?'

'Oh, I didn't tell you?' Harper's voice grew innocent, and Jamie knew his old friend was moving in for the kill. 'I asked Pat this morning. We're taking the whole family, including Brian, on vacation. Just gonna pack up our bags and go, to hell with everything. Very romantic, Pat said. She seems quite excited about it. I know I am.'

Jamie didn't say a word. He simply gripped the phone tighter and listened.

'Don't you get it yet, *sport*? Patricia loves me. She's always loved me. I do know how to make her happy, O'Donnell. I am *just her kind*. So take care of this *person*, okay? We both know that getting dirty is your line of work, not mine.'

Harper hung up. But Jamie whispered into the phone anyway. 'Yes, she's always loved you. But you've never *cared*, old sport. You got the goddamn perfect family and you've never, ever *cared!*'

He slammed down the phone. And then he simply felt tired.

Four A.M. A one-minute roundup of local news came on. Jamie watched the report of a shooting in a downtown hotel. Reporter Larry Digger was dead.

Jamie froze. Harper had not mentioned it. Jamie certainly hadn't arranged it. What was going on?

He turned up the volume. The gunman had escaped and was being considered armed and dangerous. A sketch flashed on the screen and Jamie recognized the face.

He hurled the remote across the room and watched it smash into pieces. It wasn't enough. He tipped over the glass coffee table and listened to it shatter.

'You fucker. You panicked, shitless, spineless fucker. How dare you betray me like that? *How dare you betray me!*'

The bedroom door opened. Ann Margaret stood there, wearing a white bedsheet and looking at him in confusion.

'Jamie?'

'Go to bed!'

Ann Margaret didn't move. 'Jamie, what's wrong?'

'Get away. Just get away.'

Ann Margaret moved closer. Then she said calmly, 'Nonsense, Jamie. There is nothing you can do that I can't handle. I love you, sweetheart. I do.'

Jamie hung his head and groaned.

He knew he shouldn't. He did it anyway, crossing to her in three strides, his chest thundering, his body covered in sweat. He took her in his arms and he was at once awed and humbled.

This woman had her own kind of beauty and her own kind of strength. This woman had an indomitable spirit and a tough, sensible shell. No pedigrees, no fancy words, no phony pretenses. She was right; whatever he did, she could handle. Neither of them was better than the other, and neither of them was worse.

And he loved her for that. He loved her deeply, and it was one of the few things in life that scared him.

Jamie pulled out of her arms. There were things he had to do and they were errands best done in the dark.

The TV was still on, casting its ghostly light on the room. He'd left the canning jar out in the open without thinking. Ann Margaret suddenly spotted it.

'Jamie?' she whispered.

He closed his eyes. 'It came today,' he said gruffly. 'Someone's sick idea of a joke, I guess.'

'It's about her, isn't it?'

'Annie, it was a long time ago—'

'But not long enough, Jamie. Not so long ago that someone still isn't remembering, that someone still doesn't want to see you pay.'

Jamie couldn't reply to that.

'Do you still love her?'

'No, Annie, I don't.'

'Did she get an adulterer's penis? Maybe a chastity belt?'

Jamie took her arm, forcing her to look at him. 'Annie,' he said softly, 'it's not just about Patricia.'

'How do you know? *What is going on?*'

'Harper got a note,' he said steadfastly.

'What kind of note?'

'The kind that says you get what you deserve. Plus, Larry Digger is in town and Melanie is having migraines and, Annie, William got . . . he got a note too. "You get what you deserve." '

'Oh, God.' Her tough, sensible shell shattered. 'Why doesn't it ever end?'

'I don't know. Must just be the way of things, I suppose. Some people get a good life, and some people don't.'

Jamie strapped on his gun. 'Don't let anyone in, Annie, and don't answer the phone.'

'Where are you going? What are you going to do?'

'I don't know yet.'

'Jamie . . .'

He walked to the door. Opened it. Took a step. Turned again. He came as close as he could to saying what was in his heart.

'I'll look after you, Annie. You and Melanie. I swear it.'

Brian Stokes jerked awake. It was the fifth time in five hours, and his lover finally said, 'Do you want to talk about it or should I just get you a package of razor blades?'

'Leave me alone.'

'You were dreaming, you know. I heard you call a name.'

Brian rolled away. 'Shut up.'

Nate sat up instead. Besides Melanie he was the only person Brian had ever trusted. He always pressed and he always saw too much. Now he tossed back the covers and adjusted his pajamas over his middle-aged frame, a sure sign he was gearing up for a serious discussion.

'You called out for Meagan,' he said gently. 'Brian, even when you're awake you never say that name.'

Brian thought he was going to cry. 'Fuck you.' He got up, walked to the window, and stared out at the still-sleeping city. But the images in his head were all he saw.

The funeral on the gray, dreary day. His mother keeling over halfway through the service from grief and gin. His father, stony-faced, looking at her as if he hated her.

The silence in the days afterward. The huge house empty of little-girl squeals.

Harper screaming one night, 'Where the hell were you all day? If you'd just come home . . .'

His mother replying, 'I didn't mean . . . I didn't know . . . I thought

Brian needed some time alone with me. You know how he can be, especially around her.'

'Well, he's got you all to himself now, doesn't he? He's got that, all fucking right.'

I'm sorry. I can't even tell you why I was so cruel.

Nate came up behind him. 'You're worried about your sister, aren't you?' he asked, rubbing Brian's arms. 'You've been like this ever since you went to see her.'

'I don't want to talk about it.'

'Of course not,' Nate agreed amiably. 'So how long are you going to hate yourself, Brian? And how long are you going to hate Melanie for daring to care?'

'I don't—'

'She came to you for help. You haven't even called her since.'

'You don't understand.'

Nate gave him a look. He'd seen Brian at his worst, when he was so filled with self-loathing he could barely crawl out of bed. Nate understood plenty. He said, 'Then explain it to me. Give me one logical reason for blowing off your poor sister.'

Brian shifted uneasily. 'She's better off without me. She is.'

'Hah,' Nate said. 'Your sister adores you. First sign of trouble, who does she call? Big-brother Brian. That's because she knows you care. Because you've always looked out for her. She *trusts* you. She loves you. Why are you being so difficult now?'

Brian gritted his teeth. 'It's different.'

'Your sister needs help. Not that different.'

'It's complicated, all right? She doesn't know about Meagan. No one knows about Meagan. Dammit, *I* don't want to know about Meagan!'

Nate said quietly, 'You know, you're the only person I know who came out of the closet to hide a bigger secret.'

'I did not—'

'I've been around the block a few times, I know the signs. I've watched other men come out of the closet, and it isn't easy. But generally there is a moment of relief afterward. You haven't gotten that sense of relief, have you, Brian? Six months later you are just as tense and troubled as before. Why is that? If you are finally at peace with who you are, why are you somehow *angrier*?'

Brian couldn't answer. Nate didn't need him to. 'Because that wasn't *the* secret, was it, Brian?'

Brian didn't answer.

Five A.M. dawn was just breaking over the horizon, washing Boston's streets in shades of gold. The man finally turned away from the window. He was tired from a long, hard night, but also exhilarated.

The game was in full motion now, the players not just assembled, but moving around the board. He found it interesting that for a group of people who half hated one another, for twenty-five years they had stayed close together. It made it easy to monitor them.

Harper was looking over his shoulder. William was carrying a gun. Brian Stokes was suffering from long, sleepless nights. The rest of them were working frantically to keep their secrets.

A shooter had been unleashed and the first death recorded.

And Melanie? He wasn't even sure where she was, but assumed she was safe. Otherwise he would've heard.

Melanie was the king. She was the prize in the game, the one reason it all unfolded and the only thing he had to gain.

Come on, Melanie. It's all up to you now.

Time to remember, sweetheart. Time to put the pieces together.

Time to come home to daddy.

Time to come home to me.

19

'All right,' Lairmore said crisply. 'What the hell is going on?'

At seven A.M. sharp, there was no messing with the supervisory agent. His double-breasted gray suit was impeccably tailored, his white dress shirt sharply pressed, and his military-cropped hair perfectly even. He sat behind his oversized walnut desk, while behind him, the blue FBI seal provided a halo of thirteen stars and a white banner declaring Fidelity, Bravery, and Integrity. Even during internal meetings there was always the feeling that Lairmore was conducting a press conference.

Still, David liked him.

At nearly fifty years of age, the head of the Boston healthcare fraud squad could tell you what *every* color and object in the FBI shield symbolized. He'd also go to his grave swearing that Hoover never so much as touched a pair of women's underwear; it was all a horrible misunderstanding. He was conservative, he was bureaucratic, but he also believed that health-care fraud was the worst crime epidemic sweeping the United States since organized crime – ten cents of every dollar wasted, not to mention shoddy treatment, unnecessary procedures, and the risk of human life – and he worked his ass off to do something about it. A man who believed in his job. In David's mind, a rarity these days.

Now, Lairmore stared down two agents who hadn't slept a wink.

'Oh, for heaven's sake,' he finally exclaimed, 'couldn't you two at least have showered and shaved? This isn't a bachelor party.'

David and Chenney looked at each other. They shook their heads.

'Watching Sheffield,' Chenney mumbled. His eyes lit up. 'Got a *big* break.'

'Researched Meagan Stokes,' David said. 'Dodged bullets. Talked to Supervisory Special Agent Quincy. No breaks.'

'You talked to Quincy? At Quantico?'

'Yeah, late last night. He's always at the office too. What the hell is it with this job?'

Chenney gazed at David with awe. 'Cool.'

'Ah, Jesus, Mary, and Joseph.' Lairmore stood up from his chair. 'In the hallway now.'

He stormed out. They followed. He plugged the coffee machine with quarters, then handed them the steaming cups that came shooting out. They accepted. Then chugged. Then dutifully followed their disgruntled leader back to his office, where David received a personal lecture on overextending his case team and fracturing a 'very important if not critical' investigation. David nursed the rest of his coffee and pulled his thoughts together so he could sound intelligent when he had the chance. It came sooner than he desired.

'Let's start with the Meagan Stokes case.' Lairmore slapped the Harper Stokes/William Sheffield healthcare fraud case file on the desk. 'How the hell did you end up working on a twenty-five-year-old *solved* homicide?'

David started at the beginning and ended by stating his growing certainty that the whole Stokes family had bigger secrets than fraud.

Lairmore half agreed. 'Most perpetrators do have a pattern of small-time fraud in their backgrounds. Maybe they cheated on auto insurance, then graduated to doctoring pharmaceutical billings. But in all my days, Agent, I have never heard of a person *starting* with conspiring to murder his own child for the insurance money and then trading *down* for white collar fraud.'

David smiled wearily. 'And we don't even know if Harper Stokes is committing healthcare fraud, let alone if he had anything to do with Meagan. Personally, Quincy favors the mother—'

'Harper's doing it!' Chenney burst in. 'I got it. I *got* Sheffield!'

Chenney explained his previous night's adventure in one long adrenaline rush: Harry Boer suffered chest pains and was rushed to the ER. By evening he was in ICU, under sedation but appearing to be fine. Then, bam, he had two bradycardic episodes within five hours and was now undergoing an operation for a pacemaker performed by none other than Dr Harper Stokes. And William Sheffield just happened to be spotted in the ICU ward several times, hours after his shift ended, with no patients in that ward. He was just 'around.' Conveniently around, if you asked Chenney.

'I called a pharmacist friend first thing this morning,' Chenney announced. 'She said that if you wanted to make it appear that someone needed a pacemaker, there are two drugs that would effectively interfere with the electrical conduction of the heart. They are propranolol and digoxin. Propranolol's a beta blocker, it's used to slow a racing heartbeat. Digoxin can also slow down the ventricles, but it might also accelerate the heart to lethal rates. Kinda risky, she said. Most likely, Sheffield's using propranolol.

'So,' Chenney concluded with a flourish, 'Sheffield sneaks into the ICU wards at night, that's why he's at the hospital so much. Injecting propranolol just once would cause concern but probably not lead to a cardiologist immediately recommending surgery. However, if a couple episodes happened right in a row . . .'

'Then the patients appear to have a circulatory disorder and need surgery,' David said.

'Brilliantly simple,' Lairmore said. 'Must take Sheffield two minutes for each injection. Then they're all set for an hour-long procedure that garners Harper two thousand dollars for the surgery and another four thousand in royalty dollars as he uses his own custom-designed pacemakers. If they do a couple a week . . .'

'Sheffield has no problem paying off his gambling debts and Harper can spend all he wants.' David sighed. 'One thing we are learning about Harper Stokes, he likes a nice lifestyle.'

Lairmore was nodding thoughtfully. Chenney had resumed looking troubled.

'But even if we can now prove Harper Stokes is making money from illegal surgeries, how does that tie in with what happened to Meagan Stokes twenty-five years ago?'

'That's what I want to know.' David leaned forward, planted his elbows on his knees, and though he was dog tired from a night spent poring over documents and weathering aching muscles, he got into it.

'I went through the entire Houston PD case file last night and a few key findings about the Meagan Stokes case emerged. One, in 1972, the Stokeses were in dire financial straits. They lived in a big house, but it was a gift from Patricia's father, not anything Harper could afford. He was just a resident, barely making ten thousand a year and scrounging to maintain the lifestyle to which his wife was accustomed. He'd taken out a second mortgage on the home and was already behind three payments when Meagan disappeared. Bottom line is that from a financial point of view, Meagan's murder was the best thing that ever happened to Harper and Patricia Stokes.'

'So we have motive,' Lairmore said.

Chenney was not convinced. 'If it was only about money, couldn't Harper have dreamed up his little operations back then?'

'No, residents are salaried, not paid by the procedure. One pacemaker surgery a week or a dozen, it would have been the same to him.'

Now Lairmore was the one with an objection. 'Still, Dr Stokes could have done other things – sold drugs from the hospital, sought kickbacks from pharmaceutical representatives. We all know there are many ways for healthcare providers at any level to abuse their positions for money. So I believe Chenney's point still stands. We have established that Harper and Patricia Stokes needed the money, but you haven't convinced me yet that they are the type of people to cold-bloodedly murder their little girl to get it.'

'All right, fair enough. That brings me to my second key finding. Not only did Harper have motive, but just about everyone in the family was having problems back then. To hell with having one suspect, in 1972 the police had four: Harper Stokes, Patricia Stokes, Jamie O'Donnell, and, believe it or not, Brian Stokes.' David nodded at their startled expressions. 'Exactly. This family doesn't just have skeletons, it has graveyards. So if you don't like Harper for the murder, let's look at everyone else.

'Patricia Stokes. Long before she met Harper, she was rich. Born into oil wealth, raised by a fairly domineering father, and the apple of his eye. Doesn't sound like her father liked Harper much, thought he wasn't good enough for his daughter – but that didn't stop him from giving his little girl a dream wedding and a mansion up on the hill. Unfortunately, when Patricia settled down to a future as a doctor's wife, she discovered she didn't like the scenery. Even before Brian was out of diapers, she was acting restless and bored. She took to spending lots of money. Went out partying. *And* she started spending more time with Jamie O'Donnell than with her husband, though her husband seemed to be spending more time with twenty-something nurses than his own wife.

'According to friends of the family, they did make an attempt at reconciliation. Harper started coming home more often, and they made a decision to have a second child, Meagan. This time it seemed to work. With two kids at home, Patricia gave up the party scene and finally settled into motherhood. She took up charity work, joined a few organizations, but mostly appeared content to dote on her children. According to the housekeeper, she and Harper shared a bedroom again, but the housekeeper never had to change the sheets, if you get my drift.'

'A lot of marriages turn into that,' Lairmore said mildly. 'If that's a sign of criminal activity, we'd have to arrest all husbands and wives married more than five years.'

David smiled. 'Sure, but we're not done with the Stokeses yet. So now we have Meagan Stokes in the picture. We got Harper and Patricia and the two children and happily ever after. But then, six months before Meagan's murder, Patricia and Harper start fighting every night. One maid apparently said something to friends of the family, and Patricia fired her the next day. And wonder of all wonders, Jamie O'Donnell starts hanging around again.'

'He and Patricia have a thing,' Chenney said.

'Seems that way. Police couldn't prove it, but you can't believe he's hanging around the house for the cooking. And Patricia is already starting to hit the gin. Everyone says it was the murder of Meagan that sent her over the brink, but the police can trace it back to *before* Meagan's death. Right before, which means whatever was going on, it had put Patricia in a questionable state of mind. Who knows what women do in a questionable state of mind?'

Lairmore nodded slowly, pursing his lips. 'Interesting. So we have a materialistic workaholic doctor, an unhappy alcoholic wife, and a love triangle with the family friend. Exactly what is Jamie O'Donnell's connection with the Stokeses?'

'Old friend of Harper's from college days, not that O'Donnell went to school. He's strictly self-educated and self-made. Started out working in the oil fields and took it from there. On the surface he and Harper make an unlikely pair, but they're both driven. Of course, they took entirely different routes to the top. Harper is now Mr Community and Mr Family, whereas Jamie O'Donnell *knows* people. Interpol has a file on the man.'

'What?' Now he had Lairmore's attention. David waved it away.

'Interpol has been desperate to prove that he runs guns but has never found a thing other than he keeps interesting company. Otherwise he runs a legitimate import business, pays his taxes every April 15, and puts his pants on one leg at a time just like the rest of us.'

'The rest of us aren't sleeping with Patricia Stokes,' Chenney said dryly.

David shrugged. 'Sure. So now we have the money motive and the love triangle. Maybe Harper was so angry at his wife, he decided killing Meagan would be a great way to spite her and solve his financial woes. Or maybe Jamie O'Donnell thought Patricia would never leave Harper as long as they had children together, so he tried to do something about it. Or maybe when Patricia was strung too tightly, had a little too much to drink, Meagan chose that moment to act out, and boom, bye-bye Meagan. Now we come to possibility number three – Brian Stokes.'

'This family just gets better and better,' muttered Chenney.

'Not exactly the Waltons,' David agreed. 'Brian in particular has a very troubled history. According to the Houston police report, he frequently broke items in the house and was known to reduce his mother to tears on almost a nightly basis. The interviewing officer wrote that the nanny had standing orders *not* to leave Brian alone in a room with Meagan. Apparently, he'd gone out of his way to destroy some of her toys. Then just to make it a slam dunk, Brian was seeing a therapist in 1972. It seems that Brian already had a history of playing with matches.'

'You're kidding me.' Lairmore sat up straighter. 'Don't tell me he's also a bed wetter and an animal torturer.'

Lairmore was referring to the violent triad developed by the profilers. For whatever reason, serial killers always had at least two legs of that triangle in their past. But not Brian Stokes.

'Just petty arson,' David said. 'Now, to make matters even more interesting, he and Patricia have no alibi for the day Meagan disappeared. Patricia told the cops that she took Brian to his therapist. The cops confirmed that, but the appointment was over at ten A.M. The cops got the call from the nanny at two P.M. that Meagan had disappeared from her car. At five Patricia and Brian drove up to the house, where they were both supposedly surprised by the news.'

'What about Harper Stokes or Jamie O'Donnell?' Lairmore asked. 'Do they have alibis?'

David shook his head. 'Harper claimed to be at work, but no one could ever vouch for it. O'Donnell said he was out of town but never produced any proof. Better yet, the police aren't even convinced the nanny was telling the truth about when Meagan was taken. She barely spoke English, refused to meet their gaze when answering questions, and spent most of the time sidling closer to Harper. They thought she might be a little involved with him, or at least wanted to make sure he liked what she was saying. In all probability, Meagan could've been taken at any time from any place that day. One day Meagan Stokes is simply gone. The next day the ransom note appears at the hospital where Harper works, and nothing is seen or heard from the kidnapper again. Then eight weeks later Meagan's body is found by a man and his dog out taking a walk.

'Quincy is right. Everything about the Meagan Stokes case reeks to high heaven, and every single member of the family carries the stench. If Russell Lee Holmes had not confessed, the police would've investigated the Stokeses and O'Donnell until the cows came home. And as long as the investigation was active, the insurance company would not pay out the policy. Basically, Russell Lee's last-minute confession to Larry Digger earned the family the end of a very embarrassing investigation and one million dollars.'

'How convenient, then,' Lairmore murmured, 'that Russell Lee Holmes confessed.'

'Exactly,' David said. '*Exactly!*'

'Quincy is going to reopen this case?' Lairmore asked.

'That's what he said. But I don't think he needs to officially reopen it. We're looking into it as part of our case.'

'No,' Lairmore said.

'*No?*'

Lairmore rewarded his incredulous tone with a stern look. 'With all due respect, Agent, you are in healthcare fraud. Agent Chenney here has discovered we have a viable allegation against Dr Harper Stokes and Dr William Sheffield if we can prove their activities. That case is your job. That case needs your focus.'

'But the shooter, Larry Digger—'

'Will be investigated by the Boston PD since it falls in their jurisdiction. Just as the Meagan Stokes case is in very capable hands with Quincy.'

'*Goddammit!*' David bolted out of his chair, staring at his supervisor incredulously. 'This is my case! I've worked my ass off connecting these dots, I got a terrified woman in a hotel room who doesn't even know if it's safe to go home to her family, and I got a direct link with the case I'm already working.'

'You do not have a link.' Lairmore fired back. He gave David a warning look. David didn't take it.

'The hell I don't! Twenty-five years ago, the Stokeses needed money and their daughter died, providing them with a million dollars. Now Harper is once more living beyond his means, and he's come up with another way of getting money, cutting open innocent people for profit. It's a pattern of behavior.'

Now even Chenney was looking at him as if he'd lost his mind. 'There's no pattern. Murdering your kid is not remotely close to installing illegal pacemakers.'

'One is insurance fraud, one is healthcare fraud.'

'One is homicide! The other is criminal, sure, but an unnecessary pacemaker isn't even dangerous. The pacemaker would be activated only if the person had a heart attack.'

'Someone could seize up and die on the table. Reckless endangerment of human life.'

'Which is still a far cry from murdering your own kid.'

'The rookie is right,' Lairmore said. 'You have established motive, Agent Riggs, but you haven't established character. We know Harper Stokes likes his lifestyle, maybe enough to commit fraud, but what evidence do we have that he would commit murder? Does he have a history of violence?'

'No.'

'Child abuse, spousal abuse? Neglect?'

'No.'

'By all accounts, he's raised two healthy children. No trips to emergency rooms, no arguments reported by neighbors. And in your first report on Harper Stokes didn't you write that he has a reputation for being a doting father and being exceedingly generous with his wife?'

David gritted his teeth. 'Yes.'

'And Patricia Stokes. I know Quincy has questions about the carefully wrapped body, but again, any history of abuse or neglect?'

'She has a problem with alcohol.'

'Which resurfaced six months ago. Any reports of violence then?'

David was forced to shake his head.

'Which brings us to Jamie O'Donnell. Maybe we have a criminal past there. According to Larry Digger, he visited the midwife in Texas, but again, by all reports he dotes on his godchildren and is close to the family.

'That just leaves us with Brian Stokes,' Lairmore continued. 'But by your own admission, he adores his second sister and has always been extremely protective of her. Face it, Agent, this case is over your head. The motives are there and opportunity is there, but none of the players make sense, at least not to our eyes. So leave it to the experts. Leave it to Quincy.'

'They are connected,' David said stiffly, 'and I'll tell you one last reason why.'

Lairmore and Chenney looked impatient for his little display to end.

'The caller,' David stated. 'The anonymous tipster who alerted us to the healthcare fraud at the same time he was alerting Larry Digger to Melanie. His agenda seems to be revenge for Meagan Stokes, for making sure everyone gets what they deserve. So if he's bringing us in on it, they're related, they're all related.'

Lairmore remained skeptical, but finally he sighed.

'All right, Agent. I'll give you one last shot. Establish character. Bring me any proof that Harper, Patricia, or Brian Stokes is cruel enough or cold enough or clinically unstable enough to engineer the death of four-year-old Meagan Stokes, and I'll let you work on it – in your own time. Right now I believe that healthcare fraud is the only viable case my agents have.'

'Fine,' David said curtly.

Since Lairmore didn't want to hear anything more about twenty-five-year-old homicides, they focused on the fraud angle that Chenney had uncovered. They had no hard physical evidence, so their options were limited. They could prove motive – money – and opportunity. But they needed physical evidence or a good eyewitness account. Eyewitnesses, unfortunately, were notoriously hard to get in a hospital setting. There were too many nurses and doctors around for most patients to keep straight, and nurses and doctors had a code of silence. They did not rat each other out even when they saw evidence of a crime.

The consensus was to put Chenney in the hospital undercover as a janitor. He'd prowl the ICU, ask the nurses questions, maybe even catch Sheffield in the act.

David was given the fun-filled act of building the paper trail. Going over the financial statements to prove need. Looking for evidence of payoffs between Harper and Sheffield.

Then he turned his attention to Melanie Stokes where he began his work in earnest. But by the end of the day he had merely proven Lairmore's point. Except for the migraines, Melanie was in perfect health, not a single broken bone, not a single unexplained bruise. She was reported as happy and well-adjusted, the recipient of the best birthday parties on the block.

By all accounts, her entire family simply loved her to death.

20

Melanie woke up Tuesday morning thinking of Meagan, of the family she loved so much and had assumed loved her.

She got up to stand in front of the dresser and stared at her reflection. Dammit, she *did not* look like Meagan. She was not nearly as beautiful.

She slapped the top of the dresser, then stormed downstairs.

David wasn't around but he'd left a note on the kitchen table.

Went to meeting. Will be back after five. Remember, *no going outdoors.* D.

She set down the note and roamed the room. She found frozen vegetables in the freezer and a jar of instant coffee on the counter. She boiled water to give herself something to do. While it heated up, she unburied her Day-Timer from her purse and looked up her schedule. The books were way overdue to the rare book dealer. She'd planned lunch with an old friend from Wellesley, followed by an afternoon meeting with the committee for the children's hospital winter ball. It was already nearly June and they had yet to line up entertainment. The whole thing was a disaster waiting to happen.

Melanie got on the phone and canceled everything. She had the flu, she said. Everyone was sympathetic. They encouraged her to rest. Of course they could manage without her.

She hung up feeling disappointed. She'd wanted dismay, She realized finally, cries of We need you, Melanie, we'll never make it without you.

You're special, Melanie. Indispensable. You are not *a substitute daughter.*

Dammit, how could her mother say she'd wanted Meagan again? How could she have looked at Melanie and seen *Meagan?*

Was it always just about Meagan?

Did they all feel that way? Her mother, her father, her brother, her godfather. The people who had taken her in and given her a home. The people she trusted and considered her own family.

Melanie thought to hell with questions. She was going to figure out the answers.

On a pad of paper she drew a circle and labeled it Meagan. Then around it she drew circles for her mother, her father, her brother, and Jamie. Then she drew in Russell Lee Holmes, Larry Digger, and herself. Finally she added Ann Margaret. David seemed to feel she was involved, and at this point Melanie shouldn't exclude any possibilities. Considering that, she also drew in William Sheffield.

Nine different people, all surrounding one little girl.

She drew lines connecting Meagan to her mother, father, brother, and godfather. It actually bothered her, like acknowledging another woman in a lover's life. But it was true. Meagan had come first. Melanie added Larry Digger's relationship as journalist. She could not come up with any direct lines for William Sheffield or Ann Margaret.

Russell Lee Holmes was even more troubling. She wanted to write killer, but Quincy had raised too much doubt. Russell Lee was connected not directly to Meagan then, but to the other people encircling Meagan.

And after a moment's hesitation she drew a line between Russell Lee Holmes and herself. Father and daughter. There in black and white.

After that she found that the rest flowed easier.

A little after five-thirty David rapped on the door three times, then entered. He was holding a paper bag. From the couch Melanie arched a brow inquiringly.

'Brought Chinese,' David said at last. He held out the bag, trying to gauge her mood.

'Fine,' she agreed.

He edged into the kitchen. 'Spicy orange beef and General Tsao's chicken.'

'Nice.' Despite David's fear, she was not angry with him. She'd spent the day with her diagram and it had given her what she needed most – conclusive proof that her family could *not* have killed Meagan Stokes. It made Melanie happy.

She climbed off the sofa and followed David into the kitchen.

David's jacket was off, his green paisley tie loosened, and his white shirtsleeves rolled up to his elbows. He was getting to the point of needing a hair-cut. His hair held track marks from his fingers running through it one too many times, and those lines were back at the corners of his eyes.

He looked like he'd had a very bad day, and for a moment Melanie was tempted to cup his cheek with her hand. She wondered if he would turn his face into her touch. She wondered if he would move closer . . .

She had liked the way he'd held her last night.

He said, 'The bowls are in the cupboard.'

She got them down and they dished up their dinner. They ate in silence for nearly half the meal before David spoke up.

'How was your day?'

'I watched Jerry Springer. Enough said. And yours?'

He dug deeper into his fried rice. 'I would've preferred Jerry Springer. Did you sleep at all last night?'

'A little.'

'Any more dreams of Meagan?'

'A blend. Meagan Stokes in that cabin. But you were there too.'

He glanced at her in surprise. A grain of rice decorated his bottom lip, and without thinking she brushed it away with her thumb. The motion caught them both off guard, and she quickly pulled her hand back.

'Um . . . I was in the cabin with you and Meagan Stokes,' she said a trifle breathlessly.

'Me?' He sounded frazzled himself and was studying his bowl intently. 'What was I doing there?'

'Housecleaning.'

'What?'

Melanie took another bite of food. 'Meagan Stokes was in the corner of the cabin, clutching her horse and very, very afraid. Then you walked into the cabin and started cleaning. Swept the floor, removed the cobwebs, cleaned the windows. Oh, and you hung drapes.'

'I hung drapes?' David looked stricken. 'So much for to serve and protect.'

'They were very nice drapes,' Melanie said. 'Meagan was happy.'

'Housekeeper extraordinare,' he muttered, pushing his empty bowl away. 'Give me a cape and I'll call it a day.'

He sighed, and it hurt her to see the weariness on his face. 'Well,' he said seriously, 'do you want to know what I learned today?'

She pushed back her bowl and squared her shoulders. 'Sure. Give it to me straight. What did you learn?'

'Nothing,' David said bluntly. 'The great FBI agent learned nothing. This whole case simply makes no sense.' He stood and began to clear the table.

'The shooter?'

'Jax said they checked with area hospitals and locals. So far no sign.'

'Any more evidence from Larry Digger's room? The notes?'

'Nope, not a thing.' David walked into the kitchen, slammed the bowls in the sink.

'What about Meagan's case? Did you talk more about it?'

'Sure, I reviewed it with my supervisor and Chenney. We all agree that Quincy raised excellent questions. I sure as hell don't believe Russell Lee did it. That leaves us with your family, as you know. They do have motive.'

'The money,' she said flatly, and stood herself. The subject was too aggravating to handle sitting. 'The million-dollar life insurance policy.'

'Better than that. We think your mother and Jamie O'Donnell might have been having an affair back then.'

'*What?*'

'Police notes. O'Donnell was spending a lot of time around the house and your parents were having a lot of marital difficulties. Screaming matches, that kind of thing.'

Melanie shook her head. 'My parents don't scream at each other. They have "discussions" behind closed doors.'

'Yeah, well, back then they were fighting enough to attract the notice of the hired help and friends. Seems that your father wasn't very faithful—'

'He *flirts* a lot.' She held up a hand and conceded: 'Maybe he does more than flirt, but as strange as this sounds, I don't think my mom minds. I've always had the impression she accepts my father's job and life-style as male prerogative. Boys will be boys.'

'What's good for the goose . . .'

Melanie pursed her lips, not liking this newest allegation. But these days there seemed to be more she *didn't* know about her family than she did.

She moved to the coffee table and picked up the hotel pad that revealed her work for the day.

'Then we come to your brother,' David said.

'Brian was nine years old!'

'And troubled enough to be seeing a shrink. Plus, your mom herself had given the nanny orders not to leave him alone with Meagan. He seemed to be very jealous of her and very destructive of her toys. Remember, he said that he'd thrown her toy pony against the fireplace.

'So now we have money, love, and mental instability all running in your family. But here's a twist. I did full background checks on your family, and there is simply nothing to suggest they're capable of murdering a four-year-old girl.'

Melanie nodded vigorously and waved her notepad in the air. 'Exactly! Look here. I wrote down what Quincy said about the person who did the crime, and I've done a little analysis of my own. I've been arguing that my family couldn't do it because I loved them so much. Since that doesn't carry weight in criminal investigations, I decided to look at it your way.'

She sat down on the sofa and placed the notepad on the coffee table. David took a seat next to her. She could feel the warmth of his body against her leg. She spoke faster and kept her eyes on the diagram.

'Here is Meagan and my family. Here is what we know about everyone's relationship, and here is what we know about each individual. I was thinking of what Quincy said about profiling, that you look at the psychology under the behavior. I'm not sure I can objectively say that my parents are good or bad people, but I believe I can objectively say if they are smart or precise or sloppy.'

'Okay,' David said, studying her picture. 'I can grant you that much.'

'Here is what Quincy said about the person who killed Meagan Stokes. The person is precise and knowledgeable about police procedure. Then the person has to be clever enough and credible enough to approach Meagan. Also, I guess the person has to be tough enough to deal with the likes of Russell Lee Holmes. At the same time, however, the person is maternal, at least caring and remorseful enough to wrap Meagan in a blanket and bury the body. He'd also have to feel guilty for what he did, guilty enough to, well, decapitate her.'

Even on paper that aspect of the crime still horrified her. She swallowed, and not wanting to lose momentum, for she clearly had David's full attention, she rapped the pencil tip against her diagram.

'Now, that's a unique combination of traits. Distinct, wouldn't you say? So let's look at our players. We have my father, who is very precise and smart. But frankly, as much as I love him, I can tell you he's not maternal. Hugs and kisses are definitely my mother's department. As for knowledge of police procedure, I don't think my father has even gotten a speeding ticket in his life. He doesn't watch cop dramas or read true crime, so I think he's a total washout there. Plus, tough enough to approach and/or intimidate Russell Lee Holmes? Please, this man can't bear to go a week without a manicure. Russell Lee would eat him alive.

'So, what about my mother? Now, she fits for being maternal, remorseful, and guilty. But do you really think my mother is precise? Haven't you ever seen how hard her hands shake? And while I think she's an intelligent woman, she's not this kind of clever, let alone knowledgeable about police procedure. And there really is no way she would ever approach a man like Russell Lee. Can you imagine that? So she doesn't fit either.

'Now, my godfather . . . I'll be honest. I've always had the impression that Jamie knows things. He has a way of moving, you know. If you're a female he loves, it's very reassuring, like spending time around the tough kid in school. He grew up hard and I imagine he could intimidate a man like Russell Lee Holmes. And he probably knows something about law enforcement. But Jamie isn't precise. He's blunt, physical, and rough around the edges. Also, I can't see Jamie harming a little girl. In his world that would be . . . dishonorable, I guess. He could be cruel to someone who threatened someone he loved, but he'd cut off his own hand before he'd harm a child. Actually, he's even a little maternal toward kids. Certainly he's affectionate and loving toward Brian and me. He's just not that combination of cold, precise, callousness.

'Then we have my brother.'

'He's a doctor,' David interjected. 'So he must be precise.'

'At the age of nine? And what would he know about police procedure, David? And how in the world would a nine-year-old convince Russell Lee to confess to a crime he didn't commit? Don't you see?' She turned, looking at him earnestly. 'There is no one on this page who fits what Quincy is looking for. I'm not an expert, true, but put at this level, it doesn't work. The killer simply isn't my family. End of story.'

Melanie finally relaxed. But then David took her chart from her. He took her pencil. He drew a few lines. And that easily, he burst her bubble.

'You're right, Melanie,' he said simply. 'You're absolutely right. Alone, no one individual meets all the requirements. And that's what the message has been all along. I was a fool not to see it earlier. It's not one person who's getting notes. It's all of them. And if you put them all together . . .'

He looked her in the eye. 'Your mother, father, brother, or godfather could not have committed this crime. But this *family*, on the other hand . . .'

'No,' Melanie said.

'Yes,' he replied. 'I'm sorry, Melanie. But yes.'

She had to get off the sofa. She paced around the room a few times, her thoughts in turmoil.

'It's the combination,' David murmured, making quick notes and seeming to speak almost to himself. 'As individuals they fail. But as a group they cover all the traits and areas of knowledge needed to carry out the crime. Harper devising the ransom demand, coming up with the idea to make it a copycat crime. Your guilt-stricken mother wrapping up Meagan's body. Your godfather disposing of it, I think, and handling the deal with Russell Lee Holmes when the police started asking too many questions. Getting Russell Lee to confess to Meagan's murder in return for your family providing a home for his own child. Think of how much Russell Lee would've liked that. A lifetime of hating poverty, and one day he gets an offer to transport his child to the upper class. What a deal.'

'But . . . but the murder,' Melanie protested. 'No one is cruel enough to commit the murder. You said yourself, *no one* is cruel enough to commit the murder!'

David looked up, his expression distracted. She realized with a start that this had become an academic exercise for him, a riddle for the great agent to figure out. She was shocked.

'What if it wasn't murder, Melanie? What if it was an accident? What if little Brian Stokes simply went too far with his jealous rampage one day?'

'Oh, God,' she whispered in horror.

'Think about it, Melanie. Nine-year-old Brian. He harms Meagan out of jealousy or rage and what do your parents do? They've already lost one child.'

'No.'

'Your godfather also seems loyal to him. Plus, he'd probably do anything to keep Patricia from suffering more. Finally we have a situation worthy of the three adults getting over their differences and working together.'

'But the decapitation, the mutilation.'

'Maybe they had to. Quincy said decapitation can also be about covering up a crime. They're trying to imitate a killer who strangles his victims. But what if it was an accident that killed Meagan? Maybe she fell down the stairs, maybe she was hit in the head. They must decapitate her or the real cause of death will be determined. If she was hit with a blunt instrument, there might even be paint or fiber or metallic particles buried in the wound that could be used to trace the murder weapon. So in for a dime, in for a dollar. They decapitate the body, remove the hands to hide other wounds or physical evidence, and devise a plot to imitate some serial killer they've been reading about in the paper.'

Melanie was shaking her head.

'But the police aren't convinced,' David continued. 'Harper doesn't know enough details, so his copycat attempt fails. Then Russell Lee is arrested, so they decide to go straight to the source. Jamie. Jamie pays him a visit. And they strike a deal.'

David looked at her somberly. 'I'm sorry, Melanie, but that scenario works. You are Russell Lee Holmes's child and they took you in the night he died to cover up what happened to Meagan five years before.'

'You're wrong, you're wrong,' Melanie kept repeating.

She had wrapped her arms tightly around her waist and her voice came out sounding more desperate than she'd intended.

David rose off the sofa. There was a look in his eyes Melanie had never seen before. Maybe tenderness. Maybe compassion. He took her hands, and then, in a move she didn't expect, he drew her against his body and pressed her cheek against his chest. She realized for the first time that she was trembling uncontrollably.

And then he whispered roughly against her temple, 'Maybe. But there's no arguing that Larry Digger was killed. Or that shots were aimed at you.'

She collapsed. Her knees buckled and she would've fallen if David hadn't already been holding her. Her hands grabbed his shirt for support. Her body sagged into him and he gripped her tighter.

'It's going to be all right,' David whispered against her hair. 'I won't let them hurt you. I won't let anyone hurt you.'

'My family, my family . . . I *love* them.'

She buried her head against his shoulder and held on tight.

The storm lasted a bit. Gradually she was aware of David leading her over to the couch. He lay down with her, wrapping his lean body around her. He stroked her hair, her back. Then his lips brushed her cheek, the curve of her ear. Tender. Soft.

She turned to him savagely, caught his lips full-force with her own and kissed him hard. Lips bruising lips, teeth smashing, breath labored. She arched against him, tried to bury herself in the feel and taste and sensation. He ravaged her totally, his tongue plunging into her mouth, filling her, making her whole . . .

Then, when her breasts were swollen and her nipples tingling and her whole body restless and writhing, he pulled away. She could hear his ragged breathing and the racing beat of his heart. She could see that his hands trembled.

'No more,' he said roughly.

'Why not?'

'Because it wouldn't be right. I want it to be right.'

He got off the couch in a hurry, obviously realizing that she was in no mood to be denied and he was in no shape to win. The front of his slacks bulged with his erection, and he had to fist his hands in his back pockets to keep from reaching for her again.

Melanie contemplated forcing the issue. He wanted her, and she needed to be wanted. By anyone.

But he was right. She was too desperate and she'd hate them both later.

She rose from the sofa and walked to the window. 'They've never harmed me, David. They've been so good to me.'

He didn't answer. Minute ticked into minute.

'The police should find the shooter soon,' David said at last. 'Once we get our hands on him, he'll be able to tell us a thing or two.'

'Such as who hired him.'

'Exactly.'

'And then we'll know.'

'Exactly.'

'Okay,' she said. 'Okay.'

David raised his arms above his head and stretched out his back. 'I gotta get some sleep.'

'I know.'

'You gonna stay up? Will you be okay?'

'I'll be fine.'

'We're going to get to the bottom of it,' he said again. 'We will.'

Melanie simply smiled. She wasn't so sure herself anymore. And she was wondering if there were some truths that should never be known.

David moved toward the bedroom. Then he stopped and turned, his gaze unreadable.

'You know,' he said quietly. 'You don't need them as much as you think you do. You're stronger than you know.'

'What does that have to do with the fact that I love them?'

David didn't have a reply.

Melanie stayed up long into the night. She sat on the sofa with her knees pulled up against her chest and her arms wrapped around her legs. She thought of her parents and her brother and her godfather. The way they had held her and made her laugh and doted on her. The way they had lavished their time and attention on her as if she were a long-awaited present that was finally theirs at last.

Right before she fell asleep, she thought, If I really am Russell Lee Holmes's daughter, why did Quincy say my memories of the shack weren't right? And if all this was done to protect Brian, wouldn't it matter that he's now been disinherited from the family?

The shooter, she thought groggily. The shooter will tell.

But there was no such luck. The next morning she and David awoke to the hotel phone ringing. It was Detective Jax. He'd found the shooter all right.

Unfortunately, the man was dead.

21

'It won't be pleasant,' David warned.

Melanie merely nodded, keeping her gaze out the passenger-side window, where semis barreled down Highway 93 and distant factories emitted plumes of smoke. They were approaching the harbor district of Boston. She caught the first whiff of salt.

'Jax said he was in the water,' David said. 'That always makes it look worse. Really, Melanie, you should wait until the body has been processed. You can ID it by video at the morgue.'

'But it won't be ready until tomorrow morning, correct?'

'Boston homicide is a little overworked.'

'Then I'll do it now,' she reasserted firmly, as she'd been saying since they first got the call. 'If it's him, and he's dead, then I can go home. No sense in delaying that any longer than necessary.'

'Why don't we hold off on any quick decisions,' David said vaguely, which was enough to let her know he was going to make an issue out of it. She shot him a quick glance, but he refused to meet her gaze. Obviously he didn't want to engage in the discussion then. Fine, it could wait until she saw the body. It wouldn't change her mind. She had spent a lot of time thinking since last night and formed some opinions of her own.

She turned back to the car window. The exit appeared on their right, and David careened across three lanes of traffic to take it. One tourist honked. No one else seemed to notice. The wharf came into view. As crime scenes went, this one was hard to miss.

Black and white police cruisers peppered the scene. Yellow crime tape draped across the road. One beefy officer had adopted an aggressive stance outside the perimeter and was waving them away until David flashed his creds. Like membership in an elite club, the FBI shield entitled them to a first-class viewing of a dead man.

They pulled in next to two dark sedans and one old clunker. David opened her door for her. She realized he always did that, even held out chairs. His mother's doing, she thought, and accepted his hand to pull herself out of the car. When he held out his arm for her, however, she shook her head. She preferred to walk this path alone.

They crossed to a group of plainclothes detectives and one medical examiner. The air was tangy with the scent of salt and underlined with the heavy sweetness of rot. This area of Boston's harbor was far from scenic, and Melanie had never spent much time down here. There was an old fish packaging plant that had seen better days. The dark, oily water was stagnant with dead fish, fallen sea gulls, and today, a man's corpse. In spite of all of David's warnings, Melanie recoiled at the smell.

Detective Jax turned to greet them. He once again worked a toothpick between his teeth, giving David a firm handshake and Melanie a sympathetic smile.

'How y' doin' Ms Stokes?'

'No one's shot me yet. I must be doing better than Monday.'

Detective Jax flashed a grin, then grew serious. 'Just so you're prepared, it's not pretty.'

'David warned me.'

'Sure you don't want to wait for the morgue tape?'

'As I've said—'

'Okay, okay, I got it. You're tired of Club Fed and want to go home. Fine. Then here's the drill. You don't have to memorize him or nothing. Just take a glance. Tell us if you think it's him. One look, you're done.'

'Go home and forget all about it?' she murmured, then followed Detective Jax to the body. David rested his hand on the small of her back.

There was no mistaking the dead man. He was faceup on the cracked asphalt. Puffed face gray and rubbery. Bloated hands over his head, picked ragged by feeding fish. Dark suit waterlogged and algae coated. Black holes on his white dress shirt where two bullets had fired home.

No blood this time. The water had washed it away.

'What do you think?' Detective Jax asked.

'That's him.' She kept staring. She couldn't help herself. Dead never looked the way she thought it should. With Digger it had been too bloody. With this man it was too alien. The water had turned him into something resembling a wax doll.

'Looks like he'd been shot twice, close range,' Detective Jax said conversationally. 'Probably the day before. It's gonna take a bit to ID him – no papers and not much for fingertips. Guess the fish had a real banquet. We'll send him to the state crime lab for analysis. The water will make it tougher – he's a floater and a bloater – but I've requested Jeffrey Ames for the job. Jeff's the best.'

'I know Jeff,' David spoke up. 'He's good.'

'You know Jeff?' Detective Jax switched the toothpick to the left side of his mouth and peered at David curiously.

'I'm a member of the Mass Rifle Association,' David explained. 'Jeff shoots there too.'

'You're a member of the MRA? Wait a sec, David Riggs. Are you Bobby Riggs's son?'

David nodded. Detective Jax lit up.

'Holy hell, good to meet you. I love Bobby. Man does beautiful work. Give your father my regards, 'kay? Oh, and tell him I wanna bring in my gun. Damn sight is driving me nuts.'

'I'll tell him. When do you think you'll have the initial report?'

'Forty-eight hours maybe? I'm gonna put a rush on it, but we're a little backed up these days. Spring's rough around here.'

'Do you know who killed him?' Melanie asked quietly. Her stomach was beginning to roll.

'Don't have any witnesses, if that's what you mean. We're still detailing the area, but so far no brass and no traces of blood, so he was probably shot somewhere else. Lab guys may find something on his shoes or clothing that can help us locate the murder site. It's amazing what a couple of good chemists can do these days.'

'What about the notes he took? The papers from Larry Digger's room?'

Detective Jax shook his head. 'Nope. My guess is he showed up for contact, delivering the goods and expecting to get paid. But maybe his employer wasn't so happy about the mess he made of things, or the job being only half done. So he closed out the deal with a couple of deliveries of lead. There just ain't no honor among thieves.'

'So we don't really know anything yet,' Melanie murmured. 'Sure this person is dead, but his employer could just hire another, and another, and . . .' Her voice was rising. She was losing it after all.

David and Detective Jax were watching her closely. She took a deep breath, focused on the warm, familiar feel of David's hand against the small of her back. She nodded and everyone relaxed.

'You guys care to start explaining things yet?' Detective Jax asked. 'Or should I just wait until the next dead body?'

'I don't know,' David replied. 'When are you planning on finding the next dead body?'

'Oh, holy Lord, working with G-men sucks.' Jax spat out his toothpick. 'Look, I'm going after this with all I can, Agent Riggs. I don't have the resources of the Bureau or the experts of the Bureau, but what the hell, I like to think us poor local slobs run a pretty good show. Now, do you want to give me any hints, or should I just keep gnawing away at this like a Chihuahua?'

'Larry Digger said he had proof of who my birth parents are,' Melanie offered. 'It seems someone doesn't want me to know.'

'Why? Everyone's finding their birth parents these days. It's about as popular as no-fat double lattes with whip.'

'Because maybe my birth father was a serial killer. And maybe it would be embarrassing for my family if it was discovered that they had knowingly adopted the child of such a man.'

Now she had Detective Jax's undivided attention. 'Well, shoot me, that would make a difference. So this Larry Digger, he claimed to have proof of where you came from?'

'That's what he said. We never got to see it, but we heard quite a bit of his story.'

'And he alleged your parents *knowingly* adopted you anyway? They got big hearts, or what? I didn't think the Beacon Street type liked to go outside established bloodlines.' Jax gave her a look. 'Ms Stokes, I can dance as well as the next guy, but this tango is ridiculous. If you want me to help, you give it to me clean. I'll see what I can do. Welcome to the Jax School of Justice. 'Kay?'

'Needless to say,' David said smoothly, 'it's an ongoing investigation. Listen, Detective, if you want to help, here's what we need the most: Our shooter is dead, but we still don't know who hired him, and since the job wasn't completed the first time, there's a good chance that there'll be a second contract on Melanie's life. If you hear anything—'

'I think I'll let you know.' Jax returned to Melanie, shaking his head. 'I'll work on this as hard as I can and you got Mr Personality here, too, but these things take time. It'll be days before I get the first lab report, and that's assuming the initial chem run yields findings. With bodies that have been in the water, it can take longer than that. I can already tell the bullets are soft lead, so they won't have any striations, which means the lab will have to determine gun type by class, not characteristic. That takes longer as well. Seriously, ma'am, we're looking at weeks before we start getting the first clue, and considering that you're already in danger . . .'

'He's right,' David said, having found an ally for his case. 'I'll take you back to the hotel, Melanie. We'll buy you clothes, come up with a good excuse for your parents. Hell, you can tell them you're off to find yourself. That's true enough. And it would certainly be a lot safer—'

'No.'

'Yes—'

'No! I *know* who I am, David. I'm twenty-nine years old, I have lived the last twenty years in the Stokes household, and *that is where I belong.*'

'Like hell it is. They are going to get you killed—'

'You don't know that! We don't have a shred of evidence, just a bunch of far-fetched theories. I'm not going to walk away because of that. For crying out loud, we are never going to move beyond theory with me shut up in a hotel room anyway. At the very least, you can consider my going home as the most efficient means of moving the investigation forward.'

'I will not risk you for the stupid case—'

'This isn't your choice, David. It's mine, and I'm going home!'

She pivoted, took a step toward the car, but David grabbed her arm.

'Don't you put yourself in the line of fire.'

'They won't hurt me,' she insisted stubbornly. 'They won't.'

'You are blind and stubborn and completely ignorant when it comes to your parents. You're so caught up in your romantic notion of what families mean that you're going to get yourself killed!'

'Why, thank you, David. I trust your judgment and intelligence just as much.'

She jerked her arm free and stormed back to the car.

Detective Jax let out a low whistle. 'I guess we pissed her off.'

'She doesn't understand.'

'The woman is standing in front of a corpse. I think she understands just fine.'

'No, she doesn't.' David turned on Jax. 'You don't get her yet, Detective. She was abandoned and that has skewed her judgment. Her family is perfect. Her family must need her. It's a great dream, an understandable dream. And it's gonna get her killed.'

Detective Jax shrugged. 'And if it were your family, Riggs? If it was your father we were talking about? Who would be the naïve romantic then?'

'Oh, shut up,' David said darkly, and stalked after Melanie to the car.

They drove downtown in taut silence, David tapping his fingers crossly on the wheel while Melanie stared resolutely out the window.

'You are a pigheaded fool,' he said finally.

She smiled tightly. 'I believe it runs in the family.'

They made it another half-mile, then he exploded again. 'Dammit, you can't ignore the fact that someone wants you dead.'

'I'm not ignoring it.'

'You're walking into the proverbial lion's den!'

'No, I'm not! I'm going home, which is my right. I'm going to kiss my mother on the cheek, I'm going to hug my father. I'm going to hunt down my brother for a serious heart-to-heart, and then I'm going to corner my godfather for a nice long chat.'

'Because you believe they'll magically tell you everything?' His voice lowered with scorn. 'Whatever happened to Meagan, they've kept it secret for twenty-five years. Now someone has even gone so far as to hire a paid gun. So really, I don't think they're going to simply confess. Not even to their favorite daughter.'

Melanie drew in her breath with a sharp hiss. 'They are not evil.'

'Close enough. Dammit, Melanie.' David suddenly slapped the steering wheel. 'Are you going to make me say it?'

'Maybe.'

'I'm an agent. It's out of line.'

'Then I'll take it off the record, Mr Riggs.'

He growled, but she didn't relent. She had not realized how much this mattered to her until right that moment. She was leaning toward him. She

LISA GARDNER

was staring at him intently. She'd come to need him even more than she'd realized. She really wanted to know that he cared, as well. That the last few days had not been another illusion.

He spoke in a rush. 'I care, dammit! You matter to me, Melanie, more than you're supposed to, and I don't want to see you hurt.'

'I know.'

'I sympathize, all right? They are your family, and while I certainly won't win son of the year award anytime soon, my family is important to me too. If it was my father or brother in question, I don't know that I would handle it any better.'

'I have to trust them, David. They've loved me so well.'

'Of course they've loved you, Mel. You're as close to Meagan Stokes as they're ever going to get.'

Melanie recoiled. She knew he was trying to shock her, and it worked. Her eyes were stinging. She was on the verge of tears.

There wasn't anyone in the world who didn't long to be loved for simply being herself. It wasn't fair of him to state that no matter what she did, she would always be the substitute daughter.

She turned away and looked out the window.

David got off 93, whipped through the financial district, and emerged on Beacon Street. Three blocks from home. He slowed down the car. She groped for her composure. When he finally stopped the car, she still didn't feel ready.

'Be careful,' he said quietly. The scowl had dropped. He looked genuinely worried and that touched her.

'Thank you.' She brushed his hand.

He pulled it back, shaking his head. 'I don't want your gratitude. I'm too far over the line to even pretend this is professional courtesy.'

'Yeah, it's part of your charm.'

'I *don't* have any charm. I'm old, arthritic, and cranky. Half the time I have the personality of a porcupine. Don't tell me I have charm.'

'You do, because underneath it all I know there beats a good heart.'

'Female fantasy,' he muttered.

'Truth.'

He looked like he might argue some more, but then he sighed and now he did take her hand with his own. 'Melanie, for lots of reasons I think you know, I can't just stop by your house.'

'I expected that.'

'You really will be on your own.'

'I understand that too.'

'And you're scaring the shit out of me.'

'Given.'

'Okay, fine. This is my beeper number.' He scrawled it on a piece of paper. 'If you're in trouble, I'll come. Have a bad dream, I'll come. Have a

446

bad memory, I'll come. Just dial the beeper, okay? I'll be there, Melanie. I will.'

She took the piece of paper. 'Thank you,' she said, and saw him wince once more at her gratitude. 'I need to go now.'

'Mel, wait.'

But Melanie didn't wait. She slipped out of the car. She started walking and didn't look back, not even when the car started up and drove away.

Then she was alone.

The cherry blossoms waved merrily. The scent of hyacinths was spicy and fragrant in the air. A beautiful day in a beautiful city.

Melanie looked up at the three-story brick house that was her home. She saw the solid walnut doors, the heavy iron gate. She saw the bay windows of her bedroom.

And for just a moment she shivered with fear.

Then she opened the door and stepped inside.

22

María, the maid, greeted her with a friendly nod. She looked at Melanie's wrinkled clothes and disheveled hair but took them in stride. Her parents and Señor O'Donnell were on the back patio eating lunch. Would she like anything?

Melanie shook her head and headed for the patio.

Jamie came walking through the back door. He halted at the sight of her, his face registering surprise.

'Melanie?' her godfather said hesitantly, holding out his arms as he always did but clearly uncertain.

She went into the hug, realizing she needed the contact more than she'd thought. Before she was ready, he pulled back and held her firmly at arm's length.

'What's up, lass? I hear you've been gone for two days without so much as a by-your-leave. Why are you worrying your mother like this? It's not like you.'

Melanie didn't answer immediately. Confronted by her first family member, she discovered she wasn't sure what she wanted to say. Or maybe she wasn't sure what she wanted to hear. David was right. This was more difficult than she'd thought. Her first question caught even her by surprise.

'Do you love me?'

'Of course, lass! You are my favorite woman in the whole world.'

'Why?'

'Why?' Her godfather arched a brow and regarded her more seriously. 'You are in a mood. Well, I don't know. Why do you love anything, Melanie? I suppose because you do.'

'Is it? You've always been there for me, Jamie. For my coming-home party, my first day of school, my birthdays, my charity balls, everything. That's a lot of interest in a goddaughter's life.'

'Well, you are a special goddaughter.'

'But why? Why do you love me so much, Jamie? What is it you want from me?'

Her voice was rising a notch. Her godfather immediately waved away her distress. He said simply and calmly, 'I love you for being you. And all I've ever wanted was for you to be happy.'

Melanie thought it was one of the loveliest things she'd ever heard, and a heartbeat later she knew she didn't believe a word of it. For the first time in her life she doubted her godfather.

Moments passed, the silence growing strained. Jamie's expression changed from tender to wary.

'If something was going on with you,' he finally asked, 'you would let me know, wouldn't you?'

'I don't know. If something was going on with *you*, you would let me know, wouldn't you?'

'No, I wouldn't.'

'Why? I'm twenty-nine, I'm ready to hear—'

'And I'm fifty-nine, which is still older than you and wiser.'

'Wiser about what, Jamie? Wiser about a reporter named Larry Digger, or a midwife to Russell Lee Holmes? Wiser about Brian and Meagan Stokes?'

Her godfather studied her. His eyes, she realized, were much more sharp, much more knowing than she'd ever given him credit for.

'Not Brian,' he said. 'But you, lass. You.'

'Jamie—'

He moved away, making a show of dusting off his trench coat, flicking at lint. 'I'm going to be in town a bit, Melanie. Business is booming, what can I say? So if you need anything, of course' – he looked at her meaningfully – 'call me at the Four Seasons. Day or night, I'll come.'

'Jamie—'

'I've met a woman, Mel, have I told you that? I'm thinking of settling down, maybe becoming a local. What do you think? Can you see me as a married man? Bah. You're right, you're right. What am I doing looking at myself as a family man? That's Harper's gig, you know. Pipe dreams again. I'm getting maudlin and foolish in my old age.'

'Jamie—'

'At the Four Seasons. Just call the number and your old godfather will be here. Now try to get some sleep.'

Then he was gone.

After a minute Melanie opened the French doors and walked onto the patio.

Her parents were dining alone. Harper was wearing hospital scrubs and reading the paper; he must have had a surgery this morning. Patricia sat across from him, sectioning out bites of grapefruit, which she followed with nibbles of dry toast. For as long as Melanie could remember, her mother had dined on only grapefruit and plain wheat toast.

Patricia turned at the sound of Melanie's approach and her eyes grew wide. They looked at each other uncomfortably, memories of a phone call stretching between the two of them. Melanie had never felt awkward around her mother, but now she did.

Finally, Patricia smiled tremulously and held out her arms for her daughter's embrace.

Melanie's knees almost gave way. This was what she wanted, she realized. After the last forty-eight hours, she wanted to come home to her mother. She wanted to inhale the scents of Chanel No. 5 and Lancôme face cream she'd known most of her life. She wanted to hear her mother say, as she had so many times over the years, 'It'll be all right, child. You're a Stokes now, and we'll always take care of you.'

And then Melanie thought, Oh, God, what did you people do to Meagan?

'How was your evening?' Patricia asked lightly.

'Fine,' Melanie said. She stared at the patio floor, then fingered the petals of a pink climbing rose. Her mother's arms finally came down. She turned back to her grapefruit, shaken, and Melanie felt worse.

Her father lowered his newspaper. He looked at her, then at Patricia, then her again. He frowned. 'Melanie? Are you all right? We haven't seen you in days, which is not like you.'

'I just needed some space.'

'That may be, but we're still family. Next time, make sure you call. That's common courtesy.'

'Of course,' she murmured. 'How . . . how is life around here?'

'Busy,' her father said with a sigh. He looked pale and overworked, his face showing his age. 'Got called in this morning for another pacemaker installation. I swear, that hospital never lets me get any rest.'

'Your father and I have been talking,' her mother interjected suddenly. 'We think it's time the whole family went on vacation. Even Brian.'

'Europe,' Harper said.

'What?' Melanie couldn't have been more surprised.

'I've always said we should take a family vacation,' her father continued reasonably. 'Finally I said to your mother that maybe we should just pack our bags and go. We'll spend six months traveling around France and England and the Mediterranean. It will be the time of our life.'

She was bewildered. 'I don't want to go to Europe. Not now.'

'Nonsense,' her mother said. Melanie thought her voice was too bright, as if she were placating a child. 'You need a vacation, Melanie. You deserve one. It will be wonderful. We'll relax and bask in the sun.'

Melanie shook her head. She looked at her parents, but they wouldn't return her gaze. Patricia was wringing her hands on her lap, then twisting her wedding band. Harper was tapping his foot, shifting a bit to the left, shifting to the right, in a way she'd never seen her father do before.

This wasn't a vacation, Melanie realized. This was escape. Had they gotten a shrine? Or maybe a phone call telling them they got what they deserved. Were they panicking and resorting to fleeing once more, as they'd fled from Texas to Boston?

'I won't go,' Melanie announced.

Harper frowned. 'We're offering you a vacation to Europe, Melanie. Of course you'll go.'

She shook her head. Her hands were knotted at her sides, and she realized as she spoke that her voice was climbing. 'This has nothing to do with a vacation. You *never* go on vacation, Dad. One would think if you spent more than ten minutes away from your precious hospital, you'd turn to stone.'

Her father's gaze narrowed. 'I don't know what you are talking about, young lady, nor do I appreciate your tone.'

'I'm talking about the truth,' Melanie cried. 'I'm talking about what happened to a little girl named Meagan Stokes.'

A silence descended upon the patio. Melanie saw her mother pale. Then the silence was broken by the sound of metal screeching on flagstone as her father pushed back his chair and leaped to his feet, his face an unhealthy shade of red. 'Don't you dare, young lady. Don't you dare bring this up in front of your mother!'

'Why not? It's been twenty-five years. Why don't we ever speak of Meagan? It's not like you guys don't think about her. Or that I don't find Mom staring at her portrait, or you yourself gazing at it over a glass of Scotch. Brian still calls out her name at times, Jamie used to stutter every time he had to say Melanie. Meagan's here. She's in this house and she's part of all of our lives. So why don't we ever speak of her? *What are you so afraid of?*'

'Young lady, that is enough. You will not speak to your parents like that—'

'My parents. Yes, my parents. One more thing we never mention. Why didn't we ever look for my birth parents, Dad? Why didn't you ever suggest hypnosis or regression therapy or anything that might help me reclaim my own identity? Why were you at the hospital that night and not watching the execution of Russell Lee Holmes?'

'Melanie!' her mother gasped. 'What . . . what is this?'

Melanie didn't get a chance to answer. Harper thrust up a hand, immediately silencing his wife. He stared at his daughter, and there was a cold expression on his face Melanie had never seen turned on her before.

'How dare you.' His gaze burned the way it had when he'd looked at her brother the night Brian had announced he was gay. 'How dare you stand in my own house and speak to me this way. After everything I've done for you. Goddammit, I took you in, I put a roof over your head. I've done everything a father is supposed to do, looked after your health, paid for your education, guided you through life. I've never short-changed you, young lady. I have never treated you as less than my own child, you spoiled, ungrateful—'

'What?' Melanie goaded softly. 'Killer's brat? Is that what you're trying to say? Is that how you *really* feel, Harper?'

'You little bitch.' He raised his arm and smacked her hard. Melanie fell onto the patio without even a murmur. As if from a distance, she heard her mother's soft cry of distress.

Slowly Melanie raised her head.

'It's not going to go away, Dad,' she whispered. 'The truth is out now, and not even Boston's best cardiac surgeon can control this mess. Not even you can make it go away.'

'You don't know what you're talking about—'

'Stop it,' Patricia yelled. 'Just stop it.'

They both turned to her. Patricia was getting shakily to her feet. Her body swayed tremulously, her eyes filled with unshed tears.

'Please,' she whispered. 'No more. This is our daughter, Harper. Brian is our son. They are all we have. What are you doing?'

'I'm trying to teach them some gratitude. You see what happens when you give them everything, Pat? How they are both turning out—'

Patricia placed a hand on his shoulder. 'Harper, please.'

He yanked his arm away, his expression too angry, too hurt.

'You too, Pat?' he growled. 'Goddammit, I have had enough. Who bought this house and the cars you're driving and the clothes you're wearing and the food you're eating anyway? Certainly wasn't you or your father. He left all his money to charity, remember? Told us we could earn ours. So I did. I go to that hospital every day, I work my ass off in a stressful position you couldn't even imagine, and what kind of respect do I get for that? What kind of appreciation from my own wife?'

He whirled on Melanie. 'And you. Your charity work is great, but how the hell does it pay the rent? What kind of responsibility do you show around here? You just went off for two days as if you hadn't a fucking care in the world.

'Now, what would happen if I did that? Huh? *What would happen?* Don't you people get it yet? My own children dance and play and join freak shows while *I* pay the fucking bills. My wife shops and nurses her self-pity while *I* get up and go to work every single day regardless of rain, weather, or mood. Jesus Christ, Pat, all I ever asked of you was to be a good mother. Then Meagan dies and you weren't even that. You became a mourner, a full-time professional mourner. Is it any wonder that Brian became a freak? Of course he had to turn to men. It wasn't like he was getting any affection from the women in his life!'

Patricia inhaled sharply, but her husband was far from done.

'So don't you turn on me!' He stared directly at Melanie. 'Don't you speak to me in that tone of voice! This is *my house*. Paid for by me, maintained by me, because that's what my life is all about – taking care of the rest of you whether I feel like it or not. You guys get to play. I have *never* had that luxury. Not even when my little girl was murdered, you selfish, self-centered—'

Harper's voice broke off abruptly. He was near tears, Melanie realized. Oh, God, she'd driven her father to *tears*.

He wiped his face with the back of a hand, quickly composing himself, but still angry.

'I'm going to the hospital. While I'm gone, I expect you two to give this some thought. And you, Melanie. I want an apology to both me and your mother by morning. And then you can start packing your bags. Because whether you like it or not, this whole family is going on vacation and we're all going to be happy if it kills us!'

Harper banged through the French doors. Moments later they could hear him storming down the hall and then slamming the front door. Then the house was silent.

Patricia was staring at Melanie, who tried to think of something to say, something to do. She found herself fingering her cheek; it still stung. Her mind couldn't grasp it. She'd never seen her father violent before.

'He just needs some time to cool off,' Patricia murmured. 'He's been under a lot of pressure lately . . .'

Melanie didn't say anything.

'It's going to be all right,' her mother said more anxiously. 'This is how families are. We have spells, bad spells, but we get through them, Melanie. We all get through them, and that's what makes us strong.'

'Maybe we shouldn't keep getting through them,' Melanie said tiredly. 'Maybe what this family really needs is to fall apart.'

She staggered to her feet. Her legs felt rubbery. Pain gathered behind her left eyeball. Another migraine was coming.

'You're only twenty-nine,' her mother was saying. 'Only a twenty-nine-year-old would say something like that. The bottom line is that families must forgive, Melanie, and families must *forget*.'

'Why? We have never forgotten Meagan. And you and Dad have obviously never forgiven each other, or how could he have said even half of what he did? What did you guys do back then? What did you do?'

Patricia paled again. Then her shoulders sagged and Melanie supposed she'd finally gotten what she wanted. Her mother broke, looking hurt and frightened beyond belief.

Melanie decided there was no satisfaction in it after all.

In her own room, the colors greeted her sharply. Red, green, and blue. Yellow and orange, and Lord, what a mess.

She shed her dress and climbed into the shower. And there beneath the protective spray, she sobbed simply because she needed to.

When she climbed back out, all the emotion had drained away. She was no longer scared or angry or overwhelmed. She was exhausted.

She took her Fiorinal, cocooned herself in bed, and within seconds fell asleep.

Once she woke up and saw her father standing in the doorway, his hands on his hips, his face filled with menace.

Then she was sucked back into the darkness, where she ran through a dense underbrush, thorns snatching at her hair and the scent of gardenias cloying in the air.

I want to go home. I want to go home.

Run, Meagan, run!

The sound of laboring breath coming closer . . . coming closer . . .

RUN, MEAGAN, RUN!

The gardenias, the branches, twigs, the heavy footsteps falling so close—

Nooo.

When she woke up again, Patricia sat at her bedside, stroking her hair.

'It's all right,' her mother whispered. 'I won't lose another child. I won't.'

23

David worked late. Hunched over his desk, he raked a hand through his hair and sifted through stacks of paper. His eyes were blurred by fatigue, his neck muscles ached, and his lower back had locked up. He pushed himself harder, consumed by the notion that there wasn't much time left.

Chenney had investigated William Sheffield's trash early that afternoon. He'd discovered an entire bag filled with pig organs, stained bedding, and one shiny apple. Unless Sheffield had taken up a macabre hobby, David was willing to believe the items had been left as some kind of shocking display.

After twenty-five years, had one of the co-conspirators finally had enough? Or was there a person they had yet to identify? And what other kinds of messages might have been delivered that the Bureau simply didn't know about yet?

David hated that question most of all. He was left with an overall feeling of being herded, that the messenger wasn't moving just with speed, but with competency. Hitting everyone's buttons and moving on. Advancing them all through some highly complex game where he already had an ending in sight.

That ending worried David quite a bit.

'What you got?' he demanded from Detective Jax at four in the afternoon.

'Forty-two cases and two unidentified stiffs. And how are you?'

'Overworked and underloved. Have you ID'd the shooter?'

'Nah, the tarot card reading came back inconclusive. Now I'm thinking of contacting a medium. Maybe get the guy's name and a song by Elvis Presley. You know, 'cause us local boys have nothing better to do with our time.'

'What about the pay phone records? Know who Difford spoke to?'

'Yo, Agent, keep your pants on. It takes a little time to subpoena public phone records and wade through the mess, unless, of course, you want to do the paperwork for me.'

'It's your case,' David said stiffly.

'As a matter of fact, it is. So why the hell am I talking to you?' Detective Jax hung up. Apparently forty-two cases took their toll on a man.

David was left with gnawing frustration and a really bad mood. Subpoenaing records did take time. Sorting through the records of a downtown Boston pay phone with its extraordinary high volume of calls took even longer.

He just wanted answers now.

Seven P.M. arrived.

Lairmore stopped by on his way out the door. 'Where are we?'

'Same as the morning, plus one additional corpse.'

Lairmore scowled. David raised an inquiring brow. 'Bad day, Lairmore?'

'Bad week,' the supervisory agent said. David didn't push. Lairmore's business was his own, just as David's business was his own. The red message light on his phone was already blinking with the third message left by his father.

After a moment Lairmore walked away.

David returned to the open file on his desk. He was surrounded by stacks of materials, as if they were pieces of a giant jigsaw puzzle just waiting to fall into place. He had a file on the Stokes financials, which he was dutifully compiling for his next seven A.M. meeting with Lairmore. Nothing revolutionary there. Money came in, money went out. Someone had better tell Harper there was more to life than Armani suits.

David sighed. He'd left two messages with Brian Stokes, but neither had been returned. At eight P.M. he paid a visit to the exiled son's house. No lights on, nobody home. Next David tried the private practice where Brian worked, only to be told that the doctor had called in sick.

Forty-eight hours without a single sighting of Brian Stokes. David still wasn't sure what that meant.

Nine P.M. He followed up with the lab. They didn't have conclusive news yet. No prints. Candles were a local-made brand available from a factory in Maine and sold in several hundred locations in the state. The toy did seem old. Most interesting was the scrap of dress that had yielded two blood types. They were hoping to have DNA test results by end of week, and that was considered a rush job. Of course, for DNA results to be useful, you generally needed someone to match them against.

Back to the normal investigative world of hurry-up-and-wait.

Nothing you can do anymore, Riggs. You are trying to help her, you are.

I lied to her, he thought bluntly, finally left alone with his guilt. I never told her I was investigating her father, or that we probably do have a case against Harper for healthcare fraud.

That's your job. You have to do your job. That is how you help her.

What if it makes a difference? What if knowing that much about her father would give her perspective, help keep her safe.

You don't know that, Riggs. As Chenney likes to say, there's still a world of difference between reckless endangerment of human life and hiring a hit man to kill your adopted daughter.

He finally headed back to his place.

He slipped on boxers, crawled into bed.

He fell asleep with his pager cradled against his cheek, and he dreamed he was in a wooden shack but with Melanie, not Meagan Stokes. He was cleaning, scrubbing the floor furiously, as if that would save them all.

But he could still see Melanie laid out in the middle of the floor, and no matter how hard he scrubbed, she didn't move.

In the doorway Russell Lee Holmes stood laughing.

Chenney was tired. Really tired. He'd managed to snag an afternoon nap, but between trying to track down William Sheffield's garbage and his history at some boys' home in Texas, he'd still had a long day. At least he'd learned interesting information. According to one of the nuns, Sheffield had been a bit of a monster at that boys' home. She even thought William might have poisoned one of the older boys, not enough to die, but enough to put some fear of God in the child and keep him away from William. Clearly, there was more to the thin, over-educated anesthesiologist than met the eye.

Now Chenney trudged through the dim halls of City General, pushing a cart loaded down with cleaning supplies, a giant trash can, and rolls upon rolls of toilet paper. Halls were empty, dimly lit. His cart echoed against the linoleum floor and gave him the willies. He didn't like big institutional places.

When the ICU nurse had moved on to other patients in the ward, he'd managed to sneak a glance at the charts. He couldn't understand any of the shit – that that was Riggs's department.

He'd finally focused on two older patients who were hooked to heart monitors and IVs. One looked in pretty rough shape. Toothless jaw open beneath the oxygen mask. Skin settling into folds around her neck. Flesh tone nearly gray. Chenney figured whatever condition she had, it was real.

The other man was younger, probably in his fifties. Fairly fit, actually. Good haircut. Nice spring tan, a bit of a roll around the middle and upper arms. The next time the nurse was around, he'd inquire politely about the man's condition.

Chenney turned the corner, slogging ahead, and thinking he really had to get up to speed on healthcare fraud.

'Oh, excuse me.' Chenney had been so lost in thought, he'd run into a doctor.

The man turned around, equally startled, and Chenney found himself face-to-face with Dr William Sheffield.

Chenney gripped the cart to hold himself steady. He was just a janitor, he reminded himself belatedly.

'Are you going to move?' Sheffield inquired tersely. Chenney caught a faint whiff of whiskey.

'Sorry.' Chenney eased back his cart. He had to stare at the floor now, or he was sure his face would give him away. Luckily Sheffield wasn't in the mood to chat. The anesthesiologist brushed by in a snit and kept walking down the hall.

Okay. Now what?

Chenney should swing back around to the ICU. Would Sheffield really strike two nights in a row? Anything was possible.

Chenney picked up his footsteps, never seeing Sheffield turn around with a last annoyed glance, his gaze falling to the janitor's shoes. William took one look at the retreating Italian loafers, and his stomach plunged, and his mouth went dry.

He bolted into the nearest bathroom. He vomited into the sink. He grabbed the two vials of propranolol from his pocket, wiped them clean with paper towels, and shoved them deep into the trash can.

Harper was setting him up, that son of a bitch. Looking for a fall guy so he could once again sail away into the sunset.

Well, Harper Stokes had another think coming. William was not going down without a fight. Particularly not when he knew a thing or two.

'We have problems,' Harper stated at the other end of the line.

'Would it kill you to let me sleep?' Jamie O'Donnell yawned, annoyed at being woken up for the second night in a row by Harper. Jamie glanced at the clock glowing next to his bed. Two A.M. Bloody hell.

'Hang on.' Jamie pushed back the covers and crawled out of bed, conscious of Annie sleeping beside him. Jamie touched her cheek once, then picked up the phone and carried it with him to the adjoining room of the suite, shutting the door behind him so he wouldn't disturb her.

'What's up, sport? Did you just get your tickets to Europe?' Jamie yawned again. The European vacation still rankled him. Harper riding off like the good cowboy with the tall white hat.

'Fuck Europe,' Harper said. 'This is about William. He's cracked. Called me in total panic, told me he was being pursued by a pair of Italian loafers, and that he wasn't going to let me get away with this. Then he slammed down the phone. I tried calling back twice, no answer. I went by his place. Looks as if a tornado has blown through, and both William and his car have vanished.'

'You're right. The kid's gone Humpty Dumpty.'

'Jesus Christ,' Harper exploded. 'He's ranting that I set him up. I've done no such thing. Just who the hell is behind all this? I thought you were going to figure it out.'

'I'm trying. As a matter of fact, I'd thought I'd talk to Larry Digger about it, but I couldn't. Seems that Larry boy is now dead.'

'*What!*'

'Oh, don't play dumb with me, Harper. I know you did it.'

'I did not!' Harper sounded shrill. 'What the hell is going on? Somebody is setting me up, Jamie. You have to believe me. Somebody is just plain fucking with everything. My God, even Melanie came home accusing me of doing something to Meagan.'

For a moment Jamie didn't reply. He'd never heard his old friend sound so out of control before, so genuinely afraid. He kept waiting for some feeling of satisfaction to come to him, but it didn't. He still carried the suspicion that this too was an act. It was always so difficult to tell with Harper.

'You really didn't arrange to harm Larry Digger?'

'No!'

'Well, I didn't do it.'

'But, but . . .' Harper was definitely losing it now. '*Who?*'

'I don't know.'

'You have to fix this, Jamie. Everything is falling apart. It can't just happen like this. Not . . . not after all this time. It makes no sense. This was over and done with, end of story.'

'You started it again with the surgeries, Hap. I warned you to keep your hands clean—'

'Fine, fine, I'm stopping them. Just find Sheffield for me. Work this out with him.'

'What makes you think he'll listen to me? He hates me as much as anyone.'

'Because, Jamie, he's your kind. Remember?'

Jamie was silent. Then he had to shake his head. Leave it to Harper to lash out even when he was down. There was more than a bit of the street fighter in prim, proper Dr Stokes.

'All right,' Jamie said finally, reluctantly. 'One last time, I'll take care of things. Just give me a day or two.' He added as almost an afterthought, 'Oh, Harper.'

'What?'

'Have you spoken to your son lately?'

'No. I've been meaning to call. Tomorrow I'll do it.'

'Well, I wish you the best of luck, then, old man, because I've been trying to reach him for twenty-four hours now, but Brian seems to have also disappeared. I wonder what that means, Hap. I wonder.'

24

Melanie woke up with her cheek still stinging. She fingered the bruise gingerly. Painful, but nothing that wouldn't heal. She supposed that assessment characterized much of her life these days.

When she came downstairs, the house was quiet. No Harper or Patricia. No María.

She called her brother. Brian wasn't at home. She tried him at work. He was still out sick, the receptionist informed her. Something about a forty-eight-hour flu bug. Melanie didn't believe that for a minute. If Brian was sick, he'd be at home. Now what?

The phone call, the anonymous tip that supposedly had come from her own house. In the chaos of the past few days, she'd never followed up on it. Now she dialed the local phone company and arranged for a listing of calls to be sent. That would be a start. And until then?

Melanie roamed the downstairs, feeling strange and outside her own skin. Her home looked like a setting from a play to her now, a carefully crafted backdrop. Living room hung in rose-colored silk, perfect for social gatherings. Front parlor with golden Italian marble, perfect for impressing hospital administrators. Dining room with the huge walnut table set for twelve, perfect for family dinners and long, intimate conversations as the Stokeses unwound from their day.

Back patio with its clay urns of climbing roses and wrought iron table, perfect for a father to strike a daughter.

Enough. Melanie went down to the basement, where there rested a pile of boxes that shared one common label: MEAGAN STOKES 1968–1972.

When Melanie had turned twelve, Patricia lobbied to finish the basement as a rec room for the kids. Harper denied the motion. Families needed places to hide their junk, he'd insisted. Basements served useful purposes.

It may have made sense, except the Stokeses had no junk. No boxes of old clothes, old books, jigsaw puzzles, or games. No stained carpet or too-old furniture. Harper was scrupulous – all outgrown items were cata-logued, evaluated, and sent to the Salvation Army for the tax deduction. Everything had its worth. Except these boxes, whose content was priceless.

She'd searched these boxes before, as a nine-year-old child desperate to learn more about her new parents' life. She'd run her child's hands reverently over the lace baptismal dress, the red velvet Christmas dress, the hand-knit pink 'blankie.' She'd examined the small bronzed shoes, the tiny handprint made in clay, the first works of Crayola art. She'd looked through the boxes feeling both guilty and enthralled, knowing she should stay away but consumed with the desire to know more.

This was all that remained of Meagan Stokes, and Melanie wanted to know about the real love in her family's life.

Melanie began with the box of photos.

They started with the Texas days. Jamie, Harper, and Patricia in an old white convertible; Jamie and Harper in pin-striped suits, looking like fifties gangsters; Jamie with his arms wrapped around a young, beautiful Patricia, beaming at the camera; Jamie shaking his head while a dashing young Harper kissed his future wife.

Wedding photos. Patricia and Harper inside a yawning cathedral, holding hands. Patricia wearing the perfect princess dress, flounces and flounces of white tulle cascading down her slender frame.

Outside with Jamie again, posing in a white tuxedo jacket with black trim as Harper's best man. Her god-father was still smiling, but now he stood far away from Patricia, often half cut out of the camera's lens. Despite what the three friends must have said, the wedding had changed things.

Suddenly, baby pictures. Brian Harper Stokes, February 25, 1963, 8 lbs. 10 oz. Brian being cradled in Harper's triumphant embrace. Patricia smiling tiredly. Brian crawling, Brian walking. Three-year-old Brian reaching for a figurine poised just out of his reach in a hallway. Three-year-old Brian looking stunned at the now-broken statue. Patricia's notation: 'Brian's first encounter with art. When will he learn?'

Brian dressed up for Halloween as Satan. 'Brian still in his "devil phase." At least it suits him.'

Then Patricia was pregnant. Brian faded to the background. The lens focused in on tall, slender Patricia now radiantly in bloom. Patricia cradling her stomach. Patricia in profile, looking far away at something Melanie couldn't see. Patricia at a picnic, Brian running beside the blanket. Patricia very, very pregnant, holding up a stuffed bear for the camera. Brian's face barely visible behind her. Jamie's notation, 'Pat 1968. Looking beautiful as always, lass.'

Melanie turned the page. Meagan. Patricia cradling the newborn against her breast, the ruddy face pudgy and sleepy, the tiny little hand forming a tiny little fist. Brian sitting beside his mother and newborn sister. Jamie, standing beside the hospital bed laughing, his thick finger securely caught in baby Meagan's tight little fist.

Suddenly both Brian and Meagan were growing up very fast. Picture of Brian feeding Meagan. Brian reading to Meagan. Brian pulling Meagan in a little red wagon, beaming happily.

Three Halloweens later, Brian still dressed up as the devil, but Meagan now at his side as Raggedy Ann. They were both smiling. Next photo, Patricia, Brian, and four-year-old Meagan Stokes, beaming into the camera, a beautiful young mother and her two incredibly happy, incredibly beautiful blond children.

Melanie put the album down. Her hands were shaking.

She knew what happened next. A hot, summer day in Texas. Patricia and Brian had left Meagan with the nanny one morning to go to the doctor. And something had occurred that afternoon so that Meagan Stokes ceased to exist on this earth.

They really had been such a perfect family.

There was no mention of Russell Lee Holmes in the box. No newspaper clippings of the case, not even condolence cards from the funeral. One page Meagan Stokes beamed for the camera, the next she was gone, the end of the story never given.

Melanie flipped through the book again. Jamie, Harper, and Patricia. Harper and Patricia. Baby Brian. Brian growing up. Pregnant Patricia, baby Meagan. Meagan and Brian.

Something niggled at the back of her mind.

Pregnant Patricia, baby Meagan. Meagan and Brian.

She couldn't get it. What she wanted haunted her, a word on the tip of her tongue, but she couldn't get it.

Pregnant Patricia, baby Meagan. Meagan and Brian—

Oh, Jesus! Where was Harper? Why wasn't there a single picture of her father with his new baby girl?

Abruptly a sound came from upstairs. The front door opening, then slamming shut. Footsteps on the floor above her head.

Someone was home. Melanie scrambled to replace the photo album. The Meagan boxes were sacred, and at the rate things were going these days, she didn't want to be caught rifling through them.

More footsteps. Crossing the hall into the living room, moving down the back hallway toward the office . . . Harper then. He'd returned from the hospital and was now going to catch up on his paperwork.

Melanie crept up the old wooden stairs, cracked the door, and seeing that the coast was clear, sneaked into the foyer. Seconds later she stood in front of the hallway mirror, dusting off her hands, her denim shorts, and blue and yellow top.

She could hear Harper banging around in his study; from the sound of it, he was not in a good mood.

She surveyed her reflection one last time and decided, what the hell.

Her father was never generous when backed into a corner, but sometimes, on his own, he'd been known to reach the independent conclusion that he was wrong. She could start with her own apology, see what he would do. It was worth a shot.

Melanie walked into her father's office. She expected to find Harper in green surgical scrubs hunched over his desk.

She found William Sheffield, surrounded by flying papers and holding a gun.

William was having a bad day, a bad week, a bad life. But he was coming out on top of this mess at whatever the price. He just needed proof. Surely Harper had some financial records somewhere.

'William?' A female voice called from the doorway. 'What are you doing here?'

William stilled, turned slowly. He saw Melanie standing in the doorway, with her hands stuck in her back pockets. Her gaze rested on his gun warily.

'William?' she asked again.

'You shouldn't be here, Mel,' he said. He'd thought the house was empty. He'd thought it would be a simple in and out. But now she'd seen him, and sweet Melanie always told Daddy everything. He couldn't have that.

'What are you doing, William?'

'Enjoying your house.' He gestured at the expensively paneled and decorated room. 'Quite the place. I've always wondered what it would be like to come home to this day after day. Who would've thunk my mama would've been kinder if she'd drugged me up and dropped me off at an emergency room?'

'You need to leave,' Melanie said coolly. 'Harper's not here right now, so you shouldn't be in his office.'

'Well, you know what?' William strode toward her, catching her off guard and making her gaze flicker once more to his gun. 'I don't give a flying fuck what you think. You're just Harper's adopted daughter and you don't know jack shit!'

'William . . .'

She tried to retreat. He knew she'd never seen him as a threat before – but now he charged, and had the satisfaction of seeing her gaze widen with fear. Too late. William pinned her against the wall.

'Move away,' she said.

'Why, Mel? I've already seen all of you. Already had all of you.'

'Dammit, William—'

He grabbed her hair and yanked. She yelped and immediately blinked back tears. She'd always liked to play tough, play cool. William decided it was time for a little change. Time to finally have some fun at Harper's expense.

'Getting it yet, Mel?'

'I don't . . . no.'

'Of course you don't. You know, for a supposedly smart woman, you don't know shit about your family. Yeah, that's right. Stare at me defiantly, try to think you're better than me. You're not better, Mel, you're just more naïve. After all, I figured out your father in less than five minutes, and you still haven't a clue after twenty fucking years. Who's so smart now?'

He yanked her hair again cruelly. This time she couldn't suppress the hiss of pain. He liked that.

'Your fine daddy thinks he has me beat,' William drawled. 'He thinks he can set me up to take the fall for all his little illegal operations and I'd be too stupid to figure it out. Yeah, you don't know about that either, do you, Mel?' William swept the barrel of the gun casually around the study. 'See all this, sweetheart? *Tainted.* Your daddy may be the best cardiac surgeon in Boston, but he knows nothing about money. Man digs himself in deeper and deeper all the time. But do you think that means he cuts back, keeps his family in any less style? Oh, no, not the great Harper Stokes.

'He simply concocts a plan to slice open innocent old folks and slap pacemakers in their chest. "Nobody gets hurt," he likes to say. "Insurance companies can afford it." Now, how is that for class, Melanie? How is that for your dear old dad?'

Her lips trembled. But then Melanie looked him in the eye and stated in that cool tone he hated so much, 'I don't know what you're talking about.'

He rewarded her brave words by slapping her hard. She didn't wince, which disappointed him, but her bottom lip cracked. Flecks of blood appeared. The lip began to swell.

William said, 'Well, say good-bye to Daddy, darling, because I have no intention of coming home to another surprise gift. You get what you deserve, my ass. I spotted that FBI agent at the hospital. I know what the hell he's up to, and I sure as *hell* am not going to take the fall.'

'Oh, my God. You got a note.'

'A note?' He frowned at her angrily. 'I didn't get a note. I got a goddamn message scrawled across my mirror in blood. Who would've thought your father had it in him?'

Melanie was shaking her head. 'But how are you connected with Russell Lee Holmes? Did you know Meagan?'

'What?' William didn't know what she was talking about and didn't care. He shut her up by pressing his body against hers, watching her gaze flicker more frantically.

'You want to know the truth, Mel? I'll give it to you straight, you dumb little fool. Your father is a con man who would rather slice open healthy people than admit that he's broke. Your mother is an unstable lush who can't keep her own husband satisfied, and your brother is a fucking fruitcake who can only get it up for men. And to top it all off, your godfather is little more than a dressed-up thug. Now, how is that for a sweet family portrait? Two criminals, a lush, and a fag. And what does that make you, Melanie? It makes you a patsy. The world's biggest *patsy*, conned for over twenty years. How do you like that?'

William smiled. Melanie's chin came up like she wanted a fight. But he could also read doubt in her eyes, a bit of pleading, as if she wanted him to take the words back. Like hell.

He leaned back and casually smacked her across the face. 'How dare you dump me like that, you stupid bitch.'

'How dare you treat me like shit!' she cried, and tried to knee him. He blocked her easily. Then he reached down, caught her wrist, and began to squeeze.

'I need the combination for the safe, Melanie. I need *all* of Harper's papers.'

'I don't know it—'

He let go of her wrist and pistol-whipped her. Her head hit the wall, then she slid down to the floor, her eyes blinking groggily.

'Larry Digger.'

'What are you talking about? I want the combination for the safe!'

'Did my father . . . did my father shoot Larry Digger?'

William shook his head. 'I don't even know what you're talking about. Harper's into money, not murder. Now, I want that combination.'

'What happened to Meagan?' she murmured. 'What did they do to Meagan?'

'Forget fucking Meagan. Give me the combination, or I'm going to kill you.'

He wrapped her long hair around his left hand and in one quick tug jerked her back up to her feet.

And the rest simply happened.

Sweet Melanie Stokes drove her shoulder into his gut. Air whooshed out of his lungs. She slammed the broad part of her hand into his sternum and stomped on his foot.

'Fuck!'

He hopped back, cursing, and finally getting the gun between them.

'Fuck you!' he heard himself screaming. 'I'm going to kill you, bitch. I'm going to fucking blow your brains—'

'Stop it,' she gasped, gripping his hand, wrestling for control.

The gun went off with a blast. They froze in the middle of the torn-up study. William's eyes were wide, startled. Melanie gazed at him with equal shock as he slowly slipped to the floor.

Now she could see the hole in his gut. Blood was pouring everywhere. It was on her hands, on the papers, on the floor. Just like Larry Digger, she thought.

'*Mi Dios!*' a voice breathed in the silence.

Melanie turned to find María standing in the doorway, holding bags of groceries.

'I didn't mean to,' Melanie began weakly.

María whirled and ran. Belatedly Melanie realized she was still holding the gun in her hands and her arms were splattered in blood.

All she'd ever wanted was a family. People who would love her. People who would be there for her. A place that would finally be home.

Lies and blood. Lies and blood.

Her body moved on its own.

She grabbed her purse. She burst out of the front door of her house. She started running, and she didn't stop.

25

Lairmore was ripping new assholes for his investigating agents when David's beeper went off.

'Got to take this,' David said calmly, and left the conference room. Lairmore grumbled something unkind, but David ignored him.

The number on his beeper was not one David recognized, but his call was picked up immediately. The sound of background traffic and voices filled the line.

'This is Riggs,' he said.

There was a moment of silence, then he knew it was her. 'Melanie?'

'You lied to me.'

'Melanie, where are you?'

'You told me you weren't investigating my family. You told me it was William you were looking into. I bet you slept well that night. The super agent did his job.'

'Melanie, listen to me. I'm trying to help you—'

'Fuck you, David Riggs. How dare you lie to me. How dare you not tell me the truth after everything we went through.'

'Melanie—'

'The shooting was accidental, just so you know. William was going to kill me. You can tell that to my family, but I don't know if they'll care. I don't know what they care about at this point. I guess you were right, and I didn't know them at all.'

'Melanie, tell me exactly where you are. I'll be there in minutes.'

'No. No more games. No more manipulations. From the very beginning I've let everyone mess with me. Well, now I'm doing this my way. Good-bye.'

The phone clicked. David swore furiously, earning a round of stares. Lairmore came out of the conference room, trailed by Chenney.

'Riggs!' the supervisory agent warned.

David grabbed his coat. 'Get Detective Jax on the line. That was Melanie Stokes. According to her, she just shot William Sheffield.'

The Stokes house had suddenly become a very popular place. Two ambulances and three police cars barricaded the front, blue lights flashing

467

and uniformed officers milling. Two TV stations had arrived in camera-mounted vans; the local ABC affiliate was probably not far behind.

Between the reporters, the neighbors peering from doorways and windows, and the tourists who were snapping photos, traffic on the whole four-lane street had ground to a halt.

David Riggs yanked over his car one block away and ran the rest, Chenney huffing and puffing at his heels. He'd tried calling Melanie back without success. Then he'd gotten Detective Jax long enough to be told there had been a shooting all right, and Boston homicide had a few questions for their good friends at the Bureau.

David flashed his creds to the patrolmen. Chenney simply muscled his way through. They followed the stream of crime photographers, homicide detectives, and beat officers to the study at the rear of the house. Patricia Stokes stood in a corner, her thin arms crossed in front of her and a jeweled hand fluttering at the hollow of her throat. She looked confused and frightened, as if the slightest sound would shatter her.

Her husband was in the opposite corner, scowling and rumpled. He must have just been called from surgery. He had a green mask down around his neck and his arms akimbo on his hips, the stance belligerent.

Jamie O'Donnell occupied the doorway. He had already adopted a careful expression of both concern and distrust.

'Of course María tried to clean things up,' Harper was saying tersely. 'She's a maid, it's her job.'

'She tampered with a crime scene,' Jax pointed out, standing in front of Harper.

Harper shrugged. 'How's she supposed to know that? She thought she was just doing her job.'

David saw Jax's point immediately. The blood was not in a clear puddle or splatter pattern but instead had been smeared all over the floor, making it hard to interpret the scene. On the perimeter of the streaky mess, the blood formed razor-crisp lines at random intervals, as if it had spread along the edge of pieces of paper. The paper was gone. One could interpret that scene as William being shot, incriminating documents at his feet.

Detective Jax seemed to have arrived at that conclusion himself. 'If I find out you had anything to do with this, Dr Stokes, I'll bust your rich hide for interfering with an investigation, tampering with a crime scene, and aiding and abetting. Just so you know.'

Harper smiled tightly. 'You do that, Detective, and my lawyer will eat your badge for lunch.'

'Please,' Patricia interjected in a tremulous voice. 'Can you tell me what happened to Melanie? Where is my daughter? Is she all right?'

'We're still looking for her, ma'am.'

'I'm sure she didn't do this on purpose,' she continued desperately. 'There was no reason for her to hurt William.'

'We don't know that.' Harper glanced at his wife wearily. 'After that scene yesterday? Face it, Pat, our daughter is obviously very troubled these days. Maybe she took the end of her engagement with William much harder than either of us thought. I don't know.'

'Harper!' Patricia exclaimed.

'She's been having migraines and not sleeping well! She didn't even come home the night before. I'm not going to lie to these people. You and I don't know a thing about our children anymore.'

David wasn't thinking. One moment he was standing beside Chenney, listening to Harper incriminate his own daughter, the next moment he was across the room, grabbing a fistful of Harper's scrubs and shoving the startled surgeon against the wall.

'Don't you set her up for this,' David growled. 'You don't give a rat's ass about this investigation. William's death is the best thing to happen for you and your little operations. God, this is just a game to you, isn't it? You could've gotten her killed. Do you hear me? You almost killed your daughter. *Again!*'

'D-d-dammit,' Harper spluttered. 'Let me go!'

'Easy there,' O'Donnell said softly from behind David. 'Easy there, sport.'

Slowly David became aware that the only person in the room surprised by what was going on was Patricia Stokes. Harper, who was being strangled by a man he'd met only as a waiter, was not surprised. Jamie O'Donnell, faced by two men he'd never seen before, was not surprised.

They knew. They knew who David was and who Chenney was, and probably more about the investigation than the federal agents did.

David released Harper. He stepped back briskly and split his gaze between Harper and Jamie.

'How?' David asked.

Both men gave him blank looks.

'No,' David said, shaking his head. 'I don't buy it. I don't think even you two realized what Sheffield would do when pushed too hard. I bet you figured he was a spineless shit, just like we did. But he came up with his own agenda, didn't he? Did the stupid thing and put everything in jeopardy. In fact, the only person today who's shown an ounce of common sense is Melanie, isn't it? She's outplaying you. Outplaying us all.'

A muscle spasmed in O'Donnell's jaw. 'Don't know what you're talking about, sport.'

'Sure you do. Congratulations on putting your goddaughter in danger. It's not every day a man almost gets a beautiful young woman killed. But then, you must be getting used to that feeling, huh, O'Donnell? By my calculations, this makes two. First your hired gun, and now your hired lackey. I think you're getting old.'

O'Donnell's gaze went black, confirming David's stab in the dark. 'Be careful, sport. Be very, very careful.'

David just smiled. 'I'd say ditto, *sport*, because I'm getting smarter every day and a whole lot closer. You know there's no statute of limitations on homicide, don't you? Especially of a little girl. Especially of a *poor, helpless* little girl who had no idea what you were capable of. I bet she loved her family too. Just like Melanie.'

He strode for the door. Behind him, he heard Patricia say, 'What's that man talking about? What has happened to Melanie? Has anyone thought to call Brian?'

'By Brian, do you mean Brian Stokes?' Jax inquired.

'Of course,' Patricia said, sounding even more bewildered.

'His "friend" filed a missing persons report two hours ago. Seems Brian Stokes went out for a walk two days ago and hasn't been seen since.'

The news apparently was too much. With a small cry Patricia fainted. Her husband didn't catch her. Jamie O'Donnell did.

'Would you mind telling me what is going on?' Chenney panted, barely keeping up with David outside the house. David strode down the sidewalk, his back killing him and the rest of him beyond caring.

'We got a leak. We've never met them before, and yet they knew who we were.'

'Shit,' Chenney said. 'Think Melanie told them?'

'Melanie didn't know I was investigating her father.' David reached the car. He yanked open the driver-side door with more force than necessary and climbed in. Chenney rushed to catch up. 'Don't answer to anyone but Lairmore at this point. Things are just beginning. They weren't surprised by my comments about Meagan either. They knew exactly what I was talking about.'

'They were in on it.'

'Up to their eyeballs.' David shoved the car into drive, then frowned. 'Except for Patricia. She had no idea what was going on.'

'Yo, where are we going?'

'Brian Stokes's condo, of course. Where else could Melanie have gone?'

David pulled away with a roar.

Chenney said after a while: 'You lost it back there. I mean, you *lost* it. Lairmore hears about you going after Harper Stokes like that, you'll be suspended for a month.'

David didn't reply.

26

Brian Stokes's condo reminded David of a sterile museum. He and Chenney got the building maintenance man to let them in; apparently his services came with the condo fees. Once inside the third story residence, they found themselves confronted by four rooms filled only with crystal-clear glass, chrome frames, and one black leather sofa.

'There's not even a family portrait on the wall,' Chenney said.

'He isn't so pleased with his family.'

'The adopted daughter is grateful for her parents,' Chenney murmured, 'the older son is dying to give them away. Can you imagine these guys on *Family Feud?*'

'Only if they were playing opposite the Donner party.'

They drifted from room to room. Not a speck of dust, a streak of lint, or a stray item of clothing. The man could've given David and his own brother lessons all those years ago.

'Just beer and yogurt in the fridge,' Chenney reported.

'No messages on the machine,' David said, then frowned. 'Can you really believe after two days there're no messages on the machine?'

'Maybe he calls in and checks them. Those machines let you do that these days.'

'Yeah, maybe.'

They gave the condo a second pass. Brian seemed very neat and no-frills. A troubled young man, David thought, because no sane person kept anything that sanitized.

The maintenance man claimed not to have seen any blondes entering the building that day, but he also confessed a weakness for daytime soaps. He hadn't seen Brian around. Not that he noticed the male residents much, he said with a shrug, hitching up his slacks and rubbing his beer gut. Some of them were definitely swinging on the wrong side of the field, if you know what he meant, and he didn't want them to get no ideas about him.

Chenney and David headed back downstairs. They'd just reached their automobile when a voice stopped them.

'Special Agent Riggs, Chenney.'

Both agents turned as one, Chenney going for his gun. Brian Stokes stepped out of a shadowed doorway. He looked as if he hadn't slept a minute in days.

'You can let go of the gun, Chenney,' David said dryly. 'I don't think Brian Stokes is here for a showdown.'

'I just want to talk,' Brian seconded.

'Do you know where your sister is?'

Brian shook his head. 'I just got a message. That's my role in the family.'

'And was that your role twenty-five years ago when Meagan disappeared?'

Brian looked at him curiously. 'You think Meagan was my fault,' he said, and then smiled. 'Of course. It's nothing I haven't thought myself.'

'Brian—'

'Come with me, Agent. There's something I need to show you and something I should have told you. Something I should've told everyone a long time ago.'

They followed Brian Stokes on foot, passing block after block of neat brick town houses lined up like toy soldiers. A few streets over, Brian led them into a narrow street lined with older but still stately – and expensive – homes. He let himself into the last one with a key. A flower box filled with yellow daffodils waved to them as they passed through the heavy wood door, but none of them noticed.

'My . . . friend lives here,' Brian said at last, leading them up the stairs.

'You mean your lover.'

'You could say that. In theory, no one knew the name of the man I'm seeing or the fact that I often spend the night at his house.'

'In theory?'

'Tuesday morning I received a package. Hand-delivered to my name, here, at his place.'

David and Chenney exchanged looks. 'And you've been hiding out ever since?' David asked.

'I needed some time to think.'

'And the missing persons report?'

'I asked Nate to do that. To throw him off the trail.'

'Him?'

'I don't know, Agent. I was hoping you could tell me.'

They reached the third floor. Brian unlocked the front door and led them both inside, disappearing almost immediately into the kitchen. This condo celebrated hardwood floors, a redbrick wall, and piles and piles of suede pillows and soft wool rugs – it was everything Brian Stokes's condo wasn't.

'Is Nate home?' David asked. One question was solved. This was definitely Brian's 'home,' and the other residence mere window dressing.

'At work. He's a doctor as well.'

'And Melanie. When did you see her?'

Brian reemerged from the kitchen, carrying a cardboard box and giving David an impatient look. 'I already told you, I haven't seen her.'

'But you know William Sheffield has been shot.'

'I checked my machine thirty minutes ago. Two messages. The first was from Melanie. She sounded so calm, I almost thought it was a joke. She said William had tried to shoot her, but she'd shot him instead. She wanted me to know that she was all right. Then she mentioned your name and that you were investigating our father, probably with good cause. Then she said—'

Brian's voice faltered. 'She said she knew Russell Lee Holmes hadn't killed Meagan. And then she said—' His voice broke again. He cleared his throat forcefully. 'She said that she loved me. And she thanked me for the last twenty years.'

Brian's gaze was fixed on the box in front of him. His jaw was tense, and David could see a muscle spasm. Then he got it. Brian didn't just have a small self-confidence issue. He loathed himself. He genuinely loathed himself and held himself responsible for all the bad things that happened in his family – including the fates of his sisters.

'You said you had a second message?'

'From my godfather. He's been leaving three a day. He also told me about William's shooting. He said he knew something was up and that we really needed to talk about it. Seems that he got a gift too. I think they all have.'

'They all have?'

'My mom, Dad, Jamie, Melanie, and me. Everyone who was involved back then, though some of us remember it more than others. Let me show you.'

He lifted the lid of the cardboard box. There, resting on white tissue paper was a blackened, shriveled cow's tongue.

Brian looked at them both. 'It came with a note, "You get what you deserve," but I know what it's talking about. I'd already lost my sister, you see. I didn't want to lose my father too.'

David sat down. He got out his spiral notebook and picked up a pen. 'Let's start at the beginning here, because I'm dying for answers and we got a lot for you to explain. Where were you the day Meagan Stokes was kidnapped? What did you and your mother do?'

Brian took a deep breath and then, staring at the dried cow's tongue, he began.

'I wasn't a good kid, all right? In this day and age they'd probably diagnose me with attention deficit disorder. Back then I was simply hyper and high-strung and no one, least of all my mother, knew what to do with me. Frankly, our family wasn't sweetness and light back then either. I don't know how my parents started their marriage, but by the time I came along, my father seemed to be a withdrawn workaholic who gave his best at the office and had nothing left for home. Mom was hurt and sullen half the time, spending money as a hobby, doing anything to get attention. I think I was eight when I figured out it was worse than that – that Dad wasn't always working late, that my mom knew about the other women and seemed hell-bent on becoming a bit of a party animal on her own. I don't know, it was like being raised by a robot and a sixteen-year-old. Nobody ever said anything bad about the other, but, the undercurrents when they were both in a room . . . Kids just *know* these things, okay?'

'Yeah,' Chenney said heavily, which earned him a surprised look by both David and Brian. He shrugged. Apparently he did know.

'Then Meagan came along,' Brian continued after a moment. 'She was so sweet, always smiling. No matter what happened, she'd beam and hold out her hands to you. Everyone loved her. Women in supermarkets, for God's sake, the neighbors, stray dogs. If you had a pulse, you automatically loved Meagan Stokes and she automatically loved you. Sure as hell no one ever thought that about me. And, yeah, I was jealous. I'd get angry. But . . . but I wasn't immune to her either, Agent. Even when I was jealous I loved her. Sometimes I even crept into her room at night just to watch her sleep. She was so peaceful, so happy. I never understood how my family could create a little girl who was so *happy*.

'And then I would grow afraid. I would think that my parents would ruin her too. She would love them like I did, and they would make her pay. Harper would abandon her and Patricia would grow bored, and she'd realize one day that her parents were two completely self-centered, over-indulged people. I started breaking her toys, stealing her stuff. I kept thinking if I was mean enough, she'd get strong, learn to protect herself. I hurt her and I still believed I was doing her a favor.' He smiled lopsidedly. 'Welcome to the Stokes version of family.'

'And that last day? What did you do then?'

'I had fun, Agent. I honestly enjoyed life for a moment, and that was probably my biggest sin. That day . . . that day was my fourth therapy appointment. Afterward the shrink asked to speak to my mother alone. I don't know what he said. But she took me for ice cream, though it was only eleven in the morning. She even had some, and this is a woman who's dined on grapefruit and dry wheat toast for the last fifty years. We hung out, Agent, I don't know how else to describe it.

'After a while Mom told me that things would be different. The family was having a rough spell and she understood that they'd been pretending I didn't know what was really going on. She would spend more time with me. She and my father would work things out. She realized now that her family meant more to her than anything, and she was prepared to do whatever was necessary to hold it together. She told me she loved me, she really loved me, and everything would be all right.

'We played in the park after that. She pushed me on the swing even though I was too old to be pushed, and I liked it. I remember thinking that I was almost happy, and it was sort of curious and strange. I wasn't sure I'd ever been happy before.

'Then we went home and the police officer told us Meagan was gone. Just like that. Are you a fatalist, Agent?' Brian smiled. 'I sure as hell am.'

'You were with your mother all day?'

'All day.'

'Did you see Meagan get into the nanny's car?'

'No. We left before they did.'

'Brian, do you know absolutely that Russell Lee Holmes kidnapped Meagan Stokes?'

'I honestly thought he had,' Brian said. 'I insist, if the devil had a human face, Agent Riggs, it would look like Russell Lee Holmes.'

David frowned. He believed Brian Stokes. So if Brian and Patricia were together all day and had nothing to do with Meagan Stokes's death . . .

'Then what about the tongue?' he asked in frustration. 'If you had nothing to do with your sister's kidnapping, why the "gift"?'

Brian thinned his lips. 'I'm not sure. The shrine in Melanie's room caught me off guard. That she might be Russell Lee Holmes's daughter . . . God, I don't know. All I can say is that there were some things the police didn't catch back then, and someone seems intent on getting out that info now. For example, three nights ago my godfather got a penis in a jar. Three guesses as to why.'

'Him and Patricia?'

'Yep. In spite of what people might think, not all of my parents' problems were caused by Dad's work habits.' Brian shrugged, took a deep breath. 'As for the tongue . . . My father didn't have a hundred thousand dollars for ransom money back then. He was just an overworked resident still trying to pay off his student loans, let alone keep up with my mother. So Jamie supplied the money. I was there when he arrived with the briefcase filled with one hundred thousand dollars in cold, hard cash. And—'

Brian looked up, met their gazes. 'And I was there to see that my father did not take that briefcase to the drop site. He took his briefcase instead. Empty. I know, because when I spotted Jamie's briefcase under my parents' bed, I pulled it out and opened it. All that cash, sitting right there. Do you get it? My father didn't pay the ransom. He was so damn greedy, he kept the money for himself. And Russell Lee Holmes . . . Russell Lee Holmes *killed* my baby sister.'

Brian's breath came out in angry gasps. 'And I never said a word. I never went to the cops or Jamie or my mom or anyone. I just stared at Harper night after night, watching him eat dinner and assure my mom it would be all right. Night after night. He lied through his teeth, sold out my sister for a hundred thousand dollars, and I never had the courage to call him on it. Never. Goddammit, I wanted to say it so badly and I *couldn't*. I just fucking *couldn't!*'

Brian swept the cardboard box off the oak coffee table. It didn't do him any good. The tongue tumbled out, then lay on the rug in plain sight.

'Shit,' he said after a moment. Then again, 'Shit.'

David shared that thought. So Brian and Patricia Stokes hadn't harmed Meagan. The family had not rushed into cover-up mode to protect their son. If Meagan had been harmed, it had to have been by Jamie or Harper, and it had to have been cold-blooded murder.

Of a four-year-old little girl with big blue eyes and curly blond hair.

He said, 'If it's any help, I'm ninety percent positive that Russell Lee Holmes *did not* kidnap or murder Meagan Stokes, which may explain why your father didn't take the money to the drop site. He already knew he didn't have to.'

'Come again?'

David regarded Brian Stokes seriously. 'I don't think your father was after a hundred thousand dollars. I believe he was after a million.'

'*What?*'

'The life insurance, Brian, or didn't you know? Both you and Meagan were insured for one million bucks.'

Brian Stokes hadn't known. In front of them, he went pale as a sheet, then his face twisted with rage. '*That goddamn son of a bitch!* I will kill him. I can't believe . . .'

'The ransom note that was delivered was too sophisticated for Russell Lee Holmes. Meagan did not fit his victim profile. They *never* found any physical evidence tying him with the crime. In fact, all they had was his confession—'

'Why would he confess?'

'In order to have his child raised in style. Melanie is Russell Lee Holmes's daughter, Brian. Your parents raised her to cover their own tracks. Now you tell me, for your sister's sake, does that make a difference?'

Brian was silent for a moment. 'No. Of course not. Melanie is Melanie. She is the best thing that ever happened to this family. Maybe it just figures that it takes the devil's own daughter to love the Stokeses.'

David decided to let that comment pass. 'Okay, now you have to help me. Originally we had reason to believe you or your mother might be involved. You understand that in seventy-five percent of cases, it is the family, so we have to think that way. Now we know you and your mother had alibis. What about Harper?'

'He worked. At least I thought he was at work. I don't know. My father can be a cold SOB, but I can't imagine him kidnapping . . . killing . . .' Brian shook his head. 'He's not the type to get his hands dirty.'

'Yeah? Well, what about Jamie O'Donnell?'

Brian hung his head, which was answer enough. 'He loved us, I'd swear to it. He played with us, brought us presents, spoiled us, indulged us. But—'

'But?'

He whispered, 'But there's more to him than that. He's done some things. Known some things. I get the impression – If Harper hates getting his hands dirty, then Jamie is most at home in the muck.'

'He's that kind of man,' David said.

'Yeah, maybe. But Meagan was just a little girl. I can imagine Jamie taking on a grown man, or maybe somebody who'd wronged us, but I can't see him hurting a child. Especially Meagan. Did you know that his name was the first word she learned to say? Dad was furious.'

'Let's approach this from a different angle,' David tried after a moment. 'We have two different things going on here. We have the person or persons who harmed Meagan Stokes. Most likely Harper or Jamie. Then we have someone who knows the truth, who seems intimately aware of what everyone did or didn't do twenty-five years ago. This person is trying to get out the truth, in a sick and twisted way. Maybe, if we can identify this person, we can cut to the chase and ask directly. Who knew that you saw the ransom money but didn't tell?'

Brian shook his head. 'I didn't think anyone knew. If I'd thought I'd had an ally anywhere, I would've confessed.'

David gave him a look. 'That's not possible. Someone had to have seen to know to send you this cow's tongue.'

'No kidding. And I'm telling you, Agent, no one knew!'

'Russell Lee Holmes,' Chenney said excitedly. 'He must know all the details. That Harper never delivered the money, that the family had a love triangle. Before he confessed, he probably demanded all the details. He's sick and twisted enough to enjoy a little game like that.'

'Russell Lee Holmes is dead,' Brian said flatly and with a trace of vehemence. 'I watched it.'

'Things can be switched, faked. Maybe it was part of the deal.' Chenney shrugged again. 'Why should we assume he did it solely for his child's future? Maybe he got away for *life*, huh?'

David gave the rookie a look. 'We have no proof that Russell Lee Holmes is alive.'

'We have proof we're missing some piece of the puzzle,' Chenney argued. 'You can't deny that.'

'Let's get back to the facts,' David said flatly. 'One, someone knows what happened twenty-five years ago and is intent on shaking things up. Maybe he guessed about Brian and the ransom money. He also had to know where Meagan's toy horse and clothes were all these years, so he has to be connected to the family. Hell, maybe it was William Sheffield. Maybe Harper got drunk one night and said too much and William thought this would be a great way to twist everyone for extra money. We'll have to search his place.

'That brings us to the person who actually did the crime twenty-five years ago and is desperate to keep it covered up. He hired the shooter to take out Larry Digger when he got too close and Melanie when she began to remember.'

'What?' Brian said sharply.

David filled him in. 'Whoever is doing this,' David concluded, 'is playing for keeps. I think, Dr Stokes, that having Nate declare you missing might not have been such a bad idea.

'And I'm asking you again: Understanding now that Melanie is in danger, that we are dealing with someone who murdered a four-year-old girl, do you know where she is?'

'No, Agent. I just got her message.'

'Okay, she knows she isn't safe at home, she knows she couldn't find you. She's not experienced enough or prepared enough to drop off the face of the earth, so where would she turn next?'

Brian's face lit up. 'Ann Margaret. Her boss at the Dedham Donor Center.'

It was a thirty-five-minute drive to the Dedham Red Cross Donor Center. Chenney handled the wheel, David worked the cell phone. He offered Detective Jax the tidbit that Melanie had left a message on her brother's machine saying she had to shoot William in self-defense. In return, Jax told him that they had witnesses testifying that Melanie had used a pay phone in Government Center. They had one forensics team already searching the area for the murder weapon. They'd also found the taxi driver who had driven Melanie to Brian's condo. He'd described Melanie as being pale, quiet, and 'a little spooky.'

Now the police were canvassing the neighborhood, talking to taxi dispatch stations, monitoring the airport, and getting financial records from her bank. They figured they'd turn up something shortly. How long could one debutante hide?

David said uh-huh a lot. He didn't bother to mention his current destination. FBI agents were supposed to cooperate with local law enforcement, but that didn't preclude staying one step ahead of them.

They pulled into the parking lot of the Red Cross Center a little after three. Melanie had now been on the run for over two hours, plenty of time to get down to Dedham by taxi or train.

They found Ann Margaret inside the vast white blood-donation center, sitting in a tiny office doing paperwork. The desk looked makeshift, the plastic chairs utilitarian. Industrial metal bookcases and gray metal filing cabinets.

The woman fit the office. Short, sensible, gray hair capped closely in tight curls. Lined face carrying the permanent stamp of a southern sun. Trim, neat figure clad in nurses' whites. Though not large or imposing, Ann Margaret looked like the kind of woman you could trust to get the job done.

At their approach, she glanced up, frowned, then paled as they showed their credentials.

'What is it?' she asked sharply, as if part of her had been expecting bad news for quite some time. 'What happened?'

'We'd like to ask you some questions about Melanie Stokes,' David said.

The lines of her face turned to confusion. Apparently the presence of FBI agents didn't surprise her, but FBI agents asking about Melanie did.

David motioned to two yellow plastic chairs. 'May we?'

Ann Margaret was too well mannered to refuse, so he and Chenney took a seat.

'I don't understand what you need to know about Melanie,' Ann Margaret said, setting down her pen. 'She's not even scheduled to work today.'

'She's volunteered here for a while?' David asked.

'Five years.' Ann Margaret frowned. 'Is she all right? What's going on?'

'Do you know William Sheffield?'

'Yes, Melanie's ex-fiancé. Now, see here' – she leaned forward, her lips thinning into a firm line – 'I want to know what is going on.'

'William Sheffield was found shot two hours ago. We have reason to believe that Melanie pulled the trigger.'

Ann Margaret was shaken. 'No,' she whispered.

'Yes, ma'am.'

'But . . . but . . .' She couldn't seem to find her bearings. Her hands fluttered on her desk as if seeking anchor. 'Is he dead?'

'Yes, ma'am. But we'll need you to keep that under your hat until we notify his family.'

'He doesn't have a family. He was an orphan too. It was one of the things he and Melanie had in common.'

'What do you know about their relationship?'

Ann Margaret still looked shell-shocked. 'I don't . . . I mean. Melanie is more than just a volunteer, I'm her friend. I remember how happy she was when he first proposed.'

David waited patiently.

'Her father introduced the two of them, I believe. They dated six months, seemed happy. I know Melanie said once that William was a bit jealous that she'd been adopted by such a rich family and he hadn't. She didn't understand that. He'd become a doctor after all, lived a very good life. I guess it caused a rift between them. She hasn't really talked much about him since they broke up. I assumed the parting was mutual.'

'Did she ever allude that she wanted him back or felt injured?'

'Not at all. And even if – listen to me, young man.' Ann Margaret pulled herself up. 'William and Melanie weren't a good match, but you don't kill someone over something like that. William was really a nice boy, very smart, a good anesthesiologist. And Melanie simply wouldn't hurt a fly. Plus, their breakup is ancient history. There must be some other explanation.'

'Did she talk to you about anything else going on in her life?'

'Well, I haven't really spoken to her for four or five days. She hasn't been feeling well. Problems with migraines . . .' Her voice trailed off. She seemed to realize that could be significant.

David waited, but Ann Margaret had obviously decided it would be best if she didn't say anything more.

'We really need to speak to Melanie,' David said evenly.

'I'm sure you do.'

'If you know where she is—'

'I don't know any such thing.'

'You're sure she hasn't contacted you?'

'I am her boss, Agent, not her mother.'

David said in a low, steely voice, 'If we find out you're hiding a fugitive . . .'

But Ann Margaret remained unmoved. If she did know more, she simply wasn't saying.

David placed a business card on her desk. The blue FBI shield emblazoned on the card stared up at her as he and Chenney walked away.

As he was passing through the doorway, David suddenly turned.

'Ever hear the name Angela Johnson?'

He thought she flinched.

'No.'

'What about Annie?'

A muscle flickered in her cheek. 'My name is Ann Margaret Dawson. That's all I go by, Agent – at least on a good day.'

'Of course.'

She smiled thinly. 'Of course.'

David and Chenney walked out. 'What do you think?' Chenney asked as they got into their car.

'I don't know yet.'

'She seemed to take the news rather hard.'

David tapped the steering wheel a few times, then started the engine. 'I think she may be worth watching.'

'I don't know. Melanie Stokes is spooked and frightened. If you were spooked and frightened, would you really run to Dedham?'

'No, but if my name was really Ann Margaret Dawson, I wouldn't flinch at the mention of Angela Johnson.'

'Who's Angela Johnson?'

'Russell Lee Holmes's wife?'

Chenney's eyes got round. 'You think . . .'

'Ann Margaret, Annie, Angela. Lots of Annes to be a coincidence.'

'And she's from Texas.'

'And she's about the right age.'

'Oh, my God,' Chenney said.

David just nodded and drove. He had a thousand things on his mind, but first and foremost he remained worried about Melanie.

Chenney didn't speak again until they were almost in Boston. 'Shit,' he declared. 'Riggs, we're male chauvinist pigs.'

'Probably.'

'Think for a moment. The Stokes family doesn't have motive to stir things up. We don't think O'Donnell has motive to stir things up. Melanie certainly doesn't, and you're determined to believe that Russell Lee Holmes is dead.'

'Yes, I definitely believe that.'

'So what about Russell Lee Holmes's *wife*? What about this Angela Johnson and everything she must know from back then?'

'Oh, God,' David said as the pieces started to fit. 'We *are* male chauvinist pigs.'

'She'd probably know all about the details of the crime and life in the Stokes family.'

'That would explain the shrine in Melanie's room. If you were a woman and you gave up your daughter twenty years ago to protect her, to give her a better life, you'd have to wish—'

'That she'd remember. Or someday come looking for you.'

'Christ. First thing tomorrow morning—'

'Everything I can find on Angela Jones—'

'Ann Margaret Dawson.'

'Got it.'

27

David didn't return home until ten P.M. He felt a moment of apprehension standing in front of his apartment door. Melanie knew where he lived. Would she come here on her own, give him a second chance?

He unlocked his door and pushed it wide open. Moonlight cascaded over the dingy mess that passed for his private refuge, illuminating his old green couch and the dusty collection of trophies he never could bring himself to throw away.

No Melanie. Damn.

By eight P.M. the police had traced two ATM withdrawals to her checking account. Her bank reported her coming in late in the afternoon and withdrawing an even larger sum of cash. At this point she had a few thousand dollars on her. She could get pretty far on a few thousand dollars. David wished he knew where.

He limped into the kitchen and grabbed a bag of frozen peas. His back was a mess.

His career wasn't doing so great these days either.

The press was all over the shooting of William Sheffield. Reporters were already calling the Bureau's press relations agent, stating they knew two FBI agents had been present at the scene and they wanted to know the Bureau's involvement in the case. So far Lairmore had issued the generic 'We are merely assisting local law enforcement in any way they see fit,' a party line nobody was buying.

It would be only a matter of time before someone found out about the investigation into Drs William Sheffield and Harper Stokes. Then someone would place Larry Digger at the Stokes residence, connect the dots with his recent murder, and the story would gain real momentum. While the Bureau remained looking bad. Agents leaving a trail of unsolved homicides. The Feebies – always a day late and dollar short. The potential for Bureau bashing was unlimited.

The Bureau had already had enough bad press in the nineties, Lairmore had informed Riggs and Chenney curtly after five o'clock. They'd better perform some damage control quick, or they would become the first agents in the history of the Bureau reduced to serving as meter maids.

David paced his living room. He jerked off his tie, shed his jacket. To hell with Lairmore, David couldn't stand not being able to put this case to bed.

Twenty-five years earlier Harper cut a deal with Russell Lee Holmes. Something happened to Meagan Stokes, and Harper wanted Russell Lee to take the fall. Harper gets a million dollars. Russell Lee's daughter gets a good home. Everyone lives happily ever after until one day Harper needs money again.

This time he comes up with scheme number two, slicing open healthy patients for profit. No harm, no foul, he must have thought. Piece of cake after disguising a murder.

But he didn't cover up all his tracks this time, and someone was after him now. Maybe he/she wanted vengeance for Meagan or maybe he/she wanted Melanie back or maybe he/she was simply sick to death of Harper Stokes. David sure as hell was. Killing one daughter. Adopting another and leading her on for twenty years, only to hand her over to the police on a silver platter. The man had to have ice water instead of blood in his veins.

The phone rang. David quickly snatched it up.

'Melanie?'

There was a pause. 'David?'

Not Melanie, but his father. David was disappointed, and he sounded it. 'Dad? Is everything all right? It's late.'

'Sorry. Didn't mean . . . Just couldn't get hold of you during the conventional times, you know. Did you get my messages? I've been wondering.'

His father sounded humbled and hurt. David grimaced.

'I'm fine,' he said. 'Just . . . busy.'

'Work going well?' Bobby's voice picked up. 'I got some new ideas for your gun.'

'My gun's fine, Dad. Uh, I'm doing some work with Detective Jax. He told me to give you his regards.'

'Oh, Jax. I like him. Good man. Pretty good shot, but you're better. Coming out to the range anytime soon?' Bobby asked eagerly. 'I could meet you there.'

'I don't know. I got a pretty rough case now.'

'More of that doctor stuff?'

'Yeah.'

The call drifted to silence. David shifted restlessly, cold water trickling down his back. He should say something more. *Hey, Dad, how are the Red Sox doing? No, don't tell me. It'll just break both of our hearts.*

'So,' Bobby said presently. 'Your brother is doing better. Sent his lead pitcher to the bench like I recommended. Brought up the rookie. Good kid, lots of potential. Got ten strikeouts his second game.'

'That's good.'

'I painted the house. Gray, dark blue trim. Not that different.'

'You should've told me, I would've helped.'

'No need, I have plenty of time. Business is kind of slow right now.'

Another edgy silence.

'How's your back?' Bobby blurted out.

'Fine,' David lied.

'Taking those pills the doctor talked about?'

'Nope, no need.' Lied even more.

'David,' Bobby said. 'I'm your father. Can't you at least tell me what's going on?'

David hung his head, then stared at the big trophy in the back, the state championship, won on the day his father had hugged him so hard, he'd thought his ribs would break. He hurt. He hurt too much and it had nothing to do with solidifying vertebrae and spasming muscles. He'd failed his dad. That was the bottom line. He could get over many things, but he couldn't get over that.

He said weakly, 'I'm uh . . . I'm just busy, Dad. A lot of work right now. I really should be going.'

'I see. Fraud?'

'Fraud. Homicide. I'm not doing so good at staying ahead of these guys.'

'You'll catch up.' His father sounded confident.

David squeezed his eyes shut and said tightly, 'You don't know that. Christ, Dad, it's not like I traded in a brilliant pitching career for a brilliant law enforcement career. I'm in *healthcare fraud.* I read reports, not change the world. As a matter of fact, because of me some young woman had to shoot a man to save her life today. Now she's on the run, frightened and scared and God knows what, and *it's all my fault!*'

'You'll help her,' his father said.

'*Dammit!* Listen to me, Dad, just listen. I don't save lives, okay, or the world. I save dollars and cents. That's it. I spend most of the year reading hundreds of pounds of subpoenaed documents. I don't need a souped-up Beretta with radioactive sights. *I need Wite-Out!* Wite-Out!'

The phone line fell silent. David realized what he'd just said, how much he'd said. Oh, Christ. He tried to backpedal furiously, though he knew it was too late.

'I'm sorry. I'm just working too hard. I'm not getting enough sleep—'

'I don't understand your job,' his father said somberly. 'I try, David, I do. But I'm not book-smart like you. I didn't go to college. I'm good with my hands and I'm good with guns and I'm good with a baseball. When you were doing that too, I could understand. Then you got a degree, I mean a real degree instead of going to college for ball, like we thought you would. You got into the academy. God almighty, I can't imagine ever being chosen for something like that. Now you analyze things, you take on doctors and hospitals and insurance companies, and those people aren't stupid.

'No, David, I don't get your job. I'm just good with my hands and I'm good at fixing up your gun. Because you won't play ball with me anymore, David. Customizing your Beretta is pretty much all I have left. So that's what I do. I can't advise you, I can't coach you. Half the time I can't even speak to you. So I fix your gun. Maybe that seems silly to you, but I'd rather be silly than completely shut out.'

'Dad . . .' David didn't know what to say. He should reassure his father. Play nice. Get off the phone before he made anything worse. And then, strangely, he found himself whispering, 'Dad, I failed a woman today. I mean more than professionally. She trusted me. She needed me. And I shut her out. I lied to her and told myself it was all right because of my job. I did something I know you'd never do. I don't know what I was thinking.'

His father was silent for a moment. He said quietly, 'You're a good man, David. You know you made a mistake and now you'll fix it.'

'I'm not even sure where she is.'

'Then figure it out. You're the smartest man I know, David, and I mean that. When the doc told me your condition was hereditary, caused by genetics, I had a bad thought. Made me feel guilty for days, but I think it's still the truth.'

'What?'

'I thought that if one of us was meant to get it, marked for it, then I was glad it was you. You may have had the better arm, but, son, you also just had *more*. Where would Steven be without baseball? What would I do? You, on the other hand, you took after your mother. You got her brains. And now you're an FBI agent. An honest-to-God federal agent. Haven't you ever figured out how envious your brother and I are of you?'

David couldn't swallow. He said, 'I guess not.'

'You did well, son. You did well.'

David couldn't reply. His throat had closed up on him.

'Ummm,' his dad said. 'It's getting kind of late. I know you have a lot of work to do.'

'Yeah, yeah. I'll, uh, talk to you soon. Maybe bring in my Beretta. You can play with the sights.'

'Okay. I'll even bring some Wite-Out.'

David laughed a little hoarsely. 'Thanks.'

'Good night, David.'

'Good night.'

He hung up. He sat for a while longer in the dining room, feeling a little wrung out. A little . . . reassured.

It had been a long time since he'd really *connected* with his dad. He was thirty-six years old. He kept telling himself his father's approval shouldn't mean much anymore, but that was a load of bunk. A parent's approval always mattered, regardless of age—

He stopped the thought cold. Comprehension washed over him.

Melanie Stokes on the run. Melanie Stokes feeling betrayed, as if her whole life had been a lie. Melanie Stokes wanting to know once and for all who she was.

He knew exactly where she'd gone.

He picked up the phone and roused Chenney out of bed.

28

Ann Margaret didn't go to sleep. She sat in the shadowed darkness of her little bungalow, still wearing her nurses' whites. She knew he wouldn't arrive right away, but later, when he thought no one was paying attention.

The back door finally opened. He walked quietly into the living room, hardly making a sound.

'I guess you heard,' he said at last.

She stared at Jamie from across the room. She realized there was nothing he could say that would make it right. She'd been foolish to wait up for him, but they had been through so much, first as friends, recently as lovers. She'd thought of him as her second chance at happiness. She'd thought she'd finally gotten it right. This time love would be kind.

She'd forgotten that she always fell for the wrong kind of man.

'I'm sorry, my love,' Jamie finally said softly. 'I am . . . so sorry.' He took a step forward.

'Don't.'

'Annie, please, listen to me.'

'The agents told me Melanie shot him. Why would that happen, Jamie? What could've gone wrong?'

'I don't know, Annie. You can't believe for a minute I wanted this to happen. It's a real shame. I'll do whatever it takes to make it right.'

'The omnipotent Jamie O'Donnell.' Her lips twisted. She finally rose, surprised to find that her legs would support her. 'If I said anything now, after all these years, you would kill me, wouldn't you, Jamie?'

'Don't say that, love. Don't talk like that.'

'It's true though, isn't it? You like to think you're better than Harper, but you're not, Jamie. You both piss on the people you love. Men should spend less time with guns and more time in childbirth.'

She brushed by him, her steps forceful. He tried to catch her shoulder, and she slapped him so hard the room rang with the blow. The muscle on his jaw twitched. They both knew it was in his nature to always fight back, even when in the wrong. But he checked himself now. He fisted his hands at his sides and weathered the blow for her. She supposed that meant he really did love her . . . and Patricia Stokes.

'I'm sorry, Annie,' he said again.

'Go to hell.'

'Even if you hate me, sweetheart, you struck a deal and I'll expect you to keep up your end.'

'Sold my soul to the devil.'

'Twenty-five years, Annie,' he said softly. 'Very fine life. Better than you could've done on your own, and you know it. I kept my word. I told you that very first day that Jamie O'Donnell always keeps his word, and I meant it.'

Her eyes suddenly filled with tears. The sight struck him more forcefully than her slap. He'd never seen Ann Margaret cry. Not once. He'd first respected her steel core, then grown to love that about her.

'Don't,' he said hoarsely. 'Annie . . .'

'I loved you,' she whispered. 'I thought it would make things better, but it only makes them worse.'

'It doesn't have to change.'

'But it does. You've always known, haven't you, that it would come to this?'

For his answer, he tried once more to take her hands. She pulled away.

'I don't want to see you or any of the Stokeses ever again,' she declared. 'I made a mistake back then. I paid for it, but I won't keep paying for it.'

'You can't mean that—'

'And if anything happens to Melanie,' she continued, 'I will hunt you down, Jamie O'Donnell. I will kill you with my bare hands. Don't think I didn't learn anything from the company I've been keeping, and don't underestimate me. When men are cruel, it's capricious. When women are cruel, it's serious.'

She twisted away from him and stalked down the hall.

Jamie watched her go, feeling that tightness again in his chest. In the back of his mind a little voice whispered he was having a heart attack. The rest of him knew better. His heart was breaking. He'd felt exactly this way the night Patricia walked out of his arms and told him she was going with Harper forever, going to give the bastard one last try. Jamie might be her passion, but Harper, sniveling Harper, was her kind.

It didn't change Jamie. It didn't and for that he was sorry.

Now Jamie O'Donnell whispered, 'Don't do anything stupid, Annie my love. Please don't make me kill you.'

Patricia stood in front of the liquor cabinet. She opened the door and took out the nearly full bottle of gin. Her hands moved slowly, as if weighed down by fifty-pound barbells.

She was alone. Her husband was off doing whatever it was he did at odd hours of the night, and she didn't care. She didn't care about anything anymore, and if she had been able to summon any emotion for her husband, it would have been a cold-hearted rage that would have forced her to hurt him once and for all.

She stared at the bottle of gin.

Don't do it. You don't have to make the same mistakes again. You don't have to fail again.

But maybe I do. Did we ever fix any of the problems in this family, or did we all just run away? Both my husband and my son still carry so much rage . . . and my daughter, my precious adopted daughter forced to shoot a man while still carrying the imprint of her father's hand upon her face.

The phone rang. She picked it up, uncapping the gin and saying, 'What?'

'Mom,' her son replied evenly.

'Brian?'

'Are you drinking yet? I figured that's what you would do.'

'Oh, Brian.' She started crying. 'I want my baby back. What have they done to Melanie, how could I have lost Melanie?'

'I want to hate you,' Brian said hoarsely. 'Why can't I hate you?'

'I'm sorry, I'm sorry, I'm sorry for everything.' She set down the bottle and cried harder.

'I'm standing here tonight, figuring this ought to push you over the top,' Brian announced. 'And I keep thinking, I shouldn't care. It's not my problem. I can't take care of you. I can't fix things for you and Dad, and I surely never figured out how to make either of you happy. But then I think of Melanie and how disappointed she'd be in me if I did nothing. Dammit . . . do you love her?' he asked abruptly. 'Tell me, do you at least honestly love her?'

'Completely.'

'So do I,' Brian whispered, then blurted out, 'What did we do wrong this time, Mom? How could we fail twice?'

And then he started to cry too. They cried together, in the dark, because they had been the ones who had wanted Melanie. More than Harper, they had been the ones determined to make a fresh start. And in loving Melanie and failing her, mother and son finally found common ground.

After a moment Brian pulled himself together. He told her about Larry Digger's arrival and accusations. About the altar in Melanie's room. Then Larry Digger's subsequent murder and Melanie's growing belief that she really was Russell Lee Holmes's child and that the Stokeses had somehow made a deal.

'That's ridiculous,' Patricia stammered. She reached once more for the gin.

'Is it?' her son asked. 'Come on, Mom, I know you and Dad were fighting all the time back then and both of you hate to fight. For God's sake, what could make Dad angry enough to yell?'

Her heart thundered too hard. It was unfair, she thought, that a mother would have to expose herself like this to her son.

'It was Meagan, wasn't it?' he filled in calmly. 'You were fighting about Meagan.'

'Yes.'

'And Jamie.'

Patricia closed her eyes. She couldn't say the rest.

Her son expelled a breath sharply. 'Jesus Christ, she was Jamie's daughter, wasn't she? That's why she was so happy, so pretty. I knew this family couldn't produce anyone so happy! I knew it!'

'Brian—'

'He killed her, dammit! Don't you get it yet, Mom? Not Russell Lee Holmes. The police have *proof* he could not have killed Meagan. It was Dad! He murdered her for the million-dollar life insurance. And because he knew she wasn't even his own kid. Oh, God, he destroyed our family because he needed money. And we let him, Mom. We never suspected a thing.'

'You don't know,' she said desperately. 'We don't know—'

'*I saw the fucking ransom money, Mom!* That day Jamie brought it over, but Dad didn't take that briefcase—'

'No!'

'*Yes!* I found the real briefcase under your bed. I saw Jamie's money. Dad pocketed it as well, because he knew he didn't really have to pay the ransom. *Because he knew Meagan was already dead.*'

'No, no, no! Don't say these things. You are his son, how can you say these things? He's always loved you—'

'He kicked me out of the family—'

'And he's been trying to reach you for days to let you back in. We're going to Europe. We're going to Europe as one big happy family!' Her voice had risen to fever pitch. She heard herself speak like a raving lunatic, and her bravado collapsed.

They were not one big happy family. Her own husband had kicked her son out of the family and had tried to turn her daughter over to the police. He had not paid Meagan's ransom. He had known Meagan was really Jamie O'Donnell's daughter. Oh, God, she had been living with the man who killed her own daughter and, worse, *she had loved him.* She had been grateful he brought her flowers, grateful for each crumb of attention, grateful that someday he would retire and truly be all hers.

Even now she was thinking, poor Harper, you're so desperately afraid of being commonplace, of never rising above your parents. You don't even realize how talented or loved you are.

Especially by Meagan.

Oh, Lord, she was going to be ill.

'I won't protect him anymore, Mom,' her son said quietly. 'I can't believe what he's done to us.'

'He's your father—'

'Mom, you're an alcoholic, and your own husband keeps bringing home booze. Doesn't that tell you something? I'm going after Melanie. I already failed one sister, and I won't fail another.'

Brian hung up.

Patricia was left alone in the dark. She twisted off the cap of the gin, her hands shaking. She carried the pint into the kitchen, held it upside down in the huge stainless-steel sink and listened to the gin pour down the drain.

You get what you deserve. You get what you deserve.

No! That is not true! I did not get what I deserved. I deserved two healthy, happy children. I deserved to watch my four-year-old daughter grow to adulthood. My only crime was being too human, and even that I was trying to fix. I had sent Jamie away, I had vowed to put my family first.

I told Harper that. I told him I loved him.

She found the whiskey and poured it down the sink. Astringent odors burned her nose.

The peach schnapps, the Cointreau, the pear brandy, the blackberry brandy, the Courvoisier, Kahlua, Baileys, Glenfiddich, Chivas Regal. Now the vodka, six bottles, all down the drain. She followed with vanilla extract, almond extract, and cough syrup, working her way through the kitchen, the downstairs lavette, the upstairs bathrooms. She cleansed the house of alcohol, ferreted out each and every conceivable source, dumped it out and kept purging.

He murdered her for the million-dollar life insurance. And because he knew she wasn't even his own kid.

Melanie, you were right. I should've let it all fall apart. We would have been better as a family if we'd fallen apart.

She returned to the kitchen with another bottle of cough syrup, dumped it out. It wasn't enough. She needed to do more, purge more. What else?

Her gaze fell on the refrigerator. Seconds later she ripped open the huge doors and plumbed the chilled depths. She tossed salads into the garbage disposal and ground them up. She followed with whole apples. She opened bottles of mayonnaise and ketchup and mustard and dumped it all in. Bread, beer, wine, cheese, eggs, yogurt, grapefruit.

Now she was in a frenzy, her hair whipping around her, her movements desperate.

Melanie, sweet Melanie, who deserved so much more. I will save this daughter! I will fight! For once in my life I will stand up for my children!

I am not just a drunk!

Harper walked through the kitchen door just as she stuffed half a turkey down the drain. He drew up short, staring at her with shocked, bewildered eyes.

'Are you fucking nuts?' he cried.

She snapped on the disposal and listened to it whir as it ground the bird to smithereens.

'Pat, what the hell are you doing?'

She finally turned toward her husband, her eyes falling on his bandaged right hand. He didn't seem to notice it, though, as he stared, flabbergasted.

And then he lifted his left hand toward her slightly, his expression softening into concern. Lord, he was handsome when he looked at her like that. She thought of all the years between them, the mistakes he made, the mistakes she made, her overwhelming certainty that it could all be forgiven, that they could move beyond and be happy. They both deserved at least that much.

Oh, Harper, where did we go wrong? How could we have hurt each other so much? How could you have harmed Meagan? She called you Daddy. She learned Jamie's name, but she called *you* Daddy.

She said, 'I'm leaving you.'

'Pat, sweetheart, what is going on? You've obviously worked yourself into a state.' He glanced at the floor, the empty bottles of booze. 'Please tell me you didn't . . . You've been doing so well . . .'

'I am doing well. But then, what do you care? You're the one who brings home the booze.'

'Pat! What's gotten into you? We're going to Europe.'

'Running away, that's what it was, except I was too stupid to see it. You got a note too, didn't you, Hap? That you get what you deserve.'

He stiffened, his handsome features shuttering in answer. She finally found her strength, bringing up her chin.

'No, we don't get what we deserve in the end, Harper. Because I deserved a helluva lot more than to lose my little girl. And you . . . if you really did harm her, you deserve to rot in hell!'

She charged forward, piloted by anger and desperation. She had to get out of the room. She had to get away from him before he turned those eyes on her once more and she broke.

Just as she shoved by him in the doorway, he grabbed her arm.

'Pat, let me explain . . .'

'You can't explain hurting our little girl. She thought of you as her daddy. I don't care what genetics said. You were her dad!'

'I didn't harm Meagan!'

'Bullshit. Brian said—'

Harper grabbed her other shoulder, wincing because of his bandaged hand, then shook her. 'Dammit, look at me,' he demanded. 'Look at me! I have been your husband for thirty-five years, and I swear to you, I did not hurt Meagan!'

'The million dollars—'

'She was four years old, Pat. Jesus Christ, what kind of man do you think I am?' He sounded so hurt.

She shook her head. 'I don't know anymore! You kicked out our son.

You told the police our daughter may have shot William because he dumped her—'

'I can explain it all. Oh Pat . . .' His voice gentled, he moved closer, pinning her with those eyes, those deep blue eyes. He whispered, 'You just have to give me some time. Oh God, everything is falling apart. More than you know. Don't leave me now, Pat. I need you. Don't you understand? I *need* you.'

Patricia hesitated and looked at Harper. She saw turmoil and pain in his eyes, fear and shame. She thought, this is why they had ended up together, because she knew the same emotions filled her own gaze. They were both so self-centered. Whatever had made them believe they were capable of being good parents?

'Good-bye Harper,' she said simply, and yanked out of his grasp to head upstairs.

'Everything is in my name,' he cried out behind her. 'Walk out that door and I'll cancel your gold cards, your bank cards, everything. Within ten minutes I'll have reduced you to nothing!'

She said, 'I don't care,' and five minutes later, armed with only one suitcase, she sailed out the front door.

The night wind greeted her warmly, filled with the scent of tulips. Across the street the gas lamps glowed softly in the Public Garden as taxis whizzed by.

'That is it,' Harper yelled from their bedroom window. 'Don't even try to crawl back, Pat. We are through! Do you hear me? We are through!'

On the empty sidewalk Patricia opened her arms and embraced the balmy breeze.

'I am free,' she whispered to the city. 'Melanie love, I am free!'

In the upstairs bedroom Harper slammed the window shut. He tried to take a step, and the room spun so dizzily he fell down hard on the edge of the bed. For a minute he just sat, shell-shocked, listening to the ringing filling his ears.

She'd left him. Patty had left him. Jesus, Patty had left him.

The pieces he'd been juggling for so long were falling down around him, he thought wildly. The notes in his car. The pile of organs in William's house. Jamie O'Donnell's present, the change in both his wife and daughter. William's wild accusations, Jamie's reports that the FBI was closing in on the fraud rapidly.

He'd gone too far; he'd never get out of this one. And then he thought, he had to get out of this one. He must protect his family.

He'd never meant for it all to come to this. In the beginning he'd viewed Pat as simply the perfect companion. Gorgeous, graceful, confident. A great hostess for a rising doctor, a suitable mother for his children. He'd pursued her almost clinically, armed with books on the subject and, of course, Jamie O'Donnell's advice.

And then the slow-budding wonder that such a creature truly could love him. That she believed in him more than he did. That she could look beyond his humble roots and view the man he desperately wanted to be.

Somewhere along the way he'd fallen hopelessly in love with his own wife, and it had all disintegrated from there. The mutual hurt, the mutual betrayals. The confusion on his part because he could see that he was failing her without understanding what it was he needed to do.

Then, finally, anger, when he discovered her affair with Jamie O'Donnell, anger that had turned his love to dust and made him want to smack her beautiful, lying face. He'd thought it would be better after that. He would never be vulnerable to her again. Business partners, that was the way to run a marriage.

Then they'd come to Boston. Struggled with their son's growing mood swings. Worked diligently on their adopted daughter. And he'd spotted sometimes the way his wife watched him, the quiet yearning in her face, the acceptance.

Somehow over the years the anger had also turned to dust and he'd rediscovered the love. Softer this time. Gentler.

He had wanted to give his wife the world. His son too; Brian would grow up with everything he hadn't! And maybe Melanie would as well. Because even if she wasn't his, even if he knew exactly where she came from, she had looked up to him, and he wasn't immune to that. There were weeks on end when even he was convinced they were the perfect family.

But the money ran out so quickly. Retirement looming around the corner with nothing saved, and what was he supposed to tell his former-beauty-queen wife? That at the age of sixty she might want to start thinking about getting a job?

He'd come up with a plan. No one would get hurt. A little extra money, and it helped out William too. Everything was fine. No harm, no foul. Just a little bit longer . . .

You get what you deserve!

Christ, he didn't know what to do. And the house of cards was caving in fast . . .

Earlier tonight the pretty redhead at the Armani bar, sitting in the same chair she'd occupied for the last week. Himself, going there for comfort, losing himself in the living, pulsing rush of money.

Buying the redhead a drink. Then another, then another.

They'd gone to the Four Seasons. Beneath that shimmering black top she wore something frothy and made of pure lace. He remembered struggling with the clasp. The room growing blurry, faraway . . . And then . . .

Waking up in his car in a seedy section of Boston. Doors locked, keys in the ignition, a song playing on his tape deck. The Rolling Stones, 'Sympathy for the Devil.'

The blood dewing the white bandage on his right hand. The tingling in his fingertips. Lifting the bandage slowly, gazing at what lay beneath in gauze, the pounding of his own heart.

'I didn't hurt Meagan!' Harper groaned in the room. 'Why doesn't anyone believe me? I never hurt *anyone!*'

The man in the darkened room moved quickly now, throwing everything into bags. He hadn't gotten to deliver everything he'd wanted, but the big gift had gone down today and that was good enough.

Time to move on.

William Sheffield was dead. Melanie Stokes had pulled the trigger. That was unexpected but filled him with pride. That's my girl!

No time to dwell now, though, little time to contemplate.

Things were happening fast.

He zipped up the last bag and walked out of the room. He already had his ticket for Houston. He knew for a fact that so did Brian Stokes and he guessed that very soon Patricia and Harper Stokes would have tickets as well.

The trap was set and baited. Everything would end where it began.

For you, Meagan. For you.

29

Melanie discovered that for a rich girl, she was pretty good at running away. First after withdrawing as much cash as possible from her accounts, she dumped out all her plastic but one in an alley. In a city like Boston, some thief ought to be kind enough to recover the cards, use them, and lead the police on a merry goose chase. At least one could dream.

Next, she purchased a baseball cap – thought of David, his arthritis, his baseball pictures, forced herself to dispel such thoughts – and stuffed her hair beneath it. Sunglasses, oversized T-shirt, and cheap canvas backpack transformed her into a young college student prone to furtive glances.

She proceeded to the downtown Boston Amtrak station, which brimmed and bustled with hundreds of people. Boston's South Station led her to New York's Penn Station. A taxi took her to Kennedy Airport, and there she ran into her first obstacle. Getting into an airplane required a valid ID, and she was hardly running around with a fake one. She had to use her real name after all and hope no one would think to check the New York airlines. From Kennedy she flew to Houston.

At Hobby Airport, she followed the signs to the information desk.

The man stationed there was very helpful. He got a map for her and drew out her route to Huntsville, approximately ninety minutes away. Real hard to miss, ma'am, he assured her. Stay on I-45 all the way to I-10, and follow the signs. Finding a place to stay shouldn't be a problem, ma'am. This is Houston. Everything is done to a Texas scale, with strip malls and motels and family restaurants every fifty feet. Why, it's not uncommon to witness three to four funeral processions a day, ma'am. There's that many people living here, and that many people dying. You take care of yourself, y'hear?

Melanie proceeded to the car rental booth. Renting a car required a valid driver's license and a credit card. She was on borrowed time, she thought grimly as she signed the forms.

She got out onto the interstate and drove as night began to fade to black and the world took on a vast, alien scale.

Strip malls loomed, car dealerships, and Motel 6's for as far as the eye could see. Houston sprang up on her right, tall, imposing buildings bursting out of flat land like moon craters in the falling light. The traffic halted for one funeral procession, then, twenty miles later, she stopped for a second.

It was like driving on a giant treadmill, she thought, feeling the first bubbles of hysteria. Pass a hotel, see it again five miles later. Pass a car dealership. Oh, here it is again. Everything so gray, so concrete. By the time she came to I-10 and spotted yet another Motel 6, she figured she was due to get off the road.

She paid for her room with cash. Another friendly man was behind the counter. He told her where a pharmacy was and a grocery store and a hardware store, and was doing so well she went ahead and asked him about a gun shop. He didn't blink an eye but nodded approvingly. A young lady traveling alone needed protection. Particularly this close to Huntsville. Did she know that this town, the headquarters for the Texas Department of Corrections, housed over seventy-two hundred inmates?

She hadn't known. She jotted down everything he said, and rather than going straight to her room, she headed out for the stores.

She bought fruit. It made her feel almost normal. Then she bought scissors and makeup and hair dye, and in another frenzy of activity she went into a local discount store and bought bags and bags of clothes, cheap, trashy.

She dragged them back to her room. The hour was much too late for purchasing a handgun. She locked each of the three locks on her door and finally looked at herself in the mirror.

Pale, pale face. Fine white-blond hair. Deep purple smudges framing cornflower-blue eyes.

She suddenly hated everything about herself. She looked like Melanie but she was not Melanie. She was Daddy's Girl. Abandoned, nameless. No identity, no past, no parentage.

You looked like Meagan, all right? her mother cried. I looked at you and saw Meagan! Killer's brat, killer's brat, Larry Digger hissed. Tell me, do you look at children and feel *hungry?*

She picked up the scissors and started whacking. Her hair rained down around her, and she kept ravaging. If she shed enough hair, maybe she wouldn't be Melanie Stokes anymore. If she massacred enough strands, maybe she wouldn't see William's blood on her hands or Larry Digger's body on dark blue carpet. If she cut off enough hair, maybe Daddy's Girl would show her true face and she'd finally feel some recognition.

All I ever wanted was for my family to love me as much as I loved them.

Not since she was nine years old and waking up in a white emergency room had she felt so alone.

At six A.M. Melanie got up. She ate half a cantaloupe for breakfast and a cheap cheese-filled Danish that came out of a plastic wrap. She washed it down with bitter motel coffee, black. Then she showered again and donned a new outfit. After she plastered on some makeup she was ready.

Huntsville didn't just house Texas's extensive prison system, it also housed the Huntsville Prison Museum. The museum opened at nine and Melanie planned on being the first person through the doors. If any place could tell her about Russell Lee Holmes, surely the museum would be it.

She stopped by the visitors' bureau, picked up slick, brightly colored maps, and continued straight into town. Huntsville looked surprisingly pleasant for the city that had hosted more executions than any other in the United States. Old West storefronts, clean sidewalks, wide streets. An impressive stone courthouse set atop an emerald sea of grass and the all important old-fashioned ice cream parlor.

In a town so square and quaint, it took her all of three minutes to locate the prison museum. She pulled her car into a space that still had the bar for hitching a horse. She walked up a gently sloping sidewalk on a bright warm day that promised heavy humidity and booming thunderstorms. A small family of tourists was in front of her, merrily snapping photos.

The small museum was sandwiched between a jewelry store and western shop. It wasn't much to look at. Dark walls, drop ceiling, faded brown carpet. The room mostly boasted a large model of the Huntsville prison system and many freestanding exhibits of the individual units that comprised the Texas Department of Corrections.

Melanie followed walls covered with portraits of the corrections officials who'd built the prisons. She learned of the famous prison rodeo. She got to stare at Old Sparky, appropriately on display in a fake execution chamber, the wood still rich and gleaming, the broad leather straps and metal electrodes fully functional. Next to the chair, the museum had posted the last meal requests of many men. Three hundred and sixty-two men served.

Melanie found what she was looking for in the small room marked PRISONERS' HALL OF FAME. It featured pictures of such notorious felons as Bonnie and Clyde and, of course, Russell Lee Holmes. Unfortunately the neatly typed placard next to Russell Lee's picture said very little: Convicted of murdering six children. The first prisoner to be executed by Old Sparky when the moratorium on the death penalty finally ended, and, due to his hands and feet blowing off, the last.

'Do you have any more information on specific prisoners?' Melanie asked.

'We get books and tapes donated all the time. Some of them are more specific.'

'Where would I find them?'

'Stacked against the wall, honey. Help yourself and take as long as you need. Huntsville prison has some of the most exciting history in the United States, and we're here to share it.'

Melanie sorted through the pile of old, faded novels.

Hour dissolved into hour. The curator left and a young man took over, reading *Gray's Anatomy* at the front desk until midafternoon. Then, when it became obvious Melanie wasn't going to budge, he offered to lock her into the museum while he ran across the street to grab a sandwich. Vaguely Melanie was aware of the ding as the door opened again, then the tall, ropy medical student was asking her if she wanted pastrami. She didn't.

She was reading about the deaths of men, the many, many deaths, and the intricate process that culminated in capital punishment. The book was written by the journalist who'd had the death beat in Huntsville, Larry Digger.

Melanie kept reading. Another person entered. She heard the bell and then she simply knew. In fact, she realized now, she'd been waiting for this. She'd known that of all people, he would deduce where she'd gone. After all, he was the person she'd told the most to. He was the person she'd trusted.

Melanie didn't look up. She waited until she felt the warm, hard body of David Riggs standing behind her.

'Melanie,' he began softly.

She pointed to the black and white photo in the middle of Larry Digger's book. She said, 'Meet Daddy.'

30

'Okay, Melanie, start talking.' David planted his feet in the middle of Melanie's motel room, looking harsh. He'd been up most of the night and traveling since six that morning. He wasn't in the mood for excuses and he was pissed – no, he felt guilty, scared and sick to his stomach with the worry that something might have happened to Melanie. He wasn't used to worry. He resented it. Then he looked at her face, bruised from William's fists, and he returned to feeling pissed.

Melanie wasn't helping matters. Apparently she'd decided to try out a new look – a black denim skirt that used less material than a headband, a white cotton T-shirt that was at least two sizes too small, and blue eye shadow that appeared to have been applied with a trowel.

He was afraid he knew what she was trying to prove, and it made him feel worse.

Now she arched a brow at his growling tone and shrugged. 'Sorry, Agent, but I'm pleading the Fifth.'

'Melanie—'

'What do you think? Does this outfit work for me? Very Texan, you know. Younger too. I think Russell Lee would be proud.'

'Enough, Mel. You're taking this too far.'

'On the contrary, I don't think I'm taking this far enough.'

'You are not some piece of trash! You are not this . . . this *chick*.'

'Oh, then, who am I, David? Just who am I?' She stormed away. He grabbed her arm.

'You've been dreaming again,' he stated bluntly. 'The nightmares, right?'

'Maybe I have, maybe I haven't. Maybe it's simply that I've never been to Texas before and yet everything in this damn state looks familiar.'

'Melanie, you're falling apart.'

'Yeah, well, what do you care?' She jerked her arm free and skewered him with a withering glance. 'Why are you here, David? Suffering a change of heart? Well, let me do you a favor – too late.'

'Dammit, you're wanted for questioning regarding the death of William Sheffield.'

'Are you arresting me?'

'I'm questioning you!'

'Then let me get out the thumbscrews.'

'What will it take to set things right? You want sorry? I'm sorry. You want remorse. Hey, I can do remorse. But figure it out, because I am trying to help you, and you need help! Your father has already gone on record as saying that William dumped you, that you haven't been yourself lately, and that you pulled the trigger out of spite. You shot a man and your own father has hung you out to dry. This is *serious*.'

She flinched. Her overly made up face finally stilled, but not before David caught the bleakness in her eyes. She turned away and sat down on the edge of the bed, the black miniskirt hitching up to the tops of her thighs.

'Well,' she said finally with forced nonchalance. 'Easy come, easy go.'

'Bullshit. I don't believe Harper. Neither does your mom or your brother. You have allies, Melanie. You do.'

'So you found Brian?'

'Yeah. He's sorry he missed your call.'

'Is he?' She spoke wistfully, then caught herself and fisted her hands on her lap. 'What about my mother? How is she doing?'

'She's shaken but managing. And your brother did clear her. We don't believe she or Brian harmed Meagan.'

'Which just leaves dear old Dad. You know the men in my life . . .'

'He doesn't have an alibi,' David said. 'He may have engineered Meagan's death so he could collect the million-dollar life insurance. He definitely needed the money.'

'If he did it, he didn't do it alone. He would never approach a man like Russell Lee Holmes. Jamie had to have helped him.'

'I'm getting the impression that Harper and Jamie come as a package.'

Melanie smiled thinly. Then her shoulders slumped and he could practically hear her unspoken thoughts. Two of the men who meant the most in her life plotting the kidnapping and death of a little girl. Who did the planning? Who did the murder? How much could a four-year-old child plead? How much had she screamed – or had she never seen it coming?

'William said my family was an illusion,' Melanie murmured after a minute. 'My straitlaced father has been operating on healthy people for profit, my mother is a lush, and my brother is gay. And I'm their patsy, he said. Their audience of one because I always believe whatever they show me. I'm not loved, I'm just stupid.'

'William's an ass.'

Melanie remained unconvinced. 'You knew about the surgeries, didn't you, David? You were in my house not because you were investigating William, but because you were investigating my father. White collar crime. The "case" you would never discuss with Detective Jax or Agent Quincy. And I never put it together. I was stupid for you too.'

'It wasn't that cold—'

'Of course it was! For God's sake, don't continue to treat me like an idiot. For once in my goddamn miserable life, I want to hear the *whole truth*. Why is it so hard for anyone to tell me the truth?'

David fisted his hands. His own temper was sparking, and now he found himself saying more crisply than he intended, 'Fine. You want the truth? Here you go. We have reason to believe William and Harper were selecting healthy patients and injecting them with beta blockers to make them appear to need pacemakers. It garnered your father up to forty grand a month, and your father loves money. Hell, he probably murdered his own kid for a million, so what's a simple surgical procedure for eight thousand a pop? Can we prove it? No. We have no proof. We'd hoped to catch William red-handed in the hospital and squeeze it from him. But then you shot him, so . . .' He shrugged.

Melanie bolted off the bed, stalking toward him, her eyes narrowed dangerously.

'You mean I made your life messy, Agent? Added some complications, screwed your plan? Welcome to the club, David. Welcome to the goddamn club!'

She jabbed a finger in his chest. He winced. But then he saw the tears gathering in her eyes. He stared at her bruised cheek, her swollen lip, her shaking hands, and everything in him gave way.

'I'm sorry,' he found himself saying hoarsely. 'I'm sorry, Mel, I'm sorry.'

He took her in his arms despite her protests. She kicked at him.

'I hate you, I hate you, I hate you!'

He held her closer. 'I know. Shh, I know.'

She started to sob, the grief and anger racking her frame. David pressed her against his chest. She smeared blue eye shadow and black mascara all over his white shirt. He held her tighter, but it wasn't enough. He had hurt her. He had not been the man his father had raised him to be, and this time around he couldn't blame it on his medical condition. He'd played it safe when Melanie had deserved more.

When he had wanted to give her more.

Suddenly her head angled up. Her hands dug into the back of his head as she dragged him down. There was nothing passive about the kiss. Melanie was upset and angry. She turned on him violently, seeking an outlet for her rage. He went along with it. Hell, he found himself responding to it, and then they were tearing at each other's clothes like savages.

He ripped her T-shirt off and pushed her onto the bed. Her hands grabbed his belt, cracking leather as she ripped it from the pant loops. He just managed to get the back of her skirt unzipped before she'd hooked her thumb inside the waistband of his briefs and pushed them down around his ankles.

Then she was slithering out of her skirt and sprawling on the bed in her simple cotton underwear. The sight of it grounded him, brought him back to reason.

'Easy,' he whispered. 'Easy.'

He feathered back her hair, stroked her cheek, trying to get her writhing body to relax.

'I'm sorry,' he whispered again. 'I'm sorry.' He ran his fingers down the delicate curve of her jaw to the vulnerable hollow at the base of her throat. Her pulse pounded against his thumb. He kissed her collarbone, felt her shiver a little. His lips came lower, his cheek brushing the high, firm swell of her breast. He waited a heartbeat. She moaned softly, almost a sigh. He drew in her nipple deeply and sucked hard.

She shivered. Then she tightened her legs around his waist and he went tumbling off the cliff of reason.

He kissed her breast, her waist, her navel. His hand slipped between her thighs, stroking her folds, feeling her dampen for him. She was so passionate, so responsive, and it had been a long time for him. He was torn between taking her right that instant and making the moment last.

He managed to pull away long enough to root around the floor for his wallet. He always traveled with a condom, the eternal optimist.

When he rose back up, foil package triumphantly in hand, he had a clear view of her, her slender body sprawled on the dark blue comforter, breasts high and pink-tipped, skin all cream and rose. Makeup was smeared across her face, but he could see her beneath it, her lips parted, her eyes heavy-lidded with passion.

'Look at me,' he demanded hoarsely. 'This isn't just some fling, Mel. Once this is over, I'm not ever going away.'

He smoothed on the condom, his gaze still on her face, and entered her in one fierce thrust.

She cried out.

'Melanie. Sweet Melanie.'

Her gaze darkened. 'No,' she muttered, then gasped as he began to rock. 'Not Melanie. Not anyone.'

'You're wrong. You're Melanie, sweet, loving Melanie. *My Melanie.*'

He thrust harder. Her teeth sank into her lower lip. He could feel her body tense. Then he got to see the small moment of wonder as her climax broke and brought fresh sheen to her face. She was lovely.

'David . . .'

The traffic roared and rushed beyond the curtains. He closed his ears to the sound and followed her over the brink.

Minutes later he rolled off her. Not wanting to completely break contact, he spooned her body against his. Her head rested on his arm, her gaze focused on the far wall. He was struck once more by her tiny size, the delicate shape of her arm, the long, graceful line of her back. She hardly made a dent against his own darker, larger form. He thought of her having had to take on William Sheffield, and he wished the man were still alive just so he could kill him.

Now Melanie was retreating, mentally withdrawing. He wondered if she was remembering William too. Maybe the way he'd cheated on her, or maybe the look in his face right before he struck her. Or maybe she was thinking of Harper, of the man she'd grown up calling Dad whom she knew now as, at the very least, a cold-blooded felon, if not a child murderer. Then there was Russell Lee Holmes, the genetic dad, who'd also killed little girls as a hobby.

'I'm not going back to Boston,' she said abruptly. 'I can't yet. There are answers here. I have to know what they are.'

His fingers stilled just above her elbow, his hand settling on her arm, cupping it lightly. 'If you agree to stay in my custody,' he said after a minute, 'I may be able to buy us both some time. We can work on this together, see what we find.'

'We made love.'

'Yes.'

'You're an agent. I thought they had rules about such things.'

'There are rules. I've crossed the line.'

'What will they do?'

'I don't know. I might get written up. I might lose my job. It's possible.'

She rolled over, looking at him with a fierceness that hit him hard. 'Regrets, then? Tell me, I want to know.'

He said honestly, 'No regrets, Mel. For you, not ever.'

She whispered: 'I'm ripped up, David. There aren't enough pieces left to make a whole. I'm so frightened of what I'm going to find. I'm angry and I'm scared and I . . . I can't believe what William did. I can't believe Harper hates me this much. I can't believe I loved them all and I didn't know them at all. I feel so completely, utterly *empty*, and I don't even care.'

'It's going to get better, Melanie. It will.'

'I don't even know myself anymore. Why I do the things I do or say the things I say? I want to buy a gun. I used to hate guns. What is happening to me?'

'It's going to work out, Mel,' he tried again. 'I'm going to help you.'

'David, I don't believe you.'

He had to nod. The words hurt, but she had the right. He drew her back into his arms. At least she didn't protest.

After a moment he said against the top of her head, 'Why don't you rest now, Melanie. You've been the strong one through this. Now it's my turn.'

She seemed to nod against his chest and they drifted off to silence together, then sleep. When David awoke, Melanie was untangling herself from his arms and crawling out of bed.

'I need to shower,' she said. 'I have an appointment.'

'With whom?'

She gave him a small smile and strode toward the bathroom. 'Russell Lee Holmes.'

31

When they piled into David's car, a thunderstorm was rolling across the sky. Clouds teemed and broiled, blacking out the sun and settling an eerie heaviness over the city. They drove in silence for fifteen minutes, watching the horizon crackle with lightning while the air conditioner blasted their cheeks.

David pulled over at the Captain Joe Byrd Cemetery. 'The sky looks like it's going to go.'

'It's only water.' She got out of the car and headed straight into the graveyard.

The cemetery didn't have a fence. Some flowers had been planted at the perimeter, now leaning over and panting from the heat. The rest of the cemetery was filled with rows of white crosses marching steadily backward. They rolled back as far as she could see, the last dozen rows so wind-scarred, the dates and prisoner numbers had completely eroded. Those were surrounded by hard-packed ground and thick, old grass. Then there were the front rows, the fresh new graves with the black earth still mounded from recent filling.

The sky cracked, the first fat raindrop splashing on Melanie's nose as an owl hooted and lightning danced across the sky.

'We'd better hurry,' David called above the growing wind, his dark suit glued to his lanky frame. 'The storm's almost overhead.'

'We have to look for the prisoner number,' she called back to him, and rattled off the information.

Lightning cracked again, so close they felt its charge zip through the air. The wind was whipping up now. The owl hooted again, agitated and uncomfortable. Then thunder boomed. More lightning. Melanie could feel the static electricity raising the hair on her arms, rippling up her spine, accelerating her heart. She began to feel panic. The rain hit her face. She was breathing too hard. She could feel the thunder still echoing in her belly, and suddenly she felt like a little girl lost in a sea of white death, trying to find her father.

David was suddenly at her side. He took one look at her face and ordered her head down by her knees. He grabbed her hands and gripped them tight. 'You're having an anxiety attack. Calm down.'

The sky abruptly gave up. It burst like a giant water balloon and deluged them in a sheet of rain.

David led her over to the grave he'd found. She stood beside him in front of the white cross. Prisoner number and date. That was it.

Melanie thought she should feel something. She *wanted* to feel something. This was her father's grave, her real father. Please let it mean something to her, give her some sense of closure.

She felt hollow. The marker meant nothing to her. Neither did the dead man who'd once been her father. These were abstract concepts that couldn't begin to compete with the real, vibrant, warm memories of Harper, Patricia, and Brian Stokes. David had been right, she did have a family and she missed them and she loved them. No going forward, it seemed, and no going back.

David put his arm around her shoulders. He led her back to the car through the stinging sheets of rain and held open the door for her. Then he removed his jacket, and tucked it around Melanie's shivering shoulders. Then he fastened her seat belt.

When he pulled back to close the door, his gaze was liquid gold. Understanding, she thought. Simple understanding.

'He is not what you're about, Melanie,' he said. 'You can spend your time in prison museums and graveyards if you want, but you are not the legacy of Russell Lee Holmes.'

He shut the door, and she watched him cross rapidly in front of the car to the driver's side.

He knew her, she realized, even when she had stopped knowing herself. He did have enough faith for both of them.

And then she thought, I want to go home.

She turned away so David wouldn't see her tears.

Later David helped her shower and crawl into bed, tucking the covers around her shoulders. She was too exhausted to fight him, falling almost immediately to sleep with her head buried against the feather pillow.

David got out the phone and prepared to do more work.

Their clothes were strewn all over the room, damp puddles reminding him of the choices he'd made. His suit mingled with her T-shirt, his loafers rolling over her sandals.

His FBI shield next to her makeup on the blue Formica counter.

Chenney picked up the other end of the phone line just as Melanie began to mutter in her sleep. David turned his back to her for more privacy and searched for a neutral tone of voice.

'Hey, rookie. What's the status?'

Silence over the line. Then a long, hard sigh. That told David enough.

'Lairmore didn't buy it, did he?' he said.

'I think he's gonna write you up,' Chenney confirmed. 'It's going in your files. Jesus, Riggs, you're not exactly the most popular guy around here at the moment.'

'I went after a suspect in a murder case. I wouldn't think that would be such a breach in protocol.'

'Oh, yeah, Riggs. You flew across the country without backup, discussion with your supervisor, or any solid leads. And the Bureau has such a reputation for loving cowboys. Did you sleep through the academy, or what?'

David managed a ghost of a smile. For so long he'd been convinced he hated his job. Now that he was tossing it away, however . . .

'Things blow over,' he said at last. 'Just give me an update.'

'You need to come back, Riggs, I'm serious.'

'I have a lead. I've traced Melanie Stokes to the William P. Hobby airport and a rental car agency. It's not a goose chase, Chenney. I'll leave Lairmore a report.'

'Then let me come out there and help you.'

'You don't want to come here.'

Another small silence as comprehension dawned. 'Shit. Riggs—'

'Just give me the update, Chenney.'

Chenney exhaled in fury. David waited.

'Fine. Here's where we're at, but if Lairmore drills you too hard—'

'You had nothing to do with it. Trust me, Chenney, I know.'

Chenney didn't sound mollified. Maybe he liked Riggs after all, maybe they had formed some version of partnership. Stranger things had happened.

'Well, we got some answers and some questions. Which do you want first?'

'Go in order. Where are we with the Sheffield homicide?'

'Well, I'd think you'd know more than me—'

'Chenney.'

'Yeah, fine. Okay. Jax is heading up the case, and let me tell you, he's riding Harper with a vengeance. Jax ordered fingerprinting powder over every damn square inch of the study, and every time Harper makes a condescending remark, Jax simply has more floorboards ripped up and sent to the lab. Yesterday he even tore down the curtains. Soon Harper's gonna be living in a crime lab.'

'And this is teaching us . . .'

'How to have a good time. No, we don't have many leads other than Melanie Stokes. Lairmore has us attacking it from the healthcare side. I was over at the hospital yesterday conducting the interviews on Sheffield. Interestingly enough, another anesthesiologist, Dr Whaler Jones seems to know an awful lot about Sheffield. I get the impression she was a little jealous of all the surgeries Sheffield got to pick up. She can put Sheffield at the hospital at all sorts of times he had no good reason to be there, that's for sure.'

'Still circumstantial.'

'Yeah, that's the problem we have. Too many circumstances. Lairmore is toying around with having all pacemaker patients receive a second evaluation, but from what we've heard, that won't fly. The attorney general tells us we could be sued by Harper for ruining his reputation. To be on the safe side, we got all the serial numbers of the pacemakers Harper has installed in the past five years. Quite a list, let me tell you. The FDA ran a cross-check. They've received only one complaint on the batch, which is actually well under the industry average. So we can't even go after the pacemakers that way. Everything appears perfectly legit.

'At this point, we'd have to bring in patients, remove the pacemakers, and then hook the patients to a heart monitor to see if they're truly bradycardic. Let's just say both the legal and medical experts agree that's not a great idea. On the other hand, the pacemakers naturally expire in five years and will have to be removed, so if we're willing to be patient . . .' Chenney shrugged, declaring bluntly, 'We got nothing, Riggs. At this point Harper's coming away clean.'

'What about the outline of the papers next to William's body?'

'That's the thing. There's gotta be documentation somewhere. We've ripped apart Sheffield's apartment, but no such luck. Bank shows Sheffield deposited some rather large checks from Harper, but Harper claims the money was a gift to his one-time future son-in-law, and who are we to argue? We couldn't find any propranolol in William's place, no notes, and no friends who have an inkling what he was into.'

'Jamie O'Donnell might know something.'

'Well, that brings us to the second point. Jamie O'Donnell seems to have skipped town. Checked out of the Four Seasons yesterday afternoon and nothing's been heard from him since.'

'Hmmm.' David tucked that information away. Of all the people to come after Melanie, Jamie O'Donnell would be it.

'Patricia Stokes has also bolted,' Chenney said.

'Huh?'

'Yep. I was over at the Stokes house earlier this afternoon. Harper's playing cool about it, but the maid told us Patricia packed a bag last night and walked out the front door. Boston homicide talked to the people at the Four Seasons, but they claim they haven't seen her around. Most likely she finally got sick of Harper's shit. I mean, trying to turn in your own daughter . . .'

'Not endearing,' David agreed.

'Oh, I almost forgot. Harper has on a bandage today. His whole hand is wrapped up. Seems he injured it somehow, but he won't talk about it. Jax even asked him point-blank what he'd done and Harper told him point-blank to go fuck himself. You know, I don't think Harper has that fresh feeling anymore.'

'Think if Jax pushes him hard enough, he might crack?'

'I don't think it's Jax,' Chenney said. 'I think our mystery manipulator is pulling out the stops. It's what she wants, right? All those little gifts reopening old wounds. Melanie's on the run, Brian's removed from the family, Patricia finally left her husband, and O'Donnell has gotten the hell out of Dodge. Harper's alone and feeling the strain. Ten to one, the man is frightened. I don't put anything past him at this point. I'm trying to run down information on Ann Margaret, by the way. Nothing immediate comes up on the computer though, and I haven't had time to do anything more in-depth. Kind of need more hands at this point.'

'Don't we all. What about the Texas angle? I'm here, so let's use me.'

'Actually, you may be helpful, Riggs. I think I may have a break in Texas.'

'That's my boy.'

'Okay, Jax and I went through the public pay phone records yesterday. *Nada.* I mean zip. But Jax – give him some credit here, Riggs – didn't subpoena just the Boston records, he got Larry Digger's Houston phone records as well.'

'Son of a bitch. He never told me that.'

'Of course not, we're the feds, remember?'

'Oh, yeah.'

'Well, you were the one who said Digger reported the anonymous call three weeks ago. Sure enough. Twenty-five days ago, Digger's phone records suddenly exploded with calls. I got them from Jax. Then to entertain myself this morning, I cross-referenced the names of the people Digger called with the midwives association's list of Texan members. And guess what I found . . .'

Chenney rattled off the name, David quickly wrote it down. 'I'll look her up first thing in the morning. If she remembers Russell Lee Holmes, she must remember his wife, so maybe I can tie in Ann Margaret from this side.'

'Yeah,' Chenney said, but he sounded troubled now. 'Riggs . . . I got more news.'

'That's what they pay you for.'

'I . . . uh . . . I kinda started exhumation proceedings for Russell Lee Holmes.'

'Jesus, Chenney.'

'My off-the-wall theories aren't so off the wall anymore, Riggs. I even got Lairmore scared. Remember the shrine in Melanie's room? The blue scrap of fabric with the two types of blood?'

'Of course. Come on, Chenney, spit it out.'

'Okay. They've positively ID'd one blood sample as belonging to Melanie Stokes. It's an absolute match. A lot of blood work was done when she was first found twenty years ago, so they had plenty to go on. Which brings us to the second blood sample . . . They did a DNA test, Riggs. There is a fifty percent match between the second DNA and Melanie's DNA, what you'd see between parent and child.'

'Oh, shit.' David closed his eyes. He already knew what Chenney was going to say next.

'I think we finally found the missing player in our game, Riggs. We've just sent away for Russell Lee Holmes's medical files and blood samples to confirm, but we can already tell you that the second bloodstain is an XY chromosome. We're talking Melanie Stokes's genetic dad. And, Riggs, the lab swears that bloodstain is less than one week old.'

32

Harper Stokes stood alone in the middle of his study. He had turned on the lights earlier, but the illumination had only frustrated him, revealing the glowing powder, the torn curtains, the ripped-up floorboards. For the past twenty-four hours Boston homicide had swarmed his home, investigating every carefully decorated nook, manhandling every lovingly acquired antique.

It seemed there was no place he could go anymore without being watched by a uniformed officer. No refuge left in the respectable life he'd spent his whole life building.

Jamie was gone. Patricia was gone. He wondered if she was finally happy with Jamie O'Donnell, and that thought left him gutted.

No Brian. He'd called his son's practice. They said Brian had been out for days. He didn't believe it. He'd swallowed his pride, begged for his own son's emergency number, knowing it would probably belong to some man. It had.

Nate had been polite. Brian was gone. He didn't know where. He did consider him missing.

Harper had hung up the phone feeling suddenly old and, for the first time, lonely.

Empty house. Crime-scene tape. A bandage on his hand. Once again smug Jamie O'Donnell was right. It had all come full circle.

He couldn't just stay here and mourn forever. He was a man of action. It was time to get something done. For his family. For himself.

He went up to the bedroom. From a locked safe in the walk-in closet he pulled out a gun. The bandage on his right hand made it too hard to grip, so he unwound the gauze. The fresh tattoo blazed up at him: 666.

He muttered, 'But I am not the devil. I didn't harm Meagan, dammit, and I'm not even close to Russell Lee Holmes.'

At least, not yet.

Thirty-six hours after abandoning her husband, the euphoria had left Patricia Stokes.

She'd tried to use her credit card; it had been canceled. She had tried to

512

use her ATM card; it had been declined. She was fifty-eight years old, carrying a suitcase of designer clothes, and she was penniless. A wave of fear had hit her, and she simply wanted to run to the safest place she knew – the arms of her husband.

She'd spent the previous night with friends. It had gotten her through the first few hours. With daybreak, however, had come the realization that she needed a purpose. For once in her life she needed to take control.

She'd tried the Four Seasons. Jamie O'Donnell was gone. She'd tried her son's apartment. She found her son's lover packing up her son's things and telling her that Brian had left town. He had no idea where her son had gone.

Patricia knew only one other person to try.

Now she stood with her suitcase in front of the home of Ann Margaret Dawson. She knew Ann Margaret only as her daughter's boss. Now Patricia swallowed her pride and knocked.

After a moment the door cracked open. Ann Margaret peered out cautiously, as if she were expecting something unpleasant. Then her eyes widened in surprise.

'Patricia,' she said, and opened the door all the way.

'I left Harper,' Patricia blurted out.

'Are you looking for Jamie?'

'No,' Patricia said in bewilderment. 'I'm looking for you!'

Ann Margaret closed her eyes. There was something sad about her expression. 'Do you love him?'

'Who?'

'Jamie.'

'Of course not. That was years ago. I just want my daughter back!'

Ann Margaret said quietly, almost gently, 'Patricia, I believe it's time we talked.'

Brian Stokes hunkered down lower in his seat at the airport waiting lounge. The first flight to Houston wasn't until morning, so he might as well catch some sleep. He was anxious though, already worried that he was too late.

He'd done wrong by Meagan. There was no escaping the hard, cold facts he thought. His troubled mother had had an affair with his godfather. She'd given birth to Jamie's child and Harper had found out. Harper had engineered the death of Meagan probably out of rage but also out of greed. His dad had killed his sister for a million bucks.

And Brian had never said a word.

Well, he'd been a child back then. Now, he was an adult, and he vowed to do more for Melanie.

He fidgeted in his seat, trying to stretch out his spine, then stiffened.

He could have sworn he caught a glimpse of someone familiar, but when he looked again, no one was there.

Melanie was not sleeping well. She was in the cabin. In the cabin in the middle of the woods, watching the spider ease across the window. And Meagan was behind her. Meagan was rocking back and forth, clutching her pony.

'Please let me go, let me go, let me go.'

You have no idea what he can do.

Then a shadow fell across the wood floor. A man filled the doorway and he took a step into the room. Cold wind swept through the cabin. Meagan shrank back and Melanie already knew that all was lost. He was back and it would only get worse.

'No,' Meagan whimpered.

No! Melanie cried out.

'It's okay,' David Riggs murmured in her ear, and cradled her close. 'I've got you now, Melanie. I've got you.'

She whispered, 'Too late.'

33

When Melanie woke up next, she was alone in the bed. The room was shadowed, the thick curtains tightly drawn against a blazing Texas sun. In the background came the rhythmic hum of cars racing over a concrete interstate. Closer was the rattle of a metal cart wheeling across the balcony as a cleaning woman performed her rounds.

Melanie blinked a few times. Her head was fuzzy, the impression of lingering dreams still hovering around her like a shadow she couldn't dispel. A dull throbbing had burrowed in behind her left eye. Not a full-blown migraine yet, but she should probably take some aspirin.

She finally turned her head and searched for signs of David.

Clothes were strewn across the floor. She spotted his slacks and his suit jacket, carelessly tossed by the chair.

Then Melanie heard a new sound, low, half muffled. A moan of pain.

Melanie rushed to the bathroom. She wasn't prepared for what she found.

David Riggs was writhing on his stomach on the cold tile floor.

'Oh, my God, it's your back.'

She went down on her hands and knees beside him, but David didn't reply. His face was bone white and contorted into a horrible expression as he beat the floor with the heel of his hand.

'Do you need ice? What about medication? Surely you're on something for this.'

For answer, his legs kicked out and another guttural moan escaped his lips. She leaned closer, and when she looked into his eyes she saw something worse than pain – she saw impotent rage.

'Go . . . away,' he gasped.

Melanie compromised. She threw on clothes and went running for ice. When she returned, he was still on his stomach, but he was crawling now. In many ways it was an even more horrible sight.

So this was arthritis. This was strong, capable David Riggs's world.

Melanie discovered tears on her cheeks. She put the ice in his dress shirt with shaking fingers and fashioned a clumsy ice pack.

'I'm going to put this on your back,' she told David.

David muttered something that might or might not have been a curse. Melanie plopped the makeshift ice pack on his naked lower back. Immediately his body arched, the muscles in his neck cording, and his lips curled back to bare his teeth.

'I'm sorry,' Melanie whispered. 'I don't know what else . . .'

'Leave . . . it,' David snarled. 'Time.' His head sagged between his shoulder blades, his body still convulsing.

Melanie sat beside him and waited. Eventually his limbs stopped twitching. His face relaxed more, still red and flushed. He finally got to curl his legs up, assuming the fetal position.

'How is it?' she ventured.

'Fucking . . . awful.'

'Does this happen a lot?'

'Has . . . phases.'

'Surely there's something you're supposed to do. Exercises, medication . . .'

David didn't say anything, but his gaze darted toward his travel bag. Puzzled, Melanie got up and opened it. Inside she found a bottle of orange pills. Naproxen, she read. The date on the bottle was almost a year ago, but it looked completely full.

'David, I don't understand.'

'It's arthritis,' he muttered, looking cornered. 'My spine is fusing. Sometimes I wake up at night with the muscles locked around my ribs so tightly, I can't breathe. On my really good days, maybe I can skip to work. But then I get days like this to bring me back to earth. What's a fucking pill gonna do about all that!'

Melanie touched his cheek. 'You're afraid, aren't you? You're afraid that if you take this first pill that you'll finally be giving in. You'll finally be admitting that you have a chronic disease and you will have it for the rest of your life.'

'*No, goddammit!* I'm afraid I'll take that damn pill and *it won't get any better*. That *nothing will change* and what will I look forward to then, Melanie? What will I have to hope for then?'

'Oh, David,' she whispered. 'Oh, sweetheart, you have arthritis, not cancer.'

The haunted look on his lined face undid her. He broke and she took him into her arms, cradling his head on her lap, rocking him against her.

'They put her through chemo so many times,' he muttered hoarsely. 'So many times and they never did any good, and we cleaned and it never did any good. Nothing ever did any good.'

'I understand, I understand.'

'I wanted to make my father so proud. I wanted to make him so damn proud.'

'He is, David, he is.'

'Goddammit, Melanie, I loved baseball. And there's nothing I can do. I'll never be everything I wanted to be. Never.'

'Oh, David,' she said quietly, 'none of us ever are.'

Eventually the worst passed. She remained curled up on the floor with him, still stroking his hair, neck, shoulders. And then she became aware of the smooth feeling of his skin, the distinct delineation of lean muscle and sinew right beneath her touch. His head came up. She saw his fierce blue eyes, and then she was on her back and they made love again, fiercely and with unexplained need.

Afterward they lay without speaking, intertwining their fingers over and over again, and listening to each other's heartbeats. It told them enough.

'I have a name and an address for the midwife,' David said finally, hours later.

'All right,' Melanie said.

They both got up and dressed.

The address led them to a nice neighborhood, much nicer than what Melanie expected of a woman who had once assisted Russell Lee Holmes. The modest ranch house was nestled in one of the new suburbs bursting up all around Houston, where every fourth house looked exactly the same, just painted slightly different. The yards were lush, well manicured. A few young saplings thrust toward the sun, their meager year's worth of growth marking the age of the houses around them.

A few kids on dirt bikes looked at them curiously as David pulled over. He returned their stares with a level gaze of his own and they quickly sped up. There was just something about FBI agents, Melanie thought. You could spot one twenty feet away.

David opened the car door for her. Melanie had to take a deep breath, then she walked ahead of him to the doorway.

The woman who answered on the second knock was not what Melanie expected. In comfortable beige slacks and worn white shirt, she had dirt stains on her knees and a gardening trowel in her hand. Her silver-white hair was all but hidden beneath her straw hat, making her an easy match for someone's favorite grandmother, down to the warm blue eyes and scent of fresh baking hanging in the air.

'May I help you folks?' the woman asked politely, going so far as to smile at strangers. She had an easy smile. Melanie found herself returning it.

'Mrs Applebee?' David inquired somberly.

'Yes, sir,' Mrs Applebee agreed amiably. 'Though I should tell you now, I'm a happy retired woman right down to the fixed income. No encyclopedia sets or nouveau religions for me. At my age, all I need is a pack of sunflower seeds and a few more grandkids – but but don't tell my daughter I said that.'

David grinned, then caught himself and struggled for professionalism. Melanie could tell Mrs Applebee had also taken him by surprise.

'I understand that, ma'am,' he assured her. 'Trust me. Actually, I'm Special Agent David Riggs with the FBI, and I'm here about a man you spoke to three weeks ago – Larry Digger.'

Rhonda Applebee stilled, the friendly smile replaced by wariness. She looked at Melanie curiously, then she looked back at David, who was now holding up his credentials. She said finally, 'I see. Well, then, I suppose you should come on in. I'll get us some iced tea.'

Mrs Applebee led them both through a modest, tastefully decorated house to a back patio that was surprisingly lush. Huge palm trees and brightly flowering bushes enclosed a kidney-shaped yard. The dirt was turned over in one shady corner, where Mrs Applebee had obviously been at work planting before they had arrived. She gestured to a glass patio table, where they took seats, and she adjusted the yellow and blue umbrella for better shade.

They murmured polite comments about the yard. She thanked them graciously and returned to the house for a pitcher of iced tea and a large plate of cookies.

'Oatmeal cookies?' she inquired. 'Made them fresh this morning.'

David looked at Melanie. She wordlessly agreed. This woman was so perfectly lovely, and now they were going to pick her brain about Russell Lee Holmes.

'You were a midwife?' David began finally.

Mrs Applebee gave him a brisk nod. 'Yes, I was a midwife. Retired ten years. And, yes, thirty years ago part of my practice was serving poor neighborhoods, where folks couldn't afford a doctor, medication, or hospital. Those were the days when we still put people first regardless of income. You know – the days before the HMOs.'

'Larry Digger tracked you down?' David pressed.

'Yes, but I'll tell you honestly, I didn't care much for him or his questions. The sins of the fathers, my fanny. Each child has its own right to live and let live. I really didn't want to be a part of tracking down some poor soul just because of what its father did.'

'What exactly did you tell Larry Digger?'

'Well, he had a picture, of course, of Russell Lee Holmes. And, yes, I recognized the man. Back then it didn't mean much. I made the rounds, and as much as I hate to say it, one poor, mean skedaddling father was pretty much the same as another. None of them stuck around for the birth of their child, I can tell you that much. They'd show up, give you a once-over, and then go off drinking with their buddies while their wives or girlfriends squeeze out their next progeny on dirty sheets. Childbirth is women's work, and they sure as hell don't want to be involved.'

'Where was this?' David had out his notepad now and was preparing to write but Mrs Applebee shook her head.

'That neighborhood doesn't exist anymore. It wasn't much more than a shantytown when it did, and the city bulldozed it years ago in favor of middle-income housing. Progress, you know.'

David set down his pad. 'Mrs Applebee, I understand your concern about not wanting to inflict the sins of the fathers upon a child. Frankly I think I know who Russell Lee Holmes's child is, and it doesn't bother me a bit. We need confirmation, however, and we need to know exactly what Larry Digger told you. Last week, you see, he was shot dead.'

Mrs Applebee's frank blue gaze ran David up and down. Then she gave Melanie the same appraisal. Finally she seemed to make up her mind.

'All right, Agent. What is it you need to know?'

'Let's start with Russell Lee Holmes. Did you spend much time with him?'

'No, not really. I said hi, how is she? He shrugged, told me I'd know better than him, and to call him when it was over. Then he was out the front door and I worked with his wife – at least he called her his wife, though I didn't see any wedding bands.'

'What was she like?' Melanie spoke up urgently. Rhonda Applebee looked at her curiously, and Melanie fumbled. 'His wife, I mean. The mother.'

'Oh, she made more of an impression on me than he did. A real tough one, that girl. She was already nearly fully dilated and effaced when I showed up, but she didn't so much as shed a tear. Just twisted those sheets tighter in her hands and held on for dear life. She struck me as smart – she asked good questions. She also looked me in the eye, which requires some self-respect. She mentioned that she'd been using a diaphragm and that people like her had no business having children.' Mrs Applebee murmured wryly, 'Smart *and* a realist. But I guess her husband found out about the birth control and put an end to it. She wasn't happy, but I suppose she figured the damage was already done.'

'Did . . . did she seem to want the child? Did she seem to care about her baby at all?' Melanie asked.

Mrs Applebee's face softened. 'When that baby finally came bursting out, you could tell she was tired and you could tell she was already worried about its future and hers, but, boy, the smile that lit her face, the glow that filled her eyes . . .'

'What happened next?' David said.

'When I was just cleaning up, Russell Lee finally came home. He was a bit wobbly on his feet – probably had a few congratulatory beers from his friends. Of course the first thing he did was wake up his wife and child.

'She showed him the child. He looked it over, nodded a bit, seemed satisfied. He even stroked his woman's cheek, which was about as nice a gesture I got to see in those parts. He seemed honestly proud of his kid, poofing out his chest, strutting around the house like he'd gotten a new car and done it all himself.

'Finally he asked me what he owed. I told him what he could afford. He gave me ten bucks, inspected the piles of diapers and formulas, and grunted. I told him to call me if they needed anything more, and that's the last I saw of the couple.

'Years later I pick up the paper and lo and behold, there's the same man, now identified as a baby killer. I really didn't know what to think.'

'Did you contact the police?'

'What for? I helped deliver his child, that was all. Besides, I may not be a doctor, but even a midwife values confidentiality.'

'But that wasn't the end of it, was it?' David asked shrewdly.

Mrs Applebee finally hesitated. 'No, it wasn't. Just weeks after the first article appears in the paper, some man shows up on my doorstep with a thick mane of red hair and an Irish brogue. Tells me to forget everything I ever knew about Russell Lee Holmes, his wife and child, and tries to offer me money. Well, I never. I do my job and I do it well and I'll tell you the same thing I told him – I keep my own to my own for my own and he and his dollars could take a flying leap.'

'And what did he say?' David asked.

'Why, he laughed. Very charming really, but still, you could tell . . .' For the first time, Mrs Applebee looked troubled. 'There was just something about him,' she said finally. 'In my line of work I've been about everywhere, seen about every kind of folk, some good, some bad, some kind, some cruel. You realize after a bit it's not in the clothes or the way they walk or in the way they live. You can tell a man by the look around his eyes, and that Irishman, he had that look. He was a man who knew things, who'd done things, who was capable of doing many more things . . .'

She shook her head, shivering a bit even after all the years. 'Let's just say I got the message. Whether I took the money or not, it was best that I forget everything I ever knew about Russell Lee Holmes.' Her gaze lowered, and she added more softly, 'And for a time I suppose I did.'

David was looking at Melanie. She nodded miserably, understanding his silent message. Larry Digger had been telling them the truth. Jamie O'Donnell had indeed visited the midwife. Her godfather had paid this woman a visit and had threatened to harm her if she ever told anyone about Russell Lee Holmes.

'Larry Digger implied you wanted money,' Melanie murmured finally. 'Do you?'

Mrs Applebee appeared affronted. 'Look around you, child. Why would I need money. My Howard provided for me just fine!'

'Why are you telling the story now?' David pressed more diplomatically. 'Last you knew, your life had been threatened.'

'Ah, well.' She shrugged. 'I was scared, Agent, I can admit that. But I was forty years old then and may be a bit more aware of my own mortality and my children. I'm seventy now, and my children are grown. What do I care about some Irishman? And what do I care about Russell Lee Holmes? That's all water under the bridge these days. Even you must realize that the world does not rise and fall based on the actions of one man, not even the actions of one bad man.'

'Other than that visit twenty-five years ago, and Larry Digger's visit, has anyone else asked you about Russell Lee Holmes?'

'No.'

'Have you ever seen the mother again?'

'No.'

'Do you have a name for her?'

'Angela Johnson, the name she used thirty years ago. Mr Digger told me it was an alias.'

'Can you describe her?'

'Oh, I don't know, I saw the poor thing when she was giving birth. Not a great time for a woman. She was . . . a little over five feet, I suppose. A short, tough build, like a pistol. Blue eyes. Dark hair, naturally curly. She was in her late twenties, so I suppose she's nearly sixty now.'

David was looking at Melanie. 'Does that sound like anyone you know?'

'No—'

'Ann Margaret,' he whispered.

Her eyes went wide. 'No!' But in fact, he had a point, and while Melanie was still trying to absorb that shock, David turned to Mrs Applebee and asked an even more absurd question.

'By any chance have you seen Russell Lee Holmes lately?'

'What?' asked Mrs Applebee.

'He's dead!' exclaimed Melanie.

David said, 'I'm sorry, Mel, I couldn't think of a way of saying this, but we received new information on the scrap of fabric found in your room. It contained two types of blood. The first is yours, and according to the DNA test the second sample most likely belongs to your father.'

Melanie felt the pounding pick up behind her eyeball. Wooden shack. Little girl. Shadow looming in the doorway.

'Wait a minute,' Mrs Applebee was saying. 'You believe *she* is the child of Russell Lee Holmes?'

'Yes, ma'am.'

'What in the world made you believe that?'

'Larry Digger,' David said with equal bewilderment. 'Why?'

'Because she *can't* be his child, Agent. Russell Lee didn't have a daughter. Russell Lee had a *son.*'

34

It was just after noon when Brian Stokes pulled into the Motel 6 in Huntsville, Texas. He'd been traveling since five in the morning, and after a rough night of fitful sleep in the airport, he felt tired, grimy, and anxious. At least he'd also been lucky. For twenty bucks a pop, he'd found a person at each car rental company willing to look into their records. Once he knew Melanie had a car, he'd thought to stop by the information desk, where her big blue eyes had made quite an impression on the older man who worked there. That had brought him to Huntsville, where the first hotel he encountered was a Motel 6.

He stepped out of his car. The heat and humidity slapped him fiercely, plastering his shirt to his skin. Welcome home, Texas, he thought. Christ, he didn't miss this state.

In the motel lobby he got the blushing receptionist to confess that while she didn't have a guest with Melanie's name, she just happened to have a guest matching her description.

Brian rewarded her with a wink. The twenty-year-old blushed harder and stammered she could take a message. Brian decided against leaving one. He wasn't sure what state of mind his sister was in these days and didn't want to spook her into running more. He'd wait, approach her in person.

He walked back into the parking lot feeling much better about life. He had found Melanie. He would take care of her. Everything would be all right.

Then he turned toward his car and found himself face-to-face with his father.

'What the hell are you doing here?' Harper Stokes demanded first. His white dress shirt was soaked through, his dark tie skewed. If Brian had passed a restless night, his father had suffered a completely sleepless one.

'Looking for Melanie,' Brian said, then frowned. 'What the hell are you doing here?'

'What I should've done twenty-five years ago.'

'What, tell the truth? I know what you did, Dad. I know you didn't pay the ransom. I know you sold out your own daughter for the fucking life insurance. How dare you—'

'I held this family together—'

'You ripped us apart!'

'I did what had to be done!'

'By sacrificing your own child?' Brian screamed. 'By selling out my sister?'

'You hated her! You ruined her toys.'

'*I loved her.* She was *Meagan.* She smiled at all of us, she believed in all of us. Hell, she even believed in you. How could you do that to a four-year-old girl? *How could you do that to me?*'

Harper's face darkened. He said, in a tone Brian had never heard before, 'You ungrateful little shit. You don't know anything, and I refuse to stand here and explain myself to my own son. I raised you. I did everything for you, and this is how you repay me? For the last time, I did not hurt Meagan! I didn't! And now, I've had enough.'

Harper brought up his hand. Brian noticed the white bandage. It looked like such a big wound, and on his father's hand, the place any surgeon felt most vulnerable. Then, much more slowly, the rest of the picture registered. His father was holding a gun. His own father was actually pointing a gun at him.

Brian stared at Harper and felt unbelievably calm.

He realized for the first time that all he'd wanted was his father's love and that's where he'd gone wrong. Harper hadn't been worth it. It was his mother and sister who should have counted. They were the ones who loved him, and now it was too late.

'I won't let you hurt Melanie,' Brian said matter-of-factly. 'I won't lose another sister to you.'

'I know. So trust me, Brian, I'm doing this for your own good.'

Harper Stokes ripped off his bandage. Brian saw the raw, bloody wound. A fresh tattoo: 666.

The final present, Brian thought. Then his father's hand whipped toward him with shocking force.

Brian tried to block the blow. He moved too slowly, and the handle of the gun caught him squarely on the nose. He heard a cracking sound. His own bone breaking.

He thought, Melanie, I'm sorry.

Then the world went black.

'I don't understand,' Melanie was murmuring in the car. 'I don't understand.'

'We just took a wrong turn somewhere. That happens in investigations. We need to backtrack—' David answered.

The fight had left her. She sagged in her seat, turning morosely toward the window.

'Why do I know the shack, David? I keep picturing that damn shack and

Meagan Stokes,' she whispered after a moment. 'Why can I smell gardenias, plain as day? Little girl sitting in the corner. Little girl suddenly getting a chance and bolting for the door. Running away through thick, brambly underbrush. But she won't run fast enough. I know. I know.'

David was quiet for a moment. 'Maybe Larry Digger steered us wrong. He was the one who made the big leap that you were Russell Lee Holmes's daughter. The rest of us merrily followed him into the sea like a pack of lemmings.'

'But I can see—'

'Can you, Melanie? Remember what Quincy said. He had a picture of Russell Lee's shack in front of him and he told you that you were wrong, that you were *not* picturing Russell Lee's hut. At the time we both just ignored that. Maybe we shouldn't have.'

'But then, how come I can picture Meagan and Russell Lee Holmes?'

'There's always the power of suggestion. You never knew where you came from, a whole part of you is blank and probably hungry. Then suddenly a man appears and gives you a morsel of fact. You know what Meagan looks like, Mel, her picture has hung in your house for twenty years. Maybe once you even looked up Russell Lee Holmes. His name wasn't completely new to you.'

'No,' she admitted. 'I remembered having heard it before.'

'So the seeds were sown deep in your subconscious. And when Larry Digger appeared, your impressionable mind took over. Turned his snack into a five-course meal, adding all sorts of details to round it out. But of course you couldn't get it all right.'

Slowly Melanie nodded. Larry Digger had appeared so out of the blue and had made such a big impression . . .

She was rubbing her temple. 'If that's true, David, why did the scent of gardenias work? You were the one who told me that scent would trigger memory. If it was all a fantasy, why would it be triggered by a scent?'

'Let's back up,' he announced curtly. 'What do we know? Someone murdered Meagan Stokes, and it was not Russell Lee Holmes.'

Melanie nodded.

'Your mother and brother didn't do it because they seem to have an alibi and they have been as destroyed by it as anyone.'

'Okay.'

'But your father may have been involved. We know he needed the money. And your godfather probably helped him.'

'To approach Russell Lee.'

'Exactly. So we know Meagan was killed for money, but they botched the "copycat" crime, so to speak. Thus they went to a backup plan, approaching Russell Lee to confess and get them off the hook. Now, Russell Lee did confess to the murder, so he must have been promised something.'

Melanie hesitated. 'The blood on the fabric. Maybe Russell Lee is alive.

Maybe that's what he was promised. He could be the one pulling all the strings, messing with everyone.'

'No,' David said forcefully. 'I don't buy it. The man was executed in front of witnesses. Even if the state coroner had been bribed to pronounce him dead when he was really still alive, his hands and feet blew off. You can't fake that.'

'Unless it wasn't him in the death chamber.'

'And who could they have gotten instead? What kind of moron agrees to be fried in someone else's place? It's just too far-fetched. Besides' – David's voice picked up suddenly – 'the blood on the fabric is *not* Russell Lee's. The DNA test said it was *your* genetic father's. So if you're not Russell Lee Holmes's daughter, then someone else is your father. Who the hell is your father?'

David became very excited. Melanie shook her head. Her head hurt. Dim pictures of a time and place that had been . . . Dizzy. White lights. She closed her eyes futilely and rested her forehead against the car window.

But David was obviously feeling better about things. 'You were right, Mel!' he said excitedly. 'Dammit, you were the one who was right all along.'

'I – I was?'

'Your family honestly loves you. Your family isn't violent. Your family is exactly who you thought they would be. That's why the pieces never fit. We've been trying to solve a murder that never happened. Shit!'

'What?'

David was no longer talking. He glanced over his shoulder, shot the car in reverse, and while she was still jerking forward, he put the pedal to the floor and squealed them onto the freeway.

'It's going to be okay,' he declared.

'My head hurts.'

'I know. Hang in there for me. I have one last place for you to see. And then, if my theory is correct, you'll know exactly who you are, and we'll finally get to the bottom of all this.'

'I *want* to get to the bottom of all this.'

'Of course you do, Melanie. Or should I say *Meagan*.'

35

'I can never think of Texas without feeling like a failure,' Patricia Stokes was murmuring. 'As a wife, a mother, a lover. When Harper told me we could move, I swore I would never come back. I never wanted to see Texas again. I blamed the whole state for breaking my heart.'

'I made a similar vow myself,' Ann Margaret said, 'but more out of necessity, I'm afraid. I always figured Larry Digger would keep pecking away at things, or, if not him, then someone else. When I was a child, I used to think a mistake was simply a mistake. You make it, you pay for it, you move on. Now I think some mistakes are more like a pebble hitting a pond. They start as a small ripple, then get bigger and bigger, an exploding circle of mistakes, until they become a tidal wave and you simply drown.'

Patricia glanced at her. They'd been traveling since dawn, and up talking for most of the hours before then. There were things that had finally been said and many more things each was still struggling to grasp.

'How could you love a man like that?' Patricia had to ask.

Ann Margaret smiled. 'Don't you think that's my line?'

Patricia winced. The more she learned about Harper, the less she had a right to judge others.

'When you're young,' Ann Margaret added gently, 'you love who you were raised to love.'

'Our fathers.'

'Exactly.'

'And when we're old enough to know better—'

'It's too late to do anything about it.'

'I can't believe I didn't know,' Patricia sighed. They finally reached their destination, and Ann Margaret pulled into the grand old Georgian that had been Patricia and Harper's first home. The white pillars still stood tall, but the paint was peeling and looked mildewed on the top. This house had been so beautiful to Patricia as a young bride flushed with the heady rush of newly pledged love. It was dated now, one of those tired homes real estate agents labored to sell.

The house had been on the market for a year, she and Ann Margaret had learned that morning. The rooms were empty, the owners already off to

Florida and retirement. The grass could use mowing, the flower bed needed weeding.

The house wasn't the way Patricia remembered it; its obvious age reminded her too much of her own.

'Oh, God, Annie, I failed my little girl.'

'We all did.'

'But I was her mother!'

'I know, that's why you adopted her again. Haven't you ever realized why you loved Melanie from the moment you saw her? Because a part of you knew, Patricia. Even though your mind had accepted that Meagan was dead, the mother in you knew.'

'What must she have been thinking these last few days? And then that scene with William. My poor baby, having to shoot a man she'd once cared for. How do you get over such a thing, even when you know you're right? It's too much. She shouldn't have had to go through any of that! We should've taken better care of her!'

'She's tougher than you think, Pat. Maybe she has more of her mother in her than you realize.'

'I don't want her to have to be strong. I want her to be safe. I want her back!' Patricia fisted her hands. She wanted to strike something, lash out again in hurt and rage. She could do nothing but calm herself and remain focused for her daughter's sake.

'So tell me,' she said after a minute, when she'd gotten her hands to relax. 'We're here. I know what happened twenty-five years ago. Now what do we do?'

Ann Margaret shrugged. 'If she's seeking her past, sooner or later she'll come here. And if Harper and Jamie are looking for her, sooner or later they'll try here as well. So now we wait.'

David was finally slowing the car. Melanie opened her eyes. She had fallen asleep almost the minute they reached the interstate, her mind hitting a wall and shutting down. Now, her limbs felt sluggish, her body heavy, as if a great weight were pressed against her. She could feel moisture on her face, sweat dampening her upper lip and brow. Her throat was parched.

She fumbled for a can of Coke on the floor by her feet, then took a long sip. The liquid didn't lighten the thick cloak of impending doom that had settled around her.

David quietly asked, 'Does any of this look familiar? Take your time, Melanie. We'll go slow.'

They'd arrived at a crumbling group of houses built into a curving hillside. It might have been well kept once, but it looked neglected now. Tall weeds waved along the cracked asphalt roads. Small groves of trees that might have once been pleasant, shady retreats, were now tangled and overgrown with brambles.

When Melanie rolled down her window, she caught the unmistakable scent of gardenias.

Her mind lurched. She clutched her soda as if for balance.

'I've been here,' she murmured. 'I've been here.'

'This is where your family used to live. Patricia, Harper, Brian, and Meagan Stokes.'

A minute later a tall white house emerged into view.

Big white columns. Grand Georgian style. A huge gnarled cherry tree on the front lawn, perfect for climbing. *Help me up, Daddy. Help me up.* A tall, overgrown hedge, once perfect for hide-and-seek. *You never gonna find me, Brian. I'm smart!* A graceful curving drive once marked up for hopscotch. *Look at me, Mommy, look at me!*

Two women standing next to a red rental sedan in the driveway. Crisp gray hair. Golden, gleaming blond.

Mommy, mommy, I'm going to grow up someday to look just like you.

Melanie turned toward David slowly. His eyes were concerned. And as she watched, he suddenly seemed to spin far away.

She was falling back in time, a tumbling down into a gaping black abyss . . . until she was in a dusty wooden shack and she was four years old.

'I want to go home,' she heard herself murmur. 'Dada Jamie, why can't I go home?'

'It's okay, Melanie. You're here with me, David, and you're safe. You are Meagan Stokes. Your family never hurt you, they never even abandoned you. Your father just faked it for the million dollars. Insurance fraud. Very clever insurance fraud. It's Harper's MO.'

'You don't understand,' she said. 'You don't know . . .'

In the distance, a car engine suddenly gunned and roared. Another car, coming up behind them fast. The two women turned and stared. David glanced in the rearview mirror. Melanie watched them all fatalistically. They didn't know. They couldn't understand. She had tried to run once too. She had learned . . .

'Shit,' David said. He stepped on the gas. Melanie looked at him sadly.

'You shouldn't run,' she declared softly. 'It's only worse if you run.'

'Hang on, Melanie. Dammit, hang on.'

He roared down the hill toward a grove of trees. Melanie heard shouts. The women were running. Everyone was running, even she was running in her mind. She remembered it clearly now. The fourth day, the desperate bid for freedom. Just wanting to see her family again . . .

Not fast enough though. Never fast enough. *Ah, lass, can't you see that when you run away, you only hurt yourself?*

Melanie was snapped back by a savage curse. She glanced at David and saw sweat pop out on his face as he frantically cranked the wheel. A sharp turn had suddenly appeared in the road. And they were going so fast. Much too fast. When you run, you hurt only yourself.

David swearing again. Back tires squealing, trying to break loose. David fighting them, yanking at the steering wheel so hard, the muscles on his arms bulged. David praying, maybe, then, at the last moment, glancing at her apologetically. David whispering her name.

She thought, I love him. And a heartbeat later, I'm so sorry.

The back tires won. The whole car snapped around. So much screaming. Oh, God, that was her voice, screaming.

You hurt only yourself when you run.

The other car hit them hard. Melanie had a brief impression of Harper's shocked face. Then the front of their car snapped over the top of the other and they sailed through the air.

David's hand found hers. She felt the warm, rough texture of his fingers entangling with her own.

Then the ground rushed up fast. The car landing. A new screech of metal. A scream cut short. Black.

36

Jamie O'Donnell's breath was coming out hard as he frantically focused the binoculars on the street overlooking the Stokeses' old home. He felt like he'd been running a marathon since six that morning, but more likely he was too old for this, and now that the moment was at hand, it was too real. His hands were shaking, and he had not felt this afraid in a long, long time.

First he followed Brian to the airport because he was worried about the kid. Then, when he figured he must let Brian forge his own way like a real man, he bought a one-way ticket to Houston for himself.

He'd landed at Houston Intercontinental, a place that always brought back too many memories for him and few of them good. It had occurred to him for the first time that none of them ever came to Texas. They avoided the entire state as if it carried the plague.

That was a shame in some ways. For as many of the memories were bitter, a lot were sweet. Patricia. Texas nights. Watching baby Brian grow. The miraculous birth of Meagan. Christ, the first time she'd gripped his index finger, such a tiny, tight fist. His baby. Jamie O'Donnell's girl!

Finding Melanie in Huntsville had been easy. She was smart and resourceful, he was proud to say, but it was a simple matter to trace her to the motel and set up watch. The arrival of the FBI bloke had made him nervous, but they seemed to have a thing between the two of them. Not bad really. He'd run a check on Special Agent David Riggs in the very beginning, as he'd done with all of his daughter's acquaintances. It was a father's prerogative, he liked to think, to want to know his daughter's associates.

The Riggs man had checked out well. Middle-class roots. Good rep with the Bureau, and Jamie had heard this from an inside source who hated to give praise. Shame about the arthritis, but the boy seemed to move well enough and was certainly above average in the brains department, as he'd figured out Harper Stokes quickly enough. That alone made him A-OK in Jamie's book.

The man's presence, however, had made shadowing Melanie a lot trickier. He doubted Melanie would ever think to check her rearview mirror, but Riggs was a trained professional. Jamie had had to follow them the hard way, staying three car-lengths back, occasionally turning off.

Once they'd reached the neighborhood where Mrs Applebee lived, it had been easier. He merely pulled over at a gas station on the main road and waited.

When their rental car had finally reemerged forty-five minutes later, Jamie had had a clear view of Melanie's face. She'd looked pale, shaken, and anguished.

Mother of God, his heart had lurched in his chest.

It seemed that all the times he tried to protect his daughter, he only brought her pain. And that left him with the horrible, bitter thought that maybe Harper was the better one of them after all. She'd run into his arms naturally enough when he'd adopted her. Called him Dad, went out of her way to make him smile. Seemed happy.

When Jamie had crouched down to see his daughter, his own daughter whom he'd protected at great personal risk for five long years, she recoiled from his embrace.

He still remembered the moment clearly. The way his heart had simply stopped beating in his chest. The taste of dust in his mouth. The way his reaching fingers had curled into a fist.

Harper's smug smile from across the room, enjoying Jamie's pain.

And the sudden realization of just how much he hated the son of a bitch.

From that day forward, Jamie had wanted nothing more than for Melanie to remember. She should know the true nature of self-centered, money-hungry Harper Stokes. She should know the true nature of Jamie and how honestly he had loved her over the years.

But it never happened. Melanie was happy as Melanie. Harper was surprisingly good to her, maybe because he knew it rankled Jamie so much. Or maybe he had cared for Meagan too, more than he would ever admit. Patricia and Brian adored her, falling back into their roles as mother and brother so gratefully, it had made Jamie's chest ache. And Melanie . . . Melanie grew into such a lovely, content young lady, Jamie's rage lost all momentum.

He could want only what was best for her, he discovered. And though his pride demanded action and his shame and hurt feelings rankled, he never made a move to interfere. Loving a child, he learned, was humbling. How the mighty had fallen, and how easily he'd accepted the tumble from grace.

Then, six months ago, Harper foisted William Sheffield onto Melanie. Harper kicking Brian out of the house over such a thing as being gay. And then cold, petty Harper letting Patricia dissolve into drinking again, until Melanie's whole family was once more ripped apart. Pretending to be better than his whole damn family while all the while he was slicing open healthy patients for a buck.

Jamie had had enough. He'd given Harper the world twenty-five years ago. A fresh start with a million bucks, and as soon as the time was right, his own daughter to make Harper's family complete. There was nothing more one man could give another. There was nothing more one man could do to ensure Patricia Stokes's happiness. How dare Harper piss it all away for a buck.

Even in a rage Jamie could be remarkably cold. He'd plotted his strategy, made his plan, set the wheels in motion.

Harper would finally get his due, and Jamie would finally get his triumph.

Except so much had happened along the way. Harper hiring a hit man to take out Larry Digger and his adopted daughter. Jamie had figured it out the minute he saw the police sketch on TV – that was one of his acquaintances, whom he had introduced to Harper in the past, and Jamie sure as hell hadn't hired him to attack Larry Digger, so that meant Harper must have. Jamie had to hunt the fellow down and plug three bullets into his heart simply for principle's sake. You did not mess with his daughter.

As for Harper's due . . . all in good time.

Except Harper surprised him again. Pushing William so hard the boy cracked. Then trying to finger Melanie in the boy's shooting. As if Russell Lee Holmes's son had deserved any better.

Then today, just forty-five minutes earlier, Jamie caught sight of Harper Stokes here in Houston, obviously trying to track down his daughter.

The players were assembled, but the pieces were moving faster than Jamie had expected. And for the first time since he'd started this a month before, he was genuinely afraid.

Nor for himself, but for Melanie.

Now he was parked on the road above the Stokeses' old house with a clear view of the street. He saw Patricia and Ann Margaret arrive. And then he spotted Harper, parked along a side street, waiting.

David and Melanie approaching. Harper pulling out. Harper gunning the gas. And then the cars were racing. Up over one hill, thundering down another.

The squeal of tires. The crash of metal. Jamie watched all his worst fears pass before his eyes and was too far away to do a thing about it. The car spinning, hitting the other, sailing into the air. The sickening crunch as it landed, the hood popping up.

He could hear Patricia and Ann Margaret still shouting from the house, beginning to run. Screaming.

He waited himself, breath held, for sign of his daughter.

A car door opened. Melanie staggered into view. Blood on her forehead. She seemed dazed and confused. Suddenly she plunged into the woods.

Jamie tried to call out for her, but he was too far away. Harper had spotted her from his own car. He was out. He was wielding a gun. He was plunging into the woods.

No sign of life from Riggs yet, and no time to check. His first thought, his only thought, was always Melanie.

And this is how it all comes down, Jamie thought fatalistically.

He started moving. He had a weapon, he had experience, he had training on his side. And yet as he plunged into the woods, he was thinking of his daughter, and he had never been so afraid.

You don't know enough yet, lass. You don't know . . .

Ah, Jesus God, you may take my silly life, just keep my little girl safe. Just protect my little girl from Harper.

Four-year-old Meagan was running. Running, running, running. Branches caught at her hair, cut her cheek. Low, scraggly bushes tore at her favorite blue dress, trying to hold her back.

She kept slogging forward, little legs pumping. Had to run. Had to run fast. Had to run fast, fast, fast.

She wanted to go home to her mommy. Time to go home.

Meagan pushed faster, but behind her, she could still hear the footsteps pounding closer.

Dada Jamie was going to get her. Dada Jamie was going to force her back to the shack. No, no, she wanted her mommy. She wanted Brian!

You can't go home, Meagan. They don't want you anymore. *Want to go home!* It's going to be okay, lass, I'll take care of you, we'll get you out of here and to someplace much much nicer. Why, you'll get to live like a princess in a faraway kingdom called London. *Want to go home!* I know, love, but you can't. Harper . . . your da, he's not safe for you right now. He's not even your real da, love, and I'm afraid all he really wants these days is money. *WANT TO GO HOME!* Love, no!

Footsteps, closer. Crashing underbrush, crackling branches.

Run, Meagan, run. Faster, faster.

Footsteps closer . . .

Run, run.

Breathing closer . . .

RUN, MEAGAN, RUN!

The hand whipped out and caught her hard around the middle. Melanie tried to scream. A second hand slapped over her mouth while she was yanked against a big, burly body.

'Shh, lass,' Jamie O'Donnell whispered in her ear, dragging her deeper into the thick underbrush. 'Don't make a noise.'

And for the first time, Melanie became aware of more sounds of crackling in the underbrush. Harper suddenly appeared twenty feet in front of them, making his way through the trees and holding a very large gun.

David woke up to ringing in his ears. He blinked his eyes, wondering what he was doing in the shooting range. Then he wondered why it was so bright inside the shooting range. Then he wondered why his face was so wet.

He raised a hand. Brought it back down. He had blood all over his face.

He reached for Melanie, then saw that she wasn't there. The car door was wide open, seat belt dragged out into the dirt. A second car sandwiched behind them, the driver's door also flung open into the breeze.

David shoved against his door. Nothing. Shit. His hands were shaking, a first-class lump burgeoning on his temple. For once in his life he felt pain somewhere other than his back. Jesus Christ, he had to get to Melanie.

He finally got his seat belt off. Scrambled across the passenger seat, tried to get his feet beneath him, and fell down into the dirt. The world was turning, then spinning.

He forced himself to stand up, using the car for balance. He had his gun, so he was not helpless. Melanie was still out there, no doubt dazed and confused and vulnerable.

Time to focus, David. Time to get control.

He ripped the tie from his neck and wrapped it around his forehead. That cleared the blood from his gaze. He dug his fingernails into the palms of his hands. The sharp sensation made the world stop spinning.

David took the safety off his souped-up Beretta, thanked his father for the first time in years, and plunged into the forest.

Melanie was standing stock-still, her heart thundering in her chest. The world had gone so quiet around them, every move, every sound exaggerated. Her godfather pinned her against his body until she could barely breathe. Her father, so close, stalked through the underbrush as if he were hunting small prey. The gun held in Harper's hands. The gun carried beneath Jamie's jacket, the bulge pressing against her ribs.

A single scene floated up in her mind.

She tripped over a tree root, sprawling to the ground. The air whooshing from her lungs. No more running. She was caught. Blood on her knees, twigs in her hair. Not even enough air left to cry.

Dada Jamie kneeling beside her, looking tired too. Funny that Dada Jamie should be the one with tears in his eyes. Brushing back her hair slowly, checking her for broken bones, examining her bloody knee.

Dada Jamie gently, so gently, picking all those nasty little rocks from her knees. Dada Jamie murmuring over and over again that it would be all right. She just needed time to adjust, then she'd realize he would never do anything to hurt her. Dada Jamie calling her his little girl.

Hating him anyway because he was keeping her from her family and she wanted to go home!

Something crashed in the underbrush right behind him. Jamie swiveled, Harper's head came up. Melanie saw both of them staring off at the sound, and then she moved.

She drove her elbow into her godfather's gut. He grimaced, tried to recover, and she stomped the inside of his foot. He was shocked enough to loosen his grip, and she pushed back with all her might. He tried to grab her arm. She ducked and burst free, making a beeline for the right, away from both men.

'Dammit!' Jamie swore.

'Melanie!' Harper cried.

Melanie lowered her head and ran harder.

And then it all happened at once. Sounds of crashing twigs and crackling branches. She thought she was moving quickly, but her godfather was already there, reaching for her shoulder. And then Harper was there, to her left, bringing up his gun.

She burst into the clearing just as gunfire erupted from the side.

She watched the bullet come right at her. And then she saw her godfather leap up. Jamie flying through the air, stretching out his whole body, staring right into her eyes, so earnest, so determined, so sad.

The bullet ripped into his back, bowing his body and sending him crashing to the ground.

Harper came into view, standing right in front of her with smoke still pouring from his gun.

'Goddammit,' he said, 'that man was always in the way.'

And then he leveled his gun at his adopted daughter.

David was careering through the underbrush. Leaves tangled in his hair. Roots clawed at his feet. His vision was starting to clear, but now he found he was lost and disoriented in the woods, not sure where he'd come from or where he was going.

He found himself back at the roadside, right where he'd started, except now he was aware of banging coming from the trunk of the other car.

'Hey,' a male voice was calling. 'Somebody let me out!'

David found the keys still dangling from the ignition and popped the trunk. Brian Stokes sat up.

'Are you okay?' David asked, lending him an arm to help him climb out.

Brian was fingering the bridge of his nose, which looked as if it had been attacked with a hammer. 'Harper,' he mumbled. 'Got a gun. Hit me.'

'He hit you? Why?'

'Didn't want me to . . . help Melanie. Gotta help Melanie.'

He tried to lurch forward, but he collapsed on the asphalt. 'You don't understand,' he said. 'Harper has to cover his tracks. Harper . . . has to . . . kill her.'

'Why? She's his daughter.'

'No, not his daughter. Jamie's daughter. Don't you see? She's Jamie's . . .'

The last few pieces clicked into place in David's mind, and then right on the heels of that came the thought that Harper really could be driven to kill Melanie. Shit!

As if reading his mind, a gun blast suddenly ripped through the air.

'Help Melanie,' Brian cried. '*Run!*'

David ran.

Melanie went down on her knees in the grass, ignoring Harper and his gun. Jamie's blue eyes were locked onto hers, his hand fluttering at his side, his lips searching for air. She heard a sucking sound and realized that he'd been shot in the lung. The air was literally leaking out of him.

Oh, God. Though she didn't know why, she looked at her father for help. Harper didn't move. He seemed to be in a state of shock. Maybe he hadn't meant to pull the trigger. Maybe he hadn't meant to harm any of them.

'Please,' she whispered. 'You're a doctor. Dad . . .'

He didn't reply.

Melanie gave up on him and turned her attention back to her godfather.

'I'm . . . s-s-sorry,' Jamie gasped.

'Shh . . . it's all right. You just rest, you can explain everything later.

'You . . . w-w-w-wouldn't remember. I w-w-wanted you . . . to . . . r-r-r-emember . . .'

Blood was foaming on his lips. His eyes started to roll back, and Melanie gripped his hand more tightly.

'No, dammit. You won't die on me, Jamie. I won't let you . . .'

He looked at her sadly, and she knew it was too late. He whispered, 'Selfish . . . like Harper. Annie right. I am no better. Meagan . . .'

'Jamie.'

'I love you, lass . . . my little girl.'

'No, Jamie, no—'

His body convulsed. She tried to hold him still, tried to plug the bullet hole with her shaking fingers. Blood, so much blood, leaking from his ribs, from his lips. She could feel him shudder again and again.

'God damn you,' she cried. 'Don't you dare die on me. Don't you do this to me now!'

You will always be my little girl, he had said. *And no place you go will you ever be alone.*

I forgot, I forgot. I never remembered a thing. Oh, Jamie, I am so sorry.

'M-M-Meagan,' he whispered.

'What, Jamie? What is it?'

'Say it . . . once . . .'

'Say what?'

'Call me . . . Dad.'

'Dad,' she wept. 'Dad.'

The last breath escaped him as a soft sigh and finally the struggle was over. Jamie O'Donnell lay perfectly still. He was gone.

Crashing emitted from the underbrush. Patricia Stokes and Ann Margaret suddenly burst forward, their hair filled with brambles. Another sound of scattering birds from the right. David Riggs burst onto the scene, his gun out.

Everyone stared. Jamie O'Donnell's bloody body on the ground. Melanie leaning over him with tears staining her cheeks. Harper Stokes standing there—

David pointed his gun at the same moment Harper recovered and leveled his 9mm at Melanie.

'Back away,' David said. 'FBI.'

'Harper, for God's sake,' Patricia cried.

'Shut up!' Harper snapped. 'Anybody move, and I'm going to open fire!'

How strange, Melanie thought. She felt as if she were seeing her adoptive father for the first time. The features she'd always found golden were faded and lined by strain. The square chin was really weak, the bright blue eyes uncertain.

This was the man she'd loved as a father for most of her life. A spineless, self-centered, insecure man who'd traded her away for a million bucks, and had single-handedly destroyed his own family.

She said savagely, 'Say it, goddammit. Stand right there and tell everyone once and for all what you did.'

'You don't know anything!' Harper spat out. 'I did what had to be done. I did what was in the best interest of my family.'

'You took away our daughter!' Patricia shouted. 'How was that in our best interest?'

'She wasn't *our* daughter. She was your brat. Yours and O'Donnell's, and you foisted her on me as if I'd never know. Did you think I was stupid? God, Pat, you of all people. I *loved* you.'

'Did you, Harper? It was so hard to tell, when you were always at work.'

'I was trying to build something for both of us. Or didn't you ever think about where the money was coming from when you went out shopping?'

'I went out shopping because there was nothing else to do! For heaven's sake, if you'd only said something. You stupid man, I would've lived like a pauper for you. I even gave up Jamie for you. I really did love you, and I owed it to you to make it work. I really did want – oh, God, I was planning on how to save our marriage and you were kidnapping our daughter! Did you tie her up? Did you drag her screaming from the nanny's car?'

'It wasn't anything like that! I didn't even do it. Jamie did.'

'Because he had to,' Ann Margaret interrupted. 'Because you went so far as to imply that if he didn't help you fake Meagan's murder for the insurance money, you might commit the crime for real.'

'I was hurt, I was angry—'

'You were greedy,' David stated flatly. Melanie could see him appraising the scene, moving slightly to the side so he'd have a better line of fire. He nodded toward her slightly. She realized he was trying to tell her that he was more in control than anyone thought, and it would be all right.

She didn't care. Her real father was dead at her feet. Her adoptive father had a gun pointed at her. She was feeling betrayed and angry. And then she remembered that Jamie's gun was still tucked beneath his jacket.

'How did you do it?' David was asking Harper, sidling a bit more to the left, where he could take his best aim. 'You were angry, you were broke. You decided you would have to make the situation work to your advantage. Get rid of Meagan and gain a million dollars. Very clever.'

'Brains have always been my strong suit,' Harper said. 'Don't bother, Agent. I'm not going to confess it all to you.'

'You don't have to,' Ann Margaret responded contemptuously. 'I know it all. I was there too. As Russell Lee Holmes's wife.'

She gave David a brittle smile. 'Let me start at the beginning for you. Harper hatches his horrible plan. He knew Meagan wasn't his daughter – no matter that she'd adored him for four years – and he wanted her out of the house. Jamie would do anything for the girl, so he agreed. He'd fake a kidnapping of Meagan, take her someplace safe—'

'A goddamn shack!' Harper exclaimed. '*That's* how he treated his child.'

'Well, what was he supposed to do, Harper? As a friend of the family he'd be expected to help out with the search and recovery. Plus, he couldn't very well magically have a new little girl traveling with him. If he left her with a friend, that person could blackmail you later. If he put her in a hotel, someone would surely notice a weeping girl all alone every day. You were the one insisting it be so perfect. So, yes, he locked her in a shack in the middle of the woods, where no one could find her. It was hardly ideal, and it tore him up. But it also worked.

'She was tucked away, you could fake the ransom demand, and Jamie could cough up another hundred thousand dollars to help you out.'

'The ransom money that Brian knew Harper had never delivered,' David stated. 'God, Harper, even when you're greedy, you're greedy.'

Harper wasn't looking so steady with the gun. Every time someone spoke up, he'd jerk a little in that direction. David had noticed it. Melanie too. She was sinking toward the ground, edging closer to the front of Jamie's jacket.

'The police,' Ann Margaret continued, 'started investigating immediately, just as Harper and Jamie figured. Harper was smart, however, and no one could trace the ransom note back to him. On the other hand, you immediately realized you had overlooked a few details, right, Harper? You'd gotten yourself a quick hundred thousand, but you couldn't exactly start spending it – the police would notice. No, you need money you could account for. The life insurance. Of course, for that you needed a body, and none was appearing the way you hoped. So once again you went to Jamie. To pull this off, he had to find a body for you. A body of a four-year-old girl who roughly matched the description of Meagan.'

Her hand already on Jamie's jacket, Melanie froze. 'He didn't . . . he didn't kill anyone, did he?'

'Of course not. Identifying bodies was his job, remember? He waited until he saw one that was close enough. It took four months, four nail-biting months while the police turned on your whole family. Then he stole the body from the Mississippi morgue. He mutilated the fingertips. He cut off the head so the body couldn't be ID'd from dental records. And then he wrapped the body in a blanket. He told me about it years later. Alone in the woods with that little body. Digging the shallow grave, making sure he covered his tracks. Feeling lower than low, as if he really were a child murderer. He felt so bad, he almost couldn't do it. She was so small, some beautiful little girl who would never go home. He wept. Then he placed her in the grave for the cadaver dogs to find. She was so close in height and size to Meagan, so the police simply accepted it when Harper confirmed her ID as Meagan. God, that was a sad day.'

Patricia nodded gloomily. Even Harper looked pained. Then, he swore.

'But the damn police wouldn't go away,' he said. 'We had done everything as planned and then they went and caught Russell Lee Holmes and realized he had nothing in his little shack that belonged to Meagan. Jesus Christ, how were we supposed to know they'd actually catch the bastard the next week?' He looked at Ann Margaret mutinously. 'Your husband was certainly nowhere near as smart as me.'

She replied dryly. 'Thank heavens.'

'And then what?' David said conversationally. He had gotten three feet closer to Harper. With so many people around, it was best to shorten the distance to the target. Then David realized that Melanie had moved as well. She was almost sitting on top of Jamie's body now, her hand beneath the jacket. What the hell was she doing?

'Harper sold his soul to the devil, that's what,' Ann Margaret stated. 'Sent Jamie into prison to deal with Russell Lee himself. And what a deal it was. All Russell Lee had to do was confess to yet another kid's death, and in return Harper Stokes and Jamie O'Donnell would personally guarantee that our child was raised in style. Everything we could never give him, he would magically have. And while Russell Lee was surely the devil himself, he was damn proud of that boy. What is it about men and their sons?'

Melanie looked at Ann Margaret quizzically. 'They really did agree to take care of Russell Lee's child? Then, who is that?'

'William, sweetheart. William Sheffield was my son. I turned him over to the boys' home the day they arrested Russell Lee, terrified some reporter like Larry Digger would find us both and make his life hell. I honestly thought it was for the best.

'Then, when Russell Lee and Harper agreed on the deal, I drew up papers. Harper and Jamie both had to sign a confession to all they'd done, and then I put it in a safety deposit box with instructions that it was to be opened and turned over to the police if anything happened to me. Finally I moved to Boston, where I could start over too, make something of myself, and, of course, keep an eye on Harper. As for William . . .'

She hesitated, and then she flushed. She said quietly, 'I was so sure he was better off in that boys' home. I sent money every year so he would have the best of everything. The brothers promised to take very good care of him. . . . He could get a clean start, never have to worry about some reporter connecting him with his father. And with all that money . . . I grew up so poor myself, I was so sure money was the one thing that would make a difference. I guess I'm not so much better than Harper after all.'

'No,' Melanie said. Something had come over her, and it showed in her face. Something cool. Something fearless. 'We are all better than Harper. Because it didn't stop there, did it, *Dad?* Five years later Russell Lee is finally due to be executed, then no one will ever be the wiser. But how is your family? Your family you thought would be so thrilled with a million bucks? Mom's drinking, Brian's still in therapy. You work all the time just so you don't have to face your own handiwork. And even then you didn't do the right thing.

'Jamie called you. I can remember being in the study of the hotel room in London, hearing it all but not understanding. Jamie telling you that your plan had worked, you'd done well, and now couldn't you give something back. I was so miserable without my mom. And Mom and Brian were so miserable without me. He could set it all up. Erase my memories so not even I would ever know. Drop me off at the hospital for Harper to "find." Then you could literally adopt me back. You wouldn't even have to pretend to be my real father this time. This time you could be the generous adoptive dad taking in an abandoned little girl. You liked that, didn't you, Harper? It made you look good.'

Harper glared at her stubbornly.

'And even then,' she said, 'you *fucked it up!* Kept spending, didn't you? Became a brilliant surgeon, making more and more money, but it was never enough. You learned *nothing* from ripping your family apart. Suddenly it's twenty years later and you're not the great provider you pretend to be. You're slicing up healthy patients for profit. You're violating your own doctors' oath. Why not? You've already committed a heinous act and gotten away with it—'

'I never hurt anyone!'

'*You hurt everyone!* You hurt my mom, you hurt my brother. You hurt me! And you risked your patients who trusted you with their health. And then you got mean.

'The man who shot Larry Digger, who tried to shoot me, that was your doing. Someone had found out, someone was sending you little notes, and you were afraid that finally, after all these years, the truth would come out. So you hired someone to kill me. And did you kill him too? Because you were too cheap to part with the payment money?'

'No, no,' Harper protested. 'Jamie did that. Jamie shot the man. He's the killer!'

'Jamie is the protector! He did what he had to do to keep me safe. Just like he dove in front of me when you opened fire. For God's sake, he was your friend, and you killed him!'

'He cheated with my wife!'

'You cheated with half the nursing staff. How dare you!'

'Goddammit, you don't know anything!' Harper's voice had gone too high. He lost whatever control he'd had on himself, and in a fraction of an instant David realized it was all going to hell.

He aimed at Harper's forehead just as Patricia Stokes jumped into the way.

'You will not hurt my daughter!' she cried.

'Patricia, no,' David shouted.

And now Ann Margaret was moving and Harper was leveling his gun at his wife, screaming at her to get out of the way or he'd kill her too. And how could she have hurt him when he'd loved her so much and why hadn't she just let things go, why hadn't she been able to get over the loss of Jamie O'Donnell's daughter. Because she still loved O'Donnell, that's why. She'd always loved O'Donnell more.

And while David tried desperately to get a bead, Patricia was yelling that it wasn't true, she had loved Harper more, it was his own pride that had never let him see it and she had been so certain they could have been happy together. What had happened to their dreams? How could he have brought them to this? How could he have threatened their daughter and murdered his own friend?

And then he heard Melanie. Melanie crying for her mother. Melanie realizing that Harper was beyond reason, that he really was going to shoot his own wife and David couldn't stop it, and then she was pulling something out of Jamie O'Donnell's jacket. The gun. Melanie had Jamie's gun.

'Ann Margaret, down!' David roared at the same time Harper spotted the new threat and jerked toward Melanie. Shit, Patricia Stokes was still in the way. He couldn't fire!

Harper screamed. His face twisted, something horrible and bleak passing over his eyes. Melanie rose to face him, looking calm, looking fierce.

'Melanie, no! Patricia, goddammit, get down. Get *down!*'

And Brian Stokes stepped up behind his father with a tree limb and slammed it across the back of his skull.

Harper crumpled. David rushed forward, already pulling out the handcuffs, and snapped them on. Ann Margaret and Patricia were still standing in the way, pale and dazed.

Brian stared at them all, the tree limb gripped tightly between his hands. With his bruised and battered face he looked like hell. Then his eyes found his sister.

'Meagan?' he whispered. 'Oh, Meagan . . .'

'Brian,' she cried, and then she dove into his arms. Patricia ran there too, throwing her arms around her children, cradling them feverishly against her. Together at last, the three remaining Stokeses began to cry.

David and Ann Margaret stood on the outside while the woods once again settled down, and after a minute the birds resumed chirping as if all were as it should be.

When the police arrived twenty minutes later, Patricia Stokes was still crying with Brian. But Melanie had moved into David's arms, and now he held her against him tightly and gently stroked her hair.

Epilogue

It was raining the day they laid Jamie O'Donnell to rest. It had taken weeks to get his body from the Texas medical examiner. Patricia had found a Catholic priest for the service. Ann Margaret had known he wanted to be cremated. Brian and Melanie had chosen the Newport Cliff Walk to scatter his remains; he had taken them there often where they were children, claiming he loved to listen to the sound of the waves battering the rocks. It reminded him of Ireland.

Now Melanie, Ann Margaret, Patricia, Brian, and Nate stood silently in front of the priest. Melanie found she could not concentrate on the words. Promises of hope and glory and charity meant little to her these days. She was tired of words. They were too easy to say and too tempting to believe.

She watched the dark, angry water frothing below. She thought as strange as it sounded, Harper should be here. This funeral was about him too, and whether he'd ever admit or not, she suspected he missed Jamie O'Donnell and grieved over him too.

Dr Harper Stokes was now in jail. The states of Texas and Massachusetts and the FBI were currently fighting over him, each arguing they had the best case and should get first dibs. So far the feds were winning. David's healthcare fraud squad had descended upon their Beacon Street home in a frenzy. Bank accounts were frozen, assets seized, files plundered. Melanie, her mother, and her brother had been called in for questioning so many times, the desk man at the Bureau knew them by sight.

Melanie had gotten to spend equal time with Detective Jax, going over that last afternoon with William. So far no charges had been filed against her. Her attorney assured her that the abrasions on her face, combined with the fact that the gun had been William's, made her self-defense argument plausible. Most likely the D. A. would not want to waste the state's time prosecuting the case. She supposed she should be grateful for small favors.

She would not go through life as a murderer, then. And yet she had killed a man. She wasn't sure what that made her, but then, she was unsure of so many things these days.

One day, exactly two weeks after Jamie's death, she'd awakened in a cold sweat. She'd been dreaming again about the shack and then the days in

London. Except this time Jamie said he couldn't stand to be her father anymore. She was a dreadful little girl, he hated her, and he was giving her back.

In a frenzy, she'd driven straight to the jail where they'd been holding Harper and had demanded to see him. She had to know, she had to ask him. Could he tell her if Jamie really loved her? Would he fill in the missing pieces for her? Her memory was still so hazy, and she wanted to hear that both men had cared, that Harper never really would have hurt her, even the hit man had been a mistake. He loved her, Jamie loved her, everything had simply gone awry. Two men and their jealousy, one man and his greed. It was everyone's fault but hers.

Harper, however, wouldn't see her. Since his arrest, he had refused to see anyone, even his wife.

She'd gotten back in her car, driving mindlessly. The next thing she'd known she was at David's apartment. She hadn't had a moment alone with him since the police had arrived in Texas. He was back to being Special Agent Riggs, lead investigator of the growing healthcare fraud case against Harper. Agents, of course, were not allowed to consort with witnesses in a case. She had understood. Agents had rules, and for the most part David respected those rules. That's what made him so different from her two dads.

That night, however, she'd said to hell with it. She'd banged on his door, and the moment he'd opened it, she'd thrown herself into his arms. He hadn't argued. His expression had said everything she felt, the hunger, the yearning, the need for connection, for a reminder that Texas had been real, they were real. They'd made love right there on the entryway floor. Then again in the kitchen, then finally they made it to the bedroom, where they'd started all over again.

Hours later she'd gotten up, gotten dressed, and as wordlessly as she'd arrived, she'd left. He had never called her. She expected that until the investigation was concluded, that would be the case.

She'd waited five days before showing up again. Then three days after that. They never spoke, as if both realized that would cross the line and breach the agent–witness protocol. Instead, they let their hands and mouths and bodies speak for them, urgent and hungry and fierce. Melanie trusted those silent, feverish interludes more than she trusted anything else that had happened in the last twenty years of her life.

Her mother and Ann Margaret were trying to help. Most afternoons now the three women sat out back on the patio, Ann Margaret and Patricia relating the early days in Texas to Melanie, trying to give her some perspective.

Melanie learned a lot about Jamie in those sessions. The way he had loved her mother but had never completely won her away from Harper. The way he'd loved Ann Margaret but still chose the destructive course.

The way he seemed to love his daughter, though even that love was strange and tragic.

He had made Melanie his primary heir. Swiss bank accounts holding millions of dollars were hers, ensuring that she and her mother would never want for anything. Ann Margaret was to receive a generous annual stipend for the rest of her life.

The police uncovered the electronic voice distorter he'd used for his anonymous calls. They also found ostrich feathers and a strange picture of a woman and two horrible beasts no one could explain. Last gifts, Brian said. The ostrich feathers for Patricia, for burying her head in the sand when it came to her husband's activities, and the picture for Ann Margaret, for having cavorted with not one, but two monsters in her lifetime.

According to Ann Margaret, Jamie had knowledge of everyone's crimes. The apple on William's bed symbolized that the apple never fell far from the tree. He'd even seen Brian pulling out the briefcase with the ransom money, then had waited breathlessly for Brian to blow the whistle. Of course, Brian never had.

Also, Jamie had the knack for bypassing various security systems, for ferreting out the little details of everyone's life so he could deliver the intimate gifts most intimately.

Finally, Jamie O'Donnell had had motive. According to the Texas medical examiner, Melanie's father had possessed one last secret – he'd been dying of stomach cancer, most likely with less than six months to live.

It appeared that he'd decided to use the brief time he had left to reveal the truth. That's what the FBI said.

Ann Margaret had a slightly different theory.

When you were first adopted, Melanie, you got to meet everyone again for the first time. Just as Jamie predicted, you seemed to 'know' your mother instantly. The same with Brian. You even accepted Harper quite naturally and were very protective of him.

Then your parents introduced you to Jamie. Do you remember what you did, Melanie? This was your birth father. The man who'd purposely removed you from the country to help appease Harper and protect you. The man who'd rearranged his life to care for you and then out of love for Patricia and you had given you up again. And you took one look at him and recoiled. You were afraid.

I don't think he ever forgot that moment, sweetheart. I don't think he ever stopped knowing that Harper was the one you ended up loving, while he was the one who had inspired fear.

Some things are even more powerful to a man than cancer. One of those has got to be love.

' "When I was a child, I spake as a child," ' the priest at the service intoned. ' "I understood as a child, I thought as a child: But when I became a man, I put away childish things. For now we see through a glass, darkly;

but then face to face: now I know in part; but then shall I know even as also I am known." '

That was Melanie's cue. She rose. She picked up the urn. It was amazingly heavy, substantial, and yet nothing at all compared to what Jamie had been on earth. At the priest's nod, she took off the top.

Did we ever see face-to-face, Jamie? There is so much I want to ask you. So much I wish I understood . . . So much about you to love and admire, and so much to hate.

I believe you loved me, that you did what you thought was for the best. You sacrificed for me, you sacrificed for my mother, and because of that, I love you, Jamie O'Donnell and I forgive you everything. Go in peace and God bless.

Melanie tipped over the urn. The ashes floated down in the damp, misty air, into the ocean, where they swirled and then were swept away.

Patricia and Ann Margaret walked back to the road together in the lead. Behind them came Brian and Nate, their heads huddled together and speaking quietly. That left Melanie alone in the rear. She tried not to feel lonely, but it didn't entirely work.

They arrived at the end of the Cliff Walk, where their three vehicles were parked. Melanie saw that a fourth had joined them. And as if reading her mind, a dark-suited man leaned against the passenger door and his head came up at the sight of her.

Melanie started running, and she didn't care who saw her.

'David!'

She drew up short at the last moment, suddenly self-conscious and unsure. He wore a navy blue suit, which made him look official. But then his face softened, his eyes began to glow, and she felt the knot loosen in her chest.

'Hi,' he said.

'Hi yourself.'

'Nice ceremony.'

'You heard?'

'I walked out for it but didn't want to interrupt.'

'You could have interrupted,' she said immediately. 'I wouldn't have minded.'

He smiled slightly and brushed a finger down her cheek. She closed her eyes so she could concentrate on the feel of his touch, and when she opened them again, she saw that the tip of his finger was damp. He'd brushed away her tears.

'Are you still investigating my father?' she demanded. 'Tell me, are you here as part of your special duties, because you are just killing me—'

'I'm done.'

'Done?'

'Done. Wrapped up this morning, handed over to the attorney general. I'm a free man, Melanie Stokes. So I thought I oughta find you.'

'Oh, David,' she said, and then she couldn't speak. 'Oh, David,' she tried again. She gave up words and threw herself against him. He folded her into his embrace.

'I missed you,' he said.

'Me too.'

'I wanted to know how you were doing.'

'I know, I know.'

He was suddenly angling back her head, his eyes fierce. 'I'm taking meds,' he declared in a rush. 'I can walk better, move better. Got promoted too. I have job security. But, Mel, I haven't done as right by you as I could.'

'David, I love you.'

He stopped talking and held her close. After a moment he muttered, 'Thank God. My father told me I was probably messing this whole thing up and I should've introduced you to him weeks ago. Somehow or other that would've made a difference. I don't claim to understand him. Actually, after everything I blabbered, I think he was hoping for a chance to court you himself.'

'Really? My mom asked if you were ever going to come around again. Ann Margaret told her to be quiet and mind her own business – they were in no position to give advice on men.'

He laughed. 'Interesting point.'

She grabbed his lapels. 'Say it, dammit! It's been a bitch of a month and I want to hear it. All of it!'

'I love you, Melanie. I want to settle down with you, raise two point two children, and grow old together. I want to be with you every single day of my life.'

She melted against him. The knot left her chest completely. The haze of the last month cleared from her eyes. Now she could see it all clearly. Herself, him, probably two point two children. Maybe a golden retriever.

Family. At last, a family of her own.

Funny, but in her mind she saw Jamie O'Donnell beaming and four-year-old Meagan Stokes finally happy.

Melanie Stokes whispered, 'Yes.'

The Third Victim

Author's Note and Acknowledgements

When I first proposed this book to my editor, it was the winter of 1998 and nearly seven months since the last shooting – Kip Kinkel's May rampage in Springfield, Oregon. That tragedy had followed close on the heels of another, in Jonesboro, Arkansas (March 24, 1998), which had followed West Paducah, Kentucky (December 1, 1997), Pearl, Mississippi (October 1, 1997), and Bethel, Alaska (February 19, 1997). Like many Americans struggling to grasp five shootings in fifteen months, I wanted to understand why these mass murders had occurred and what could be done to prevent them.

After fine-tuning what would be appropriate to cover in a work of fiction whose goal must also be to entertain, I began researching this novel. One Monday, while wrapping up weeks of interviewing, I asked an expert if he believed that the rash of incidents indicated a new trend in juvenile behavior. While this point is controversial, the man did not hesitate to answer. 'Absolutely,' he said. 'As for future shootings, the question is not if but when.'

The very next day, Littleton, Colorado, joined the sad list of shot-up schools in a scope and scale that was staggering. I watched the news clips, and like people all around the world, I gave my thoughts and prayers to a community I had never met. Every time one of these shootings occurs it is heartbreaking, but as Supervisory Special Agent Pierce Quincy tries to explain in the following pages, it does not have to be hopeless. With each tragedy, we have learned and are learning. In addition to Littleton, Springfield, and Jonesboro, there is Burlington, Wisconsin, where police responded to an anonymous tip in time to arrest three teenage boys plotting to assassinate a target list of 'in' students, and there is Wimberly, Texas, where concerned students contacted police in time to foil a plot by five eighth-grade boys to blow up the junior high. People are learning to listen, and it does work.

In the end, I believe we owe an enormous debt of gratitude to each of the communities that has suffered this tragedy. By sharing their experience with us, and their sorrow, they are teaching us to be better people, students, families, and neighbors. May there come a day when white lilies and red roses are not piled against schoolyard fences. May there come a time when we are not haunted by the image of teenagers signing farewell notes on white caskets. May there be a future when our schools once again know peace.

The following people helped me tremendously with my research. I appreciate their help and patient explanations. Of course, all mistakes are mine, and some facts are subject to artistic license.

Gregory K. Moffatt, PhD, Professor of Psychology, Atlanta Christian College
Thomas Grisso, PhD, Professor of Psychiatry (Clinical Psychology), Director of Forensics Training and Research, University of Massachusetts Medical School
Steve Ellis, Officer, Amity Police Department
Rudolf Van Soolen, Chief of Police, Amity Police Department
Jonathan McCarthy, Paramedic, New Orleans Health Department
Amy Holmes Hehn, Senior Deputy District Attorney, Juvenile Division, Multnomah County
Stacy Heyworth, Senior Deputy District Attorney, Multnomah County
Michael Moore, Attorney-at-Law
Lorenz, teacher
Bruce Walker, computer whiz extraordinaire
Chad LeDoux, gun aficionado and fellow writer
Debra Dixon, author

1

Officer Lorraine Conner was sitting in a red vinyl booth at Martha's Diner, picking at her tuna salad and listening to Frank and Doug gossip, when the call first came in. She was sitting alone in the booth, eating salad because she'd just turned thirty-one and was beginning to notice that the pounds didn't magically melt away the way they had when she was twenty-one, or hell, even twenty-seven. She could still run a six-minute mile and slip into a size 8, but thirty-one was fundamentally different from thirty. She spent more time arranging her long chestnut hair to earn those second glances. And for lunches, she traded in cheeseburgers for tuna salad, five days a week.

Rainie's partner that day was twenty-two-year-old volunteer police officer Charles Cunningham, aka Chuckie. Known in the lingo of the tiny police department of Bakersville, Oregon, as a 'green rookie,' Chuckie hadn't yet gone to the nine-month-long training school. That meant he was allowed to look but not touch. Full authority would come when he completed the required academy courses and received his certificate. In the meantime, he got to gain experience by going on patrols and writing up reports. He also got to wear the standard tan uniform and carry a gun. Chuckie was a pretty happy guy.

Before the call came in, he was up at the lunch counter, trying to work some magic on a leggy blonde waitress named Cindy. He had his chest puffed out, his knee crooked forward, and his hand resting lightly on his sidearm. Cindy, on the other hand, was trying to serve up slices of Martha's homemade blueberry pie to six farmers at once. One cantankerous old man muttered at the rookie to get out of the way. Chuckie grinned harder.

In the booth behind Rainie, retired dairymen Doug Atkens and Frank Winslow started placing their bets.

'Ten dollars says she caves,' Doug announced, slapping a crumpled bill on the pink Formica table.

'Twenty says she dumps a glass of ice water over Romeo's head,' Frank countered, reaching for his wallet. 'I know for a fact that Cindy would rather earn good tips than Clark Gable's heart.'

Rainie gave up on her salad and turned around to face the two men. It was a slow afternoon and she had nothing better to do with her time, so she said, 'I'll take a piece of that.'

'Hello there, Rainie.' Frank and Doug, friends for nearly fifty years, smiled as a single unit. Frank had bluer eyes in his sun-weathered face, but Doug had more hair. Both men wore red-checked western shirts with pearl snaps – their official dress shirts for an afternoon spent out on the town. In the winter, they topped their shirts with brown suede blazers and cream-colored cowboy hats. Rainie once accused them of trying to impersonate the Marlboro Man. At their ages, they took that as a compliment.

'Slow day?' Doug asked.

'Slow month. It's May. The sun is out. Everyone is too damn happy to fight.'

'Ahh, no juicy domestic disputes?'

'Not even a quibble over whose dog is depositing what souvenirs in whose yard. If this good weather continues, I'm gonna be out of a job.'

'A beautiful woman like you doesn't need a job,' Frank said. 'You need a *man.*'

'Yeah? And after thirty seconds, what would I do?'

Frank and Doug chortled; Rainie winked. She liked Frank and Doug. Every Tuesday for as long as she could remember, she would find them sitting at that booth in this diner at precisely one P.M. The sun rose, the sun set. Frank and Doug ate Martha's Tuesday meatloaf special. It worked.

Now Rainie tossed ten bucks into the pot in Chuckie's favor. She'd seen the young Don Juan in action before, and Bakersville's young ladies simply loved his dimpled smile.

'So what d'you think of the new volunteer?' Doug asked, jerking his head toward the lunch counter.

'What's there to think? Writing traffic tickets isn't brain surgery.'

'Heard you two had a little encounter with a German shepherd last week,' Frank said.

Rainie grimaced. 'Rabies. Damn fine animal too.'

'Did he really charge Romeo?'

'All ninety pounds.'

'We heard Chuckie 'bout peed his pants.'

'I don't think Chuckie likes dogs.'

'Walt said you took the shepherd out. Clean shot to the head.'

'That's why they pay me the big bucks – so I can counsel drunks and shoot household pets.'

'Come on, Rainie. Walt said it was a tough shot. Those dogs move *fast.* Chuckie indebted to you now?'

Rainie eyed the rookie, still puffed up like a rooster at the lunch counter. She said, 'I think Chuckie's scared *shitless* of me now.'

Frank and Doug laughed again. Then Frank leaned forward, a gleam in his old blue eyes as he started fishing for real gossip.

'Shep must like having more help,' he said meaningfully.

Rainie eyed the bait, then refused the offer. 'All sheriffs like getting people willing to work for free,' she said neutrally. It was true enough. Bakersville's modest budget allowed for only one full-time sheriff and two full-time officers – Rainie and Luke Hayes. The other six patrolmen were strictly volunteers. They not only donated their time for free, but they paid for their own training, uniforms, vests, and guns. Lots of small towns used this system. After all, the majority of calls dealt with domestic disputes and crimes against property. Nothing a few good people with level heads couldn't handle.

'I hear Shep is cutting back his hours,' Doug prompted.

'I don't keep track.'

'Come on, Rainie. Everyone knows Shep and Sandy are having their differences. Is he working on patching things up? Getting more comfortable with his wife having a job?'

'I just write up civil incidents, Frank. No spying for the taxpayers here.'

'Ahh, give us a hint. We're going to the barbershop next, you know. Walt gives free haircuts if you provide fresh news.'

Rainie rolled her eyes. 'Walt already knows more than I do. Who do you think *we* call for information?'

'Walt does know everything,' Frank grumbled. 'Maybe we should open up a barbershop. Hell, any kind of moron oughtta be able to cut hair.'

Rainie looked down at the two men's hands, twisted from a lifetime of hard work and swollen by a decade of arthritis. 'I'd come in,' she said bravely.

'See there, Doug. We could also pick up chicks.'

Doug was impressed. He began contemplating the details, and Rainie decided it was time to exit stage right. She swiveled back around in her booth with a parting smile, then glanced at her watch. 1:30 P.M. No calls coming in, no reports from the morning to be written up. An unusually slow morning in an already slow town. She looked at Chuckie, whose cheeks had to be aching from that smile.

'Wrap it up, rookie,' she muttered, and drummed her fingertips restlessly.

Unlike Charles Cunningham, Rainie had never planned on becoming a cop. When she'd graduated from Bakersville High School, her first thought had been to get the hell out of dairyland. She'd had eighteen years of claustrophobia building up inside her and no family left to keep her chained. Freedom, that's what she needed. No more ghosts, or so she'd thought.

Rainie had boarded the first bus to Portland, where she'd enrolled at Portland State University and studied psychology. She'd liked her classes. She'd liked the young city brimming with cooking schools and art institutes and 'alternative lifestyles.' She'd gotten involved in a heady affair with a thirty-four-year-old assistant district attorney who'd driven a Porsche.

Nights spent taking over the wheel of the high-performance vehicle with the windows rolled down. Putting the pedal to the metal and streaking up the sharp corners of Skyline Boulevard with the wind in her hair. Climbing higher, higher, higher, pushing harder, harder, harder. Searching for . . . something.

Then, when they finally crested the top of the hill, the city spreading out like a blanket of stars, pulling over and stripping off clothes as they furiously fucked amid gearshifts and bucket seats.

Later, Howie would drive Rainie home, where she'd pop open a six-pack of beer alone, though she of all people knew better.

Rainie glanced at her watch again. 'Come on, Chuckie. It's not like Cindy's going anywhere.'

The radio on Rainie's belt crackled to life. Finally, she thought with genuine relief, some action.

'One-five, one-five. Calling one-five.'

Rainie picked up the radio, already sliding out of the booth. 'One-five here, go ahead.'

'We have a report of an incident at the K-through-eight school. Wait . . . hang on.'

Rainie frowned. She could hear noises in the background, as if dispatch had her own radio up very high or a phone next to the radio receiver. Rainie heard static and shouts. Then she heard four distinct popping sounds. Gunshots.

What the hell?

Rainie strode toward Chuck, turning him around just as dispatch came on again. For the first time in eight years, Linda Ames sounded frazzled.

'All units, all units. Reports of gunfire from Bakersville's K-through-eight. Reports . . . blood loss . . . blood in the halls. Calling six-oh . . . six-oh . . . Walt, bring the damn ambulance! I'm securing channel three. I think it's a school shooting. Oh my God, we're having a school shooting!'

Rainie got Chuck out of the diner. He looked pale and shocked. She waited to feel something but came up empty. There was a faint ringing in her ears. She ignored it as she slid into the old police sedan, buckled up, and reached automatically for the sirens.

'I don't understand,' Chuckie murmured. 'A school shooting? We don't have school shootings.'

'Keep the radio on channel three. That's the designated channel, and all information will pass through there.' Rainie slammed the car into gear and pulled out. They were on Main Street, a good fifteen minutes away from Bakersville's K-8, and Rainie knew that a lot could happen in fifteen minutes.

'We can't be having a school shooting,' Chuckie continued, babbling. 'Hell, we don't even have gangs, or drugs, or . . . or *homicides*, for that matter. Dispatch must be confused.'

'Yeah,' Rainie said quietly, though the ringing was growing in her ears. It had been years since she'd heard that sound. Years since she'd been a little girl, coming home from school and knowing from the first step into the doorway, the first note of foreboding in her ear-drums, that her mother was already drunk and this was going to be bad.

You're a cop now, Rainie. You're in control.

Suddenly, she desperately needed to hold a bottle of beer.

The radio crackled again. Sheriff Shep O'Grady's voice came on as Rainie cleared the first light on Main Street. 'One-five, one-five, what is your position?'

'Twelve minutes out,' Rainie responded, weaving sharply around one double-parked car and barely squeaking by the next.

'One-five, switch to channel four.'

Rainie looked at Chuckie. The rookie made the switch to the private channel. Shep's voice returned. He didn't sound as calm anymore. 'Rainie, you gotta get there faster.'

'We were at Martha's. I'm coming as fast as I can. You?'

'Six minutes out. Too damn far. Linda sent the rest of the officers scrambling, but most gotta run home for their vests and sidearms. Nearest county officer is probably twenty minutes away, and state a good thirty to forty minutes. If this really is a major incident . . .' His voice trailed off; then he said abruptly, 'Rainie, you need to be the primary.'

'I can't be the primary. I don't have any experience.' Rainie glanced at Chuck, who appeared equally confused. The sheriff was always the primary on the case. That was procedure.

'You have more experience than anyone else,' Shep was saying.

'My mother doesn't count—'

'Rainie, I'm not sure what's really going down at the school, but if it's a shooting . . . My kids are there, Rainie. You can't ask me not to think about my children.'

Rainie fell silent. After eight years of working with Shep, she knew his two children as well as a favorite niece and nephew. Eight-year-old Becky was horse crazy. Thirteen-year-old Danny loved to spend free afternoons at the tiny police station. Once, Rainie had given the boy a plastic sheriff's star. He'd worn it for nearly six months and demanded to sit beside Rainie whenever she came over to dinner. They were great kids. Two great kids in a building filled with two hundred and fifty other great kids. Not one above the age of fourteen . . .

Not in Bakersville. Chuckie was right: These things couldn't be happening in Bakersville.

Rainie said quietly, 'I'll be the primary.'

'Thanks, Rainie. Knew I could count on you.'

The radio clicked off. Rainie hit another red light and had to tap the brakes to slow. Fortunately, cross-traffic saw her coming and halted right away. She was vaguely aware of the other drivers' concerned expressions. Police sirens on Main Street? You never heard police sirens on Main Street. They still had a good ten-minute drive, and now she was genuinely concerned that that might be too long . . . too late.

Two hundred and fifty little kids . . .

'Turn back to channel three,' she told Chuckie. 'Order the medics docked.'

'But there's a report of blood—'

'Medics are docked until the scene is secured. That's the drill.'

Chuck did as he was told.

'Get dispatch on. Request full backup. I'm sure the state and county boys have heard, and I don't want there to be any confusion – we'll take all the help we can get.' She paused, sifting through her memory to classes taken eight years ago in a musty classroom in Salem, Oregon, where she had been the only woman among thirty men. Full-scale mobilization. Procedure for possible large-scale casualties. Things that had seemed strange to be studying at the time.

'Ask local hospitals to be on alert,' she murmured. 'Tell the medics to contact the local blood bank in case they need to boost supply. Linda needs to request SWAT coverage. Oh, and tell the state Crime Scene Unit to be ready to roll. Just in case.'

Dispatch returned before Chuckie could pick up the radio. Linda sounded shrill. 'We have calls of shots still being fired. No information on shooter. No information on casualties. We have reports of a man in black at the scene. Shooter may be in the area. Proceed with caution. Please, please, proceed with caution.'

'A man?' Chuck said hoarsely. 'I thought it would be a student. It's always a student.'

Rainie finally hit the rural highway on the edge of downtown and opened the car up to eighty miles per hour. They were on their way now. Seven minutes and counting. Chuck picked up the radio and ran through the list of orders.

Rainie started thinking of the other communities and schools she'd seen in the news without completely understanding. Even Springfield, Oregon, had seemed far away. It was a city, and everyone knew cities had their problems. That's why people moved to Bakersville. Nothing bad was ever supposed to happen here.

But you already knew better, didn't you, Rainie? You of all people should've known.

Chuckie was done with the radio. Now his lips moved in silent prayer. Rainie had to look away.

'I'm coming,' she murmured to the children she could see clearly in her mind. 'I'm coming as fast as I can.'

On Tuesday afternoon, Sandy O'Grady was trying hard to get some market-research reports done and was failing miserably. Sitting in a small corner office – a former bedroom of a converted Victorian home – she spent more time gazing out the window than at the stack of reports piled high on her scarred oak desk.

The day was beautiful, not a cloud in sight. A true rarity in a state with so much rain that the locals affectionately referred to it as liquid sunshine. The temperature was mild too. Not as cool as it could be in spring, but not so warm that it started pulling in all the tourists and spoiling the mood.

The day was perfect, a rare treat for all of Bakersville's citizens, who endured all the other days too – the rainy autumns, the icy winters, the mudslides that sometimes closed the mountain passes, and the spring floods that threatened to destroy all the fertile fields. One good day out of a hundred, her daddy would have noted ironically. But he would've been the first to say it was enough.

Sandra had lived in Bakersville all her life, and there was no other place she'd want to raise her family. Nestled between Oregon's Coastal Range on the east and the Pacific Ocean on the west, the valley boasted lush, rolling hills dotted by black and white Holsteins and ringed by towering green mountains. The dairy cows outnumbered the people two to one. The family farm still endured as a way of life. People knew one another and took part in their neighbors' lives. There were beaches for summer fun and hiking paths for fall glory. For dinner, you could have freshly caught crab, followed by a bowl of freshly picked strawberries topped off with freshly made cream. Not at all a bad life.

In the end, the only complaint Sandra had ever heard about her community was the weather. The endlessly gray winters, the thick, pea-soup fog that seemed to weigh some folks down. Sandy, however, even loved the gray, misty mornings when the mountains barely peeked over their flannel shrouds and the world was wrapped in silence.

When she and Shep had been newlyweds, they would go on walks in the early morning hours, before he had to report for duty. They'd layer up in barn coats and black rubber boots and wade through dew-heavy fields, feeling the fog like a silky caress against their cheeks. Once, when Sandy was four months pregnant and her hormones were raging out of control, they'd made love in the mist, rolling beneath an old oak tree and soaking them-selves to the bone. Shep had looked at her with such awe and wonder. And she had wrapped her arms tight around his lean waist, listening to his fast-beating heart and daydreaming about the child growing in her belly. Would it be a boy or a girl? Would it have her curly blond hair or Shep's thick brown locks? How would it feel to have a tiny life nursing at her breast?

It had been a magic moment. Unfortunately, their marriage had not seen many of those since.

A knock at her door. Sandy pulled her gaze guiltily from the window and saw her boss, Mitchell Adams, leaning against the old bull's-eye molding. He had his ankles crossed and his hands thrust deep into the pants pockets of a three-thousand-dollar charcoal-colored suit. Dark hair just brushed his collar in the back, and his lean cheeks were freshly shaved. Mitchell Adams was one of those men who always looked good, whether he wore Armani or L. L. Bean. Shep had hated him on sight.

'How are those reports coming?' Mitch asked. In spite of Shep's concern, Mitchell was one-hundred-percent business. He had not hired Sandy because she remained lithe and beautiful even at forty. He had hired her because he'd realized that the former homecoming queen had a brain in her head and a need to succeed. When Sandy had tried explaining this to Shep, he simply hated Mitchell more.

'The meeting with Wal-Mart is tomorrow,' Mitch was saying. 'If we're really going to convince them to move into our town, we have to have our numbers in order.'

'So I'd better get the numbers in order.'

'How far along are you?'

She hesitated. 'I'm getting there.' Code for she hadn't gotten a damn thing done. Code for she'd had another big fight with Shep last night. Code for she'd be staying late to get the reports done, and that would generate yet another argument with her husband, and she didn't feel as if she could win anymore. But she was too Catholic to do anything different, and so was Shep.

They just kept going around and around, and now Becky was spending all her time sequestered in her room with an army of stuffed animals she believed could talk, while Danny spent more and more time playing on the Internet in the school's computer room. He'd told Sandy that he was earning extra credit from Miss Avalon. But both Sandy and Shep suspected that their son didn't want to come home anymore. Then last month there had been the incident with the lockers . .

Sandy was unconsciously rubbing her temples. Mitchell took a small step into the room, then caught himself and moved back.

'By tomorrow morning,' he said quietly.

'Absolutely. First thing in the morning. I know how important the meeting is.'

He finally nodded, though Sandy could tell he wasn't satisfied. She didn't know what else she could say. That was her life these days. No one was completely satisfied – not her boss, her husband, or her kids. She kept telling herself that if she could just hang in there a little longer, things would work out. The meeting with Wal-Mart was something they'd been working on for nine months. Keeping late hours, burning the midnight oil.

But if it went well, a lot of money would be pouring in. The commercial real estate company could finally hire more employees. Sandy would probably take home a nice-size bonus. Shep might finally notice she had real abilities and ambitions, just like him.

One forty-five P.M. Sandy got up and closed the blinds on her window, hoping that would help her focus. She poured herself a glass of water, picked up a pen, and prepared to get serious.

She'd just started reviewing the market data when the phone at her elbow rang. She picked it up absently, one half of her mind still processing numbers. She was not prepared for what she heard.

Lucy Talbot sounded hysterical. 'Sandy, Sandy! Oh thank God I reached you! There's been a shooting, at the school. Some man, they claim he's run away. I heard it on the radio. There's blood in the halls. Students, faculty, I don't know who. People are running in from everywhere. You gotta get there quick!'

Sandy didn't remember hanging up or grabbing her purse or yelling to Mitchell that she had to go.

What she remembered was running. She had to get to the school. She had to get to Danny and Becky.

And she remembered thinking for the first time in a long time that she was glad Shep O'Grady was her husband. Their children needed him.

2

Bakersville's K-8 looked like a scene out of bedlam. As Rainie came to a
screeching halt half a block away from the sprawling, one-story building,
she saw parents running frantically across the parking lot while children
wandered the fenced-in schoolyard, crying hysterically. Fire alarms were
ringing. Walt's 1965 ambulance siren as well, damn him. More cars came
careening dangerously around the residential streets, probably parents
called from work.

'Damn,' Rainie muttered. 'Damn, damn, damn.'

She could see teachers gathering up their charges into small groups. A
man in a suit – maybe Principal VanderZanden; Rainie had met him only
once – took up a post by the flagpole and seemed to be trying to organize
the chaos. He wasn't having much luck. Too many parents were running
from group to group trying to find their children. Too many children were
circling aimlessly in search of parents. A young boy with blood-soaked
jeans staggered away from the whirling madness and collapsed on the
sidewalk. No one seemed to notice.

Rainie jumped out of her car and ran. Cunningham was right behind
her. As they cut through the sea of people, pushing toward the school's
glass front doors, Rainie spotted Shep's patrol car, strategically parked to
block off the west entrance of the parking lot. The sheriff himself, however,
was not in sight.

The front doors had been thrust wide open. Rainie could just make out
Bakersville's two volunteer EMTs, Walt and Emery, hunched down at the
end of the wide hallway, where they were already ministering to a victim.

'Dammit,' she swore again. The two men had no business being in the
building before it had been secured.

A parent came running up, heading straight for the open doors. Rainie
grabbed his arm just as he tried to push by, and she shoved him back
forcefully.

'My kid,' he started.

'Into the parking lot,' she yelled. 'No one enters the building! Hey you,
you there in the suit. Come here.'

Rainie snagged the younger man in mid-run. He had a look of authority about him, his olive suit nicely tailored and his black shoes freshly polished. He was frowning at Rainie, clearly anxious and in a hurry.

'Are you from the school? What's your name?' Rainie demanded.

'Richard, Richard Mann. I'm the school counselor, and I need to get to the students. We've had some injuries—'

'Do you know what happened in there?'

'There were shots. Then the fire alarm sounded; then everyone was running. One minute I was in my office doing some paperwork, the next minute it was chaos.'

'Did you see who was shooting?'

'No, but someone said they saw a man run out the west side doors. I don't know.'

'What about the students? Is everyone out?'

'We followed basic evacuation procedure,' Richard Mann replied automatically. Then his face fell. He lowered his voice so only Rainie could hear. 'Two teachers said they saw some students down in the halls. They had to attend to their own classes, though, so they didn't feel they could stop . . . and they didn't want their kids to notice. I've also seen some wounded children out here. I tried to grab the EMTs, but they were already heading into the building.'

'Do you have any medical training?'

'I learned CPR from the Y.'

'Good enough. Here's what you're going to do: Form a first-aid station on the school lawn. Gather up all the injured kids – I just saw a boy collapse by the sidewalk, so you need to send someone over there. Then ask among the parents. There's gotta be other people here who have some sort of training – CPR, animal husbandry, camping first aid, I don't care. Have them assist the kids and hold the fort the best they can. Walt looks to have his hands full inside, and we probably have another good ten or fifteen minutes before Cabot County's ambulance arrives.'

'I'll do my best. It's just so hard to be heard above the noise.'

Rainie pointed a finger at Shep's patrol car. 'See that? In the backseat is a bullhorn. Knock yourself out. Now, once you get a first-aid area set up, I have another job for you. Are you listening?'

The young counselor nodded intently. His face was pale, and his upper lip was beaded with sweat, but he seemed to be paying attention.

'See all the people clogging the parking lot?' she said. 'We need them all moved across the street. Tell the teachers to line up their classes and conduct a head count. When they're done, they can match up students with parents. But everyone except the wounded clears this parking lot, for safety reasons, okay? And nobody goes home until they've been dismissed by the police. Got it?'

'I'll try.'

'Did you see Sheriff O'Grady?'

'He ran into the building. I think he was looking for his kids.'

Richard Mann took off for Shep's car. Rainie eyed the sprawling white school building, which she gathered was still unsecured, then looked at her rookie, who was nervously stroking his gun.

Rainie took a deep breath. She had only classroom training in these things, and that had been years ago, but she didn't have any other choices. Walt and Emery were already in the school. Shep too. She and Chuckie might as well join the fray.

She turned to him. 'Walk *right* behind me, Chuckie. Eyes open, hands off your gun. Walt's acting without authority, but he still doesn't deserve to be shot.'

Chuckie nodded dutifully.

'There are just three things to remember at a crime scene: Don't touch a thing. Don't touch a damn thing. Don't touch a goddamn thing. Okay?'

Chuckie nodded again. Rainie glanced at her watch. 1:57 P.M. The parking lot was still a mess, and it was hard to think over the din of sirens and crying children. It was hard to look too closely, because now she was noticing the red spots on the sidewalk, the unmistakable trail of blood from the school into the yard. The injured children fleeing for their lives. And the others? The ones Richard Mann said the other teachers had seen?

Rainie couldn't think about that yet.

She had her Glock in her right hand and her backup .22 holstered at her ankle. She hoped that was enough. She gave Cunningham a reassuring nod, and entered the building with her walkie-talkie in her left hand.

The noise was louder in the building, the long hallways funneling the relentlessly pinging fire alarm and raining the sound down upon their heads. 'Dispatch,' Rainie yelled into her walkie-talkie. 'One-five calling dispatch. Linda, come in.'

'Dispatch to one-five.'

'Get me Hank on the wire. I need to know how to turn off the damn fire alarms.'

'Ummm, okay. One moment.'

Rainie and Chuckie paused in the front lobby, wincing against the steadily increasing noise.

Ahead of them, the main hallway was surprisingly clean. No backpacks scattered, no books thrown across the vast white-tiled floor. To the right loomed the admissions office, where the glass windows were covered with pastel cutouts of paper flowers and the cheery word *Welcome!* Rainie still didn't see any signs of violence.

The walkie-talkie crackled to life. Rainie held it up against her ear to catch Linda's instructions. Inside the main office. A master panel. Rainie eyed the closed door. No telling what was on the other side. And impossible to hear. That was the whole problem.

She motioned Chuckie to the side. No time like the present.

Ducking low. Leading with her gun. Kicking open the door and rolling inside. Coming up . . . Nothing. Nothing. Nothing. Office secured.

She crossed to the main control panel, and a second later the fire alarms abruptly broke off.

Chuckie blinked sharply. The silence was stunning after the noise. Stunning, and eerie.

'That – that's better,' Chuckie said after a moment, working on sounding confident when his face had turned the color of parchment.

'Major learning from Columbine,' Rainie muttered. 'The fire alarms obscured all sound. Made it impossible for the SWAT team to pinpoint where the shooters were in the building.'

'You've been trained in school shootings?' Chuckie asked hopefully.

'No. I read *Time* magazine.' Rainie jerked her head. 'Come on. Keep your head on straight. Use your ears. You'll be okay.'

They returned to the main hall, both of them holding their sidearms and moving gingerly. After the office, rows of blue lockers began, the doors closed. The shooting must have happened after all the students were back in class after lunch, Rainie decided. She wondered if that was significant. Then she wondered what she would find in the classrooms.

She noticed a few misshapen slugs on the floor as they moved farther in. Probably stray shots from the main area of incident, or maybe debris kicked into this area when people stampeded out. She stepped carefully around all the objects, though she had no illusion about the situation in front of her.

An officer's first priority when approaching any crime scene was to preserve human life. The second objective was to apprehend the perpetrator, if still in the vicinity, and secure the scene. Third was to detain witnesses and protect the evidence, for it was always the officer's job to look beyond the tragedy of the moment. In the days to come, the people of Bakersville would be clamoring for answers. They would want reconstructions of the day, who did what to whom. What had gone wrong. Who was to blame.

Rainie already knew that those questions would not be easily answered. The school was located in a residential area, and too many civilians had beaten officers to the building. Between them, the EMTs, and the students, the hallway was contaminated. And now here were Rainie and Chuckie, two armed and inexperienced officers at their first major crime scene. She was in trouble before she started, and she still had no choice but to continue.

Rainie could hear Cunningham breathing hard behind her, while Walt cursed fifty yards in front of her. 'Goddammit, Bradley,' the volunteer EMT was muttering. 'Don't you cut out on me now. Hell, man, we got poker on Friday.'

Rainie and Cunningham quietly came up behind Walt and took

inventory. Custodian Bradley Brown lay at a main intersection of two wide hallways. From this vantage point, Rainie could see nearly a dozen class-room doors to the left. They were all shut, which immediately made the hairs on the back of her neck prickle to life.

She glanced at Chuckie, but the rookie was looking to the right, where the hallway led to two glass side doors, shattered and streaked with a dark substance that was probably blood. More lockers dented here, a great deal more damage. The primary area of incidence.

A body lay not far from the doors. Long dark hair, a flowing summer dress. Probably a teacher. Closer in, Rainie saw two more shapes. Smaller, motionless. Not adults.

Cunningham made a hiccuping sound.

Rainie turned away.

'Already looked,' Walt said tightly from the floor.

'You shouldn't even be in here.'

'They're kids, Rainie. Just kids. We had to.'

Rainie didn't bother with any more chastising. Walt was a former army medic and an experienced volunteer EMT. He knew the considerations, and what was done was done. She turned her attention to the custodian.

Bradley was an older man, his gray hair bristly, his brown pants and blue chambray shirt well worn. He wore a modest gold watch, the kind you might get as a reward for twenty years of service. And he had been shot high in the chest: blood relentlessly seeped through the white gauze bandages.

'Others?' the janitor whispered.

'Everyone's fine, Bradley,' Walt answered crisply. 'Just gotta worry about your miserable hide. What are you doing, getting yourself shot like that?' Walt slipped an IV needle into Bradley's arm, trying to get fluids into the man as his own drained out.

'You're doing great,' Rainie reassured the janitor, kneeling down beside his head and giving him a smile. 'So what happened here, Bradley?'

'Got . . . shot.'

'No kidding.' She forced a chuckle, as if they were sharing a small story over lunch. 'See who did it?'

'Came . . . around . . . the corner.'

She nodded supportively. Bradley's skin was turning blue. He was going cyanotic. Then would come hypovolemic shock from blood loss, followed by unconsciousness. If the bleeding still didn't stop, he would die. Walt and Emery were working furiously, but bandage after bandage continued to turn red.

'Heard shots . . .' Bradley gasped. 'Wanted . . . to help.'

'You're a brave man, Bradley.'

He grimaced. 'Came around . . . boom. Never . . . saw . . .'

'What hit you?'

'Yeah.' His breath escaped as a hiss. 'Toured in 'Nam. Funny . . . thought it'd be . . . there.'

Bradley's eyes suddenly rolled back in his head. Walt swore sharply.

'Dammit, I need more gauze. Emery.'

Emery held open an empty kit. 'We've hit bottom.'

'Load and go,' Walt directed, reaching for the gurney as Rainie scrambled out of the way.

'Won't do any good,' Emery countered. 'Hospital's too far away.'

'Chopper?' Rainie asked.

'Called it in seven minutes ago. Probably got another five-minute wait.'

'Well, shit,' Cunningham cried from behind Rainie. 'Stop the bleeding, do something for him. He's dying, can't you see?' The rookie looked at them all, then in a burst of movement ripped off the tan shirt he'd bought with pride just two months ago. 'Here, here, use this.'

'We need more,' Walt said. 'To bandage the wound up tight.'

'The janitor's closet,' Rainie exclaimed. 'Right there. It must have something.'

'Sanitary napkins,' Walt declared. 'They work like a charm!'

Chuck was closest. He grabbed the metal doorknob and pulled hard. The door was locked. He pounded it once with an open hand. When that didn't work, he leveled his gun.

'Jesus Christ!' Rainie hurtled herself at his outstretched arm and knocked the Glock .40 from his grasp just before he could fire. Then she turned on him with hard eyes.

'Goddammit. Don't you ever draw down like that! Not at a crime scene where you'd contaminate all the evidence, and not in a building where everyone is scared out of his mind. Half the parents out there would've come running in with their shotguns and blasted you to bits.'

'We gotta get it open!' Chuckie yelled.

'Then throw your shoulder into it! You're not made of glass.'

Chuckie's eyes lit up. He took a running leap at the closet as Rainie stepped to the side and prepared to cover. All those closed-up classrooms. Who took the time to shut a door when they were running for their lives? Who sealed up each room neat and orderly, as if they had all the time in the world? Not schoolchildren, she thought. Not teachers. Which left only one option.

The closet door split open. Cunningham crowed his triumph and plunged into the black depths before Rainie could stop him. Then he froze her heart with a cry.

'Oh my God! There's a kid in here!'

Walt and Emery rushed forward. Rainie pushed them back. 'Let me check it out,' she said tightly. 'Jesus, Walt, you've already used up your nine lives.'

She stepped into the walk-in closet, blinking three times as her eyes adjusted to the gloom. Cunningham was in a corner, leaning over a little girl who had scrunched herself into such a tight ball that Rainie could make out only her golden blond hair. Then the child looked up. Rainie knew her instantly.

'Becky O'Grady! Oh honey, are you all right?'

Rainie motioned for Walt and Emery to enter, then holstered her gun and fell to her knees in front of Shep's youngest child. At first glance, Becky seemed to be fine. Rainie ran her hands down the little girl's arms, searching for any signs of injury. No cuts, no bruises. No signs of powder burns or bullet holes, or God knows what under these circumstances. Then she noticed the glassy look in Becky's bright blue eyes. Carefully, Rainie drew her forward, and the little girl collapsed bonelessly into her arms.

Rainie rushed Becky out of the closet and laid her out on the cool floor. Emery took over.

'Dilated pupils,' he declared. 'Lack of response. Can you tell me your name?'

Becky said nothing.

'Can you hear me?'

She remained silent, but when he snapped his fingers, she turned her head toward the sound.

'Shock,' Emery said after a moment. 'Probably caused by the trauma. She just needs time.'

Rainie hunkered down in front of the child, less convinced and still worried. Becky had a smudge of dirt across her nose, cobwebs in her hair. She was wearing a green Winnie the Pooh T-shirt, with Pooh and Piglet dancing and a caption saying how merry it was to have a friend.

Rainie gently rubbed one of the sooty marks from Becky's cheek. She cupped a hand against the girl's pale face. 'Honey,' she said quietly. 'How did you end up in the closet?'

Becky just looked at her.

'Were you hiding?'

Slowly, the girl nodded.

'Becky, do you know who you were hiding from?'

Becky's bottom lip began to tremble.

'Was it someone you knew?'

Becky looked down.

'It's okay, Becky. It's all over now. You're safe.' Rainie glanced at all the closed classroom doors. 'No one can hurt you anymore. I just need to know who did this so I can do my job. Can you help me do my job, Becky?'

Becky O'Grady shook her head.

'Just think about it, honey. Just think.'

Minute passed into minute. The little girl remained silent, and finally she turned away from Rainie and rolled back into a ball. Frustrated, Rainie rose to her feet. Walt and Emery had loaded Bradley onto the stretcher. Chuck's shirt held a thick pile of sanitary napkins to the man's chest. Bradley's skin was still pale blue, but he seemed to be breathing more easily. Score one for the good guys.

Rainie looked around. The closed door was splintered. Walt had tossed half its contents into the hallway in his quest for sanitary napkins. He and Emery had tracked bloody footprints everywhere. The hall doors remained ominously shut, and Becky O'Grady was curled into the fetal position at Rainie's feet.

Then farther down the hall. The fallen teacher. The two smaller forms . . .

Jesus Christ, what had happened at Bakersville K-8?

Rainie pulled Chuckie aside and spoke quietly. 'We need to get Becky out of here. Why don't you carry her outside and see if you can find Sandy? By now the other officers should be arriving. Have them set up a perimeter around the grounds. You tell them for me: Nobody gets inside the perimeter, and that includes the press, the mayor, and the richest parent in town. Then tell Luke he's in charge of the crime-scene log.'

'Press will be here soon,' Chuckie muttered, his face already scrunching with distaste.

'We'll let Shep deal with them.'

'Okay.' He was looking around the hallway now, the quiet, still hallway, with the shattered doors at the end. 'Rainie? Why are all the classroom doors closed? I thought the counselor guy said they evacuated like a fire drill. Seems like none of the kids would close the doors or turn out the lights when they were running from the building. So who'd do such a thing?'

'I don't think it was the kids or the teachers.'

'The man in black?'

'Would you take the time to close each door as you were fleeing from your crime?'

Chuckie's brow furrowed. 'Probably not, but who does that leave?'

Rainie smiled at him wryly. 'I don't know, Cunningham, but I guess I'm about to find out.'

3

Sandy O'Grady took the S-corners of the residential street at forty-five miles per hour. The tires of her loyal Oldsmobile squealed their protest, but she didn't notice. Her hands were tight on the wheel. Her blue eyes were locked forward.

All around her, people were running. Sprinting out of their houses, charging down the neat little sidewalks, their faces white with shock, their mouths already yelling the grim news to their neighbors. They carried first-aid kits and blankets, towels and water bottles and anything else they thought might be of use.

Sandy screeched around the next corner, hit a speed bump hard, and finally had to brake. Just as well. Two blocks from the school the street was clogged with hastily parked automobiles and frantic parents. Sandy drove halfway up the sidewalk, slammed her Olds into park, and joined the fray.

So much noise. Walt's old ambulance braying. Children crying *Mommy, Daddy*, parents screaming children's names. She heard police sirens and revving engines. She heard a sharp, loud keening, as if the soul had been ripped from a mother's heart, and her own blood went cold.

This couldn't be happening. Not in Bakersville. Not in her children's school. Oh God, couldn't someone make this all go away?

She waded through the sea of people and cars. She didn't know where to go. She just kept slogging toward the school, trying to get closer. Where were her children? Where was her husband? Wouldn't someone tell her what to do?

Up ahead, she saw a police officer in a Cabot County uniform. He seemed to be simultaneously ushering people away from the school building and asking who was in charge. No one had an answer for him. Parents just wanted to find their children.

Sandy finally arrived at the chain-link fence that surrounded the schoolyard. She pressed herself against it, peering into the parking lot, where she could now see children stretched out on the blacktop, some holding cold compresses to their heads, others lifting scraped elbows and knees to be bandaged. Five adults were manning the makeshift first-aid station, using emergency kits and towels as fast as other people handed them in. Sandy

570

recognized Susan Miller, Johnny's mom and a nurse at Cabot Hospital. She saw Rachel Green, the head of the PTA and a stay-at-home mom, wrapping an eight-year-old's wrist. She saw Dan Jensen, the town vet, hunched over a boy whose jeans were caked with blood. Sandy could just make out the hole ripped through the tough fabric. The boy had been shot in the leg.

God, a bullet wound. The shooting was real. Everything was real. Someone had opened fire in Bakersville's school.

Sandy thought she was going to be sick.

Vice Principal Mary Johnson raced by. Sandy snagged her arm.

'Mary, Mary. What happened? How is everyone? Have you seen Becky or Danny?'

Mary looked frazzled, her normally neat hair in frizzy disarray, her faced covered with a sheen of sweat. Her expression was blank for a moment; then she recognized Sandy and clasped her hand.

'Oh Sandy, I am so sorry. We're doing everything we can.'

'Has something happened to my children? Where are Danny and Becky? *Where are my kids?*'

'Shh, it's all right. I'm sure it's all right. I have to ask you to step away from the school. All the children were led across the street with their teachers. We put them in each yard in order of grade. So Becky's class is in the fourth yard down. Danny's would be four yards down from there.'

'You've seen them? They're okay?'

Mary Johnson hesitated. Something flickered in her gaze. Sandy felt her breath catch in her throat again.

'I don't know,' Mary said. 'There have been so many children—'

'You haven't seen them.'

'We evacuated most of the children from the school. It's just taking us a bit to get it all sorted out.'

'Oh my God, you haven't seen my children.'

'Please, Sandy—'

'Are there fatalities? Just tell me. *Are there fatalities?*'

Mary Johnson tightened her grip on Sandy's hand. Then Sandy saw it all in her somber gaze, the news the vice principal didn't want to say out loud, the news they would all be struggling with for the next few days, months, years: Children had been shot and killed.

It really was happening here.

Sandy couldn't breathe, couldn't think. She wanted to turn back the clock six hours, when she had been at home, pouring bowls of Cheerios for her children before kissing them on the head. She wanted to turn back the clock to ten hours before that, when she had been tucking their wiggling forms into bed and reading stories of little boy wizards and magical spells. That was what their lives were supposed to be like. They were just children, for God's sake. Just children.

A shout rose up from the crowd. Sandy and Mary turned toward the school doors just in time to see Walt and Emery come racing out with a stretcher.

'Move, move, move,' Walt was shouting.

The Cabot County officer yelled at people to clear the street. A car was in the way. No one seemed to know who owned it. The officer opened the door and popped the car into neutral. Two young men ran over to help push the vehicle out of the way. People cheered the small victory. Walt was already firing the ambulance to life.

Then Sandy saw Chuckie Cunningham running across the parking lot with a towheaded little girl wrapped tight in his arms.

Becky.

Sandy leapt forward before Mary Johnson could stop her. She raced across the parking lot and opened her arms just as Becky saw her and cried, 'Mommy!'

And then her little girl was in her arms. Sandy was holding her close, inhaling the sweet scent of apple shampoo. She was squeezing her tight, tight, tight, and Becky was holding her neck so hard it hurt.

'My baby, my baby, my baby.'

'Mommy, Mommy, Mommy.'

'My baby.'

She raised tear-filled eyes to Chuckie, who she now realized was half naked and streaked with blood.

'Danny?' she asked hoarsely.

'I don't know, ma'am.'

'Shep?'

'I'm sorry.'

Sandy sank to her knees. She had one child with her, one child safe. But it wasn't enough. The foreboding was grabbing hold of her again. Something cold and dark flowed through her veins. She raised her head pleadingly to the sky.

'Where is my son? Oh God, *where is Danny?*'

Alone in the school, Rainie gripped her Glock .40 with moist palms. Her breath came in shallow gasps. She could feel her heart pounding unnaturally in her chest. She did her best to ignore the sensations as she walked to the far left side of the school – the end farthest from the bodies – and prepared to conduct a methodical search of classrooms she was already sure weren't empty.

She turned her mind to dim memories of lessons learned in police courses taken years ago. Some kind of acronym thing. ACCESS . . . AGILE . . . ADAPT. That was it. ADAPT.

A: Arrest the perpetrator, if still at the scene.

(Was the perpetrator still at the scene? The reports of a man in black. All these closed doors.)

D: Detain and identify witnesses and suspects.

(The herd of students who'd already raced out of the building. Bradley Brown, still fighting for his life. Witnesses maybe, but other people's responsibilities now.)

A: Assess the crime scene.

(The clean halls and untouched front office. The dented lockers farther in, the spent shells on the floor. Don't overlook the obvious, that's what they said in class. What was obvious in a school shooting? The dead on the floor?)

P: Protect the scene.

(Rainie winced. The EMTs, the battered closet, the shells Cunningham had kicked across the floor. The parents who'd taken over the parking lot. The state Crime Scene Unit was going to arrive, and her career would be over.)

T: Take notes.

(Rainie stared at her gun. She thought of the spiral notepad in her breast pocket. She wondered how she was supposed to hold that and the gun.)

Forget taking notes. She had to focus on step one, arresting the perpetrator if possible. God knew what it meant that she was doing things out of order. At least she was doing them and trying the best she could.

Her mind moved forward. She was searching a particularly large and complex crime scene for a suspect. She had a vague recollection of a lecturer explaining how to work a grid at a large site. Start in, spiral out, slowly expanding the area searched. She couldn't remember much more beyond the theory and decided she would have to approach this scene as a horizontal strip. She would work left to right. Quiet, calm, prepared.

Rainie put her back to the wall, tucked her chin against her chest to make herself a smaller target, and led with her gun.

Stay calm, stay professional. Do your job.

The first room was the hardest. The top half of the closed door was glass but decorated with so many cutout pictures of bunnies and tulips that she couldn't see inside. The lights were off as well, as in all the rooms in the school.

Rainie slowly twisted the doorknob with her left hand. From the crouch position, she pushed the door open into the room. Shadows, long and gray, in the back of the room. Sunshine, bright and fierce, in the front. She rolled across the threshold and came up with her Glock held in the two-handed Weaver stance. Right. Left. Front. Back. Nothing.

Rainie finally rose to her feet in the empty room. She turned on the lights and propped the door wide open to keep the premises exposed. And then she prepared for the next room.

Bit by bit she worked her way down the hall. Then she was at the intersection, where bloody gauze still covered the floor and the dents on the bright blue lockers grew worse. She saw more blood splatters. A big dent on a bottom locker, where a body must have careened into it hard. Casings scattered across the white-tiled floor as if someone had flung a handful down the hall.

She could picture things now. The loud crack of gunshots, followed by the panicked screams of schoolchildren. Little girls and little boys streaming from classrooms as the fire alarm sounded; teachers begging them in shaking voices to remain calm. The chaos of bodies running for the front doors, pushing, shoving, tripping, falling. Blood in the halls.

She took a deep breath, forced her pulse to slow.

Stay professional, Rainie. Do your job.

She checked out the fifth-grade classroom, then the sixth. Next the library, big and sweeping with endless rows of books. Nothing.

Finally she was at the end of the hall, where shattered glass was strewn across the floor from the broken doors, where three bodies lay quiet and still.

Rainie didn't want to look at the victims, especially not the children. She understood that the sight would hurt her, scar her someplace deep, where even tough guys like her were vulnerable. She knew it would make her think of other times, too, after she had worked years to forget those scenes.

But this was bigger than her. It had needs that had nothing to do with her own. It was about the rights of the victims and the needs of the parents outside, though she knew that from here on out nothing anyone did for three sets of parents would ever be enough.

The first victim, a little girl, lay on her side. Rainie felt for a pulse, though Walt had already warned her and blood stained the entire front of the girl's shirt. Rainie swallowed hard and moved on, trying not to disturb the scene.

The second victim was also female. Looked approximately eight years old. She had also received multiple bullet wounds to the chest. She was lying just ahead of the first victim. Their arms stretched out toward each other, their fingers nearly touching. Had they been holding hands walking down the hall? Best friends giggling together? Rainie wanted to brush back the little girl's hair. She wanted to whisper to her that it would be all right.

Her vision blurred, tears burned hot in her eyes. She couldn't afford that.

Be professional. Move on.

She noted positioning. She noted victimology. She crossed to the third body.

Lying just outside the computer-lab door, this victim, also female, appeared to be a teacher. Three female fatalities – coincidence or plan? She had long dark hair and exotic features. She was also young, her smooth skin making her appear as if she were simply sleeping. Then Rainie noticed the small, neat bullet hole in her forehead.

Small-caliber weapon, Rainie thought. Probably a .22. Christ, the teacher didn't look a day older than herself. Late twenties maybe. Early thirties. No wedding band, but beautiful enough that you had to think some man would be sitting alone tonight, holding her picture with shaking hands while trying to forget the future that would never be. Christ.

Rainie had to take another deep breath. Only three more doors. All near the epicenter of violence. All dark and waiting. Time to get on with it.

Rainie backed up against the wall and sat in a crouch until her hands stopped shaking.

Only the teacher had a head wound, she thought. A single-entry shot, dead center, delivered with a great deal of precision. The two girls sported a multitude of wounds, high, low, left, right, as if they had walked into a firestorm. But the teacher . . . the teacher was different. Perhaps the intended target? Shooter went for her first, then encountered the two girls walking down the hall?

Or maybe he started with the girls in the hall, and upon hearing the noise the computer-lab teacher opened her door. She would've been right in front of the killer. Had he gotten up his courage by then? Decided it wasn't that different from a video game? Figured why waste bullets if he could do it with a single shot?

Either scenario bothered Rainie. For the little girls to have so many wounds and the adult victim only one. There was something to that. She just didn't have the time to think about it now.

Suddenly, she heard a noise. The faint screech of a metal chair slowly being pulled across the floor.

Rainie scrambled across the hallway. She threw herself against the wall next to the classroom door just as the metal handle turned and the door eased open.

'Don't do this,' a man said. 'We can still fix everything. I swear to you, son, there's nothing that happened today that we can't handle.'

Shep O'Grady came into view, tan uniform stretched tight over his burly frame. His buzz-cut hair glistened with moisture, while his bulldog features were unnaturally pale. From her angle, Rainie could see that he'd managed to unsnap his holster, but he'd never had time to draw his weapon. Now his hands were held in front of him in a gesture of submission. He worked frantically to plead his case.

'I'm sure it's all a big mistake. A misunderstanding. These things happen. Now we gotta work together, clear things up. You know there's nothing I wouldn't do for you.'

Shep took another step back, his hands still up, his gaze focused ahead. Being forced into retreat? Rainie didn't know. Then she glanced fifteen feet behind Shep, where the three bodies lay. Shep was being herded into the scene of carnage, she realized. And when he got there . . .

It was amazing how steady her hands felt, how calm her nerves had become. Shooting was something she'd done all her life. Never in the line of duty, but Shep was her boss, her friend. They went way back, had a history together few could appreciate. Everything felt natural after all.

One last thought: commit to the shot, for hesitation was the number one killer of cops.

Rainie pivoted sharply away from the wall and simultaneously shoved Shep out of the doorway. Her gun went level, her legs braced for recoil, and her fingers found the trigger just as Shep screamed, '*No!*'

And Rainie found herself face-to-face with thirteen-year-old Danny O'Grady, pale as a sheet and bearing two handguns.

4

Oregon state homicide detective Abe Sanders had just sat down to a late lunch, a big Italian sub with double pepperoni and double cheese. His wife would yell at him if she saw him, lecture him about jeopardizing his health and turning her into a cholesterol widow. Most of the time he agreed with her, and at the ripe old age of forty-two, he had the trim waistline to prove it. But not today. Today was just one of those days.

Margaret Collins, an attractive blonde who manned the department phones, came walking by his desk and did a double take. 'Wow, Abe. Next thing we know, you'll be drinking beer.'

'They were out of turkey,' Abe muttered, and unconsciously held his Italian sub closer to him, as if he feared someone would take it away.

'The Hathaway case turned sour, didn't it?' Margaret deduced sagely. She was a true-crime buff and often had better instincts than any of the detectives.

'Damn judge,' Abe said, and took a huge bite of sandwich.

'Inside a drawer isn't plain sight.'

He chewed busily, too polite to talk with his mouth full. After a choking swallow, he declared, 'The drawer was already open.'

'By another homicide cop.'

'Damn cop,' Abe said, and took a bite of cheese.

Margaret laughed. She winked, making him momentarily forget his wife, then sauntered away, leaving him alone with his feast. Abe chewed down another bite, but his heart wasn't really in it. Brown deli mustard had dripped onto his desk. He shook his head and set down the sandwich in favor of a napkin.

Truth was, he always ordered indulgent food when cases went bad, and he rarely ate any of it. He'd fantasize about just what he'd like to order, salivate while in line, and get the largest size possible. Then he'd take it out, think about the calories, the fat content, the cholesterol level, and set it aside. Decadence just wasn't in him. He was a type-A control freak to the core, even when confronted with a loaded Italian sub or a plateful of double-chocolate brownies. He'd even been known to put the lid back on a pint of Ben & Jerry's chocolate-chip cookie-dough ice cream after only one bite.

When Abe Sanders was young, he'd been the Boy Scout with all the merit badges, the student with the good report card, and the track star with the fastest time. He'd read the classics 'just for the hell of it.' He'd gotten the girl every guy had wanted. And he'd bought a four-bedroom ranch in an older, 'nice' section of Portland with an impeccably manicured lawn.

Then he'd finally shocked his family. He'd become a cop.

His parents joked that their neat-freak son had decided to clean up the whole world. His two brothers, one older, one younger, told him he suffered from an overdeveloped hero complex. His chess buddies gravely informed him that the entire accounting community had wept the day he headed for the academy, that spreadsheets would never be the same.

Abe himself never really talked about why he became a cop. Maybe he simply understood better than most that life was messy, even for type-A control freaks. There was his wife, whom he loved and adored and who finally discovered, after five years of trying, that she could never have children. There was the tidy house they'd chosen as their home in the early eighties, only to have gang-bangers and crack addicts move in down the block. There was Abe himself, anal, precise, obsessive-compulsive, learning that his planned path as a CFO simply couldn't hold his attention.

He wanted a sense of accomplishment, a sense of change. Hell, maybe he did just want to make the whole world as orderly as his desktop files.

Didn't matter in the end. Detective Sanders was a damn good cop.

Other detectives rode him hard. They shook their heads at his manicured hands, told jokes about his polished loafers. Tried to drive him nuts by replacing his expensive, personally purchased black stapler with a cheap gray government issue that always jammed. One day they even rotated the tires on his car to see if he'd notice (he did).

Then they worked with him.

Abe Sanders with a case was a man obsessed. Abe Sanders with a case was passion and drive and, for reasons not even he could explain, anger. Pure rage at the injustices of life and the goddamn shit-faced pea-for-brains numbnuts who took away good, honest, hardworking lives.

Maybe other detectives didn't understand the value of a good stapler, but all cops knew rage. It was the common denominator no one ever spoke about and everyone understood.

Abe carefully rewrapped his sandwich, placing it in the middle of the triangle-shaped paper, folding in the corners, and rolling it tight. He dabbed at the mustard on his desk with a wet napkin. Then he threw everything away.

The Hathaway case had burned him. Not that it was really the judge's fault. Snickers had written the search warrant too loosely, so the cops had to improvise. That never worked anymore. Lawyers ran the world, and smart cops had to learn to anticipate the fine print. That was just the way of things.

Abe could count on one hand the number of warrants and arrests he'd had problems with. Being anal was good.

He got up to go wash his hands, and his lieutenant stuck his head out of his office.

'Sanders? Need a word.'

Abe walked in curiously. He sat on the edge of the hard plastic chair in his lieutenant's office. And a moment later he heard about a small town called Bakersville, two hours southwest of Portland, that didn't even have its own homicide force. He sat, quiet and stunned, as his lieutenant described what they believed to be the second school shooting in Oregon in just a matter of years. Already reports of casualties. Crime Scene Unit was on its way, county officers on their way, and state officers rushing in. No word on the shooter yet and, oddly enough, no one could locate the sheriff.

'The call has come down from the governor,' his lieutenant said. 'This case is high profile and, by all accounts, already out of control. The brass wants a good front man, someone with experience, solid organizational skills, and the ability to coordinate city, state, and – most likely – federal resources.'

'Absolutely.'

His lieutenant looked at his neatly tailored gray suit and strong, trim figure. 'Someone who looks good to the media.'

Abe smiled wolfishly. He liked the press. He knew just how much to feed them and then he devoured them alive. It made him happy. 'Absolutely!' he said with more enthusiasm.

'You'd have to be on the road. Probably two to three weeks straight at the beginning, then all the return trips.'

'Not a problem.' It wasn't. Sara hardly noticed his presence these days. He'd finally given in to her pleas and gotten her a ten-week-old puppy. Now she was busy coddling the pup and feeding the pup and chucking it under the chin. One day he was going to come home and find the dog decked out in baby clothes and a bonnet. The damn thing would probably grin and take it, too; so far, the sheltie seemed remarkably even-tempered.

Sometimes Abe found himself petting the creature. The little guy's downy coat was remarkably soft to the touch. Not that he wanted to get that close to anything that had no bladder control, for chrissakes.

'Then you're on the case,' his lieutenant said. 'Tackle it as if you'd gotten there yesterday. And Sanders . . .'

Abe halted at the door.

'The EMTs reported at least two children dead. It's gonna be a tough one, for everyone.'

'Is the shooter a kid?'

'No word on the shooter yet.'

'But most of them are kids.'

'We're assuming that's the case. Play it tight. And quick. That would be best for everyone.'

Abe understood. When kids were harmed, people went a little nuts. Sometimes, cops did too.

Sanders commandeered a car. He phoned ahead for a hotel room, as he always did, grabbed what little information the department had on the still-evolving scenario, and hit the road.

'One measly sheriff and two semi-trained officers,' he muttered as he headed home to pack his bags. 'Kids killing kids, and not even a homicide department to manage the mess. Good thing I'm heading out there, 'cause these yokels have got to be shitting their pants.'

Rainie jerked her finger off the trigger just before she pulled it back.

'Danny,' she gasped.

The boy stood, shell-shocked. His right arm was extended halfway, pointing the .22 somewhere around Rainie's kneecaps in a sure grip. He held a .38 in his left hand, down by his side, and for a moment Rainie wasn't certain where to look.

She kept her weapon trained on him, then Shep took a step toward her.

'Stop!' she yelled to no one, to all of them. Shep was still armed, and though she trusted him as a friend, she couldn't count on his actions as a father. If he thought Danny was threatened or if Danny felt threatened . . .

Rainie could feel the situation spiraling dangerously out of control. She reined in her panic.

'You,' she said to Shep, keeping her gaze on Danny. 'Are you okay?'

'It's a mistake,' Shep said desperately. 'All of this is one big mistake.'

'Fine, but until this mistake is over, keep your hands where I can see them.'

'Rainie—'

'Danny, I want you to listen to me. You must put down your guns. Okay? I want you to move very slowly and place your weapons on the floor.'

Danny didn't move. His gaze swung wildly from side to side, and Rainie could nearly smell the panic roiling off his skin. He was dressed in black jeans, a black T-shirt, and white running shoes. She couldn't see any more weapons on him, but it was hard to be sure. He came from a house loaded with firearms, and she knew Shep had taken him hunting from the time he could walk.

'Danny,' she said in a more commanding voice. 'I'm going to count to three, and then you are going to place your weapons on the floor.'

'Rainie—'

'Shut up, Shep. Danny, are you with me?'

'He didn't do anything!'

'*Shut up*, goddammit, or I'm going to make you flatten out on the floor too!'

Shep shut up, but it was already too late. Danny's expression had grown wilder, and his right hand was beginning to tremble. Rainie shifted her stance for better balance. She slid her finger back on the trigger, just in case.

'Danny,' she said more loudly. 'Danny, are you listening to me?'

The boy turned his head slightly toward her.

'This is pretty intense, isn't it, Danny?'

He nodded shortly, both his hands shaking now.

'I think you'd like this to end, Danny. I know I'd like it to end. So I'm going to tell you what we're going to do. I'm going to count to three. You are going to slowly lower your weapons to the floor. Then, when I tell you to, you're going to kick the guns over to my feet. Then you simply lie down with your hands and feet spread. That's it. Everything will be over, Danny. Everything will be all right.'

Danny didn't say anything. His gaze flickered past her, to where the two girls were sprawled with their hands still outstretched toward each other. He seemed to notice the teacher as well, and a deep tremor snaked through his thin frame.

Christ, he was going to go. Shoot himself or suicide by cop. Rainie didn't know which, but the end would all be the same. Dead bodies. Dead kids. Jesus, no.

'Danny,' Rainie said desperately.

It was too late. His right arm lifted.

'No!' Shep sounded wild.

'Don't do it, Danny!' She had no choice, her finger pulling back on the trigger.

And Danny turned his gun toward his head.

'*Goddamn!*' Shep hurtled toward his son. Rainie jerked her gun up and blasted her shot into the ceiling, just as Shep sent himself and his boy tumbling to the ground. Danny's handguns disappeared from view, trapped between two bodies. Then one came sliding out from between them. Rainie kicked it away and looked in time to see Shep grab the .22 in Danny's right hand. He squeezed hard. His son cried out. Shep jerked the weapon free and flung it down the hall.

That quickly, it was over. Danny collapsed on the floor, the fight gone out of him, as his father sat up. The burly sheriff was breathing hard and tears streamed down his cheeks.

'Goddamn,' Shep gasped. 'Goddamn, goddamn. Ah, Danny . . .'

Belatedly, he tried to pull his son into his embrace. Danny pushed him away.

Shep's head fell forward. His big shoulders continued to shake.

Quietly, Rainie took control. She rolled Danny onto his stomach eight feet from where three people would never move again. She spread his arms

LISA GARDNER

and legs and patted him down. Finding no additional weapons, she curved his arms behind his back and handcuffed his wrists.

'Daniel O'Grady,' she said as she hauled him to his feet, 'you are under arrest. You have the right to remain silent. Anything you say can and will be used against you in a court of law—'

'Don't say a word,' Shep ordered roughly. 'You hear me, son? Don't say a thing!'

'Shut up, Shep. You can't invoke silence for your child, and you know it. Do you understand these rights as I've said them to you, Danny? Do you understand that you're under arrest for what you did here at school?'

'Don't say a word, Danny! Don't say a word!'

'Shep,' Rainie warned again, but it didn't matter.

Danny O'Grady didn't even look at his father. He stood with his shoulders hunched, his oversize black Nike T-shirt too big on him, his features haggard. He said finally, 'Yes, ma'am.'

'Did you do this, Danny?' Her voice softened. Rainie heard her own confusion, her need for reassurance. She'd known this boy most of his life. Good kid. Used to wear her deputy's badge. *Good kid.* She said more firmly, 'Did you shoot these people, Daniel? Did you hurt these little girls?'

And he answered, in a faraway voice, 'Yes, ma'am. I think I did.'

5

Rainie and Shep remained silent, each trying to process what they had just heard. Shep didn't argue with Danny's statement, didn't try to say it was a misunderstanding, didn't try to remind her that Danny was just a kid. He appeared too overwhelmed.

Rainie herself couldn't think of anything more to say. She was a cop; she had heard a rough confession. Her duty was clear.

Rainie led her handcuffed murder suspect to the front doors of the school, where a dozen flashbulbs promptly went off in her face. The media had arrived. Shit.

She backpedaled furiously, yanking Danny away from the glare of hot lights and frenzy of shouted questions. He looked at her in dazed confusion, meekly submitting to her will. She wished he wouldn't look at her like that.

'You can't be seen walking out with us,' she told Shep after a minute, the three of them pressed against the hall walls like fugitives.

'I'm not leaving you alone with him.'

'You don't have any say in the matter. I can interrogate him without you, and I can sure as hell stick him in jail without you, and you know it.'

Shep absorbed this with a scowl. Oregon law didn't give much special consideration to juvenile murder suspects. As long as Danny was at least twelve years of age, he could be held criminally liable for his actions and would be eligible for waiver to adult jurisdiction. His rights were the same as those of any person under arrest, and his parents had no say in things. The best Shep and Sandy could do was hire a good lawyer for their son. And be happy that he wasn't fifteen years old, in which case he'd fall under Measure II and automatically be tried as an adult. And be happier still that Oregon didn't have so-called CAP laws, which would hold Shep or Sandy criminally responsible for allowing guns to fall into Danny's hands.

'What do you want to do?' Shep asked.

'Take off your shirt.'

Shep glanced at his son, followed her train of thought, and unbuttoned his sheriff's uniform. Underneath it was a plain white T-shirt, worn in places and bleached white by Sandy every Sunday when she did the laundry. The sight of him in just his undershirt made him look all too human and tore at Rainie's emotions a little more. She resented that.

Shep carefully draped his shirt over his son's head, as if his boy were made of glass and Shep couldn't bear to break him.

'It will be all right,' he whispered. He looked at Rainie again, humbled and waiting for her next command.

'Go find Luke,' she said, her voice coming out unsteady. She jerked her head toward the east exit. 'Have him bring the patrol car around to the side.'

'I want to ride with Danny.'

'No. Luke's going to find a state guy, someone we don't know, and he's going to interview you. Don't look at me like that, Shep. You know it has to be done. You and Danny have been alone together. He's your son. . . . We have to know what he said to you. What he did. Why you entered a crime scene alone, and' – she smiled thinly – 'why you appointed your second-in-command the primary officer the minute you got the call.'

She met Shep's gaze and, for the first time, saw him flush. 'You didn't think I'd picked up on that, did you? Or were you hoping I'd let it go?'

He didn't say anything.

'Did you know, Shep? Did you hear the news and already know?'

'It wasn't like that.'

'I don't even believe you and I'm your friend. Dammit.' Rainie was suddenly fed up. She *was* the primary. She had hours of work ahead of her, processing a thirteen-year-old boy, testing his hands for gunpowder residue, demanding to know why he'd shot up his school. Then she'd return to the crime scene, wade through it again and again in order to get into a mass murderer's head. Finally, worst of all – tomorrow morning, most likely, or evening at best – she would personally attend the autopsies of two little girls who'd died holding hands. She would have to listen to the inventory of the trauma to their bodies. She would have to imagine once again what their last moments had been like. Then she would have to contemplate that another child, one she'd known personally, one she'd been proud of, had done that to them.

'Get out of here,' she told Shep. 'Find Luke and get this show on the road.'

'I need to find Sandy first,' Shep said stubbornly. 'We have a friend . . . a lawyer. She can give him a call.'

'Get out of here!'

Shep finally relented. He gave his son one last glance. It looked like he wanted to say something more but couldn't find the words.

The sheriff turned and walked out the front doors. Flashbulbs flashed. A roar rose up from the crowd at the sign of fresh activity. Then Rainie caught a new sound – the faint beating of helicopters bearing down upon them. The medevac choppers had finally arrived to carry the wounded away.

And Rainie couldn't help thinking that it would be much later before the ME's office came for the bodies.

Officer Luke Hayes was thirty-six years old, balding, and shorter than most women. His trim build, however, was a compact one hundred fifty pounds that turned many ladies' heads and became useful in a fight. In Rainie's opinion, however, Luke's biggest asset was his steely blue eyes. She'd seen him stare down drunks twice his size. She'd seen him hypnotize enraged housewives into lowering their favorite knives. Once she'd even watched him reduce a growling Doberman to a groveling mass with a single, relentless look.

Shep was smoke and steam. Rainie got restless and moody. Luke balanced out their tiny department with his steady presence and slow, curving smile.

Rainie had never seen him ragged. Until today.

Leading Danny to the east-side exit – the one opposite the area of incidence – Rainie caught up with Luke just outside the door. His head was covered in sweat and he'd soaked his uniform through. For the last fifty minutes, he'd been trying to keep panicked mothers from rushing the school building, while collecting names and witness statements, and the strain showed on his face.

'Are you okay?' he asked Rainie immediately.

'Good enough.'

His gaze flickered to Danny, and his strong shoulders slumped. Rainie understood his thoughts. Luke and Rainie playing with five-year-old Danny in the one-room sheriff's department while Shep took care of something or other. Let's play cops and robbers. *Rat-a-tat-tat.* Or maybe cowboys and Indians. *Bang-bang-bang.*

'You know why big cities have so many problems, Rainie? 'Cause they can't do anything like this. Can't bring their kids to the office. Don't have others helping them out. No wonder our jobs are so slow in Bakersville. We're too busy taking care of our own to have time for trouble.'

'We need to get going,' Rainie said softly.

Luke sighed, nodded slowly, and squared his shoulders. He was ready.

Luke took up the post on the right side of Danny's hunched form. He looped his hand through the boy's bound arm. Rainie did the same on the left. On the count of three, herding Danny between them, they ran the gauntlet to the waiting patrol car.

Compared to the relative quiet inside the school, the sounds and sensations of the outside yard hit Rainie as a one-two punch. Reporters yelling questions as they spotted two cops hustling a cloaked person out of the school. EMTs shouting orders as they frantically loaded up the next injured student. Children crying, crying, crying in their parents' arms. A mother, alone on her knees on the ground, weeping hopelessly.

Rainie and Luke kept their attention focused ahead as other officers rushed to assist them.

'Move, move, move,' someone was yelling. Rainie thought that was stupid. They were all moving as fast as they could.

'Clear out, clear out. Come on, people, back off!'

The reporters were closing in, photographers fighting maniacally for the front-page shot.

Rainie heard a new scream and made the mistake of turning her head. Shep had found his wife. She was holding Becky tight against her chest and turning toward the running police line.

'No,' Sandy cried, took a step, and was caught from behind by her husband. 'No, no, nooooo!'

A muffled sound emerged from beneath the shirt. Danny had heard his mother and started to cry.

Finally, they arrived at the patrol car. Rainie hastily stuffed Danny in the back, the shirt still wrapped around his head. The reporters were shamelessly trying to jostle in, but the officers forced them back.

Rainie rounded the driver's side. Luke jumped into the passenger's seat. With two slams of the car doors, they shut out the chaos and were alone with their murder suspect. Shep's shirt had slipped down. Danny didn't seem to care, and it was too late to fix it now.

Luke turned on the sirens. Rainie pulled away from the curb.

A moment later they hit a wall of people clogging the street. Rainie prompted them with the horn and they reluctantly parted, all craning their necks to peer at the suspect in the back of the car. A few people looked stunned and saddened.

Others already appeared murderous.

'Damn,' Luke murmured.

Rainie stared in the rearview mirror at her young charge. Danny O'Grady, suspected murderer of three, had just fallen asleep.

6

Rainie worked another six hours.

Together, she and Luke formally processed Daniel O'Grady for aggravated murder. They took his fingerprints and photograph. They tested his hands for gunpowder residue (GSR) and had him exchange his clothes for an orange corrections-department jumpsuit that was twice his size. Later his clothing would be tested at the state crime lab for gunpowder, hair, fiber, and bodily fluids – anything that would further tie him to the crime.

With the Cabot County DA present, they conducted a ten-minute interview before a lawyer, Avery Johnson, showed up and coldly put a halt to further questions.

He berated them for interrogating a child, informed Rainie that his client was obviously not in a stable frame of mind, and demanded that Danny be immediately moved to the county's juvenile facilities, where he could be examined by a medical doctor and treated for shock.

During this whole exchange, Danny sat listlessly and appeared to be a million miles away from the sheriff's office where he had once played after school.

Luke and Cabot County DA Charles Rodriguez made arrangements to drive Danny the forty-five minutes to the juvie facilities. Rainie had to return to the school grounds, where the CSU had finally arrived and some state homicide detective named Abe Sanders was ordering everyone about as if he owned the place.

She exchanged one last batch of nasty stares with Avery Johnson. He told her she would be hearing more from him. She told him she could hardly wait. He told her this was a travesty of justice. She just stared at him harder, because she knew what her next line was supposed to be and her heart wasn't in it.

She sent the lawyer on his way and, with Danny in Luke's custody, headed back to the scene of the crime.

For the next five hours, Rainie walked the scene with the technicians from the state CSU. She reviewed with them what she knew of the EMTs' intrusion on the scene, as well as her own activities, which had left gunpowder residue and ceiling plaster in the key incidence area. The technicians were not amused. They took her Glock .40 to compare GSR found on it with GSR found at the scene. Then Rainie helped collect more than fifty-five spent cartridges from a shooting that had left three dead, six injured, and an entire town devastated.

Police officers recovered four empty magazines for the .22 and three speed loaders for the .38 revolver. None of the cops liked finding the rapid loaders – they were a tool designed to make a police officer's life easier, and it reminded them that this crime hit close to home.

At eight P.M., Rainie held an impromptu briefing out in the playground. She introduced herself as the primary officer and related her experience capturing Danny O'Grady in the afternoon. She thanked the various state and county officers who'd responded to the call and stayed for hours after their shifts had ended to assist with the case.

Then Detective Sanders, the state liaison, took over, discussing the theory of the crime, which they were developing as they processed the scene.

It appeared to be a blitzkrieg style of attack, he said, occurring shortly after one P.M., when the students had returned to class. According to the third-grade teacher, the two girls, Alice and Sally, had asked for a bathroom pass. Shortly after they stepped into the hall, everyone heard the first sounds of gunfire.

It was unclear whether they had been the first victims or if that had been the computer-science teacher, Melissa Avalon. She had been alone in the computer lab, so no one knew if she stepped out after hearing the shots or if she was shot first, then the girls. It was doubtful the medical examiner could shed any light on things, as time of death wasn't an exact science. What they were working on now was figuring out the exact path the shooter had walked and the trajectory of the shots so they could extrapolate a logical sequence of events.

No material witnesses? Rainie asked.

None, the other officers agreed. Most students registered the sound of gunshots, then started running toward the exits with no clear idea where the shots were being fired. Six students reported seeing a man in black, but these were the younger children and none of them could be more specific. Where had this man come from? Where had he gone? How tall? How short? Fat, thin? Asked to be more exact, the kids quickly grew confused.

Two officers had followed up at the houses immediately around the school grounds. Those neighbors hadn't spotted any strange man cutting across their yards.

'Ergo,' Sanders concluded, 'this man-in-black thing is a dead end. Probably just the boogeyman, conjured up in traumatized minds. It happens.'

'Wait a minute,' Rainie said. Sanders shot her an annoyed glance. She could already tell he was assuming control of the case. He was the state guy with a pretty suit and a bigger police shield than hers. He obviously had no use for small-town cops or small-town theories. The big-city guys never did.

'There's still the issue that six children reported seeing a strange man,' she said firmly. 'That must mean something.'

'That hysteria is contagious,' Sanders said.

'Or that they saw something out of place, *someone* out of place. Look at the shootings. You're saying it's a blitzkrieg attack. Most victims are sprayed with bullets and we got holes all over the school to match. But then there's Melissa Avalon. Single shot to the forehead. That's a very precise wound for a random attack.'

'Maybe he had it in for her. Do we know about Danny's relationship with the teacher?'

Officers flipped through their notebooks. No one had followed up on the victim's background yet.

'Look,' Sanders said graciously, obviously deciding that Rainie wasn't a complete idiot, 'the Avalon angle does appear interesting. I'll make note of it. And tomorrow, when we start getting the case team assembled, I'll assign a couple of guys to check it out. Hell, there's still plenty of footwork to do. This is just the stuff off the top of my head.'

'Then off the top of my head, I don't think we should be dismissing anything yet.'

Abe rolled his eyes. 'Yes, ma'am.' Then he muttered, 'Of course, you were the one who arrested the kid.'

Rainie stiffened. She'd had a long day; she didn't need this kind of bullshit. The anger that welled up in her chest was dangerous. It was also out of proportion, not just because Abe Sanders was obviously some kind of putz, but because she'd arrested a kid she knew and, dammit, she liked.

You stupid, selfish little boy, how could you be so cruel?

Abe Sanders was still looking at her, waiting to see if she'd take the bait. If she ranted and raved, she'd look unprofessional and he could feel better about things. Rainie had no intention of giving him that kind of satisfaction.

She said, 'We need to have a conversation tomorrow.'

'Yep.'

'First thing in the morning.'

'Absolutely.'

'Seven-thirty?'

'Seven.'

'Fine. See you then.'

They returned to the CSU technicians still working the school. The building was now ablaze with lights, covered in a swath of yellow crime-scene tape and littered with plastic strips from Polaroid film. In the hallway, sections had been cordoned off to form a grid. The most 'active' areas were handled by men in white space suits with special vacuums to suck up every last particle of dust. In other places, technicians scraped blood off windows into tiny vials or sprayed down walls with Luminol in hopes of bringing more carnage to light. Officers stood by, carefully recording all findings into a crime-scene log that would probably fill three binders by morning.

Rainie walked into a classroom and, with a magnifying glass, resumed combing the walls.

She didn't leave for another two hours, and then the feel of the pine-scented air against her cheeks was shocking, and the stars appeared almost too white in the clear night sky.

She needed to do at least two reams of paperwork. The DA wanted to file charges by noon tomorrow and would need the first wave of police reports. Rodriguez would be taking an aggressive stance. Five counts of aggravated murder for three deaths. A crime so heinous, Daniel O'Grady should be immediately waived to adult court to stand trial. The thirteen-year-old was a menace to society. He had killed little kids. He had betrayed his community. He had reminded his neighbors that evil could be the person next door. Let's lock him up for the rest of his life.

Never to date, attend a prom, fall in love, get married, have children. To be alive until he was eighty or ninety years old, but never to live.

Rainie didn't go to the office. She drove home, where she could sit on her back deck beneath the clear night sky and listen to the owls hoot. She went home, where she could strip off a uniform that smelled of death and grab a cold beer.

She went home, where, finally free from prying eyes, she rested her forehead against the neck of the cold beer bottle, thought of those two poor little girls, of the schoolteacher, of Danny, of herself fourteen years ago.

Police Officer Lorraine Conner went home and, alone at last, she wept.

Not that far away, a man watched.

He was dressed completely in black and held a pair of high-powered binoculars to his eyes. The binoculars were a recent purchase, made when the need to see her face, her expression, her clear gray eyes, had become too much to bear. Now the view made him giddy. He could see everything on her back deck, every nuance of her slender body, backlit by the moon and topped off by the porch lights. She was *crying*. Crying.

In all the times he watched, he'd never seen such emotion from her.

It excited him.

It was hard to imagine, but all those years ago when Bakersville had first captured his attention, it had had nothing to do with Officer Lorraine Conner. He'd been reading an article on the Internet, 'Small Dairy Community Destroyed by Floods, Promises to Rebuild.' The journalist began with a melodramatic litany of rising river waters, torrential downpours, and thundering mud slides that descended upon a tiny coastal town during one week in February. How neighbor banded with neighbor to drive their cows to higher ground. How the water kept rising, deluging the lower farms, lifting entire houses off their foundations, and still rose, heading up the rolling hills.

Doe-eyed cows, trapped for days in frigid chest-high water, bawling in fear. Entire trailer trucks, bravely trying to reach more cattle, swept off inundated roads. Pinch-faced wives and children, finally retrieved by boats from their huddled last stands on metal barn roofs. Stoic dairymen, shooting their own herds to put the fragile beasts out of their misery.

As the journalist assured all the readers, here was a town that had met the wrath of God.

And then rebuilt. Bake sales, bingo drives. Innovative programs such as Adopt-a-Cow, which encouraged city kids and large corporations to support individual cows with money for food and shelter. Half a dozen operations, built on higher ground and spared the flood, opening their barns, hay-lofts, and milking parlors to their neighbors for as long as they needed. The town was making a comeback.

At the end of the article, the mayor was quoted as saying, 'Of course we're helping each other. This is Bakersville. We're strong here. We care about our town. And we know what's right.'

The man had known then that Bakersville would be next. A perfect little place, with perfect little people extolling their perfect little values. Where everyone loved everyone, and everyone was a friend. He wanted them all dead.

He was a patient man. He understood better than most the importance of planning. Good reconnaissance, his father had always barked. A smart soldier does his homework.

His father was a shit-for-brains asshole. But the man did his homework. He identified his target. He researched. He learned. Politicians, school officials, reporters, major organizations. Sheriff's department. He planned. He had all the time in the world, as far as he was concerned. What was more important was doing things right.

He would show this town the wrath of God. He would show them the wrath of him.

Then Officer Lorraine Conner. The first time he saw her in person, casually walking by during one of his many recon visits, he'd nearly stopped in his tracks. High cheekbones, an uncompromising chin. Bold gray eyes that possessed a hard, direct stare. Not pretty, but striking. Arresting, if you were into puns.

Here was a woman who knew how to get things done. Not a trace of stupidity, which he'd come to expect in small-town cops. Not even a wide girth or beer gut to show how she really spent her Friday nights. She was fit, fighting trim, and supposedly hell on wheels with a rifle.

Then he heard the rumors.

Her mother. Fourteen years ago. The brutal slaying that had never been solved. The woman drank, you know. Used her daughter as a human punching bag. Shameless, the old biddies hissed, their eyes bright as they imagined their own hands connecting with firm, young flesh. Everyone knew Molly Conner would come to no good.

They say the shotgun blast ripped off her whole damn head. Not a trace of flesh left above the neck. Just some headless torso in cheap, four-inch heels, clutching her bottle of Jim Beam. Told you she'd take the booze with her to the grave. Chortle, chortle, chortle.

Young Rainie came home from school and found the mess. Least that's what she told the cops. Came inside to find the body, walked back outside to see a squad car pulling up to the drive. That young deputy – you know, Shep, before he became the sheriff – he was the first at the scene. Reported Rainie had brains dripping down her hair, all over her back. Handcuffed her right away and took her in.

Later they dismissed the charges. Experts claimed the fact the brains were dripping down proved they'd fallen from the ceiling, that she walked in when the scene was still fresh, not that she'd pulled the trigger, which would have caused the gore to blow back onto her body in horizontal streaks. Or some such nonsense.

Let me tell you, no one can get convicted in this damn state. I mean, the girl's covered in fresh guts and somehow that ain't enough? Lawyers. That's the problem. Lawyers.

'Course, Rainie turned out all right in the end. Sure as hell a damn sight better woman than her mom. She's not even that bad a cop.

The man agreed with them there. A few taps on the keyboard and he'd learned quite a bit about Rainie Conner. Had received a bachelor's in psychology from Portland State University. Upon returning to Bakersville, she'd become the first female officer in the sheriff's department. She'd passed her academy courses the first time around. She had a file of excellent reviews. She stayed fit by jogging three to four times a week, and she always read the current issue of the *FBI Law-Enforcement Bulletin* the minute it arrived. She was dedicated, thorough, and, according to various drunken rednecks, she moved fast for a girl.

The man had also learned things about Rainie's intensely private personal life. She did date men (which was subject to some debate within town) but always from an outside community. She didn't go out often, nor did she keep any one man around for long. She never let her dates pick her up or bring her home. Instead, she would meet them at the chosen restaurant, possibly return to their house, and rise and depart long before they even woke up in the morning.

She seemed to have some basic need for sex but never for sharing. That fascinated the man.

She also had another quirk. Every day when she came home from work, she opened a bottle of Bud Light. And every evening before she went to bed, she emptied the full bottle of beer off the back of her deck. An ode to her dead drunken mother, the man figured. Did she picture Molly Conner dead then? Remember the headless torso and gray matter on the ceiling?

It was one of the reasons he'd bought the binoculars. Because sometimes her lips moved as she poured out the booze, and he was beyond general interest now, beyond objective reconnaissance. He desperately, desperately needed to know what she said.

Up yours, Mom?

Fuck you?

The man was enamored with Rainie Conner. She had become his personal hero. And she had added something to his particular venture. She was the police officer destined to find him out, he'd decided. She alone could recognize his genius, his mastery. Finally, ten years later, here was an adversary worthy of his talents.

In the beginning, his plans for Bakersville had been modest. They had changed since then.

Now the man carefully retreated into the cover of low-growing shrubs. He put away his binoculars. He took one last, admiring look at his gun and allowed himself the luxury of remembering how good it had felt . . .

Then he moved on. He still had many more things to do before the long drive back to his hotel.

7

INTERVIEW OF DANIEL JEFFERSON O'GRADY
MAY 15, 2000

This is Officer Lorraine Conner, conducting an interview of Daniel Jefferson O'Grady, who is suspected of murdering three people at the Bakersville kindergarten-through-eight school, on Tuesday, May 15, 2000. Assisting me is Officer Luke Hayes. Also present is District Attorney Charles Rodriguez. O'Grady has been advised of his rights and has refused counsel. The time is 4:47 P.M.

CONNER: Danny, can you tell us what happened today at your school?
Silence.
CONNER: Danny, are you listening? Do you understand my question?
Silence.
CONNER: What day is it today, Danny?
Pause.
O'GRADY: Tuesday.
CONNER: Very good. Is Tuesday a school day?
O'GRADY: Yes.
CONNER: Did you go to school today?
O'GRADY: Yes.
CONNER: When did you go to school, Danny?
O'GRADY: This morning.
CONNER: With your sister? With Becky?
O'GRADY: Yeah. My mom drops us off. Becky doesn't like the bus. It ran over a cat.
CONNER: That's sad. Becky likes animals, doesn't she?
O'GRADY: Yes. She's freaky.
CONNER: Are these the clothes you wore to school today? The black jeans, black T-shirt?
O'GRADY: Yes.
CONNER: Do you wear a lot of black clothes?
O'GRADY: I don't know.
CONNER: Is there a special reason you wore all black today?
Silence.

CONNER: Did you go to class this morning, Danny?

O'GRADY: Yes.

CONNER: You're in seventh grade, aren't you? Who's your teacher?

O'GRADY: Mr Watson.

CONNER: Is he a good teacher? Do you like him?

O'GRADY: He's all right, I guess.

CONNER: What did you study this morning?

O'GRADY: We have English in the morning, then math. Then we were going to have a geography game this afternoon. Map games, the capital cities . . .

CONNER: The game didn't happen this afternoon, did it, Danny?

Silence.

CONNER: Do you bring a backpack to school?

O'GRADY: I have a backpack.

CONNER: What did you have in the backpack today?

Silence.

CONNER: Danny, did you have two guns in your backpack? Did you bring guns to school?

Pause.

O'GRADY: I guess so.

CONNER: Where did you get these guns? Are they yours?

O'GRADY: No. *(pause)* My father's.

CONNER: Did you take them out of a drawer?

O'GRADY: The gun safe.

CONNER: The safe? It wasn't locked?

O'GRADY: The safe was locked. My father always locks the safe.

CONNER: Then how did you get the guns out?

O'GRADY: I'm smart, all right? I'm very smart.

Pause.

CONNER: All right, Danny. You're smart enough to open the safe, get two guns, and bring them to school. Then what were you smart enough to do, Danny?

Silence.

CONNER: Did you fire your guns at school? Did you start shooting in the hallway?

Silence.

CONNER: Danny, I'm trying to help you. But to do that, I need to know what happened this afternoon. Those little girls and that teacher are dead, Danny. Do you understand dead?

Pause.

O'GRADY: My grandma died. We went to the funeral. That's dead.

CONNER: And did your parents cry? Did it make them very sad? As sad as they were today? You saw your father cry, Danny. Do you understand why he was crying?

O'GRADY: Yeah. *(barely audible)* Yeah.

CONNER: What happened this afternoon, Danny? What did you do? Were you just so mad, was that it?

Silence.

O'GRADY: I'm smart.

CONNER: Danny, did you kill those girls? Did you open fire on your classmates?

O'GRADY: I'm smart, I'm smart, I'm smart, I'm smart!

CONNER: *Did you kill those girls, Danny?*

O'GRADY: Yes! Yes, okay? I'm smart!

CONNER: Why, Danny? Why did you do such a thing?

Sound of door bursting open.

JOHNSON: My name is Avery Johnson, and I'm here to represent Daniel O'Grady. This interview is over.

CONNER: Why, Danny, why?

JOHNSON: Don't answer—

CONNER: Tell me why! *Why did you kill those little girls, Danny?*

O'GRADY: I'm scared.

On the Boeing 747, Supervisory Special Agent Pierce Quincy finally took off the headphones and set aside the tape recorder. He'd listened to the interview of America's newest mass murderer three times since taking off in Seattle. Now he took a moment to jot down his thoughts in a notebook he had hastily purchased at Sea-Tac airport. On the outside of the red spiral book he had written: CASE STUDY #12, DANIEL JEFFERSON O'GRADY. BAKERSVILLE, OR.

The stewardess came up, took his empty cup to give him more room, and smiled charmingly. Quincy returned the smile automatically, then broke off eye contact before she would be tempted to start up a conversation. He was still preoccupied with schoolboys and the forces that drove them to kill.

Over the years, Quincy had received many charming smiles from flight attendants. At the age of forty-five, he had dark hair that was graying at the temples, but he was tall, lean muscled, and well dressed. He also carried himself well. He'd been there, done that, knew where he was going, believed in always being polite, and had absolutely no patience for fools. He made his living flying to four different US cities in five days and hunting down the worst predators the human race had to offer. And he had a direct, probing gaze that people found either deeply compelling or completely intimidating.

Especially on business trips, when his briefcase was filled with crime-scene photos of some of the most brutal slayings on earth. After fifteen years in the business, Quincy was prone to shuffling the photos like playing cards, an act that made him both proud of his objectivity and saddened by his callousness.

It had been pure coincidence that Quincy was on the West Coast when Quantico called about the Bakersville shooting. In theory, Quincy was on personal leave from his job of researching killers and teaching homicide-investigation classes at the FBI Academy in Virginia. Last week, however, he'd received word of a strangled prostitute's body found along Interstate 5 in Seattle. Local police were concerned the case might have connections to another string of murders committed in the eighties by the notorious Green River Killer, who was never caught. Quincy had revisited that case last year as part of a project to close out cold-case files. Unfortunately he'd not found any fresh leads. Then the new murder.

The FBI's deputy director had personally given Quincy the news and told him to stay home.

'These are the times when you need to be with your family,' the deputy director had said. 'We understand that. This case is probably unrelated. I don't want you worrying about it.'

Quincy had thanked the man for his concern. Then he had gone to Dulles airport, purchased a ticket to Seattle, and boarded the plane. His youngest daughter was returning to college the next day, his ex-wife had no intention of speaking to him even if he did stay, and as for his daughter Amanda . . . There was nothing Quincy could do anymore for Amanda. What was done was done, and frankly, Quincy needed his work.

Before transferring to a research role with the Behavioral Science Unit five years ago, Supervisory Special Agent Quincy had earned his stripes as one of the Bureau's finest profilers. Each year, he'd taken on roughly one hundred and twenty serial rapists, murderers, and child kidnappers. He'd pursued men with IQs well above genius level and ensnared them in traps of their own making. He'd analyzed crime scenes awash with blood and found the case-breaking clue. He'd saved lives and he'd made mistakes that sometimes cost lives.

He knew how to handle that kind of stress. In fact, his ex-wife, Bethie, routinely claimed he didn't know how to live without it. According to her, his world had become as dark as the murderers he analyzed, and without a brutal slaying to unravel, he simply didn't know what to do with himself.

Quincy didn't care for that image of himself, but neither did he refute it. His line of work did take its toll. He spent so much time enmeshed in cases of extreme violence, it was easy to lose perspective. All county fairs became places where child molesters lay in wait for new victims. All basements housed human remains. All charming, good-looking law students were secretly psychopaths.

Frankly, Quincy would never, ever take a ride in a Volkswagen Bug, the vehicle of choice for many serial killers. He just wouldn't do it.

Nor, he had found, could he watch his daughter die.

In Seattle, the prostitute's murder turned out to be a one-off crime, eventually traced to a trucker passing through the area. Quincy had gone so far as to peruse Homicide's cold-case files, ostensibly to offer fresh perspective but really to delay going home, where he would no longer be Super Agent, capable of capturing even the most vile of villains, but instead Helpless Parent, resigned to waiting by a hospital bed like any other person for the inevitable to occur.

Then a young boy had walked into his Oregon school and opened fire. And Quincy, in a manner of speaking, had been saved.

Like most Americans, Quincy had only peripherally noticed a small but tragic shooting that occurred in November 1995 at Richland High School in Lynnville, Tennessee, leaving two dead and one wounded. The tiny town, population 353, seemed too remote to have any connection with Quincy's life, and the small murder spree seemed an isolated occurrence. But just three months later another shooting occurred: Frontier Junior High, Moses Lake, Washington. Three killed, one wounded, by a fourteen-year-old student. Almost exactly a year later a new shooting, in Bethel, Alaska. Two killed, two wounded, by a sixteen-year-old gunman who had lined up a gallery of friends to watch his rampage. Eight months later sixteen-year-old Luke Woodham murdered three people and wounded seven in Pearl, Mississippi. Two months after that three more students died at Heath High School, in West Paducah, Kentucky. The pattern was clear. Jonesboro, Arkansas; Springfield, Oregon; Littleton, Colorado; Fort Gibson, Oklahoma. Other schools, other tragedies seared into the national consciousness.

Headlines screamed of an epidemic of violence sweeping across America's youth. Video games, some cried. Too many guns, not enough parents. Or maybe it was Hollywood or Capitol Hill or Jerry Springer. But something had to be done to stem the tide. Ban guns, censor cartoons, install metal detectors, enforce dress codes, something.

In the FBI's Behavioral Science Unit, researchers such as Quincy were less certain. Were the shootings a genuine trend or a statistical anomaly? Were these 'normal' children motivated by outside forces such as the media, or did this point to a deeper, developmental issue?

What really drove teenagers to kill, and how could shootings be prevented?

Even at Quantico, the leading criminal experts didn't have ready answers. And that frightened them, for they had children too.

Six months ago Quincy had begun a major research effort to dissect the minds of juvenile mass murderers and identify ways to help them, as well as to prevent future shootings. The goal was to devise a system that would help identify potential mass murderers for school officials and law-enforcement agencies. Also, Quincy hoped to formulate action steps to help parents and teachers deal more effectively with potentially violent teens.

Identifying future shooters, however, was easier said than done.

Unlike serial killers, mass murderers were not a homogeneous bunch.

People went postal because they'd had a bad day, because they were mentally unstable, because someone influenced them, because they were high/drunk/stoned, because they were in love/out of love/confused by love, because they sought glory, because they sought revenge, because they sought death. Mass murderers could be young, old, rich, poor, well educated, poorly educated, well adjusted, or loners. Their attacks could be random or well planned.

In addition, many mass murderers ended their rampages by taking their own lives, making it difficult to get more information. What had brought that person to the breaking point? What had the shooter been thinking during his rampage? Would he repeat his act given the chance, or was it a onetime homicide spree? Most of the time, no one ever knew.

The best experts could do currently was a 'risk assessment' of individuals, a checklist of behaviors statistically found in mass murderers. Mass murderers:

1. had a history of violence, e.g., wife-beating, child abuse, brawls, etc.
2. inspired 'subjective fear' in people. After shootings, there were always a few neighbors or coworkers who had a 'bad feeling' about the person. They avoided the man at work, didn't let their children play with the boy, were sure never to be alone with the guy, etc.
3. exhibited antisocial behavior, either a longer-type personality or someone who deliberately violated societal rules.
4. had poor social skills.
5. liked to make threats, realistic or idle.
6. lacked a support system, e.g., came from a fractured family, had few friends, etc.
7. felt wronged – by life, the corporation, peers, spouse, etc.
8. were under severe situational stress, e.g., recent job loss, impending divorce, death in the family, etc.

Quincy felt that the checklist was not a bad tool. Human resources departments of many major corporations routinely used it to identify potentially dangerous employees. In the wake of school shootings, school counselors across the country had also requested the information for their offices.

Unfortunately, the checklist was proving too vague when applied to youthful offenders. What was 'situational stress' for an eleven-year-old? Getting braces, having a pimple, breaking up? What was a 'history of violence' for a grade-school boy? Throwing rocks, tearing wings off flies, engaging in rough sports?

Add to that the significant number of children who came from broken homes, and that every teenager worth his salt felt deeply and grievously wronged by life, and a statistically improbable number of youths emerged as future homicidal maniacs – hardly an encouraging thought.

Children were simply too hard for adults to understand or predict in the best of circumstances. Their coping skills were limited, they were a bundle of hormones, and they generally believed everything must happen now, today, immediately, with no thought of long-term consequences.

Finally, juveniles were highly motivated by peer pressure, a rare factor in adult homicide. Children were also proving more susceptible to media images and outside influences such as cults and hate groups.

In short, the more Quincy learned, the more he realized how much he had left to learn. This would be a long assignment. Years, he was beginning to think, of spending quality time with kids who killed kids.

He was both intrigued by the task and repelled by it – in other words, his general state of mind.

The fasten-seat-belt light came on. The plane was preparing for descent. Quincy gathered up Danny O'Grady's interview tape and notes. His brow furrowed.

He did not have much information on the case yet, but already there were a number of elements that bothered him. The shooting of the teacher seemed so exact, for one thing. He wanted to know more about her and Danny's relationship. Then there was the timing of the shooting. Why when all the students had gone back into class? That struck him as an attack strategy devised to *limit* the amount of damage, as if the shooter didn't want many people hurt.

Finally, there was the interview. Judging by the tone of the child's voice, Quincy would bet he'd been in a state of shock, not the best time for a thorough interrogation. Plus, while the investigating officer had done a nice job of trying to open the boy up by resorting to simpler questions, she had used too many leading questions. That was always dangerous with children, as they were prone to giving the answer they thought the adult desired, instead of the right answer. Danny's repeated reference to being smart bothered Quincy as well. Something else needed to be asked.

He wondered what the chances were of the boy's lawyer agreeing to an interview. Then he wondered what the chances were of the local police welcoming his assistance with the case.

Supervisory Special Agent Pierce Quincy smiled.

A local police officer welcome a fed with open arms? Hardly. He was already placing bets on which expletive Officer Lorraine Conner would use first.

8

'You little shit. Go behind my back to the DA one more time, and I'll tie you up, take you out into a field, and personally introduce you to Bakersville's home-grown cow pies. Got it?'

'I simply needed some information—'

'You tried to yank my case!'

'Only when it became clear that you weren't qualified to handle it.'

Rainie's eyes bugged open and she nearly foamed at the mouth. She was having a bitch of a morning, which had already included one very terse conversation with Abe Sanders at seven A.M. Apparently that had not gotten the job done, however, because here it was just after eleven and she was going to have to take her scissors and cut him down to size. How dare he ask the DA to remove her as primary officer on the case! How dare he try to claim state jurisdiction of her homicide!

Didn't he know better than to mess with a woman who'd gotten only four hours of sleep?

Rainie moved out from behind the hastily erected desk – actually a piece of plywood laid atop two sawhorses – that had just been placed in the brand-new 'op center' for the Bakersville case team. Sure, the command post was really the attic of the Town Hall, stifling and dusty and hot, but she'd managed to commandeer a coffeepot and a water cooler from the mayor's office. Already, that made these quarters luxurious compared to the twenty-by-twenty headquarters of the sheriff's department.

Rainie had been working her damnedest this morning. Up at four-thirty to burn the knots out of her muscles with a good, hard run, she then typed up the police reports from the night before, met with the mayor about getting more space for her case team, and prepared for her first meeting with Abe. She'd thought they'd made the ground rules perfectly clear at that time. The case would require state and local cooperation. Abe would serve as point man for the state's resources, handling the physical evidence, managing the CSU, and adding his own considerable experience to the investigative efforts. Rainie's department would provide the ground troops – herself, Luke, and three volunteer officers – to conduct interviews and pull records. They knew the people in their town the best and would get more cooperation from the school and parents than state officers would.

Abe was welcome to process the crime scene and commandeer the school computers in search of further evidence. Rainie knew she needed help. But she would not, could not, should not, give up jurisdiction of the case. End of story.

Or so she'd thought at seven this morning.

'You messed up,' Sanders said now, obviously worried she hadn't gotten the message the first time. 'You're inexperienced and it showed.'

'I secured the scene and arrested a murderer. Shame on me.'

'You trampled the scene,' he corrected with a grimace. 'My God, you let in the EMTs. Haven't you ever seen what they do to a place? Why not just invite the fire department and throw a party?'

'I ordered Walt docked. He chose to violate those orders. Something Bradley Brown is still very grateful for.'

'He might have lived anyway.'

'Might have lived? Are you guys paid by the body or what?'

Sanders remained unswayed. 'EMTs ruin scenes, simple fact of life. So do concerned parents running after their children and school bureaucrats to do head counts—'

'We got there as fast as we could. Geography is another simple fact of life, and geography places that school in the middle of a residential area and us fifteen minutes away. Can't stop what we aren't there to manage.'

'Fine, what about once you were there? Discharging your weapon? In the middle of the scene?' He raised a brow.

'An armed murder suspect drew down on me!' Rainie snapped. 'Value a crime scene. Don't plan on dying for it.'

'Oh, now I get it. You were afraid for your life, so you shot up the ceiling. I stand corrected, Officer. That makes perfect sense.'

'You insufferable—'

Rainie fisted her hands at her side. She counted to ten a second time and noticed that another man had just appeared in the doorway, also wearing a sharply pressed suit. God help her, the state men were multiplying.

She forced her fists open and managed in a more reasonable tone of voice, 'As I wrote in my report, Detective – which you have no doubt read, edited, and found fault with the font size – at the last minute the suspect's father threw himself in front of me, forcing me to alter my fire.'

'So you're trigger-happy? That's how you want to go on record?'

'Hey, have you ever pulled your weapon on the job? Have you ever been in the line of fire? What the hell do you know about being trigger-happy?'

Sanders scowled. Apparently, Mr Perfect never had been at the front lines. Look who was the inexperienced one now? Rainie's triumph, however, was short-lived.

'Well,' the state detective said briskly, 'that brings us to all the problems with the arrest.'

'What?'

'First off, the confession. Have you talked to the DA yet about the confession?'

'Hell, I called Rodriguez in to listen to the confession. Everything was by the book.'

'Apparently not everything. O'Grady's lawyer is already seeking to have the confession tossed—'

'You thought he'd ask to have it entered into evidence instead?'

Sanders ignored her sarcasm. 'He claims the boy was in shock at the time and in no state of mind to waive his rights. He also points out that your questions were leading, which is inappropriate when interrogating a minor. He has a score of experts lined up to contend that you put words in Danny's mouth, getting him to say exactly what you wanted to hear.'

'Like I wanted to hear that my boss's son killed three people,' Rainie grumbled, then waved her hand in a dismissive motion. 'Fine. It doesn't matter. We still have the positive GSR results and the two handguns. We can build one helluva case off that.'

Sanders smiled thinly. For the first time, Rainie understood that they really were in trouble.

'Yes. The gunpowder residue found on Danny O'Grady's hands and clothing.' Sanders adopted the demeanor of a thin-lipped defense attorney. 'Is it true, Officer Conner, that you discharged your weapon at the scene?'

'Yes, as I explained—'

'Isn't it true that anytime a gun is fired, it emits gunpowder residue?'

'Sure, but I was hardly standing over Danny—'

'But it would get on your hands, wouldn't it, Officer? And then didn't you pat down the suspect, Danny O'Grady? Didn't you touch his clothes, his arms, his hands as you searched for weapons, as you twisted his arms behind his back for the bracelets? In fact, couldn't all that gunpowder found on his person really have come from *your* hands from discharging *your* weapon?'

Rainie was stunned. Christ, she hadn't thought of that. Everything had happened so fast. First trying hard not to kill Shep or his kid. Then needing to get Danny immediately restrained. What was she supposed to do? Tell a murder suspect to stay there like a good boy while she ran to the lavatory to wash her hands?

'The lab can do more tests,' Rainie mumbled desperately. 'There are different kinds of gunpowder. They could prove what's from my weapon, what's from his.'

'Oh, they're trying to,' Sanders assured her, resuming his normal punching tone. 'We don't know yet if it's possible, however. Looks like Danny was using his father's ammo, and wouldn't you know it, Shep does his ordering for the department and for himself all from the same manufacturer. Tricky, huh?'

Rainie had a headache. She almost rubbed her temples, then realized she couldn't afford to give away that much. Plus, that man was still standing in the doorway, taking everything in with no apparent regard for their privacy. If he was a reporter, she would have to kill him.

'Do we at least have the murder weapons?' she asked Abe, since he was the one in charge of evidence.

'ATF took the weapons for ballistics testing. We don't have results yet.'

'But what else could they be? If all else fails, we've got Danny's prints on the guns. That's something.'

Abe said, 'No prints on the guns.'

'*What?* No way. I *saw* him holding those guns. I made Shep leave the building before me. There is no way the weapons were wiped clean.'

'Not wiped clean – smeared beyond lifting one clean print. Such as what might happen when an experienced police officer pretended to wrestle a handgun from his child's grip.'

'No,' Rainie said.

'Why not? Because Shep is your boss? Because you feel indebted to him?'

'Don't go there. That has no bearing on anything.'

Sanders, however, had no learning curve. 'Everything has bearing. In the hands of a good defense attorney, Conner, the Andy Gibb poster you kissed every night when you were twelve can have relevance. I asked around. You were arrested for murder fourteen years ago, at the tender age of seventeen. Arresting officer, one Shep O'Grady. And the man who worked to have the charges cleared, one Shep O'Grady.'

'Because he realized he made a mistake.'

'Who cares? Fact remains that you work together, you have dinner at his house, and fourteen years ago he helped you out of a bind, then six years after that gave you a job some people still question. You think that won't come up during trial? Shep's got loyalty to Danny; you've got loyalty to him. And you three are alone at the scene. Face it, chain of custody on this case is screwed.'

'Nothing inappropriate happened in that building, Detective. You weren't there. You don't know how things went down.'

Sanders was silent for a moment. Then he said quietly, dangerously, 'No, I don't think *you* know how things went down. Shep made you the primary officer before ever arriving at the scene. Why? When you arrive at the school, Shep's car is there, but for forty-five minutes there's no sign of him. Where's the sheriff? What's he doing?'

'He already stated that Danny was holding him hostage in that classroom.'

'Do you know that? Do any of us really know that? From where I'm sitting, you search this whole school without them ever peeking out their heads. Then, when you're due to enter that classroom anyway, they finally show themselves. Next thing you know, you're front-row center for a little display that magically makes you discharge your weapon – obliterating a key piece of evidence – while giving Shep O'Grady a chance to handle the other two key pieces of evidence. Damn convenient if you ask me.'

Rainie was incredulous. 'You think Shep staged an *armed* confrontation between a police officer and his son on the off chance it would eliminate some of the evidence against Danny?'

'He didn't stage it for *any* officer, Conner. He staged it for you. You've known Danny for eight years. Hell, according to everyone in this town, you and Luke helped raise Danny O'Grady, watching him every afternoon in the office. What were the chances you'd open fire?'

'Shep is a good cop. He wouldn't tamper with evidence.'

'He's a father. Don't kid yourself.'

'I was there, I saw it go down. I know what happened.'

'Yeah, well, Shep's already going all over town claiming there's trouble with the evidence and that he's certain his kid will walk. Who do you think pointed out that you'd discharged your weapon before frisking Danny? Who do you think is claiming the scene is FUBAR? Shep's got his own agenda. You just don't want to see it, and that's why you need to hand over the case. To someone who is perfectly objective. To someone who has experience.'

'To someone who loves looking good in front of a camera.'

Sanders shook his head. He appeared disgusted. 'Conner, I got a ninety percent conviction rate. Hate me if you want to, but show me a little respect. You're the one keeping the case out of ego. I just want to push it ahead to conviction, so everyone can get on with their lives.'

'Then you're an idiot,' Rainie told him flatly. 'You really think locking away a thirteen-year-old kid will make us feel better? Give us a sense of closure? Personally, I'll be driving by that school for the rest of my life, wondering what really happened yesterday afternoon. And all the parents and teachers will be wondering the same thing. What drives a boy to kill? Why did two little girls have to die? Why *didn't* we prevent this from happening?

'More than an arrest, my town needs an explanation, and I'm going to get it for them. Now get out of my office, Detective, and the next time you talk to Rodriguez, pull that stick out of your ass. It's really not helping.'

Rainie returned to her desk and sat down. A moment later she had the satisfaction of hearing Sanders storm away. It didn't improve her mood, however. She was already growing weary of their battles.

And disheartened. Sanders was right: she had fucked up yesterday. She'd done her job earnestly, and that meant nothing in the criminal justice system. She had captured a suspect but destroyed the evidence. Soon she'd only be fit for a job with the LAPD.

And her credibility would come into question. People still whispered. Of course, it was a small town. If people didn't whisper through the long, rainy winters, everyone would lose their minds.

Rainie Conner's tough. Gotta watch out for her. Killed her own mother.

Rainie sighed, then became aware that the man in the navy blue suit was still standing there, watching.

'Can I help you?' she asked sharply.

'Officer Lorraine Conner?'

'I don't know. Who's asking?'

The man smiled, a wry tilt of one corner of his mouth. The gesture crinkled the corners of his eyes and momentarily startled Rainie. Lean hunter's face. Penetrating blue eyes. She did a quick double take before she caught herself. Then she was embarrassed. Whoever the man was, she already wished he'd turn and walk away.

He said, 'I'm Supervisory Special Agent Pierce Quincy of the FBI.'

'Ah shit.'

He smiled dryly again. And it got to her again, even now, when she definitely knew better. She wished for a bottle of beer.

The agent moved into the room and, without waiting for an invitation, took a seat. 'I take it that gentleman is with the state?'

'Mr Perfect is a state homicide detective. God help us all.'

'A ninety percent conviction rate is impressive.'

'So is his spelling ability. You still want to deck him after a five-minute chat.'

'Problems with the case?'

'I screwed it up royally,' she assured him.

'And now you're resting on your laurels?'

'Hardly. I'm planning my next line of attack.'

The corner of the man's lip twitched. Rainie was happy to see that she had amused him, but she still wasn't in the mood for a chat. She sat forward and cut to the chase. 'What do you want, G-man? I'm tired, I have a triple homicide to investigate, and I'm not giving up jurisdiction of my case. Just so you know.'

'I'm here to help—'

'Bullshit.'

'Okay, I'm one more bureaucrat placed on this earth to mess with your mind and question your abilities.'

'Finally, some honesty in law enforcement.'

'I also want to talk to Daniel O'Grady.'

Rainie leaned back. That answer she believed. She just wasn't sure what it meant.

She tilted her chair onto its back legs, absently placing one foot on top of her desk, then crossing her other foot over it. Her legs still ached from running this morning. She stretched out her calves while she gave Supervisory Special Agent Pierce Quincy another appraising stare.

Experienced, she thought, well established in his career. Probably in his forties, graying slightly at the temples. Worked well with his short-cropped hair and distinguished suit. Added to his power. She was willing to bet money Supervisory Special Agent Pierce Quincy consciously did a lot of things to add to his image of power. He didn't need much help, though. It was all in his eyes – that piercing, steady stare. This man had seen some things on the job. He'd taken on a few things more. Nothing overwhelmed him anymore, and for a moment Rainie was envious.

'You a profiler?' she asked, though she already knew the answer.

'I do some profiling. I also teach classes and research various subjects for the Behavioral Science Unit.'

'You study serial killers.'

'Serial killers, rapists, and child molesters,' he said with a straight face, then added, 'It makes for very pleasant dreams.'

'What do you want with Danny? He's a suspected mass murderer. That's different from a serial killer.'

'Very good, Officer. Plus, he's a juvenile mass murderer, which is distinctly different as well. Unfortunately, we don't understand these distinctions, hence my new research assignment.'

Rainie's brows shot up. 'You're researching school shootings?'

'Correct.'

'You're going from town to town, investigating kids murdering other kids?'

'Yes.'

Rainie shook her head; she didn't know whether to be amazed or appalled. 'Traffic accidents I can handle,' she told him. 'Drunken brawls, stabbings, even the occasional domestic incidents. But what went down in that school yesterday . . . How can you focus on something like that full-time? How can you keep from waking up screaming every night?'

'With all due respect, Officer, I have a bit more experience with violent crime than you.'

Rainie grimaced. 'Thank you. Words I haven't already heard twelve times this morning.' She straightened up in the chair and let her feet hit the floor. 'Well, sorry to break it to you, Agent, but I doubt you'll get to speak with Danny. His parents got him a crack defense attorney who's placed him off-limits to all interviews. Despite the fact that Danny has confessed twice and was found holding the murder weapons, he's pleading innocent.'

'Do you think he's guilty?'

'I think I have a case to put together.'

'That's a careful answer.'

She smiled at him wolfishly. 'I may be inexperienced, SupSpAg, but I learn quick.'

'Soup Spag?'

'Supervisory Special Agent, in local law-enforcement terms. We're not big on titles, you know.'

'I see.' Quincy appeared a little dazed. Rainie had a feeling he wasn't sure what to make of her yet, or how to handle her. The thought pleased her. She liked keeping the feds guessing. In the end, it might be the only thing she had to show for her day.

So she supposed she should've known. She'd no sooner started feeling smug than the FBI hunter went on the attack.

He said calmly, 'I don't think Daniel O'Grady shot up his school. And I don't think you're certain of it either, Officer Conner. I think we're both still wondering what really happened yesterday afternoon. And better yet, how we can prove it.'

9

Rainie drove Quincy to the school.

Quincy sat in the passenger's seat, gazing out the window with what he was afraid must be an incredulous stare. He had not been to Oregon in many years and had forgotten its stunning beauty. They drove through rolling verdant pastures liberally sprinkled with black and white Holsteins and topped by red farmhouses with bunches of yellow pansies. He could smell freshly mown grass and the salty tang of ocean air. He could see towering mountains ringing the valley, their summits carpeted in dense Douglas fir.

King-size cab trucks whizzed by, their powerful V-8 engines gunning. People waved to Rainie as they passed, and about half a dozen black Labs lolled their tongues as they panted merrily out the window. Up ahead, everyone slowed for a John Deere tractor that was laboring down the road. No one honked at the aging farmer or yelled at him to pull over. They simply waited and waved politely when they finally had room to pass. In answer, the farmer touched the brim of his faded red baseball hat.

'That's Mike Berry,' Rainie said, as they swung wide around the green tractor, breaking her silence for the first time since they'd gotten into the patrol car. 'He and his brother own the two biggest dairy farms around here. Last year they bought out three family farms that were destroyed by the floods. One belonged to Carl Simmons, who's sixty years old and has no family left. Mike arranged for a living trust, so Carl can stay in his home until the day he dies and never worry about a thing. The Berry brothers are good people.'

'I didn't think there were many places like this left,' Quincy said honestly.

Rainie turned to look at him. 'There aren't.'

She went back to driving. Quincy didn't bother her again. He could tell that her mood had turned pensive, and in truth he was growing troubled himself. For all his talk of objectivity and professionalism, it was difficult to look at such beautiful countryside and contemplate the savagery that had gone on in the grade school. So far, few things in Bakersville were as he'd anticipated.

That included Officer Conner. All PC platitudes aside, most female cops he'd known were broad-shouldered, thick-waisted, and, frankly, butch. He would not use those terms to describe Officer Conner. Her five-foot-six figure appeared fit and pleasantly curved. Her long chestnut hair, worn unapologetically loose, framed a startling, attractive face with wide cheekbones, firm jaw, and full lips.

Then there were her eyes. Not blue, not gray, but somewhere in between. Quincy imagined that the color shifted with her mood, becoming soft flannel when she was contemplative, icy blue when enraged. And when she was intrigued? Her head tilted slightly, her lips parting in anticipation of a kiss?

Quincy skittered away from his thoughts and shifted uncomfortably in his seat. It wasn't like him to think of a police officer that way. Business was business. Especially these days.

He moved his analysis to her qualities as a cop. She was inexperienced. Her handling of the crime scene and the suspect proved as much. But he didn't think she was dumb. In his thirty-second appraisal, she had struck him as stubborn, smart, and naturally analytic. He already understood she was fiercely loyal to her community and, at times, proud to a fault. He suspected she lived for her job, had few close friends and few outside interests. This, however, was cheating. He was drawing heavily on the profile of the surviving child of an alcoholic, which could go one of two ways – an underachieving drunk or an overachieving workaholic. Since Rainie obviously wasn't the former, he imagined she was the latter. She had yet to prove him wrong.

All in all, she was a different sort of police officer from what he'd expected. Probably different from what Detective Abe Sanders had been expecting as well, and thus they were butting heads. With all due respect to Bakersville's sheriff's department, most small-town police officers had good people skills but weren't the brightest bulbs on the Christmas tree. They made roughly twenty thousand a year. Their cases were routine. They had a tendency to settle into ruts as masters of their tiny domains, and what analytic abilities they did have atrophied as they patrolled Friday night football games.

Of course, Quincy was an arrogant federal agent, paid extra to look down at all other forms of law enforcement – especially those mental midgets in ATF.

Rainie turned off the rural route, and farmland gave way to a neighborhood. Minutes later a sprawling white school building came into view. Yellow crime-scene tape roped off the parking lot, and mounds and mounds of wrapped flowers threatened to bury the chain-link fence.

Rainie pulled the patrol car over.

'You haven't been here yet today, have you?' Quincy asked quietly.

She shook her head, still looking at piles of flowers, balloons, and teddy

610

bears. Two feet deep, stretching along a good ten feet of fence. Loose roses and pink ribbons and tiny, tiny crosses. Handmade signs saying *We love you, Miss Avalon,* and a large red carnation heart reading, *For my daughter.*

Rainie's eyes had grown overbright. She sniffled roughly, and Quincy knew she was fighting hard not to cry. He turned to the makeshift memorial.

'It's one of the amazing things,' he said after a moment. 'On the one hand, these incidents are so tragic, they make us fear the worst about humanity. What kind of society produces children who attack other children with assault rifles? On the other hand, these incidents *are* so tragic, they bring out our humanity. The small acts of courage that get the kids through the day, from the EMTs entering a war zone to the teachers risking their lives to tackle a shooter. From the brother who protects his sister with his own body, to the mother who administers first aid, setting aside her fear for her own child to help someone else's. And all around the globe it strikes a nerve – people feel a need to send flowers, poems, candles, anything to let your town know it's not alone. Bakersville is in their thoughts and their prayers.'

Rainie wiped the corner of her eye, then blinked a few times. 'Yesterday,' she said thickly, 'the call went out that the hospital needed more blood to handle the casualties. The Elks immediately opened up their lodge to the Red Cross. Next thing you know, there was a line of people extending four city blocks waiting to give. The grocery store sent out their bag boys with free lemonade for everyone. A couple of older ladies set up play stations for the kids. There were people in that line for two or three hours and they never complained. Everyone just said it was the least they could do. That was the story the *Bakersville Herald* carried today on the front page. The news of the shooting was in a smaller box in the lower right-hand corner. Not everyone agreed with that prioritization, but I thought they might have a point.'

'The shooting is about an individual. The aftermath is about a town.'

'Something like that.' Rainie unfastened her seat belt. 'If you don't mind, Agent, I spent most of yesterday in that building, and now I'd just like to get this over with. Not being an experienced profiler type, there are many things in that school it hurts me to see.'

Quincy followed her into the school. He already had his notepad out and his mind working overtime.

Earlier, in her office, Officer Conner had agreed to walk Quincy through the crime scene for his notes, as well as to refresh her own. He would not say that they were working together, more that Rainie shared his concerns about Danny's innocence. Thus, she was allowing him to tag along as a quasi-observer, quasi-expert. Of course, she'd told him frankly, the minute he tried to claim the case as his own, she reserved the right to cut him off at the knees. At the time, she'd looked at his kneecaps quite seriously.

Quincy had the feeling that Officer Conner was not known for playing nice with others. Perversely enough, he liked that about her.

Now they walked down the yawning hallway toward the back of the school. Quincy noted the floors dusted with printing powder, the small sections of cutout tiles that must have been spotted with blood and been carted away to the lab.

According to Rainie, the CSU had finished up round one of processing the scene this morning. There would be future visits as the task force sought to finalize a thorough 'walk-through' of the events on that day. Then there were the mounds of evidence it would take months to sort through. Quincy estimated that a school of this size would yield hundreds of footprints to sort and thousands of fingerprints to match. The crime-scene log would probably grow to six or seven volumes.

'This is where I found Walt and Emery assisting Bradley Brown,' Rainie said, pointing to a bloody area at the intersection of two main hallways. She looked at him expectantly.

'Was Brown conscious?'

'Yes. I asked him if he'd seen anything, and he said no. He heard the shots, came running up this hall, turned right, and boom.'

Quincy turned right, where the level of violence was clearly depicted by the outline of three bodies on the floor. 'Everything happened down there?'

'That's what we think.'

'In the hallway, not a classroom.'

'That's correct.'

'How did Danny end up in the hallway?'

'According to his teacher, he never returned to class after lunch. Mr Watson said he'd wondered what was going on, but Danny was hardly ever late, so he figured there must be a good reason he hadn't returned yet.'

'What time was that?'

'The school runs three lunch periods. Danny's is the last, ending at one-twenty. Students have five minutes to get to class, signaled by a bell at one-twenty-five. Danny wasn't in his classroom at one-twenty-five. At one-thirty-five, dispatch received a call about shots fired.'

'So Danny skips his class. And the girls are in the hallway because?'

'Alice needed to use the rest room. Sally was her buddy – in the third grade, you travel in pairs. Their teacher gave them a hall pass.'

'What about the other fatality, Melissa Avalon. She's alone in the computer lab?'

'Yes, it's her lunch break. She keeps the lab open for students to use during cafeteria hours, then closes up shop at the one-twenty bell.'

'And that's scheduled, correct? At one-twenty, she's always alone in the lab?'

Rainie nodded, easily following his train of thought. 'It's looking more and more like she was the target, isn't it? Sally and Alice just happened to be at the wrong place at the wrong time.'

'That's my assumption at the moment, but let's not jump ahead.' Quincy moved to the janitor's closet, arching one brow at the mess. 'I take it Officer Cunningham is one big boy,' he murmured.

Rainie grimaced. 'He was doing his best at the time. Things were intense.'

'Becky O'Grady was hiding in the back of the closet?'

'Yes, all the way in the back. Curled up in a ball. She appeared to be suffering from shock, and I couldn't get her to answer many questions. I understand that Sandy took her to the emergency room, but the doctor said she just needed time.'

'Do you think she saw what happened?'

'I don't know. Luke talked to her teacher this morning. She claimed Becky was in the classroom right up to the time of the shooting. Mrs Lund thinks she got separated from her class during the mad dash to exit the building. It was a good thirty or forty minutes before Mrs Lund even realized Becky was gone.'

'So now we have two questions.' Quincy ticked them off on his fingers. 'First, what happened to Danny O'Grady between the end of lunch – one-twenty P.M. – and when you finally confronted him at . . .'

'Two-forty-five-ish.'

'Over an hour unaccounted for.' Quincy frowned.

Rainie smiled thinly. 'Not completely unaccounted for. Shep was with him. He claims he arrived at the school a little after one-forty-five. Students had already fled the premises. He went inside to offer help and encountered Danny, dazed and confused and picking up the guns.'

'Picking up the guns? Oh, I like that. As if the boy simply stumbled upon them.'

'You don't believe Shep either, do you?'

'He's not the most objective witness,' Quincy observed. 'I'll stick with my analysis for now: we don't know what Danny did between one-twenty and two-forty-five. The next question we have is what happened to Becky O'Grady from roughly one-thirty-five to your arrival at around one-fifty.' He frowned again. 'I don't like the fact that the two students unaccounted for just happen to be brother and sister. I don't believe in coincidence.'

'You don't think Becky's part of it, do you?' Rainie was startled. 'For heaven's sake, she's eight!'

'Has someone followed up with her yet?'

'Luke Hayes and Tom Dawson are going to try to interview her this afternoon. I'm not optimistic, though. Shep and Sandy are pretty hostile right now, and we don't have the right to question her away from her parents. I doubt anything will come of it.'

'You could ask the DA to subpoena her as a witness for the grand jury.'

Rainie shrugged, then surprised him by saying, 'I looked into that this morning. According to Rodriguez, there's still no way of enforcing testimony. Her parents could simply coach her to say she doesn't remember, and that would be that. My guess is that if we hope to get anywhere with her, we need to play nice. Who knows? Shep and Sandy have to be wondering what really happened yesterday. Maybe sooner or later they'll be willing to let Becky talk. Perhaps they'll even let Luke ask her questions this afternoon. I'm just not betting on it.'

'How well do you know them?' Quincy asked.

'Well.'

Quincy nodded and let her move away. He didn't think she was aware of it, but she had wrapped her arms tightly around her middle, as if she was trying to block out the scene. The stance made her appear younger, more vulnerable. She was looking at the outline of Melissa Avalon's body. By all accounts, Miss Avalon had also been beautiful, compassionate, and dedicated to her job.

Wordlessly, they moved down the hall to the shattered doors. Quincy stopped at the door across from the computer room.

'Danny came out of this classroom?'

'Yes. He was backing Shep through the door at gun-point.'

'Holding both the .22 and the .38?'

'Yes.'

'How did he seem?'

'Agitated. Wired.' Rainie's brow furrowed as she contemplated his question further. 'He seemed hostile toward his father.'

'Holding him at gunpoint would appear hostile.'

Rainie shook her head. 'There was more to it than that. Shep was telling him that everything would be all right, then he was trying to tell him not to speak to me. But everything kept coming out as a command, and that made Danny withdraw even more. I think he has a big chip on his shoulder regarding his father. Shep rides him hard.'

'How so?'

'Shep was a big football star in his high school days. Superjock. Danny . . .' Rainie shrugged. 'He's small for his age, not good at sports. I think Shep believes he just needs to try harder, and I think Danny wishes his father would leave him alone.'

'Have you ever heard Shep call his son stupid?'

Rainie shook her head. 'You're talking about the interview tape, aren't you? Danny's obsession with being smart. That's the oddest thing. See, Shep's not the kind of father to worry that much about grades. Bad day on the football field, yes. Bad day on the report card, hey, these things happen. I don't know where that was coming from.'

'Does Danny have any close friends?'

'We're still working on that.'

'We'll want a complete list of all students absent yesterday, plus notes on whether they knew Danny O'Grady and can account for their time.'

'Alibis for children,' Rainie muttered, and rolled her eyes. 'Why the ones who were absent?'

'Because no one says the shooter had to be in attendance that day. Plus, they still might be involved. In several of the shootings, other students played a role, either encouraging the main suspect's actions or enjoying the show.'

'*What?*'

'Bethel, Alaska,' Quincy said. 'Evan Ramsey did the shooting, but two fourteen-year-olds encouraged him. One went so far as to teach him how to use the shotgun. Both assembled some of their other friends to join them in the cafeteria for a "show." '

'Wonderful.'

'Luke Woodham also appears to have been influenced by other kids,' Quincy reported. 'In this case, I'm wondering if that's where Danny's obsession with "I'm smart" is coming from. It sounds rehearsed and overly vehement. Either it's a phrase he's using to compensate for genuine doubts about his intelligence, or it's a cover for something else. Something that's still too frightening or overwhelming for him to say. How did he seem after the shooting?'

'Distant. Withdrawn. He sobbed a little when he heard his mother's voice. Then he fell asleep like a baby in the back of the patrol car.'

Quincy nodded, not surprised by her description. 'He's dissociating, keeping himself distanced from the events until he's able to deal with them. That's a normal reaction to any kind of trauma. The question becomes, how long will the dissociation last, and how will he react when his mind does start to process what happened.'

'He's on suicide watch,' Rainie volunteered. 'I understand that's standard procedure for a case like his.'

'It's not a bad idea. Unfortunately, Danny is probably suffering from post-traumatic stress disorder and now will go through its various symptoms. One day he might talk about everything very matter-of-factly, then collapse, weeping, the next day. He might sound cold at times as he repeats the day's events over and over again. He will probably refuse to call victims by name. All of this can be interpreted one way or another by well-meaning people. And none of it means he's guilty. It simply means he's experienced a trauma, whether as a perpetrator or a witness, and his mind is struggling to cope. That fact, however, can get quickly lost.'

Rainie sighed. 'I don't know,' she said. 'Maybe we're making this too complicated. On the one hand, some things don't make sense about the shooting. On the other hand, what shooting makes sense? And who else could've done it? All the students present that day were in class when the shots were fired, so they're accounted for. The only two students with time lapses are Danny and Becky, and neither choice is appealing. Maybe in the end it's just too hard to believe a child did it, so I focus on the question because it's easier than the answer.'

'It's good to focus on questions,' Quincy said. 'It's your job.'

'Well, it's not a good job today, Agent. Maybe tomorrow it will be, but I'm not particularly enjoying it today.'

She headed for the side doors, obviously disturbed again. Quincy wasn't surprised when she stopped by the broken windows and gazed out on the rolling green hills and afternoon sun. Recharge, he thought. Sometimes he had to do that himself.

He bent down and inspected the shooting area more closely. He noted the way the bodies had lain and tried to picture in what direction they'd fallen. Then he explored the door frame around Melissa Avalon's computer lab for telltale holes.

Ten minutes later he was done making notes. Now he had many questions for the medical examiner.

He turned back to Rainie, who was still standing by the broken doors. She was no longer looking outside, however, but staring at the outline of Melissa Avalon's body. Her gray eyes were impossible to read, her features stilled.

Quincy wondered how few hours of sleep Rainie Conner had gotten last night. And for just one moment, he was tempted to ask her. To step over the line and into her space, because once upon a time he'd been the inexperienced agent with a homicide and he understood how some images stayed in your head long after you turned out the lights.

Some nights he did wake up screaming.

But that was neither here nor there.

He said, 'I'm done now.'

Rainie led him from the building.

10

Outside, Rainie and Quincy encountered Principal Steven VanderZanden. A slightly built man with an expressive face and twinkling eyes, he now appeared subdued as he surveyed bloodred roses piled against the chain-link fence. The wind ruffled his dark, thinning hair and pressed his gray suit against his frame. He didn't seem to notice. He walked the fence line, adjusting arrangements so that names showed more clearly, then pushed back two teddy bears to reveal a framed portrait of Melissa Avalon.

Rainie and Quincy walked up to him quietly. Principal VanderZanden and his wife were relatively new to Bakersville, having moved into the area three years earlier when VanderZanden accepted the job at the K-8. Not having kids, Rainie had never met him until last summer, when they'd rubbed shoulders at a town function. VanderZanden had impressed her then with his enthusiasm for his students and his rapport with their parents. No project was too big in his eyes, no student too small for his attention. He had been giggling like a schoolgirl over having secured the federal grant for Bakersville's first computer lab and could barely wait to surf the Web himself.

He also seemed a little bit flirtatious, but he had a few glasses of wine under his belt when she'd run into him, and, frankly, the whole crowd was pretty loose by then.

'Principal VanderZanden.' Rainie shook his hand. She could tell he was preoccupied. Yesterday evening he'd returned to the school to survey the damage and inquire as to when he might have the building back. With only one month to go before school was out for the summer, no one knew what to do about classes. They could bus the kids to neighboring Cabot, but that town was nearly forty minutes away, and after everything that had happened, parents wanted to keep their kids close to home.

'How are you, sir?' Rainie made the introduction between VanderZanden and Quincy. She still wasn't sure what she thought of the federal agent's presence, but so far he was proving less annoying than the state detective. There was something to be said for that.

'Are you an expert?' VanderZanden homed in on Quincy's credentials. 'Can you tell me what happened in my school?'

'I don't think there's any such thing as an expert when it comes to these crimes.'

'Maybe we should've gone with metal detectors.' VanderZanden turned back toward the building. 'After the Springfield shooting, Oregon educators were warned. But even then I thought of it as an issue for the high schools to address. We have kindergarten students here. I didn't want them starting their educational experience passing through giant security stations and being patted down by armed guards. What kind of message would that send?'

'Personally, I don't believe in metal detectors,' Quincy said, but added before the principal could be too encouraged, 'They would simply make the students better targets by creating long lines in front of the building.'

'Oh, this is ridiculous!' VanderZanden shook his head and expelled a gust of pure frustration. 'I've been up all night with calls from frantic parents, wanting to know what to do. The teachers are frightened, the school board overwhelmed. On top of all that, Alice's parents asked me to give the eulogy at her funeral. Of course I'll do it, I'm honored. But still . . . You go into education, you fantasize about watching your students grow up, maybe even attending their wedding or admiring their firstborn child. You certainly don't expect to give the eulogy at their funeral. Did you know that Sally's and Alice's parents are going to pay the burial expenses with money from their college funds?'

VanderZanden obviously didn't expect an answer. He turned away to adjust another bouquet. Quincy and Rainie exchanged looks. They would just let the man talk. Apparently, he had a few things to say.

'The flowers started arriving first thing this morning,' VanderZanden added after a moment. 'I've seen pictures of the flowers sent to the other schools, so I expected something like this. Still, to see it. Notes and cards from all over the country. Teddy bears and balloons from hundreds of strangers.' He turned to them, sounding angry again. 'I received calls from two other principals who've been through this and half a dozen child experts who are experienced in this area. It's like we joined some club. I don't want to be part of a club! I wish we were alone. I wish we were the only place this had ever happened. Instead, we're what? The eleventh, twelfth, thirteenth school to go through this? Dammit, we should've known better!'

He pinched the bridge of his nose, clearly trying to pull himself together and not having much luck. His gaze returned to the picture of Melissa Avalon. He pinched his nose harder.

'I'm sorry. It's been a long twenty-four hours.'

'It's okay,' Rainie said. 'Take your time.'

'I needed time last night. Now I need a vacation. Well, that's neither here nor there. I'm sure you have more questions, though I already told Detective Sanders the little I know about things.'

'Detective Sanders?' Rainie inquired sharply. Warning lights went off in her head. She didn't ignore them. 'What did you tell Detective Sanders?'

'Not much.' VanderZanden shrugged, obviously caught off guard by her tone. 'I was in my office when I heard the shots. I came out to the main entranceway to see what was going on and heard someone scream. The next thing I knew, the fire alarms went off and everyone began running for the door. At the time I figured it was something minor. A student had fired a cap gun in the halls and the smoke had triggered the alarms. Or someone had lit a few firecrackers as a prank. These things happen.

'The first time I realized it was serious was when I saw the face of Mrs McLain, the sixth-grade teacher. She was white as a sheet; her hands were shaking. I told her to calm down, it was just a drill, and then she *looked* at me. She looked at me and she said, "I think some students have been shot. I think someone just shot at us. I think he's still there." Even then it wasn't until I saw Will's bloody leg in the parking lot that I realized she'd been right – someone had opened fire in our school.'

'Did you hear anyone say Danny's name?' Quincy asked.

VanderZanden shook his head. 'I heard Dorie screaming about a man in black coming to get her. Of course, Dorie is only seven years old, and we've had problems with her imagination before. Once she had the entire second-grade class convinced they couldn't go to the bathroom because little trolls hid inside the toilets to snatch children for lunch. You have no idea how messy it can be when twenty-one seven-year-olds won't use the rest rooms. I had parents calling me for weeks.'

'Were a lot of children around when she was going on about the "man in black"?' Rainie asked.

'Everyone was around. We'd evacuated the whole school into the front parking lot, as specified in our fire-drill manual.'

Rainie blew out an exasperated breath. 'Well, that explains that batch of interview answers,' she muttered to Quincy. 'One hysterical girl, two hundred and fifty impressionable minds.' She returned to Principal VanderZanden. 'Are you sure none of the teachers saw anything? What about Mrs McLain? I can't believe someone was shooting a gun in the hallway and no one noticed.'

'I don't think the shooter was standing in the hallway. One of the teachers said that it sounded like the shots were coming from a room at the end of the west wing. Maybe the computer lab. I know that from where I was standing in the main entranceway, I couldn't see a thing.'

Rainie glanced at Quincy. He nodded faintly, sharing her thought. The killer started with Miss Avalon, then turned to see Sally and Alice. Shot them as well, then ducked into the now-empty computer room as all hell broke loose. It would explain the lack of witnesses as well as the random firing pattern.

'What can you tell us about Danny O'Grady?' Quincy asked Vander-Zanden. 'Was he a good student? Did he get along well with others?'

'Danny's a fine student. He's made the honor roll several times. He was hardly ever sent to my office with discipline issues. Melissa – Miss Avalon was just telling me the other day that she'd never seen anyone so good with computers. He has a natural talent for it.'

'What about enemies?' Quincy pressed gently. 'Was Danny picked on by other students? Was he considered popular by his classmates – or was he often a target of their unwanted attention?'

Rainie nodded her head at this question. She should've thought to ask it herself last night. Rightly or wrongly, most school shooters felt painfully persecuted by their peers. Rainie had even read somewhere that these homicides weren't that different from teen suicide – the less popular kid felt an unbearable amount of pain and decided to do something about it. In the case of a school shooting, however, the kid didn't just plan to end his own life but to take some of the offending parties' lives with him. That's the thing with teenagers – they came up with sentences that didn't always fit the crime.

VanderZanden seemed to be struggling with Quincy's question. He finally shook his head. 'I wasn't aware of anything,' he said, then added more reluctantly, 'I'm an adult, however, and an authority figure. In other words, while I try to be in touch with my students, I'm still probably not the best judge of what really goes on among twenty adolescents during a thirty-minute recess.'

'What about close friends of Danny's who might be able to tell us more?'

'I don't think Danny has close friends. He's quiet, keeps to himself.' A thought seemed to strike VanderZanden all at once. 'You know, there was this incident, not too long ago . . .'

Quincy and Rainie perked up.

'There's this older boy, Charlie Kenyon. Do you know him?'

'Oh, sure.' Rainie supplied for Quincy: 'Charlie's the son of our former mayor. Nineteen now, a bit too much money, way too much free time. He was sent off to military school back east four years ago, but he returned last spring no worse for the wear. Now he fancies himself some kind of minor hood. Hangs out where he's not wanted, drives under the influence every other weekend. We've brought him in half a dozen times, but it's always misdemeanor stuff and his father's quick with bail money and high-priced lawyers. I don't get the impression Charlie's feeling a need to reform anytime soon.'

VanderZanden nodded his head with real emotion. 'That's Charlie. About two months ago he started hanging around our school after hours. Teachers would see him lounging outside the fence, talking to kids on the playground. As long as he was on the street side of the fence, however, there was nothing we could do. Then one day Mrs Lund saw Charlie hand Danny a cigarette through the fence. She immediately took the cigarette away from Danny and wrote him up, but there was nothing she could do about Charlie. He told the boy not to sweat it. "Detention is when all the fun stuff happens," or something like that. We sent a note home to Danny's parents, and we never caught him smoking again, but we'd still see Charlie around. I don't know why he insisted on bothering us at the K-through-eight. You'd think he'd be more interested in the high school.'

'Did Charlie know Miss Avalon?' Quincy asked.

'I don't think so. She moved to town just last year, when we got the federal grant. Then again . . .' Principal VanderZanden flushed. He looked at Rainie with something akin to embarrassment.

'She was very pretty,' Rainie filled in for the tongue-tied principal. 'Very, *very* pretty.'

'She's a very good teacher,' VanderZanden added immediately, but his dark eyes appeared wistful. Melissa Avalon had been beautiful.

'How old was she?' Rainie inquired.

'Twenty-eight.'

'Young enough and pretty enough to attract a nineteen-year-old,' Rainie concluded, and looked at Quincy. He appeared deep in thought.

'Miss Avalon moved to Bakersville recently?'

'Last summer. We hired her in August. Frankly, we'd given up on getting the grant, and then boom. You know the feds. Obviously.'

'Where did Miss Avalon come from?'

'She'd just gotten her master's from Portland State University.'

'Was this her first job?'

'Her first full-time teaching position. She subbed in Beaverton's school district before that. That's one of the reasons we hired her.' VanderZanden gave them the apologetic look of a veteran civil servant. 'We have a very tight budget here, and new teachers are cheaper than experienced ones.'

'Do you know anything about her private life?' Rainie asked. 'Where her family lives, anything?'

VanderZanden hesitated. He looked self-conscious again and wouldn't meet Rainie's gaze. 'I believe she has parents in the Portland area.'

'What about past relationships? Maybe an old boyfriend she left behind? A current beau who wanted more of her time?'

'I think . . . I think you should ask her parents about that sort of thing. It's not appropriate for me to be commenting on the private lives of my staff.'

'Principal VanderZanden, we don't have a lot of time.'

'Phone calls are fast, Officer,' he said firmly. 'It's the advantage of modern life.'

Rainie frowned, not liking the principal's sudden lack of cooperation, but before she could push harder, Quincy pissed her off by taking over the interview.

'What about Danny's relationship with Miss Avalon? Did they get along well? Did he have any problems in her class?'

'Oh no,' VanderZanden said emphatically. 'That's the crazy thing about yesterday. I would've sworn Miss Avalon was Danny's favorite teacher. Certainly he loved being in the computer lab and was one of our most adept students on the Internet. Before school, during lunch, after school. It seemed he was always in the lab. Sometimes Miss Avalon even stayed late just for him.'

'On the Internet?' Rainie jumped in. 'Do you know what he'd do on the Web, where he'd go?'

'I'm not sure. Visit Web sites, look things up.'

'Did he go into chat rooms?'

'Probably. Miss Avalon had it set up so students couldn't access X-rated sites – she had one of those filters installed. Otherwise, students were free to roam. The whole point was to encourage them to be more computer savvy.'

'Did he play computer games?' Quincy asked. 'Any specific ones?'

'I don't know. In all honesty, the only person who would is Miss Avalon.'

Rainie nodded, chewing on her bottom lip. Danny loved the Internet. That put a new spin on things. An adept user could go just about anyplace, learn just about anything. The Springfield shooter, Kip Kinkel, had used the Internet to learn how to build bombs and rig booby traps. Right before they were murdered, his parents had even commented to friends that they were happy to see their troubled son take an interest in computers. Finally, something nonviolent . . .

It also meant Danny could've been exposed to any number of crackpots and loose cannons. Forget just Charlie Kenyon. Danny was a young, troubled boy whose family was going through a hard time. His vulnerability would've been boundless.

'We need to search those computers,' Rainie muttered.

'Detective Sanders already has them. Didn't he tell you?'

'Oh, you know Detective Sanders. He's such an efficient little – It must have slipped his mind.' Rainie smiled sweetly for VanderZanden, though her sarcasm was not lost on Quincy.

'Did Danny often stay late after school?' Quincy returned to the original line of questioning.

VanderZanden glanced at Rainie. She shrugged. 'It's a murder investigation. Everything is going to come out sooner or later.'

VanderZanden sighed. He appeared tired and worn again. A man due to have many more sleepless nights and ethical struggles over how to best serve his students. He said quietly, 'Danny's parents have been having marital difficulties.'

'Sandy got a new job,' Rainie told Quincy bluntly. 'She likes it, but it's a lot of hours. Shep didn't want her to work in the first place, let alone if it came in the way of getting dinner ready.'

'Are they separated?'

'Nah. They're Catholic.'

'Oh, got it.'

'Sandy came in one day to meet with Danny and Becky's teachers,' VanderZanden explained. 'She expressed that there was a great deal of tension at home and she knew it was hard on the children. She wanted their teachers to understand what was going on and keep an eye out for the kids. Becky has certainly been more withdrawn this year. And Danny has had a few . . . issues.'

'The smoking,' Rainie prompted. 'And . . .'

'Three weeks ago Danny came to school agitated. He couldn't remember his locker combination, and something in him just went. He started pounding on the door with his fists and yelling how much he hated the locker and the school and how was he supposed to remember anything when everyone knew he was stupid—'

'Stupid?' Quincy interjected. 'You heard him say he was stupid?'

'Oh yes, I was there, Agent. It took both myself and Richard Mann to subdue him. Danny was yelling "Stupid, stupid, stupid" over and over again. I was very worried about him.'

Quincy looked at Rainie. She shrugged. She didn't know where this was coming from either, but Danny seemed to have an issue with his intelligence.

'He was on the honor roll?' Quincy asked the principal again.

'Yes.'

'You considered him a good student? His teachers were pleased with his performance?'

'Yes. He wasn't the best in some subjects, but, then, when something interested him . . . I don't think there was anything he couldn't do on a computer.'

'Principal VanderZanden, did you ever hear his parents call him stupid?'

'Sandy? Never. She loves those kids. As for Shep?' VanderZanden arched a brow. 'Let's just say he was more concerned about the size of his son's muscles than the power of his brain.'

'Did Danny do many after-school sports?'

'Shep made him try out for football. He got on the team, but sports aren't Danny's forte. He's small for his age, a bit awkward. Unfortunately, his father can be rather . . . forceful. He wanted his son to play football, so Danny played football. In all honesty, however, Danny mostly warmed the bench. He just wasn't any good. You know, you really should talk to the school counselor, Richard Mann, about these things. He met with Danny a few times after the locker incident and would know a lot more about his state of mind.'

'We'll be sure to do that,' Rainie told the principal. She remembered Richard Mann from yesterday. He'd been very efficient in setting up the first-aid station and clearing the parking lot. She also remembered him as being on the young side, and that made her immediately wonder about him and pretty Miss Avalon. More food for thought.

'We're going to need a copy of Danny's school records from you,' Rainie told the principal. 'His report cards, incident slips, everything.'

'I'm not sure—'

'We can get a subpoena if we have to. I'm just asking you to save us all some time.'

'All right, all right. There's just so much to do . . .' VanderZanden looked at his school building. The front doors were closed, the interior seeming shadowed and foreboding from this distance. Yellow crime-scene tape still roped off the parking lot and wove through the chain-link fence, while dark red stains spotted the school sidewalk – blood from the wounded students who had clutched neighbours' hands while waiting for the medevac choppers to arrive. It was impossible now to look at the building and not think of death.

'I understand that Columbine had to completely refurbish the inside of the high school,' the principal murmured. 'After the shooting they ripped out the carpet, repainted the walls, redid the lockers. They even changed the tone of their fire alarm, which had sounded for hours that day. And their library – that poor, tragic library – simply doesn't exist anymore. They covered up the entrance with a new bank of lockers and brought in a trailer to house the books.'

He looked at Rainie and Quincy. There were no twinkling lights in his eyes. 'I'm not sure what I'm supposed to do here,' he said honestly. 'The damage isn't that extensive, and yet it is. I want the children to feel safe again, but in this day and age, schools can be scary places. I want the building to be welcoming, but I don't want to pretend nothing happened. I want us to move on, but I don't want us to forget.

'I don't know how I'm supposed to do all that. When I was training to be a principal, the biggest threat we could imagine was an earthquake. They certainly hadn't started the duck-and-run drills in the LA schools for drive-by shootings. Nor had they ever envisioned that schools would become war zones for rival gangs and street disputes. Now we have teachers and students dying in the halls. Small towns, big towns, black, white, upper class, lower class – it doesn't seem to matter. And the human in me wants to rail against that, wants to live in denial, while the principal in me knows I can't do that. I have an obligation to my students. If this is the world we live in, then this is the world I must prepare them for. But how do I do that? I'm not sure *I'm* prepared for this world. I know Miss Avalon wasn't.'

'Have you arranged for grief counseling?' Quincy asked gently.

'Of course. Several child psychologists are coming into town.'

'I didn't mean just for the students. I meant also for you and your staff.'

'Of course, of course.' Principal VanderZanden's attention drifted back to the memorial. It rested on the poster that said, *We love you, Miss Avalon.*

His figure swayed. He suddenly looked small to Rainie. A slight, vulnerable man growing old in front of her eyes.

'She really was trying to help him,' VanderZanden said to no one in particular. 'She really cared for her students, especially Danny. If you could've seen the time she spent with him, all those hours after school because she knew he didn't want to go home. She helped him learn basic programming, she laughed with him over Internet jokes. She was so patient, so caring . . . Sometimes I hate Danny O'Grady. And that makes me feel worse. What kind of principal hates a student? What kind of man fears a child?'

Principal VanderZanden obviously didn't expect any answers. He squared his shoulders. He walked back to his car while clouds finally moved over the sun and the first drops of spring rain began to fall.

After a moment Rainie said, 'I think he needs some help.'

'You would, too, if you'd just lost the woman you loved.'

'Principal VanderZanden is a happily married man!'

And Quincy said, 'Not when he was with Melissa Avalon.'

11

Sandy O'Grady kept thinking that Danny was dead.

Small communities had their rituals, their established ways of dealing with the major passages of life. Almost all involved food. Someone was getting married – bake the bride's favorite bread and tape the recipe card to the baking tin for her future kitchen. Someone was having her first child – pile up the homemade sugar cookies cut into the shape of little booties. A graduation barbecue – bring Mama's award-winning three-bean salad. The yearly race to bale hay before the Oregon rains ruined the crop – bring fresh corn and tomatoes from the garden, plus bags of sugar and rock salt for the ice cream maker. Maybe include a package of chocolate chips.

Someone died – bring out the casseroles. Dad's ham and potato surprise. Grandma's seven-layer taco supreme.

Bake a ham, baste a turkey. Make it big, hearty, and rich. And deliver it with plenty of Kleenex and a shoulder for the widow to lean upon. Then return two days later with a pan of brownies or a couple of apple pies. Sooner or later even the most stoic survivors turned to sugar for solace. It's simply a way of life.

Yesterday evening, on the O'Grady front doorstep, the first casserole had appeared. It was accompanied by a note that said *Deepest sympathies.* No name attached. Sandy realized then how bad the days would be. Neighbors understood their torment. Some even sympathized. But in these circumstances no one knew what to do.

When Danny had been transported to Cabot Country's juvenile detention hall, he'd been wearing a bulletproof vest.

The police had spent the evening in the O'Gradys' home. Men Sandy and Shep had never seen before, wearing grim expressions and navy blue windbreakers emblazoned with the letters CSU, cordoned off Danny's room. They pulled apart his bed, disemboweled his closet. They tore into his desk, dismantled his furniture, and boxed up everything he had ever touched. They shredded Danny O'Grady's bedroom, dusted it down with fingerprint powder, then left as somberly as they came.

Becky hid in the coat closet.

Sandy's parents came over. They hugged Sandy and wept. They pulled

626

Becky from the closet and cried harder. They looked at Shep stonily, so he would know that whatever had happened, it was his fault. Then Sandy's mother moved into the kitchen and started baking. Her father sat on the couch and did his best to look strong.

The parish priest had paid a visit. He sat with Sandy and Shep. He reminded them that the Lord gave no burdens that could not be borne. He assured them faith would get them through this time of sorrow. He took to speaking of Danny in the past tense, which at once seemed natural and nearly drove Sandy out of her mind.

Danny was not dead. Danny was not a burden. He was a confused and frightened boy, lying now in an institutionally gray juvenile hall with bars on the windows. He was in a state of shock, the doctors told Sandy and Shep when they tried to visit this morning. Curled up tight with his arms wrapped around his knees, as if he was so exhausted by life he was trying to return to the womb.

No, they couldn't see him yet. He needed more time and more sleep. Maybe tomorrow.

Sandy didn't want to leave. She didn't want to return to a house that magically produced casseroles and to a mother who was turning out row after row of pies as if a properly fluted crust was the secret to managing life. She didn't want to spend another minute with the priest who had married her and Shep and who now looked at them with the solemn compassion usually reserved for lepers. She didn't want to stare at her garage, where early this morning someone had scrawled *Baby Killer* with dripping red paint.

Danny was not a stone-cold killer. He was a child. He was *her* child, and she wanted her family back! She wanted to be a warrior mom, slayer of all dragons for her children.

Except no one could tell her which dragon to slay. No one could tell her what had happened yesterday afternoon to turn her eight-year-old daughter into a silent ghost and her thirteen-year-old son into a mass murderer.

Now their lawyer, Avery Johnson, was speaking with them in their kitchen. They had just returned from the preliminary hearing in front of the juvenile court judge, where Sandy had been shocked by the informality of the proceedings. The room had looked little different from a high school classroom, with its plain white walls and linoleum-tiled floor. The judge, wearing a dark robe, clearly was surprised to see two lawyers in suits. His opening comment had been 'You guys don't come here often, do you?'

In this very simple room with very simple proceedings, the county DA, Charles Rodriguez – a man Shep had worked with for years, a man Sandy had invited to her house for dinner on numerous occasions – formally filed a petition for waiver to adult court given the 'heinous nature of Daniel O'Grady's crimes against the community.'

He'd charged their son with five counts of aggravated murder, one count for the first victim and two counts for each additional victim as they were part of a multiple homicide. If found guilty in adult court, Danny could receive five consecutive thirty-year-to-life sentences. He had gone into the care of the county yesterday evening. He would never come home again.

Sandy kept thinking that Danny was dead.

'Now, you have to look on the bright side,' Avery Johnson was saying. 'Danny's only thirteen years old. He has statistics on his side.'

'Statistics?' Sandy asked weakly. She was mangling a piece of freshly baked apple pie. Her mother had served it with a giant scoop of vanilla ice cream just ten minutes ago. Sandy watched the ice cream melt into little flowing rivers, then she formed dams with bits of baked apple. After a moment Shep took her plate and ate the pie himself. In times of crisis, he always gained an appetite while she lost hers.

'In the upcoming hearing,' Avery was saying, 'we must argue what's in the best interest of the child and the community. Basically, a waiver hearing focuses on two key aspects of Danny's personality: Does he pose too great a risk to others to be sufficiently handled by the juvenile system, and is he amenable to rehabilitation? Naturally, the DA is going to argue that Danny's act proves he's a dangerous felon beyond all hope of rehabilitation, thus he falls outside the jurisdiction of juvenile court. The judge should cart the child away to adult court, which has the means to handle a master criminal.

'Our job is to prove otherwise, and the good news is that the statistics are in our favor. The majority of children who commit violent acts won't reoffend in adulthood. Furthermore, and we must emphasize this, studies show that there is a *higher* chance of recidivism with a child who is incarcerated with adults than with a child who is held in juvenile facilities. Thus, it is in the state's own best interest to keep Danny in juvenile jurisdiction, where he can be rehabilitated and then start over on his twenty-fifth birthday as a productive member of society.'

'You're assuming Danny is guilty,' Sandy said shortly. 'Why are you assuming that my son is guilty?'

Avery, an older man with wire-rimmed glasses and expensive suits, gave her a faint smile. He had eaten his pie within minutes, then gently patted his upper lip with his paper napkin as if it had been made of the finest linen. Sandy wasn't sure if she liked him yet. She thought he might be too pompous, too rich and oozing of success for her taste. But Shep had been taken with him since they first met at some law-enforcement function where Avery was the keynote speaker. Shep went so far as to call him a 'friend,' though Sandy knew that wasn't really true. Avery Johnson moved in circles beyond them. He lived in a gorgeous home in Lake Oswego and was hardly taking this case out of the goodness of his heart. Sandy imagined the man charged five hundred dollars an hour and was racking up billable time even as he ate their pie.

She did not know how they were going to pay him. She had no idea what kind of lies Shep must have fed the man about their financial circumstances to even get him to show up. She just knew that Shep wanted Avery Johnson. He was the best there was and Shep wouldn't hear of anything less for his son. That was his idea of fatherhood, and it both enraged Sandy and broke her heart.

'Sandy, you can rest assured that I will never let a jury think your son is guilty.' Avery smiled at her again. 'But we're not at a jury trial yet. Six months from now it will be Charles Rodriguez and myself "discussing" Danny's future with Judge Matthews, who, frankly, is a miserable old fart who would like to bring back corporal punishment to public schools. He probably does think Danny is guilty. He probably thinks Danny should hang. Fortunately, that's not germane to the hearing. At this point we're simply addressing which court should have jurisdiction over the case. So I need to argue that, guilty or not, Danny's – and the community's – interests are best served by keeping this case in juvenile court.'

'Because even if he's a mass murderer now, when he grows up he'll be magically cured?'

'Exactly. And there's nothing magical about it. I've been reading articles on juvenile crime all night, and the experts call it the "desistance phenomenon." From ages twelve to eighteen, male teens exhibit a spike of criminal activity as their rise in hormones and developmental changes outpace their coping skills. Then at eighteen, as they become adults, get jobs, and find more permanent relationships, they settle down. Criminal activity falls off, and even teens once described as "troubled" go on to lead normal lives.'

'So if Danny is innocent, he's innocent. But if he's guilty, he's merely going through a phase? That's what we're going to argue in court?' Sandy's voice was becoming shrill. She couldn't help herself. It sounded ludicrous. It sounded insane.

Shep shot her an impatient stare. 'For God's sake, Sandy, what do you want to hear? He just told you his job is to keep Danny out of adult court, and this is the way he can do it.'

'Sandy—' Avery began soothingly.

Sandy cut him off. 'I don't know what I want to hear! Maybe that my only son is not capable of killing three people. Maybe that my firstborn child is not a murderer, it's all been a big mistake.' She slammed her hand down on the table.

'Look at you two, discussing legal theory as if it makes a difference. This isn't a ball game. It doesn't boil down to who wins or loses at the end of the night. This is our son! This is our community! How are we going to walk down the streets if Danny is found guilty? What are we going to tell Becky? My God, Shep, didn't you see what they wrote on our garage? They're going to kill him. Our neighbors hold Danny responsible for the murder of two little girls, and sooner or later someone is going to kill him. Dammit. Dammit, dammit, *dammit!*'

Sandy pushed back from the table. She got up, paced four steps around the tiny kitchen, then realized she was crying uncontrollably. Shep did not get up to console her. Last night he had tried to come to her bed after months of sleeping on the sofa. His voice had sounded ragged. He'd told her he just wanted to hold her. Maybe they could put aside their differences for a while. Once, they'd been good friends.

Sandy's anger had been too tight in her chest. She had looked at her husband, the father of her children, raw and vulnerable with his big shoulders sagging, and all she could think was that if Danny had been driven to murder, it was Shep's fault. He pushed the boy too hard. He had never appreciated that Danny was different, more intellectual, more like her. Instead, Shep had tried to force him into his arrogant, macho world.

He had broken their son. He had broken their family. Sandy hated him.

And then, as abruptly as the emotion had overcome Sandy, it ripped through her body and she had nothing left. She stood in their kitchen empty, exhausted, and swaying on her feet.

She turned toward the doorway and there was Becky, watching her with somber blue eyes.

'Don't let the monster get you, Mommy,' Becky said. Then she turned and walked back into the family room, where Sandy's parents were watching TV.

Sandy returned to the table and had a seat.

'I know this is an emotional time for you,' Avery began.

'Jesus fucking Christ,' Sandy said.

Shep sighed heavily, got up, and cut himself a third piece of pie.

'Look,' Avery said briskly, 'let me walk you through the whole process. Maybe by the end it will be clearer to you what we're trying to accomplish. The next six to twelve months are going to be crucial to Danny's future.'

Sandy held up a hand. 'Why do we have to wait six to twelve months?'

'Because it's going to take that long for everyone to prepare for the waiver-motion hearing. It's not a small thing.'

'But Danny can't come home, can he? You said there's no bail for juveniles accused of murder. So what is this? My son isn't even on trial yet, isn't even found guilty of murder, and he's going to spend at least six months locked up in a juvenile detention hall? For God's sake, how can that be legal?'

'It's the way the system works.'

'Well, fuck the system!' Sandy was beyond reason and knew it.

Avery Johnson gave her that small, soothing smile again. Then his voice got sharp. 'Mrs O'Grady, I know you don't want to hear this, but there is a good chance that Danny committed these crimes. He was found holding

Shep at gunpoint. He brought your family's guns to the school, and, furthermore, he confessed *twice*.'

'He's in shock. You said so yourself. He doesn't know what he's saying.'

'The guns, Mrs O'Grady. The guns. How did two handguns get from your safe to the school?'

Sandy looked at Shep helplessly. He stabbed the air with his ice-cream-covered fork. 'My son didn't do it,' he said stoically.

For the first time, Sandy felt a rush of warmth toward her husband.

Avery Johnson said sternly, 'You're a police officer, Shep, and not even you can prove your son's innocence—'

'I will—'

'You can't—'

'I got six months.'

Avery Johnson sighed. He clearly thought they were both in denial. He tried again:

'Even if you manage to explain away how *your* guns came to be at *that* crime scene, why *your* son held *you* hostage, and why your son confessed twice to *three* murders, the fact remains that Danny is a troubled boy. He obviously has issues. Thus, all legal necessities aside, as parents you should be able to see the value of the next six months as an opportunity to get Danny the help he needs. He'll be examined by child-development experts. He'll take a battery of psychological exams. He'll have his childhood, his family, his friends, all thoroughly explored. While I'm sure it may be awkward at times, the result should be a better understanding of who Danny is and what problems he's facing. Does that make sense?'

Sandy finally considered the matter. She glanced at Shep, who was rolling a bite of pie around in his mouth in a manner that indicated he didn't really taste it. She could tell the lawyer's words had depressed him; his shoulders had slumped again. Danny had problems. Danny had issues. It was Shep's way to deny all things he didn't like to hear, but he had no more words left. The lawyer's comments had struck too close to the secret doubts in their hearts. What if Danny was troubled? What if they had turned their little boy into a monster?

There were such dark shadows beneath her husband's eyes. Sandy had to look away.

She knew that after leaving her room last night, Shep had lain down on the floor next to Becky's bed. Their little girl had refused offers to sleep in her parents' room, instead building a wall of stuffed animals around her bed. Big Bear, her favorite doll, was reserved for special bodyguard duty. Hannah the horse was positioned at the door. Twelve Beanie Babies cordoned off the windowsill. Pugsley the dog was handed over to Sandy, just in case she needed protecting too.

Becky whimpered many times in the middle of the night. Once, around three A.M., Shep caught her leaping out of bed and running for her closet.

When he tried to shake her awake, she whimpered harder, so he finally carried her back to bed with Big Bear. Becky mumbled for him to look out for monsters before falling more deeply asleep.

At six A.M. Shep moved to the couch in the family room. At seven A.M., when Sandy went to check on Becky, she found her curled up in the far corner of the closet, four dresses pulled down to hide her gleaming blond hair.

Becky still hadn't said anything about what had happened yesterday, and the doctors predicted she never would. Whatever she had experienced was too traumatic for her eight-year-old mind, and she was now working resiliently to lock it all away. Sandy and Shep were instructed to make their daughter feel safe, while being careful not to sound dismissive of her fears. Whatever that meant.

Sandy had the feeling she and Shep were aging exponentially these days. She would dearly love to pick up the phone to speak with Margaret or Liz or Margie about it, the way the four mothers had been comparing notes on their children for the last six years. Except she couldn't do that. Her children might be suffering, but her son was supposedly the cause of everyone's pain. It was now her job as his mother to pay his dues.

'What . . . what if Danny did do it?' Sandy ventured for the first time, staring tremulously at the rich, successful Avery Johnson, who held their future in his hands. 'What if all the experts study Danny and conclude that he is a killer?'

'This is what I've been trying to explain. The point of this trial isn't to say that Danny is a killer; it's to evaluate whether he will kill again. Juvenile court is going to appoint a forensic psychologist to evaluate Danny, his personality, past behavior, violent tendencies, et cetera. There is a whole range of parameters this psychologist will analyze, hence it takes some time. When he's done studying Danny, the expert will write up a report. In this case, given the seriousness of Danny's alleged crime, the forensic psychologist will probably make two statements. One will say, presuming Danny did commit mass murder, he has X percent chance of killing again. If he didn't commit mass murder, he has Y percent chance of being rehabilitated.'

'I don't understand. If Danny didn't do the crime, then he should have a one-hundred-percent chance of leading a normal, healthy life. How can there be a second statement?'

'The forensic psychologist is looking beyond this moment, Mrs O'Grady, to Danny's entire life, not just this one act, which he may or may not be guilty of.'

'Danny has always been a very good boy,' Sandy said automatically.

Avery Johnson looked at her sympathetically but firmly. 'Danny suffers explosions of violent rage. He spends a lot of time with guns. He has a reputation for being antisocial. These things are going to come up, Mrs

O'Grady. The forensic psychologist will be looking at all sorts of factors, including tensions in your family and other sources of stress.'

Shep bowed his head. Sandy knew what he was thinking. Their crumbling marriage. Shep's raging temper – not a great model for dealing with aggression, though Shep, God bless him, had never lifted a hand against her or the children. The furniture, however, was not always so lucky.

Shep finally spoke up. 'What if we don't like the expert's findings? Can't we get our own shrink?'

'Absolutely. First thing tomorrow morning I'll petition juvenile court for our own forensic psychologist. They'll still appoint the expert, but he'll work for us.'

'What does that cost?' Sandy asked hesitantly. 'I mean . . .'

She glanced at Shep; she could tell he was angry she'd brought up money. But she couldn't help herself. Sheriff paid only twenty-five thousand a year, and Sandy barely made nine dollars an hour at her job. She'd been hoping for more, she'd been hoping to be salaried after this new deal with Wal-Mart closed, but that already seemed a million years ago. She'd run out of the office and never looked back. In the evening Mitchell had left her a very nice message telling her to take all the time she needed, but she could tell he was disappointed. He needed help for the meeting now. With her gone, he'd have no choice but to find someone else. That was business.

'The juvenile court pays for the experts. It comes out of the court's funds.'

'It won't cost us anything?' Sandy asked.

Her husband growled. Avery Johnson assured her it wouldn't. For the first time she saw some compassion in his eyes. He probably understood a great deal more about their finances than she'd thought.

'The advantage of having our own expert is that he'll be subject to patient–client confidentiality. Danny can be perfectly honest with him, and if we think that's too damning in the end, we simply won't have our expert testify. No one will be the wiser.'

'But us,' Sandy said.

'If you have the information, you can get Danny help,' Avery said calmly.

'If you keep him out of adult court,' she countered.

'That's the challenge,' he agreed. 'For a thirteen-year-old boy, adult court spells doom.'

They were all silent for a moment, contemplating the road ahead and the young life at stake. Sandy rubbed her aching temples.

'Danny didn't do it,' Shep said stubbornly. 'I'm going to prove it.'

The phone rang. Shep automatically picked it up. He said hello, then his face froze and he slammed the phone down.

'Wrong number,' he muttered, but they all knew he was lying. The phone had been ringing all morning. Disembodied voices yelling, *'I hope they rape the bastard good. I hope in prison they fucking tear him apart. Baby killer, baby killer, baby killer.'*

Sandy had lived in this town all her life. She had loved it with her whole heart.

She turned back to Avery Johnson. 'What are our chances? Tell me honestly. What happened to the other boys accused of mass shootings?'

'Nearly all are in jail for life. But most of the shooters were sixteen, which made them fall automatically under the jurisdiction of adult court.'

'But not everyone? There's been an exception?'

'Jonesboro. Those two boys were too young, and Arkansas didn't have a statute for sending juveniles to adult court.'

'They remained in juvenile custody?'

'I believe they were ordered held until their twenty-first birthdays.'

Sandy felt hopeful for the first time. 'And did that work out, Mr Johnson?' she asked anxiously. 'Are they safe, productive members of their community now?'

'Nobody knows yet, Mrs O'Grady. Nobody knows.'

12

Wednesday, May 16, 5:57 P.M.

The man's favorite service provider was AOL. He liked the way it grouped headline news and made it easy to jump from story to story. Double-click on news summary, *Sheriff's Son Suspected in Small-Town Slayings.* Two paragraphs later, double-click again for the *in-depth* report. Whole world mourns. Three families devastated, president cries out for greater gun control, yada, yada, yada. A sidebar gave him additional options. He could chat with others on the subject. See a timeline of all the recent school shootings. Read an interview of other school-shooting survivors discussing how each new incident reopened their wounds and ripped out their hearts. He read that article. Open wounds, bleeding hearts. God, he loved journalism these days. For that matter, he kept the December 20, 1999, edition of *Time* magazine under glass. Anything for inspiration.

Two hours before he'd downloaded the most recent articles on the Bakersville story. Not as much coverage as he'd hoped. Only three dead, that was the problem. Front-page news had become a lot more competitive than when he'd first started. He'd have to remember that.

Six P.M. The man pushed away from his laptop. Damn, he was hungry.

This motel didn't offer much in the way of amenities. He'd hoped for a larger hotel, a nice innocuous chain. No such luck within driving distance of Bakersville. He'd had to go with a cheap, privately run place. On the one hand, the owner seemed overly interested in his guests. On the other hand, there wasn't a large staff working all hours of the night to notice the man's activities. Win some, lose some.

The man's stomach grumbled again. He decided to try the local bar.

Fifteen minutes later, coat and hat in place, he journeyed down the tiny main street into a dimly lit tavern. Three local men, clustered around the single TV, looked up curiously. The lone, balding bartender gave him a small nod of greeting. The man took a seat in front of three silver keg levers and ordered a beer.

'Anything good on the news?' he called down to the other men.

'Senate wants some new gun law. Hold the parents accountable for whatever damage their kids do with guns.'

'About time,' the man's friend mumbled. 'As they say, the apple never falls far from the tree; these kids had to get their ideas from somewhere.'

The third man eyed the first two levelly. He had an old, weather-beaten face from a lifetime spent riding a John Deere. He said quietly, 'Shep's a good man.'

The other two shrugged and almost immediately began studying their feet. Apparently they felt in no position to argue.

So the man at the bar drawled, 'Shep's a good sheriff, sure. But a father – don't you think a father is a separate thing?'

The three men turned away from the TV. For the first time, they truly studied him. The older man, Ruddy-Face, spoke first. 'I don't think we caught your name.'

'Oh, I'm just passing through. Business, you know. Generally I love traveling down the coast. Pretty countryside, nice people. But this time . . . A thirteen-year-old boy shooting two little girls. Then murdering that poor teacher . . . Such a beautiful woman, such a horrible waste.' He turned back to the bartender, whose welcoming demeanor had already disappeared. 'Can I get an order of buffalo wings? Extra hot. Extra blue cheese.'

'Nobody knows if Danny O'Grady did it,' Ruddy-Face said stiffly. The bartender nodded.

'Come on, Darren,' one of his friends said softly. 'My wife heard it straight from Luke Hayes's mother that Danny confessed.'

'And I'm telling you that the O'Gradys are good people.'

'Any other suspects?' the man at the bar asked casually.

'Some kids reported seeing a man in black,' Ruddy-Face said instantly.

'Come on, Darren, no one believes that. They're kids. They're frightened and they got a big imagination.'

'Doesn't mean it's not true.'

The other men frowned but once again deigned not to argue.

'I heard the O'Gradys have marital problems,' the man at the bar said next.

Ruddy-Face tried his cold stare on him. He was large, barrel-chested and thick-armed even now, from a lifetime of work. The man at the bar was not impressed. Old men like Ruddy-Face didn't engage in bar fights. They used their age and position to shame their opponents into silence. Well, he'd finally met his match. The man at the bar had no shame.

'I'm just saying what I heard,' he said evenly.

Ruddy-Face took a step forward. One of his companions caught his arm.

'Leave him alone, Darren. Man's got a right to his opinion.'

'Last summer,' Ruddy-Face said in a clipped voice, 'I drove to Bakersville for the weekly auction. Damn if I didn't blow out a tire on my trailer and nearly kill us all. Shep O'Grady was passing by in his patrol car, his son sitting in the passenger seat. They pulled over and helped me out. And Danny didn't just sit there. He got out of the car, helped line up the spare, and worked on tightening the lug nuts like a fine young man. When I thanked them both, he told me, no problem, sir, and shook my hand. I don't know what happened in that school. But I wouldn't be too quick to judge a boy, or two parents, the rest of you have never met.'

The man at the bar said, 'Really, that's interesting. 'Cause I heard Danny O'Grady has a nasty temper. Hangs out with the wrong crowd, trashed his own locker. My client has a son at Bakersville K-through-eight, and he said everyone knew Danny O'Grady was not right in the head.'

Ruddy-Face drew his bushy white brows into a thick, thunderous glare. His friend once more caught his arm.

'Face it,' his friend said in a placating voice. 'Tragedies like this aren't meant to make sense. Makes me wonder sometimes if each generation don't need a war, simply to have a way to vent.'

'You think war makes for better youths?' Ruddy-Face asked incredulously.

The friend shrugged. 'I remember shooting up Germans and Koreans, but never our schools.'

'That's a load of horseshit, Edgar.'

'I'm just saying—'

'Drug addictions and double amputees, that's what you're saying. Yeah, war works wonders for young men.'

'Well, what do you think is going on, Darren? These shootings keep happening! Jee-sus, how many has it been now!'

All the men fell silent, even the one at the bar, who was fighting not to grin.

Ruddy-Face said shortly, 'I guess we'll just have to see what happens.'

Edgar snorted. 'If anything happens. Bakersville doesn't even have a sheriff anymore. I hear that woman's in charge.'

'Officer Lorraine Conner,' the man at the bar said, and the bartender eyed him curiously.

Edgar nodded. 'Yeah, that's right. She's taken over the case, and God knows she's barely old enough to vote.'

'They also brought in a fed,' the man at the bar offered. 'Some expert in school shootings.'

'The feds got an expert in school shootings?' The bartender spoke up for the first time.

The man grinned at him. 'Interesting, isn't it?' he said. 'Now we just have to find out if the man is any good.'

Eight P.M. the streets of Bakersville had descended into dusky shades of gray, and Rainie's mood had grown tense.

After speaking with Principal VanderZanden, Rainie and Quincy had paid a visit to Melissa Avalon's tiny apartment, hoping to learn more about her life. By all appearances, Melissa Avalon was specifically targeted in the shooting. Perhaps she'd even been the only intended victim, and Rainie was having a hard time believing Danny O'Grady would purposely shoot the one teacher who'd been kind to him. Which raised the question of who Melissa Avalon was and, better yet, who might have wanted her dead. After hearing Quincy's suspicion of an Avalon–VanderZanden romance, Rainie was starting to lean in the principal's direction. Or maybe his betrayed wife . . .

Quincy, on the other hand, wasn't convinced of anything yet. He seemed to buy Melissa Avalon as the primary target, but he didn't think that meant the shooter had to know her. He'd murmured something about plenty of strangers having murdered plenty of young pretty women simply for being young pretty women. Rainie really didn't want to know what the agent read at night.

Unfortunately, Sanders had halted their investigation cold by getting to Avalon's apartment first. Drawers were rifled, the kitchen dismantled, the bed ripped apart. The crime-scene technicians had even pawed through the woman's tampons.

Rainie would have to wait for the state's report on the evidence or beg Sanders for information about her own damn case. It didn't leave her feeling amused.

She had stormed back to the task-force center with Quincy just in time to meet Luke Hayes and Deputy Tom Dawson. They had hoped to interview Becky O'Grady before dinner. They had failed. Avery Johnson had been at Shep's house. He had demanded to be present for the interview, and Sandy and Shep had insisted on sitting in as well. That had put an eight-year-old witness in a tiny family room with five scrutinizing adults.

Becky did the logical thing. She held her stuffed bear tight, curled up in a ball on the sofa, and fell asleep.

After fifteen minutes Luke and Tom headed for the door. Shep didn't see them out. The lawyer took care of that, after informing the officers that the O'Gradys would be changing to an unlisted number immediately due to harassing calls. Also, he wanted patrols to guard the family's safety. Hadn't they seen what some hostile redneck had written on the O'Gradys' garage?

The graffiti had really bothered Luke. He took two Polaroids for their files. Then he drove straight to the hardware store, where he purchased one bucket of primer and one bucket of white paint. He and Tom had spent the last hour personally repainting Shep's garage. Neither Shep nor Sandy ever came out to thank them.

Rainie didn't know what to say. Tragedies brought out the best in towns. But they could also bring out the worst.

Luke and Tom had no sooner left than the mayor paid Rainie a visit. He'd just received a call from Sally Walker's parents. What was this about the autopsies being pushed back until the next day? Why couldn't the families get their daughters' remains back so they could get on with the funerals? The parents were furious.

Also, had Rainie managed to catch George Walker on the five o'clock news? That's right. The father had appeared on camera stating to anyone who would listen that Danny O'Grady was getting away with murder. He'd killed three people, and the Bakersville sheriff's department would never go after him because he was Shep's son. Favoritism plain and simple, so all you mothers out there had better round up your children and lock the doors. One day soon, Danny O'Grady would be back in town.

All afternoon long there had been a run on rifles at the sporting-goods store. Not just in Bakersville but also in neighboring Cabot County.

People were frightened, the mayor stated bluntly. People were angry. So Rainie had better wrap this case up quick. Or there would be a hell of a lot more violence in these small-town streets.

Right after the mayor left, Rainie got out a new box of number-two pencils. She sat across the sawhorse desk from Quincy and methodically broke every single one in half. Then she broke the halves in half. Then she composed her thoughts.

It did her no good. Day two of the investigation and she had nothing but a longer list of questions. Why had Danny shot the one teacher who had apparently been trying to help him? Had Charlie Kenyon influenced Danny to act? Or maybe someone Danny met on-line? It seemed far-fetched to think that a stranger could influence a teenager to kill, but by all accounts Danny was a vulnerable kid and, God knows, stranger things had happened.

The single, small-caliber shot to Melissa Avalon's forehead. The scattered wounds on the others.

It seemed as if she ought to know more by now, but instead she had no answers, and she had worked herself into a state where the mere sound of Quincy's pen scratching against paper made her want to grab his notebook and beat him over the head with it. He'd laughed when she broke the pencils in half. The fed guys never knew how to have any fun.

He wasn't so bad, really. Cool in his detached FBI sort of way. Curious in how he kept staring at his cell phone, as if he was both expecting an important call and dreading it. And intense. More intense than she would've guessed this morning.

There was something about the way he had moved through the scene at the school, something about the way he had meticulously picked through Melissa Avalon's ravaged apartment, as if every bit of information was going into his brain and by sheer force of will he'd make the pieces fit. She had the impression that Quincy might be a little bit bright, and a little bit serious, and a little bit *strong*. That made her stomach tighten, which was something she needed right now about as much as a hole in her head.

Damn FBI agent. Damn state detective looking to prove a point. Damn Danny O'Grady. And damn a bunch of drunken fools who'd decided the only answer to violence was more violence. Christ, didn't they know how much paperwork they were going to cause her?

Rainie glanced away from the window and the night descending upon Bakersville's streets. She looked down at her new sawhorse desk, found that her hands were still fisted at her sides, and knew that her jumbled thoughts were all just noise. She could handle an FBI agent and a state detective. She honestly didn't give a rat's ass about what the mayor wanted for some press conference, and she wasn't afraid of a few local boys full of too much beer and not enough common sense; she'd dealt with that before.

What she didn't know, what she genuinely feared, was tomorrow morning at five A.M., when she would drive to Portland to watch the chief medical examiner cut open two little girls.

The thought of it unnerved her. She didn't want to see Sally and Alice again. Not now, when she knew their names and their families and that they had been best friends from birth. She didn't want to think of their final walk down that hall or the single cemetery plot that would now hold twin coffins.

Last night, for the first time in over five years, Rainie had dreamed of her mother's death. The blood and brains on the wall. The smell, the godawful stench of seeping human fluids and fresh gunpowder settling into the carpet. The headless body slumped on the floor, looking so strange and alien Rainie wouldn't have known it was her mother except for the bottle of Jim Beam still clutched in her lifeless hand.

And as she'd been staring, seventeen years old again, gray matter dripping down onto her hair, Danny O'Grady had come walking out of the kitchen and calmly handed her the smoking shotgun.

'I only did what you wanted done,' he'd said, then exited out her front door.

Rainie had woken up in a cold sweat at four in the morning, shivering uncontrollably. She forced herself to walk into the tiny living area, where the brown carpet and gold-flowered wallpaper had long ago been replaced. She studied every single aspect of the room – new, modern, fourteen years later – and she could've sworn she saw blood on the ceiling.

Rainie went back to bed, but she knew from the trembles in her hands when she woke up an hour later that her dreams had still been unkind.

This case was getting to her. She hadn't expected that after all these years. It frightened her. And it made her mad.

'I want dinner,' she stated abruptly, standing up at the crude desk and beginning to gather her things.

Quincy looked up from his notebook. His expression was mild, but he'd discarded his jacket, rolled up his sleeves, and loosened his burgundy tie. It made him look more approachable. It also emphasized the dark circles beneath his eyes. Apparently, superagent hadn't been sleeping much even before arriving in Bakersville.

'They have food in this town?' he asked with feigned surprise. 'And here I'd thought we skipped lunch out of necessity.'

'Lunch is for sissies,' Rainie said. 'Come on. I'll take you to Martha's Diner. Best chicken-fried steak in town.'

Quincy raised a skeptical brow, maybe questioning Martha's claim to fame, maybe already anticipating his arteries hardening. Either way, he grabbed his navy blue jacket and followed.

Martha's Diner was quiet at this hour. Most working folks had already eaten, and most farmers would soon be in bed. Nothing like several thousand cows to ruin a town's nightlife. Rainie recognized the credit union's president, Donald Leyden, eating alone after his divorce. Then Rainie spotted Abe Sanders.

Sitting alone in a corner booth, Sanders was holding his cell phone with one hand while picking at a skinless chicken breast with the other. In between comments on the phone, he chewed raw carrots from a Ziploc bag. Then Rainie noticed the Tupperware container of lettuce. The state detective traveled with salad. If she hadn't known before, she definitely knew now – Abe Sanders was the Antichrist.

'Yes, I hear the puppy,' he was saying with some exasperation into the cell phone. 'No, Sara, you don't need to put him on the phone. No, no. Hey—' His voice suddenly changed to a higher pitch. 'Hi there, Murphy. Yes, you're a good dog. You're such a good dog. Now put your mom back on the phone. Really, put your mom – Sara. Sara, there you are. Yeah, yeah, I said hi, but he's a dog, for chrissakes. He doesn't understand the modern miracle of AT&T.

'Wait a minute. Is he whimpering now? Why is the puppy whimpering? What happened? What? Really?' Sanders sounded surprised, then sheepishly pleased. 'Murphy goes around the house each morning looking for me? He misses me. Huh. I'll be damned. He really is a smart little guy.'

Sanders finally noticed Rainie and Quincy staring at him.

He sat up quickly, looking caught red-handed, and hastily said good-bye. He was still blushing when he snapped shut his flip phone.

'New puppy,' he muttered. 'My wife . . . she's kind of nuts about the thing. You know how it is.' He swallowed, then nodded toward the empty side of the booth. 'Want to have a seat? I got some news.'

Rainie already felt wary, but she slid into the red vinyl booth while introducing Quincy to Sanders. The two had obviously heard of each other, and the handshake was perfunctory.

'So what brings you to Bakersville?' Sanders asked after Quincy blew off Rainie's suggestion of chicken-fried steak and ordered a Caesar salad. Rainie shook her head to let him know he was making a mistake, then ordered the steak, mashed potatoes, and an extra helping of gravy. She hadn't eaten all day, and she'd be damned before she was shamed by two men into eating salad. She was still trying to decide if a chocolate malt would be overkill, when Quincy answered.

'I'm researching school shootings for the Behavioral Science Unit. Naturally I'm interested in this case.'

'You're observing?'

Quincy looked at Rainie. 'Something like that.'

'We don't need federal help,' Sanders said bluntly.

Quincy smiled. 'Don't worry, Detective. I wouldn't dream of stepping on Officer Conner's toes by claiming jurisdiction over the case. I hear she has very strong feelings on the subject – and that she's very good with her sidearm.'

Rainie grinned at the unexpected compliment. Sanders scowled.

'Well,' the state man said briskly, wiping his hands on his napkin, 'the whole thing will probably be moot by morning. As a matter of fact, I'm pretty sure I wrapped up the majority of the case today.'

'Really?' Rainie gave him a dubious glance. 'And here I thought I'd destroyed the case just this morning.'

'Sometimes the evidence comes together in spite of an officer's best intentions,' Sanders assured her.

'I'll remember that. What new evidence?'

'Oh, didn't I tell you?' Sanders feigned surprise. 'Got some info back from ATF today. Tracing Danny's .38 revolver and .22 semiauto was simple. Both registered to one Shep O'Grady. Furthermore, the CSU recovered five .38-caliber slugs from the area of incidence last night. Today the ME confirmed that blood and fiber on the slugs are consistent with the two juvenile DOAs, and – drum roll here – ballistics determined that rifling on the slugs matches Danny's revolver. You were right, Conner, we got at least one of the murder weapons.'

'So the .38 was used to kill the two little girls,' Rainie said with a frown. 'That still doesn't prove Danny was the one who pulled the trigger.'

'Yeah, but we also got Danny's prints on all the casings recovered at the scene. A good lawyer will still argue that only proves Danny loaded the guns, not that he fired them, but at this point the circumstantial evidence is overwhelming. We can tie Danny to the murder weapon. He has no alibi for the time of the shooting, and we have a witness – you – who places him in the school immediately after the shootings, holding his father hostage. Even if we can't get his confession entered into evidence, I think we have enough for a jury to connect the dots.'

'What about Melissa Avalon? So far, the evidence ties him only to the girls.'

'Don't know about Avalon yet. It appears she was shot once in the forehead with the .22 semiauto. No exit wound, of course, so we have to wait for the ME to retrieve the slug during tomorrow's autopsy. Cases like this generally aren't promising, though. Twenty-two-caliber slugs are only forty grains and made out of soft lead. Most of the time they're too deformed from ricocheting around the skull to yield any rifling marks. We'll have to see. On the other hand, I learned some dirt today when I got my hair cut. According to the rumor mill, Avalon and the principal were really tight . . . if you know what I mean.'

'Big deal,' Rainie said. 'Quincy figured that out after a ten-minute chat with the principal. Go, fed.'

Quincy shrugged modestly. Sanders looked chagrined. 'You knew he was stepping out on his wife?'

'His reaction to Miss Avalon's death seemed overly intense for the circumstances.'

'Huh.' Sanders scowled, grabbed a fresh carrot stick, and then recovered. 'It doesn't matter to the investigation,' he said firmly. 'I checked with the administrative staff, and Principal VanderZanden was in his office when the shots were fired. From what I can tell, Danny is the only one unaccounted for at the time. Something else to put in our reports.'

'There are still the students who were absent yesterday to consider,' Rainie said.

'Twenty-one students out sick,' Sanders reported. 'Sixteen already have alibis in the form of anxious parents. I bet you the other five are cleared by tomorrow afternoon.'

'What about the computers?' Quincy asked. 'Principal VanderZanden said Danny spent a great deal of time online. I'm curious about that.'

Sanders looked at him shrewdly. 'You're thinking outside influence,' he said.

'It's been a factor in several of the shootings. And I am surprised by Danny's sophistication in breaking in to what I would presume to be a state-of-the-art gun safe.'

Sanders grunted. 'Don't know enough yet about the gun safe to determine how hard he had to work to get into it. I do know Shep had a helluva gun collection. We're lucky Danny went with two small handguns instead of the rifles. God knows what kind of damage he could've done then.'

'Do we know why he chose the .38 and .22?' Quincy asked.

Sanders looked at Rainie. She shook her head. 'He didn't comment and I didn't think to ask. I guess I assumed because they were easier to fit into a backpack. Concealment.'

'But Danny was a hunter, wasn't he?' Quincy asked.

'Sure. Since he was very young.'

'Did he spend a lot of time with handguns as well?'

Rainie had to think about it. In the meantime, their dinners arrived. Quincy's salad looked fresh and crisp – the advantage of being in farm country. Rainie's chicken-fried steak, on the other hand, was smothered in thick gravy, with a pat of butter melting on top. The smell made her stomach growl, but when she picked up her fork, she discovered that the conversation had already destroyed her appetite.

'Shep generally tells hunting stories,' she said after a moment. 'I know Danny has some marksmanship awards, but I think they were with a .22 rifle.'

'First place, junior division,' Sanders confirmed. 'We seized the trophy from his bedroom.'

Rainie grimaced. She didn't want to think what it must have been like for Sandy and Shep to watch their son's room be boxed up by Crime Scene Unit personnel. Or what kind of impression that must have made on Becky.

Quincy was talking. 'So Danny's most comfortable with a rifle but selects two handguns. He has a love–hate relationship with sports but goes after the teacher of the computer lab, whom he supposedly adores. He hides in a room so nobody will see him but never leaves the building after the shooting. Interesting.' He turned to Sanders again. 'About the school computers . . .'

'Techies are examining them now,' Sanders said. 'Looks like a main computer and three workstations. The school had a firewall server, so the good news is that it probably has a record of which workstation visited which Internet sites at what time. In theory, the lab rats will have a complete rundown for me of all the sites visited by the end of the week. I did get a call this afternoon saying that the computers have been messed with – the cache file purged, the Web browser's history file deleted, et cetera – so it appears that someone made an effort to cover their tracks. The techies weren't too concerned. Something about probably being able to find things in the cookies, or God knows what. They were going to start work on it in the morning.'

'If there are any problems, we have excellent recovery agents at the Bureau,' Quincy mentioned casually.

'Yeah, yeah, yeah.' Sanders definitely had no intention of parting with his evidence. He waved his hand dismissively. 'I'm sure we'll be fine. We already got a lot of evidence in place. At this point, the computer stuff will just go to state of mind.'

'We don't have anything connecting Danny to Melissa Avalon,' Rainie pointed out.

'Then the DA just pursues the charges for killing the girls. That's fine by me. There are only so many consecutive life sentences a man can serve.'

'A boy can serve,' Rainie said absently, giving up on her dinner altogether and stealing a piece of Quincy's lettuce. 'Only so many consecutive life sentences a boy can serve.'

Sanders rolled his eyes. 'Like age has anything to do with it these days. We're about to be overrun by an entire generation of juvenile psychopaths. Isn't that right, Quincy? Dual-income families have turned out a batch of superpredators who have no sympathy or remorse. Blast 'em up on Nintendo; blast 'em up on the streets. Murder pregnant women; run home to watch Bugs Bunny on TV. *The New York Times* ran a whole article on it.'

'I wouldn't believe everything you read,' Quincy said.

'Why not? I read that article in the early nineties and we've had how many school shootings since then?'

'Half a dozen, I'm sure,' Quincy said mildly, 'but we still had one of the safest school years on record in 1998.'

Sanders gave Quincy a dubious look. The FBI agent returned it levelly. 'In the 1992–1993 school year,' Quincy said, 'a time frame I'm sure that article quoted, there were fifty-five fatalities. As you point out, however, this is before we experienced the rash of school shootings. In the 1997–1998 school year, we saw three school shootings. And yet, total fatalities for that year were only forty, nearly a thirty-percent decline. The truth is, violence in schools is a lot like airline crashes – tragic and shocking and headline-grabbing, but by no means indicative of the whole sector. Children are still safer at school – and in planes – than in the family's minivan.'

'But then again, these incidents aren't magically going away,' Rainie countered. She stole a crouton from Quincy's salad and gave him her own version of his hard, direct stare. 'In the beginning, maybe you could dismiss this as a phase, but it's been years now. One shooting is scary. Seven are downright terrifying.'

'We face troubling issues,' Quincy agreed, 'but we shouldn't lose perspective. Overall juvenile criminal offenses have declined in the last five years. And as we've cracked down on drugs and gangs, schools have become safer. That's the good news.

'On the other hand,' he added as he saw their growing skepticism, '*some* teenagers are shockingly violent and lacking in remorse. And, unfortunately, the media distorts that fact. *Normal Boy Kills Ten. Perfect Family Murdered by Fourteen-Year-Old Son.* It leads us to rampant paranoia and, if we're not careful, fear of all children. The truth, however, is that the overwhelming majority of children who commit these shootings aren't, quote unquote, normal. Several have suffered from recognized mental disorders and were supposed to be on medication. Even the ones who weren't under a doctor's care probably had a strong degree of attachment disorder, making it easier for them to contemplate murder.'

'What's attachment disorder?' Sanders asked.

'It's the failure to bond,' Rainie said instantly, then shrugged and helped herself to more of Quincy's salad. 'I studied psychology in college. I remember a thing or two.'

'Very good,' Quincy assured her, then frowned and pulled his salad protectively to him. She stole another crouton. He gave up.

'Everyone needs to bond,' Quincy explained to Sanders. 'In theory, as children we bond with our parents. We cry, our parents respond to our cry by feeding us, and we decide our parents are good people and love us – we bond. As we grow older, this bond extends to the rest of society, helping us be good friends, neighbors, husbands, et cetera. Unfortunately, not all children form bonds. The baby cries and is hit. In that case, instead of learning to trust or care about others, the child becomes egocentric, lying compulsively, manipulating others, being incapable of feeling empathy. For the most part, we see this phenomenon in abused or abandoned children. Lack of bonding, however, can happen in "good" households too. It's just not as common.'

'Good parents have bad kids?' Sanders asked, and rolled his eyes to show his opinion. Quincy wasn't fazed.

'Absolutely. A mother suffers from severe postpartum depression and is unable to meet her infant's needs. Or the newborn suffers from a painful medical condition and it's not in his mother's power to meet his needs. Or the newborn simply isn't amenable to bonding. No matter how hard the mother tries, the baby pulls away. It's rare, but it happens. So yes, good parents can end up with one child who is very social and one child who is very antisocial.'

Sanders gave Quincy another dubious look. 'I don't buy it,' he said bluntly. 'You're saying these kids are little freaking psychopaths from birth. Well, if that's the case, why doesn't anyone notice? Why do all the headlines read *Normal Boy Kills Ten?*'

'Think Ted Bundy,' Rainie offered conversationally. 'Everyone thought he was a handsome, charming man. Only problem was that he raped and murdered young girls as a hobby. Oops.'

'Exactly,' Quincy said, and gave her an approving nod. Rainie found herself smiling back. The fed had warm blue eyes when he smiled like that – dazzling, Paul Newman eyes.

'Still sounds like psychobabble to me,' Sanders was harrumphing. 'The kids are murderers. End of story. The best solution is to lock them up and throw away the key.'

'Age doesn't matter?' Quincy asked mildly. He was still looking at Rainie. Belatedly, they both returned their attention to the salad.

'Nope,' Sanders said. 'If the kid is capable of doing the act, he's capable of paying the price.'

Quincy shrugged, obviously less convinced. He stabbed another bite of salad, then surprised both Rainie and Sanders by saying, 'Maybe. God knows I've seen some things.' He paused. 'Some kids are dangerous,' he said finally, more forcefully. 'Some of the youths I've interviewed probably are beyond all help, let alone our ability to imagine. But not all of them are like that. And our legal system is based on the philosophy that we'd let a hundred guilty men go free before sending one innocent man away. It seems clear to me, then, that we have an obligation to try to identify which youths are amenable to rehabilitation. Not to simply lump all offenders together, then ship them out of sight.'

'Can you really help a kid who's committed murder?' Rainie asked curiously.

'Sometimes. The younger the child is, the better the chances. Also, attachment disorder is a range. Some of the kids I've interviewed represented the extreme end of the spectrum. To put it in Sanders's terms, they are "little freaking psychopaths." And I'll agree with him there – it's safer for us all to lock those ones up and throw away the key.' Quincy smiled dryly at the state detective. Then his voice dropped. He appeared more somber. 'However, that's not the case for all of our teenage offenders. As we discussed before, Officer Conner, mass murderers are not homogeneous. Some of the school shooters were definitely more followers than leaders. They were troubled, they were vulnerable. They let themselves be manipulated into performing a violent act, because they were hurt and disturbed and didn't know how to deal with that. They did what they did, but afterward they also felt remorse and regret. I think these kids probably could be reformed. Given their ages, it seems a shame not to try.'

'And if we're wrong and they kill again?' Sanders quizzed. 'You gonna be the one visiting the family's home to tell them how your failed science experiment murdered their wife, sister, mother? You gonna be the one on TV trying to explain why we thought it was such a great idea to let a known killer loose on society?'

Quincy gave him a faint smile. 'It happens. Some of our more prolific serial killers – Kempner, for example – are graduates of the juvenile system. Killed young. Were sentenced to rehabilitation. Came of age. Killed even more people.'

'At times like this, I'm glad I don't have a kid,' Sanders said.

Quincy finally sighed. He set down his fork and seemed to lose interest once and for all in the salad. 'Things are becoming more complicated,' he murmured. 'Do you know we're now using our serial-killer profiling techniques in high schools?'

Rainie arched a brow. Sanders exclaimed more eloquently, 'You're shitting me.'

'I shit you not, Detective. In the wake of the recent shootings, several school districts have implemented "student profiling." School administrators have a checklist of "suspicious" behavior to use to evaluate each student's potential for violence. Things like animal cruelty, abusive language, writings containing graphic violence. A few of our agents are now teaching classes in behavioral science and psychological profiling to teachers.'

'What happens if a student is profiled as potentially dangerous?' Rainie asked with a frown. 'Do they call the cops, pat him down, and confiscate his video games?'

'Most districts have a policy to notify the parents, then the student can be sent to counselors or be expelled. It's being taken quite seriously.'

'So were the Salem witch trials.'

'Yes, but the witches never killed thirteen people. Schools are under pressure. Three years ago Principal VanderZanden rejected the notion that a shooting could happen here. How much do you want to bet he's regretting it now? And if the school board hears of profiling next week, how much do you want to bet your teachers will be searching for future homicidal maniacs in between grading papers?'

They all grew silent. Sanders shook his head. 'Man, I could not be a teacher,' he said vehemently. 'I see two to four homicides a week, nice fresh kills, and still the thought of what's going on inside the classroom scares me to death. Half of these teachers are being bullied and harassed by their own students, and now they're supposed to actively wonder which little boys are cold-blooded killing machines. Yeah, they'll sleep well at night.'

Rainie shrugged. 'Teachers should be used to it by now. When was the last time the PTA called for better parenting? It's always the school's fault. No matter what happens, my God, why aren't schools doing a better job of raising our kids?'

Quincy smiled dryly. 'Spoken as two people who don't have children.'

'I wonder what did it for Danny O'Grady,' Sanders mused out loud. 'He doesn't seem so different from the other school shooters to me. Bit of a loner, spends all his time in a computer lab, and can't cut it on the football field. I haven't found a teacher yet who knows of any close friends. Then you throw in the fact that his father seems to have a God complex, his parents are fighting all the time, and little Danny pretty much cut his teeth on a hunting rifle . . . Hell, maybe profiling would've saved the school from him. Seems like it was only a matter of time.'

Quincy shook his head. 'I don't think profiling would've identified Danny O'Grady. He was a good student, polite with his teachers, diligent in his studies. We've heard no stories of torturing pets and not even a fascination with fire. Danny is angry. But there's still no evidence that he's homicidal.'

'Oh, the kid did the deed,' Sanders said confidently. 'Conner caught him red-handed with the murder weapons, and he's confessed twice. Case closed. Now we just got to wrap everything up before this whole frigging town explodes. Redneck assholes. There oughtta be an IQ requirement for owning a gun.'

Rainie didn't say anything. It was after nine-thirty, the diner was nearly empty, and in spite of Sanders's big words, they all appeared pensive.

'Food for thought,' Quincy said in the hushed solitude of the restaurant, wiping his hands on his paper napkin and getting ready to stand. 'All of the school shooters craved notoriety. They walked openly into their schools and pulled out their guns in plain sight. They wanted their classmates to know it was them. They wanted full recognition of their vengeance. But Danny O'Grady managed not to be seen by a single person. In fact, one of the teachers claimed the shots were fired from within the computer lab, as if the killer was deliberately seeking to remain unnoticed.'

'He panicked, he was scared,' Sanders said.

'Second thought. School shootings are about displaced rage. Now, by all accounts, Danny has a domineering, intimidating father. I imagine he does have some displaced anger. So why didn't he target the football coach, a macho man like his father, or star athletes, who would represent the kind of boy his father wants him to be, or the school principal, a classic father figure? Why would he deliberately seek out Melissa Avalon – young, female, and an expert at the subject he loved the most? What about her would incite his rage?'

'Maybe he developed a crush on her. She refused his attentions and he snapped.'

'Third thought. Most shooters go after as many victims as possible. Overkill and inciting terror in their peers is part of their fantasy. They want to feel powerful. So why did Danny wait until after lunch, when everyone was back in their classrooms? And why choose smaller handguns when he's comfortable with rifles and they'd inflict more damage?'

'Maybe it wasn't a real school shooting,' Sanders said with a scowl. 'Maybe he just wanted to get back at Miss Avalon because she hurt his feelings or looked at him the wrong way and it was more than he could take. So he snaps, plots his revenge against her, and the other two girls simply get in the way.'

'Not a bad theory, Detective, but you have one problem.'

'What?'

'You can't tie him to Melissa Avalon's death. You're saying that she's what this was all about, and yet she's the one victim you can't prove he killed. How do you explain that?'

Sanders finally spluttered to a halt. He was wide-eyed and thinking hard.

Quincy's lips curved into an ironic half smile. 'I don't know what happened yesterday afternoon in that school, Detective, but I think there's more to it than meets the eye. We need to keep our minds open at this point. And we need to know what's in those computers. Especially after what your technicians said.'

'What did my technicians say?'

'That somebody tried to erase the Web browser history and cache files. You don't erase what isn't important.'

'Shit,' Sanders said.

Quincy smiled again, but the shadows were darker around his eyes.

They all rose from the table. Rainie reached for money, but Sanders surprised her by picking up the tab.

Then they were outside, where the night air smelled of pine needles and fresh spring rain. No one had anything more to say. Sanders walked back to his car. Rainie and Quincy remained standing alone. She studied his face again, his blue eyes that could be both warm and hard. She wondered if he was right about Danny, and the fact they still knew so little frustrated her.

She wanted answers for her community. She wanted answers for Shep and Sandy. She wanted answers for herself, so she could finally get visions of the school out of her head and the night would stop closing in on her.

The fed was watching her, the look on his face hard to read. She studied his hands again. Those hard-earned calluses. The absent wedding ring.

'I need somewhere to sleep,' Quincy said at last.

She said, 'I know just the place.'

13

Ginnie's motel hotel wasn't seedy. The mattresses were twenty years old and the scarred maple dressers had been picked up at garage sales, but the flowered curtains were hand-sewn, the worn white sheets freshly laundered, and the rugs vacuumed vigorously each day.

Ginnie ran the front desk, her gray hair in pink sponge curlers and her massive frame covered by a dark blue muumuu with an orange-flowered print. She explained to Quincy that she had opened the Motel Hotel ten years ago when her fourth husband, George, had passed away. After so many years of taking care of men, she'd decided to run a business where she could have a new man over every night. She winked flirtatiously when she said this. Quincy hoped she was joking.

Ginnie went through her spiel. She served homemade muffins every morning, Toll House cookies every night. She'd wash your laundry for two bucks a load; please leave the dirty clothes piled by the front door. Finally, the Motel Hotel was not as rustic as it seemed. She'd installed state-of-the-art data lines so she could check her stock portfolio every hour on-line.

She slapped a laminated list of access numbers for local Internet providers on top of the desk. Then she invited Quincy to visit her site at BigMama.com.

Rainie suppressed a smile. Quincy began to back away slowly from the muumuu. Moments later he and Rainie were in the parking lot, where the tiny string of rooms spread out in a pink-painted V.

'Where the hell have you brought me?' Quincy asked Rainie as he found his door and fumbled with the key.

'Local color,' Rainie told him. 'Only tourists stay at the Motel 6.'

'Can't I be a federal tourist?'

'Of course not. Ginnie knows the best gossip in Bakersville – after Walt, of course. Show up for breakfast tomorrow morning. Down a few bran muffins. You'll be amazed how much you'll learn.'

'And how clean my colon will be,' Quincy muttered, and shoved the old door open.

Inside, Rainie watched as Quincy set his duffel bag on the single queen-size bed, placed his computer beneath the pine table, and identified the location of the phone jack. She imagined that she was observing a ritual the agent had performed in hundreds of hotel rooms in hundreds of small towns. He checked the closet, grabbing the extra pillow for the bed, then hung his jacket neatly on the back of a chair. Next he entered the tiny bathroom, inspecting the stock of soap and shampoo. Finally he returned to the front of the room, studying the window and the door locks.

A single curved latch, which appeared older than dirt, held the window shut. Quincy grimaced. The door cheered him up about as much. One chain, easily snapped. One bolt lock that could be jimmied by a two-year-old. He shook his head.

'Is anyone around here aware of basic safety?'

'And spoil our small-town charm? The city council would never hear of it. Besides, what kind of idiot robs a fed?'

'I'm going to need a broom handle to jam this window,' he said seriously. 'And a chair to stick under the door.'

'Don't you carry a gun, SupSpAg?'

'Yes, but requisitioning sticks involves less paperwork.'

Quincy went outside, found a suitable twig to jam the lower window casing, and jury-rigged the room the best he could. Apparently, he did take safety seriously. Then again Rainie had caught a glimpse of the photos he carried in his computer bag. She supposed if she did nothing but stare at murder victims all day, she would be obsessed with bolt locks and window guards as well.

Finally, Quincy dusted off his hands. He'd done all he could do with his accommodations. Now his gaze drifted to the phone. Rainie watched him quickly look away. Unfortunately, there was little else in the room to hold his attention. Ginnie didn't believe in TV.

The night was thick outside. The room filled with shadows. Nothing left to do but say good night and hope they didn't wake up too many times, dreaming of little boys armed with assault rifles and little girls fleeing down long, dark hallways.

'Rainie,' Quincy said after a moment, 'can I buy you a drink?'

Rainie was startled. She hadn't seen the offer coming. She stared at him harder and tried to decide what it meant. A drink. Just a drink? With smart, capable Supervisory Special Agent Pierce Quincy. He struck her as the kind of man who lived his life by certain rules. But his gaze was softer now. Not an agent anymore, she thought. A man addressing a woman.

She honestly wasn't sure what to do with that.

She felt restless, edgy. She'd seen too much death, and tomorrow morning she would rise at the crack of dawn to examine it some more. She should be alone. Sit on her back deck, cradle an icy bottle of beer, and listen to the hoot owl mourn. But she wanted to go to a bar. Someplace where the music was loud and the dance floor crowded and all the women were pretty, while all the men had a gleam in their eyes. She could pick a date. She could pick a fight. On nights like this, she wasn't sure which she preferred.

She just knew that sometimes she was her mother's daughter, and she never trusted herself when she was in this kind of mood. *Go home, Rainie. You know the drill.*

She studied Quincy instead. The firm set of his lips. The strong line of his shoulders. That blue, blue gaze of a man who knew what he was about.

Goddamn him.

Thirty minutes later, she'd changed into civvies and they were sitting at a bar.

Tequila's was a happening place. Plank floor covered in peanut shells. Tiny booths covered in scarred brown vinyl. Pitchers of beer that went for a buck fifty on Wednesday nights and all-you-could-eat mozzarella sticks during happy hour. The jukebox belted out country favorites. On the dance floor, half the couples moved easily to the rhythmic steps of line dancing. Deeper in the shadows, other couples moved to other rhythms in perfect time.

Rainie yelled her order for a bottle of Bud Light over the din. Quincy surprised her by ordering the same. He struck her as a Heineken man, but live and learn.

For a while they simply sat, watching the dance floor, absorbing the noise and loosening up until the lessons of Bakersville's K–8, and Danny O'Grady, seemed far away.

'Nice place,' Quincy said shortly.

'Fun,' Rainie said.

'Come here often?'

'Careful, SupSpAg. Next thing you know, you'll be asking my sign.'

Quincy grinned. It was a good look on his face, especially with his shirtsleeves rolled up and his silk tie loosened. He took a long pull from the beer bottle.

'Nice and cold,' he said. 'How's yours?'

'Don't know. I'm an alcoholic, Quince. Came from an alcoholic mother. Probably had an alcoholic father. I'd know if my mother had sobered up long enough to remember his name.'

He gave her a curious look. 'We didn't have to come to a bar.'

'Not a problem. I've been sober ten years. I know what I'm doing.'

'But you still order a beer?'

'Yep. I like holding the bottle in my hand and knowing I can set it down again. It's the sense of power, I'm sure. Plus' – she slipped him a wink – 'beer bottles are a goddamn phallic delight.'

Quincy burst out laughing. She grinned back at him. She bet he didn't laugh often, which was too bad. He sounded good laughing. He looked good too.

'And you?' she asked, setting down the bottle. 'Tell me the truth, SupSpAg, what really brings you to Bakersville?'

'The job, of course. So much crime, so little time.'

'Travel a lot?'

'Three or four cities a week. I'm either a federal agent or a rock star.'

'Hell on relationships,' she said casually.

His lips curved at one corner. She hadn't fooled him. 'I was married,' he said. 'Lasted fifteen years, which was probably seven more than I deserved. I used to carry a photo of her in a silver frame in my briefcase. Every hotel room I stayed in, the first thing I would do was place her picture on the table. Unfortunately, that didn't match her idea of quality time. We divorced. I learned to work without her photo on my desk. And you?'

'I don't do relationships. Have a strict policy against them. I figure if half of the American people are getting divorced, that's good enough for me.'

Quincy gave her a skeptical look. She could tell he was trying to evaluate her statement for truth versus bravado. 'You're young, intelligent, beautiful. What about starting a family?'

'Oh no. I don't do children. They're small, needy, easily destroyed. Let's be honest. I've come a long way from my family history, but I'm still the child of an abusive alcoholic and we don't make great parent material. For the Conners, the cycle ends here.'

'You shouldn't underestimate yourself, Rainie.'

'I don't underestimate myself. I'm simply honest.'

She watched him take another swig from his beer. He was definitely interested. She could see the light in his eyes. He was reluctant, bemused, but interested. Call her a fool, but it made her smile.

She leaned forward, sweeping her long hair to one side as she prepared to get serious. 'So tell me more, Quincy. We're here in a bar, a long way from crime scenes, and you're almost through your first beer. Tell me all the baggage. I like starting with the junk out in the open. It saves time later.'

'I don't have interesting baggage.'

'Everybody does.'

'No, I just have typical law-enforcement stuff. The ex-wife. The two grown children who barely know I exist. Too much dedication to the job, not enough attention at home. The usual mistakes.'

'Yeah? So why are you avoiding phones?'

He jerked, caught off guard. Then he gave her a more measured stare. It pleased her to surprise him. She was beginning to realize that with an academic like him, it was a form of flirtation.

'I didn't realize it was that obvious.'

'Pierce?'

'Don't call me that. Only my ex-wife uses my first name. Everyone else calls me Quincy, like the medical examiner from the old TV show. Serial killers and their sense of humor,' he murmured.

She kept looking at him. He finally set down his beer.

'One of my daughters,' he said abruptly, 'is in the hospital.'

'Is it serious?'

'She's dying. No, that's not true,' he corrected himself. 'She's dead. She's been dead for four weeks. Twenty-three years old and involved in such a bad automobile accident that the front windshield carries an imprint of her face. I know. I made the police show it to me.' He looked off in the distance a moment. Rainie was struck by how haggard he appeared. Then how exhausted.

'Now she lies in a hospital room,' he said quietly, 'where machines breathe for her and pump her heart and feed her food, while the rest of us sit by her side day after day, desperate for some miracle to save her. Except that her brain is dead and the machines can't fix that. The miracles of science take us so far, and yet not nearly far enough.'

'Jesus. Shouldn't you be there?'

'Yes.'

'Well, why aren't you?'

'Because if I had to spend one more minute sitting in that room, watching that mockery of human life play out in front of me, I was going to lose my mind.' His eyes suddenly glinted with moisture. He brushed it away with the back of his hand and looked at her almost impatiently. 'Rainie, my daughter doesn't have a *face* anymore. Her vehicle hit a telephone pole going thirty-five miles per hour without her seat belt on. Do you really want to hear how the force of impact pushes a body not just forward but up in the air? That steering-wheel columns are designed to collapse so they won't crush a person's chest or internal organs, but that they also can't halt all the G forces once they've been unleashed? How the body keeps going forward, keeps going up. How the person's skull now slams into the metal frame of the windshield, which isn't designed to collapse, which isn't designed to give way? And then comes the nose and face, slamming into the windshield, shattering all those bones, while the skull is driven deeper into the person's brain . . .

'My daughter doesn't have a head anymore. She has a pulpy mass carefully held in place by staples and thread and miles of fluffy white gauze. The only reason she was even put on life support was that the doctors were waiting for permission to harvest her organs. But now she's there, a grotesque doll animated purely by machines, and my ex-wife, Bethie, keeps mistaking that for life, so she won't let go. And I don't think it's right. I don't think there's any . . . dignity . . . in that. And I don't think my younger daughter, Kimberly, should have to sit at her sister's side and listen to her mother and me fight over when to pull the plug. My feelings on the subject are clear. Now it's up to Bethie to figure out when she can let go.'

'So you arrived, you gave your expert advice, and you left.'

Quincy blinked several times. 'You know, you could at least pretend not to see through me,' he said at last. 'Particularly when you're sober at the time.'

He took another swallow of beer, looking as if he needed it now. His bottle was nearly empty. The waitress stopped by to ask him if he wanted a second. He hesitated, his gaze clearly thirsty, but then shook his head.

'Surprised you didn't go to whiskey,' Rainie commented.

'I did, for a week. Then I had to give it up due to irony. Amanda was killed by a drunk driver.'

'Ah.'

'I tried eating. Potato chips, candy bars, Gummy Bears. Anything that came out of a hospital vending machine. But I kept forgetting to chew, and that made things difficult. I resumed jogging. That seems to do the trick. You?'

'Twelve miles, four days a week. Bet I could run you into the ground.'

'I'm nearly fifteen years older than you, Rainie. I bet you could run me into the ground.'

'Quincy, you're not that old.'

The space between them sparked again. He looked away first.

'Now it's your turn,' he said abruptly. 'Tit for tat.'

'All right.' She brought up her chin gamely and got a good grip on her Bud Light. 'My mom was a drunk. A mean drunk. A promiscuous drunk. Trailer trash, you know the type. She got into a lot of brawls, hung out with men who beat her, and, following the trickle-down theory of family management, returned home to beat me. Except one day when I came home, she'd been decapitated by a shotgun blast to the head. And unfortunately for me, I was the first person at the scene.'

'Did Shep O'Grady arrest you?'

'Yep.' She shrugged. 'I would've arrested me too. The whole town knew what she was doing. Now here she was dead, and I had her brains in my hair. I made a great suspect. But I was the wrong one.'

'And who was the right one?'

'Officially, it's still unsolved. Unofficially, they're pretty sure it was her man of the moment. A neighbor saw him at the house right before she heard the gunshot. Maybe it was some kind of lover's quarrel, or maybe he was just too drunk to think straight. My mother didn't exactly date rocket scientists. He was a trucker, I think. They put out an APB, but no one ever saw him again. Just some guy passing through. And now it's been so many years I don't even remember his name.' Rainie shrugged again. 'Given the way my mother lived, I don't think the story could have ended any other way.'

'And for you?' Quincy said quietly. 'After all that, I'd think you would've left Bakersville for good.'

'I tried. Went to Portland. Enrolled in the university. Got drunk. For four years. Then joined AA. When I finally graduated, I decided I might as well go home, because for all of my running I was ending up in the same place I began. Besides, I like it here. I inherited my mother's house, all paid for, which is good when you're making fifteen grand a year.'

'You still live in the house where you grew up?' He gave her a skeptical look.

'I don't mind. It's the deck I like the best anyway.' She gave him a funny smile. 'Honestly, I like small-town police work. I get to deal with people, not paper. And Bakersville is a good community. We have a lot of nice folks.'

'Excluding the neighbors who never said a word about your mother beating you each night. And excluding the neighbors who still believe that you're a murderer.'

'Oh, the ones who think I killed my mother don't mind. In their opinion, what goes around comes around.'

'But you don't think that, do you, Rainie? And these last two days, staring at Danny O'Grady – that must have been very difficult for you.'

She stiffened. Her hands tightened around her Bud Light. 'Don't psychoanalyze me.'

'I'm not,' he said evenly. 'I can't help noticing, however, that today you gave an instant explanation of attachment disorder. Combine that with the fact you grew up in an abusive household, in circumstances not that different from those experienced by most violent kids. These issues aren't new to you. You've given it some thought. Long after this case is over, you'll still be giving it some thought.'

'Well, at least my interest is personal and not some misplaced hero complex.'

She had lashed out reflexively. It did not occur to her just how bitter and vicious she sounded until she saw him wince.

'Touché,' he murmured.

Rainie promptly looked down, embarrassed. It was in poor taste to ask a man to share his troubles and then hold them against him. She wanted to be a better person than that, but she knew she wasn't. She had a quick temper and a bristly personality. Apologies came hard to her.

'I don't mean to make you self-conscious,' Quincy said quietly.

'Danny bothers me,' she said abruptly, before she changed her mind. 'I saw his eyes. Trapped. Angry. Confused. I know that stare, and I looked at those bodies and I wondered . . . Everyone says kids can't be that angry, homicidally angry, but I know they can be. Sometimes it's hard not to be. To be young and helpless and defenseless . . .' Her voice broke off. She sat there, holding the rest of the words in and feeling her heart beat against her chest like a trapped bird.

'You worry you could've been Danny O'Grady?' Quincy asked.

She didn't say anything.

'You're not Danny,' he said firmly.

'I know that! I'm a woman, and women don't displace rage. We don't become mass murderers or serial killers. We focus our anger instead, going after whoever hurt us, or self-destructing. It doesn't matter, though. That's not what this is about. It's the violence, I think. Because it's a shooting and not an automobile crash or combine accident. I'm not sure. But it's bringing it back. Everything. Like it happened yesterday. And everyone was just so busy wondering that day if I'd killed her or not, no one bothered to ask me how I felt. I'm not sure I even bothered to wonder how I felt. All those times, all those nights, the screaming fits. But she was my mother, and it took so much bleach to get the blood out of the ceiling. I think I scrubbed for days and still you could see the pink stains and she was my *mother*, for God's sake. The only family I had.'

'Rainie, are you okay?'

'Yes, fine. Dammit, I need to shut up.' He had taken her hand at some point. She didn't remember when, and the fact she hadn't noticed such a thing jolted her. She always noticed when she was touched. All these years later, she was very careful about physical space. She took her hand back, raking it through her hair and discovering that she was more agitated than she'd realized. Quincy was looking at her again with concern. It made her want to laugh flippantly, but that would do no good.

'I'm sorry,' she said shortly. 'I accuse you of treating me like a patient, then I treat you like a shrink.'

'I'm not your therapist,' he said evenly. 'Let's keep that straight.'

'Of course not. I don't need a therapist!'

He raised a brow. She grew more flustered. He took back her hand.

His gaze was reassuring. 'Rainie, listen to me. What you're going through is very real. It's called post-traumatic stress syndrome. Fourteen years ago you suffered a major trauma. And even though you've dealt with that trauma on many levels, it still affected you. Now you're going through a similar situation and that's bringing the first one back. It happens to everyone. When the Gulf War happened, the Veterans Administration had to set up hotlines for the Vietnam vets who were suddenly experiencing flashbacks to twenty-year-old firefights. Sadly, every time one of these school shootings happens, it puts all the other families in all the other communities through the wringer again. Flashbacks, nightmares, anxiety attacks. All part of the drill.'

'I'm a professional. It's my job. Will attend homicide. Won't bat an eye.'

'You're human.' His fingers squeezed hers. 'You're an intelligent human. Your brain is going to work in spite of you.'

'Well, take this brain back. It's stuck on instant replay and I've had enough.'

He smiled faintly. 'The older the trauma, the sooner it will fade. In the meantime, it might help to talk to someone. Does the sheriff's department provide any mental-health resources?'

'Our department doesn't even provide coffee.'

'Perhaps some of the professionals flying in to help the kids.'

'Yeah, perhaps.' But her tone of voice told them both she'd never go. Seeking out a real professional would be too much like admitting a weakness. She didn't do that anymore.

'It's getting late,' Quincy said.

Rainie looked around. The music was dying down and tables had cleared out. He was right; they should both be going. Separate rooms, she knew. She had said too much, and you couldn't hook up for a one-night stand after baring your soul.

She rose on her own. After a moment Quincy followed suit.

'Quincy . . . Sorry about your daughter.'

'Thank you. It doesn't help, but it does.'

'I know.' She hesitated. 'I'm also sorry for what I said earlier. The misplaced hero complex. I'm not the best at playing nice with others.'

'And here I thought it was part of your charm.'

Quincy placed his hand on the small of her back and guided her toward the door.

Outside, the night was cool and Rainie was back to watching him expectantly. His hand still rested on her back. His body was close. She could smell his aftershave, subtle and expensive. She didn't know what it was about him. He was strong, intelligent, sophisticated. She'd never tried finding someone who challenged her. She'd always just gone with the unquestioning young stud, the kind who wouldn't ask too many questions. It was safer.

Now she studied the exposed hollow of Quincy's throat, where a light smattering of dark hair rippled across it. Now she gazed at his other hand with those long, deft fingers. Now she looked up into his face and peering blue eyes that saw too much.

She took an instinctive step back, confused and suddenly spooked. His head had already dropped forward and his lips brushed her cheek.

'I'm not your therapist, Rainie.'

'I know.'

His lips brushed her other cheek, warm, firm, dry.

'I don't know what I'm doing here. I have policies about these things.' His lips fell to the hollow of her neck. Her head had fallen back. She knew better, but she didn't. The kiss was light. It teased her.

'No fraternizing?' she murmured.

He raised his head. 'No one-night stands. No passing through. I'm too old for that shit, Rainie. I've been to too many towns, spent too much time studying the worst that men can do. I've tried marriage and I've tried fatherhood and I have all the things I'm proud of in my life and all the things I wish I'd never done. I don't believe in one-night escapism anymore. I don't see the point.'

She tried to open her mouth to argue, but he cut her off by brushing his lips over hers. She startled in surprise. He stopped, lingered, his mouth moist, seeking. His hands were splayed across her back. He held her lightly, giving her plenty of room, and that made her both grateful and disappointed.

She had just started to lean forward when he broke off the kiss.

'I'm interested in you, Rainie,' he murmured against her ear. 'You're not what I expected. You're smart. You're complicated. And I already know you won't go home with me tonight.'

'I won't,' she whispered.

'You're going to torture yourself with the drive to the ME's office tomorrow. You're going to dream of your mother and dead little girls.'

'Don't—'

'I'm not your therapist, Rainie. I'm simply a man who's been there.'

His hands fell from her back. He stepped away and she felt the night intrude bitterly. Her arms grew cold. She shivered as she watched him walk over to his car, but she didn't call him back. She had her own vehicle to drive home. One of her rules. One of her many, many rules designed to keep herself safe.

Supervisory Special Agent Pierce Quincy drove away.

And, after another moment, Rainie went home alone.

14

Shep was waiting for Rainie on her back porch when she got to her house. Judging by the pile of empty beer bottles at his feet, he'd been there a while, and the wait had done nothing to improve his mood.

'Where the hell have you been?' he demanded when she finally walked through the sliding glass door.

Rainie eyed him for a minute. It was late, well past midnight, and she didn't have the patience for this conversation. On the other hand, she supposed she should've seen it coming.

She loosened the cuffs of her worn chambray shirt. 'Go home, Shep.'

'Aren't you meeting with the ME first thing in the morning? Christ, Rainie, this is a murder investigation. What are you doing running around till the small hours of the morning?'

'I believe I'm acting as primary on the case. Now get the hell off my back deck.'

Shep pretended not to hear her. He set down his beer and stood authoritatively, as if he was still acting sheriff. The fact that he swayed on his feet didn't help. Rainie shook her head.

'We gotta talk about this case.'

'You're drunk, you're not thinking straight, and if anyone sees you here, George Walker will have even more ammunition to take to the five o'clock news. Suspect's father cavorting with police.'

'Danny didn't do it!'

'We got his prints on the casings, Shep.'

'Not all of them.'

'What the hell does that mean?'

'Oh, Sanders didn't tell you, did he?' Shep got a smug glow in his eyes. He pounded his chest. 'I got my own contact at the state crime lab. When I talked to him this afternoon, he told me they'd found prints on the shell casings from the .38 and the .22 – except for one .38 casing. A single casing with no smudges, no dirt, no prints. In other words, wiped clean. And get this, there's something odd about the shell casing. My contact couldn't tell me what, but he'd sent it out for further analysis. So there you go. Something's odd about the evidence, Rainie. Something else went down in those halls, and this proves it.'

'Oh, Jesus Christ, Shep. Not all shell casings will yield prints and you know it. Now, for the last time, go home.'

'One casing wiped clean, Rainie! I'm telling you, someone else was at that scene. This proves it. Maybe Danny helped. Okay, okay? I can see that much. He got the guns, maybe he thought that he was helping a friend. But someone else pulled the trigger. You gotta help me with this, Rainie. You gotta believe me.'

'I don't have to do any such thing.'

'What does that mean?'

Rainie looked her boss in the eye. She said crisply, 'First you appoint me primary, Shep. Not even at the school yet, and you already know something's up. Then there's that whole confrontation with Danny. You get me to discharge my sidearm. You manage to get your prints all over the guns. Thirty seconds later most of the physical evidence is destroyed. And you made sure everyone knew it. Officer Conner screwed up the case. Danny will walk away scot-free. What the hell went down in that hallway, Shep? You want me to help you, you tell me what was really going on that afternoon.'

'Rainie, I swear to you—'

'*Bullshit! Cut the crap.*' Her temper went. She was suddenly bone-weary and deeply resentful of Shep. He'd made her part of this tragedy. And now he was on her back deck, begging for her help, after playing her like a fool. How dare he do that to her? Especially when she'd considered him a friend.

'You knew what was going on, Shep. You suspected Danny. Why?'

'Don't you yell at me, Lorraine Conner. I may not be on active duty, but I'm still sheriff of this town!'

'What the fuck happened, Shep? What did you do?'

'This is no way to treat me! Didn't I help you out all those years ago? All those questions I could've asked. All those questions that have still never been answered about what went down that day. I never followed up. I let sleeping dogs lie. Now it's your turn to do the same.'

'*Get off my property!*'

'He's my son! Goddammit, Rainie, he's my son . . .'

Shep's shoulders suddenly convulsed. He stood on her porch, surrounded by half a dozen empty beer bottles, and wept into his hands for his child.

Jesus Christ. Rainie went into her house. She fetched two fresh bottles of beer from the fridge. Back outside, she wordlessly handed one to Shep. The other she cradled in her hands, waiting for that feeling of power, of control. It didn't happen tonight. Jesus Christ.

After a moment Shep pulled himself together. He wiped his face with the sleeve of his shirt. He twisted off the cap of the bottle and downed half the contents in a single swallow. Then he downed the other half.

'How'd you get here, Shep?'

'Drove.'

'You're not driving home.'

'I know.'

They stood in silence. Rainie looked up at the night sky. It was clear following this afternoon's rain. The stars were like pinpricks of silver against black velvet. She loved this kind of night. Perfect for sitting on her deck, listening to the owls and imagining the waves crashing against the rocky shore. The inside of her house might hold all the bad memories of her childhood, but the outside held the few precious things that had been good. The land and the trees and the sky. The knowledge that no matter what happened, she was only a small part of it in the end and the stars would be here long after she was gone and the last tears had dried.

Maybe other people were overwhelmed to think of their tiny size in relation to the cosmos. She was comforted by it.

'I gave Danny the combination for the gun safe,' Shep said quietly. 'He asked for it two weeks ago, and I gave it to him.'

'You went to all the trouble to get a state-of-the-art gun safe and then you gave your child the combination?'

'Sandy's gonna kill me.'

'Shep, you're in such a world of hurt.'

'I didn't know! Danny said he wanted practice breaking down handguns since he'd already mastered his rifle. Hell, I was happy he was interested. You gotta understand, Rainie, guns are about all Danny and I have left. I tried football – he's just no good. I tried basketball, baseball, soccer. The boy has no athletic ability. He just wants to read or surf the Web or some such garbage. . . . You don't know what it's like to be a father, Rainie, and realize one day that you got the son you always wanted and, somehow, he turned out to be his mother.'

'Did you know the pistols were missing?'

Shep was silent, which was answer enough.

'Jesus, how can you be so smart and yet so dumb?'

'Don't you think I just got punished enough?'

'No, I think George Walker got punished enough. I think Alice Bensen's parents got punished enough. Dammit!'

'I didn't *know*, Rainie. Three days ago I checked the safe for the pistols. They still weren't there. So I asked Danny about it. He said he hadn't gotten them back together yet, that was all. The minute he reassembled them, he'd put them in the safe. I didn't think about it again.'

'Until you got the call.'

'But Danny didn't do it! I swear to you, Rainie, that boy doesn't have a single aggressive bone in his body. Hell, if he was more like me maybe I could imagine it. But he's his mother's son. He wouldn't hurt a fly.'

'What did you find when you got to the school; Shep?'

'It's just like I said in my report. When I arrived, the building was already evacuated. Someone said they saw the shooter run from the building. Someone else said there were still wounded kids inside. So I went in. And in the computer lab I found Danny holding the revolver and semiauto—'

'Holding them? Not picking them up. Holding them.'

'He'd just picked them up—'

'Shep!'

'All right! He was holding them, dammit. Holding both guns and looking faint. The minute I said his name, he pointed them at my head.'

'And that doesn't tell you anything?'

'He was panicked, Rainie! Frightened and, ah hell, he'd been crying. I swear to you, there were tears on his cheeks. For chrissakes, this is Danny. Danny who used to wear your deputy's badge. Danny who liked to play under the desks. Danny who always wanted to sit by you at dinner—'

'Shut up! I don't want to hear it anymore.'

Rainie walked away from him. She stood at the edge of her deck, her arms wrapped tight around her middle for warmth. In the distance, she saw a flicker of light, as if the moon had caught a piece of glass. It troubled her, and she was trying to focus in on the source, when the trees rustled abruptly and a large bird took flight.

'If Danny's involved,' Shep said from behind her, 'it's only because someone else got him into it. He's been . . . troubled lately. And maybe he's impressionable. At thirteen all young boys are impressionable.'

'We know about the lockers, Shep. And we know about Charlie Kenyon. The Danny in my mind is a sweet little boy, and just yesterday morning I would've agreed with you, but I'm not sure anymore. There is a lot more to him than meets the eye. And these kids . . . they're always somebody's sons, Shep. They're always somebody's children.'

Shep's head fell forward. Rainie had told him the truth with the best of intentions, but she couldn't stand to see him look so defeated.

She offered quietly, 'We're trying to learn more from the school computers. Maybe if we can find a record of him talking to someone online . . . hooking up with an outside influence . . . I don't know.'

'Good, good.' Shep's voice had picked up. 'That's the thing. Find out who really did all this.'

'You really want to know what happened, Shep, let us talk to Danny. The FBI agent, Quincy, he's a trained psychologist and an expert in mass murderers. He'll know how to handle Danny. He'll get to the bottom of this.'

'No.'

'Shep, you want me to help Danny, but you don't. Make up your mind.'

'No interviewing him! He's confused right now. Maybe he even wants to take credit for things – some kids are like that, you know. But I don't want my kid spending the rest of his life in prison because he felt a need to brag.'

'What about Becky? She might have seen something—'

'The doctors say she's in shock.'

'Quincy's an expert.'

'Since when did you start thinking so much of an outsider? Wait a minute. That's where you've been, isn't it? You went out with the Fed!'

'Well, tie stones to my feet and drown me in a river.'

'That's not funny.'

'Shep, if you want answers, give me some help. At least let Quincy interview Becky.'

'Our lawyer will never go for it.'

'It's not his call.'

'I can't. I don't – I gotta talk to Sandy first. Let me talk to Sandy.'

'Thank you, Shep,' Rainie said seriously. 'Sandy has a good head on her shoulders. She'll do the right thing.'

Shep, however, didn't look convinced. He said wearily, 'I got a son in juvenile detention for murder. I have a daughter sleeping in closets, and I have neighbors spray-painting *Baby Killer* on my garage. The right thing? I don't know what that is anymore. I already heard from the mayor that we're not allowed to attend any of the funerals. He thinks it'll upset people too much. For God's sake, this is my town, Rainie. I know George Walker. I used to bowl with Alice's uncle. Now – now it's come down to *this*.'

Rainie didn't say anything. She didn't have the words to comfort him.

'Someone else pulled that trigger,' Shep said tiredly, stubbornly. 'Mark my words. And you gotta help me prove it, because a state detective and a federal agent aren't going to care. They don't live here. They don't know Danny the way we do. So it's just you and me. The way it was fourteen years ago. Just you and me again.'

'You didn't do me any favors fourteen years ago, Shep.'

Shep's gaze simply fell to the deck.

Rainie sighed. She moved over to the deck railing and dumped out her bottle of beer. She said what she needed to say, soft, so no one could hear.

Shep didn't pry. He knew better after all these years.

After a moment she turned back to him. 'Come on, Shep. I'll drive you home.'

Crouched behind a dense cover of trees, the man finally released his breath. It had been no good. She always ducked her head when she spoke, so even with the binoculars he couldn't see clearly enough. Maybe if he brought a video camera one night. He could record her actions, then play them back for someone who specialized in lip-reading. An expert might be able to see enough.

But that would be sharing. He didn't want to share. Rainie was special. His.

He planned to keep it that way.

The man rocked back on his heels, pursing his lips as he considered his options. His head was buzzing a bit. He'd stayed in the bar long enough to have two beers, even though he shouldn't have. But Ruddy-Face had still been standing there, looking down at him all stern and tough. It had punched buttons better left alone and he'd found he couldn't back down. So he'd stayed, drinking down beer he couldn't taste and feeling that measured, hateful stare.

Then he'd simply started to laugh. The whole thing was too damn funny for words. Old men thinking war would be good for kids. Give 'em a Hitler and they won't have to kill one another.

The man had started to laugh, and he was still laughing when he left the bar, watching old Ruddy-Face shake his head. Fuck Ruddy-Face. Fuck 'em all. If only they knew . . .

The first time the man had picked a town for one of his projects, he hadn't been anxious. More like curious about what he could do. He'd had a vision. It started as a dream late at night, a way to pass the hours when he was alone and no one cared. Then it took over his waking hours. It became an obsession, a fierce, burning need gnawing away at his gut.

Show the old man. Show up the old man. Fucking show up the old fucking man. He'd head out to the cemetery, guzzling hundred-dollar bottles of the fucker's precious brandy and feeling the fury beat like a drum in his veins. *You think I'm weak? You think I'm dumb?*

Well, let me show you . . .

The first time he'd been very careful. No ties between himself and the community. He'd selected the town by computer, researched it by computer, approached the players by computer. When it had finally been necessary to conduct some on-site activities, he'd worn disguises and used only cash. The three *Ps* of a successful mission: Patience, Planning, and Precautions. *See, I was* listening, *you old fuck.*

In the end, it had been easy. Screams and smoke and blood. Beautiful, fantastical death.

Not a tremor in his hand, not a care in the world.

But then it had been over. Police came, investigated, arrested, moved on. Case closed. He returned to everyday life, visited the cemetery again, guzzled another bottle of brandy.

Who's weak now, old man? Who isn't feelin' very smart?

And then . . .

Nothing. Story faded from the news. Town got on with things. People moved on with life. And he was alone again, feeling his power, knowing the things he knew, and . . . bored.

Time for a second strike. Raise the stakes, prove his point, elevate the game.

He picked the next town more carefully, spent longer reconning in the area, studying the rhythms of life. Still lots of patience and planning. Still many, many precautions. Computers were a wonderful tool.

Then one day everything was in place. Screams and smoke and blood. Beautiful, fantastical death. This time he lingered afterward – from a way away, of course, using binoculars – but still he lingered, adding an extra zing.

Cops arrived on scene. Dull, unimaginative small-town yokels. Saw what he wanted them to see, thought what he wanted them to think. Made their arrest, felt good about themselves.

In fact, everything went so well, the man decided not to go home right away. He hit upon the hotel plan – in a separate city, of course, though frankly he wasn't convinced even that precaution was necessary. He rented a car, drove back into town. Hung out in the local bars and listened to the local folks talk. He had so much fun, he even went to the funerals and watched the mothers cry.

Who's smart now, you old fuck?

Five days later it was all over and done. Reporters packed their bags. Lawyers worked out some deal. He returned to the ordinary world of his 'acceptable life,' and eventually this film also faded from his mind.

He needed something more. His plans worked, but the thrill was lacking. From what he could tell, he was too smart (*Hear that, old man?*). He could make the cops dance on a pinhead and they'd fucking thank him for the floor space.

He needed a place more challenging, a target more riveting, and an opponent more worthy. He needed to expand the playing field.

Bakersville had come to him like a goddamn wet dream.

The perfect place, the perfect target, and the perfect cast of Keystone Kops hot on his trail.

Finally, he was having some fun.

Big, burly Shep, crying over his son. Smart, pretty Officer Conner, worrying about her town. And now Supervisory Special Agent Pierce Quincy. Quantico's best of the best.

Finally, he had a game worth playing. Which was good, because as far as he was concerned he was no longer producing a single-act play. This game was just beginning.

Do you remember what it felt like when you pulled the trigger, Officer Conner? Do you still dream about the wet sound of your mother's exploding head?

Someday I want to hear all about it.

But not tonight. Tonight he had to drive to Portland. He still had work to do.

The first time Becky O'Grady fell asleep, she dreamed she stood up to the monster in her school. She planted her feet in the hall. She yelled, 'Bad, bad monster. Leave my brother alone! Don't you hurt my friends!'

The monster was ashamed. He crawled away. Then Alice and Sally hugged her and cried. Pretty Miss Avalon kissed her on the cheek and told her she was very brave. Everyone was happy, including her mommy and daddy, who never fought again, and Danny, who gave her a kitty.

The second time Becky fell asleep, she dreamed she stood up to the monster and he bit off her head.

At five in the morning, Becky O'Grady crawled to the hall closet and piled coats on top of her shoulders. But she knew it wouldn't do any good.

The monster was coming. She had not saved Danny, and she and the monster both knew it. Soon he would come for her. Soon it would be her turn.

Becky whimpered for her mother. But mostly she cried for Danny, because when he had needed her most, she had not saved him.

15

Sandy stood at the kitchen sink, washing the same flower-bordered plate over and over again. Outside, the sun was shining. She had cracked the window to let in the fresh morning air, and now she could hear the sounds of her neighborhood preparing for a new day. Somewhere down the street a lawn was being mowed. Probably Mr McCabe. He was a retired school principal who took religious care of his yard. In June, people drove in from miles around just to admire his roses.

A dog barked three or four houses over. Then came the sounds of a mother yelling for her child. Andy? Anthony? Maybe Andrea, the Simpsons' four-year-old daughter. Last Halloween she'd dressed up as a cowboy – not a cowgirl, she'd told everyone, a *cowboy*. Sandy really liked the child, even if she insisted on calling her Mrs O'Grady, which made Sandy feel old.

She turned the plate in her hand and rhythmically washed the back.

When she and Shep had first moved into this neighborhood eleven years ago, they were one of the few couples with kids. Since then the neighborhood had grown and so had the families. There must be five toddlers on this block alone. Two of the girls in Becky's class lived just four blocks over. There were a number of boys as well, though most of them were too young for Danny. Sandy had always thought that was a shame. It was so easy for Becky to find someone to play with, whereas Danny had to be driven to someone's house. That took planning. That took having a parent home to serve as chauffeur.

Danny had never complained, though. He seemed content to read books or stay at school or play on the computer. Later in the evenings she'd sometimes go on walks with him around the neighborhood. They'd wave at the other families. Danny would check out houses with DirecTV. Or sometimes she'd walk and he'd ride his bike around her and show off stunts like riding no-handed for her amusement.

She'd always liked those walks. She'd felt safe, passing through their modest community where everyone worked hard and knew one another's name.

This morning Sandy didn't feel comfortable enough to step outside to

669

get the morning paper. She was too afraid people would stop and stare. And she wasn't sure which bothered her most, the looks of anger or of pity.

She stayed in her kitchen, a prisoner under house arrest, and scrubbed her appliances until they sparkled. Then she attacked the kitchen floor, all the while pretending it was just another day in the neighborhood and her life hadn't really ended two days ago.

This morning Sandy had called the detention center at promptly seven A.M. It had been forty-eight hours since she'd last spoken with her son, and she desperately needed to see him. Was he frightened, was he scared? Did he understand what was happening to him? Did he miss her or call out her name in the middle of the night?

What if he was having nightmares? What if he wasn't getting enough to eat or the blankets scratched or the sheets itched? For God's sake, she was his mother and she needed to be with her son!

The head of the detention facilities, a Mr Gregory, had firmly but politely informed her that Danny had already begged them not to let his mother in. The director had located Danny in the cafeteria first thing this morning to mention that his parents wanted to visit. Danny had immediately grown so agitated that staff members had had no choice but to return him to his room.

It appeared he was too traumatized to deal with his parents. Maybe in a week or two.

Sandy had never heard of anything so ridiculous. If her son was traumatized, all the more reason for her to come. She could bring his favorite toy, bake his favorite cake. Please, something, anything . . .

Don't leave me on the outside like this. Don't leave me feeling so helpless.

Mr Gregory informed her that her son was still under suicide watch. And they'd had to return Danny to his room because, at the mention of seeing his parents, he grabbed a fork from another youth and tried to puncture his own wrist.

She and Shep were not to visit. Period.

The sound of the lawn mower stopped. A sharp bang as Mr McCabe removed the clippings bag. He was probably dumping the grass on his flower beds. Sandy had seen him do it a hundred times. Churning the grass clippings into the beds to replenish the nitrogen. Working the soil tenderly with his old, gnarled hands.

She finally set the plate in the drying rack. The dishes were done. Her countertops sparkled, her floor was freshly mopped. She'd even cleaned the stove and wiped down the microwave. Now it was eight in the morning and Sandy didn't know what to do.

She turned toward Becky, who was eyeing her somberly from the kitchen table.

'Would you like more cereal, honey?'

Becky shook her head. The bowl of Cheerios placed in front of her fifteen minutes ago still appeared to be untouched.

'What about some fruit?' Sandy coaxed. 'Or what about pancakes? I can make you chocolate chip pancakes!'

Sandy regretted the words the moment she said them. Chocolate chip pancakes were Danny's favorite.

Becky shook her head.

Sandy resiliently turned toward the refrigerator, searching for more options. Becky hadn't eaten in nearly two days.

'I know,' Sandy said brightly, 'how about some salad!'

She eagerly pulled out the clear glass bowl. The salad had been among four dishes that had arrived on their front porch yesterday. The others had contained macaroni and cheese, a ham-and-potato dish, and some kind of mystery-meat surprise. This bowl had impressed Sandy, however. The mixture of strawberry Jell-O, apples, bananas, walnuts, and whipped cream was a favorite children's salad, and it touched her that others were thinking of Becky. God knows, the little girl was suffering too.

Sandy held up the brightly colored salad for Becky's inspection. Becky had always loved Jell-O and whipped cream . . .

A slight hesitation, then finally Becky nodded. They had a winner!

Sandy dished up a large bowl for her daughter, humming slightly to herself in honor of having scored a victory. She poured a glass of orange juice to go with Becky's breakfast. After another thought, she poured a glass of juice for herself as well and joined her daughter at the table.

From the living room came the sound of Shep snoring. He'd been out most of the night and returned at some small hour of the morning, reeking of beer. Sandy knew without asking where he'd gone. Rainie's house. Whenever he was troubled, whenever he had something on his mind, he always went there.

Once Sandy had entertained wild notions of what must be going on at the Conner residence. Everyone had heard stories of Rainie's mother and what kind of woman she'd been. Sandy had imagined her husband and his deputy rolling around in a torrid embrace. She had fantasized about them laughing together and giggling madly over what an idiot pretty little Sandy Surmon must be not to suspect a thing.

One night in a fit of jealous rage, she'd hightailed it over to Rainie's tiny home in the middle of the soaring woods. She'd driven up the dirt driveway at full steam, already formulating a bold confrontation in her head.

She'd discovered her husband and Rainie sitting on the huge back deck in complete silence, each just staring out into the woods and holding a beer.

Sandy had gone back home without ever saying a word.

Over the years she'd come to realize that she simply couldn't fathom her husband and Rainie's relationship. She didn't know what caused the long silences between them or the unspoken exchanges. She didn't understand how Shep could sometimes seem to belong more to Rainie than to her, when Sandy had borne him two children and, as best as she could tell, Rainie only handed him bottles of Bud Light.

Whatever bonded them was deep, but at least it wasn't sexual. So Sandy did her best to fight her nagging, painful wish that Shep would come to her when he was troubled, instead of heading to another woman's house for hours of companionable silence.

'Mommy, what happened to school?'

Sandy looked at her daughter, genuinely startled by the question and the sound of her daughter's voice. Becky had barely spoken since the shooting, and when she did, it was generally a one-word statement. 'What do you mean, honey?'

'There's no school today.'

'No, Becky, there's no school today.'

'Tomorrow?'

'You don't have to go to school tomorrow either, sweetheart. I don't want you to worry about school. It's all done for a bit.'

Her daughter continued to eye her intently. 'Are the other kids going to school?'

'You mean your classmates? No.' Sandy was trying to pick her words carefully. 'They're all done with school for a bit as well.'

'It's not summer.'

'It's almost summer.'

'Mommy, it's not summer.'

'Becky . . . You know something bad happened at school, right? You understand that?'

Becky nodded.

'Well, that bad thing has made everyone sad. You're sad, aren't you?'

Becky nodded again.

'I'm sad,' Sandy said softly. 'Daddy's sad. And the other kids, they're sad too. So for a little bit, because everyone is so sad, there's no school.'

'But someday?'

'Someday, Becky, yes, there will be school. But it's okay, honey! It won't be until you're ready, and we'll make sure the school is very safe. So the bad thing—'

'The monster.'

Sandy hesitated. 'Yes, so the monster can't happen anymore.'

Becky stared at her. Her eyes were big and serious. Sandy hadn't realized until now just how old her little girl had become. Then Becky returned her attention to her bowl of whipped cream and Jell-O. Sandy understood. Becky didn't believe her. She already assumed her world wouldn't be safe again. Not in a time when monsters could go to school.

Sandy returned to the kitchen sink, downing the last of her orange juice and then carefully, methodically washing the glass. The light on the answering machine blinked madly at her, but she'd already heard the message yesterday. Mitchell trying to find her, before Shep had changed their phone number to end the relentless calls. Mitchell, so sorry to disturb her at a time like this, but he was desperately trying to get his hands on the Wal-Mart reports. Could she please give him a quick buzz and tell him where he might find the files?

Sandy knew what he was looking for. She could picture the files perfectly in her mind. But she hadn't picked up the phone and called him back.

Maybe Shep was right. Maybe she'd been working too much, putting her own needs in front of the children's. If she'd been home more, paying more attention . . . If Danny had felt safer, more important, more loved . . .

If . . . if . . . if . . .

Sandy shut off the water. Her hands were shaking on the faucet; she had tears in her eyes.

Mommy, what happened to school?

I want to make the world safe. Oh God, honey. I wish I could make the world safe for you.

'Mommy.'

Sandy turned back to Becky. For a moment, she thought she saw blood on her daughter's face and she nearly screamed. Strawberry Jell-O, her mind filled in belatedly. Strawberry Jell-O.

But then she saw the tears in her daughter's eyes.

'My tongue hurts.'

Sandy rushed across the kitchen. She looked at her daughter's mouth, and to her dismay, she realized it was bleeding. Poor Becky's tongue was bleeding.

'What happened? Did you bite your tongue? Ah, honey, let me get you a washcloth and an ice cube. Hang on a second.'

She picked up the salad, carrying it over to the sink. It wasn't until she was running a fresh washcloth under the tap that she looked in the bowl and noticed the way light glinted off fragments of Jell-O.

Very slowly, Sandy got out a spoon. She dug through the salad. She pulled out five shards of glass.

Baby killer. Baby killer. Baby killer.

It's a children's salad! Even if you hate us, what kind of animals put shattered glass in a fucking children's salad!

She returned to Becky with surprising calmness. She wiped off her little girl's face; she gave her an ice cube to suck on. Already the bleeding appeared to have stopped. The glass shards were small. Maybe they hadn't done much damage.

Tenderly Sandy feathered back Becky's fine blond hair. 'How are you feeling, honey?'

'Okay.'

'Did you eat much?' she asked lightly.

Becky shook her head. 'Not hungry.'

'If your tummy hurts, you'll tell me, won't you?'

Becky nodded. Sandy decided to let it go. Becky seemed fine and Sandy didn't want to frighten her with another trip to the emergency room.

'I know,' Sandy said briskly, 'let's make some snicker-doodle cookies! I'll bring out all the ingredients and you can help me measure everything. How does that sound?'

Becky shrugged.

'Wonderful. Let me just clean this stuff up and we'll be on our way.'

Sandy gave her daughter a bright, reassuring smile. She kept her chin high and her features composed. Then she returned to the kitchen sink, where she spooned all the Jell-O salad and the three other casseroles into the garbage disposal while she swore to herself that she would not, would not, *would not cry.*

'Don't let the monster get you, Mommy.'

'Becky, I would never dream of doing any such thing.'

16

Thursday, May 17, 6:33 A.M.

Quincy did not dream of his daughter. In the gray hours of the morning, he tossed and turned in the pink Motel Hotel, caught in a case that had happened nearly a decade ago. Thirteen-year-old Candy Wallace, with the pretty blond hair and hundred-watt smile. Beautiful, sunny Candy Wallace, who was raised a devout Baptist and had no idea of the true evil that lurked in men's hearts.

She was snatched on her way home from school on a normal Wednesday afternoon. One minute she was walking down the street. The next, a pile of books was all that remained.

But Candy's captor hadn't really wanted Candy. He wanted Polly, her sixteen-year-old sister, and getting the wrong sibling angered him. So he took to calling the Wallaces' home. He would put Candy on the phone. And then he would do things to her while her sister and parents listened.

After the first phone call, Quincy was brought in to listen as well. They considered him to have expert ears.

Now, in the throes of his dream, he did not remember Candy Wallace's screams or the agonized face of her mother. He did not recall her sister Polly begging for the man to stop, to please come take her instead. She would willingly go with him if he would just let her little sister go. Please, please, please . . .

Mostly, Quincy remembered Candy's last words, after five days of endless agony.

'Please don't be sad, Mom and Dad. It'll all be over soon and I know I'm going to a better place. God loves me and will take care of me. I'm going to be fine. I love you. I love even this bad, bad man. My heart is true.'

Quincy woke up with tears on his cheeks.

He lay in his bed for a long time, thinking of the strength of a thirteen-year-old girl, thinking of God and faith and the things he'd left behind after too many years on the job.

A day after the last phone call they found Candy Wallace's body, naked, bruised, and mutilated. Three weeks after that they arrested the man who did it, an unemployed handyman who had once worked on the air-conditioning unit at the Wallaces' home. He said Candy had insisted on telling him that God loved him, so he'd cut out her tongue. Quincy had thought that there was nothing they could do to this man that would ever be enough.

He'd flown back to Virginia feeling isolated and worn to the bone.

He'd entered his home but walked away from his family, because he'd never learned to go from a crime scene to the people he loved. At times like this, he couldn't look at his daughters without seeing all the horrors that could befall them. The handymen, the drifters, the charming law students. He couldn't look at his family without seeing pain and suffering and death.

Now Quincy got out of bed. He called the hospital to learn that Amanda's condition hadn't changed. His ex-wife was asleep in the room if he wanted to speak with her. Quincy told the nurse not to wake her. His other daughter, Kimberly, was not at the hospital. She had probably returned to school. Like him, she seemed to have accepted that her sister was gone, a defection to Quincy's camp that Bethie couldn't bear.

Of course, things between his ex-wife and their younger daughter had been tense ever since last year, when Kimberly had announced she was studying sociology at New York University. Someday she wanted to be a profiler with the FBI. Just like her dad.

Quincy pulled on an old pair of running shorts and a gray FBI T-shirt. He hit the street, inhaling sharply at the cold sting of morning. Then he was off and running, still thinking of a young girl's dying screams and unfailing love. Still thinking of his own daughter, and the tragedy he hadn't protected her from after all those years of trying to make the world a safe place.

And then he was thinking of Rainie and her shadowed gray eyes and strong, stubborn chin. The way she took her punches. The way she still got up for the fight.

Once he'd made the mistake of thinking that isolation was protection, that focusing solely on his work would make a difference for people, for his family. He had listened to a young girl die, but he had not heard what she was saying.

Quincy was old, but he was learning.

He ran for a long time, with the mountain air cool and clean against his cheeks. He greeted a beautiful morning in a lush, coastal valley and he understood why Rainie Conner still lived here, perfectly.

Shortly before one, Quincy showed up in the tiny task-force center in the attic of city hall. He hadn't expected Rainie to be back yet from the autopsies scheduled in Portland, but she was already sitting at her sawhorse desk when he arrived. She didn't look up right away, scribbling intently on some piece of paper.

He took a moment to study her. Her face was paler than yesterday, the shadows deeper under her eyes. Another sleepless night, he presumed, coupled with a brutal morning. Autopsies were never easy, particularly when they were of children.

Judging from her focused movements, however, Rainie still had no intention of slowing down.

She reminded him of someone else. It took him a moment to place the name. Tess. Tess Williams. Another case, years ago, but with a better ending. Tess had made the mistake of marrying the perfect man, the kind other women always said was too good to be true. In Jim Beckett's case, they were right. The handsome, dedicated police officer had had a small sideline activity. He pulled over beautiful blondes for speeding, and then he murdered them. Tess had been the first person to figure out her husband's evil doings, and she'd slowly gathered the evidence against him while still sharing his bed.

Jim Beckett did not go down without a fight. He cut a long, bloody swath through the task-force team, including putting some fresh scars on Quincy's own chest. But Tess proved to be tougher than anyone had suspected. When Beckett hunted her down after he escaped from prison, Tess made sure the Massachusetts taxpayers never had to pay for his room and board again.

Quincy hadn't thought of her in years. He tried to do the math on how old her daughter Samantha would be now. Ten years old? It had been a bit. He wondered how she and Tess were doing.

He never followed up on the people in his cases. Even in the ones that went well, he was still a reminder of a dark time. Somehow, it didn't seem appropriate to be sending out Christmas cards.

'Are you going to stand there mooning all afternoon?' Rainie asked from her desk, still staring down at her paper.

'Just admiring the view.'

She looked up long enough to shoot him a hard glance. 'Oh, please.'

'The autopsies went that well, I see.'

'Everything I ever feared, plus ten. For heaven's sake, either get in the room or shut the door. I can't stand people loitering in the doorway.'

Quincy took his time entering, eyeing her more cautiously. She was more ragged than he'd expected. When she spoke, her voice carried the edge of someone teetering on the brink of a dark place. He would bet she hadn't let herself cry. That was a bad sign. Sometimes you had to cry after autopsies. It was the only way to release the pain.

'Writing up the report?' he asked neutrally.

'Nope. Writing up a list. What do you think of the mysterious man in black?'

'Pardon?'

'The man in black, the figure various kids reported seeing at the school. Fact or fiction?'

'I don't know.'

'What if he exists? Could a stranger be involved in shooting up a school?'

'You would be amazed at the things a stranger can do,' Quincy said slowly, 'even one met over the Internet. Witness all the young kids currently being lured from chat rooms into real-life meetings with pedophiles.'

'Fine.' She scribbled furiously. 'Man in black. Connection to Danny through the Internet, then tries to cover tracks by erasing the hard drives of the machines. Except then we're back to Melissa Avalon. Why one precise gunshot to her head? I hate that fucking wound.' Rainie caught herself, blew out a breath of air, and briskly started writing again. 'We can work on that angle later. Next up, school counselor Richard Mann.'

'What about Richard Mann?'

'He's young, thirty-three according to his file, though he doesn't look a day older than fifteen if you ask me. If we go back to assuming that Melissa Avalon was the intended target, he could have motive. Maybe he had a thing for Melissa Avalon and didn't like learning about her private staff meetings with VanderZanden. Plus, as a counselor, he'd know what buttons to push to drive Danny over the edge. That takes care of means.'

Quincy finally got it. 'You're working on a list of other possible suspects.'

'Yes, the fed can be taught.'

Quincy arched a brow. She wasn't just edgy this afternoon, she was brutally cutting.

'May I ask who you have listed?'

'Charlie Kenyon, Principal VanderZanden, the mysterious man in black, and now Richard Mann.'

'I thought the principal had an alibi.'

'At first glance, but you never really know until you start applying pressure.'

'Charlie Kenyon makes sense,' Quincy mused after a moment, deciding it would be most productive to play along. 'An older, influential kid. We already know he has trouble with authority and likes to hang around the school. I'm less convinced about the principal. Even if it was a love affair gone awry, I have a hard time seeing him shooting two students and an even more difficult time seeing him coerce Danny into taking the blame.'

'Strong authority figure. Danny can't stand up to his own father, so why should he be able to stand up to the school principal? Plus, you heard his last words in the interview. The kid's scared. When you're in elementary school, who seems more all-powerful and all-knowing than your principal?'

Her logic wasn't bad. 'But then there is VanderZanden's reaction to consider. He appears genuinely grief-stricken.'

Rainie granted that. Then her eyes lit up. 'What about his *wife*?'

Quincy exhaled slowly and watched her scribble it down. Her movements were feverish. She was trying too hard.

'Rainie, why are you making this list?'

'Focus. This investigation lacks focus.'

'You already have a suspect in custody. That appears very focused to me.'

'Yes, but we don't know if he's the right suspect.'

'His fingerprints on the casings haven't convinced you?'

'They didn't convince you.'

'I'm paid more to be skeptical.'

Rainie set down her pen. She paused long enough to look him in the eye, and Quincy was startled by the sight of her pale skin stretched taut over her gaunt face. Apparently she was forgoing food as well as sleep. It was only a matter of time, then, until she crashed.

'Shep visited me last night,' she said abruptly.

'Ah,' Quincy said. Things became much clearer for him. 'Laid on the personal guilt.'

'Of course. What are friends for? Even better, he contacted the crime lab himself through a friend. Turns out Abe Sanders has been holding out on us.'

'I can hardly wait.'

'There's a problem with one of the .38 shell casings. Not only does it completely lack prints or smudges – as in it appears to have been wiped clean – but ballistics found something strange about it. When I followed up this morning, I learned that it had some kind of residue inside, probably a polymer.'

'Plastic? As in perhaps threads of polyester fabric?'

'Who knows? But *inside* a shell casing is a weird place to find traces of fabric, plus Danny was wearing one hundred percent cotton when I brought him in. They're conducting further tests, of course, but we're back to having more questions than answers.'

'You're going to kill Detective Sanders, aren't you?'

'Yes. At three this afternoon. You're welcome to watch.' Rainie smiled tightly. 'Then I had the most fascinating chat with the ME at seven this morning. She conducted Avalon's autopsy late last night so we could get straight to the girls this morning. Lucky me. And get this: the .22 slug that killed Melissa Avalon was not deformed. In fact, the damn thing traveled in a nice straight line through the center of her brain and stopped at the base of her skull. No ricocheting. Nice, recoverable slug with an intact base. Should yield plenty of rifling marks for ballistics. Except it has none.'

'No rifling marks? Is the ME thinking a smooth-bore gun?'

'I don't know what the hell Nancy Jenkins is thinking. The woman is definitely intrigued and, unfortunately for me, coy. Let me see if I can get her exact words right. Something like "The slug would appear to have come from a .22, but I don't think it has".'

'She doesn't think it has?'

'Turns out Nancy Jenkins is a gun buff. She's not commenting officially until she gets the ballistics report back, but there's something funny about the slug that killed Melissa Avalon. And she's pretty clear it's not your average funny. It's your smart, clever funny.'

'Too smart and clever for a thirteen-year-old boy?'

'Now you're getting it.'

'And the bullet came to rest at the base of Avalon's skull?'

'Exactly. At the base of the skull. As in a downward trajectory. As in how can a four-foot-ten boy shoot down at a five-foot-six woman?'

'Who was not on her knees,' Quincy filled in for her, 'considering how the body fell.'

Rainie nodded angrily. 'So there you have it. At this point it looks like there's something rotten in Denmark. At the very least, it's doubtful that Danny killed Melissa Avalon, which also raises questions about Sally and Alice.'

'There was probably someone else present and a murder weapon we have yet to identify.'

'Yep. A murder weapon we have yet to identify and a motive. Why Melissa Avalon? I can't get it out of my head. Why young, beautiful Miss Avalon?'

'And now you're building the new theory of the case.'

'Since I am primary officer, I thought I'd give it a shot.'

'Rainie, can I make your day?'

'By all means, give it a whirl.'

'I have a one-thirty appointment with Richard Mann to ask him about Danny O'Grady. Come with me, Rainie. I'll be good cop, you be bad cop. Together, we'll ambush him.'

A feral gleam came into Rainie's eyes. The satisfaction in her face was enough to make him smile. And unfurl something slow and tender in his chest.

'I get to be bad cop?'

'You are the most qualified.'

'SupSpAg, I could kiss you.'

'Promises, promises,' he said lightly, and led his favorite law enforcer from the room.

17

They met Richard Mann in his office at the battered school, which had finally been opened up to staff members. He'd told Quincy he needed to catch up on paperwork, and Rainie's impression of the young counselor was of someone deeply disheartened. His face was pale, his eyes bruised. He'd made an effort to dress up for the meeting in tan khakis and a sage-colored sweater, but he maintained a certain rumpled air that spoke of sleepless nights and unanswered questions. Did he wonder if he should've seen the shooting coming? In the dark hours after midnight, did he think there was more he should've done?

Rainie didn't know much about the man. She'd asked a few parents, all of whom said he seemed very nice. Inexperienced, a few commented, but hardworking in an earnest sort of way. Tuesday, when things had been hairy at the school, he'd certainly stepped up to the plate and done what she'd asked. There was something to be said for that.

But Rainie still wondered about him and Miss Avalon. Even tired, Mann had that clean-cut, all-American look going for him. Trim figure. Short-cropped brown hair. Blue eyes. In a high school he would've inspired half a dozen juvenile crushes. And at Bakersville's K-8?

'Officer Conner,' Mann said with obvious surprise when she showed up in the doorway alongside Quincy. 'How nice to see you again.' He smiled at her, clearly not alarmed by her presence, and held out a hand.

'Mr Mann.' Rainie accepted his handshake. Weak grip, she thought. Definitely young. Then added, unnecessarily, not at all like Quincy.

'Oh, call me Richard. Mr Mann is my father.'

'I know the feeling.' She and Quincy took seats. Located off the admissions office and next to VanderZanden's room, Richard Mann's space was small but tidy. The main attraction was one large window overlooking the side of the school parking lot, which let in lots of sun. The floor was blue Berber, the walls stark white, and the multitude of filing cabinets industrial gray. Except for two plants and one poster of cartoon faces demonstrating different human emotions, there wasn't much in the way of decorations. Definitely a bachelor's office, Rainie decided. She'd bet his apartment looked equally utilitarian.

At the moment, empty cardboard boxes and discarded files littered the floor.

'Cleaning house?' Quincy inquired.

'Going through old files,' Mann confessed. He waved his hand apologetically over the pile. 'We're starting to run out of room, and most of these files are from before my time.'

'That's right. You're new here.'

'It's been a whole year. I don't feel so new anymore.'

'Bakersville is a big change from LA,' Rainie observed.

'That's what I was looking for.'

'Small-town life?'

'Someplace with no drills for drive-by shootings.' He smiled weakly. 'Of course, that didn't work out quite like I had planned.'

'Where were you when the shooting started?' Rainie asked.

'In my office. It was my lunch break.'

'You don't eat during normal lunch hours?'

'No. I have an open-door policy for the kids. You know, anyone can walk in if there's something they want to talk about. That sort of thing.'

'We understand Melissa Avalon also left her door open for the kids during lunch.'

'That's right.' He nodded.

'So you both took lunch at the same time.' Rainie narrowed her eyes suggestively and watched Richard Mann grow confused. He'd been expecting an interview about Danny O'Grady, not his own activities on the day of the shooting.

'Yes, I believe so,' he said with less certainty. On his lap, his hands were already beginning to fidget. This, Rainie decided, was going to be like shooting fish in a barrel.

'You two ever do lunch together?'

'Well, we *were* coworkers—'

'We understand Miss Avalon liked to get to know some of her co-workers.'

'I don't understand . . .'

'She and Principal VanderZanden. Or didn't you know about that?' Rainie hardened her voice, and Richard Mann squirmed in his seat.

'I thought we were going to talk about Danny.'

'How well did you know Melissa Avalon?'

'We worked together, that's all.'

'She was very beautiful.'

'I suppose . . .'

'Young, about the same age as yourself?'

'Yes, I guess.'

'Also new to the area. Come on, Mr Mann, don't tell me you two didn't have anything in common.'

'Wait a minute. You think Melissa and I—' Mann made a little gesture with his hand, looked at them with shock, then vigorously shook his head. For the first time since the start of the interview, he visibly relaxed. 'I'm sorry, Officer, but if you guys think I was involved with Melissa, then you don't know much about her.'

'What do you mean?' Quincy asked smoothly.

'Melissa had issues – Freudian issues.'

'You mean with her father?' Rainie demanded sharply.

'I don't know all the details,' he replied, 'but she mentioned once that she was estranged from her family. Her father was a hard man, she said, very demanding and not very forgiving. Then you consider that she took up with VanderZanden in a matter of weeks and the man's nearly twice her age . . .'

'A substitute father figure,' Quincy filled in.

'That was my analysis, yes,' Mann said, and flashed Quincy a grateful smile. He was obviously pleased to have a chance to show off his own psychological training to a big-shot profiler.

'The father ever visit?' Rainie pressed.

'I don't know.'

'What about her mom?'

'I don't know.'

'For someone you worked with for a whole year, you don't know a lot about her, do you?'

'She was very private about her family!'

'Not with Principal VanderZanden.'

'I was not involved with Melissa Avalon,' the counselor said through clenched teeth. 'We were coworkers, that's all. If you people are so concerned about her private life, talk to Steven. Or, better yet, call her father. I've heard a rumor he hasn't even bothered to claim her body yet.'

'We'll be sure to do that,' Quincy said.

'So what about Danny O'Grady?' Rainie pounced. 'We understand you'd been seeing him as a counselor.'

'Only for a few weeks—'

'Oh yeah? And precisely how long does it take to figure out that a boy who trashed his school locker has problems managing rage?'

'His parents are going through a rough time. There was no reason to think Danny's anger was anything more than an adjustment phase. When marriages turn sour, kids get mad.'

'Where were you again when the shooting happened?'

'In my office!'

'Do you have witnesses?'

'How dare you!' Richard Mann lurched out of his chair, his handsome face beet red and his expression injured. 'I did everything I could to help those kids, Officer. Don't you remember? *I'm* the one who arranged the first-aid center. *I'm* the one who got the parents cleared out of the parking lot so the emergency vehicles could get through. And now *I'm* the one fielding dozens of calls from parents whose children are waking up screaming. So how dare you imply that I had something to do with this? My God, this is breaking my heart!'

'Officer Conner doesn't mean to imply anything, Mr Mann,' Quincy said calmly, holding up his hands in a soothing gesture. 'It's simply her job to ask these kinds of questions. Of course we appreciate the help you gave on the day of the shooting.'

Mann turned to Quincy, obviously still unsure. Quincy smiled warmly.

'I just thought we were going to be speaking about Danny,' Mann said after a moment. 'I wasn't expecting this kind of . . . attack.'

'Police interviews can be intense,' Quincy said diplomatically. 'Of course, we consider everyone innocent until proven guilty.'

Mann looked pointedly at Rainie. She lifted one shoulder in a negligent shrug. Pretty boy had no alibi and got really defensive really fast, she thought. Then again, the student he'd been counseling had allegedly murdered three people. It probably didn't let him sleep well at night.

'Back to Danny O'Grady,' Quincy encouraged.

'I don't know what I can tell you there,' Mann said sulkily. 'Some of it is privileged.'

Quincy beamed at him. He said with a saccharine sweetness that nearly made Rainie roll her eyes, 'Of course, I would never ask a psychologist to violate his oath by breaching client confidentiality. Even general information would be helpful.'

Mann had to think about it. He finally sank back down into his seat, steepled his hands in front of him, and regarded the FBI agent more intently. 'I honestly don't know much,' he said at last. 'I'd just started talking to Danny a few weeks ago, and the first few sessions were small talk. You know, establishing trust, building a rapport. We hadn't had a chance to get into things.'

'These things take time.'

'We talked a little bit about Danny's interest in computers,' Mann offered. 'Danny really loved surfing the Net, playing around with programming. He never flat-out admitted it, but I got the impression he might be involved with hacking. The computer was exciting to him, but also a challenge. He might have been pushing the envelope a bit.'

'Maybe going places he wasn't supposed to?'

'Maybe. I think it's obvious to everyone that Danny has issues with self-esteem. His father is too hard on him. He berates Danny, tries to force him into doing things he doesn't want to do. He's hardly a model of support.'

'He makes Danny feel dumb?'

'Dumb, inferior, weak, helpless. Honestly, I think people should be required to get a parenting license before they're allowed to have children.'

'Shep may not be the perfect parent,' Rainie interjected with a frown, 'but he loves his son and wants the best for him.'

'Fine, but that and a quarter still won't get Danny a cup of coffee.' Mann waved his hand to silence her next round of protests. He was back on sure footing, and the parents had been right – his earnestness was compelling. 'Look, Officer. I'm the one in the trenches, and I can tell you whole-heartedly that intentions don't matter in parenting. Kids don't understand what you mean. They understand what you do. And most of the things Shep does make Danny feel powerless and incompetent. Computers, on the other hand, make him feel strong.'

'Did he ever talk about people he might have met online? Places he might have gone?' Quincy pressed.

'I can't comment on that.'

'Hey, Mann—' Rainie began impatiently.

He cut her off primly. 'Danny is my patient and I won't violate privilege.'

'Can you really exercise privilege if you're only a school counselor?' Rainie asked Quincy.

He gave her a look that clearly told her not to take the bad-cop thing too far. Mann was getting edgy, and they needed to get more information from him.

'You should try the computers,' Mann said abruptly. He leaned forward, saying in almost a whisper, 'I want to help, but I can hardly start my career by breaking confidentiality. On the other hand, Danny was using the school computers. Now, I'm not a computer person, but I thought cops had the ability to trace anything these days . . .'

Quincy and Rainie exchanged glances. Mann had done everything but the wink, wink, nudge, nudge. So they were back to the computers. Okay.

'Is there one person Danny mentioned a lot?' Quincy tried probing. 'Maybe a new friend he'd made recently?'

'Everyone knows about him smoking with Charlie Kenyon.'

'But what about someone on-line? Maybe an adult figure from a chat room or e-mail loop. That sort of thing?'

Mann hesitated again. His gaze went from Rainie to Quincy to Rainie again. What the hell. She let her features relax and gave pretty boy a smile.

'It would be helpful, Mr Mann. Coupled with what you did in the school parking lot on Tuesday, how quickly you helped manage the situation – that would make you something of a hero in this whole affair.'

Hero, apparently, was the right word.

'There was someone,' Mann confessed. 'Danny thought it was another kid, a fellow hacker he'd befriended on-line. I read a few of the e-mails, and the language seemed more sophisticated, though. I was betting it was really an adult male passing himself off as a teenager.'

'And you weren't concerned by this?' Quincy asked.

'Oh, I was concerned,' Mann told him vehemently. 'That's why I asked

Danny to start bringing me the e-mails. I know the things that can happen on-line – child molesters, pornographers, terrorists. The Internet isn't any safer than a walk through New York City at night. But what Danny showed me was harmless. They were friendly notes, admiring his accomplishments on the computer, sharing information about other programs to try, Web sites to visit. On the other hand . . .' He paused. 'I've heard rumors that Danny said something right after the shooting. That he was saying over and over again that he was smart.'

Quincy glanced at Rainie. She gave up that information with a nod.

'The notes Danny got, they always ended with this guy telling Danny how smart he was. Stuff like *I can't wait to see what the whiz kid does next. You're so smart.*' Mann shrugged helplessly. For the first time, Rainie thought he looked miserable. 'That strikes me as coming from this guy. So maybe there were other notes, other things that Danny didn't tell me. I don't know . . .'

Mann's voice faded. Then he said more quietly, more somberly, 'I really wanted to help Danny O'Grady. I was concerned about the Internet relationship and concerned about his parents' marital problems, but I thought I could reach him. Even reading the e-mails, I didn't see it coming. I thought . . . I thought kids who did this sort of thing were supposed to have a history of violence. Torturing household pets, starting fires, playing violent video games. Danny didn't do any of those things. To me, he seemed to be a decent boy going through a hard time. I honestly had no idea. I swear, I had no idea . . .'

Richard Mann's shoulders slumped. He simply sat there, shaking his head.

Quincy leaned forward. 'Mr Mann, do you happen to have a copy of any of the e-mails?'

'Danny wouldn't let me keep them. He worried he was already violating the person's trust by even showing them to me.'

'Do you remember anything about them? A name, a chat room, an e-mail address?'

'I don't – wait a minute. The e-mail address. I remember trying to understand what the guy meant. Something about no fires. Volcanoes. Lava. That was it: No Lava. Isn't that odd for a signature?'

'No Lava. No Lava what? Do you remember the carrier, the Internet provider?'

'One of the major ones, I think. AOL maybe, or CompuServe. Something like that.'

Rainie scribbled it down. She looked at Quincy.

'We have some federal agents who specialize in undercover Internet operations,' he said. 'We could send someone on, pretending to be a teenage boy, see if No Lava takes an interest.'

Richard Mann sat back. He ran a hand through his short hair and expelled a pent-up breath. 'I really am trying to make things right. Sally and Alice were sweet girls. And this . . . it just shouldn't have happened here.'

'We'll see.'

Rainie rose. She handed Mann her card and gave him the usual spiel to call the sheriff's office if he thought of anything else, though she seriously doubted he'd be in the mood to talk to her anytime soon. As she opened the door of the office, however, he spoke up again.

'Officer Conner.' Rainie halted, and the counselor motioned to the space behind her, which housed a large desk for the school's secretary. 'As you can see, my office is directly off the main administrative space. While I might have been eating lunch alone at the time of the shooting, there is no way I could have left without someone noticing. Ask our secretary, Marge. I'm sure she can confirm that I took one roast beef sandwich into my office at the start of the period, and I hadn't gone anywhere by the time the first shot was fired. Just so you know.'

Rainie nodded. She knew when she was being put in her place. Then her gaze fell to the old files strewn across the floor and she read the two names on top. *Sally Walker. Alice Bensen.* Of course. They wouldn't need permanent records anymore.

Richard Mann had followed her line of sight. His expression had become equally subdued.

'I should take those,' Rainie murmured after a moment. 'For the victimology reports.'

Mann gazed at her curiously. Was he startled by how she could think that way? Or was he wondering, as she was, when she had learned to be so cold?

He picked up the two files. He handed them over to her.

After that, there was nothing left to say.

18

Thursday, May 17, 3:12 P.M.

By the time Rainie and Quincy grabbed lunch at Dairy Queen and headed back to the task-force center, Abe Sanders was waiting for them. The state detective was sporting a sharply pressed gray suit and shiny black shoes, making Rainie suspicious that the man who traveled with salad also packed an iron and a shoe-polishing kit. Just what did he do for fun in his spare time?

He had made himself at home behind Rainie's desk and was reading a fax. Rainie snatched the paper out of his hands without preamble.

'I doubt that's for your eyes.'

'You mean we're not all part of one big happy family?' he drawled innocently.

Rainie skewered him with a glance, then scanned the fax. It was from the law offices of Johnson, Johnson, and Jones. Those office Christmas parties must be a hoot. The fax informed her that she and her deputies were not to contact Shep, Sandy, or Becky O'Grady without legal counsel being present. If any member of the task force insisted on violating this order, a harassment suit would be filed against the Bakersville sheriff's department. Sincerely, Avery Johnson.

'Wonderful,' Rainie muttered. That conversation between Shep and Sandy had obviously gone well. Or had Shep mentioned her interest in interviewing Becky to Avery Johnson as part of his desire to do everything absolutely right for Danny? You would think an experienced sheriff would know better.

'Looks like we won't be interviewing Becky O'Grady anytime soon,' Sanders commented.

'We'll see,' Rainie said. She handed the fax to Quincy, who appeared unconcerned.

'Routine,' he said.

'Just the beginning,' Sanders agreed, speaking with the confident air of one experienced officer to another. 'By the end of this case, the whole town will be swimming in lawyers representing, protecting, and suing the masses. I'm surprised George Walker hasn't already filed a notice to sue the sheriff's department. God knows he thinks this whole thing is Shep's fault.'

Rainie chewed her bottom lip. She hated to admit this with Sanders present, but she was out of her league. 'You think I'll be sued?'

'Sure,' Sanders said matter-of-factly. 'The Walkers and the Bensens will probably launch civil suits against the sheriff's department for either not warning the community about Daniel O'Grady or botching the investigation against him. That, of course, will involve you. Then they'll probably file a civil suit against the O'Gradys personally, just in case things don't work out in criminal court. I wouldn't be surprised if Melissa Avalon's parents do the same. Finally, you have all the kids who were injured, though none of them sustained wounds that are that serious. They'll probably fall into two camps: those who would just as soon put this all behind them and those who will pool their resources and go for blood.'

'But why sue a sheriff's department?' Rainie asked with a scowl. 'We're so broke most of our officers work for free. And the money we do have comes straight from the city, which means people are just suing their neighbors in the end.'

'The city and department carry liability insurance,' Sanders explained. 'Those policies run into the millions, so a good lawyer will argue that there's money to be had with only the insurance companies to be hurt.'

'But the premiums go up, and taxes go up, and again all the neighbors foot the bill.'

'You're thinking too logically, Rainie. Kids got hurt. The system let people down. Now they want someone to blame. Didn't you learn anything in the nineties? Law enforcement is both the first line of defense and the best scapegoat in town.'

Rainie shook her head. She hated lawyers. They took everything and made it too complicated. And they seemed to think that money healed all wounds. Don't just mourn your child, cash in on the loss.

Rainie crossed behind her desk, nudged Sanders to get the hell out of her seat, and did her best to focus on the matters at hand.

'So,' she said shortly, folding her hands in front of her and regarding both men. 'I met with ballistics, as well as the medical examiner in Portland this morning. Sanders, is there anything you've been meaning to tell me, or should I shoot first and ask questions later?'

The state detective shrugged. 'Oh, you mean about the so-called mystery casing.'

'What the hell, let's start with that.'

'Ballistics has an odd duck, that's all. One casing that has no prints on the outside and some kind of substance on the inside.'

'A polymer,' Quincy said.

Sanders shot him a look. Then he gave Rainie a stare of disgruntlement. He obviously didn't like her sharing information with the fed. Rainie couldn't care less.

'Yeah, a polymer,' Sanders said finally. 'I didn't tell you about it, though, because we don't know anything yet. They need to run more tests. Until then we don't have any new information.'

'Sanders, a strange casing is information—'

'Conner, a case of this size with this much evidence has a million and a half things like a strange casing. We got debris that can't be categorized, footprints we can't match, and bodily fluids out of place. It goes with the territory. If I tell you about every single question that comes up, you're gonna go nuts.'

'I'm the primary officer, Sanders. Going nuts is my problem, not yours.'

'All right, all right.' Sanders held up two hands in a gesture of peace. 'I was honestly trying to be helpful.'

'Bullshit. You just want to keep this case quick and simple.'

'Yes! Quick and simple is better for everyone. For God's sake, this whole town is knee-deep in firearms.'

'All the more reason for us to be making sure we get at the truth. And right now I'm really not sure Danny did it.'

'Because of a stupid casing?'

'Because of a stupid casing, a stupid slug, and a stupid trajectory that indicates Melissa Avalon's killer was at least a few inches taller than her!'

'What?'

Abe Sanders appeared genuinely startled. Rainie also drew up short. Then she got it. The detective didn't know about the medical examiner's report yet. He'd only been communicating with the crime lab, not the ME's office.

'Didn't you know?' she couldn't help drawling in mocking imitation. 'The .22 slug followed a downward trajectory from the victim's forehead to the back base of the skull. In other words, an undersize thirteen-year-old boy did not shoot a standing grown woman.'

Sanders looked stunned, then perplexed, then thoughtful. Rainie could see him turning over the facts in his mind. Was there any way Danny could've reached up with his arm and held the gun at a downward angle? What if Danny had been standing on something? What would he have stood on, and why?

She understood Sanders's mental musing, because she'd gone through it all herself at seven this morning. The ME and her assistant had even demonstrated the logistics to Rainie. The only way they could recreate the approximate trajectory of the slug was if someone at least the same height fired the shot.

'Shit,' Sanders said after a moment.

'Exactly. So now this mystery casing isn't as unimportant as you thought. Plus we have the issue of a .22 slug with no rifling marks. In short, none of our evidence matches anymore.'

'Wait a minute, wait a minute,' Sanders said quickly. 'Let's not throw out the baby with the bathwater. We recovered a .38 revolver at the scene, which was used to kill two victims. We have Danny's prints on the majority of the .38 shell casings, plus three rapid loaders. I don't know about Melissa Avalon, but we still have a case against Danny for Sally and Alice.'

Rainie stared at the state detective incredulously. 'This doesn't change things? We have a major hole in the case and it doesn't change anything for you?'

'It raises some questions we need to answer,' Sanders said levelly, 'but no, it doesn't change the case for me.'

'*How can it not change everything?*'

'Because everything isn't changed! Look, I know this is your first homicide, Conner, but the truth is, they don't all wrap up in neat little boxes. You end up with questions and sometimes the evidence is a mess. Our job is to make a case, and we still have enough to argue that Danny killed two girls. Now, maybe he didn't kill Melissa Avalon, maybe there was somebody else at the scene or someone who decided to take advantage of the chaos for his own agenda, but from where I stand, Danny O'Grady killed Alice Bensen and Sally Walker, case closed.'

'No,' Rainie insisted vehemently. 'Case is not closed. The minute we get a mystery person at the scene, case is shot to hell. Enter defense lawyer Avery Johnson. See Avery Johnson argue that Danny procured the guns and Danny loaded the guns but that somebody else – say, the five-foot-eight man on the grassy knoll – pulled the trigger. Watch jury lap it up like a cat at a creamer. The minute we have a mystery person at the scene, our case, as it were, is officially dead in the water.'

Sanders scowled. He opened his mouth to argue, then shut it, then started to speak again, then finally settled for scowling harder. It was obvious he genuinely believed that Danny had done the shooting. But he also couldn't fault Rainie's logic. A mystery person provided reasonable doubt; they no longer had enough for the DA to make his case.

Sanders turned to Quincy. 'Feel free to step in at any time,' the state detective growled.

Quincy shrugged. 'I thought Officer Conner was doing a nice job.'

'Well, you're the expert, dammit. Tell us what we're missing.'

'Honestly, I believe we're back to investigative basics. It seems to me we have a number of key questions. One, why Melissa Avalon? Her murder bears unique elements, so one theory would be that she's the linchpin behind what happened. We know that she and VanderZanden were probably involved. According to Richard Mann, she had fractured relations with her family, particularly her father. Now, I wonder if her father has access to a computer.'

'Luke Hayes is in charge of the victimology reports,' Rainie said. 'I can ask him to focus on Melissa Avalon for now and try to have something for us tomorrow.'

Quincy nodded. 'Second area of focus: the school computers. We know

Danny spent a great deal of time online, possibly talking to someone called No Lava. Who is this person? And what was his agenda when he contacted a thirteen-year-old boy? Learning what's on the computers should help us with a second possible theory of this case, that the man in black is a stranger who Danny met on-line.'

'Speaking of which,' Sanders interjected gloomily. Both Rainie and Quincy turned to stare at him. He focused on Rainie, saying defensively, 'I was going to tell you. There just hasn't been time.'

'Spit it out, Sanders.'

'I got a call from our technicians this morning. They're having problems recovering data from the school computers.'

'What kind of problems?'

Sanders smiled tightly. 'You'll like this. As I mentioned before, there were some signs that Danny—'

'That someone,' Rainie corrected.

'Fine, that someone made an attempt to clean the machines. The history file for the Web browser had been deleted and the cache file had been purged. But that's pretty obvious stuff that most computer-literate people know how to do, so the techies weren't that worried.'

'I gather it gets worse.'

'In a nutshell. I guess anytime you visit a Web site, the site puts a small piece of information in the computer's "cookie" file so that the next time the user visits the site, the site can "remember" information about the user. A good technician can bring up the cookie file from the hard drive and get fairly complete records of every place the user has been. Nope. On all four computers, the cookie files had been deleted as of six P.M. Monday, May fourteenth. The only cookies present are new ones from Tuesday morning, and they're a hodgepodge collection of eToys.com and various Pokémon sites, probably from the kids that morning.'

'What about e-mails?' Quincy pressed. 'I know I can go on-line and retrieve old e-mails, even ones I've read and deleted.'

'Generally yes. *Someone*, however, cleaned out the old and the saved e-mails, then compacted the files so they're unrecoverable. Finally, the person accessed the firewall server and deleted all the data logs. In short, the four computers are wiped clean.'

'I want them,' Quincy said simply.

'You can have them,' Rainie agreed.

'Wait a minute,' Sanders protested. 'We have good people—'

'The FBI has better.'

'Dammit, our technicians have already started work—'

'Then the FBI's data-recovery agents will be all that much faster at finishing.'

'It's true,' Quincy told Sanders, who looked ready for a full-blown snit. 'Even after everything you've described, the information is somewhere on the computers. When a file is deleted, the computer generally only deletes the directory reference to the file, not the actual data. So unless our infamous someone thought to use a Department of Defence-approved deletion program that overwrites the data with zeros, the information is on the machine. We need this information. Whatever Danny was doing on-line with No Lava is highly relevant to what went down Tuesday afternoon. So let our data-recovery agents handle it. We'll get answers sooner versus later.'

'We can get the information too,' Sanders insisted curtly. 'I can put a rush order on it. There's no reason for the FBI to get involved.'

'Too late,' Rainie said.

'Dammit, it's just an excuse to steal jurisdiction—'

'I don't give a rat's ass!' Rainie yelled back. She slapped her hand against the top of her desk. 'Someone else was in the school. Someone else shot Melissa Avalon. I want to know who, goddammit, and for the last time, Sanders, it's *not* your call.'

Sanders fell back into steely silence. He crossed his arms over his chest. He muttered, 'Man, what I'd give for a hot fudge sundae right now.'

Rainie glared at him harder. They all fell silent. The seconds ticked off. After a moment Quincy said, 'Third action step.'

He looked at them both. Rainie nodded to show she was paying attention. Sanders returned to the conversation more grudgingly.

'We go back to what you were doing this morning, Rainie – a complete list of other possible suspects. VanderZanden, Charlie Kenyon, Richard Mann, Melissa Avalon's father, this computer person, No Lava.'

'I'm working on that. I just don't have a lot of manpower.'

'Fine,' Sanders interjected crossly. 'Let's divvy it up between us. What the hell, we can pretend cross-jurisdictional investigations really work. I'll take VanderZanden. The fed can have No Lava, since he's stolen my computers. Luke Hayes has Melissa Avalon's father—'

'I'll take Charlie Kenyon and Richard Mann,' Rainie volunteered.

'Perfect,' Sanders said flatly. His eyes met Rainie's with open challenge. 'That just leaves us with one last suspect: Shep.'

'No way! He's the sheriff—'

'Whose time at the school is completely unaccounted for! We know he's got problems at home. We know he's an older man, which makes him exactly Melissa Avalon's type. And we know he goes way back with you, Conner, which makes this whole damn case even more interesting.'

Rainie decided to ignore that last comment. She said tightly, 'Shep called me from his radio after the shots were fired, meaning he was in his patrol car, not at the school.'

'Or he did the deed, returned to his car in the parking lot, and made the call.'

'Shep would not frame his own fucking son!'

'We don't know that he did! Come on, the evidence is all over the place. Danny did it. Wait, no, a second person's present, maybe he did it. You said it yourself, Conner, Danny's got the perfect defense right now – the man on the grassy knoll. Looks to me like he's about to walk. Meaning Shep's either really clever or really lucky.'

'You,' Rainie said hotly, 'have been watching too many Oliver Stone movies.'

'I'll do it,' Quincy said calmly. They both looked at him belatedly, as if just now remembering he was there. 'I'll look into Shep,' he repeated, then quickly cut off Rainie's objection. 'It's due discipline, Rainie. There are too many things about this shooting that don't make sense. Until they do, everyone must be a suspect – mysterious men in black and, yes, the town sheriff.'

Rainie sat back. She wasn't happy, but there was no more point in arguing. Quincy returned to the general conversation.

'One last thing,' he said. 'If the UNSUB is a stranger, we need to cast a wider net because chances are that he's still in the area.'

'You mean in Bakersville?' Rainie asked incredulously.

'No, this town is too small to hide in. He'd look for a neighboring town, maybe a larger tourist resort. Someplace where he could go to bars and local establishments and watch all the news coverage. He's probably following the investigation very closely and asking others about it. It's his way of reliving the moment, of still having fun. We should make contact with neighboring police departments. Have their officers ask hotel workers and bartenders. Any new faces showing a lot of interest in Bakersville's tragedy? Any mid-twenties to mid-forties white males who've been mouthing off on the subject or asking a lot of questions? That sort of thing.'

Sanders nodded. 'I can make a few calls,' he said, then shrugged dubiously. 'I don't want to lose my own men to a wild-goose chase, though. You guys may like the notion of some mystery man, but I keep coming back to the victim's injury. I've seen a lot of homicides, and a single gunshot wound to the forehead – that's a targeted victim any way you look at it. Maybe it wasn't Danny, but *somebody* specifically wanted Melissa Avalon dead.'

Quincy didn't argue. Neither did Rainie. It did seem to come back to Melissa Avalon, and the fact that they still couldn't understand why made them all very uncomfortable.

'Well, at least we have one lucky break on our side,' Quincy said finally.

Sanders and Rainie exchanged startled glances. Sanders did the honors. 'We have a break?'

'The recovery of the .22-caliber slug. You said it yourself, Detective. Most .22s become too deformed for a ballistics test. My guess is our shooter knew that too. So he tells Danny to bring a .22. Chances are, his slug will ricochet inside the skull, obliterating trajectory and rifling marks. Given all other circumstantial evidence, Danny will be blamed for Melissa

Avalon's death as well. Except the bullet doesn't ricochet. It holds a trajectory that immediately lets us know the shooter must have been another adult. And it keeps enough of the base intact to reveal its little secret – it's perfectly smooth, indicating a unique weapon. One 40-grain slug later, we know something else happened at that school.'

Rainie slowly nodded. Without the slug and its trajectory, there would never have been any reason to look beyond Danny O'Grady. Especially with the boy confessing each and every chance he got.

Sanders, however, was frowning. 'I don't get it. You're saying someone asked Danny to bring a .22 to cover for his own .22. But why the hell would he do that? Why wouldn't he simply use Danny's gun?'

Rainie stopped. Stared. She looked at Quincy, who for once appeared completely flummoxed.

'The .22 slug is smooth,' she murmured. 'It definitely didn't come from Danny's gun. And that poses another question: If the shooter brought his own weapon to kill Melissa Avalon, why a .22? It's not that powerful, particularly for a head shot. Frankly, many people survive that wound. And yet he fired only one shot to her forehead with his own gun. Risking her living to tell the tale. Risking someone seeing him armed. I don't understand . . . Something here doesn't make sense.'

They all looked at one another. No one had an answer. A preselected victim. A mystery slug. An unidentified man who had cajoled a thirteen-year-old boy into taking part in murder.

They had come a long way from a mindless act of rage, and now, suddenly, Rainie didn't know where they were going anymore. She thought about her small, peaceful town. She thought about the towering trees and the gentle rolling hills. She thought about Danny, so scared and frightened and determined to take credit for murder. She thought of the school halls, still streaked in blood.

And for the first time in fourteen years, Rainie was frightened.

19

Danny sat alone in his eight-by-eight room, staring at a spider that was slowly working its way across the thin-carpeted floor.

The door was open. Every morning at 6 A.M., the doors were flung wide by burly staff members who yelled, 'It's that time, boys and girls.' The doors stayed open all day, joining a series of look-alike rooms to a main hallway until nine o'clock at night, when everyone prepared for bed. More staff people – not guards, Danny was told, but *guides* – came by and locked everyone in from the outside. At ten o'clock came lights-out. Danny would find a face peering in through the Plexiglas window, making sure he followed the rules.

Danny followed the rules. He didn't make any trouble. He got up when he was supposed to. He let the *guide* escort him to the cafeteria. He stared at his tray. He let another *guide* lead him to a classroom, where twenty boys, ages ranging from twelve to seventeen, pretended to be studying under the eyes of some chipper lady who insisted that they could be whatever they wanted to be. Later they were allowed to *socialize.*

Danny always came back to his room, where he sat alone. No one cared. Cabot County's Juvenile Center was a newer facility. It operated as a giant, beige-colored dorm, unlike the other places kids whispered about. Old prisons converted into youth facilities where the walls and floors were slabs of concrete and everybody got to watch everybody pee. Cabot County wasn't anything like that. Some of the kids got to wear their own clothes as long as they didn't sport gang colors or offensive T-shirts. The social room had lots of Plexiglas windows and real live plants. If kids earned enough merit points, they could watch TV or even rent movies for the VCR.

For the most part, the guides led them through their days, a careful schedule of meals, classes, and rec time. As long as you did what you were told and went where you were told, no one made a fuss. You could even be alone during the social time. Sit in your room. Stare at your blue hospital scrubs. Watch spiders. Didn't matter.

The whole point was that you were never going to make it any farther. The nice rooms had Plexiglas windows for a reason. And all the outside doors were inch-thick steel. Then there was the ten-foot-high fence ringing the yard and topped with coils of barbed wire. The searchlights. The guides who had keys to rifles loaded with rubber bullets.

When Danny first got there, the older kids had been fascinated by him, and they told him stories of juvies who'd run for it. Kids who had been flattened by mattresses, gassed with pepper spray, or, rarely, if they made it beyond the fence, hunted down by growling Dobermans. If the dogs catch you, they're each allowed one bite as a reward, kids said. The guides pick the place.

Danny thought the kids were full of shit, but he didn't say anything. Since the day he'd come in, that had been his motto. Don't give up a word.

I'm smart, I'm smart, I'm smart.

I'm scared.

Now he watched the spider laboriously climb toward the barred window, thirsty for sunlight or maybe the wind in its hairy little face.

Danny fingered his scrubs – no laces, no buttons, no belts for a kid under 'SWatch' – and tried to get his mind to shut up.

The lawyer came to talk to him yesterday. Danny hadn't wanted to see the man. He had a fancy gray suit and an expensive watch and Danny knew he must cost a lot of money, which made him feel worse. His mom would be stressed about that, trying to figure out how to pay. His father would yell at her that it didn't matter, because good old Shep didn't get how the world worked. He was still lost in his football fantasies where he and/or his son were scoring the winning touchdown during the big homecoming game.

Danny hated worrying his mom. He knew she had cried. He'd heard her himself. Late at night he tried to cover his ears with his hands to block out the sound, but then he'd have to move his hand and stuff it in his mouth to keep from whimpering.

The lawyer made small talk. He told Danny what a lawyer did and what a trial was about. What his role would be and what Danny's role would be. He spoke as if Danny was four years old, and Danny let him. He stared at a point just beyond the lawyer's ear while the man babbled for an hour.

Danny wasn't supposed to talk to the counselors, he was told. They technically worked for the detention center, so it could be argued that they were law enforcement and anything he told them might be used against him at trial. To be on the safe side, Danny should ask for a chaplain or a pastor or a rabbi if he felt like spilling his guts. Priest–penitent privilege was absolute.

Danny didn't talk. He knew absolutely he could not talk, could not trust anyone, even during the quiet hours of the night when the words bobbed up inside him and lodged as a fierce, hard knot in the center of his chest. That's when he saw what had happened again, clearly but somehow distanced, as if it had all been a dream and had nothing to do with him. Then he'd raise his hand, see that he wasn't even trembling, and want to scream and scream and scream.

The lawyer told him two experts would be visiting him as well. There were more rules about talking. One of them couldn't be trusted. Danny was to be careful. The other – Schaffer, maybe? – worked for his parents. He could tell him everything. Maybe he should think about telling him everything. Maybe he would feel better about getting it off his chest.

The lawyer looked at him kindly.

Danny thought about Miss Avalon. The expression that had washed over her face. The way she had turned toward him. Her last words, not understanding.

'*Danny, run! Run, run,* run!'

The spider reached the window. Danny watched it race happily over the warm, unbreakable glass.

So many things in his mind. All these images, but so far away. Blood. Noise. Smells he'd never imagined. Hot guns in his hands. But so far away. Maybe just a dream. Snap, open your eyes and it's gone. Maybe a bad TV show. *Click,* turn it off, go to bed.

Sally and Alice and Miss Avalon. Sally and Alice and pretty Miss Avalon.

'*Run, Danny, run!*'

Danny got up. He raised his hand and slammed it down on the spider. Smash. He had happy spider guts all over his hand. He studied his fingers. They still wouldn't tremble. He stared at his hand and he willed it to shake. Nothing.

Danny, the stone-cold killer.

He went back to his bed.

Rainie swooped down on Charlie Kenyon like a bat out of hell. She'd had four run-ins with the nineteen-year-old, and this time around she didn't have the patience. She spotted him riding a small Huffy dirt bike down a bumpy logging road on his father's wooded estate, she flipped on her lights, and she went after him.

Quincy was riding shotgun. He didn't blink an eye at the display of sirens, lights, and billowing dust as Rainie pulled Charlie over to the side of the road and fishtailed to a stop. She got out of the car with her hand resting on the top of the baton in her heavy utility belt.

'Off the bike, Charlie.'

'Holy shit, Officer, was I speeding?' Looking cool in a black leather jacket and too-tight jeans, Charlie remained standing over the dirt bike. He gave her a mocking grin. Rainie worked on not smashing in his face. She needed to get more sleep. Even for herself, she was short-tempered these days.

Charlie's gaze flickered behind her, to where Quincy was climbing out of the car.

'Who's the suit?' Charlie asked.

'None of your business.'

'Breaking in a new partner? Shouldn't you have told him about the dress code? Man, I've seen guys killed for wearing silk ties in these parts.'

Rainie ignored his comments. 'Whose bike, Charlie?'

'Why? Gonna make me an offer?'

'Whose bike, Charlie?'

'Mine—'

'It's sized for an eight-year-old.'

'I'm nostalgic.'

'Really? And here I thought you were just a lying piece of shit. Get off the bike, Charlie, and put your hands in the air.'

Charlie finally dropped his James Dean routine long enough to scowl and whine. 'Hey, I won the bike fair and square. It's not my fault the kid never learned to dodge left in a fight.'

'I said *now*.'

'I'm on my father's property—'

'*Now!*'

Charlie finally went quiet. He stared at her. He stared at Quincy. Then he grudgingly swung a leg over the bike and let it drop to the ground. 'All right, all right, don't get your panties in a wad.'

'Hands in the air. Turn around. Place them against the tree trunk. Spread your legs.'

'You're gonna pat me down? Over stealing a bike?'

'Who said this had anything to do with a bike?'

'What the—'

He was too late. Rainie had already gotten close enough to hook her foot around his. She twisted him straight into the tree trunk, planted his hands above his head, and frisked him. A minute later she was the proud owner of a corkscrew, a switchblade, two hundred dollars cash, and a roll of quarters.

Quincy helped himself to the coins. He hefted the roll in his hand, fisted his fingers around it, and admired the weight. Charlie Kenyon knew how to pack a punch.

'Slow nights, Mr Kenyon?' he asked Charlie.

Rainie released her pressure on the teen's back. He turned around unhurriedly, making a big show of shaking out his arms and fussing with the collar of his leather jacket. After smoothing back his brown wavy hair, he gave Quincy a disdainful stare.

'I'm sorry,' the teen said with bracing sarcasm, 'but I didn't catch your name.'

'Supervisory Special Agent Pierce Quincy. FBI.'

'Ah shit,' Charlie said.

Rainie finally smiled. 'Funny, your father said the same thing when I spoke to him this afternoon. It appears it's one thing to tangle with the locals, but not even your father feels like messing with the feds.'

'You can take the bike.'

'No kidding. Charlie, tell us about Danny O'Grady.'

'What?'

'You heard me. We want to know everything you ever said to Danny. And if I were you, I'd give us absolute cooperation, because a few eyewitnesses have already told us enough to book you as an accomplice to murder. You're nineteen, Charlie. You end up aiding and abetting a mass murder, and there's nothing your pissant ex-mayor father can do to help you anymore. You graduate to a whole new league of adult delinquency. We're talking hard time, and not even at one of those lovely country-club prisons. You'd get the real thing.'

'Hey, hey, hey, hey.' Charlie held up two hands and made a big show of backing off. 'You think I was involved with hurting those girls? No way, no how. I got an alibi.' He gave Quincy a look. 'And she's real sweet, if you know what I mean.'

'Why were you hanging out at the elementary school? Are high school kids too tough for you? Bigger, stronger, might actually put up a fight?'

'I don't know what you're talking about. I just got a thing for jungle gyms.'

'I'm getting angry, Charlie. I'm not getting a lot of sleep these days, and the mayor told me this morning to do whatever's necessary to solve this case, so I wouldn't make me angry right now.'

'I got a federal witness,' Charlie said promptly.

Quincy looked at the sky. 'Where?'

'Shit, I thought you guys had standards.'

Quincy eyed Rainie balefully. 'I guess that explains Waco.'

Charlie flinched. 'This just burns me, man.'

'My heart's breaking,' Rainie assured him. 'Why were you at the elementary school, Charlie?'

''Cause I get bored, okay? 'Cause there's nothing to do in Bitchville, USA, and sometimes I need a little distraction.'

'Is that what Danny O'Grady was to you? Distraction?'

Charlie shrugged. 'Danny was interesting. Real potential, if you know what I mean.'

'No, I don't. He was a good student, smart, stayed out of trouble. The only potential I saw in him was to get a lot further in life than you ever will.'

Charlie turned away from her. He looked at Quincy slyly. 'You know what I mean, don't you, fed? I've heard about you. You're some big-shot profiler. Best there ever was, put away the infamous Jim Beckett. Dazzle me, fed. It's damn slow around here. I need someone to say something interesting just so I can stay awake.'

'I think you should keep doing the talking,' Quincy said evenly. 'Us law-enforcement types have a hang-up about hearing things in your own words. Besides, I'm sure you love to listen to yourself speak.'

'You're no fun.'

'It's a job requirement.'

'Charlie, what were you doing with Danny?'

'*Nothing*, okay? Exercising our First Amendment rights. You come down on me for that and I'll sic the ACLU all over your small-town ass.'

Rainie turned to Quincy. 'This isn't working for me.'

'He seems very belligerent,' Quincy agreed.

'I think we're going to have to do something about that.'

'Harm a single dead-skin cell on my head and my father will sue you back to the Stone Age.'

'At this point, your father would have to get in line.' Rainie turned back to Quincy. She said thoughtfully, 'I'm thinking hair or jacket.'

Quincy carefully scrutinized Charlie's black biker jacket and meticulously styled hair.

'Jacket,' he said.

'Okay.' Rainie stepped forward. Charlie saw her coming and tried to duck right. She countered, found a sleeve, and neatly spun Charlie around. A second later she held the black leather jacket and Charlie stood stunned.

Rainie smiled at him. She was in such a dark mood these days. She didn't want to deal with punks. She was sick of kids who wielded guns and switchblades with no real concept of death.

'We're going to play a game, Charlie. I'm going to ask questions. You're going to answer. Quincy, the expert, is going to evaluate your answers for truthfulness. If he doesn't like what you say – or you make me angry again – I'm going to start slicing up your coat. You give me lip, your jacket loses a sleeve. Got it?'

'It's just a dumb jacket. I can buy a new one.'

'Okay.' Rainie opened his switchblade and found the collar.

'Wait, wait, wait, wait, wait!' Charlie was panting. His gaze was locked down on the collar, and perspiration beaded his upper lip. The jacket was old and sported a biker gang's symbol on the back. The kid could deny it all he wanted, but Quincy and Rainie had him pegged. The jacket was part of Charlie Kenyon's costume, and he felt overexposed without it. They might as well have snatched Superman's cape.

'First question, Charlie. Why were you hanging out with Danny O'Grady?'

'Because he was cool, all right?'

'Danny is a computer geek. How is that cool?'

'No, no, no.' Charlie was shaking his head. 'You don't get it. You had to look in his eyes. He was *old*, man. And . . . and . . . angry. At his father. I know these things.'

'Danny's a kindred spirit?' Rainie asked dryly.

'Something like that.'

'What about Melissa Avalon?' Quincy interjected. 'What was she?'

Charlie's answer was more forthcoming. 'She was hot! Jesus, fed, did you look at her? Whoa, mama.'

'You ever approach her?'

'Sure, I tried.' He shrugged, his hands digging into his pockets. He was definitely self-conscious without his jacket. 'She, uh, was intimidated by my good looks. Besides, I heard later I violated her age rules. Avalon had a geezer fetish.'

'Was she a kindred spirit?'

'What d'you mean? Oh, was she angry? I don't know. Didn't seem angry to me. You should ask Danny. He was the one spending so much time with her.'

'Did he ever mention his feelings for Miss Avalon to you?'

'Didn't have to. The boy was lovesick for her. You could see it all over his face.'

'Did Avalon know this?'

'Probably. I don't think puppy crushes were new to her.'

'How did she treat Danny?'

'I don't know. I hung around the school grounds, not the freaking computer lab.'

'Did Danny know about her "geezer fetish"?'

'Sure, I told him. What, you guys think Danny killed her in a jealous rage? Nah, you don't get it.' Charlie shook his head, sounding honest for the first time. 'Danny's smarter than you think. He knew he liked her, but hell, she was a teacher. He understood what that meant. Worship from afar, end of story. He wasn't imagining white picket fences or the mother of his children. The kid's thirteen, for chrissakes.'

'What about the other two girls?' Rainie asked. 'Sally and Alice?'

'Couldn't pick them out of a lineup if I tried.'

'Are you going to go to the funerals, Charlie?'

He shrugged. 'The old man's making me.'

'Do you think it's sad that they're dead?'

'Don't know them. Don't care.'

'You're a real hard-ass, aren't you, Charlie Kenyon?'

'You're the one threatening my jacket.'

'Did you ever talk to Danny about killing people?'

'We talked about lots of stuff.'

'Charlie.' She held up the switchblade, then his jacket.

Charlie's jaw hardened. She thought he was going to freeze up on her. Then she moved the blade closer to the collar and he surrendered again.

'Yeah. Sure. You wanna know? Sometimes I dream of blowing this whole freaking town off the map. I dream of getting my hands on a big mother-fucking nuke and saying *sayonara*, babe. You know, plant life grows back bigger and stronger after a nuclear holocaust. Maybe that's what this town needs.'

'You told all this to a thirteen-year-old boy?'

'Only after he told me he wanted to hack his father into twenty different pieces and run him through a blender.'

Rainie stared at him. A muscle worked in her jaw. She said with more anger than she wanted to give away, 'A child tells you he fantasizes about murdering his own father, and you didn't think to go to the police?'

'Who am I going to go to? Shep, his dad? Or, better yet, you?' Charlie chuckled unkindly. 'Isn't that a pretty picture? Half this town still talks about what you did to your mother. What would you have done with Danny? Mail him a shotgun?'

'I never harmed my mother,' Rainie said hotly. 'And if I had done such a thing, I'd be in prison where I'd belong, not standing here talking to you.'

But Charlie had that sly look back on his face. 'I know, I know,' he said with a conspirator's wink. 'The fed's here. You don't want to blow your cover. That's all right. But you don't have to lie to me, babe. I'm telling you, I can see these things. And you're a member of the cool-kids club too. Hell, around here, you're probably the charter member.'

'One last question,' Quincy interjected quickly, because the shotgun comment had pushed Rainie to the brink and they all knew it. 'Did Danny ever mention an on-line friend to you? Someone named No Lava?'

'Computer geek? Yeah, maybe. Danny was always into something. I didn't know how one person could spend so much time staring at a screen.'

'Did you ever see any of the e-mails?'

'What the hell would I want with them?'

'Danny really liked No Lava. Maybe you were jealous.'

'Look, I've never even heard of this No Lava, and frankly, the name sounds like an impotent dude to me. Danny liked mail, okay? Six months ago, eight months ago, I don't remember, he was all excited about someone he'd met on-line. He was always having to go check his frigging e-mail. That's all I know.'

'You encouraged him,' Rainie said softly. 'Danny was troubled and you helped push him over the edge. Now three people are dead, and some of that's on your head, Charlie. You're going to have to live with that.'

'Who gives a fuck? Legally, I'm free as a bird. Now, give me my jacket back. As much fun as this has been, I got places to go and people to see.'

'Sure,' Rainie said. She smiled at him. Then she raised the switchblade and sliced the collar clean off his coat.

Charlie shrieked. Quincy took a shocked step forward.

Rainie retrieved the severed piece of leather. A moment later she squeezed the long plastic bag of white powder from the collar onto her palm.

'Heroin. About three ounces of it, which would make a little more than simple possession. Congratulations, Charlie. Legally speaking, your troubles are just beginning.'

'Goddamn cunt! How dare you! You're no better than me! You're no better than any of us!'

'Sure I am, Charlie. There are two choices for angry people in this world, and only one of them wears a badge.'

Charlie shrieked again. Rainie enjoyed loading him into the car.

20

It took Rainie four hours to process Charlie Kenyon. She had to catalog the heroin into evidence. Then she had to store it in the safe that passed as the department's evidence locker. She'd just finished fingerprinting Charlie when his father's lawyer arrived and tried to tell her she'd used entrapment to find the drugs. Rainie volunteered an FBI agent as her corroborating witness. FitzSimons turned downright abusive. She'd had no right to search Charlie Kenyon, no justification for mutilating his jacket, and she'd violated every constitutional law ever envisioned by the forefathers and then some.

Rainie took it in her stride. It amazed her how comforting the drug bust felt after the relative chaos of the past three days. She knew Charlie, she knew FitzSimons, she knew Charlie's dad. All the usual suspects, all the usual paperwork, all the usual crimes. She could've done this arrest in her sleep.

She spent two hours carefully wording the arrest report and building the file against Charlie. Then the paperwork was done and she returned to the task-force center, where the shadows had grown long and the attic office was eerily quiet. Well past ten o'clock; another long day in a long, strange case.

Luke Hayes had gone to Portland, where he would hopefully interview Melissa Avalon's parents. Sanders was out doing God knows what Sanders did. Maybe arranging the soup cans in the grocery store or crashing a Tupperware party for more stay-fresh seals. Quincy was following up on No Lava. Or maybe he'd started in on Shep. Whatever he found, she'd probably be the last to know. She was both frustrated by that and grateful.

Now there was just her and the hum of the old computer and the buzz of all the thoughts still crowding her head.

Charlie had rattled her today. Not just with his accusations against her. Rainie knew what people thought and said. She accepted that salacious rumors would always be more appealing than cold, hard fact. It didn't get to her.

He had spooked her with his comments about Danny.

'Only after he told me he wanted to hack his father into twenty different pieces and run him through a blender.'

705

Rainie couldn't let the statement go. So much violence. So much rage. She knew these things happened. God knows, some nights . . . Huddled in the closet, bruised and shaking and still tasting the blood on her split lip. Wishing it would go away. Wishing she'd have the strength to make it stop.

The fantasies. That she'd rise up and her mother would finally cower before her. That just once she'd strike back, maybe slap her mother hard, and then her mother would repent, weeping, 'I never knew how much it hurt. I swear I never realized. Now I know and I'll never do it again.'

Maybe that was the difference. Through all of her pain, Rainie never forgot that Molly was her mother. And the kernel of her fantasies was still about love and forgiveness. That her mother would realize what she was doing. That she'd give up the bottle. That she'd take her little girl in her arms and swear never to hurt her again. That for once Rainie could relax in her mother's embrace and feel safe.

Even at the worst of it, she had not wished her mother dead.

It had taken a great deal more than that to push her over the edge.

Rainie paced the tiny attic. Her body ached and her mind ached and she couldn't stand being alone with her own thoughts anymore. She needed sleep, a decent meal, a good hard run. It was too late to jog, she had no appetite, and she was honestly afraid to close her eyes.

'What would you have done with Danny? Mail him a shotgun?'

No, she would've told him that she understood. She would've taken him to her back deck, where the mountain pines towered above them and owls hooted deep in the shadows and it was difficult to take yourself seriously when you were so small in the general scheme of things. She would've let him talk. Get it all out, angry child to angry child, if that's what it took. Then maybe she would've talked. Perhaps she would've told him things she'd never told anyone else. Sitting on her deck with the trees around them and the clean mountain air fresh on their faces.

Maybe she would've saved Danny O'Grady.

But she hadn't done any such thing. She'd seen him just two weeks before the shooting. She'd thought he was pale and jumpy and curt with his father. And in the next instant she'd shrugged it away because, just like everyone else, she thought it was a phase. Trouble happened only in bad families. Not to a nice, ordinary kid like Danny.

She, a kindred spirit, had failed him. And she didn't know yet how she was going to live with that.

Quincy was hunched over his laptop in his cramped hotel room when knocking sounded at the door. He'd been working for two hours, scouring various on-line carriers for any record of a member named No Lava. His eyes were blurry. His shoulders carried knots the size of small boulders. Every time he shifted to get more comfortable, the rickety desk threatened to collapse and take his laptop with it. Thirty minutes ago he'd started cramming crime-scene photos under the uneven legs for better support. He did not want to know what this said about his life.

The knocking came again.

Quincy pushed away from the table, rubbed the back of his neck, and self-consciously checked the mirror. His white shirt, pressed crisp just this morning, was now a wrinkled mess. His tie was somewhere on the floor. His cheeks sported a five o'clock shadow, and his dark hair was rumpled from running his fingers through it over and over again. If memory served, this look had worked for him in his thirties, when it made him sexy in a dark, brooding sort of way. He was in his mid-forties now. He thought he simply looked tired.

Some decades were definitely better than others, he thought. What the hell.

He checked the door's peephole and was not surprised to see Rainie standing there.

He opened the door, and for a moment they simply studied each other.

She'd changed out of her officer's uniform. Now she wore faded straight-leg jeans and a loose hunter-green sweater with a turtleneck collar that framed her face. Her chestnut hair was down and freshly brushed, gleaming gold and red beneath the hotel's outdoor lights. She didn't appear to be wearing a drop of makeup, and Quincy liked her that way. Her pale skin fresh and untouched. No barriers between his hand and the feel of her cheek, or his lips and the corner of her mouth.

He had spent the latter part of the afternoon learning things about Lorraine Conner he had not anticipated. Certainly he was starting to understand that her past held a great deal more than met the eye. Maybe nothing, but maybe something. He doubted she would tell him the whole truth yet, and he wondered about the dangers of learning it all at the last minute, when it might be too late for both of them.

He should be careful. He was a smart, logical man who knew better than most the dark potential of human nature. The warning did him no good. She was here, at his hotel room, and he suspected his face now held a giddy smile.

'Hey,' she said after a moment.

'Good evening, Rainie.'

'Working?'

'Just finishing up.'

'Really?' She stuck her hands in her back pockets and studied the pavement. She was clearly self-conscious, and that touched him.

'I was just about to order take-out Chinese,' he said politely. 'Would you like to join me?'

'I'm not that hungry.'

'Neither am I, but we can pretend together.'

She entered his hotel room. He made an effort to clear his paperwork off the bed, since the room was small and there was no place else for her to sit. She studied his laptop while he shoved manila files back into his black leather briefcase/computer carrier.

'Looking for No Lava?' she asked.

'Yes. Most Internet providers have member directories where you can enter your on-line name and vital statistics. Lots of people fill out the forms, so I thought I'd see if we could get that lucky. Unfortunately, we're not that lucky. Next step is to get a subpoena and contact the carriers directly.'

'Did you run a background check on Shep today?' she asked.

Quincy stopped, still holding four files, and blinked. She wasn't wasting any time. He put the files in the bag, zipped it shut.

'Do you like lo mein?' he asked lightly.

'Order whatever you want.'

'Lo mein it is.' He picked up the batch of take-out menus Ginnie had left next to the phone and sorted through them until he found one for the Great Wall of China. He placed an order for lo mein and green tea. Rainie was still studying him.

'I don't think we should have this conversation,' he said presently.

'That means you found something.'

'No. It means I have professional standards and this is a clear case of conflict of interest. Shep is your friend. You and he go way back.' He regarded her steadily.

'I never slept with Shep,' Rainie said matter-of-factly.

'You know most people think that you're the reason his and Sandy's marriage is falling apart.'

'We're not involved. Never have been, never will be.'

'He spends a lot of time at your place.'

'I know.'

'Rainie—'

'People talk. Don't you get that yet? It's a small town, it rains eighty percent of the year, and the cows outnumber the people two to one. Most of the time there's nothing else to do around here but talk. That's just the way it is.'

'Why didn't you tell me about the shotgun, Rainie? The shotgun that killed your mother had your prints on it until it disappeared from the police evidence locker. Then one day it was magically back in custody, but completely wiped clean. Why didn't you tell me it disappeared from evidence?'

Her face went cool, her chin coming up, her gray eyes turning the color of slate. He recognized that expression. Her fighter's stance.

'Do you think I killed my mother?'

'No.'

'Do you think I shot her in cold blood? Came home from school one day and blew off her goddamn head? I'm just a female version of Charlie Kenyon? No better than Danny O'Grady?'

He said gently, 'No, Rainie, I don't.'

'Then what does it matter, Quincy? It was fourteen years ago and I didn't do it, so just let it go. It's one thing to deal with all the stares and rumors from my neighbors, but I don't expect that from you!'

'Give me some credit,' he countered sharply. 'I'm not a small-town deputy you can snow under with a few loud words. I know something happened, Rainie. Something happened, Shep helped you with it, and that's what binds you, isn't it? I still don't know what. Maybe I don't need to know, but there is something between you and Shep. And it's beyond professional ties and it makes the fact that you were alone in the school with Shep and Danny very shaky. Sanders was right. You should've surrendered jurisdiction over this case. And I suspect you know that as well.'

She fell silent, her lips thinning. He'd caught her off guard. He had wondered in the beginning what a woman as smart as Rainie was doing working such a limited job, and today he'd gotten his answer. Because it kept her in control. She worked with nice people, but none of them was the type to pry. He suspected she dated men of more brawn than brains and kept the relationships short. No one could question her too much. No one could get too close. She had turned protecting herself into a way of life.

'I couldn't give up jurisdiction,' she said abruptly.

'Because you promised Shep you'd be the primary in the case?'

'Yes.' She hesitated. 'I owe him that much.'

'Just how much do you owe him, Rainie?'

'Shep had faith in me. He's been a good friend and I feel loyalty toward him. But I have professional standards, too, Quincy, and I don't compromise them. We all go through life making our choices and we're all responsible for what we've done. If Danny shot those girls, then by God, he needs to be held accountable for that.'

'You're sure of that?'

'Of course I'm sure! Covering up doesn't do him any favors. Why don't people realize that? We have a basic human need to make restitution in order to absolve our guilt. Letting kids walk away scot-free or shielding them from the consequences of their actions doesn't help them. A moment's mistake, a moment of bad judgment could fester into a lifetime of hatred and self-loathing and destructiveness. Until it's become a dark spot you can't forget and can't let go and it builds and builds—'

She broke off. She was breathing hard. Her gaze had become locked on the blue floral bedspread and her hands were fisted at her sides.

'The nightmares are worse, aren't they?' Quincy asked quietly.

'Yes.'

'You're not eating.'

'I can't.'

'You're too smart to be doing this to yourself.'

'I can't seem to stop.'

'Why did you come here tonight, Rainie?'

She looked at him with frustrated, troubled eyes. 'I think I need to talk.'

'Then talk. But say something new, Rainie, because I no longer have the patience for lies.'

The Chinese food arrived. Quincy split the lo mein, though he suspected she wouldn't eat. She didn't. She set the white container aside but accepted a cup of tea. He took a bite of his own dinner. He wasn't that hungry either, but he'd learned a long time ago that letting himself get run-down during a case, especially a very difficult case, didn't do anyone any favors.

'Sally and Alice's funeral will be held tomorrow afternoon,' Rainie said shortly. 'The mayor just called and told me. The bodies were retrieved from the ME's office this evening, and the families don't want to wait. Everyone thinks it would be best to get this behind us.'

'That will be a rough afternoon.'

'Yeah. We've called for backup from Cabot County. Extra patrols both during the funeral and afterward. Patrol cars stationed outside of the bars, you know.'

'Emotions are already running high, add to that a little booze . . .' Quincy trailed off. They both knew what could happen. Young men and guns, vigilante justice.

'We'll be doubling up the guard around Shep's house,' Rainie said quietly. 'Luke asked to lead the effort.'

'And you?'

'I can't. There would be more talk.'

'George Walker isn't very happy with you.'

'No. A lot of people aren't. I was hoping . . . I wanted to be able to say that Danny didn't do it. Before we got to the funerals, I wanted to have so much evidence I could look George Walker in the eye and say, "A thirteen-year-old boy didn't murder your daughter, sir. Some other bastard did it." As if that would make a difference.'

'You're not so sure about Danny anymore, are you?'

Her expression grew strained. She said softly, 'No.'

'Charlie Kenyon?'

She slowly nodded. 'His account of what Danny told him. That he wanted to cut his father into pieces, run him through a blender. . . . So much anger. I didn't realize . . . I didn't know things had gotten that bad.'

'It's not your fault, Rainie. It's hard for any of us to believe that people we personally know and care about are capable of violence. People seem to forget: Murderers don't come from test tubes. They're born into this world like the rest of us, and they also have family and friends.'

'That's just a platitude. I don't *want* any more platitudes. I'm sick of easy answers or thirty-second analyses of complicated crimes. Kids are shooting up their schools, grown men are walking into offices and mowing down their coworkers. And I understand your point that schools and businesses are still safer than driving on the highway, but that explanation is not enough. These shootings are happening everywhere, even places like here, where they don't belong. And they are happening to everyone, even to Danny O'Grady, who just three days ago seemed like a normal kid going through a hard time. And . . . and I feel like I missed something. I should've seen this coming. But then I look at it again, and I know I still never would've expected violence. Because I don't understand it, Quincy. Even I, who was raised by a woman who lived by her fists, can't imagine shooting up strangers. And I need to know why this happened to my town, because no matter how hard I try, I just can't get to sleep.'

'It's not your fault, Rainie,' he said again.

She shook her head impatiently. 'Explain the shootings to me. I need to know. Is it because of guns? As an officer, should I be banning them from my community? Or is it video games and violent movies, and books. . . . Is it all because of that?'

'Those things are factors. On the other hand, do I think censoring Hollywood and banning guns would end all the crime? No. Some people, even kids, are that angry.'

'Then it's inevitable? We've become a violent culture and there's nothing we can do about it?'

'I don't think that. There's always something we can do. We're an intelligent society, Rainie. Nothing is beyond our grasp.'

'Tell that to George Walker. Tell that to the parents of Alice Bensen. I'm sure they're sitting home right now thinking about how capable society is.'

Quincy fell silent. She was in a mood tonight.

'Do you want a solution, Rainie,' he asked after a moment, 'or do you want an excuse to be angry?'

'I want a solution!'

'Fine,' he said crisply. 'I'll give you my two cents, for what it's worth. Society is not filled with evil souls. But it is filled with people who are mobile, fractured, overworked, overweight, overcrowded, and overtired. That's a potent combination, particularly for people with poor coping skills and volatile tempers. And we're seeing the proof of that in the increasing number of impulsive, angry acts, such as mass murders and road rage.'

Rainie sighed. She rubbed her temples. 'It's a sign of the times?'

'It's a sign of stressful living,' Quincy said, then shrugged. 'In the good-news department, some of the solutions are fairly simple. Why not teach rage-management classes and stress-coping skills in school? While we're at it, we could emphasize good communication skills and self-monitoring. Physical care also makes a big difference. In fact, the first thing a child psychologist does when he begins treatment of a new client is address sleep, exercise, and eating habits. You think you have trouble with rage? Try getting eight hours of sleep at night, eat more fruits and vegetables, and enjoy a good workout. Ironically enough, very few people bother with these basic steps anymore, and then they wonder why they're tense all the time.'

He gave her a pointed look, his gaze sliding to the untouched carton of food by her side. Rainie nodded slowly. She said, almost hesitantly, 'I took a class in anger management.'

'In Portland?'

'Yes. After I'd enrolled in AA. When I was still struggling. Alcohol numbs a lot of emotions. Then you give it up . . .'

'I think that was a great thing for you to do,' Quincy said honestly. 'I wish more people would think that way.'

Rainie immediately shook her head. 'I'm not so great, Quincy. Don't admire me too much.'

He didn't say anything, waiting to see if she would elaborate. The darkness still rimmed her eyes, and she was clutching her cup of tea as if she wished it were a bottle of beer. Apparently, however, she still wasn't in the mood to share.

'How's your daughter?' she asked shortly.

'The same. I called this morning.'

She regarded him curiously. 'That doesn't make you feel worse? She's your daughter, she's dying, and you're not there for it. A phone call doesn't seem like much in the face of all that.'

'Rainie, when I said my daughter was killed by a drunk driver, I was being a little misleading.'

She froze. 'I see.'

'My daughter wasn't hit by a drunk driver,' Quincy said matter-of-factly. 'She *was* the drunk driver. She loaded up at a friend's house, then tried to drive home at five-thirty in the morning. And she killed an elderly man out walking his dog before she wrapped her car around a telephone pole. My daughter is dead. The man is dead. The dog is dead. And yes, a phone call to a hospital room is completely inadequate.'

'Quincy, I'm sorry.'

He smiled roughly. 'So am I. I'm not perfect either, Rainie. Some things, like what really matters in life, we all learn the hard way.'

She nodded. Her expression was still troubled, though. She had more things to say; he could feel the words churning just below the surface. He leaned forward as if he could will the truth out of her. He hadn't lied to her last night. She fascinated him. She had worked her way into his mind, and now he wanted to cup her cheek with his hand, brush her lips with his fingertips . . .

She was a fighter, and he had so much respect for that.

Her face relented a fraction. Yearning burgeoned in her soft gray eyes. A need to share. A need for connection. He wished he could reach out and touch her. He was too afraid she'd bolt at the first sign of movement.

'Rainie—'

'I should go.'

'I'll listen.'

'I don't have anything to say! I just need a little time.'

'Another fourteen years? Or maybe just five, until the next homicide comes along? It's eating you up inside. Get it out! What happened with your mother? What did you do with that shotgun?'

She stood abruptly. He was stung by the fire in her eyes, the sudden hard set of her chin.

'Don't bring up my mother again.'

'No dice.'

'It's not your business—'

'Too late. You should've stuck with dating rednecks, Rainie. Because you have a real man now and I'm not going anyplace.'

'You arrogant son of a bitch.'

'Yes. Now, tell me about your mother, Rainie.'

'The number one line most abused by psychologists. That's what I am to you, aren't I, Quincy? A very interesting case study. Something you can write up for the American Society of Shrinks – otherwise known as ASS – later on in the year.'

'Shut up, Rainie.'

'Oh, good comeback.'

Quincy frowned angrily. Then he shocked them both by striding forward and grabbing her arms.

'Brute force?' she whispered, and her lips parted. He saw something dark come into her eyes.

'It's what you want, isn't it?' he countered levelly. 'A pattern you recognize, a way to bring me down to the level you think you deserve. If you can keep it physical, then you'll never have to feel. Right?'

She stared at him mutinously. He brought her even closer, until her lips were a mere inch from his.

'Let me go,' she muttered.

'You're only going to leave here to pace your house all night long. You're terrified of sleep. You're terrified of nightmares. You want them to end, but you still won't do what it takes to make them go away.'

'Let go of my arms or you'll never sing baritone in the church choir again.'

'Talk to me, Rainie. I *want* to listen. I might even understand.'

She shuddered in his arms. He saw the conflict in her eyes again. Some part of her wanted to talk. Some strong, fierce part of her took good care of herself even in spite of herself. But he also saw the layers of fear and doubt and confusion. Years of baggage, accumulated every time her mother opened a fresh bottle and turned on her daughter with an open fist.

Her face shuttered. One moment he thought he might be on the brink of discovery, the next she was gone. Her jaw settled, her eyes went flat, and he knew the battle was over. He released her. She stepped back, shaking out her arms.

'Not bad,' she drawled with a clear edge in her voice. 'I wouldn't have picked you for a tough guy, SupSpAg.'

Quincy didn't bother with a reply. She had retreated behind her brittle shell. From here on out, all he'd get from her would be attitude. Her mother had taught her well.

'I'm leaving,' she said defiantly.

'Good night, Rainie.'

She faltered, then scowled. 'You can't stop me.'

'Sweet dreams, Rainie.'

'Son of a bitch,' she told him flatly, and stalked to the door.

She opened it with more force than necessary. He didn't interfere. She slammed it behind her. He didn't move.

Long after the sound stopped ringing in the room, he was still standing by the bed, thinking of Rainie Conner and all the things that could've happened fourteen years ago. He thought of shotguns and Danny O'Grady and his own daughter, whom he loved with all his heart.

The world needed more kindness, he thought not for the first time. The world needed more faith.

'Isolation is not protection,' he murmured. But he wondered sometimes if his epiphany hadn't come too late.

Rainie's house was dark when she got home. She never remembered to turn on the patio lights before leaving for work, and now her tiny house was hard to see as it sat nestled in the woods. She parked outside on the dirt driveway and fumbled with her keys.

When she finally stepped inside, no one came to greet her. This was the way she wanted her life, but tonight the emptiness deepened her mood.

She went around the two-bedroom ranch, turning on lamps. The space still seemed oppressive. She couldn't get Quincy's words out of her head or the scent of his cologne off her skin.

'Why didn't you tell me about the shotgun, Rainie? Why didn't you tell me it disappeared from evidence?'

She entered the kitchen and opened the fridge. She was the proud owner of twelve bottles of Bud Light, one pound of Tillamook cheese, and an expired quart of milk. She closed the refrigerator.

She went out to her deck.

The woods were dark around her. The moon was in its waning phase, and it was hard to see where the tops of the pine trees ended and the velvety night sky began. The bracing air brought goose bumps to her skin, and she hugged her middle for warmth.

She walked around her deck, then walked around her deck again.

'*Why didn't you tell me about the shotgun, Rainie? Why didn't you tell me it disappeared from evidence?*'

She couldn't. She'd been an idiot to go see Quincy in the first place. He just radiated such strength. All those lines in his face. It made her believe there was nothing she could tell him that he couldn't handle. And she was so very tired these days.

But there *were* things she couldn't tell him. She'd been naive to think it would be enough to talk around the issue. She'd forgotten that Quincy was not the kind of man who would settle for less. Damn him for grabbing her like that, making her breath catch in her throat and her stomach turn tiny flip-flops.

One more inch and her body would've been pressed against his. She could've run her hands all over the lines of his face. She could've felt the steel bands of his arms and legs. She could've been just a woman and he could've been just a man and maybe that would've been easier in the end.

She could've crept out of the room the minute he fell asleep. Some habits were hard to break.

Rainie went back inside. She found every picture of her mother that she owned. She turned them all facedown. It still wasn't enough. Tonight she didn't think anything could be enough.

She finally curled up on the sofa, fully dressed and desperately needing sleep. She was thinking of Quincy again and his intense gaze. She was thinking of Charlie Kenyon and Danny O'Grady and all the things that wouldn't give her peace.

She finally fell asleep.

And an hour later she woke up screaming. She was on the floor and her mother's body was splayed out in front of her and someone was standing on her back deck staring in at her. The man in black! The man in black!

Rainie bolted for her bedroom. She needed a gun. The CSU had taken her Glock .40. She tore through her closet until she found her old 9 mm in a shoebox, then went storming out into the night. But the deck was clear and the air was cold and it was all in her mind after all. No man. No intruder. Just the lingering effects of a very bad dream.

She went back inside shakily. She kept her 9 mm. She curled up with an afghan. And she stared at the white ceiling of her family room and willed the blood to stay away.

You're too smart to be doing this to yourself, Rainie.

But apparently she wasn't, for the night went on and on.

She finally fell asleep around five. At six-thirty, the phone woke her up, ringing shrilly. Sandy O'Grady sounded frantic on the other end.

'I have to talk to the FBI agent,' Sandy said at once. 'Oh God, Rainie, I don't know what else to do.'

Rainie got up to face another day.

Twenty minutes later, walking out to her patrol car, she found a note tucked under her windshield wipers. It said: *Die, bitch.*

She crumpled it up and threw it away.

21

Ed Flanders had been a bartender for thirty-five years. He hadn't meant to do that. In the beginning it had been just a gig, a mindless summer job that would let him hit on girls while making a ton of money in tips. He was passing down the Oregon coast on his way to LA, where he was going to make it big. Hanging out in Seaside to catch a community play, he'd first seen the Help Wanted sign and decided what the hey.

It had been a long time since.

In the beginning, he told himself he stayed for his art. Seaside had a decent community theater program and enough tourists passing through to make it worthwhile. Each summer he'd audition for a lead role and work on building his resumé. Then, when he never moved beyond parts such as Peasant #3, he told himself he stayed for the money. A bartender could make a little dough during the wild summer months. Then he told himself he stayed for the benefits, because he'd finally hit thirty and realized the true joy of a good HMO. Truth was, he'd met Jenny by then and, stick a fork in him, he was done.

Next thing Ed Flanders knew, several decades had passed, he was now a grandpa and pretty little Jenny was still the love of his life.

Ed Flanders didn't have any complaints.

Until two days ago. That man, coming into the bar and ordering his buffalo wings. That man, getting Darren all riled up, though God knows it didn't take much anymore.

That man, talking about those poor little girls and all the things that had gone wrong over in Bakersville.

Ed Flanders had met a lot of people in his time, and that man bothered him.

Not the questions, he decided after a bit. Everyone in town was talking about the shooting that happened just an hour and a half away. Some people claimed to know Shep personally. Lots of people had some sort of family involved.

Oh, people talked about the shooting, all right. In the bars, in the churches, in the streets.

But not that many locals, let alone strangers, went around spouting some

717

junior officer's name. Lori . . . Liz . . . Lorraine. Lorraine Conner. She wasn't even the one on TV. That was the mayor, and some state guy named Sanders.

So how'd this guy know Conner's name like that?

And worse, why did Ed Flanders think he'd seen the guy before? Something about the eyes, or maybe it was the nose. Take away the years, maybe soften the hair . . .

Damn, he couldn't quite place the face.

That strange, uncomfortable man who had walked into his bar and made everything *wrong*.

Ed didn't like him. Didn't trust him. He just didn't know what to do about that yet.

Back in the hotel room, the man finally allowed himself to collapse. Damn, he was tired. The pace of the last few days, the things he still had to get done . . . People who thought murder was easy had obviously never tried it.

The man fished around in his pockets until he dug up a cellophane wrapper of pills. He ripped it open with his hands and downed four herbal diet pills, one after another, then poured a glass of water. The caffeine made him a little light-headed, but he needed the pick-me-up.

Lots of things done, lots of things left to do.

Last night he'd almost botched the whole affair. Lorraine Conner had looked so wiped out when she'd finally returned home, it had never dawned on him she'd wake up. One minute he thought he'd safely made it from her bedroom closet to the back deck, the next she was flying off the couch like some banshee.

Holy shit, he'd barely cleared the deck railing in time. Even then he'd been about to crash through the woods like a maniac, when something about her movements drew him up cold. She was acting stilted, surreal, looking at things that weren't even there. A second later he figured it out. She was still asleep, chasing some phantom in her twisted dreams.

Maybe he'd triggered something. Maybe night turned her into a raving loon. Hell if he knew. He'd taken cover in his normal spot and simply waited her out. After another moment she'd gone back into the house and he'd been free and clear.

He'd gotten a little giddy after that. He even remembered laughing, one of those high-pitched sounds like you hear in movies. He'd have to watch that. Can't lose control.

Not just yet.

Today, after all, was the funeral. And then . . .

He was a very smart man. Someday soon Lorraine Conner would get to appreciate that.

Lorraine Conner, Pierce Quincy, Shep O'Grady, and little Becky.

Now this, he told his old man silently, this is how you have some *fun.*

22

'Danny called me this morning. I know it was him.' Sandy O'Grady sat on a metal folding chair in the task force's HQ, twisting her hands on her lap and trying very hard to sound calm. 'I could hear clanging in the background and people talking. Institutional noises. But the caller was silent. I said, "Danny, I know it's you. Please talk to me, Danny. I love you."'

'What did Danny say?' Quincy asked. He was sitting in a chair beside her, impeccably dressed, which immediately made her think of Mitch, her boss. She pushed the thought to the back of her head.

'He didn't say a word. He just sighed. Heavily. Like . . . like someone hopeless. Then he hung up.'

'You're sure it was Danny?' Rainie spoke up for the first time. She was leaning against the windowsill all the way across the room. Her arms were crossed over her chest. Her cheeks were gaunt. Frankly, she looked the worst that Sandy had ever seen her.

Not that Sandy was in a position to talk. She'd quickly grabbed a nearby OSU sweatshirt after receiving Danny's call, and it turned out to be stained in four different places with old yellow baby spit-up and new white patio paint. Her normally bright blond hair was dull and matted from sleep. She hadn't showered, let alone put on makeup. She didn't have the energy anymore to worry about these things.

'It was Danny,' she told Rainie firmly. 'Shep changed our number to an unlisted one two days ago. Only family members and Danny's lawyer know how to reach us now. We haven't gotten one of *those* calls since.'

'Are you getting a lot of pressure from your neighbors?' Quincy asked gently.

'Some.' Sandy kept her chin up. 'Others, our good friends, are still there for us. One couple on our block – I don't even know them that well – came over last night with a plate of brownies and sat with us. There are . . . bad moments, but there are good ones too. Danny's innocent until proven guilty, you know.'

Unable to help herself, she turned once more toward Rainie.

'It's official police business,' Rainie said curtly. 'I can't talk about it.'

'Rainie, he's my son. He's upset, he's suicidal. Just yesterday he tried to gouge his wrist with a fork, for chrissakes. I'm not sure how much longer he can take being locked up in the detention center, and I don't know what to do. Shep tells me there's proof someone else was involved – mysterious shells, I don't know. Can't you do something with that? Drop the charges? Bring Danny home? Please—' Sandy's voice broke off pleadingly. She didn't know Rainie well. She would call her a friend, but more because they had Shep in common than because they'd ever spent any time talking. Still, Rainie had come to their house for dinner at least once every few months. She played with Danny and Becky. She seemed to honestly enjoy time with the kids. Surely she wouldn't forget those moments now. Surely she wasn't completely immune to Danny's plight.

The woman in question, however, remained impassive. Her uniform suddenly loomed as a wall between them, and for the first time, Sandy got it. Rainie wasn't looking at her as the sheriff's wife. This morning Sandy was in the task-force center as a mass murderer's mother.

Sandy threw out desperately, 'Maybe Shep can help find out who did it.'

'We don't want Shep,' Rainie said flatly. 'We want Becky.'

'What do you mean?'

'Is she still sleeping in closets, Sandy?'

'That's not anyone's business—'

'She saw something; we all know it. You and Shep keep saying you want the truth. Let us ask for it.'

'Avery Johnson would never permit it.'

'It's not his call.'

'Yes, it is! He's our lawyer. My God, we're going to have to mortgage our home just to pay his fees. After all that, how can we not listen to what he says? He's acting in our best interests.'

'What about Becky's best interests?' Rainie pressed relentlessly. 'The girl only feels safe in enclosed spaces. She's having nightmares, and Luke says she's as pale as a sheet. How long are you going to let that go on?'

'The doctor said she'll grow out of it with time—'

'We can make it sooner versus later.'

'You can't have Becky! Dammit, Rainie, she's all I have left!'

Rainie pressed her lips into a thin line. She gazed at Sandy disapprovingly. Sandy returned the stare. Rainie didn't understand what she was asking. She wasn't a mother.

'We can prove that Danny didn't shoot Miss Avalon,' Rainie said abruptly. 'We can tell by the slug that was recovered and the trajectory of the shot that it was done by someone other than Danny.'

'Oh thank God.' Sandy sat back in the metal chair. For the first time in three days, she felt weight lift off her chest. 'So there was this man in black at the scene. He's the killer, and Danny's just confused and traumatized by what he saw. Can't you drop the charges now?'

'Mrs O'Grady,' Quincy said quietly, 'I think there are some things about

Danny you need to know. I suspect you're beginning to wonder about them, too, or you wouldn't have called this morning.'

Rainie supplied bluntly, 'We're not sure he didn't kill Sally and Alice.'

'But the man, the man in black—'

'Ballistics matched the slugs that killed those two girls to the .38 revolver Danny brought to school. And we have his prints on the other .38 shell casings recovered at the scene.'

'That just means he loaded the guns,' Sandy countered. 'Shep explained this to me. The prints don't prove a thing.'

'Danny's fingerprints are on over *fifty* shell casings. That means he also reloaded the guns during the shooting.'

'Shep told me that rapid loaders were used. So Danny prepped the guns and the rapid loaders. This other person did all the shooting.'

Rainie finally pushed away from the window. She shook her head impatiently. 'Listen to yourself! Danny brought a revolver and a semi-automatic weapon to school. He loaded them, and he prepared additional ammunition. Does that sound like an innocent bystander to you?'

'He's just thirteen—'

'You don't have to be old to pull a trigger.'

'He's confused—'

'He confessed multiple times!'

'He's frightened! He's angry, he doesn't understand—'

'He told Charlie Kenyon he wanted to hack Shep into twenty pieces and run him through a blender! Jesus, Sandy, we're beyond simple acting out. You didn't catch Danny smoking a cigarette or staying out after curfew. He's involved in a triple homicide. At the very least, he supplied the murder weapons. At the most, he may have massacred two eight-year-old girls. For God's sake, wake up!'

'My son is not a killer!'

'But maybe he is! Now, what the *hell* are we going to do about it?'

Rainie drew up short. She was breathing hard. Sandy was breathing hard too. She glared at her husband's most senior officer, and she thought she had never hated anyone more. How dare she talk about Danny that way. After all those dinners in Sandy's home. All those times Danny had asked to sit next to her, sweet and adoring. The cold, unfeeling—

And then she realized that Rainie's eyes were overbright. And then she realized that Rainie Conner had thinned her lips in order not to cry.

The air left Sandy's lungs in a whoosh. In Rainie's frustrated gaze she saw all the truths she'd been working diligently to deny, and suddenly she had no defenses left.

Her son was a loner. And subject to fits of rage. And he struggled with Shep and struggled to fit in at school and, dear God, he was good with guns. Learned everything straight from his father.

The world began to spin. Sandy grabbed her chair and held tight.

'Mrs O'Grady?' Quincy asked.

'Give me a moment.'

She locked her gaze on the floorboards, concentrating on making them stay in focus. Minutes passed. She didn't know how many. Time had grown slow, and she was mostly aware of an oppressive cold stealing into her body and making her tremble.

'I don't know what to do,' Sandy whispered. 'I don't . . . I don't know what to believe anymore.'

Quincy spoke up first. 'I imagine your lawyer has arranged for a forensic psychologist to examine Danny?'

'Yes. And the court has appointed a second. They haven't started yet. He said it would be months before they delivered their reports. Maybe even six months before we know anything.'

'He's your son, Mrs O'Grady. What do you think Danny did and what do you think he needs now?'

'I can't tell you.' Sandy gave a hollow bark of laughter. 'That's the truth, you know. I'm under orders from my lawyer and my husband not to talk to you – an expert on these things – because you're also part of law enforcement and you could testify at trial. And my suicidal son isn't allowed to speak with anyone either. Testimony might be used against him, better not to say anything at all. Oh my God. *What am I supposed to do?*'

Quincy didn't say anything. Neither did Rainie.

Sandy's eyes filled up. She said through her tears, 'I don't understand how this can be legal. They took away my son. They've locked him up for murder, but with the waiver hearings and pretrial motions it could be years before he goes to court. In the meantime, Danny has to stay in a place where he's not supposed to talk to anyone and he's surrounded by other convicted juvenile delinquents. Even if he's found innocent one year or two years later, how can he possibly be better off? I'm worried that the county is ruining an innocent boy. And I'm terrified that they've imprisoned a guilty one. Oh my God, Rainie, what if he did it? What will we do then?'

Quincy had squatted down in front of her. He had such compelling eyes. Deep, and heavily crinkled at the corners, as if he'd seen a thing or two. Sandy hadn't expected to like the man. Shep had positioned him as an enemy in their lives, to be avoided at all costs. But Sandy discovered that she was comforted by his presence. Supervisory Special Agent Quincy seemed sure of himself and the situation, whereas she felt as if the entire world were made of quicksand and she was sinking down, down, down.

He took her hand and placed it between his own. His palms were warm and rough. 'It's not hopeless,' he said.

'How? Our lawyer already said that if Danny is found guilty in adult court, they'll lock him up and throw away the key. No one cares that he's only thirteen.'

'But the fact that he's thirteen does put him below Oregon's automatic waiver to adult court. He is going to get a hearing designed to look at his *specific* case, and thank goodness, because Danny's case has some elements worth considering.'

Sandy gazed at him. Quincy ticked off the points with his fingers.

'One, we have evidence that somebody else was involved. If we can identify that person, we may be able to prove that Danny was manipulated, perhaps even threatened, into acting.'

Sandy nodded faintly.

'Two, we have to look at Danny himself. The fact that he's now under suicide watch may be a positive sign. It could indicate that Danny feels remorse for his actions, that he's a troubled boy but not a budding psychopath.'

'Or it could mean he's traumatized,' Sandy said after a moment, her voice gaining strength. 'There is someone else involved. You all agree on that. So maybe Danny was just doing as he was told by bringing the guns. Maybe he didn't understand what was really going to happen, and then by the time it was all over and done with, there was nothing he could do anymore.'

'But confess,' Rainie said dryly.

'That's the good news, Mrs O'Grady,' Quincy said levelly. 'Now you have to face the other facts.'

Sandy hesitated. She bit her lower lip. She knew where he was going to go, and she wished he wouldn't. Deep in her heart, she'd already gone there. Danny was troubled, and it was her fault as his mother for not doing something about that sooner. That's what everyone said when these shootings happened. Where were the parents?

I'm sorry. I was at work.

'Danny is subject to mood swings, isn't he?' Quincy said matter-of-factly. 'He goes for long periods of time without reacting, then explodes with rage.'

'You mean the incident with the school lockers.'

'He's alone a lot.'

'There are not a lot of boys on our block the same age.'

'He doesn't have many friends at school.'

'He's really into computers.'

'Mrs O'Grady, Danny has problems coping. His anger is over-controlled, which I think you realize. He also doesn't have a good support network, and given the issues with your marriage, he's under a lot of stress. Then we get to the issues between him and his father. Danny's mad at Shep but also intimidated by him. This sets the stage for displaced rage, where Danny takes all that emotion and turns it on someone else, someone who doesn't scare him.'

'You mean like two little girls?' Sandy whispered.

'Or a cat or dog.'

'Danny has never hurt animals,' Sandy said immediately. 'Becky would never stand for such a thing, and he's very protective of his sister.'

'It's good that Danny's symptoms aren't that extreme. But he still exhibits some of the warning signs we see in kids prone to do these types of shooting. For his sake, we need to deal with that.'

Sandy hesitated. 'How?'

'Let's start with Danny's overcontrolled rage. He needs to learn to vent his anger steadily and constructively instead of letting it build to dangerous heights. Most experts would recommend daily physical exercise as a starting point.'

'He's not athletic.'

'What about a family walk, Mrs O'Grady? Or some teens like martial arts.'

'I . . . I could look into that.'

The agent nodded encouragingly. He continued, 'Also for a child like Danny, violent books, video games, and movies are not appropriate. They only fuel angry thoughts.'

'Danny's never really been into violent movies. But in all honesty, I don't know what he does on the Web.'

'If you have a troubled son, you need to know what he's reading or surfing on the Internet, Mrs O'Grady. It can make a difference.'

Sandy hung her head.

'Danny's issue with his father is more involved,' Quincy said quietly. 'He and Shep need family counseling, or Danny needs private counseling, or both. You also might want to find additional family relationships for Danny with a grandparent or aunt or uncle. That way if things are strained at home, the child still has other sources of comfort and support.'

'I never thought of that,' Sandy said honestly. 'Our family's not that big. Shep's parents passed away years ago. My own . . . God knows they love my kids, but they aren't the warmest people in the world. It's not their way.' She paused. 'Do you think . . . Do you think Danny's troubles are caused by the fact that I went back to work?'

Quincy smiled at her kindly. 'No, Mrs O'Grady. Being a working mom doesn't mean you're a horrible mom. Stay-at-home parents have troubled children too.'

Sandy nodded. She would never admit it out loud, but she was relieved. She hesitated, then asked, 'My son was already troubled. Now at the very least he's witnessed three violent murders. What will that do?'

'He needs to get it out. Keeping the experience bottled up will only make it worse.' Quincy's gaze drifted toward Rainie.

'And if . . . if he did do something bad?'

Quincy was silent for a moment. 'He's going to need a lot of help,' he said at last. 'Chances are that he's experiencing a great deal of guilt and self-loathing. Someone needs to help him come to terms with that. Otherwise, there is the danger that he will simply shut down that part of himself. He will start actively considering himself to be a remorseless killer. And he will become one.'

A knock sounded on the door. Luke Hayes stuck his head in. His gaze went straight to Sandy.

'It's time,' he said.

'Already?'

Sandy glanced at her watch. It took her a moment to read the dial, for her hand was still shaking violently. Nine A.M. The joint funeral for Alice and Sally wasn't due to start until one. But the whole town was probably turning out, and people wanted to get good seats.

She had no choice but to go home. By the mayor's orders, she and her family would be spending the day under virtual house arrest. He didn't want them to upset the town, and that hurt Sandy almost more than the threatening phone calls, messages, and casseroles combined.

She slowly rose and gathered up her purse. She had hoped for easy answers this morning. Of course, there were very few such things anymore. Just more questions. And more doubts to torment her through all the long days to come.

She loved Danny so desperately. Was it right to actively wonder if her son was a murderer and still love him? Was it right to mourn for Alice Bensen and Sally Walker but still want the best for her child?

Suddenly, she felt so exhausted, she wasn't sure how she was going to make it down the stairs.

She turned to Rainie one last time. 'Do you know who this other person is yet? Do you have any leads on who did this to us?'

Rainie seemed to hesitate. 'Danny ever mention anyone named No Lava to you?'

Sandy regarded her curiously. 'Of course he did. *No Lava@aol.com*. That was his teacher's account. It's Avalon, spelled backward.'

23

Rainie and Quincy climbed into Luke's patrol car at a little past ten. Since Luke and Chuckie were sitting in the front seat, they took the back. Chuckie immediately looked self-conscious about having a commanding officer and federal agent behind him. He kept glancing nervously over his shoulder, as if he thought Quincy might goose him at any moment. After the second time, Quincy placed his face against the patrol car's mesh divider. When Chuckie turned again, he discovered Quincy's nose up close and personal. The rookie literally squealed.

Luke sighed heavily. Rainie shook her head. Quincy sat back, contented.

'You're riling my partner,' Luke said at last. He was slouched low behind the steering wheel, studying Sandy and Shep's quaint neighborhood with a deceptively lazy gaze. His hat was on the seat beside him; the brim limited his line of sight. The top of his head came to just above the dashboard; the lower vantage point expanded his field of view. Mostly, he watched the residential street for signs of out-of-place traffic, but from time to time he also perused the rooflines of the surrounding houses with his narrow gaze. Luke was an ace sniper.

'Any activity?' Rainie asked.

'Quiet as a church mouse.'

'How are you holding up?' Rainie asked Chuckie. He had his baton on his lap and was stroking the handle as if it were a favorite pet.

'All right,' Chuckie muttered.

He studied his lap, refusing to meet her gaze. His broad face was haggard, his hair uncharacteristically mussed. Rainie hadn't given the green rookie any thought during the last three days. Now she regarded him intently.

'Cunningham,' she ordered more sharply.

Chuckie's gaze reluctantly rose to meet hers. She held it for a minute. Chuckie was messed up. He had dark circles under his eyes and a nervous twitch in his hand. Apparently, seeing real action was different from boasting about it, and it was wrong of her not to have thought about him before now.

'You did well on Tuesday,' she said curtly.

727

'I broke a freaking door,' Cunningham muttered. 'Left footprints every-where. The state technicians yelled at me. That man Sanders said I was a disaster.'

'Sanders is full of shit. You acted with heart, Chuckie. The rest you'll learn with time.'

Chuckie's gaze fell to his kneecaps. He still looked troubled. When he had volunteered for this job, he had probably envisioned saving lives and protecting his community. He had not expected the debilitating frustration of arriving too late or the hard truth that today his job was merely processing the damage. Rainie understood. She knew one of the reasons George Walker hated her was that she hadn't paid him the respect of personally visiting his family. She should've done that the very first day, except that she couldn't bring herself to go, sit on a worn sofa, and make small talk while a father sat hollow-eyed and a mother wept. She just couldn't do it.

Rainie turned back to Luke. He was still studying Shep's house. It was a tidy, three-bedroom ranch with an attached two-car garage. Soft gray paint. Crisp white trim. One garage door was a brighter white than the other, obviously the one vandalized on Wednesday. Rainie wondered if Shep and Sandy could look at the bright white paint without remembering what was written underneath.

'We need to talk,' she said to Luke.

He nodded. He looked tired from his long trip yesterday, his cheeks not as freshly shaven as usual and his uniform rumpled. But his eyes were sharp and his hands steady. You could always count on Luke.

'How'd it go in Portland?' Rainie asked.

He frowned. 'Thought we were debriefing after the funeral.'

'Something came up. You can watch and talk.'

'Apparently.' He slapped Chuckie's leg with his hand. 'Go get us some coffee, Cunningham.'

'Again?'

'Three cups. The good stuff this time. We gotta impress the fed.' Luke shot Quincy a look in the rearview mirror.

'I take mine black,' Quincy offered.

Chuckie grumbled, but he knew when he wasn't wanted. He got out of the patrol car and started walking to the grocery store around the corner.

'Chuckie needs some personal time,' Luke said the minute the rookie disappeared from view.

'I noticed.'

'He's a good kid, Rainie. Just saw too much.'

'What do you suggest?'

Luke shrugged. 'Kid that age? We should take him out shooting a few times. Then take him drinking after that. He'll work through it.'

'Stress, guns, and alcohol,' Quincy said dryly. 'Makes me wonder why the Veterans' Administration hasn't thought of it.'

Luke grinned at him. 'You're thinking quality time on the shrink's couch, huh? Yeah, uh-huh. Chuckie boy will open up to some hundred-dollar-an-hour suit the day pigs fly. Sorry, feebie, but sometimes the locals know best.'

'All right, all right.' Rainie held up a hand. 'I want to know about your meeting with the Avalons in Portland yesterday. Tell us everything.'

Luke's face immediately fell. He released his breath as a sigh, his gaze returning to Shep's house and looking troubled. 'Jesus, Rainie, why don't you start with the easy questions?'

'Do you like Mr Avalon as a suspect?'

'I spent three hours in the man's company, and hell if I know. First off, Mrs Avalon isn't Melissa's mother. Guess she died in childbirth. So I met with Daniel Avalon and Melissa's stepmother, Angelina.'

'*Daniel* Avalon?' Rainie asked sharply.

'Yep,' Luke said gloomily. 'Weird, Rainie. Real weird. Mr Avalon comes from old money. Invested heavily in real estate in central Oregon and made out like a bandit in the recent boom. He and Mrs Avalon live in an old Victorian in Lake Oswego. Nice house, I guess. It was crammed full of so much junk, I was afraid I'd break something if I sneezed. They served me tea. In real china. With Mrs Avalon all fussed up in some buttoned-up, lace-collar, cameo-brooch outfit that I think she bought at Jane Austen's garage sale. Mr Avalon favors tweed and doesn't permit his wife to speak unless spoken to. Need I say more?'

'Stuffy and pretentious wasn't a crime last I checked.'

'May I?' Quincy intervened.

'By all means,' Rainie assured him. She was sitting as far away from him as she could in the backseat. They were both pretending not to notice.

'Did Mr Avalon wait many years before remarrying? Say twelve to fifteen years?'

'Thirteen,' Luke said. He looked at Quincy curiously.

'Did he speak of his daughter glowingly, but always as a child? "When Melissa was eight years old she was the best dancer . . . Oh, little Melissa always had the sweetest smile. She used to charm everyone in grade school." Little acknowledgment of her life now?'

'Yeah, as a matter of fact, he had pictures of her all over the place, but they were mostly little-girl stuff. First ballet class, ten-year-old piano recital, that sort of thing.'

'No photos of her mom?'

'Not that I saw.'

'Her room still a little girl's room? Lots of pink ruffles and teddy bears?'

'And clowns.' Luke shuddered.

Quincy nodded. 'I'm guessing Mr Avalon had inappropriate relations with his daughter.'

'Incest?' Rainie looked at Quincy incredulously. 'Jesus, SupSpAg, how do you sleep with that mind?'

'I can't be sure,' Quincy said modestly, 'but it has all the classic signs. Domineering father alone with his young daughter for the first thirteen years of her life. Seems very doting on the outside. I'm sure if you conducted further interviews you'd find plenty of neighbors and teachers telling you how "close" Mr Avalon and his daughter were. How "involved" he was in her life. But then she hits puberty and the jig is up. To continue risks pregnancy, plus she's starting to get a woman's body, and many of these men aren't interested in that. So Mr Avalon goes ahead and takes a wife, some poor, passive woman to serve as window dressing and help him appear suitable to the outside world. Now he clings to the fantasy of what he once had. And protects it jealously.'

'Does Mr Avalon have access to a computer?' Rainie asked Luke.

'In his office.'

She turned to Quincy. 'If Mr Avalon was involved with his daughter, would he have problems with her relationship with VanderZanden?'

'He'll have problems with any of her relationships. In his mind, she's his.'

'That's it then. He found out, got angry—'

'And got an alibi,' Luke interrupted flatly.

They looked at him sharply. He was nearly apologetic. 'I tried, Rainie. I stayed in town till eleven last night trying to break this guy's story. I've probably pissed off every blue blood in the city and it still holds. Mr Avalon was in a business meeting all day Tuesday. His secretary swears it, and two high-powered muckety-mucks agree. They were working on some resort deal from noon until nearly seven o'clock at night.'

Rainie chewed on the inside of her lip. 'Have you had time to run background checks on the supporting witnesses?'

'You mean between midnight and six A.M.?'

'Could be about money,' Rainie theorized. 'Sounds like Mr Avalon has a lot. If they do regular business with him . . . Maybe they'd be willing to vouch for his time in return for a few favors.'

'Possible. Don't know how we can prove it, though. There is one other thing. I asked Mr Avalon if he'd ever been to Bakersville. He said absolutely not. But I ran a background check before interviewing him, and according to state tax records he owns a cabin in Cabot County, just thirty minutes away. When I pushed him on it, he said it was merely a hunting cabin. He never used it himself but kept it for business associates. His wife nodded, like that means a damn thing. I don't know. Something's wrong there, Rainie, seriously wrong, but I don't know what to make of it yet.'

Luke's gaze returned to the street, where a teenage boy on a bicycle was coming into view. In sagging jeans and a loose jersey shirt, the kid seemed pretty nondescript. But he wore a green canvas backpack and he was staring at the O'Grady home intently.

'Here's my question,' Luke muttered, tapping a finger on the steering wheel as he followed the kid with his gaze. 'Why now? Melissa Avalon was twenty-eight years old. If Quincy's right and Daddy was going to melt down, wouldn't it have happened years ago?'

'Not necessarily,' Quincy answered. He had noticed the cyclist as well. Then Chuckie came into view, carrying a cardboard box with four cups of coffee. 'Was this Melissa's first time away from home?'

'Yep,' Luke said.

'That would do it.'

'I wonder if we're making this too complicated,' Rainie murmured out loud, shifting in the backseat for a better view. 'Mr Avalon's got motive. Mr Avalon's got money. His daughter just happens to die from a single gunshot wound to the head—'

'Assassination,' Quincy filled in.

'What if it wasn't supposed to be a school shooting? What if Danny was being enlisted to create a diversion, something that looked like a shooting to disguise Melissa Avalon's death. Except—'

'Except he accidentally killed two little girls,' Luke supplied dryly. He opened his mouth to argue more, then suddenly said, 'Shit.'

The boy was in front of Shep's house. His bicycle had slowed. His body shifted. The backpack slid down . . .

Luke fumbled for the door handle. He shoved it open with his shoulder just as Rainie tried to bolt, realizing too late that the doors had shut and she and Quincy were trapped in the back of the police cruiser. Down the street, Chuckie saw the commotion and dropped his coffee. Rainie watched him reach immediately for his gun.

'No,' she yelled uselessly, and pounded the unbreakable window. 'Dammit, Chuckie, *no!*'

The boy saw Luke bearing down on him. He turned slightly and spotted Chuckie fumbling with his holster. His expression promptly shifted from purposeful to petrified.

Luke ordered, 'Stop!'

And the boy shoved his backpack at Luke with all his might and took off, while the officer staggered back in surprise. Down the street, Chuckie was still juggling his handgun. Rainie couldn't be sure from this distance, but it looked like the rookie had tears on his cheeks.

'Damn, damn, damn,' Luke shouted. He regained his footing and let the backpack fall to the ground, but the kid ran from the street to dart between the multitude of houses. A second later he was out of sight. With another sigh of disgust, Luke stalked back to the patrol car and settled for bailing Quincy and Rainie out of the backseat. They gathered around the backpack on the sidewalk just as Cunningham came running up, panting heavily.

'What'd he do?' Cunningham demanded breathlessly. He rubbed his cheeks. 'What's in the bag? What happened? Did he try anything?'

'One thing at a time, Cunningham,' Rainie growled. She looked at Luke. He shrugged, hunkered down, and placed his ear over the green canvas bag.

'I don't hear ticking.' He hefted up the backpack and frowned. 'No clinking. Hell, it feels like books.'

He resolutely unzipped the main pouch. Out poured two weighty volumes with fine leather binding and rich gilded edges – the Bible, Old and New Testaments. The note attached to the front said: *To the O'Gradys. Jesus forgives.*

'Oh my God,' Chuckie said desperately. 'I almost *shot* that boy.'

Quincy said softly, 'I think it's time we took a deep breath.'

Luke picked up the two volumes. He carried them gently to the front porch and placed them in front of the door. Then, without a word, he went back to the wheel of his patrol car, slouched down to the level of the dashboard, fingered his hat on the seat beside him, and resumed keeping guard.

24

Becky O'Grady placed her finger carefully over Big Bear's black-stitched mouth. He regarded her steadily with his big golden eyes.

'Shh,' she told him. 'We have to be very quiet.'

Big Bear helped her out. Becky knew he didn't like the closet. He'd always been afraid of the dark. But now he was a very brave brown bear. He didn't make a single noise as she gently twisted the knob on the closet door and eased it open.

There was a break in the argument in the family room. Becky froze instantly. Her mommy and daddy had been fighting for a long time now. Something about some man her mommy had talked to this morning. She shouldn't have done that, Becky's daddy said. Why didn't she trust him to take care of things?

Becky's mommy wasn't happy. She told Becky's dad he was in denial. Becky didn't know what that meant, but she was sad it made her mommy so angry, because Becky was in denial too. The doctors had said so.

Maybe it was a bad disease. That would explain why Becky's best friend, Jenny, no longer came over to play. Like the time Becky had the chicken pox. No one could play with her then either. And her skin had itched so bad. She'd wanted to scratch and scratch, but her mommy made her sit in a bathtub filled with hot water and oatmeal. Becky hated the chicken pox. Of course, Grammy Surmon had made her her very own pie. Banana cream, and Danny hadn't been allowed to eat any of it unless Becky said it was okay. She'd kinda liked that.

Now the thought of Danny made Becky's chest hurt. She held Big Bear closer.

The fighting started again. Daddy was yelling that Mommy didn't care enough about Danny. Mommy was yelling that it was all Daddy's fault. 'How did Danny get the guns, Shep? Tell me how Danny got the guns.'

Becky slipped inside the dark hallway closet. She shut the door. The light and the voices disappeared. She hunkered down on the old blanket her mommy had put in there for her and held Big Bear close.

Sometimes, when she was alone in the dark like this, just her and Big Bear, she could almost breathe again. The funny weight would leave her

733

chest and she would feel not so bad anymore. She was safe. She was okay. Here in the dark, nobody could hurt her.

She could close her eyes and the bad things would go away. She could float, peaceful, thinking of kittens and clouds and all the things she liked best.

Today she tried the trick. She screwed her eyes shut. She pressed her cheek against the top of Big Bear's woolly head. But nothing happened. No floating. She was just a little girl sitting on a hard floor in a closet that smelled like old shoes.

She kept seeing Sally and Alice. She saw them on the floor. Then she saw pretty Miss Avalon.

And then she raised her eyes . . .

Becky whimpered in the closet. She turned her face into Big Bear's neck.

'Be brave,' she told him. 'Be brave. Be brave. Don't make a sound.'

Big Bear was a very brave brown bear. He didn't make any noise as she rocked with him on the floor while her parents fought in the living room. He didn't make any noise as she whimpered and warred with evil monsters. And he didn't make any sound as she cried and still saw too many things, like what had happened to pretty Miss Avalon.

Becky's mouth hurt from the Jell-O salad. Her shoulders sagged from too many nights without enough sleep. She didn't give up, though. She was tough. Her daddy liked to say that she was just like him, a real *trouper*.

Becky didn't know what a trouper was. But she wanted to be like Daddy, big and strong and brave. She needed to be like Daddy.

She had to be tough. She had to keep Danny safe.

The funeral service for Sally Walker and Alice Bensen was originally scheduled for one P.M. at the tiny white Episcopal church on Fourth Street. By noon, however, when the pews, the foyer, the lawn, and the parking lot were filled to standing room only with somberly dressed neighbors, Reverend Albright moved everything graveside. Groundsmen hastily erected canvas tents, and a fierce ocean breeze whipped the blue awnings frantically above everyone's heads.

No one complained. Cars continued to arrive. Weathered dairymen, clad in their Sunday best, escorted their wives slowly up the hill, heads bowed against the wind. Bakersville High's basketball team, which heralded Alice Bensen's brother as star forward and Sally Walker's uncle as coach, gathered in full uniform to serve as honor guard. The men of the Elks Lodge, where George Walker belonged, also wore dress colors, standing formally to one side and waiting for the service to end, when they would be in charge of transporting the mountain of flowers back to the families' homes.

The ladies of the Episcopal church gave out programs. Neighbors supplied a steady stream of condolence cards and homemade pies for the luncheon to follow.

Rainie took it in from a distance. Even from two hundred feet away, the sight of two freshly dug graves, side by side on an emerald green hillside and framed by mountains of red and white flowers, haunted her. She noticed that Quincy kept to the perimeter as well. She was surprised he'd even come. Given recent events with his own daughter, she couldn't imagine that the next hour wouldn't grab his heart and squeeze it dry.

Then again, the federal agent seemed to thrive on pushing himself to bear the unbearable.

Sanders was also present. He had taken up a post on the east side of the hill, where a side street offered cemetery access. Standing in a dark blue suit with his hands clasped in front of him, he blended with the crowd of gathered mourners.

By agreement, Rainie was the only officer in uniform. Sanders and the county men all roamed the crowd wearing traditional mourning clothes. That way they could monitor the services without intruding unnecessarily on the families.

No one expected any trouble during the ceremony. Rainie and the mayor, however, were concerned about the hours afterward, when people would leave the service with emotions running high, find a bar for a few drinks with their buddies, and work themselves into a state of pure testosterone. Alcohol and guns were never a great mix, and God knew Bakersville had plenty of both.

The county men had orders to work the crowd, listen sharp. Particularly vocal attendants would be monitored later in the evening. The mayor didn't want to take any chances, not after the recent run on rifles at the sporting-goods store.

At Quincy's suggestion, the men were also looking for 'someone out of place.' Maybe a middle-age white male who seemed strangely removed from the gathering of family and friends. Maybe a man who appeared to enjoy funerals too much. Any man stupid enough to look at twin coffins and smile.

Rainie didn't think they'd get that lucky, but Quincy insisted. If it was a stranger-against-stranger crime, there was a good chance the man would attend.

Rainie found herself thinking of the dream she'd had last night. Jerking awake. Tall, imposing shadow on her back deck . . . She was unnerved these days.

A hush suddenly descended over the crowd. Rainie jerked her attention back to the rolling green cemetery in time to realize that a train of cars had just arrived. The families, with their daughters, were here.

George Walker got out first. A heavyset man, his broad face flushed and his eyes bloodshot, he came around to open the door for his wife. Jean

Walker was as petite as her husband was large, and she swayed against his thick arm as he led her to the grass. They waited together for the Bensens, who took much longer to climb out of their vehicle. Rainie had never met Alice's parents, Joseph and Virginia. She knew only of their son, Frederick, whom Frank and Doug avidly declared to be the best basketball player ever to pound the boards at Bakersville High. Most of the town followed his career and college aspirations.

Now Rainie was immediately struck by the Bensens' strong Nordic looks. They held their heads high as they approached the Walkers. They kept their gaze steady as they watched the honor guard step forward. They remained unflinching as their son bent his lanky legs to carry his eight-year-old sister to her final resting place.

Ten minutes later both coffins were delivered to the front of the tent and the minister formally began the service.

Rainie glanced over at Quincy. He wasn't watching anymore. His gaze was far off, where distant trees framed the blue horizon. She didn't know what he was thinking, but tears streamed down his cheeks.

The minister concluded his introduction. A young man Rainie didn't recognize rose and helped an older woman work her way to the microphone. The wind blew hard, flattening the woman's black silk dress against her rounded frame, but she fought forward. At the front, she opened a book and cleared her throat. She introduced herself as Alice Bensen's aunt. Then she read a passage in Alice and Sally's memory. It was a selection on the meaning of friendship, from Winnie the Pooh.

That was it for Rainie. She also turned away until VanderZanden rose to give the eulogy.

He appeared somber as he stood in front of nearly eight hundred people. He had written out his speech, and the piece of paper trembled in his hands. Rainie discovered, however, that she couldn't muster any sympathy for the man. She was too busy staring at his wife, who had been patting his hand supportively for the last forty-five minutes. Abigail VanderZanden was a little plump from the years and a little dowdy in a square-shaped, navy blue JC Penney dress, but she had a generous smile and sparkling blue eyes. She also appeared genuinely proud of her husband, and that made Rainie like VanderZanden even less.

There were no winners today, Rainie thought, and that realization wore her down a little bit more. She had had hopes of big discoveries. Fantasies of standing in front of her community and telling them exactly what had happened on Tuesday afternoon and why. No more driving by the school in pained bewilderment. No more staring at your children over breakfast cereal, wondering what might happen to them that day. No more horrible questions, like why were young boys suddenly prone to murdering their classmates.

Instead Rainie stood on an emerald hillside in Bakersville's only cemetery, feeling the blustery wind against her face and listening to the haunting echo of 'Amazing Grace' sung by fourteen adults while Frederick Bensen broke down sobbing against his mother, who cradled him in her arms.

Long after the final note died away, people remained standing. Reverend Albright came back up. He cleared his throat and said that concluded the services. People still didn't move.

Danny should be here, Rainie realized. Danny and Shep and Sandy and Becky, and, hell, Charlie Kenyon and the mysterious second shooter, and any boy who'd ever picked up a gun and thought about pulling the trigger. This was death. This was loss. This was the moment when everything became real. And why weren't there more children at this funeral? Most of the kids in Bakersville had the power to take a life. Why didn't their gun-owning parents think to show them what that meant?

The stillness finally broke. The first few people reluctantly trickled out of the tent. Then, like a dam breaking, the others followed suit.

Rainie looked around, trying to pick out the state men. She still saw nothing suspicious and nothing out of place. She sidled up to Quincy, whose cheeks were dry and face carefully composed.

'Ready?' he said.

She figured they both knew she wasn't. 'Mann first. Then VanderZanden.'

'Deal.'

Rainie hesitated one last moment. Her gaze was still scanning the crowd. It finally occurred to her that she was checking out the profiles of the various men. She was studying their silhouettes. Middle of the night. The figure in black on her back deck . . .

She shook her head and forced the image away. As she and Quincy moved down the hillside, however, her gaze continued to work the crowd.

They found Richard Mann off to one side of the tent, huddled together with four other faculty members, all female. Without being asked, he stepped discreetly away from his companions, joining Quincy and Rainie behind a cluster of pine trees.

'Nice to see you again, Mr Mann,' Rainie said politely. Her bad-cop role was probably a little much for a funeral.

'Did you talk to Charlie Kenyon?' Mann asked curiously. 'Was Charlie involved?'

'We talked to him.' Rainie regarded him coolly. The more she tried to study the counselor, the less she knew what to think. 'I'm afraid that's a dead end, though, Mr Mann. Charlie doesn't appear to be involved.'

'Really? I was so sure . . .' Mann's face fell. He sighed heavily, then rubbed his face. That quickly, he looked haggard, and Rainie was shocked to realize that he was much more upset than she'd realized. 'I'm having real issues with this,' he said abruptly.

'What kind of issues, Mr Mann?' Quincy inquired.

'I've been turning things over and over in my mind, and I just can't see Danny instigating a murder. And not just because I'm his counselor and I feel guilty. It's more. . . . Yes, Danny had rage issues.' The counselor made a groping motion with his hands, as if searching for better words. 'But physical action just isn't his style. Danny's a computer geek, not a school-yard bully. If he was angry with the school or even authority figures in general, I could see him doing something sophisticated. Maybe hacking into the school's databases and giving everyone straight As. Or working his way into the DMV computers and revoking Principal VanderZanden's license. Something clever. I just . . . I just can't see him resorting to murder.'

'Danny was raised with guns,' Rainie said. 'He's as comfortable with them as he is with computers.'

'I guess.' Mann, however, didn't look convinced. 'What about Mr Avalon?'

'He claimed the body,' Rainie said. 'It appears he's planning services for his daughter.'

'Oh.' Mann appeared surprised again. 'I guess I heard wrong. Isn't Melissa an only child? How horrible for her parents.'

Rainie nodded, but her attention was already beginning to drift. Richard Mann knew as little as she'd suspected in the beginning. No doubt he'd thought to make up for his guilt – or, hell, make up for his youth – by appearing to be some kind of expert. But in the end he was simply one more overwhelmed public servant caught with his pants down. Basically, he was like her.

'We have reason to believe someone else was involved in the shootings,' Quincy said abruptly.

'Really?' Mann's brows shot up, just as Rainie gave Quincy the evil eye. She didn't see the need for him to be giving up this kind of information.

'So I was right! Danny wouldn't do such a thing. But who, then? Another student? I don't remember Danny talking about anyone in particular. He didn't have many friends in school. You know, though, there's still this Volcano person from on-line. Internet relationships can be very powerful.'

'We think the contact might have been more than over the Internet, Mr Mann. We think Danny might have also met No Lava in person. Would you know anything about that?'

Rainie nearly stepped on Quincy's foot to shut him up. What the hell was he doing? But Quincy's gaze was still boring into Richard Mann's. He looked like a hound dog on a scent.

'Oh no,' the school counselor said quickly, his gaze dropping. 'I never heard mention of that.'

'Really? That's odd,' Quincy mused out loud, 'Here you are seeing this child twice a week. You know he's getting e-mails from someone, but he never mentions seeing him in person? And you never pried?'

Richard Mann began to squirm.

'Do you own a gun?' Rainie piped up, finally catching on. 'How tall are you, Richard? Five-ten, five-eleven? Yep, that would fit.'

'That would fit? What?'

Rainie turned casually to Quincy. 'Didn't he say he's from LA? Chances are, he knows more about guns than you and I put together.'

'I don't know *anything* about guns! Frankly, all LA taught me was to be wary of loud noises. Why are you two looking at me like that? What is this about?'

'Someone else shot Miss Avalon,' Rainie said flatly. 'We have hard evidence she was killed by someone who's at least five-foot-six. Where were you again Tuesday afternoon? And what was the exact nature of your relationship with Melissa?'

'You think I—'

'I thought you'd be happy. You said it broke your heart to think of one of your students committing murder. Well, now you can rest easy.' Rainie's voice went hard. 'Tuesday afternoon. Where were you, Richard?'

'In my office, like I said. This is nuts! Every time I try to help—'

'Did Danny ever mention meeting someone in person?' Quincy continued relentlessly. 'A new friend. Someone from out of town.'

'I don't remember—'

'No Lava, Mr Mann. You knew Danny was getting e-mails. And you suspected more, didn't you? Danny said something that made you wonder, but you never told anyone. You never told anyone and now you're afraid. You messed up. You were his counselor and you failed him.'

Richard Mann had started panting. Beads of sweat covered his upper lip. 'I . . . I . . .'

Quincy leaned forward. He was firmly in control, and now he said with a trace of steel, 'You're standing one hundred feet from the graves of two murdered children, Mr Mann. You helped bury them today. You said prayers for them today. Help us solve their murders. Finally tell us the truth.'

The school counselor shuddered. His gaze darted all around them, looking for escape, but there was none. There was just him and two law-enforcement officers and the secret truth Quincy had finally ferreted out from the dark corners of Mann's conscience. Richard Mann looked up. He was clearly ashamed.

'He didn't say enough for me to do anything with it,' he murmured. 'I swear, if I'd known what was going to happen—'

'Spit it out,' Rainie ordered.

'I asked Danny once what he really knew about No Lava. I told him my concerns about him befriending someone who was only an e-mail address.

What if he was really a six-year-old boy or a dirty old man – though I didn't put it quite that bluntly.'

'What did he say, Richard?'

'He said she wasn't anything like that. And when I tried to explain to him that was exactly my point, she might not even be a she but a he, Danny got this funny look on his face. He blew me off. At the time I thought it was attitude. But after Tuesday I started to wonder. What if it wasn't attitude? What if he was simply positive that he knew the truth – for example, if he'd met No Lava in person, so he'd seen for himself that she was female?'

'Why the *hell* didn't you tell us this earlier?'

'It was just a theory!' Mann protested.

'You told us all your other theories.'

'No Lava isn't a theory – I saw the e-mails! And I was honestly saying what I'd heard about Melissa and her father. How was I to know it was a rumor?'

Rainie blew out an exasperated puff of air. Leave it to an amateur head shrink to fuck up a critical investigation. She gave him a remorseless stare. He bowed his head.

'Anything else you'd like to tell us, Richard?'

'No,' he said meekly. 'That would be all.'

'Do you know when Danny might have met this person? Or when they started talking?'

He shook his head emphatically, still not daring to make eye contact.

'Are you on-line, Richard? Have you ever received an e-mail from Miss Avalon?'

'I just bought my first personal computer. I'm pretty good with some of the software, but I'm not that comfortable on the Web yet. In fact, I was thinking that maybe one afternoon I'd have Danny show me the ropes. It could be a way of bonding.'

'You never received an e-mail from Miss Avalon?' Rainie repeated.

'No. Why would I?'

'That's all. We're done with you.' Rainie gave a little shoo-shoo motion with her hands. Richard Mann nodded gratefully, hesitated one more moment as if he thought she might change her mind, then made a beeline back to his companions. No doubt he'd tell them he'd just been an invaluable source of help to the police investigation into this hideous crime. No doubt they'd smooth pretty boy's ruffled feathers and puff him back up to the image of the man he wanted to be. Personally, Rainie was fed up with his incompetence.

She turned back to Quincy. She rubbed her temples, where she was starting to get one hell of a headache. 'Female, huh? Female influence, using Melissa Avalon's own e-mail address to contact Danny. We're not thinking Miss Avalon helped plan her own death with an unmarked bullet, are we?'

'No. We're thinking e-mail addresses are a very easy thing to hijack, and what better way to impress a budding young hacker like Danny.'

'Oh good. I'd hoped that's what we were thinking. Now, just out of curiosity, who do we think did it?'

'We don't have a clue.'

'But he might be a she? I don't know. The kids reported a mysterious *man* in black, not a woman, and even seven-year-olds ought to know the difference.'

'Unless she dressed up as a he.' Quincy had a strange smile on his face. 'Cross-dressing psychopaths aren't as uncommon as you would think.'

'Great, more ambiguity. That's just what this case needs. VanderZanden next? Maybe Mrs VanderZanden?'

'By all means. Lead the way.'

Rainie had no sooner turned back toward the crowd than she ran into a man. She had just started to apologize when she looked up and realized who he was. George Walker stood before her. His beefy face was flushed red. His cheeks were covered in moisture. He raised his hand to point at Rainie, and she was struck by how hard his massive body was trembling.

Rainie's throat went dry. She tried to swallow, muster a coherent greeting. She was pinned by the ravaged look in George Walker's eyes.

'What – have you – *done* – for my – *daughter?*' he bit out.

'We're . . . We're working very hard, sir.'

'*You fucked up all the evidence!*' George Walker roared. People glanced their way at the sudden noise. His wife saw them, went ashen, and hurried over.

'I'm sorry, Mr Walker. I know this is very difficult—'

'That little bastard killed my daughter and you're not even trying to put him away. You think I don't know? You think we haven't heard? He killed our little girls and you're protecting him. He butchered our little girls and you're trying to clear *his name.*'

'George, George.' His wife had arrived. She put her tiny hand on his arm as if she could hold him back. She gave Rainie a pleading look.

'I'm sorry,' Rainie whispered.

'*Sorry! You haven't even come to our house. Our children were murdered in cold blood and you didn't even pay your respects!*'

'George, your heart. George—'

'Mr Walker,' Quincy tried.

'*How many times have you been to the O'Gradys' house?* How many times to visit that murdering little bastard? My girl, my girl. My little, little girl. He killed her and you don't care.'

'We're working . . . so hard, Mr Walker—'

'You sympathize with him, don't you, Rainie Conner? You're nothing but a murderer too!'

'George!' Mrs Walker appeared genuinely stricken.

Rainie just stood there and took it. She didn't have a good reply anymore. And she didn't have the strength to move.

'I'm going to sue your ass,' George Walker railed. 'I'm going to sue you and the school and Shep O'Grady. You harbored a murderer in your midst, and it's gone on long enough. Bakersville deserves justice! My little girl deserves justice! Sally and Alice and Miss Avalon. Sally and Alice and Miss Avalon. Sally and Alice and Miss Avalon—' His voice broke off. His shoulders started to heave. He turned back to his wife, wrapped his giant arms around her frail shoulders, and wept.

And Rainie just stood there and took it.

She was aware of everyone staring at them now. Hundreds of people devouring a scandalous scene, searching for each nuance, already thinking how they'd repeat the story to their neighbors later. And she was aware of Quincy watching her as well. His gaze was kind, understanding. Somehow it hurt her the most.

'You need to go,' he murmured.

'I can't.'

'Rainie, you aren't doing him any favors.'

Rainie nodded slowly. George Walker still sobbed in his wife's arms. Jean Walker looked directly at Rainie, trying to second Quincy's motion with her gaze. *Go, get out of here, before you make things worse.*

Rainie turned away and walked down the hill with Quincy at her side. People were still staring. For the first time in her life, she didn't return their gazes.

She kept walking, and for reasons she couldn't talk about, she was ashamed.

25

Rainie, Luke Hayes, Sanders, and Quincy assembled in the attic of city hall for the task-force meeting. Rainie had already been in the headquarters for the past thirty minutes, gathering paperwork and breaking any #2 pencil she could find. The hardwood floor was now covered with slivers of yellow debris, earning concerned looks from both Sanders and Quincy. Luke, on the other hand, barely registered the mess. He had been working with Rainie for years.

Rainie took a seat behind her sawhorse desk and briskly shuffled together her notes.

'Ready?'

The three men unfolded their metal seats and nodded.

'Let's start with updates on the suspects first, since I know we have progress there. Next we'll move on to evidence, then revisit our theories of the case. Got it?'

Everyone nodded. Rainie began:

'At our last meeting I was assigned Charlie Kenyon and Richard Mann as possible suspects. Charlie's a bust. He was out of town on Tuesday, visiting his girlfriend in Portland, which was corroborated by the girl's parents. As you'll see in my notes' – she handed out three copies of her handwritten interview with Charlie – 'he hung out with Danny O'Grady on occasion, but I'm willing to believe he didn't know anything about plans to attack the school. Mostly because we have Charlie arraigned on possession charges right now, and if he did know anything specific, he'd be dealing that information to save his hide.'

'Charlie, Charlie, Charlie,' Luke murmured.

'Exactly. So count Charlie out. That leaves us with Richard Mann. I've run a basic background report.' Rainie passed around more copies. 'Mann has no record of criminal activity and no handguns registered in his name in Oregon or California. I called the LA school where he worked as a student teacher last year, and they rave about the guy. They're sending me a copy of his personnel file, but I'm not sure it's gonna lead anywhere. Finally, the school's secretary, Marge, confirms his alibi: She saw him go into his office with a sandwich at the beginning of the period. And she was

743

there, right outside his and Principal VanderZanden's offices, until shots were fired. She also said that to the best of the rumor mill's knowledge, there wasn't anything one way or another between the school counselor and Miss Avalon.'

'Does that seem odd?' Sanders spoke up. 'They're both young, both new in town. Seems like if anything they'd be friends.'

'Sure, why not?' Rainie agreed. 'Or maybe VanderZanden entered the picture right away, and after that Avalon wasn't interested in expanding her social circle. Don't know. I'll keep asking around, I'm just not optimistic. On a scale of one to ten, ten being the son of a bitch we're going to lock up for life, I give Richard Mann a three, but it's a weasel factor three, based more on the fact that he's held out information on us than anything concrete.' Rainie shrugged. She'd tried, but at the moment her suspects looked no good. 'What about Principal VanderZanden? Sanders?'

'Still inconclusive,' Sanders reported, opening a color-coded file and also dispensing copies. Rainie noticed that his notes were typed – and he had chosen a nice font. 'VanderZanden's alibi for the shooting is also the school secretary, Marge. She said she saw VanderZanden go into his office and shut the door at the end of lunch. Minutes later, when the shots were fired, he came running out of his office and joined her in the hall.'

'Sounds like an alibi to me,' Luke said.

Sanders shook his head. 'Yes and no. When I checked out the offices' – Sanders gave Rainie a pointed glance – '*I* happened to notice that both Richard Mann's and Principal VanderZanden's offices have windows big enough for a grown man to exit. That raises the possibility of either man departing his office through the window, reentering the school through the side door, and surprising Miss Avalon in her classroom. In theory, he could've used Danny to create a large diversion by continuing the gunfire while he ran back out of the school and reentered his office through the window.

'The good news with this scenario is it would explain why some children thought they saw a man in black but none of the neighbors saw anyone flee through their yards. The bad news is that the office windows overlook the school parking lot. What are the chances of a grown man climbing in and out of that window without anyone noticing?'

'Stranger things have happened,' Luke said with a shrug, but no one jumped on that bandwagon. The chances were pretty slim.

'For the sake of argument,' Sanders continued, 'we do have motive. According to Avalon's diary, she was starting to have doubts about being involved with VanderZanden. In her last entry she talks about wanting to find a therapist. You know, to resolve her father-figure issues.'

'Had she told VanderZanden this?' Quincy asked.

'Don't know. We haven't found any correspondence between them. Plus, I can't find any close friends or confidantes to tell us more about

Avalon's state of mind. According to her coworkers, she was nice but kept to herself. Her phone bills are a bust. I can't even find records of her calling VanderZanden, so they either communicated strictly in person or she did it all by computer. Of course, the computers are wiped clean.'

'So we have one possible scenario,' Rainie summarized. 'Avalon wanted to end things with VanderZanden. He retaliated by arranging her murder, disguised as a school shooting. Which involved intimidating Danny into being his cover, wiping all lab computers clean to cover his tracks, and sneaking in and out of his office to do the actual crime.' She frowned. 'It's elaborate, but not impossible.'

'Give him a six,' Sanders said. 'He has motive and opportunity. The VanderZandens only have a .22 rifle registered in their name, but it's not impossible to get your hands on an unregistered gun. I mean, as long as you're climbing out your office window, why not stop at the street corner for a black-market semiauto?'

'Point taken,' Rainie observed dryly. She was about to turn to Luke when Quincy interrupted.

'What about Mrs VanderZanden?'

'What about her?' Sanders asked.

'Any evidence that she knew about the affair? Neighbors report any tension in the marriage?'

'Umm . . .' For once the superefficient detective was caught off guard. 'I'd have to get back to you on that.'

Rainie was impressed. So Sanders wasn't all-knowing, after all. Who would've thought?

She returned to their rundown of current suspects. 'Luke, bring Sanders up to date on Daniel and Angelina Avalon.'

Luke turned to Sanders. He didn't have notes or handouts, and his expression made it clear he thought Sanders's color-coded binders were a deep-seated cry for help. 'Angelina Avalon is Melissa's stepmom,' Luke reported off the top of his head. 'Her real mom died during childbirth. Daniel waited thirteen years to remarry, and Quincy thinks he was having "inappropriate relations" with his daughter.'

'Incest?' Sanders asked incredulously.

'Bingo,' Luke said. 'Daniel Avalon gets a weasel factor of fifteen, if you ask me. Unfortunately, he currently has an alibi.'

'What kind of alibi?'

'Important business meeting. Two clients vouching for his time. One possibility is maybe he hired someone to do it, but I don't know. Mr Avalon has a hunting cabin in the area, and for the record, the Avalons have five guns registered in their names, though none of them is a .22.' Luke recited easily: 'Smith & Wesson .357, a Glock .40, a Beretta 9 mm, and two Mossberg 12-gauge shotguns.'

'Holy shit, what are they preparing for?'

'Y2K. The guns were purchased in the fall of '99. Mrs Avalon probably feared for her china. Or maybe she's afraid of all those clowns in Melissa Avalon's room.' Luke shuddered again.

'In other words, we can't count out the Avalons yet,' Rainie concluded. 'You'll push harder on it, Luke?'

'First thing tomorrow morning I'm paying a visit to the hunting cabin, then heading back to Portland and seeing if I can't finagle some bank records.'

Rainie nodded. Luke planned on spending the rest of the evening guarding Shep's house. He didn't take his friendships lightly.

'That brings us to you, Quincy. Where are we with No Lava and Shep?'

'What?' Luke sat up tensely. He'd been absent during their last discussion, when Shep's actions had been questioned.

'It's okay,' Quincy said, raising a calming hand. 'Nothing came of it—'

'Damn right!' Luke spat out.

'According to the school staff,' Quincy continued evenly, 'no one saw Shep enter the building before the shooting. Plus, his patrol log puts him at Hank's hardware store a little after one, which Hank confirmed. At that point, it's questionable whether he had the time to drive to the school and commit murder before one-thirty.'

'You examined his patrol log?' Luke was still offended.

Quincy ignored him. 'So we can count Shep out. That brings me to the person writing e-mails to Danny from No Lava@aol.com. I did learn a few things there. One, according to Sandy O'Grady, the No Lava address was actually Melissa Avalon's account.'

'Melissa Avalon was the one writing Danny e-mails?' Sanders interrupted.

Quincy shook his head. 'I don't think so. Melissa saw Danny every day, so there wouldn't be a need for her to be sending him lots of mail. Plus, I tried checking AOL's member directory on Thursday to see if I could find a record of a No Lava and nothing came up. This afternoon I followed up with an AOL technician. According to service logs, No Lava was listed in their directory until Monday at six P.M., when the account was canceled and the caller ordered all traces of the member name removed. I'm willing to bet that our shooter made that call at the same time that she was purging the hard drives of the school's computers.'

'She?' Luke questioned.

Quincy pursed his lips. 'According to Richard Mann, Danny had implied that his pen pal was female. It's an interesting possibility. I just don't like Mann as the sole source of information. On the other hand, that might explain a few things. We've certainly looked at a lot of suspects without coming up with any strong candidates. Maybe we are looking at the wrong gender. God knows Danny gravitates more toward women – both his mother and Melissa Avalon. In many ways, he'd be more vulnerable to a manipulative female than a male.'

'Maybe Mrs VanderZanden found out what her husband was doing,' Sanders said slowly, finally understanding Quincy's earlier line of questioning.

'And maybe Angelina finally caught on to her real role in her husband's life,' Luke filled in. 'Can't be fun to figure out you're nothing but a place holder for a too-old daughter.'

They all turned and stared at Rainie.

'What? Because I got double-X chromosomes I magically know what drives women to kill?'

Luke appeared abashed. Sanders, on the other hand, nodded matter-of-factly.

Rainie rolled her eyes. She said briskly, 'Let's bring this all together. Fact one, someone else was involved in the shootings on Tuesday.'

Everyone nodded.

'This person is at least five-foot-six, proficient with computers, and also gun savvy.'

'And how.' Sanders flipped to a gray-colored tab. Gray for guns? Christ, these state boys had too much time on their hands. 'Got an update on the ballistics info. You'll like this – at least, the ballistics department is very pleased with themselves. They want to write this up as a case study. Okay, so the ME identifies one .22-caliber slug with no evidence of rifling but containing a polymer residue. Also found, one .38-caliber casing with faint traces of polymer residue. Finally, also discovered – once the crime-scene technicians were told to look for it in the debris bags – three tiny pieces of plastic, which fit together to form a single unit about the size and shape of a pen cap. Anyone, anyone? What do we have?'

'I hate riddles,' Rainie said flatly.

But Luke Hayes breathed, with near reverence, 'A sabot.'

'Nice work, Officer.'

'What the hell is a sabot doing in a school shooting?' Luke said with a frown.

'What the hell is a sabot?' Rainie asked.

Sanders looked at Luke, who did the honors. 'I've heard of them for hunting. Basically you take something like plastic and wrap it around a smaller-caliber slug so it will fit in a larger-caliber gun. Then a big gun can fire smaller bullets with greater velocity and mushrooming capacity. You know, for large-game hunting.'

'Oh, Jesus Christ.' Rainie looked at them all as if they'd gone mad. 'You mean to tell me that someone is applying techniques for large-game hunting to *school grounds?*'

'We don't think this has anything to do with hunting techniques,' Sanders supplied. 'The ME is the one who first thought of the possibility, and that's because she'd read about it once before – in a mob shooting in New Jersey. The other advantage of making a sabot, you see, is that it makes the slug hard to trace. No rifling marks, no matching with a murder weapon. Also, this answers Rainie's question about why only one shot to the forehead – hardly a sure kill with a .22. Well, the slug was fired by a bigger gun, meaning greater velocity, more force. Whoever we're looking for isn't dumb.'

Rainie turned this over in her mind, trying to see how it was done. She spared a glance at Quincy, who had a curious look on his face, as if many things were becoming magically clear. She was happy for him. Personally, between the little scene with George Walker and now this, her temples were pounding and her hand had a tremor she hoped no one would notice.

'How do you make a sabot?' she asked Sanders.

'It's involved. In this case, ballistics has determined that the .22-caliber slug recovered from Avalon's body was actually fired from a .38-caliber gun.'

'Danny's .38 revolver.'

'No. Rifling doesn't match. Give me a minute, we'll get to it. Okay, so we have someone, Quincy's UNSUB, who wants to cover his tracks. He hits upon a great idea. He'll shoot a .22-caliber slug from a .38 revolver. Given the entry wound and weight of the recovered projectile, everyone will be looking for a .22 semiauto. He'll never get tied to the crime.

'But how to make a .38 fire a .22-caliber bullet? That's where the sabot comes in. The UNSUB takes a plastic rod and turns it until it's the diameter of a .38-caliber bullet. He then cuts the rod to the same length as a .38 slug and – this isn't child's play – center-drills the piece of plastic with a .22-caliber hole. He cuts the piece of plastic lengthwise in three equal pieces, then glues the pieces back together at the base. Voila, he has made a sabot. Now he removes a .22 slug from its casing. Then he simply pushes the slug into the center of the sabot from the top, inserts the entire thing into a .38-caliber casing, and loads a .38-caliber-size bullet into his revolver. Upon being fired from the barrel of the gun, the sabot's three pieces will fall apart, leaving the .22-caliber projectile to continue on and strike the victim. And the UNSUB ejects the shell casing, then walks away with his .38 revolver, leaving no one the wiser.'

'We're talking serious thought here,' Rainie said.

'And knowledge of guns. Sabots have been around since the earliest firearms, but it's not like everyone's using them.'

'Now that we know what it is, can we trace the bullet?'

'Not the slug,' Sanders said, and got a wicked gleam in his eye. 'But you can sure as hell trace the plastic. Ballistics has already reassembled the three pieces and they form a perfect model of a .38 projectile, right down to the rifling marks.'

'Don't be an ass, Sanders. Tell us what we've got.'

The state detective's face fell. 'Yeah, well, that brings me to the bad news. So far the sabot doesn't match with anything we have. Not with the .38 revolver recovered from Danny or with any other revolvers or slugs whose rifling marks we have on file.'

'Drugfire,' Quincy said.

'Noooo,' Sanders groaned. 'Not again!'

'Absolutely,' Rainie overruled him. 'Face it, Sanders, you can only check statewide. Through the drugfire databases, Quincy can cover the whole country for a match with another .38 slug used in a crime. The sabot goes to the fed.'

'And what has he done with my computers lately?'

'It's only been twenty-four hours,' Quincy said mildly.

'I'd have given you updates within twenty-four hours. Hell, I just delivered a sabot to you in fifty-six!'

'Let it go, Sanders,' Rainie told him kindly. 'The feds have better toys. It's a fact of life.'

Luke had a perplexed look on his face. He leaned forward, planting his elbows on his knees, and peered at Sanders intently. 'You're saying this person went out of his – or, I guess, her – way to make a special bullet to kill Melissa Avalon. A bullet that couldn't be traced back to . . . the person?'

'A bullet that conceivably couldn't be traced back to him or her. Yes.'

'Why?' Luke asked bluntly. 'Danny's there. Danny's brought two guns covered in his fingerprints and registered to Danny's father. What's with the third weapon? Isn't that more dangerous? Someone might see this person armed and mention it later. Or maybe something goes wrong and this person ends up dropping the gun, or dropping the sabot, or God knows what. Seems to me that the margin of error is higher with the additional .38.'

They all studied one another. Sanders had brought up the question before. They still didn't have an answer.

'Symbolism?' Rainie tried after a moment. She glanced at Quincy, the resident expert in criminal behavior. 'Maybe there was a personal reason behind the .22 slug as well as a practical one. The person had a reason to kill Melissa Avalon, and the choice of bullet is tied in to that.'

'Christ, it's not like she was a werewolf and had to be killed with a silver bullet,' Sanders muttered. 'A .22 slug is as common as it gets.'

'What about the gun? Maybe the .38 revolver was a special gift from her husband, with the barrel engraved, *To the One I Love*, which had really touched her heart – until she found out he'd given it to her out of guilt over doing the hokeypokey with another woman.'

'Doing the hokeypokey?' Sanders pressed with a raised brow.

'Fine, fucking. He was fucking another woman. Does that work better—'

'I think we're missing something,' Quincy said quietly.

Rainie and Sanders shut up. They all turned to him. His face was remarkably composed, but there was a light in Quincy's eyes Rainie had never seen before. He was excited. He had figured out part of the riddle, and he was thrilled to death.

'Let's look at the elements of this crime,' Quincy began evenly. 'First, our UNSUB utilizes manipulation. He or she identifies a troubled youth – Danny O'Grady – and approaches him, probably first via the Internet but then meets him in person to cement the relationship. This person needs someone like Danny. He learns his buttons, and he begins to push.

'The UNSUB also enjoys complexity. I think Luke and Sanders are correct. Why use a sabot when Danny's .38 would've done? Maybe because he or she could. In all probability, the .22 slug would deform, making it impossible to test and leaving us none the wiser. But in case it didn't, the UNSUB left another little riddle for the police to solve. Another way for law enforcement to be impressed by his or her skills.

'Which also brings us to the computers. It would appear that the UNSUB has been using Melissa Avalon's e-mail account to contact Danny. So why erase the school computers? Any correspondence, downloads, et cetera, would only show Danny talking to his teacher. Even if the contents of the e-mails were questionable, Melissa Avalon is dead. How is she going to defend herself? But again, one level of diversion is not enough for our UNSUB. He or she also tampers with the school computers. I'm almost positive now that when data-recovery agents delve into the hard drives, they will find everything overridden by zeroes. Our UNSUB seems obsessed with being thorough.'

'But what about Danny?' Rainie objected. 'Once you've introduced another person into a crime, it's no longer efficient. He's scared now, sure, but sooner or later he's bound to talk. That seems like a huge loose end. If the UNSUB really wanted to be untraceable, he or she should've acted alone.'

'No.' Quincy vehemently shook his head. 'This UNSUB absolutely *would not* do everything alone. After all, what's the point of being so ridiculously clever if no one ever learns about it?'

Rainie went still. She saw comprehension slowly washing over Luke's and Sanders's faces, and she knew they had arrived at the same conclusion she had when their eyes suddenly widened in horror.

'You mean . . . you mean this person wanted someone to admire his efforts?'

'Yes.'

'And if Danny does crack, does one day tell everything . . .'

'What's one of the biggest factors we're already seeing in school shootings? Ego. Boys trying to assert their identity in a crowded world. Confused children who equate being infamous with being famous. Are you kidding? The UNSUB is *hoping* that someday Danny will crack. Not right away. Our shooter needs time to get out of Dodge. But one day he hopes to pick up the paper and read about a thirteen-year-old boy whose sole line of defense in a triple-homicide case is that the bogeyman made him do it. And all the crime experts will say this proves how today's youths refuse to take responsibility for their actions, and the legal experts will say this proves how today's defense attorneys go out of their way to confuse juries with conspiracy theories, and our UNSUB will have a good laugh. Our UNSUB will clip every article on Danny O'Grady's trial and have a ball.'

'We're no longer talking a crime of passion, are we?' Rainie asked weakly.

'No. Not at all.'

'But why Melissa Avalon then? The special bullet. The single shot to the forehead. Those are all signs she wasn't a random victim.'

'Oh, she wasn't random. The selection process was simply different from what we thought. I should've seen it earlier, when everyone kept saying how close Danny was to Miss Avalon and how patient she was with him.'

'I don't get it—'

'Danny loved her, Rainie. That's why the UNSUB chose her. Because what better way to demonstrate your control over a troubled child than to make him assist in the murder of the one person who's been good to him. The only other person he trusted.'

'But that doesn't make any sense,' Sanders burst out. 'No one's going to turn on someone they like. You want to lead a kid over to the dark side, you play on something he already hates. You know – "You think your daddy's an asshole? Well, so was mine. Now, let me tell you what I did about it, little boy".'

Quincy shook his head. 'You can do that, Detective, but the bond isn't as strong – not as strong as our UNSUB needs. In classic indoctrination technique, you get the initiate to turn on the things he loves the most. That's when you know you have him. In fact, a Canadian serial killer cemented his homicidal partnership with his wife by making her participate in the rape and murder of her own sister. After that, she couldn't turn against him. That would mean having to face what she'd done. The guilt's too high.'

'Danny,' Rainie whispered. 'Already under suicide watch. Oh my God, the things that must be going on in his mind.'

'He did it? Danny did it?' Luke was rocking back and forth slightly. His face held newly etched lines, and he looked at Quincy almost in agony. 'You're saying Shep's son killed those girls. And this son of a bitch made him.'

'Yes. I think that's how it probably happened.'

'*Who is this bastard?* Can't you tell us that? Can't you stick data in some fancy feebie database and give us something practical to work with?' Luke jumped to his feet. The tendons in his neck stood out like cords, and he looked at them all almost wildly.

None of them said anything. Rainie thought of Luke, night after night, sitting in his patrol car outside Shep's house, determined to protect the O'Gradys' honor. Little Danny, who played in their office after school. Little Danny, playing shoot-'em-up cops and robbers with Bakersville's finest. *'Bang, bang, bang. Good shooting, Danny. Way to go, kid.'*

'One other thought,' Quincy said in the tension-filled attic.

They stared at him, wondering how it could get worse and knowing that it would.

'Murder is like anything else. It has to be learned. The first time is messy, the second time more systematic. These homicides, they're very sophisticated.'

'Oh shit,' Sanders said.

Rainie closed her eyes.

'This isn't the first time this person has done it,' Quincy concluded quietly. 'I would bet my career on it. And if the UNSUB is using the Internet to identify vulnerable teens . . . It's a wide, wide world out there, ladies and gentlemen. God knows where he'll strike next.'

A phone rang. Sanders flinched in the unsettled silence of the room. Luke recovered first and picked up the receiver. He said yes. He nodded. He said yes again. He took some notes.

He hung up the phone, and there was already something about his face that made Rainie cold.

'That was some bartender in Seaside,' Luke said shortly. 'Some guy just walked back into his joint. He's asking a lot of questions about the shooting. And he's talking about you, Rainie. He's talking all about you and how he personally knows you shot your mother fourteen years ago.'

'We got action,' Sanders said crisply. Luke and Quincy nodded, muscles tensing, clearly ready to roll.

Rainie's reaction was slower in coming.

'Yeah.' She sighed softly. Nodding her head. Thinking of Danny. Thinking of psychopaths. Thinking of that night, all those years ago. 'Yeah,' she said with resignation. 'Here we go.'

26

Dusk blanketed Bakersville. Homeowners flicked on porch lights, scattering pinpricks of silver illumination against the darkening hillsides. Dairy cows clustered under trees for warmth, forming rocky contours as they hunkered down for sleep.

In some houses, parents held their children close, thinking of the schools they had attended in their days and the seeming battlegrounds their children attended now. You don't want to raise your kids to be afraid. Everyone goes to school. No sense in making a big deal about it. But to button them up each morning, kiss the soft down at the top of their heads, and send them out to their day – unarmed, defenseless, terrified of the kid in the next seat . . . Oh God, oh God, what has happened to our schools?

In some bars, young men kicked back extra shots, talking about the fucking lawyers who could get anyone off and the dumb-ass juries who cried harder for the murderers than their victims. Ain't no justice in the world. Ain't nobody trying to keep our families safe. This kid will probably walk away by the time he's twenty-one, just like those boys in Arkansas. Doesn't seem right. Not like those two little girls can magically crawl out of the ground when they come of age. Why should he get better than them just 'cause he's a kid too? A murderer is a murderer. Don't do the crime if you can't serve the time. Yeah, that's it. The kid's a killer – let's make him pay!

In Seaside, Ed Flanders nervously towel-dried beer mug after beer mug and hoped the cops would show up soon.

The man's own glass was long since emptied. Ed had asked him if he wanted another. The man had declined. Ed suggested buffalo wings. The man said no. Now the man watched TV. Some news-magazine story on how a volunteer group, Cyber Angels, worked to protect unsuspecting Internet users from on-line stalkers. The man wore a strange smile.

Ed rubbed the beer mug harder. Though he wasn't the type, he was learning to pray.

Seventy miles away, Rainie tore up Route 101 with her lights flashing. Quincy gripped the dash but didn't say a word. Sometimes he would glance

753

at her. She always looked away. Sanders and Luke were in a car behind them, Luke at the wheel and having no trouble matching Rainie's pace.

Sometimes they used to make this run up the winding coastal route just for the hell of it. To keep sharp, they told Shep. Practice their skills. Now those days seemed so far away.

The radio crackled. Suspect was on the move, dispatch relayed. Please advise.

Rainie had to think about it a minute. A crowded bar, a suspect they knew nothing about . . .

'Don't make contact. Just follow him,' she said shortly, then annoyed herself by looking at Quincy for confirmation. The FBI agent nodded. She scowled, replaced the receiver, and drove faster.

An hour later they were in town. Dispatch guided them to a small hotel, and just around the corner, tucked behind a grove of trees, they encountered a ring of police cruisers.

'Looks like we found the party,' she muttered.

Quincy nodded. His face appeared calm, but he still had that light in his eyes. He unfurled from her police cruiser like a boxer about to step into the ring, up on his toes and light on his feet. Rainie watched him a moment too long. The lean line of his body. His graceful, self-assured ease.

She felt a sense of doom she couldn't shake. The night was closing in on her while the others geared up for the chase. Let's get the stranger, let's get the evil man in black.

He's talking all about you . . . personally knows you shot your mother fourteen years ago.

Stranger? She didn't know anymore. She had bad thoughts about bad things that had happened way too long ago.

Quincy was looking back at her curiously. She forced her attention to unfastening her seat belt.

Sanders had already located the officer in charge. She and Quincy walked up in time to hear: 'Suspect appears to be approximately forty years old, graying brown hair, five-ten, five-eleven, approximately one hundred and eighty pounds. He's wearing a long trench coat, so he could be carrying weapons. The motel owner gives his name as Dave Duncan, supposedly some kind of traveling salesman. Said the man's quiet and a nonsmoker, if that's any help.' The officer rolled his eyes.

'Time he returned to his room?' Sanders asked.

'Forty-five minutes ago. We have a pair of officers interviewing the bartender, Ed Flanders, right now. I guess the guy's been in twice. The first time he seemed to be picking a fight with a few locals over whether Danny O'Grady had done the shooting or not. We'd gotten the bulletin yesterday to be on the lookout for strangers who seemed to be following the shooting, so we'd already reached out to the bartenders. Then tonight this guy shows up around seven and starts back in. Except tonight he seemed to be focused on Officer Conner.' The officer's gaze slid over at Rainie. 'Ahh, begging your pardon, ma'am, but Mr Duncan was saying that he knew for a fact you'd killed your mom, you'd killed Mrs Conner' – the officer seemed to decide that was a more polite way of saying it – 'some years ago. He said he had proof, but when Ed tried to ask more questions, the guy blew him off.

'We haven't been able to get a good look at him yet – we were following him in the dark – but Ed swears he knows him from somewhere, just can't think of where.'

'Older man?' Quincy probed. 'Heavyset?'

'Yes, sir.'

Quincy looked at Rainie. She shrugged. ' "Older man" could be several possibilities. Principal VanderZanden, Melissa Avalon's father. Or, what the hell, maybe even Mrs VanderZanden or Mrs Avalon in drag. The UNSUB was clever enough to disguise a bullet. God knows what he or she could do with physical appearance.

'Why don't we just get this over with?' she said stiffly, and everyone nodded. A few of the young men had their batons out. They had a lot of experience breaking up bar fights during the hot summer months, and now they were good to go.

Officer Carr ran them through the drill. The manager of the hotel would call the room and say there was trouble with the bill, would Mr Duncan please come to the lobby. The minute Duncan stepped clear of his room, the officers would descend. They were all wearing flak vests and were prepared to use necessary force. The goal was to be so fast and quick, Duncan would never have time to react. Once they had him in handcuffs, they could begin questioning.

Rainie nodded her consent and pretended Sanders wasn't doing the same. She could tell Officer Carr was proud of his role in hunting down a key suspect. Years later this would be one of those stories repeated over and over again in all the good cop bars.

They settled down behind the trees and prepared to watch the show.

The hotel manager nervously picked up the phone and dialed the room. Rainie could see everything through the uncovered lobby windows and was happy Mr Duncan couldn't say the same, because the hotel manager was sweating bullets. Poor man looked like he was going to have a heart attack, while beside him a somber young officer had dropped into a crouch and had his gun pointed at the front door. Rainie understood it was just a precaution. She was less sure the hotel manager appreciated that.

The manager set down the phone. He was frowning. He said something to the officer and then Carr's radio crackled to life.

'No one's picking up,' Carr muttered. 'The manager can't get Duncan to answer.' He appeared worried. He glanced at Bakersville's quartet for advice.

'Think he's figured it out?' Sanders murmured.

Rainie took in the half-dozen cars and sixteen milling men. 'Jeez, I don't know how.'

'What about having the manager approach the room in person, knock on the door?' Sanders asked. 'The moment the door cracks open, we'll push him aside and force our way into the room.'

Quincy looked at the hotel manager, who had sweated through his white shirt and was now swaying on his feet. 'I don't think so.'

'I'll do it,' Rainie said.

They all stared at her. She shrugged. 'I swear to God I have no real desire to be shot. But do you see any other maids around?' She gestured to the all-male crowd. 'I thought not.'

Five minutes later Rainie was trying to pull a too-small threadbare gray blouse over her bulletproof vest. The skirt came to mid-calf and honestly didn't do a thing for her legs. Then she thought of her mother, dying in three-inch heels.

Jesus, her head was a mess tonight. Would somebody please get her a beer?

She finally got the blouse buttoned, sucked in her gut, and walked out to the men.

'You all right?' Quincy asked promptly. Those federal agents didn't miss a thing.

'Fine and dandy.' She performed a pirouette, looking for a place to stick her 9 mm.

'Back waistband,' Sanders said.

'Can't.'

'Why not?'

''Cause the skirt's too fucking tight!'

'Okay.' Sanders raised his hands and walked away.

Quincy formed a pile of six clean white towels and tucked her gun in the middle, with the handle sticking out of the back for easy access. He handed it to her, his dark eyes calm.

'He makes a move at all . . .' Quincy said.

'I can't shoot him.'

'If he goes for a gun, you do what you have to do.'

'I can't shoot him,' she repeated more forcefully. 'Quincy, if I wound up killing him . . .'

She didn't have to say the rest. It simply hung there between them. The doubts, the suspicions, the rumors that fourteen years later still hadn't gone away.

'Chances are that he knows we're out here,' Quincy said softly.

'Then let's just get it over with. I'm tired of his games.'

She nodded at Sanders, who looked mighty curious about what would happen next, then at eager Officer Carr. Everyone assumed their positions.

Rainie didn't allow herself to think anymore. She lifted the towels high enough to obscure her face and got on with it.

March one, two, three. At the door now. Pause. Deep breath. *Hey, mister, want some towels?* Or maybe shoot first and ask questions later . . .

She knocked on the door.

No answer.

Did you know what you were saying in that bar? Or were you making this stuff up just for me?

She knocked on the door again.

No answer.

The rest happened very slowly. She set down the towels. She picked up her 9 mm. She twisted the door handle, not surprised to find it unlocked, and led with her shoulder into the room.

Behind her, men yelled, *Down, down, down.* Others cried, *Go, go, go.*

Rainie tumbled into the room, bringing up her gun, though she didn't know what she expected to find – or maybe she did. Maybe some part of her knew what body she would find there on that bed. Except . . .

Empty. Empty. Empty.

Officers jostled her aside. Seaside's finest pumped into the room. 'Police! Police! Police!'

Still nothing.

More scattered voices. 'What do you mean, nothing? Where the hell could he have gone? I thought you said you were watching this room.'

'I don't know, sir. I swear to God, *I don't know.*'

Rainie didn't look at any of them. She was staring into the bathroom at the mirror over the double-basin counter and the large words scrawled there: *Too Little, Too Late.*

A lock of hair was taped beneath the red words. It was long, black, with just a hint of curl. Rainie didn't need a lab report to guess its owner.

Beautiful Melissa Avalon, lying dead in a pool of hair.

'Too little, too late,' Rainie read aloud, her voice coming out shaky. She finally looked at the men in the room. 'Would somebody, anybody, like to explain this to me?'

No one replied.

After another moment Sanders picked up his cell phone. He called the CSU.

'Hey,' he said shortly. 'We got another crime scene.'

27

Two hours later Rainie and Quincy drove back to Bakersville. They had finally figured out how Dave Duncan vacated the room. He had cut a hole in the back of the closet, creating a small escape hatch that opened up behind a rhododendron bush at the side of the hotel. The police closed in. He squeezed out, taking his minimal baggage with him.

Quincy was right: The UNSUB liked to have contingency plans.

While the technicians dusted for prints, bagged the hair, and documented the words written in lipstick, Quincy gave them a more detailed profile of the person they were looking for. In his experience, an UNSUB of this type would most likely be male, middle-aged, and unmarried. The crime was highly organized, indicating above-average IQ and professional skills. The UNSUB also utilized manipulation, meaning he felt comfortable being around others and might even have a serious relationship, though chances were his partner often felt she didn't understand her man very well.

According to profile statistics, the UNSUB had probably tried to join the police force or the military at one time but had been either turned away or dishonorably discharged. He was obviously mobile and would still be following the case quite closely.

Common wisdom held that the UNSUB's name wasn't Dave Duncan – he'd paid for the room with cash and showed a barely legible driver's license. Perhaps he was finding a new motel even now, someplace a little more populated, where a 'traveling salesman' would be hard to locate. He knew the net was closing in, and yet – they all shared the hunch – the man wasn't done. The man wouldn't flee.

Seaside would work to write up all the information they could find on David Duncan's visit to their town – description, places he'd been, things he'd said. Sanders would once more coordinate processing the evidence with the CSU.

Luke still planned on watching Shep's house for the rest of the night. Then he was heading to Portland to finish interviewing Mr and Mrs Avalon. This time he'd take a composite sketch with him. Maybe sit across from Mr Avalon. Maybe push the drawing under the man's nose and see what kind of reaction bubbled to the surface.

Rainie would inherit the fun-filled task of generating lists of hotels up and down the coast. Someplace not too far from Bakersville. Someplace not too far from Seaside. Maybe even a rental room in a house run by a little old lady. Or a rarely used hunting shack.

She'd never realized how many places there were to hide around her small town. No one would envy her task.

It had been a long day. They were all exhausted beyond words. Sanders and Luke hit the road. Rainie and Quincy rode back in silence.

Inside the city limits, Rainie stopped at a small convenience store for a six-pack of beer. Then, by unspoken consent, she and Quincy went to his hotel.

There was an awkward moment. Rainie stood in the doorway with the Bud Light. Quincy stood in his room, surveying the space as if realizing for the first time how small and intimate it was.

He pulled out two chairs from the rickety table. Rainie pointedly bypassed them and headed straight for the bed. He didn't say anything. After another moment he shed his jacket, drew off his tie, unbuttoned the top of his shirt, and sat on the mattress, not far from her.

It was hard to read his face from her angle. Half was lit by the lamp next to the bed, half was hidden in darkness. She didn't know what he thought after days like this. Was he still excited, thrilled by the hunt? Or was the adrenaline fading now, leaving behind the sobering realization that another monster roamed the world? One more predator on top of last month's predator and the one the month before that.

Did he get tired? She was tired. She was restless and back to the kind of mood where she didn't trust herself. George Walker's words echoed in her head. So did Officer Carr's nervous look when he tried to figure out how to mention the accusation that she'd killed her own mother. She should have a thicker skin. Tonight she didn't. She felt vulnerable and weary, sick of pretending she knew what she was doing, when she hadn't known for days and the case was only getting worse.

She was soft tonight, a little bit aching. She looked at the hard plane of Quincy's chest, the exposed smattering of dark chest hair, and she wanted to lay her head on his shoulder. A strong, capable man. She wondered how his heartbeat would sound against her ear. She wondered if he would curl his arms around her and hold her the way leading men always held leading ladies in the movies.

She had never been held. Slapped on the shoulder in good-natured ribbing. Even patted on the butt in pickup games of hoops. Lack of comforting touches wasn't something she dwelled on. But tonight it bothered her.

Rainie got out a beer. She tossed a bottle to Quincy, placed her own against the top edge of the bedside table, and whacked it once with the base of her palm to pop the top off. A cool mist rose immediately from the neck.

LISA GARDNER

She took a deep breath, pulling the scent of hops inside her mouth and rolling it over her tongue. Damn. What she would give for just one drink. One long, soothing, numbing drink.

She slouched back against the old wooden headboard instead and cradled the bottle against her belly.

Quincy's own bottle was unopened in his hand. He was watching her with a tight, dark look in his eyes.

'Talk to me,' she murmured.

'Rainie, that display had nothing to do with conversation.'

'Shut up and talk to me.'

He arched a brow pointedly at that clear statement.

'What's your ex-wife like?'

'Christ, you're trying to kill me.'

Rainie sat up. She gazed at him more frankly. 'I mean it. What's your ex-wife like?'

Quincy sighed. Apparently he decided she was serious, for now he took the cap off his beer bottle and drank deeply. Then he settled back on his elbows in the middle of the queen-size bed. Her curled feet loosened enough to nestle against the side of his hip. She admired the line of his throat against the open collar of his white dress shirt.

'Bethie's a good mother,' he said finally. 'She takes wonderful care of our daughters – daughter. Daughters.'

'How did you meet?'

'College, when I was pursuing my doctorate in psychology.'

'Is she a psychologist?'

'No. Bethie's from a wealthy family. College was a means of meeting an appropriate husband. A shame – she has a wonderful mind.'

'Is she pretty?' Rainie asked.

Quincy took more care with his answer. 'She has aged well,' he said at last, his voice neutral.

'Pretty, smart, and a good mother. Do you miss her?'

'No,' he said firmly.

'Why not?'

'My marriage is old news, Rainie. When we met, Bethie admired my background as a Chicago cop, while fully expecting me to settle into a more socially elevated lifestyle as a private-practice psychologist. Hell, I expected the same thing. But then the Bureau started recruiting me. I didn't say no. And poor Bethie ended up with an armed FBI agent for a husband. If I wanted to be fair to her, I should've stayed a psychologist. But I was true to myself. I got into this stuff, and then my marriage faded away.'

'Why don't you say anything bad about her?'

'Because she's the mother of my children and I respect that.'

'You're a gentleman, aren't you?' Her voice suddenly gained an edge. She didn't plan on sounding bitter or looking for a fight, but she took a step

760

down that road anyway. Fighting was what she did best, conflict more second nature to her than kindness. She thought of George Walker again and her eyes began to sting. She wished they would stop.

'I believe in the importance of civility,' Quincy said quietly. 'I see enough inhumanity in my job without needing to add to it.'

'I'm not civil.'

'No.' He smiled wryly. 'But somehow it works for you.'

Rainie stuck her beer on the nightstand. Her movements were restless. He had given her a gracious out. She couldn't take it. The mood ruled her now, and she only knew how to go toward dark and dangerous places.

'You come from money, too, don't you, Quincy? The nice suits, the expensive cologne. This stuff isn't new to you.'

'I don't come from money. My father is a Yankee swamp rat, born and bred. Owns hundreds of acres of God's own land in Rhode Island, works it with his own sweat and will take it with him to the grave. He taught me the importance of manners. He taught me to love fall, when the leaves change and the apples grow crisp. And he taught me never to tell the people close to you that you care.' The corner of his mouth twitched wryly. 'The suits I picked up on my own.'

Rainie got on her hands and knees on the bed. Her gaze was locked on his. She moved closer. 'I'm white trash.'

He didn't take his eyes from her. 'Don't degrade yourself.'

'I'm not. I'm telling you who I am now, so you can't hold it against me later.' She kept advancing. He didn't retreat. 'I'm not civil. I hate to apologize. I have a bad temper, bad dreams, and a bad mood, and I shouldn't be doing this, but dammit, I'm going to do it anyway.'

He said quietly, 'Liar.' Then he reached up with his broad hand, cupped the back of her head, and dragged her down to his mouth.

She'd invited the kiss, but the first contact still shocked her. She felt cool, strong lips against her own hot, angry mouth. She tasted hops, smooth golden hops, and she opened her lips greedily, as if she would gladly get drunk off him. Then his tongue pushed into her mouth, strong and commanding, and in spite of her best intentions, the old panic reared hard.

She drove her fingernails into her palms. She did her best to control her mind. Yellow-flowered fields. Smooth-flowing streams. So many techniques she'd learned over the years. Keep it simple. Keep it quick. Never lose control. No one was ever the wiser.

Quincy's palm was rough against her cheek. It tickled her and brought a flood of unexpected heat low in her stomach. She halted, a bit frightened. His lips whispered across her neck. She let her head fall back. She exposed her throat to him. His breath was warm and tantalizing across her collarbone.

He'd go lower, she thought. Must remember to moan. Yellow-flowered fields and smooth-flowing streams. She could feel his lips, firm and skillful. But she could also feel the dark places hovering just out of sight. Yellow-flowered fields and smooth-flowing streams. He would touch her breast. She would arch her back. Get it over with. Get it *done*.

She felt suddenly, unspeakably sad. She had started this, but it would not be what she needed in the end. And she'd been wrong to do this with Quincy. He wasn't like the other men. With them it had been cheap and mindless. With this man, it would be blasphemy.

She lowered her head. Don't let him see her eyes. Don't let him see her stark and gray and thinking so hard about yellow-flowered fields and smooth-flowing streams and Danny O'Grady holding the shotgun that had blown off her mother's head.

She ached. She suddenly ached so hard she didn't know where the pain ended anymore and Rainie Conner began.

Quincy's hands came up. He feathered back her hair with his fingers. He swept the long, fine strands from her face. And then he kissed the corner of her eye where the first of her tears had gathered.

Rainie scrambled off the bed. 'For God's sake, don't be so damn *nice*.'

She came to a halt in front of the rickety table, holding the collar of her shirt shut with her hand and breathing much too hard.

On the bed, Quincy sat up slowly. His dark hair was mussed. She didn't remember doing that. His cheeks were raspy with five o'clock shadow. She slapped a hand against her throat and belatedly felt the warm flush of whisker burn.

Shit. She was an idiot. She just was. And now she was going to cry, and that would be adding insult to injury. How could one person be so dumb? That was it. She grabbed her coat and headed for the door.

'Stop!'

Quincy snapped the word, shockingly loud in the silent room. Rainie froze.

'Please sit down,' he said more quietly.

'No.' She had her hand on the doorknob and she wasn't letting go.

'*Dammit, sit down!*'

She sat in the hard wooden desk chair by the door.

'I'm sorry,' Quincy said shortly. 'I didn't mean to yell at you. I didn't mean to let things get this far. I didn't mean a lot of things tonight.'

That made her feel better. Rainie pasted a smile on her face that could've shattered glass and said, 'Ah, thanks, fed. Now, if you'll excuse me, I'll be on my way.'

'Shut up, Rainie. And give the attitude a rest.'

Quincy rose tiredly off the bed. For the first time Rainie noticed that his hands were trembling. The lines were more pronounced around his eyes. His mouth carried a fresh, grim set. The sight of him like that hurt her. She had done that to him, and she knew it was wrong of her.

She wished she was the type of person . . . She wished she could erase the grimness from his face.

Instead, she sat, like a bad pupil who'd been caught red-handed and now waited for the blow to fall.

'Don't look at me like that,' he said impatiently. 'I'm not your mother, I'm not some abusive husband. Sometimes I feel like wringing your neck, but I'm not going to hit you.'

'Too well bred for that, Quincy? Don't know how to get down and dirty?'

A muscle leapt in his jaw. She thought she might have pushed him over the edge and she actually felt triumphant. *What the hell are you doing, Rainie? Why won't you just shut up?*

She couldn't help herself. She rose out of her chair, driven by demons she was smart enough to explain but too worn down to control. She walked toward him slowly, watching his eyes narrow again, feeling powerful because of the way his gaze fell to her lips. She undid the button at the top of her breasts.

'No more foreplay,' she whispered. 'Let's just do it. How do well-bred Yankees fuck? Missionary? On top? On bottom? Doggy-style? Sixty-nine? Oh, what would your daddy say?'

She slid loose another button, revealing her worn white cotton bra. Her hands weren't shaking anymore. She felt giddy. Not part of her body, but far, far away, where she could watch it all unfold as if they were merely characters in a play. How many times before? It didn't matter. There was always the morning for repentance.

Quincy caught her hand in a tight grip. She smiled and pressed her body against his, wriggling her pelvis suggestively against his erection.

'Fuck me, Quincy,' she murmured in a voice she barely recognized. 'Fuck me good.'

And he said harshly, 'What was his name? How old were you? Did your mother know, or was she too drunk to care? *Goddammit!*' He broke off contact, shoving her away and striding across the room as if he could barely contain himself. One moment she was next to his hard form. The next he was gone. She had to put out her hands to steady herself.

'You've never told anyone, have you?' he demanded. 'And now here I am, and I need to be impartial to help you and there's not an impartial bone in my body. I want to hunt him down. Christ, I want to break every bone in his body. How many of these assholes can I put away, *and it still isn't enough!*'

'I don't know what you're talking about.'

'Bullshit.'

'Do you treat all your women this way? No wonder your life is all work and no play.'

'Rainie, what happened fourteen years ago?'

'Look at the time. Clock has struck midnight. Gotta run.'

'Fourteen years ago. So long, but not long enough, is it, Rainie?'

'Are you going to be around in the morning? We have a lot of work to do, but then you're not really part of this case team, are you? One phone call and you're out of here, and we both know it.'

'Rainie—'

'*Let it go, dammit!* Why the fuck can't you let it go?'

'*Because I'm me!* Because I'm not stupid and, so help me God, I'm interested in you! And because some part of you is interested, too, or you wouldn't keep coming back to my room night after night, looking for conversation. Now here we are. Let's have the conversation, Rainie. You need to talk. I need to listen. Let's go. Let's get it done!'

'I don't believe this crap.'

'And I don't believe that you forgot the name of the man who supposedly killed your own mother.'

He delivered the words with brutal force. Rainie drew up short. For a moment she thought she'd heard him wrong. He couldn't. Nobody – How did—

Her heart hammering so loud in her chest.

But he was Quincy, of course. That's how he knew. Because he was Quincy, Quantico's best of the best, and she kept coming to him night after night, feeding him bits and pieces.

'You don't know what you're talking about,' she said weakly.

Quincy just looked at her.

'I'm not going to simply stand here and take this,' she tried.

Quincy set his lips.

'This is bullshit! I'm going home.' She strode for the door.

He still didn't say a word.

She got the door open. She threw her coat over her arm with more force than necessary. And she realized for the first time that she wasn't looking out into the night. For all her bold words, her attention was focused behind her, in the room, on Quincy, who still stood quiet and motionless in the middle of the floor.

So help me God, I'm interested in you . . . and some part of you is interested, too.

Call me back, she thought suddenly, wildly. That's what I needed to hear; I just didn't know it at the time. So call me back. One more time. I can't do it on my own. I've spent too long keeping everything under control. And I'm tired and there was this man on my back deck last night, in black, and you don't know what that did to me.

The yellow-flowered fields. The smooth-flowing streams.

She was crying. She felt the tears trickle down her cheeks, and it shamed her. She hated tears. Her mother had told her years ago there was no use in crying, and she'd been right. Tears didn't change a thing. Oh God, they didn't change a thing.

The yellow-flowered fields. The smooth-flowing streams.

Call me back . . .

Quincy remained silent. And then she realized she wasn't in the doorway anymore. She stood alone in the parking lot. Her coat was on and the hotel room door was shut. Once more her subconscious was working faster than she was.

The night was thick and cold around her. She looked up and counted the stars until the tears dried on her cheeks.

The vast night in the vast world. She was probably one of the only people on the planet who was comforted by feeling small.

Call me back . . .

Rainie crawled into her patrol car. She realized there was crap all over her window. Someone had glued newspaper over the driver's side and written: *We'll show you justis, bich!*

Rainie got out of the car. She used her keys to tear the love letter from her windshield. Night still silent. No movement from Quincy's room.

She drove home.

28

The dirt driveway leading up to Rainie's house twisted darkly through a river of night. She'd forgotten to turn on the outside lights again and with her glue-smeared windshield she couldn't see a damn thing. Maybe she'd take a wrong turn and die in a fiery car crash twenty yards from her front door. Or hit a tree and wind up paralyzed. She could be the next Ironside.

Christ, she needed sleep.

Finally pulling up to her home, she retrieved a flashlight from the glove compartment and used it to trek around in the overgrown weeds until she found her hose. Her lawn needed to be mowed. The edges could use some quality time with a weed whacker. Her kitchen still didn't contain any food. Someday soon she was going to have to return to the more mundane matters of life.

Now she stood outside at two in the morning and rinsed sticky glue and old newspaper from her patrol car, until it gleamed faintly beneath the scrutiny of her flashlight.

Once she was done, the weariness hit her hard. She returned the hose slowly. She let the loose coil fall against the earth. She dragged herself to her front steps.

In the last few days she'd let post-traumatic stress syndrome get the better of her. She'd realized this during the drive home. She'd gone too long with too many nightmares and not enough sleep. She'd stopped eating well and started turning toward Quincy as if he could magically make it all go away. Big mistake. But what was done was done.

Tonight she had bottomed out. Tomorrow she would get back on her feet. She'd been here before and she knew how these cycles worked.

She mounted the front steps and, after a bit of fumbling with her keys, got the door open. She was struck all at once by the cross breeze that hit her face. What the—

She snapped on the hall light, her hand reaching automatically for her sidearm as she searched for other signs of danger. Her gun hand came up empty. She'd locked the 9 mm and her backup piece, a .22, in the trunk of her patrol car. Nothing she could do about that now. She flipped the light back off and waited for her eyes to adjust to the gloom. Still no sounds out of place. Just the breeze upon her face. She finally pinpointed its source – her sliding glass door was wide open. She could peer straight through to her back deck.

Shep?

He'd turn on a light and sit in plain sight. He would know better than to risk getting himself shot as an intruder.

Dave Duncan.

Rainie slid along the wall until she came to the open space of her kitchen and adjoining family room. Two bedrooms and a bathroom to her left, one big space to her right. No sign of life.

And then her gaze fell on her sofa, and everything inside her plummeted.

It couldn't be. Definitely not. And just after that conversation with Quincy . . .

Who would know how to reach inside her deepest, darkest nightmare and rip out her heart?

She scrambled for the light. Scraped the plaster wall with her fingernails and still couldn't find the damn little switch. Light, light, she had to see. Had to know. It couldn't be . . .

And then she had it. The single overhead light flooded the family room. Her old round kitchen table with the pedestal base. Her overstuffed chair. Her faded, comfy blue sofa. And the shotgun. Propped up against the back cushions of the sofa. Five long scratches still scarring the old wooden stock.

Time slipped backward. She couldn't stop it. She ran into the kitchen, fumbling with knives, but in her mind she was seventeen and had just come home from school.

Stop it stop it stop it. Couldn't be. The gun had gone to evidence storage in Portland. She knew. She'd looked into it. She'd consoled herself with the knowledge that she'd never have to see the damn thing again.

She grabbed the first knife she came to, a small paring knife, and yelled wildly, 'Come out, come out, you bastard!'

But no one answered. Even the owls were silent, while her mother was a headless corpse in the family room and, oh God, what was that on the ceiling? Oh God, what is this, dripping down on me?

'Who are you? Who the fuck are you? Come out where I can see you!'

She tore down the hallway to the two bedrooms. No one. She ripped open the bathroom door. Empty. She raced onto her deck, trying hard not to notice the shotgun but of course staring at it, while time grabbed her by the throat and dragged her down viciously.

Her mother screaming, 'You liked it, didn't you? You no-good whore!'

Herself whimpering, 'I just wanted him to stop.'

Shut up, shut up. She was not seventeen anymore. She was not helpless. She was a police officer. She was strong. She squared off against the towering pine trees, threw back her shoulders, and roared, 'I know you're out there. I know you're watching, Mr Dave Duncan or whatever the fuck your name is! You want me? Face me like a man, you miserable piece of shit!'

Her mother: 'Liar. I should've known a daughter of mine wouldn't turn out any better.'

'He raped me!'

'You're pregnant, aren't you? Well, don't look at me to help. I'm not paying for your mistakes.'

'I just want him to stop . . .'

'Then rub his balls, honey. That always works for me.'

He had to be out there. She could feel him. The goddamn man from her deck, the big-mouthed stranger reviving old rumors in the bar. The stupid man in black who'd gone from manipulating mere schoolchildren to thinking he could mess with the likes of her.

Rainie ran inside. She grabbed the barrel of the shotgun with both hands, like it was a serpent ready to strike. But she was ready now. Prepared. Back outside. She hefted the gun overhead. She lofted it against the black velvet sky.

'Is this your idea of a joke? You think you can rattle me! Fuck you! I'm on to you, you son of a bitch. I'm on to you, so fuck you!'

She heaved the shotgun into the air. She watched it whip around and around. Heard it smack hard against a tree trunk. Her breathing was labored. She could hear faint ringing in her ears. Nothing good ever happened when she heard that ringing in her ears.

A moment passed. Then another moment. No sound in the trees, though she knew he had to be there. He'd driven a troubled little boy to murder, and now apparently he was looking for a new source of fun. What was it Quincy had said? The UNSUB would try to manipulate law enforcement for sport. He prided himself on clever acts.

Rainie would show him. Hell, she'd just thrown a shotgun at him and now stood with only her fists and her rage for protection. Oh, and a small paring knife.

She started to laugh. She didn't know how it happened. She was standing with her legs apart and her hands balled into fists, ready for a fight, and then she was laughing and thinking of what her mother had yelled at her fourteen years ago.

'Then rub his balls, honey. That always works for me.'

She got it. Fourteen years later, she finally understood her mother's crude advice. And she had to slap her thighs and hold her middle as the laughter ripped out of her in savage gasps.

She was crying. Tears ran down her cheeks. Second time in one night. Jesus, it sucked to be her.

She was climbing off the deck. Knowing she shouldn't do it. It was just what the bastard wanted. Having to do it anyway.

Burrowing under the boards into the crawl space, where the soil was rich and dark and she scratched at it with her bare hands. Deeper and deeper and deeper. Still here. Still horrible. All was safe. Still here.

Oh God, she'd had no idea laughing could hurt so much. Oh God, was that her face in the mirror, with the sunken cheeks and mud splatters in the shape of tears?

An hour later she had her 9 mm and her flashlight. She went into the woods. She started to hunt. She had no illusions about what she would do if she found the man, and that both terrified her and left her calm.

About two hundred feet from her house, she discovered the hollow. Behind some low shrubs for cover, leaves flattened down from long vigil. Ground was cold now, but she knew he'd been there. Watching. It seemed very clear to her. A man who enjoyed manipulating children to kill. A man who was obviously angry but didn't have the gonads to do anything about it himself. Who would appeal to him more than a police officer rumored to have killed her own mother?

That was what tonight had been about. First setting the scene at the bar, then supplying the props in her living room. He was inviting her to the party.

'Come back one more time,' Rainie murmured. 'Let me show you what I can do, you twisted son of a bitch. Let me show you *everything*.'

She collected the battered shotgun on her way back in.

Fifteen minutes later the trees rustled as a figure leapt down to the ground not far from where Rainie had been standing. The man touched the dirt that still held her footprints. Then he brought his fingertips to his mouth and licked them.

And then he smiled.

Perfect.

29

Sandy O'Grady wasn't asleep when the phone rang. She was lying on her back in bed, staring at the gray shadows shifting on her ceiling. She'd been dreaming that she was a little girl again. She'd been out in fields, lounging back in the thick grass with her best friend, Melinda. They were identifying the shapes of clouds.

'Look, that one's a dragon.'

'Oh, oh, an elephant!'

'A two-headed dog!'

Sandy had woken up with tears on her cheeks and the nearly unbearable need to call Melinda. Except she knew that wasn't really it. Melinda had moved to Portland nearly fifteen years ago. She'd gotten married – Sandy had attended the ceremony seven months pregnant with Danny – and she and Sandy hadn't spoken since. Their lives had moved on, the way lives did. They both had new friends who lived closer, had more in common, and required less effort to keep in touch.

She didn't honestly miss her childhood friend that much. She supposed, however, that she missed her childhood.

To be young and carefree. To be so sure that you had all the answers.

Snoring came from the living room, where Shep slept on the sofa. Rustling came from the front-hall closet, where Becky slept on the floor. And silence came from the bedroom where Danny used to be.

Six A.M. Staring at the ceiling. Wondering where her life had gone wrong. Wondering how to make sense of things. She was a mother now, and it was her job to know the way.

The phone rang.

Sandy picked it up before it completed the first highpitched peal.

She said, 'Hello, Danny.'

He didn't reply. She heard the now-familiar background noises. Clanging metal, distant hum of voices. Sandy had seen some of Cabot County's facility the first time she'd tried to visit Danny. New, modern, really not so bad compared to how some youth detention halls could be. In Sandy's imagination, however, the youth center remained a grim, gray prison, and these noises fit that place.

'How are you doing, Danny?' she asked, keeping her voice light. She shifted to get more comfortable on the bed. She had him on the phone. She might as well keep him, for it seemed this would be as close to contact as she would get with her son.

'We're doing okay,' she said conversationally. 'We miss you. Your father is working very hard to help you. We hired a lawyer, Avery Johnson. I know you've met him. He's very good, the best of the best. Your father and I are pleased he took your case.'

Still nothing.

She took another deep breath. 'Becky is starting to come around. She got a new stuffed animal yesterday. A white and gray kitten. You know how much she likes cats. In fact, we might get a real cat soon. Would you like that? Your father is thinking maybe he could handle a pet after all, and Becky has sworn up and down she'll take care of everything. He'll never have to know it's around. Of course, now we need to go to the pound to pick out a kitten, and I'm not sure how Becky will handle that. She'll take one look and want to bring home every animal in the place. We could end up with a zoo. Can you imagine your father knee-deep in puppies and kittens?'

Silence.

Sandy's eyes began to burn. She blinked the tears away. 'I wish I could see you, Danny,' she said. 'I miss you. Very much. I'll be honest. I've – I've been better. But there are a lot of folks around here who believe in you. The church has started a fund-raiser to help with the legal bills. Your grandma and grandpa, they've been by every day to help out, and they keep saying how much they can't wait to get this whole misunderstanding behind us. The neighbors have brought over food. Why, yesterday we even got a brand-new set of Bibles! – Danny?'

Still no answer.

She sighed quietly. 'I miss you. I wish I could give you a big hug right now. I wish I could kiss the top of your head. I wish . . .' Her voice had grown thick. 'I wish I could make everything all right. Because I know whatever happened, you didn't do it on purpose. You're a good boy, Danny. You're *my* boy, and I love you very much.'

More silence. Sandy couldn't take any more of this; her son was breaking her heart. She went to hang up, and Danny finally spoke.

He said dully, 'So much noise. And this horrible smell. Not like the movies. I pulled the trigger. So much noise.'

'Danny?'

'They jerked. The lockers went pop. People fell down. So much noise. I did such a bad thing, Mommy.' His voice rose abruptly. '*I did such a bad thing!*'

Sandy's chest tightened. She had suspected this was coming, and still, hearing the long-feared words out loud nearly ripped her in two. She whispered helplessly, 'I'm sorry, honey. I am so sorry it came to this.'

'The noise. So much noise . . .'

'Danny—'

'He's going to kill me.'

'Who, Danny? We want to help you—'

'I want to die, Mommy. I wish I could lay down my head and just . . . die.'

'Don't talk like that! You're young, you made a mistake. It's this other person's fault. He tricked you, Danny. Can't you see that? He manipulated you. Now tell us who it is. Please, Danny.'

But Danny had pulled himself back together. She could hear his ragged breathing quiet, then a long snuffle as he wiped his nose with the back of his hand.

'I can't,' he said at last, and his voice sounded surprisingly mature, surprisingly resolved. 'I can't tell you anything, Mommy. I'm too damn *smart*.'

30

Quincy was already up and moving when the old rotary phone shrieked to life next to his bed. At first he was startled by the sound, then he was confused. No one called him here. The office used his cell phone, and the locals – namely, Rainie – seemed to prefer to simply show up. Then a new thought struck Quincy. He froze at the bathroom sink, one half of his face still lathered, the other half shaved.

The phone squawked again.

Funny, but he couldn't get his feet to move.

He'd been so sure that when the call came it would be on his cell phone. God knows he lived and breathed through its digital lifelines. But he'd also given the office the hotel number, and if Bethie had asked some hospital assistant to please track him down . . .

The phone kept ringing. He forced himself to get moving.

Thirty seconds later it was over and done. And it was as horrible as he feared and as simple as he'd expected. If he would just come to the hospital. They would unplug the machines, pull the ventilating tubes. It could be over very quickly or very slowly. You just never knew.

He started packing his bags. When white foam splashed his carry-on, he realized he hadn't finished shaving and returned to the sink.

He had phone calls to make. The first few, to Quantico, were easy. The last one, to Rainie, he realized he didn't know how to do. His expertise was in the professional world. When it came to his personal life, he still had a lot to learn.

The case here needed him. Things were moving fast now, and with a sophisticated killer things generally got worse before they got better. He found himself thinking of Jim Beckett and another young, beautiful law-enforcement officer whose attempt at stopping the serial killer hadn't even broken his stride. Oh God, he hoped it didn't come down to that here.

Rainie needed him. She was resilient, but she was going through things no one should go through alone. Last night, right before she turned on him again, he'd seen the ache in her eyes. One more moment, one last defense, and she'd be ready to open up completely. He wanted to be there for that moment. They had the start of something rare and special, he thought. God knows, he did not meet enough people in his life who both challenged and captivated him.

Except his family needed him, too, and as happened so often in his life, he couldn't be in two places at once. He was not Superagent or Superfather. He was just a person leading a complicated life, and sometimes he did fail the people he loved.

Rainie was tougher than Bethie, he thought. And she was trained in the field. Weak comforts, but he would take what he could get.

He picked up the phone and dialed. Rainie answered on the fifth ring, just when he was beginning to give up. Her voice sounded distant and not at all like her.

'Rainie? I'm sorry, did I wake you?'

She mumbled something that might have been yes.

He waited, and when she didn't offer anything more, he kept the conversation simple, for there was no way to make it kind. 'Rainie, I have to return to Virginia now.'

Stunned silence. He'd expected as much.

He continued with more calmness than he felt. 'The hospital just called me. Apparently, Bethie has agreed to shut off life support. She's already signed the forms to donate Mandy's organs, and there are people who are waiting . . . It's . . . it's time.'

Rainie didn't say anything.

'I'll come back,' he said quickly. 'I had the sabot couriered to the crime lab yesterday and pulled a few strings to make it a priority project. I can apply even more pressure while I'm local.'

She remained silent.

'And I'd like to do some additional research while I'm back there,' he added briskly. 'I was thinking about it early this morning. I'm willing to bet the person we are looking for is what we call an authority-complex killer. The most famous example is Charles Manson, of course.'

He thought he might be babbling. She still wasn't talking and he couldn't seem to stop.

'An authority-complex killer generally comes from a family with an extremely domineering parental figure,' he heard himself say. 'This parent either physically or verbally abuses him as a child. The child grows up fantasizing about facing down his parent but never has the ability to do so. Instead, his rage becomes focused on other people in power. Except rather than seek out direct violence against them, the killer manipulates others into acting. This, of course, makes him feel powerful and omnipotent.

'I need to look up additional case studies, but authority-complex killers are generally charismatic, verbal, and possess excellent socialization skills. The interesting thing about them is that they are mental. Even more than violence, they enjoy toying with people in charge, creating elaborate ruses such as we've seen. This person doesn't want things quick or easy. He wants to watch the police sweat and gloat over our seeming stupidity. In other words, the more I think about it, the more I'm sure Dave Duncan is still in the area.'

'There's a chance he's still in the area,' Rainie intoned dully.

'But don't underestimate him,' Quincy added hastily. 'He'll kill directly if he has to. Particularly established authority figures, such as cops.'

There was a noise over the phone, as if Rainie was dragging something heavy across the bed.

Quincy frowned. He grew silent and for the first time heard the gulf looming between them. He had a sudden image of her sitting alone on her bed in the dark, cradling her gun for comfort. Things had ended badly last night, and now he couldn't stay to make them right.

'Rainie?' he asked.

No answer.

'I'm coming back.'

No reply.

'I'm not bailing on you and I'm not bailing on this case. Isolation is not protection,' he said adamantly, though he was definitely babbling, now and didn't expect her to understand what he meant. 'Dammit, Rainie—'

She said quietly, coolly, 'Have a nice flight.'

Abe Sanders sat down to a hearty three-egg omelette in the back booth of Martha's Diner. One big advantage of working in the middle of Hicksville, USA – fresh produce. His omelette oozed with plump mushrooms, premium Tillamook cheese, and, best of all, fresh spinach. Too many places in the city ruined that. They offered canned spinach or, even worse, creamed spinach. Abe shuddered. Not even Popeye would touch that stuff.

No, Bakersville definitely offered good food, including buttermilk pancakes made from scratch. Abe loved pancakes made from scratch. This morning, however, he'd cheerfully gone with what he considered to be the healthy, high-protein choice. The case was progressing well, albeit in a different direction than he'd originally assumed, and he didn't want to slow himself down by carbo-loading.

He finished his omelette, tipped the cute waitress generously, and drove the short distance to City Hall.

The attic sounded quiet as he climbed the narrow wooden staircase. That surprised him. It was nearly eight A.M., late by the last few days' standards, and he'd assumed that at least Rainie would already be in the task-force center. Seemed she was always the first to arrive and the last to depart. He definitely couldn't fault her work ethic. Now, if only she'd stop tormenting #2 pencils. He'd bought. three boxes before he learned to keep them in the glove compartment of his car.

He opened the attic door, swept the small space with a quick glance. Apparently he was the first one in.

He set about brewing coffee and picked up a banded pile of mail delivered by the mailroom clerk first thing this morning. One overnighted envelope for Rainie, postmarked Ca. Probably Richard Mann's personnel records from the LA school. One pink phone-message slip. According to a hard-to-read scrawl, Agent Quincy had to leave on pressing family business and would be gone for a few days. Most likely his daughter. Abe thought with genuine sympathy. Bad break, that. The agent didn't talk about it, but the word was all over town. Quincy's daughter had been KO'd by a drunk driver. Abe had already heard the story four separate times while eating in the diner.

The rest of the mail appeared to be junk. He threw it on the corner of Rainie's desk. She could deal with it later.

Since he seemed to have a moment to himself, he pulled out his cell phone and called home. His wife was in a state. The puppy was having trouble attending to his business this morning. She wanted to take him to the vet.

'For God's sake, feed him some bran cereal and be done with it.'

She cheered up at that idea. Then, of course, she insisted on putting the puppy on the phone.

'Yeah, yeah, yeah,' Abe said.

The puppy barked enthusiastically.

'You got no bladder control,' Able told him.

More vigorous barking.

'You're peeing all over my rugs.'

Very cheerful barking.

'Yeah. Fine. I love you too. Now gimme back my wife.'

His wife came back on. Heaven help him, he was blushing.

'How's it coming?' she asked.

'It's coming.'

'Going to be home soon?' He knew she tried her best, but she sounded wistful.

His voice softened. He said, 'I love you, honey. And I miss you too.'

Sanders hung up the phone. He was sorry Dave Duncan had slipped through their fingers last night, but now that they knew who they were looking for, it was only a matter of time. The guy was on the run, after all. Probably panicked and scared and thinking he had no place left to hide.

Damn right. Sanders had personally issued the statewide APB late last night. If Duncan was in the area, some local eager beaver would get him in his sights.

Sanders got to work on his report. He didn't look up again until noon. Then he was startled by the time and the fact that Rainie still hadn't shown.

Something niggled at him. Something he didn't like.

Abe Sanders tried her house. Then he tried the radio in her patrol car. And then he started to panic, because he didn't get answers anywhere.

For all intents and purposes, Officer Lorraine Conner had disappeared from the face of the earth. And even if Abe didn't care for Rainie's methods, he knew that just wasn't like her.

31

Becky sat on her skinny bed, surrounded by stuffed animals and holding Big Bear against her tummy. Her parents were talking unhappily in the family room. They were trying to keep their voices down, the way they did when they were mad at each other but didn't want anyone to know. Becky thought that her mommy had been crying. And her daddy was in one of his Very Bad Moods. He'd boarded up the hall closet when Becky got up this morning. He'd told her that little girls were supposed to sleep in beds, so by God she had better get used to hers.

Becky didn't think her mommy agreed with that. Becky didn't care. She had a closet in this room too. She'd picked the hall closet only because it was closer to where her daddy slept. And as much as Becky liked Big Bear, she didn't know if he'd be any good in a fight. He was only made out of stuffing, after all, with a button for a nose.

Her mommy and daddy were arguing about Danny.

'He needs help, Shep! Serious help that he's not going to get from a youth detention facility.'

'I know that! But we have to be patient, Sandy. You heard what the lawyer said. If Danny talks to the wrong person, it could wind up in court. Then what kind of help would he get? We have to wait until the forensic exams are done. We'll know more then.'

'In six months to a year? For God's sake, he's already under suicide watch—'

'They're taking good care of him.'

'There's no one for him to talk to. You had to hear him this morning. He was begging to die. Goddammit, this is our son!'

Becky slid off her bed with Big Bear. Careful not to make any noise, she crept closer to the family room and pressed herself against the hallway wall.

'There is nothing more we can do,' her daddy was saying roughly. 'We gotta just . . . trust him to get through this.'

'No.'

'Sandy—'

'There is another option.'

'Like hell there is!'

'He did it, Shep! Oh for God's sake, don't cover your ears like a child. This is Danny, and he called me at six in the morning to tell me that he'd pulled the trigger and he can't get it out of his head. He's only thirteen years old. I don't know how it all came to this. I wish I did. But somehow . . . He went in that school, Shep. And he did what he did, and now it's tearing him up inside. And we can sit here in denial or we can climb into the trenches with him. I think . . . I think that's all we have left.'

'Trenches? There are no trenches. There is prison. And he goes in alone and he dies there alone. Christ, haven't you been following the other cases? There aren't any second chances for mass murderers. Not even for a thirteen-year-old. Danny goes away for more multiple life sentences than years he's got left to live. End of story.'

'Avery Johnson said that if Danny was willing to plead guilty, the county would probably be willing to work out a deal. It would spare everyone the anguish of trial.'

'My son is not a murderer.'

'Yes, he is.'

'I'm warning you, Sandy.'

'Danny shot two little girls! Danny killed Sally Walker and Alice Bensen. Those parents have to walk by empty bedrooms for the rest of their lives. Because of our son. What about that, Shep? *What about that?*'

'Goddamn you, Sandy—'

Shep's voice broke off savagely. Becky peeked into the room and saw that her daddy's face was swollen and ugly red. He had his hand drawn back, like he was going to hit something. Except it was her mommy who stood in front of him. She had her chin up and was staring at him like Danny did when he was daring someone to do something bad.

Becky was frightened. She wanted to yell stop, but just like in the school, she was too scared to make words come out of her mouth. She didn't recognize these people, with their flushed faces and mean hands. She wished they would go away so her real parents could come home. She missed when they all used to eat dinner together, even Danny, who would sneak his peas onto her plate.

'If you beat your wife, will that make you feel better, Shep?' Sandy said quietly. 'Or maybe, right at this moment, are you getting some idea of where we went wrong?'

Shep shuddered. His hand slowly came down.

'I'm trying,' Sandy continued softly. 'I'm trying harder than I've ever tried in my life to make this family whole. But I can't do it anymore. We failed, Shep. Somewhere we went wrong, and Danny went wrong, and poor Becky – God knows what's even going on with her anymore. But the way I see it, we have two choices. We can pretend it never happened and not act too surprised when we get the call someday that our son is dead, or we can give up on what we wish had happened and start dealing with what did.

'Danny was involved in the killings. Danny has problems dealing with his rage. Danny is a deeply troubled boy. But he's a good boy, too, if that makes any sense, and the guilt is tearing him up inside. If we don't let him talk, and talk soon, I don't think he's going to make it. He'll either finally find tableware he knows how to use or, worse, he'll shut out his emotions. He will become cold and remorseless.

'He's only thirteen, Shep. I want him to have a chance to become the man we dreamed about, not a newspaper headline. I don't know about you, but for me that makes our choice pretty clear.'

And Becky's father said tiredly, 'What choice, Sandy? Danny's not ours anymore. He belongs to the legal system, and I know that beast. The minute he says he's guilty, he'll be locked away for life. And even if he gets counseling and becomes our good boy again, what the hell is our good boy going to do locked away with violent felons for the rest of his life? Why don't we just buy him a T-shirt that says RAPE ME NOW and let him wear it at the fucking trial?'

'Shep!'

'Sandy, what do you think is going to happen? *Why do you think I'm so scared!*'

Her mommy fell silent. Becky thought she looked like she was going to cry. Becky was crying. She had tears all over her cheeks.

'There must be other options,' her mommy said at last, but she no longer sounded so certain. 'We need to talk to Avery Johnson, raise the possibility. See what can be worked out . . .'

'He can't go to prison, Sandy. I won't let that happen. I won't.'

Sandy rubbed her arms. 'I don't know what to do anymore,' she murmured. 'I feel . . . like the worst is still to come.'

'I'll think of something, Sandy. He's my son. Give me time, and I'll come up with something.'

Becky's mommy finally nodded. Becky clutched Big Bear hard and slid away from the doorway. Her heart was pounding hard in her chest now. She had the heavy feeling, where she could barely breathe.

She wanted to run into the family room. She wanted to throw her arms around her daddy's legs and beg him to leave Danny alone. But just like at the school, she was too frightened. Her mouth wouldn't work.

She went back to her bedroom. She started throwing blankets and clothes in her closet for cover. Big Bear would need a place to hide. And Mrs Beetle and Polly the Pony and her new kitten.

Becky had a lot of work to do.

Bad things were gonna happen if people pushed Danny. Very bad things. The monster was still out there, and if Danny wasn't smart, if Becky wasn't smart, he'd kill them all.

He had promised.

*

Rainie started her preparations the minute she got off the phone with Quincy. First she mowed her lawn. Then she took care of the edging. The high grass would make the tracks too easy to see for what needed to happen next.

She put on a mask. She grabbed a shovel. She ignored the ringing phone and went to work, not letting herself think about what had to be done. Afterward she raked the grass back up to cover the marks. Then she took a long hot shower and steamed the rich, moist earth from her hands.

Another hour, toiling with the shotgun, just in case.

A little after two, as she returned from the trunk of her patrol car with her substitute 9 mm and backup .22, her phone started ringing again. She didn't answer but then heard Luke's voice on the machine.

She picked up the receiver as he was still calling her name.

'I'm here.'

'Jesus, Rainie. Where the hell have you been? Sanders is going nuts trying to find you.'

'I mowed my lawn. How are things in Portland?'

'Muddled.' Luke sounded confused. She could hear the sounds of traffic, so he must be using his cell phone. 'You took the morning to do yard work?'

'The grass didn't seem to realize murder was a good excuse not to grow. Why are things muddled in Portland?'

'Daniel Avalon has disappeared. We were supposed to meet at his office this morning, but his secretary's been stalling me with one feeble excuse after another. I finally tried his wife. Looks like Mr Avalon didn't come home last night. And, get this, I drove by his hunting cabin on the way to Portland. It's definitely been recently used.'

'You think he's Dave Duncan.'

'Well, with the right disguise . . . Hell, anything's possible.' Luke sighed. 'I put out an APB with his "normal" description, plus a description of his car and the cabin. It's the best I can do for now.'

'I'm sure he'll turn up shortly,' Rainie said neutrally. Her eyes had already gone to her back deck.

'Rainie . . . I made Angelina show me the gun cabinet. One of the shotguns is missing. I don't think that's a good thing.'

'Fire with fire,' Rainie murmured.

'I'm coming back to Bakersville, okay? There's nothing for me to do here anymore and I'd feel better if I were back in town.'

'Whatever you think is best, Luke.'

'Good.' He hesitated. She could hear the unspoken questions still in his voice. She and Luke went way back. He would come if she asked him to. He would die for her if it came to that; he was that kind of man.

But she was who she was, too, and she couldn't ask anyone to pay for her sins.

He said, 'Rainie . . .'

And she said, 'I'm a big girl, Luke. I know what I'm doing.'

She recradled the phone. The hour was growing late and she didn't have much time to waste. She went with a simple white cotton shirt, covered by a light jacket, perfect for concealing her handgun. She paired the top with long jeans that flared at the ankle. Perfect for disguising her backup .22.

She took her ID. She would need it to get into the Cabot County Youth Detention Facility. After that, however, she considered herself on her own. Not Officer Lorraine Conner but simply Rainie, doing what she should've done days ago.

She prepared one last surprise in her family room, just in case. Then she glanced at her watch. Danny was due to be moved at five P.M. Shep had decided he wanted Danny to be examined at the nearby psychiatric hospital. That didn't give her much time.

Rainie hit the road in her own beat-up Nissan. An hour later she sat across from Danny O'Grady, whose thin, gaunt face was a close match for her own.

'Danny,' she said quietly, 'I think it's time we talked.'

She didn't leave until he'd told her everything.

Quincy walked tiredly down the hospital corridor toward the room he'd hoped never to see again. He'd had to pass through Chicago on his way to Dulles, and his damn flight from Portland had landed forty-five minutes late, forcing him to run for his gate. He'd been terrified of missing his connecting flight, terrified of being stranded at O'Hare. Terrified of having to call Bethie and tell her he was missing another momentous occasion in his daughter's life. This one, though, would definitely be the last. Ha ha ha.

His thoughts were raw. He felt both exhausted and wired, the way he did when he approached a fresh crime scene, and that unsettled him even more.

A few nurses saw him walking and nodded in greeting. He recognized their faces but didn't remember their names.

Finally he was at the door. That damn smell again. And the over-whelming sense of white. He had been raised to believe that death wore black. He felt needlessly betrayed.

He put on his game face, for he knew no other way to enter the room, then briskly opened the door.

Bethie was curled up in a chair next to the bed, sound asleep. Her dark hair had lightened in the last few years but curved gracefully around her shoulders. With her taupe slacks and fine silk sweater, she looked much too nice to be spending her days in a hospital room. Quincy felt instantly guilty, his most common emotion when it came to his ex-wife.

He cleared his throat. She woke up slowly, blinking her blue eyes and looking startled to see him.

'Pierce? Done saving the world already? I figured it would take you at least another week.'

Quincy ignored her sarcasm and gazed upon his elder daughter. Amanda's face was still covered in white gauze. Tubes and needles bristled across her prostrate form and nearly obscured a body that had once been defined by slender grace. The violence of keeping her alive shocked him once more. It slowed his steps.

'I came as fast as I could,' he told Bethie as he picked up Mandy's hand. He squeezed gently. There was no response. He studied her small pale fingers against his palm. He marveled at her fingernails, dutifully growing long and pink while the rest of her withered away. It seemed like only yesterday those were baby fingers, gripping his thumb tight.

'I don't understand,' Bethie said from behind him. 'I thought you'd had enough.'

'I wasn't going to miss this, Bethie. I'd always planned on being here, once you were ready.'

'When I'm ready for what?'

Quincy turned around. He was still holding Mandy's hand, but now he was registering the genuine confusion on his ex-wife's face. His stomach plummeted. Someplace deep inside him had just gone cold.

'Someone from the hospital staff called. You're ready to turn off life support—'

'I most certainly am not!'

'Bethie—'

'Is this some kind of trick of yours, Pierce? Do you think this little melodrama will force my hand? Because it won't work. I am not killing my daughter just to convenience your schedule.'

'Bethie—' But he didn't say anything more. She had no idea what he was talking about. He'd been set up, and he'd walked into the trap as meekly as a mouse.

Oh God, Rainie.

Quincy replaced Mandy's hand on the sheet. He kissed her temple. His hands had started to shake.

'No changes?'

'No changes,' Bethie said stiffly.

'And Kimberly?'

'Settled back in at college, I suppose. Not that she bothers to call.'

Quincy nodded and tried not to appear too hasty as he headed for the door.

'Thanks for visiting,' Bethie called out sarcastically behind him. 'Do come again.'

Quincy stopped for just a moment in the doorway. 'It's not your fault,' he said honestly. 'What happened to Mandy, it was not your fault.'

'I don't blame myself,' Bethie said thickly. 'I blame you.'

Quincy headed down the hallway. The minute he was in the parking lot, he flipped open his cell phone. His first call was to his friend in the crime lab, who had received the sabot late last night.

'Did you enter it into drugfire?'

'Jeez, Quincy, nice to hear from you too.'

'I don't have time, Kenny. Where are you with the sabot?'

'Well, if you'd bothered to check your voice mail, you'd know I worked on it all friggin' night. The rifling matches with two other shootings, Quince. Two other school shootings. And both those cases are considered closed, with two kids in jail. So if these crimes are still happening . . . Get your butt to Quantico, Quincy. You're kind of in demand.'

'I'm going back to Oregon. Fax everything to the Bakersville number as soon as you can.'

'Are you nuts? We have the same gun used in three separate *school shootings* in three separate cities over a ten-year span. What do you think is going to happen next?'

'He's going to kill Rainie,' Quincy said simply. 'It's part of his game. Drive her over the edge, then attack when she's down. And I didn't see it coming. Shit, I didn't see it coming, and now I'm *all the way across the fucking country!*'

And then he was off the phone and in a taxicab, where he yelled at the driver to go fast, fast, *fast*, while he thought of his daughter and all those moments in his life when he hadn't done enough.

32

Danny was exhausted. Long after Rainie left, he lay on his bed, curled in a ball, staring at the same spot on the floor. He had told her everything. He shouldn't have, but he had, and now he was drained.

She had told him that secrets made things worse. She had told him that secrets gave the man power over him. Danny didn't know anymore. He had so many pictures in his mind. He wished he could turn off his brain and make everything go away.

This morning his hands had started trembling, and now they wouldn't stop. This morning the cold had left him and now he was filled with a burning pain. He hated the feel of his own skin. He hated the sight of his face in the mirror. He wanted something sharp so he could slice away his fingers. Then he wouldn't have to see them holding a gun or pulling a trigger. Then he would hurt outside the way he hurt inside, and somehow that would be more right.

He was tired. But he couldn't sleep. He was worried about Becky. He should make himself move, do something. He didn't know what.

Footsteps came down the corridor. One of the guides appeared. He was smiling, jolly, like a clown. 'It's that time,' he said cheerily.

Danny looked at him blankly.

'You're going on a field trip, Mr O'Grady. Your parents are sending you to the funny farm.' Mr Jolly laughed at his joke.

Danny curled up more tightly on the bed.

Two men materialized behind Mr Jolly. They wore uniforms and looked vaguely familiar to Danny. They held up shackles. If you left the walls of the detention center, you had to be shackled. There was no point in avoiding it anymore. They would take him one way or another.

Off to the funny farm. His insides burned. He wished he had something sharp.

Danny stood as ordered. He held up his arms. The younger guy did his ankles first. He didn't make it very tight. Not as tight as the last guy had done. That guy had cut into Danny's skin and left welts. Danny had known from the look on the man's face that that was what he wanted.

785

Danny kept quiet. The younger guy had the belt around his waist now. His hands were chained in front of him to the belt. He was done.

The older man nodded. 'Danny,' he said roughly, familiarly.

Danny figured he must know the man. Maybe a friend of his father's. Good old Shep loved the brotherhood of the uniform. Couldn't be easy to be a cop now.

The patrol officers led him out to a Cabot County police cruiser. They stuck him in the back, then climbed into the front. The two men kept looking at each other but didn't say much.

Danny didn't ask any questions. He didn't know why he was going to the funny farm or for how long or what happened when he got there. He still didn't ask any questions. He just wished he had something sharp. Cut away his fingers. Never have to gaze at his hands anymore. *Miss Avalon, Miss Avalon, Miss Avalon.*

'Run, Danny, run!'

The car started moving. The older man studied Danny in the rearview mirror. Danny didn't like his look. He hunched his shoulders and tried to be small.

Ten minutes later the older man said to the younger man, 'What do you think?'

'I guess it's as good a spot as any.'

'Hey, you,' the older man said to Danny. 'Hold on, kid.'

Suddenly, the car swerved. One minute they were on the road, the next the car went bouncing down the embankment. Danny thought the man would try to brake. Instead he hit the gas. *Boom.*

The impact slammed Danny forward into the divider. He blinked his eyes. It took several seconds more for the dust to clear. When he finally had his senses together, he realized the patrol car was smashed against a tree. Steam came from beneath the hood. The two cops looked bleary, and the younger one had blood on his forehead.

'Shit,' the kid cop murmured, touching the cut and wincing. 'Shit, that's gotta be authentic.'

'Get out,' the older man was saying. His lip was bleeding and his cheek appeared bruised. He spoke with more urgency. 'For God's sake, kid, grab the keys and get the hell out of the car. Didn't your dad tell you anything?'

Danny finally realized that the back door had opened. Had one of them done it, or was it from the crash? He couldn't remember how things had happened, and already his feet were moving, though through no will of his own.

He got out of the car. Both cops were moaning. Someone squawked over the radio. They pretended to moan louder while the older one pointed at the keys dangling from his utility belt.

Danny took the keys and undid his shackles. Now he saw another police car coming, except this one wasn't from Cabot County. It was from

Bakersville, and Danny knew immediately who was climbing out of the front seat.

Danny threw the keys into the grass. He leapt forward, catching the older cop by surprise, and grabbed his sidearm.

The man's eyes turned white with fear. He started to babble; Danny didn't stick around to hear. The fog had lifted. He had no more doubt in his mind.

He ran. Straight into the ravine, crashing through the underbrush. He heard the cops yell and his father yell. '*Wait, wait, we're just trying to help.*' '*Son, please . . .*'

Danny ran faster.

He had a gun now, and he knew exactly what he had to do next.

He was *smart*.

At a little after five-thirty in the evening, Principal Steven VanderZanden turned his car up the rounded driveway to his house. Abigail was sitting beside him, holding his hand. Ever since the shooting, she'd had a need to touch him. She stroked his cheek more often, cajoled him out of his recliner onto the love seat, slept with her body pressed up against his.

It had been years since she'd been so affectionate, and right after the shooting Steven hadn't known how to feel about that. His sadness and guilt over Melissa left him needy, grateful for the contact. And yet the nicer his wife was, the worse he felt.

Today he had realized he needed to tell his wife the truth. Just get it all out in the open. Then see what she did to him.

Except this morning his wife had suggested that they drive to the beach, get away for a little bit. The days had been long since the shootings, so many people who needed his guidance and so many doubts to keep him up late at night. It would be months before he sorted through the aftermath. Months before he understood his role as a principal and guardian of students again.

His wife wore a new sundress she'd apparently bought yesterday at Sears. The bright blue made her eyes vivid, and he found himself watching her, noting the way she smiled. She was flirting with him, he'd realized finally. Gently, subtly, in order to give him plenty of space.

And he found himself thinking about other times, when the marriage was new and they thought nothing of spending hours giggling on the sofa. He thought of the way he'd always appreciated his wife's common sense and how she made him feel strong, when he'd spent his whole life as a five-foot-eight runt who was never the hero on the football field. He remembered the way he liked his wife, particularly in the days before Melissa Avalon had arrived in Bakersville and stunned him with her smile.

By five this afternoon he had made his decision. He'd made a mistake, an error in ego and judgment. He hoped his wife would never have to learn how much he'd hurt her. And now he just wanted his old life back.

They approached the house.

The first sign of trouble was just a flicker of movement out of the corner of Steven's eye. The next minute the back window of the car exploded in a hail of glass.

'Oh my God,' Abigail cried.

'Duck!' Steven yelled.

He floored the gas pedal on instinct and overshot the driveway. The car tumbled down the side of the hill and came to a halt in a tangle of underbrush. He fought for reverse. No such luck. He tried to shoot forward. They were stuck.

Another gunshot. The side window exploded.

Steven looked at his wife of fifteen years. He thought he knew what was going on. There would be no escape. Melissa had warned him.

He said quietly, 'Run, Abigail. Run as fast as you can.'

And then he got out and prepared to meet his fate.

In the attic of city hall, Sanders was restless again. Six-thirty. Christ, for how long could one woman take care of her yard? That was a local for you. Perfectly good as long as the case was exciting. Once it got down to the grunt work, bailed out through the closest window.

He grumbled some more, strolling around the tiny attic and rolling out the knots in his neck. Luke Hayes had checked in briefly, but he was now back in the main office of the sheriff's department, writing up the day's worth of paperwork under Sanders's orders. Sanders didn't know how they generally did things around here, but in cross-jurisdictional investigations you needed up-to-date written reports or things fell through the cracks.

Speaking of which.

Sanders picked up Rainie's mail from the California school. Since she wasn't here, he'd just have to take matters into his own hands.

He opened the flat envelope and began to skim the contents.

'Oh shit,' he said thirty seconds later. 'Oh *shit!*'

And then, in the corner of the room, the police scanner crackled to life with the first reports of gunfire.

33

'Hello, Richard.'

Rainie stood on her back deck in the gathering gloom. It was late, nearly eight o'clock. She'd stopped on her way back from Cabot to grab a sandwich and turn things over in her mind. She hadn't eaten much, but things had become clearer to her. Why the shadowy figure of a man on her back deck? Why some stranger spouting off about her mother in a Seaside bar? Why the shotgun on her sofa? Because, somewhere along the line, this had become about her.

And having found her, the killer would not magically go away. Quincy was right. He wasn't done yet.

Rainie had parked her car at the bottom of her driveway. She'd already known who she was looking for. When Danny had finally, brokenly uttered the name, she'd realized she wasn't even surprised.

She had carefully made her way up through the woods to the back of her house. Her efforts were not disappointed. Mann sat calmly on her back deck with her mother's shotgun cradled in his arms.

She boarded the stairs, then leveled her 9 mm at his chest.

'Hello, Lorraine,' he said conversationally. 'Hope you don't mind, but I'm tired of foreplay.'

'Fine. Stand up and I'll shoot you.'

'Lorraine.' He gave her a chiding look. 'Didn't you learn anything fourteen years ago?'

'Yes,' she said honestly. 'Don't wait so long. And confess sooner – it does a body good.'

Richard Mann grinned at her charmingly. He wore black jeans and a black turtleneck, making him harder to distinguish in the falling night. His brown hair was different. He'd bleached it blond and touched up his eyebrows and lashes. The effect was startling – from conservative young professional to aspiring rock star. Rainie understood what that meant. Richard wasn't planning on continuing his starring role as Bakersville's school counselor. In fact, he was merely attending to one last loose end before he rode off into the sunset.

'I went under your deck,' Richard said. 'Why did you move him?'

'I had my reasons.'

'You visited Danny today, didn't you? Surely by now you know you can talk to me. In fact, I'm probably the only person in town who can truly understand.'

'You're a sick, twisted bastard, Richard. I'm a cop. There's nothing you understand.'

He laughed with genuine amusement. 'You honestly believe that, don't you, Rainie? How clever. You've manipulated your conscience into allowing yourself to live. But I'm curious. This beer thing. I've been watching you for months now, and I just have to know. When you dump the beer over your deck railing, what is it you say?'

'None of your business.'

'And once again you disappoint. I had such aspirations for you in the beginning, but then you became prickly and dull. I'm not sure I like you anymore.'

'It's probably the gun,' she told him. 'Stand up and surrender. We'll see if that improves your feelings at all.'

He smiled. 'No, thank you. I'm more comfortable the way things are. I'm good at my job, you have to admit that. A good school counselor should be able to lead and inspire. And boy, did I lead and inspire. You should've seen Melissa's face at the end. She really hadn't a clue.'

'Is that why you came here? To gloat?'

'You know why I came here.'

'I'm not as easy to manipulate as a thirteen-year-old boy,' Rainie said stiffly.

Richard stood abruptly. 'No. You're even easier.'

He took a step forward.

'Stop or I'll shoot.'

He threw the shotgun aside. 'But, Lorraine, I'm an unarmed man.'

'Don't call me that!'

He took another step forward. 'You know you want to do it. Killing gets in the blood. Hard the first time, so much easier after that. I've read it releases powerful chemicals in the brain. No other high quite like it. Believe me, I know.'

'Freeze!'

'Come on, Lorraine. Just pull the trigger. You've been talking to Danny, you know how good it feels. You hate me. You hate me for manipulating the boy. You hate me for helping him kill those girls. You hate me for putting him in your dreams. Yeah, I've watched you sleep. I know it's all back in your mind. So pull the trigger, Lorraine. Do it one more sweet, satisfying time. Remember the power. Celebrate your rage.'

'Goddammit.' She dropped the handgun to his kneecap, and when he took another step toward her, she fired.

And the automatic weapon uttered a hollow little click.

Richard laughed. He picked up her mother's shotgun, holding it loosely in his arms. 'Keeping a gun in a shoe box in your closet? You don't even make my life that difficult.'

Rainie was still staring at her Beretta. 'How? I just cleaned it, loaded it . . .'

'The firing pin. Filed it down a fraction of an inch, just enough so it can't hit the firing cap. That was the night you woke up, but I was already outside by then.' He held up the shotgun to her gaze. 'You removed the firing pin. I know, I checked. Take it from me – too obvious. Never do a lot, Lorraine, if just a little will get you by. It's grand deceptions that always come back to haunt you.'

'I wouldn't be polishing up your lectures just yet,' Rainie countered. She let the 9 mm fall from her fingers, then eased back, trying to give herself more time for her next move. Her ankle holster. She'd kept the .22 locked in a box in the trunk of her police cruiser. She couldn't believe he'd been able to get to that. 'You're not doing too well this time. The clean shot to the forehead for Melissa Avalon—'

'Have done it three times now. Always the information teacher, always a single shot to the forehead. No one's ever put the pieces together. Once a mass murderer is in custody, who starts comparing his work to other homicides? Ask your friend Quincy. Shooting rampages are considered one-off crimes.'

'But we knew you were involved—'

'Please, the sabot was a calling card. Sooner or later I needed someone to pay attention in order to have any fun. For God's sake, I gave you No Lava. I even invited you to personally visit my office so you could stare at the window I used to exit the building and rendezvous with Danny outside. You could've at least considered the possibility.'

'We did. It seemed far-fetched.'

'Yes, well, cops have singularly linear minds,' Richard conceded with a shrug. 'It's where you go wrong. Violence is a creative act. It requires patience and care. I've been nursing Danny O'Grady along for over a year, you know. Slowly making him feel comfortable on-line. Letting him know his feelings of rage and inadequacy are common and acceptable. Then it was easy. Met him in person. Showed him I'm a legitimate guy – his own school counselor, in fact. How can you doubt what the school counselor is telling you? "You need to stand up for yourself, Danny. Show everyone, including your father, who's boss."

'Of course, I never mentioned Melissa Avalon. I left that as a last-minute surprise. He just had to bring the guns and his backbone; I'd help him take a stand. When we walked into the side entrance of the school, the boy was shaking like a leaf. But you should've seen the look of determination on his face. Man, I was proud. Ironically enough, I kind of felt like a father. And then I walked into the computer lab and drew down on pretty Melissa Avalon.'

Richard's voice lowered. He leaned forward conspiratorially. 'The trick is to hesitate,' he confided. 'Let the kid apprise the situation. Let him understand he has the chance to intervene. And then, while he's still shocked and dazed and trying to find his conscience, bam! Pull the trigger. Down goes the precious little teacher. And the kid is all yours. He didn't stand up for good. Now he's gotta be evil. I told the boy to let it rip, and he bawled like a baby, but he didn't disappoint. Not bad shooting, really, considering he was too frightened to leave the doorway of the computer room. Shep might be a decent teacher after all – at least when it comes to guns.'

Mann rocked back on his heels. He sighed and finished up contentedly, 'Danny killed himself two little girls. And as soon as everyone left the building in a wave of mass confusion, I calmly exited stage right. Piece of cake, just like the times before.'

'Not quite. Becky saw you.'

Mann merely shrugged. 'Guess she tried to play hero and find her brother. Bad break for her, when she ran down the hall and discovered her own brother and school counselor holding the proverbial smoking guns. But not so bad for me. I simply threatened to kill Danny if Becky talked, and threatened to kill Becky if Danny talked. Voila. If people would raise children who were *more* callous, my job might actually be difficult. Without a guilty conscience, of course, there is very little to manipulate.'

'And is that why you created Dave Duncan, some stranger running around Seaside? More need to manipulate?'

Mann smiled wolfishly. 'Come on, Rainie. A murder has been committed – what do the brilliant cops do? They line up the locals. Now before, that was my whole advantage. I had no apparent ties to what happened, so no one ever thought to even question me. But that got boring. This time I became a local – quite nicely, if I do say so myself. But now I will be subject to questioning, and I kind of stole an identity, which might come up if somebody pushes too hard. How to cover? I know. I'll create some out-of-town stranger for you to chase. Clever and ironic. Someday I'm gonna have to write a book.'

'Not to burst your bubble, Richard, but if you're so good, why do I know you're the shooter? And Danny's admitted that you are. For that matter, I've already called and left messages for the others about you. Face it, the jig is up.' Rainie was lying about having left messages for Sanders and Luke, but Mann didn't seem to care.

'They aren't coming, Lorraine. Don't you understand that yet? Your hero Quincy is rushing into the arms of his ex-wife. And your friends Detective Sanders and Officer Hayes are dealing with another shooting across town. Or didn't you hear? It seems that someone sent Daniel Avalon a copy of a private tape his daughter made of her and her new lover, in flagrante delicto. I guess it was a little much for Mr Avalon. He looked up good old Principal VanderZanden. He brought his favorite shotgun.' Richard covered his lips delicately. 'Oops. It's just you and me, Lorraine. Let's talk.'

'Why? You had your fun. What do I have to do with anything?'

'Tell me how it felt that afternoon. Tell me how much you enjoyed killing the man who shot your mother.'

'Go to hell.'

'It felt great, didn't it? You don't like to admit it, but it gave you a secret thrill. And you like to relive it, don't you, Lorraine? Every time you step onto your back deck. Every time you raise your beer in a silent toast to the man you blew away.'

'Richard, I changed my mind.' Rainie sat down on a nearby bench. She watched him still. 'I will tell you what I say each time I dump out a beer.'

'What?' He was honestly breathless.

'I toast my mother.' Her fingers trailed down to her ankle.

'You tell her off? You send her a giant, postmortem fuck you? Oh, I like that. I do the same thing once a year.'

'No.' Her hand closed around the small handle of her gun. 'I don't tell her, Fuck you. She tried to stop him, you asshole. She was slow to believe, but she finally told him a few choice words. And then he blew off her head. So no, I don't tell her, Fuck you. I tell her I'm sorry. I tell her I should've killed him sooner. And then I tell him I hope it's hot enough down there in hell.'

She whipped out her .22. 'Bye-bye, Richard.'

'Too late, Rainie. Danny's right behind you.'

Rainie heard a board creak. She turned reflexively, saw Danny's shocked, pale face. Too late she realized her mistake. She tried to turn back around. She squeezed off one wild, desperate shot.

Then Richard savagely slammed her mother's shotgun into the side of her head.

Richard stepped forward quickly. He leveled the unfirable shotgun at Danny and said, 'Gimme the gun.'

Danny looked at Rainie's crumpled form. The boy handed over his firearm.

Richard smiled. Like candy from a baby. He tucked the gun in the back waistband of his jeans and left Rainie's shotgun on the deck. 'Your daddy sprung you, didn't he?'

The boy didn't say a word. He simply gazed hungrily at Richard's gun. Richard wasn't worried, however. Danny was too browbeaten by his father to ever do something bold. That had been half the fun.

Now Richard bent over and, with some difficulty, hefted Rainie onto his shoulder.

'You squealed on me, didn't you, Danny? Didn't I tell you that smart boys don't squeal? Smart boys stay quiet, if they want to keep their families safe.'

Danny remained wordless.

'Well, there's only one thing to do now,' Richard said with a sigh. 'We're going to have to kill your sister. Rules, Danny. Just ask my old man. You gotta live by the rules.'

Quincy's flight didn't touch down in Portland until nine P.M. Luke met him at the gate and started briefing him as they both half-walked, half-jogged to his illegally parked car.

'Her neighbor reported hearing a gunshot a little after eight P.M.,' Luke was saying. 'Frankly, we didn't get that call until nearly nine P.M.'

'Why so late?'

'Because we had our hands full with another shooting, and dispatch got confused. Daniel Avalon had disappeared as of yesterday afternoon. Today he surfaced in Bakersville, trying to blow off Steven VanderZanden's head.'

'Casualties?'

'Not yet. VanderZanden ended up bruised and battered, but fortunately Avalon's a lousy shot. On the other hand, VanderZanden's wife figured out what it was about from all the cursing and swearing. I don't know yet how VanderZanden will fare with her.'

'Hell hath no fury like a woman scorned,' Quincy murmured. Someone came barreling toward them with a cart filled with luggage. They both swerved wildly and kept running. 'When did officers arrive at Rainie's house?'

'Fifteen minutes ago. So far there's no sign of Rainie, but there are blood splatters on the deck. Sanders thinks he got her.'

'Any phone calls, any gloating? He loves games. This whole thing has been one giant adventure for him.'

'Yeah, well, we're trying to cut off his amusement ride. In the good-news department, Sanders opened up the personnel file for Richard Mann around six-thirty. First thing he saw was a black-and-white photo of the real Richard Mann, which certainly didn't match our favorite counselor. He'd already called for a couple of uniforms to descend upon Mann's house when the shooting started at the VanderZanden residence.'

They arrived at Luke's patrol car. Quincy threw his bags on the floor and climbed in. Luke flipped on the sirens. Off they went.

'What did they find at Mann's house?' Quincy asked, gripping the dashboard as Luke took a corner hard.

'We found one computer. A cop hit the space bar. The monitor came up with a screen that said: *Love you too, Baby.* Then the whole thing blew up. Luckily, it was a small charge and no one was hurt.'

'Fuck!' Quincy slapped the dashboard. 'We've spent this whole dance two steps behind.'

'Yeah, and now the dance floor is getting crowded. In other news, Danny disappeared at five-thirty this evening. Two Cabot County cops were transporting Danny to a mental facility when they ran off the road. Supposedly when they regained consciousness, he'd already stolen the keys to his shackles and disappeared into the mist.'

Quincy looked at Luke. He said, 'Shep.'

Luke said nothing, which coming from him was a yes.

'Is he in custody?'

'They're still questioning him. But there's no sign of Danny, and I know Shep. He'd do anything for his son, probably even this. But something's gone wrong. He looks like a giant bowl of jelly. If I didn't know any better, I'd say he's scared out of his mind.'

'You think Danny ran off on his own?'

'I don't know.'

'You think he went to Rainie's house?'

'We're dusting for prints. Ask me when the reports come back.'

'How well does Danny know the area?'

'He's hunted here all his life. He'd do all right.'

'Get your hands on Shep. Have him meet us at Rainie's place.'

Luke didn't bat an eye. 'Okay.'

'Ask Sanders to send two state troopers to the O'Grady house. I want Sandy and Becky under full police protection. According to the preliminary information, Richard Mann – or whoever he is – has done this three times. On each occasion it's been a mass shooting. And on each occasion there have been no witnesses. I don't think he's going to start now.'

Luke paled but nodded soberly.

'Luke, do you have a vest?'

'Yes.'

'Put it on. Make sure everyone puts theirs on.'

'You don't think he's left town.'

'I know he hasn't left town. It's the nature of the beast. Each time, he has to raise the stakes in order to get the same thrill. And, heaven help us, he's tired of being bored.'

34

Abe Sanders ran up to meet Quincy the minute he arrived at Rainie's house. The CSU was tearing up floorboards, dissecting the deck in search of trace evidence. Giant floodlights illuminated the grounds, while men in navy blue windbreakers swept the premises inch by inch with bobbing flashlights. Quincy had seen this scene hundreds of times by now, and it still struck him as surreal.

He'd never even been to Rainie's home. There should be nothing here to connect to her in his mind. But when he saw the back deck framed by soaring trees, he could picture her at once, and pain socked him in the gut. Her vulnerable eyes, her stubborn chin. So much unfinished business.

He had to reach out a hand to steady himself. Then he got on with the matters at hand.

'What have they found?' he asked Sanders.

'It's under the deck.'

Quincy followed Sanders around. Shep was back there as well, hunched with his chin tucked in the top of his coat against the night's chill. Luke was right. Shep looked on the verge of being ill. If he'd been behind the jailbreak, things had not gone as planned.

Then Quincy noticed that men were furiously working the dirt beneath the deck like a promising archaeological site. They dusted, fluoresced, and categorized. They carted away piles of dirt.

'It looks like a fresh grave,' Sanders was saying. 'Right under the deck. But all we've found so far are some old threads and gravel. They're still working on it.'

Quincy looked at Shep. The sheriff had thinned his lips. Quincy understood. They were looking at the final resting place of the man who had killed Rainie's mother. And Quincy also understood who had put him there.

'Anything else?' Quincy asked.

'We found an old shotgun,' Sanders said. 'Shep already identified it as the gun that was used to kill Molly Conner fourteen years ago. In theory, it's an open case, so all evidence has been held in the state police's storage locker in Portland. Then two days ago a young man claiming to be from the Bakersville sheriff's department checked out the evidence. He gave Rainie's badge number, which the doofus officer in charge never followed up on. And gee, Bakersville's newest police officer just happens to match Richard Mann's description.'

'He gave this some thought.'

'No kidding. We got a ton of fingerprints from his house, but it's going to take a while to work through the system. We've been calling him Mann, though apparently the real Mann is teaching in some remote village in Alaska and has no idea someone stole his identity. When he gets back to civilization, he's in for a little surprise.'

'Mann's still around here,' Quincy said.

'He'd be an idiot to remain in the area. We got guys everywhere.'

'He's an adrenaline junkie. He's taken it this far. He'll see it all the way through.'

'What do you think he's doing?'

'I'm not sure anymore. In the beginning, I think he was planning on business as usual. He identified a kid who was troubled. He found an identity he could use as a ruse. It's not rushed. He's executed three complicated crimes in the space of ten years. He takes his time. He's cautious. Think of what we talked about earlier: He operates with a double contingency plan. So even if you penetrate the first wall, you simply encounter the next layer of defense.

'My guess is that he was too good. Two spectacular crimes and no one came close to figuring them out. Where's the thrill in that? Where's the rush? So this time he started to take more chances. He lingered after the shooting. He gave us more hints, but I just didn't see them. His whole little diatribe on what makes a good father. He was referring to his own issues with his father, of course. Then that little speech at the funeral on how he'd decided Danny couldn't be the shooter. Danny was too smart, too sophisticated to use blatant force. He wasn't talking about Danny. He was talking about himself.

'And then we get to Rainie. He brought her the shotgun, the gun most of the town believes she personally used to kill her own mother. That must have captivated him. Here's a woman who is rumored to have done exactly what he fantasized about every day of his childhood. She probably seemed glorious to him.'

'You think he wanted her to run away with him? Become his partner?' Sanders asked incredulously.

Quincy shook his head. 'No. I think he made the same mistake everyone else in this town has made. She didn't shoot her mother. And that deeply, deeply disappointed him.'

Sanders could fill in the rest. 'And if he's disappointed . . .'

'If we don't find them soon,' Quincy said quietly, 'I doubt she'll live through the night.'

A voice suddenly came from deep in the woods. 'Over here, over here,' a technician cried. 'I got something!'

They ran. There on the ground, a tiny piece of white cotton, as if torn from a T-shirt.

'They went into the woods,' Sanders said triumphantly. 'Quick, somebody get some dogs.'

'Adjoining roads,' Quincy said immediately. 'Logging roads, rural routes, dirt roads, anything. Get your men on them, because he didn't come all this way on foot.'

Abe excitedly began making the calls, and then they were plunging into the underbrush, desperate to find a trail, desperate to find Rainie.

'Shit!' Richard Mann said for the fifth time in about as many minutes. He staggered to a halt, wiping the heavy sweat from his brow and giving Rainie a look that was rapidly growing ragged.

She pretended to ignore his hatred while lowering herself gingerly to the ground, not the easiest thing to do with her hands tied behind her back. Her head hurt. She had regained consciousness quickly, but that hadn't done her any favors. When Richard had smacked her with the shotgun, he'd done a good job of it. Her jaw throbbed; she suspected it was broken. Her eye had swelled shut; she thought the socket might be fractured. She was starting to see double with what vision she had left, and the pain was becoming less constant but more acute. Hemorrhage, maybe? Blood clot? The possibilities were endless.

At least she was having the last laugh. Her wild shot had caught Richard Mann in his right buttock as he'd swiveled around to swing the shotgun. He'd dismissed it as a mere flesh wound, but after hiking up the steep mountain for a bit, he'd taken to favoring his right leg. His walking was no longer steady; his face had become flushed. They were taking more and more breaks and stopping for longer periods of time. It was hard to tell in the dark, but she suspected he was bleeding heavily. He'd stuffed his windbreaker down his pants to bandage the wound, but he must have begun to doubt that system, for he kept pausing now to check the ground for signs of blood.

Mess with me, get shot in the ass, Rainie thought. She smiled at her own dark humor, then promptly winced in pain.

Danny was still with them, now sitting quietly beside Rainie. He had yet to say a word. He simply walked, his head ducked low and his hands stuck in the pants pockets of his blue surgical scrubs. The night was cold. He kept fidgeting with his white cotton undershirt as if trying to get warm. Rainie wished there was more she could do for him.

Hell, at this point, with the trees swaying sickeningly in front of her eyes, she wished there was more she could do for herself.

How had Danny gotten out of the detention center? And why had he come to her back porch? Had he suspected Richard Mann might show up there? Had he wanted to help her?

Or was he still Richard's accomplice? She thought of what Quincy had said yesterday. Once the dominant partner got the other to kill, it became too difficult for the weaker one to walk away. And Danny had killed. He had told her about it today in a thin, high voice that sounded as fragile as a reed.

She didn't know anymore. She was trying to hold the thoughts together in her mind, sort through them, come up with a plan. Her face was on fire, and the pain was becoming more intense.

Mann staggered back to his feet. His flashlight swung wildly. It illuminated two dark spots on the dusty trail and made him curse. The man was bleeding quite nicely. He kicked up dirt over the blood, grabbed a tree limb to rake over their trail, and gave Rainie a look that was downright feral.

'Up,' he snarled.

'I think I'm going to vomit,' Rainie murmured.

'*Up!*'

'Okay,' she said. She leaned forward and threw up on his shoes.

'Fuck me!' Mann leapt back two feet, kicking furiously at bushes and needles in a vain attempt to get the puke off his shoes. His arms flailed. His face had gone purple. Rainie didn't hesitate. Maybe it wasn't a pretty plan, but it was as good as it was going to get.

'Run,' she yelled at Danny. '*Run!*'

And then she hurled herself at Mann.

They went down in a tangle of bodies, the gun flying from his grasp. She heard Mann thrashing and swearing. It seemed his legs and feet were everywhere, and she instinctively tried to protect her head. Her eye, her eye. Oh God, her cheek was exploding on her. But she couldn't bring her hands up. They were tied behind her back, leaving her churning on the ground like a helpless worm.

Richard went after her with a vicious kick. She barely rolled out of the way; then he abruptly backed off.

Shit. He was going for the gun. She rolled back and kicked him as hard she could in the back of his knee. His legs folded beneath him. She went after his shot-up hip with her pummeling feet.

She couldn't see any sign of Danny. Please let him have run. If she could buy time, give him a chance to get farther away . . .

Richard was trying to get to his feet again. She saw his gaze go to the handgun he must have snatched from Danny, which was now lying just four feet away in the dust. He gritted his teeth and lunged. She rolled to the right as quickly as she could and managed to kick him in the side of the head.

'Damn bitch,' he swore. Then he suddenly got a curious smile on his face.

He reached out and curled his hand around a big helping of pine needles and dirt. Rainie ducked her head. She closed her eyes to protect herself, but she had no hands to hide her bloody face as he flung the dust and needles at her head.

She spluttered, blinked reflexively, and buried eight tiny needles in her one good eye.

'*Goddammit!*'

It hurt. Hurt worse than she'd imagined pain feeling. Hurt even worse than all those years ago, when she'd been so small and helpless. Fuck that. She would not be small. She would not be helpless.

She went after Richard Mann with her pummeling legs and realized for the first time that he was laughing. He was standing now, not even going after the gun. He just stood there, watching her writhe on the ground and finding it funny.

'Going someplace, Lorraine?'

'Bastard!'

He laughed again.

She rolled toward Richard Mann with a kamikaze yell, and he calmly kicked her in the damaged side of her face.

Lights exploded. She saw blazing, fantastical colors, followed by a white-hot blur. And then the corresponding agony ripped a scream from her lips.

'Had enough yet, Lorraine? Want to taste a little more?'

She started rolling again. She couldn't see. Just felt him coming after her and knew what kind of pain he'd like to inflict next. She wanted to be fierce and brave, but the pain was too much and now she fled in the dirt. Rolling, rolling, rolling, seeking some desperate way out.

Her kneecap smacked into a tree trunk. She howled. Mann laughed. Footsteps coming closer. Faster, faster. She switched directions suddenly, working on memory only, and ripped her way across the earth. The gun, the gun, the gun. Somewhere around her, the gun.

'No!' Richard Mann yelled suddenly.

And then she knew she had him. She rolled on top of the 9 mm and grabbed it with her bloodied fingertips.

'What are you going to do, Lorraine?' Mann taunted breathlessly. 'Shoot it with your kneecaps?'

She said hoarsely with her back to him, 'Halt. Police.'

'Hand it over, Lorraine. Be a good girl, and I promise I'll kill you quickly.'

Footsteps coming closer.

Her wet, slippery fingers frantically trying to orient the heavy pistol, find the trigger.

The sound of Mann's ragged breath, bearing down on her. She couldn't see him, had little hope of aiming. Just try to find the trigger. Pull it back.

Do something, even if she only ended up winging his big toe. The gun slipped again. She was doomed.

Mann bending over her. Mann rearing back his leg to kick her in the face—

'*Halt! Police!*'

Flashlights suddenly flooded the area. Rainie tried to focus her dirt-filled eyes. The lights were too bright, the voices too far away. Her fingers reclaimed the gun as she turned her head and saw Richard Mann gazing toward the lights. He was breathing hard. So was she. His face was ugly and mottled with rage. And hers?

'Fuck them,' Richard Mann snarled. He reared back to wallop her in the head—

And Rainie pulled the trigger.

Richard Mann dropped to the earth, just as three other officers opened fire. Rainie rolled over. She lay three feet from Mann's body and watched the hate slowly dim and die out in his eyes.

A moment later, Quincy came forward. Rainie knew him by his smell as he bent down and cradled her against his chest.

'I came as fast as I could,' he murmured. 'I told you that I would.'

She could see the others now. Abe Sanders. Luke Hayes. Shep O'Grady. And Danny, standing with his father's arm around his thin shoulders and tears on his cheeks.

'How did you find us?' she asked.

'Danny left us a trail with pieces of his T-shirt. He's been ripping them off and dropping them down his pants leg.'

Danny said simply, 'I'm smart.'

Rainie turned her face into Quincy's embrace then. His arms were warm. His heartbeat strong. He felt so nice.

I'm finally being held, she thought.

And then she started to cry. She wept for Danny, who had caused so much death, and she wept for herself and what she knew she must do next.

Epilogue

Two weeks later

The sun was out when Rainie descended the stairs of Cabot County's courthouse. She wore jeans and a simple white T-shirt, tucked in and belted at the waist. The days were already warm with the promise of summer, and after four hours in an office, she enjoyed the feel of spring on her still-healing face. In the good news department, the swelling in her jaw and eye socket had finally gone down. In the bad news department, her face was now approximately eighteen different shades of yellow and green. At least Richard Mann had not inflicted as much damage as he'd originally thought. Rainie's doctor assured her that she'd be fine within another few weeks – after he muttered that this proved once and for all that she was thick-skulled. Wiseass.

The Bakersville task force had been busy in the days since Richard Mann's shooting. Abe Sanders had gotten his wish – formal jurisdiction over the case. He'd also gotten more federal agents breathing down his throat than any one man could handle.

The fingerprint results had been stunning. Richard Mann was really Henry Hawkins of Minneapolis, Minnesota. Born to a domineering army lieutenant and his meek librarian wife, Hawkins had moved a dozen times in his childhood. He'd grown up hard, according to his journal, steeped in guns and his father's quick fists. He'd mastered a chameleon personality as he'd shuffled from town to town, school to school. And he'd honed his rage. At his father's harsh ways. At the other children who always saw him as an outsider. At his mother, who never stood up for herself or him.

At the age of twenty, Hawkins's parents died unexpectedly in a car crash, robbing him of any chance for retaliation or forgiveness. And his homicidal rampage began.

At this point, the FBI had linked him to two other school shootings. They were revisiting those cases now, interviewing the boys who'd craved notoriety so badly they'd gone to prison rather than admit someone else had been involved. The feebies were also looking into a handful of other shootings, where children had lashed out unexpectedly while Hawkins was living in their town. No doubt some cases were coincidences. They weren't sure, however, that would be true for them all.

Hawkins still owned his parents' house in Minnesota. He had armed it with a number of pipe bombs and booby traps to make the investigators' lives more interesting. It slowed down efforts but did not stop them. Sanders was leading that raid, and Hawkins had met his match in the state detective's meticulous nature.

It would probably be months, maybe even a year, before the last of the evidence was processed. Not that it would matter to Henry Hawkins. With no one to claim his body, he had been laid to rest in Potters' Field.

Danny's case was also being revisited. Shep and Sandy were now working with Charles Rodriguez on a plea arrangement. There was still a long road ahead for Danny. He had killed two little girls, and even understanding that he had been influenced by a savvy outsider didn't change that fact. There should be barriers in all of us, the DA had argued this morning, lines we should know better than to cross. And one of those barriers should be resistance to taking human life. Danny hadn't possessed that barrier, and that had to be addressed.

In the end, it appeared that Danny would enter an admission to the charge of aggravated murder in return for a guarantee of remaining under juvenile court's jurisdiction. There he would receive a disposition of serving at a youth correctional facility for a period not to exceed his twenty-fifth birthday. The Oregon Youth Authority would formally assume custody over him, conducting a new mental-health assessment and providing resources for his treatment. It would be up to the OYA to determine when he was ready for parole.

Sandy and Shep put their house up for sale. Chances were that Danny would end up at the Hillcrest facility in Salem, so they were looking to relocate there. Shep was interviewing with various security companies. Though most suspected that he'd engineered the 'car crash' that allowed Danny to escape, there was no proof of wrong-doing, so his record remained clear. Sandy wanted to focus on her children and become more active in reforming juvenile law. Technically, they remained married, though the last time Rainie had seen them, she'd witnessed few moments of intimacy. She had a feeling they'd reached a point of living together but separately. Maybe they thought it was better that way, for Becky.

Rainie reached the bottom of the courthouse steps. She was trying to decide whether to head immediately to her car or spend the rest of the sunny afternoon walking around town, when she heard a voice behind her.

'Hello, Rainie.'

Rainie turned and spotted him immediately. She smiled before she thought to stop herself, and then it was too late to take it back.

Quincy leaned against the stone wall, wearing one of his expensively cut suits and a conservative blue tie. It had been two weeks since she'd last seen him. Following the scene on the mountainside, he'd flown immediately to the sites of the other Hawkins school shootings to handle the reopening of those cases. She imagined he'd been flying all over the country since, interviewing youths and juggling more crime-scene photos.

Now he was in front of her, and she no sooner looked at him than she realized she'd missed him. He was smiling at her. Maybe he'd missed her too.

'Hey,' she said.

'Shep told me you'd be here.'

'I didn't know he spoke to federal agents.'

'Neither did he.'

Quincy motioned to the empty spot beside him. She made a big show of wandering over, trying not to move too fast. He smelled good. Someday she'd have to ask him about his cologne, because, damn, she liked that scent.

'How are things going?' she asked.

'That was going to be my question.'

'Things are looking up for Danny,' she offered. 'A lot of people have come out to support him. Not that they condone his actions, but Henry Hawkins/Richard Mann/Dave Duncan fooled the entire town, including the school district. After that, it's easier to understand his impact on one troubled child.'

'And Becky?'

'Better. The minute Sandy told her Richard Mann was dead, the weight lifted off her shoulders. Apparently in the confusion of the shooting, she ran to find her brother. Unfortunately, she spotted him and Richard together in the computer lab, not far from Miss Avalon's body. Richard told her if she talked, he'd kill Danny. And if Danny talked, Richard would kill Becky. He was right, you know. Simple strategies can be highly effective.'

'Well, now he and the devil can debate the matter to their hearts' content.' Quincy's smile lifted the corner of his mouth. The familiar expression tugged at her. She wished she didn't feel so awkward. She wished she could touch him.

'Rainie?' he asked quietly. 'How are you?'

She shrugged. There was no point in lying anymore. This was the new and improved Lorraine Conner. Telling the truth until it hurt. 'I've been better.'

'Is the DA going to press charges?'

'Don't know.' She jerked her head toward the court-house. 'My attorney and I just had a meeting to hear our options. Funky thing, Oregon law. I thought since I shot Lucas when I was seventeen, it would fall under juvenile jurisdiction. Nope. In Oregon, it's the age I am when it comes to the attention of the court that matters, not the age when I committed the crime. That means Man One, up to five years' jail time. The DA said that "given the nature of the extenuating circumstances," he might be willing to deal down to less than a year, served locally. All I have to do is plead guilty to a felony murder charge. I wasn't – I wasn't expecting that.'

Rainie didn't have to say anything more. Quincy understood. A felony charge would bar her from law enforcement for the rest of her life. She wouldn't be able to get a job working security. She wouldn't even have the right to carry a gun.

'Can't you fight it?' Quincy asked after a moment. 'Plead not guilty due to diminished mental capacity. Or argue you acted in a dissociative state, brought on by the trauma of your mother's murder.'

'You sound like my lawyer. She doesn't think the state has a leg to stand on. Frightened seventeen-year-old girl. Rampaging suspected murderer with more tattoos than morals. She considers this case a slam dunk.'

'So you're pleading not guilty,' Quincy said.

Rainie merely smiled. She peered up at the blue sky, turning over facts that were still new and troubling to her. 'I think I want to plead guilty and give full allocution,' she said quietly.

'Why? You have a need to eat jail food?'

'I think I just need to tell, Quincy. I need to get it out in the open. What I did fourteen years ago was horrible. And you were right: no matter how long it has been, it will never be long enough.'

'He raped you, Rainie.'

'Yes.'

'Did you try to go to your mother?'

'Yes.'

'But she didn't believe you.'

'No. And then I went to Shep.'

For the first time, Quincy was surprised. 'He knew?'

'I wanted to press charges, but Shep didn't believe me. He was just starting out, and I was a seventeen-year-old girl from the wrong side of town. No one gets out of life without a few regrets.'

'So you went back to your mother,' Quincy deduced.

'No. I just went home. I didn't know what else to do. But I guess she just needed time to think about it. I'm not sure. Later that night Lucas came over. Drunk – what else was new? They had a huge fight and she threw him out, yelling at him to keep his stinking hands off her daughter. I think that's the first time I felt proud of my mother. The first time I had hope that things might be better.'

'Then I came home the next day, and Lucas had shot off her head.'

'And Shep was remorseful?'

'Not when he arrested me. But Bakersville didn't have any female officers, so he had to take me to Cabot County for processing. There a woman made me strip so she could bag my bloody clothes as evidence. And I . . . And I was pretty damaged from what had happened. When she left the room, I heard her tell Shep that either my boyfriend really liked it rough or I'd spent a long night with the Hell's Angels. Poor Shep. It couldn't have been fun to realize what a mistake he'd made.'

'Did he give you the shotgun, Rainie?'

'No. At that point, I think he simply saw the error of his ways. Between my condition and the neighbor's report on the time of the gunshot, they put out an APB on Lucas. They figured he'd flee the scene, but I wasn't convinced. He didn't have a lot of money, he specialized in being a mean son of a bitch. I think . . . I think I just knew he'd come back. That had been the point. My mother was dead. Now he could do as he pleased.

'I didn't have any more weapons. I wasn't old enough to legally buy a gun. The shotgun was the only thing I knew about. So I went downtown. I waited until six o'clock when the sheriff locked up the office for the night. I knew the volunteer officers were out on patrol. If any other business came up, the department's answering machine told you how to reach the sheriff at home, so everything was deserted and safe. I broke into the sheriff's office.'

'There wasn't an alarm?'

Rainie raised a brow. 'In Bakersville? Who's dumb enough to break into a sheriff's office, anyway? Even now, one of us forgets to lock up half the time. It's not like we have a decent coffee maker to protect.'

'You have evidence, though.'

'In a separate evidence locker in the back. These days we use a safe. Very solid, hard to penetrate. Fourteen years ago, however, it was a basic lockbox. I picked it open with a hairpin. And I took my shotgun home.'

Quincy sighed, rubbed the bridge of his nose. He obviously knew where things were going from here. 'Lucas showed up,' he said.

'He walked right up to the sliding glass door before seeing me. And then . . . he smiled, like this was going to be even more fun than he'd thought. He slid open the door. I shot him at point-blank range in the chest. Wouldn't you know it? He died with that same goddamn grin on his face.'

'Why didn't you call the cops, Rainie? You could've claimed self-defense.'

'I was a kid. I didn't know the legal system. I just knew my heart, and in my heart it wasn't self-defense. He had hurt me. He had taken away my mother. And I wanted him dead. I wanted him wiped from the face of the earth. And I'd taken my mother's shotgun home, just for that.'

'You buried him under the deck.'

'Took me all night.'

'And then you ran away,' Quincy concluded.

She nodded. 'I took off for Portland and spent the next four years trying to drown every image in my head.'

'What about his car, Rainie? What about any neighbors reporting the sound of a gunshot—'

'My neighbor had left for a fishing trip. There was no one around.'

'Fine, what about the fact that one minute Lucas was in Bakersville and the next he disappeared? What about the fact that your mother's shotgun just happened to disappear from the evidence locker one night, only to magically reappear sometime later? This doesn't sound like rocket science to me. Shep should've been searching your place by the end of the week, tops. You didn't even hide the body well.'

Rainie didn't say anything.

After a moment Quincy sighed. 'He let it go, didn't he? No harm, no foul. Remind me never to let Shep feel as if he owes me a favor.'

'It's a small town, Quincy. And small-town policing . . . The rules are sometimes different. What goes around comes around. It's not always just, but it can be right. For the record, to this day Shep and I have never spoken of it.'

'Of course not. That would make it conspiracy.'

'I was prepared to pay for what I'd done,' Rainie countered immediately. 'In many ways, that might have been better. I could've gotten it out in the open. I could've faced it, put it in perspective, paid my dues. Instead . . .' She faltered for the first time. 'Lucas had a wife and a kid. I took him from them. For fourteen years, they haven't even known what happened to him. I should've known that. Even if I hated him, I shouldn't have forgotten that he was human. Rodriguez is right: there are certain barriers we shouldn't cross, and one of them is the willingness to take a life.'

'He would've gone after you that night,' Quincy said gently.

'But that's the point, Quincy. I'll never know. I killed him first, and that makes me no better.'

'Rainie—'

She held up a hand. 'No platitudes. I did my deed. Now I'm going to get to pay for that. Responsibility and accountability. They're not such bad things. You know why I dug him up that night?'

'Why?'

'Because I was afraid Richard Mann would take him away from me. When we first got the call about a man bragging that he had proof I'd killed my mother . . . I don't know. I just flashed to Lucas, under my deck, and this strange dream I'd had the night before of a man standing there, the man in black. Suddenly, I was terrified. That it had been the killer on my back deck. That he had discovered the body and when I walked into Dave Duncan's hotel room, that would be the first thing I'd see – Lucas's corpse waiting to greet me. But then I walked in, and the room was empty, and . . . I realized I wasn't relieved. In fact, I was even more anxious. What if he still knew, what if he'd taken the body, and then . . . then I'd have no proof of what I'd done, and I needed that proof. I needed to confess what happened. Danny had made that clear to me.'

'So what happens now, Rainie?'

She had to take a moment. In spite of her best intentions, the answer to that question made her throat close up. She worked on clearing it. She still sounded husky as she said, 'The mayor asked me to resign last week.'

Quincy looked immediately pained.

'You know,' she said more briskly, 'there's just something about a cop with a corpse under her deck that people don't like. And here I'd finally managed to impress a tightass like Sanders. But Luke's in charge now. He'll do a good job.'

'You could move, start over someplace else.'

'Not if I plead guilty. Things like that are hard to explain away during a job interview. "What do you feel is your biggest weakness?" "Uhh, last time I was pissed off and under stress, I shot a man".' She shook her head in disgust.

'Is that why you want to plead guilty?' Quincy asked levelly. 'To punish yourself further?'

'I *killed* someone!'

'Who raped you and shot your mother, all within forty-eight hours. Post-traumatic stress syndrome. Dissociative state. These aren't magical terms psychologists have come up with to confuse juries, Rainie. They are genuine syndromes, well documented and well known, as your lawyer can tell you. You were seventeen years old. You were frightened. And Lucas came back to get you. Your lawyer is right – there isn't a jury in this world that will find you guilty. Now how can twelve strangers have more faith in you, Rainie, than you do?'

Rainie couldn't answer. Her throat had closed up again. She looked down and resolutely studied the cracks on the sidewalk.

'If you really want to move on with your life, Rainie,' Quincy said gently, 'move on. Forgive yourself. Go to trial and give the jury a chance to forgive you as well. You're a good person. You're a great police officer. Ask anyone in Bakersville. Ask Sanders. Ask Luke. Ask me. I'm an arrogant federal agent, and I would be honored to work with you again.'

'Oh shut up, Quincy. Now you're making me cry.' He was. She dabbed at the corners of her eyes and sniffled roughly. Damn fed.

'What are you going to do?'

'You might have a point.'

'Of course I have a point. I'm the expert.'

'I still have so much to learn.'

'Rainie—'

'No, don't say it.'

'How do you know what I'm going to say?' He tried to reach for her. She stepped out of his grasp, already shaking her head.

'Because I do! Because for a man who's been to so many crime scenes, you still have a romantic view of life. But it'll never work, so just don't say it.' She made a firm no-crossing signal with her hands.

'I want to take you out to dinner,' he said calmly.

'You are such an ass!'

'I'm promising lo mein, with green tea. I'm hoping this time we'll both eat.'

'For chrissakes, you're not staying, Quincy. You're an agent. You love your job. You're good at your job. I'm just a stop along the way.'

'I could stop a lot. It's the advantage of being a big shot.'

'Why? To watch me cash my unemployment checks?'

'Rainie—'

'It's true and we both know it! You're . . . you, Quincy. You know who you are and where you're going and that's great. But I'm me. And me is a mess. I liked being a cop. God, I liked being a cop. I don't . . . I don't know what comes next. I have to figure it out. And I guess I have to go through a trial. And I can't do that with you watching. I liked being your coworker. I won't be your charity case.'

'Rainie.' He sounded exasperated. Then he simply sounded sincere. 'I *missed* you these last two weeks. I drove myself crazy thinking about you. People said only civil things to me, and I honestly resented it. I wanted you instead.'

Rainie shook her head again. He was not making this easy for her. She felt longing. In all honesty, she felt pain. The scent of his cologne haunted her. It made her want to lean into his hard frame. He would hold her. He had done so that night, and it was one of the few precious memories she had.

But she still knew better. He had a hero complex, and she was too proud to be a damsel in distress.

Another minute passed. Quincy's shoulders finally slumped. He shook his head, and it was his turn to stare at the ground. Rainie stuffed her hands in the back pockets of her jeans.

'I gotta go,' she said after a moment, looking at everything but him.

He didn't say anything, and she figured that was that. She started walking back down the cheery street, and the sun was so bright in her eyes, it brought on tears.

She turned at the last minute. She shouldn't do it. She did it anyway.

'Quincy.'

He quickly, hopefully looked up.

'Maybe . . . maybe someday, when things are going a little better. Maybe I could come visit.'

And he said honestly, 'I can hardly wait.'